DR. BEAGLE
AND MR. HYDE

© 1952 United Feature Syndicate, Inc.

Peanuts Parade Paperbacks

---

1. Who's the Funny-Looking Kid with the Big Nose?
2. It's a Long Way to Tipperary
3. There's a Vulture Outside
4. What's Wrong with Being Crabby?
5. What Makes You Think You're Happy?
6. Fly, You Stupid Kite, Fly!
7. The Mad Punter Strikes Again
8. A Kiss on the Nose Turns Anger Aside
9. Thank Goodness for People
10. What Makes Musicians So Sarcastic?
11. Speak Softly, and Carry a Beagle
12. Don't Hassle Me with Your Sighs, Chuck
13. There Goes the Shutout
14. Always Stick Up for the Underbird
15. It's Hard Work Being Bitter
16. How Long, Great Pumpkin, How Long?
17. A Smile Makes a Lousy Umbrella
18. My Anxieties Have Anxieties
19. It's Great to Be a Super Star
20. Stop Snowing on My Secretary
21. Summers Fly, Winters Walk
22. The Beagle Has Landed
23. And a Woodstock in a Birch Tree
24. Here Comes the April Fool!
25. Dr. Beagle and Mr. Hyde

DR. BEAGLE AND MR. HYDE

© 1958 United Feature Syndicate, Inc.

by Charles M. Schulz
Holt, Rinehart and Winston / New York

PEANUTS comic strips by Charles M. Schulz
Copyright © 1980, 1981 by United Feature Syndicate, Inc.

All rights reserved, including the right to reproduce this book or portions thereof in any form.

Published by Holt, Rinehart and Winston, 383 Madison Avenue, New York, New York 10017.

Published simultaneously in Canada by Holt, Rinehart and Winston of Canada, Limited.

First published in book form in 1981.

Library of Congress Catalog Card Number: 81-80708

ISBN: 0-03-059862-1

First Edition

Printed in the United States of America

10 9 8 7 6 5 4 3 2 1

© 1952 United Feature Syndicate, Inc.

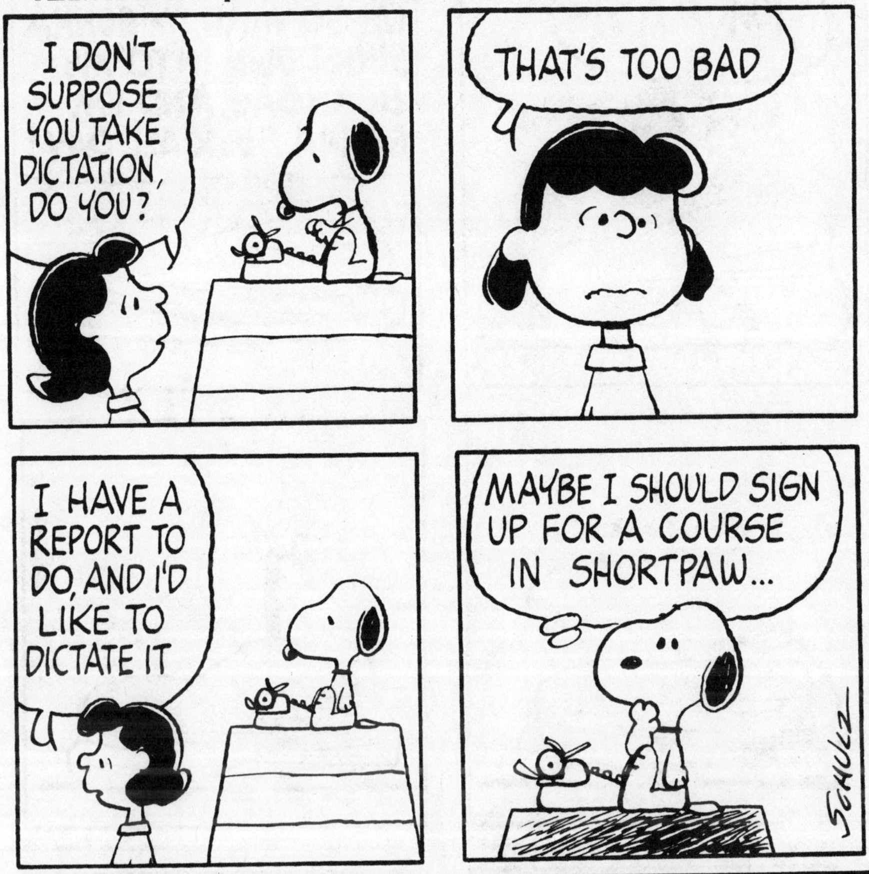
I DON'T SUPPOSE YOU TAKE DICTATION, DO YOU?
THAT'S TOO BAD
I HAVE A REPORT TO DO, AND I'D LIKE TO DICTATE IT
MAYBE I SHOULD SIGN UP FOR A COURSE IN SHORTPAW...
SCHULZ

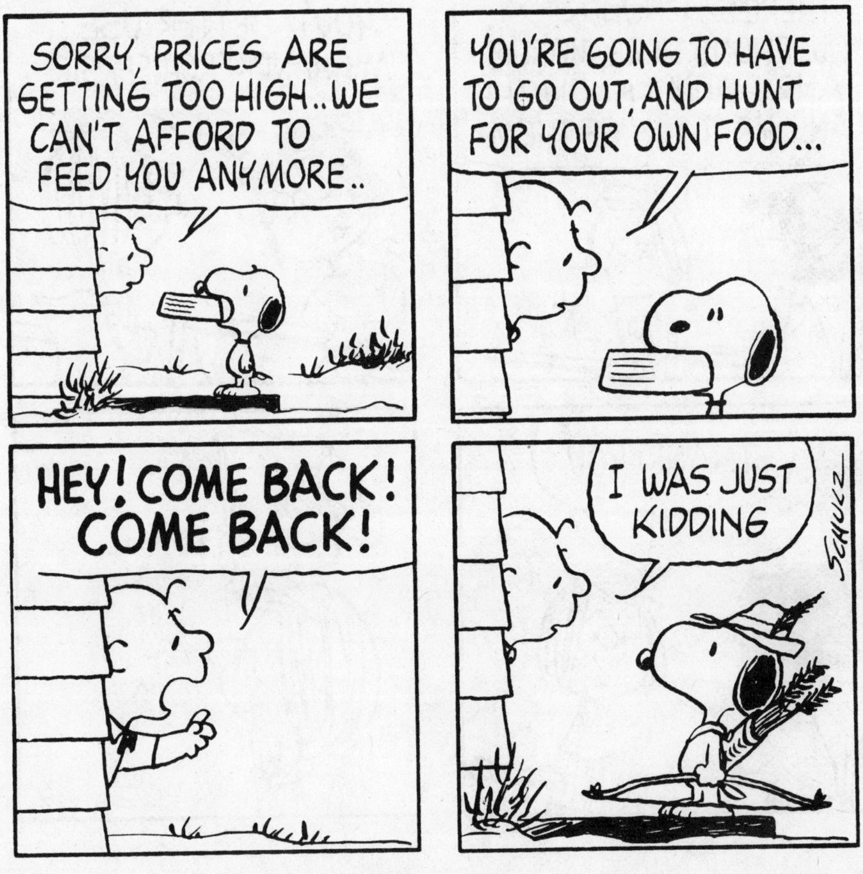
SORRY, PRICES ARE GETTING TOO HIGH..WE CAN'T AFFORD TO FEED YOU ANYMORE..
YOU'RE GOING TO HAVE TO GO OUT, AND HUNT FOR YOUR OWN FOOD...
HEY! COME BACK! COME BACK!
I WAS JUST KIDDING
SCHULZ

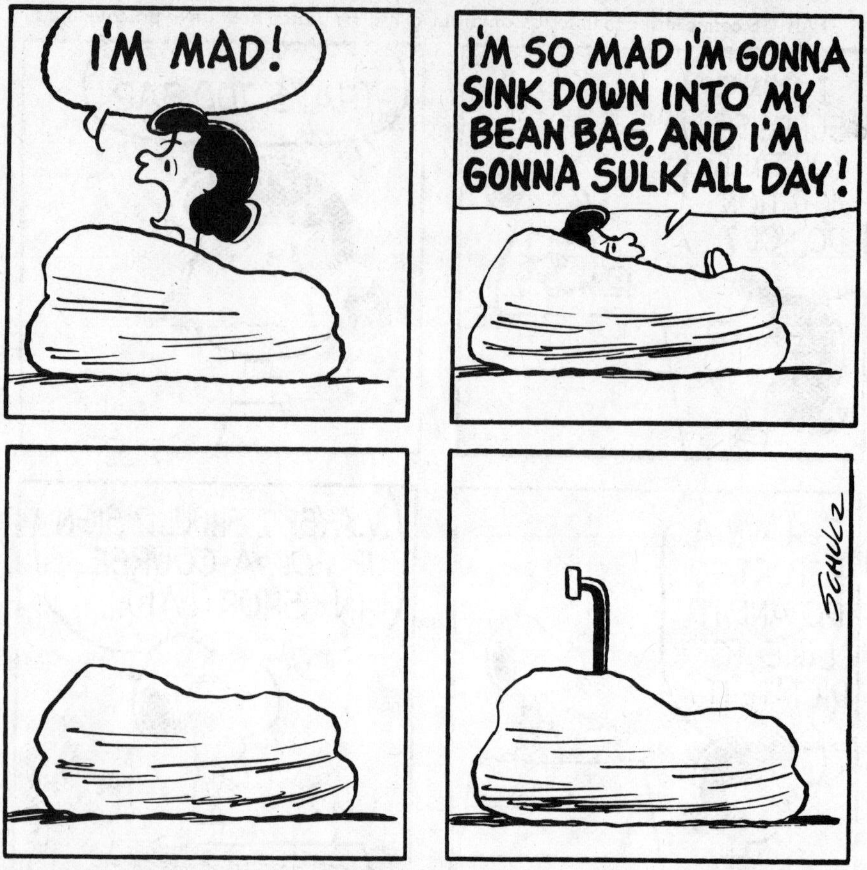
I'M MAD!
I'M SO MAD I'M GONNA SINK DOWN INTO MY BEAN BAG, AND I'M GONNA SULK ALL DAY!
SCHULZ

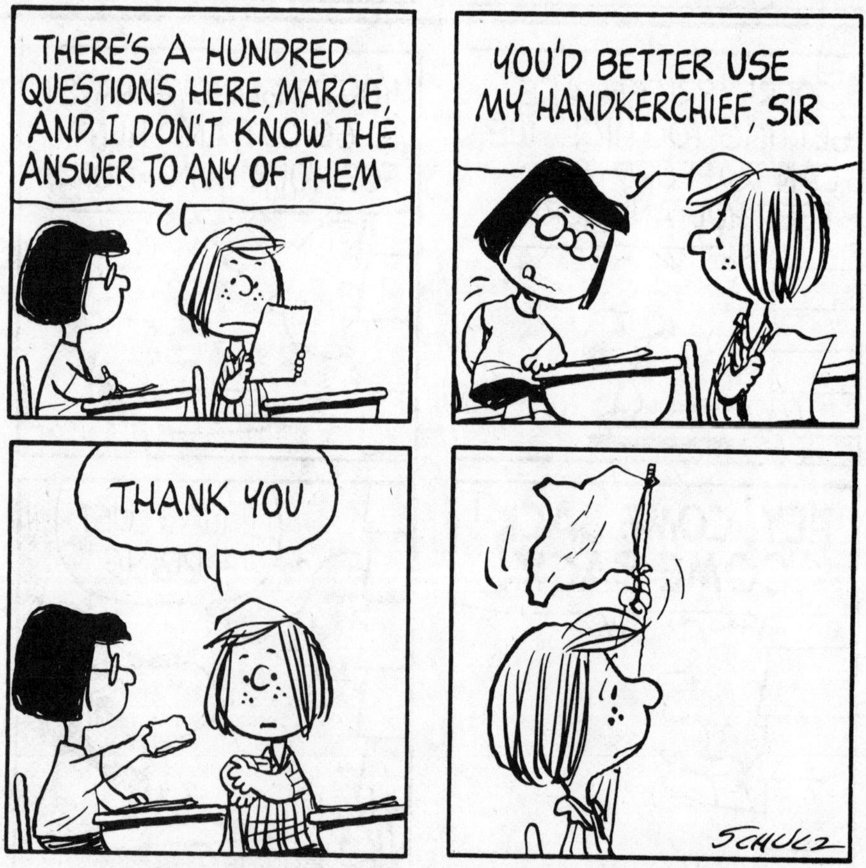
THERE'S A HUNDRED QUESTIONS HERE, MARCIE, AND I DON'T KNOW THE ANSWER TO ANY OF THEM
YOU'D BETTER USE MY HANDKERCHIEF, SIR
THANK YOU
SCHULZ

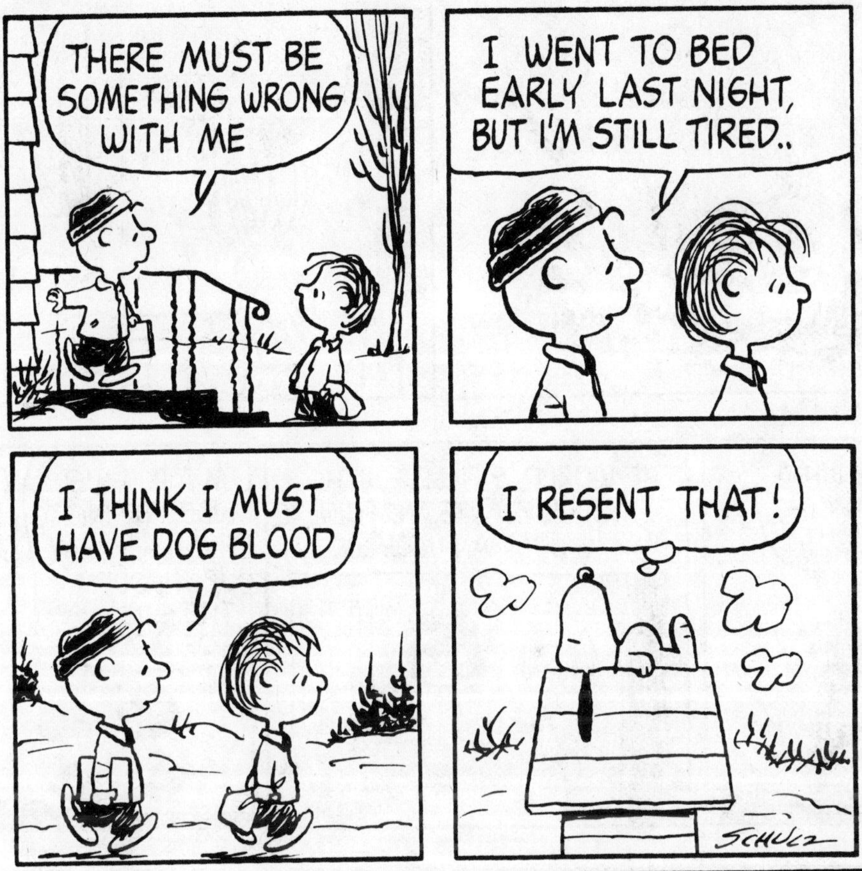
THERE MUST BE SOMETHING WRONG WITH ME
I WENT TO BED EARLY LAST NIGHT, BUT I'M STILL TIRED..
I THINK I MUST HAVE DOG BLOOD
I RESENT THAT!
SCHULZ

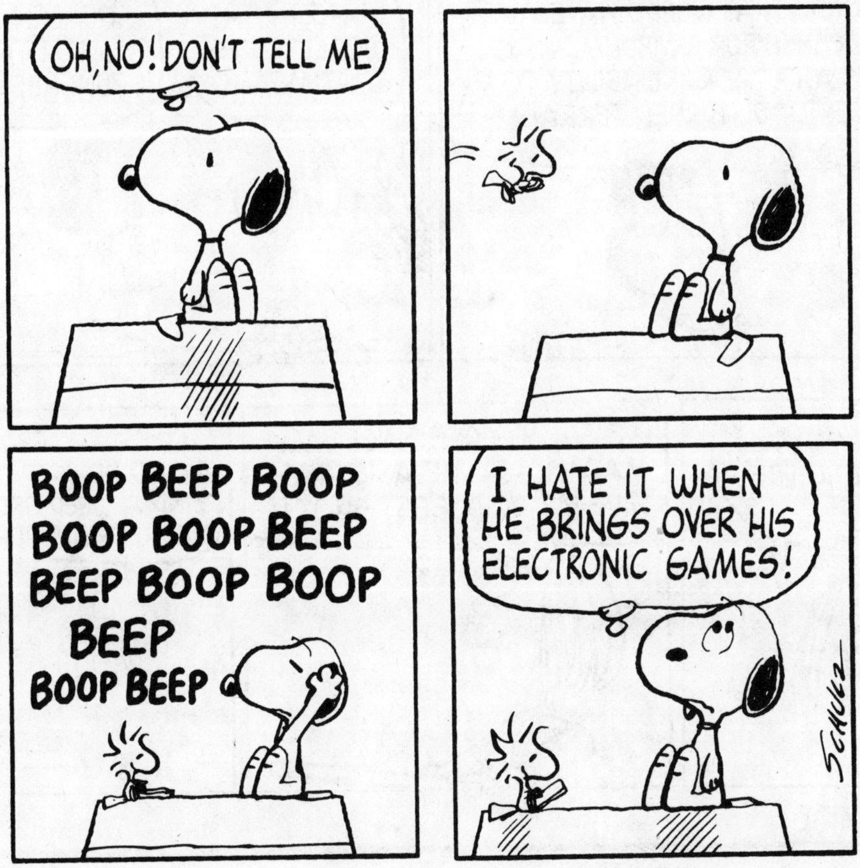
OH, NO! DON'T TELL ME
BOOP BEEP BOOP BOOP BOOP BEEP BEEP BOOP BOOP BEEP BOOP BEEP
I HATE IT WHEN HE BRINGS OVER HIS ELECTRONIC GAMES!
SCHULZ

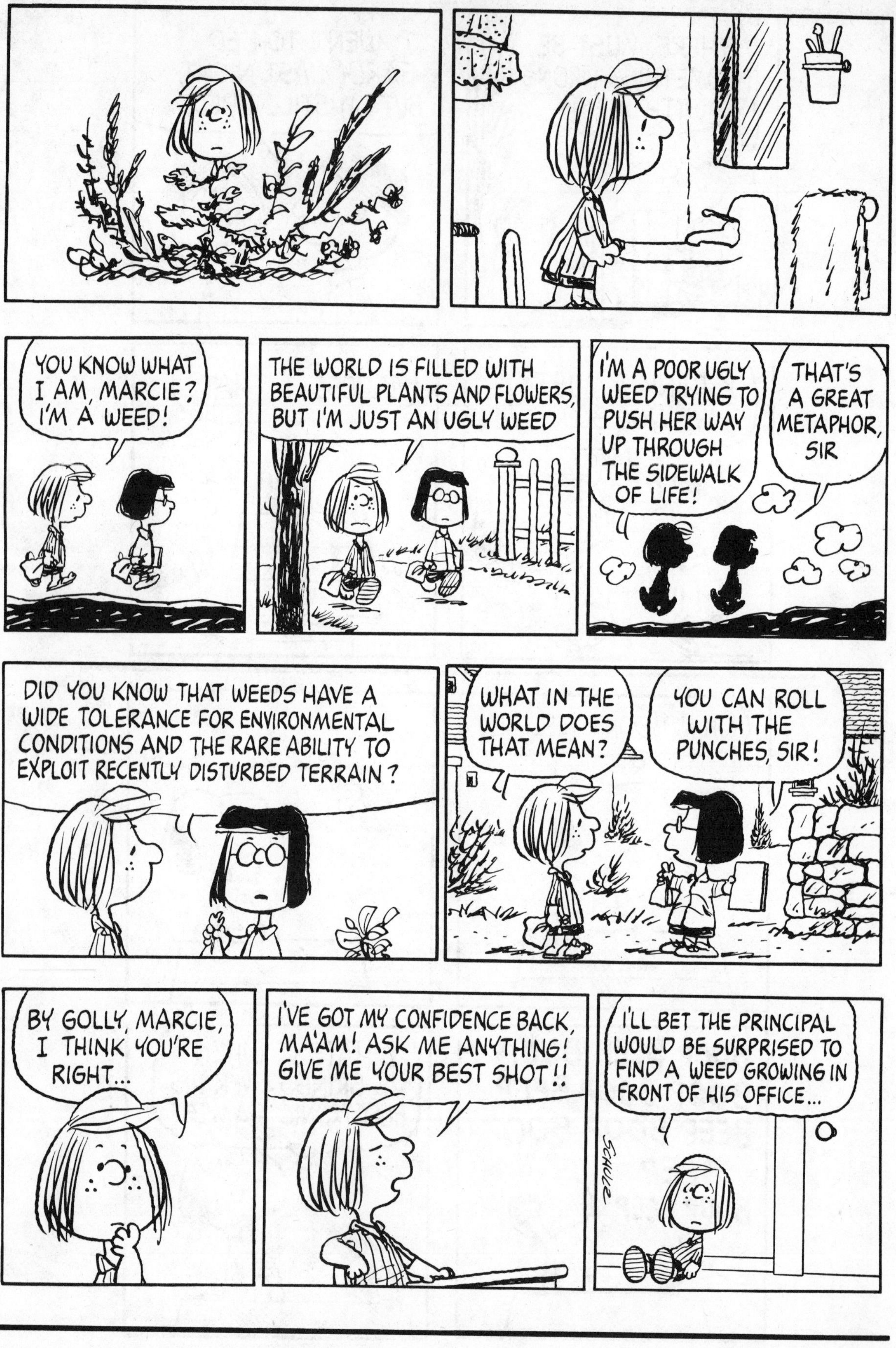
YOU KNOW WHAT I AM, MARCIE? I'M A WEED!
THE WORLD IS FILLED WITH BEAUTIFUL PLANTS AND FLOWERS, BUT I'M JUST AN UGLY WEED
I'M A POOR UGLY WEED TRYING TO PUSH HER WAY UP THROUGH THE SIDEWALK OF LIFE!
THAT'S A GREAT METAPHOR, SIR
DID YOU KNOW THAT WEEDS HAVE A WIDE TOLERANCE FOR ENVIRONMENTAL CONDITIONS AND THE RARE ABILITY TO EXPLOIT RECENTLY DISTURBED TERRAIN?
WHAT IN THE WORLD DOES THAT MEAN?
YOU CAN ROLL WITH THE PUNCHES, SIR!
BY GOLLY, MARCIE, I THINK YOU'RE RIGHT...
I'VE GOT MY CONFIDENCE BACK, MA'AM! ASK ME ANYTHING! GIVE ME YOUR BEST SHOT!!
I'LL BET THE PRINCIPAL WOULD BE SURPRISED TO FIND A WEED GROWING IN FRONT OF HIS OFFICE...
SCHULZ

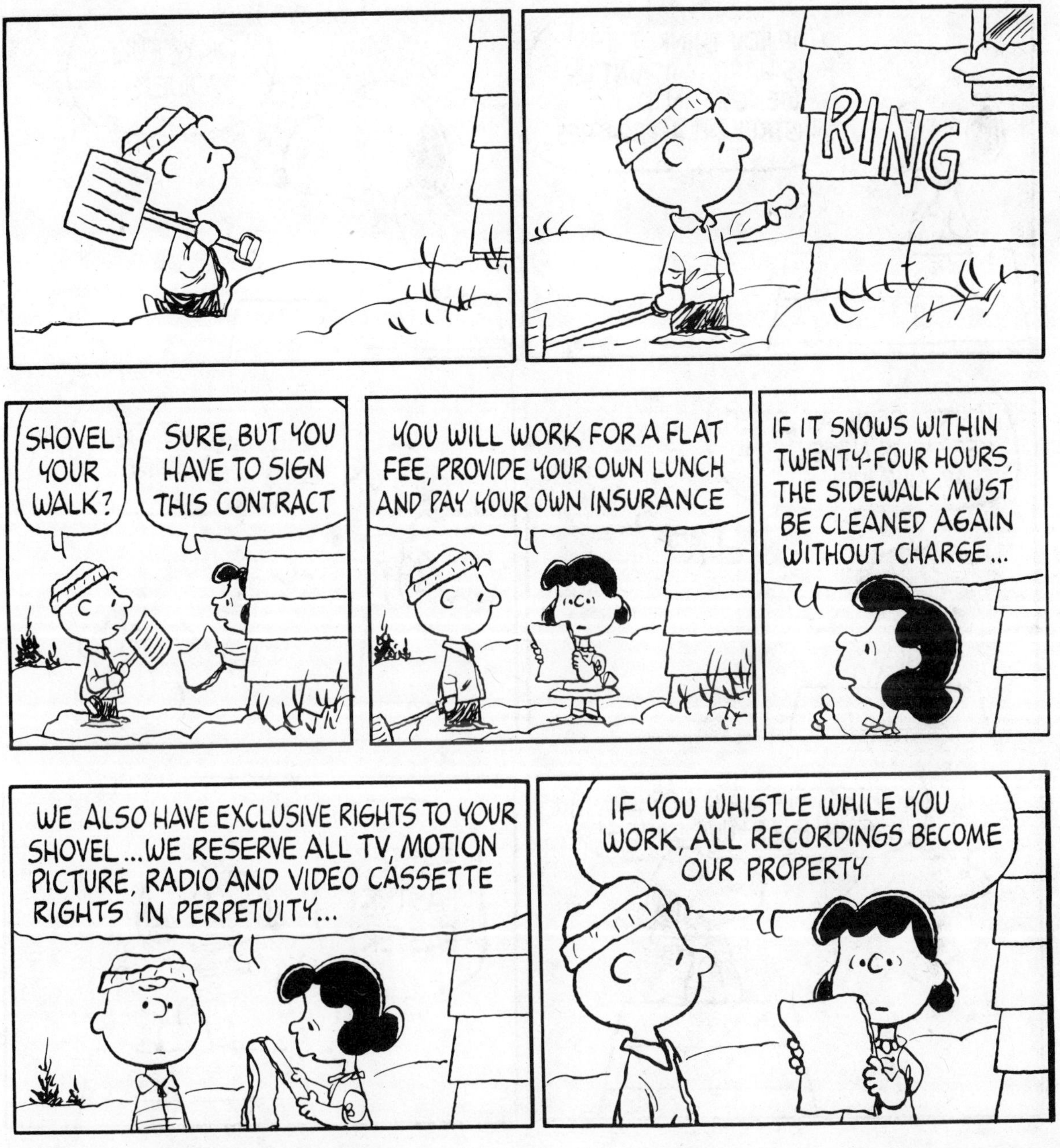
RING
SHOVEL YOUR WALK?
SURE, BUT YOU HAVE TO SIGN THIS CONTRACT
YOU WILL WORK FOR A FLAT FEE, PROVIDE YOUR OWN LUNCH AND PAY YOUR OWN INSURANCE
IF IT SNOWS WITHIN TWENTY-FOUR HOURS, THE SIDEWALK MUST BE CLEANED AGAIN WITHOUT CHARGE...
WE ALSO HAVE EXCLUSIVE RIGHTS TO YOUR SHOVEL...WE RESERVE ALL TV, MOTION PICTURE, RADIO AND VIDEO CASSETTE RIGHTS IN PERPETUITY...
IF YOU WHISTLE WHILE YOU WORK, ALL RECORDINGS BECOME OUR PROPERTY
THE AREA TO BE SHOVELED RUNS FROM THE PORCH TO THE STREET... HERE, SIGN ON THE BOTTOM LINE...
THE CONTRACT IS LONGER THAN THE SIDEWALK!
SCHULZ

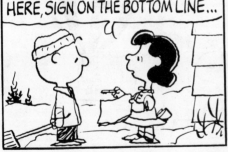

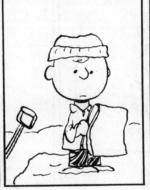

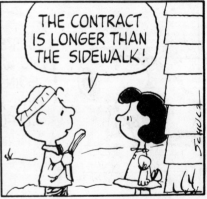

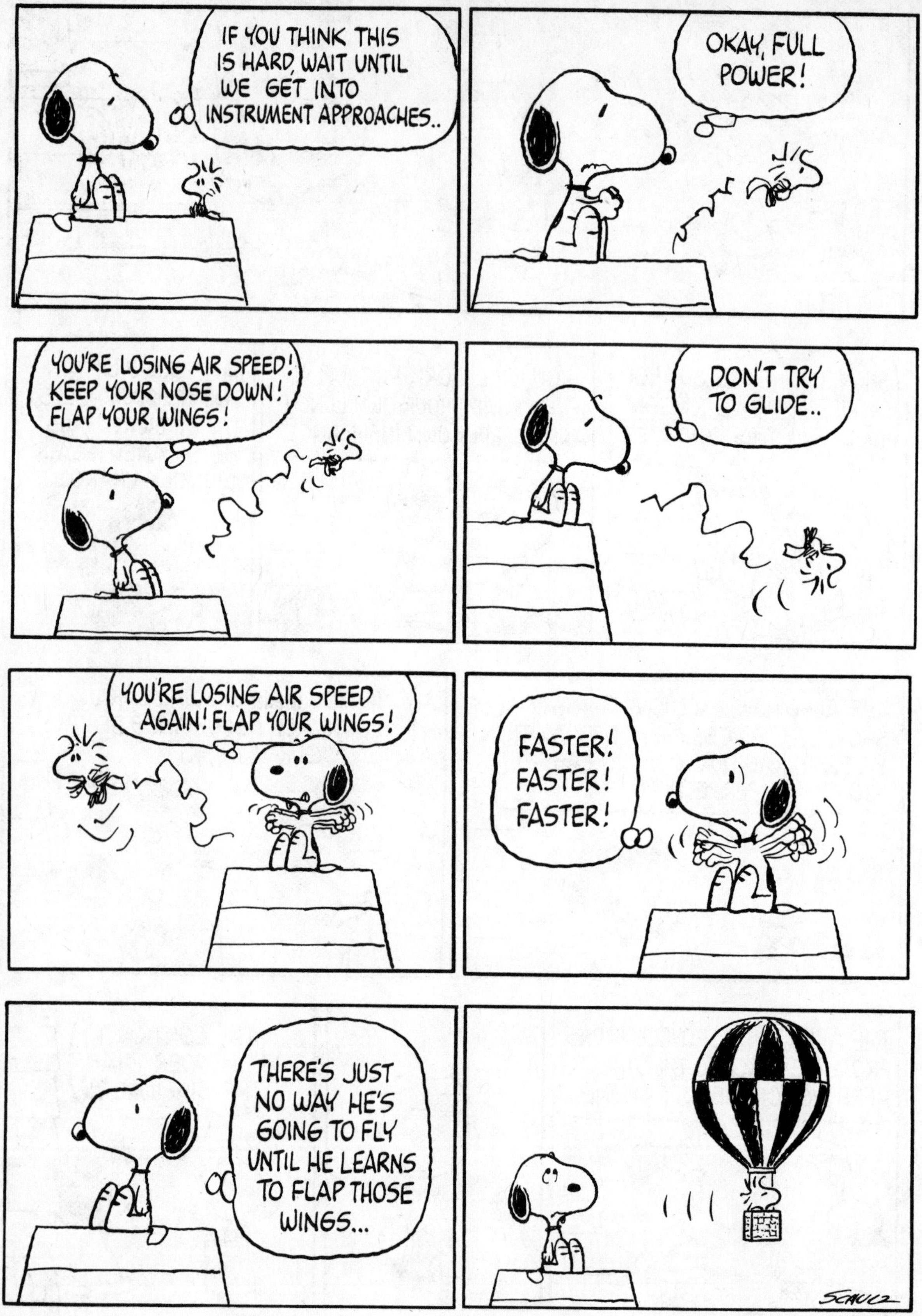
IF YOU THINK THIS IS HARD, WAIT UNTIL WE GET INTO INSTRUMENT APPROACHES..
OKAY, FULL POWER!
YOU'RE LOSING AIR SPEED! KEEP YOUR NOSE DOWN! FLAP YOUR WINGS!
DON'T TRY TO GLIDE..
YOU'RE LOSING AIR SPEED AGAIN! FLAP YOUR WINGS!
FASTER! FASTER! FASTER!
THERE'S JUST NO WAY HE'S GOING TO FLY UNTIL HE LEARNS TO FLAP THOSE WINGS...
SCHULZ

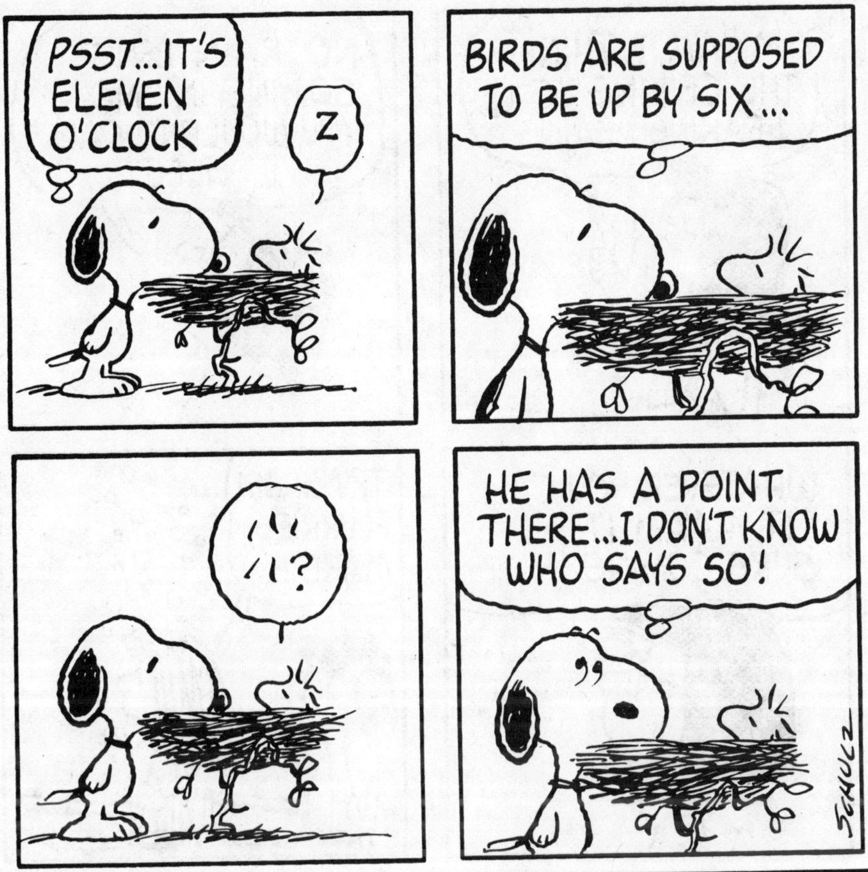
PSST...IT'S ELEVEN O'CLOCK
Z
BIRDS ARE SUPPOSED TO BE UP BY SIX...
HE HAS A POINT THERE...I DON'T KNOW WHO SAYS SO!
SCHULZ

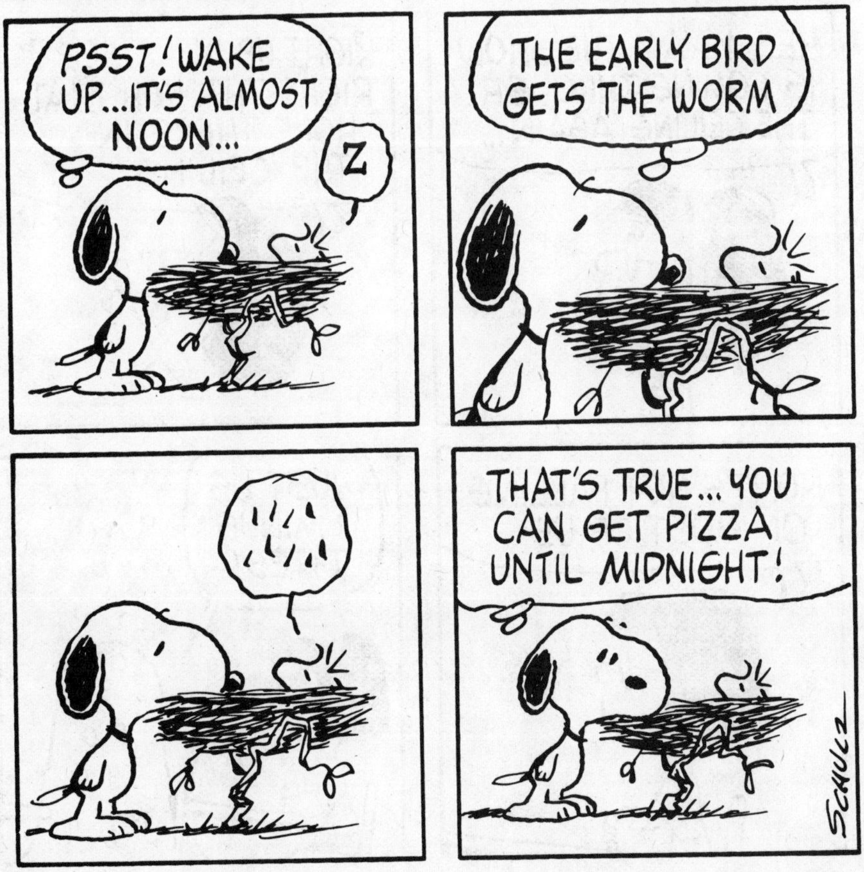
PSST! WAKE UP...IT'S ALMOST NOON...
Z
THE EARLY BIRD GETS THE WORM
THAT'S TRUE... YOU CAN GET PIZZA UNTIL MIDNIGHT!
SCHULZ

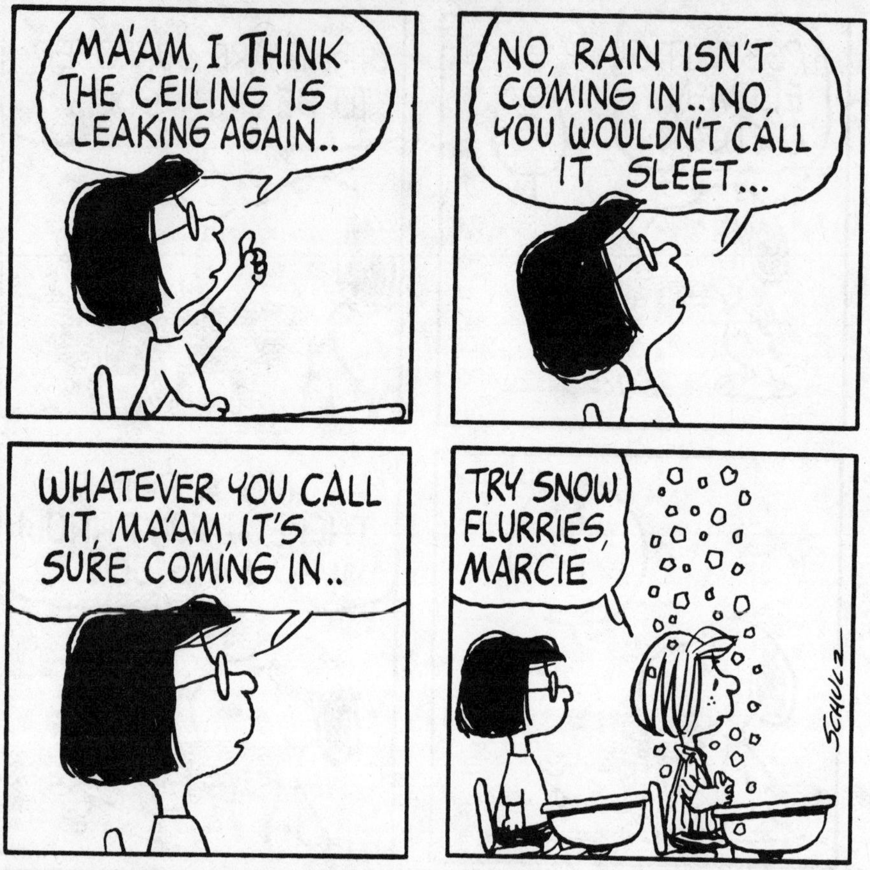
MA'AM, I THINK THE CEILING IS LEAKING AGAIN..
NO, RAIN ISN'T COMING IN.. NO, YOU WOULDN'T CALL IT SLEET...
WHATEVER YOU CALL IT, MA'AM, IT'S SURE COMING IN..
TRY SNOW FLURRIES, MARCIE
SCHULZ

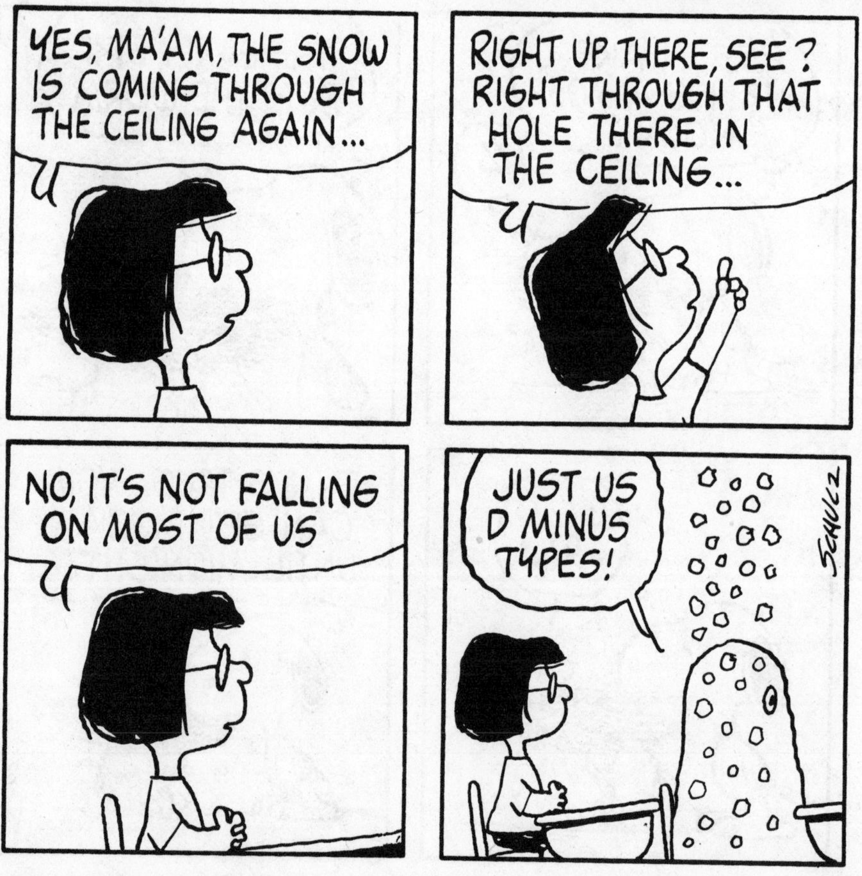
YES, MA'AM, THE SNOW IS COMING THROUGH THE CEILING AGAIN...
RIGHT UP THERE, SEE? RIGHT THROUGH THAT HOLE THERE IN THE CEILING...
NO, IT'S NOT FALLING ON MOST OF US
JUST US D MINUS TYPES!
SCHULZ

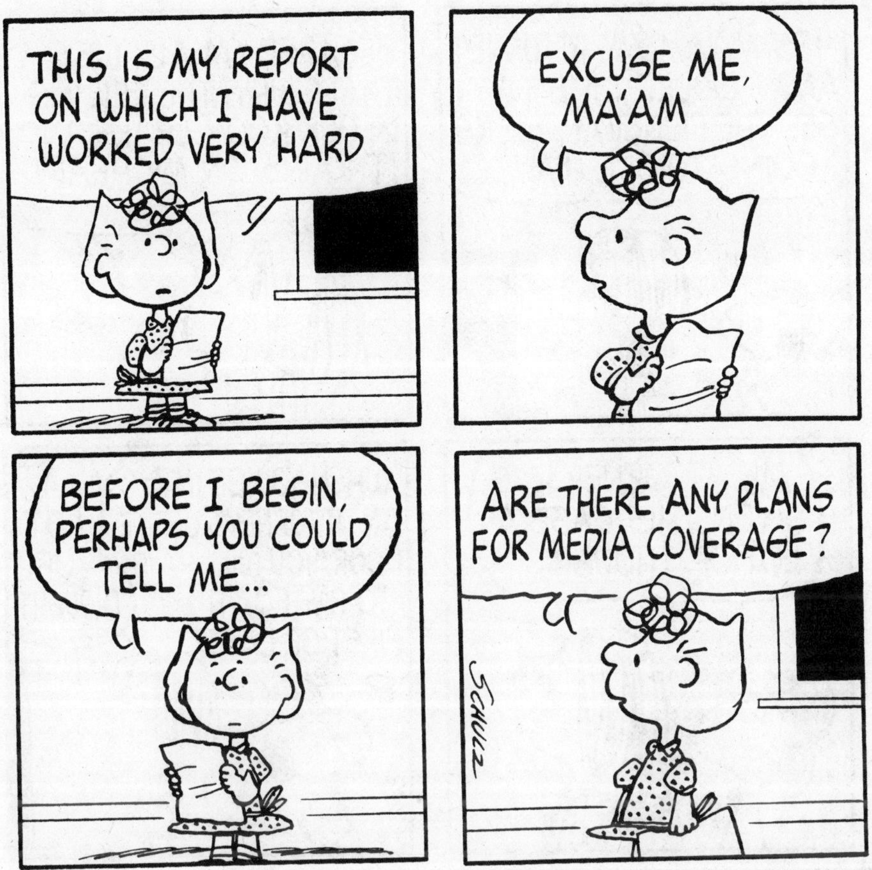
THIS IS MY REPORT ON WHICH I HAVE WORKED VERY HARD
EXCUSE ME, MA'AM
BEFORE I BEGIN, PERHAPS YOU COULD TELL ME...
ARE THERE ANY PLANS FOR MEDIA COVERAGE?
SCHULZ

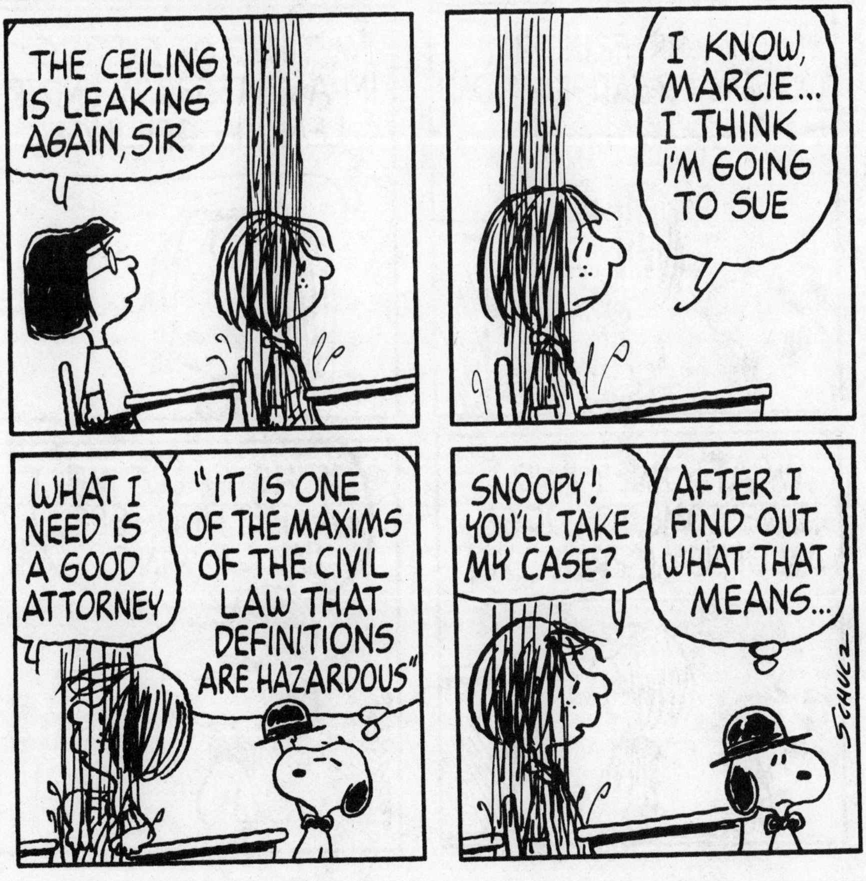
THE CEILING IS LEAKING AGAIN, SIR
I KNOW, MARCIE... I THINK I'M GOING TO SUE
WHAT I NEED IS A GOOD ATTORNEY
"IT IS ONE OF THE MAXIMS OF THE CIVIL LAW THAT DEFINITIONS ARE HAZARDOUS"
SNOOPY! YOU'LL TAKE MY CASE?
AFTER I FIND OUT WHAT THAT MEANS...
SCHULZ

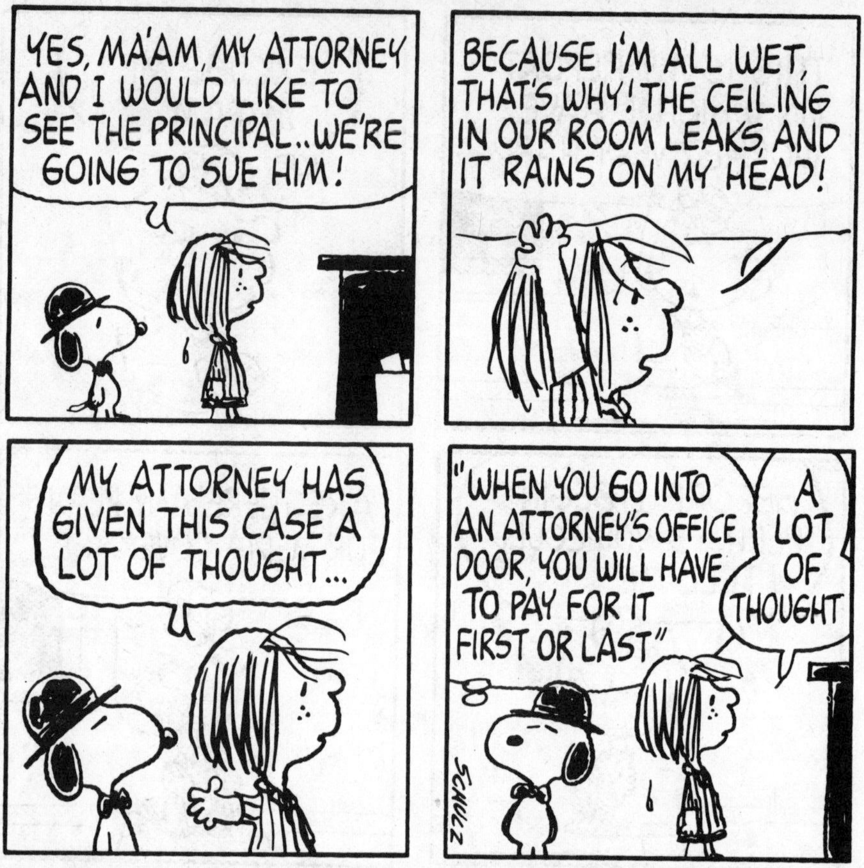
YES, MA'AM, MY ATTORNEY AND I WOULD LIKE TO SEE THE PRINCIPAL..WE'RE GOING TO SUE HIM!
BECAUSE I'M ALL WET, THAT'S WHY! THE CEILING IN OUR ROOM LEAKS, AND IT RAINS ON MY HEAD!
MY ATTORNEY HAS GIVEN THIS CASE A LOT OF THOUGHT...
"WHEN YOU GO INTO AN ATTORNEY'S OFFICE DOOR, YOU WILL HAVE TO PAY FOR IT FIRST OR LAST"
A LOT OF THOUGHT
SCHULZ

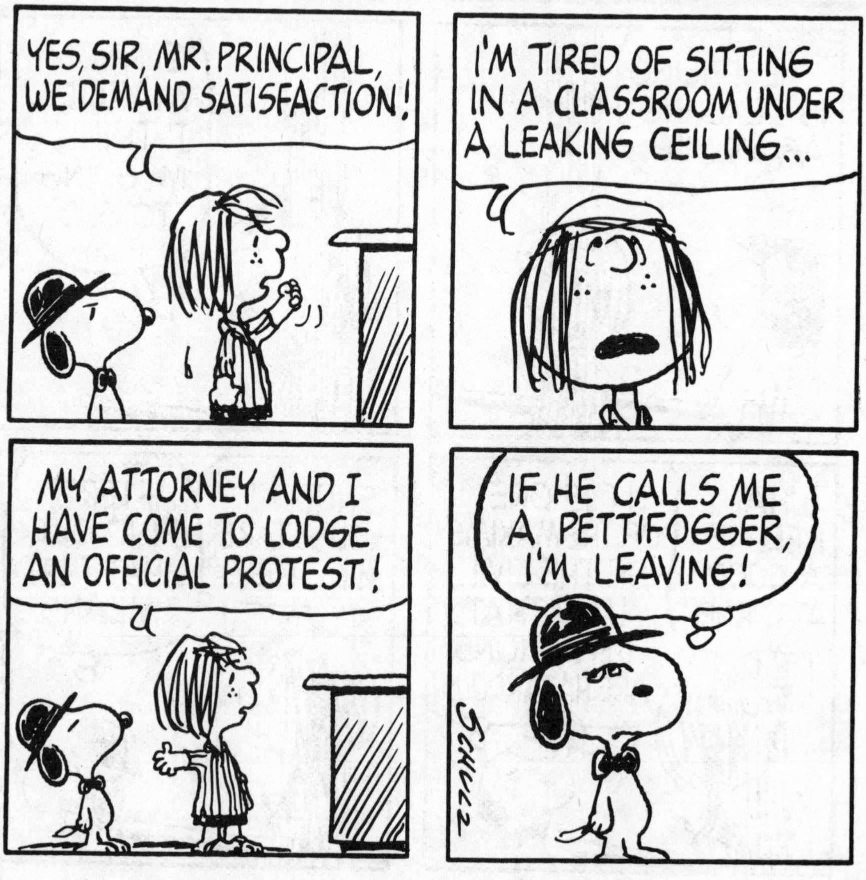
YES, SIR, MR. PRINCIPAL, WE DEMAND SATISFACTION!
I'M TIRED OF SITTING IN A CLASSROOM UNDER A LEAKING CEILING...
MY ATTORNEY AND I HAVE COME TO LODGE AN OFFICIAL PROTEST!
IF HE CALLS ME A PETTIFOGGER, I'M LEAVING!
SCHULZ

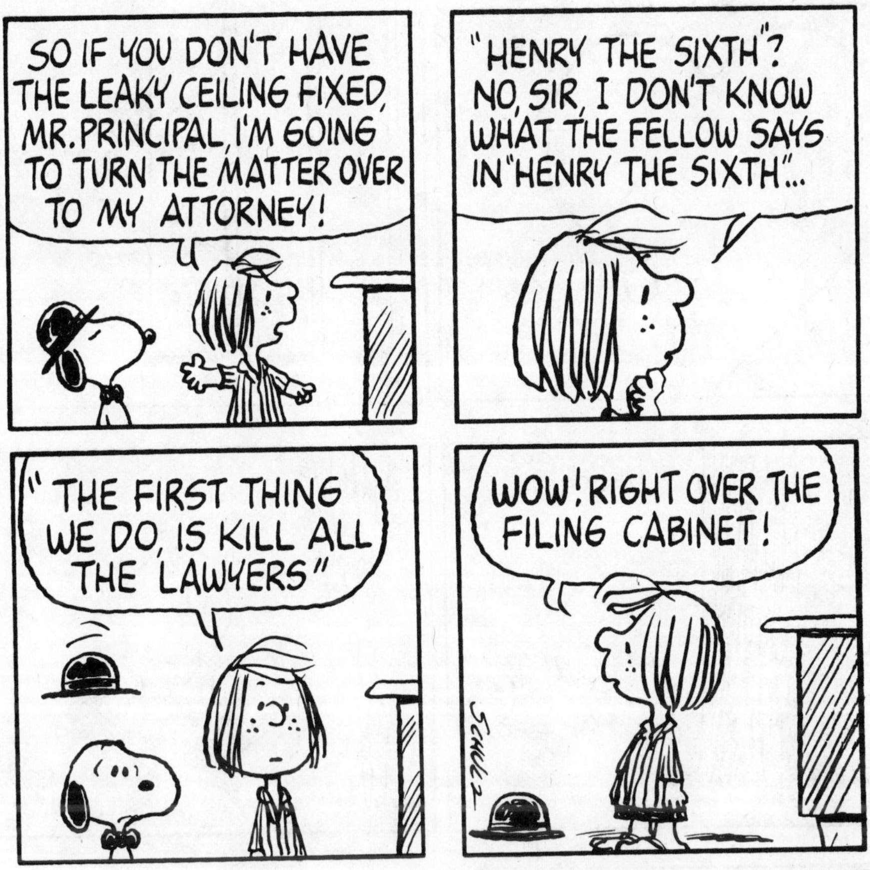
SO IF YOU DON'T HAVE THE LEAKY CEILING FIXED, MR. PRINCIPAL, I'M GOING TO TURN THE MATTER OVER TO MY ATTORNEY!
"HENRY THE SIXTH"? NO, SIR, I DON'T KNOW WHAT THE FELLOW SAYS IN "HENRY THE SIXTH"...
"THE FIRST THING WE DO, IS KILL ALL THE LAWYERS"
WOW! RIGHT OVER THE FILING CABINET!

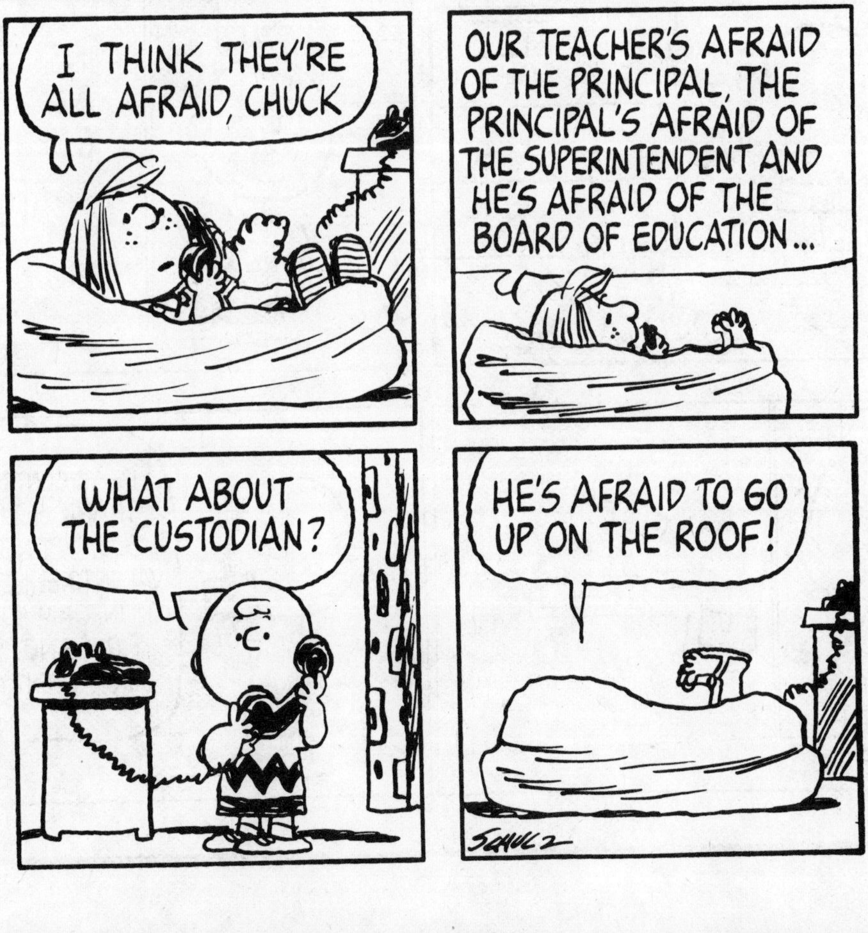
I THINK THEY'RE ALL AFRAID, CHUCK
OUR TEACHER'S AFRAID OF THE PRINCIPAL, THE PRINCIPAL'S AFRAID OF THE SUPERINTENDENT AND HE'S AFRAID OF THE BOARD OF EDUCATION...
WHAT ABOUT THE CUSTODIAN?
HE'S AFRAID TO GO UP ON THE ROOF!

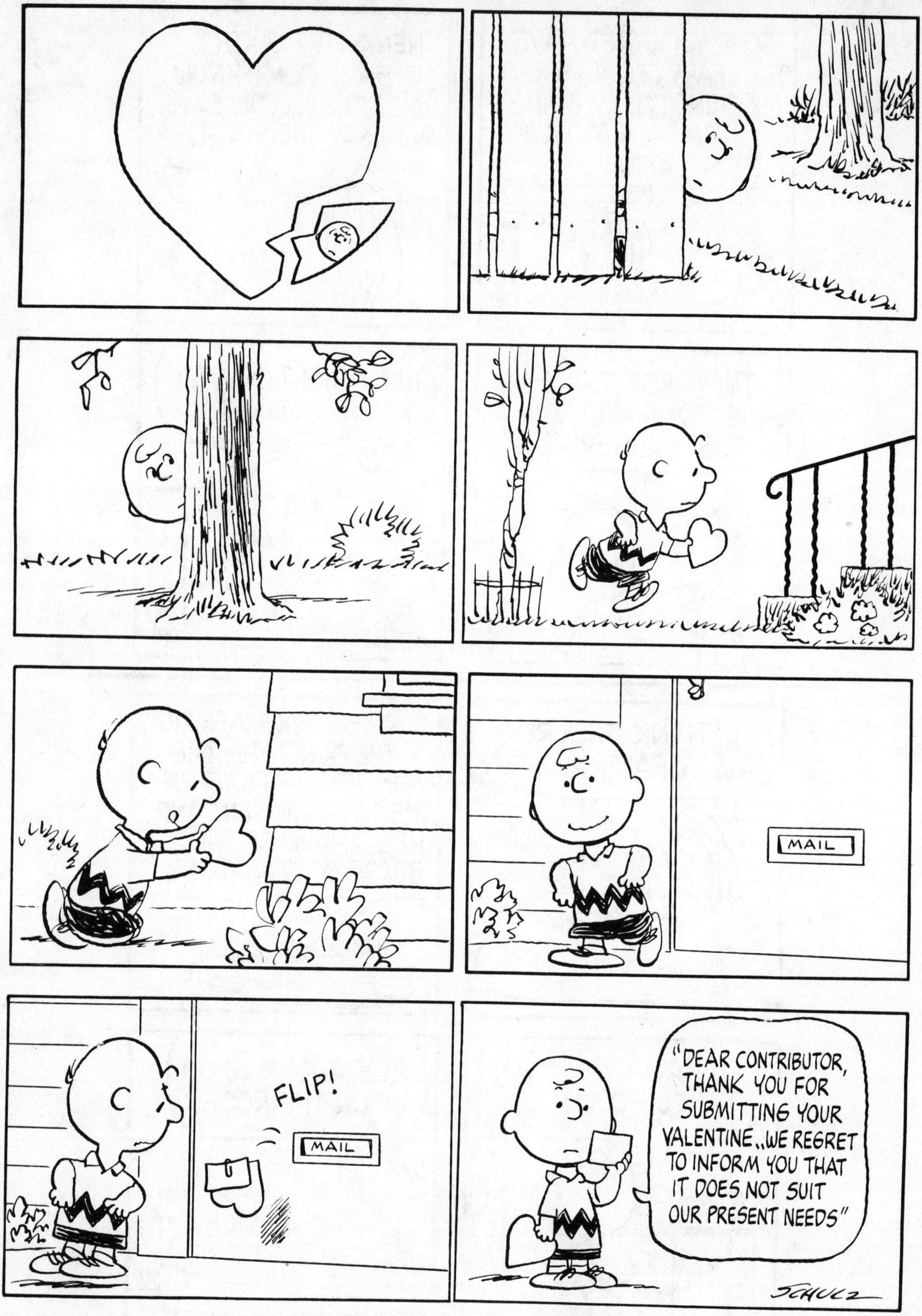
MAIL
FLIP!
MAIL
"DEAR CONTRIBUTOR, THANK YOU FOR SUBMITTING YOUR VALENTINE..WE REGRET TO INFORM YOU THAT IT DOES NOT SUIT OUR PRESENT NEEDS"
SCHULZ

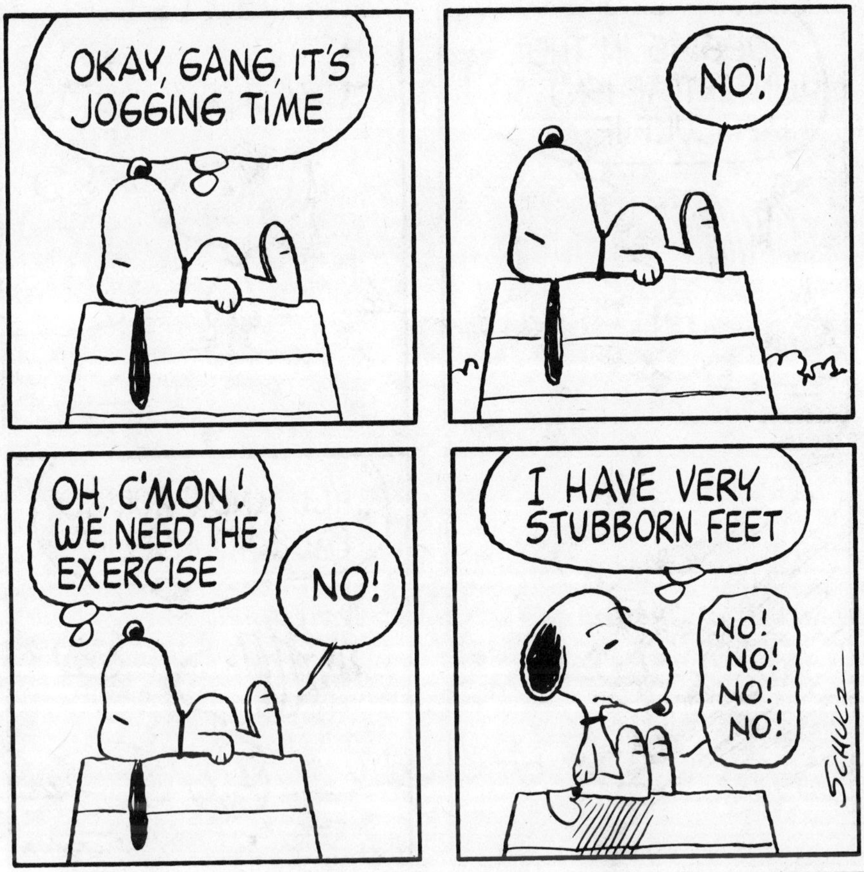
OKAY, GANG, IT'S JOGGING TIME
NO!
OH, C'MON! WE NEED THE EXERCISE
NO!
I HAVE VERY STUBBORN FEET
NO! NO! NO! NO!
SCHULZ

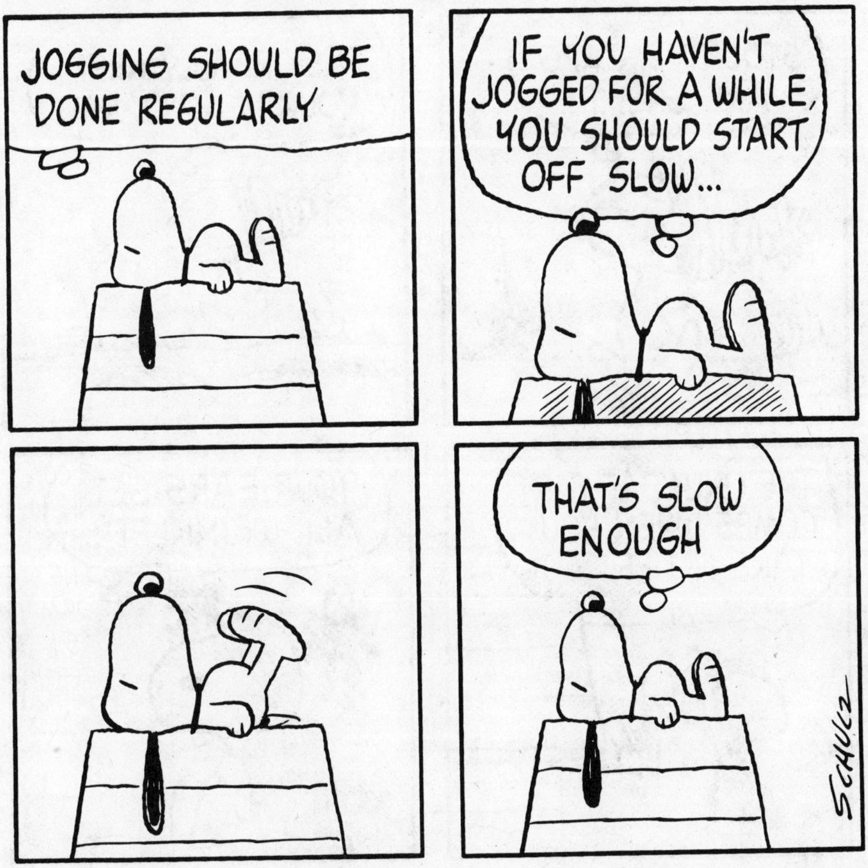
JOGGING SHOULD BE DONE REGULARLY
IF YOU HAVEN'T JOGGED FOR A WHILE, YOU SHOULD START OFF SLOW...
THAT'S SLOW ENOUGH
SCHULZ

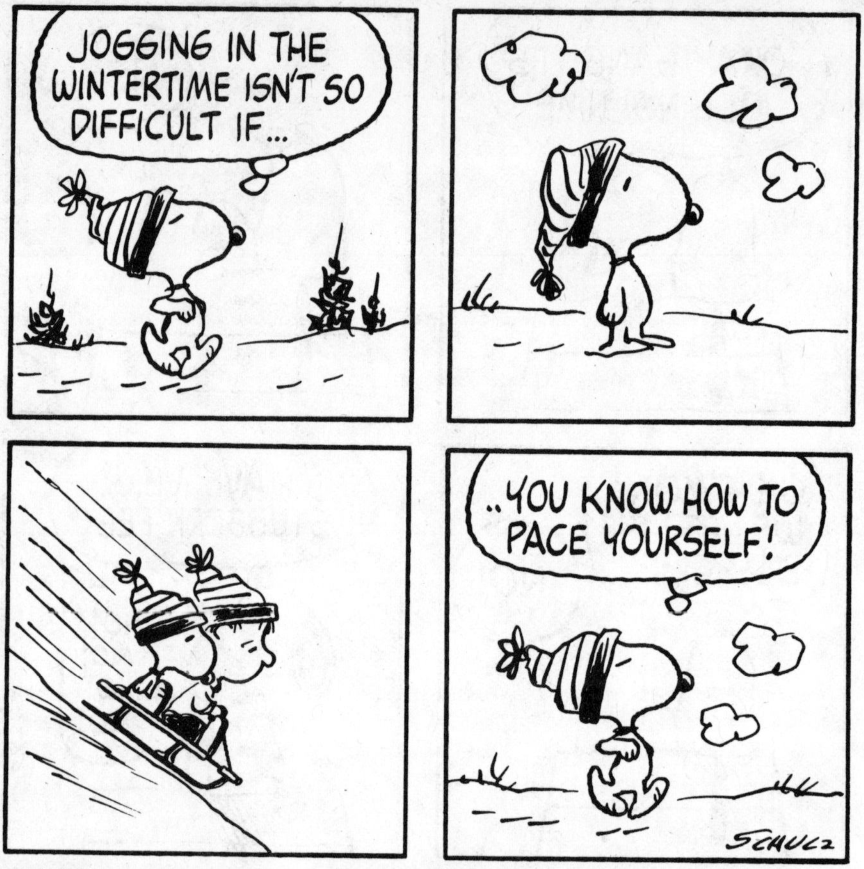
JOGGING IN THE WINTERTIME ISN'T SO DIFFICULT IF...
..YOU KNOW HOW TO PACE YOURSELF!

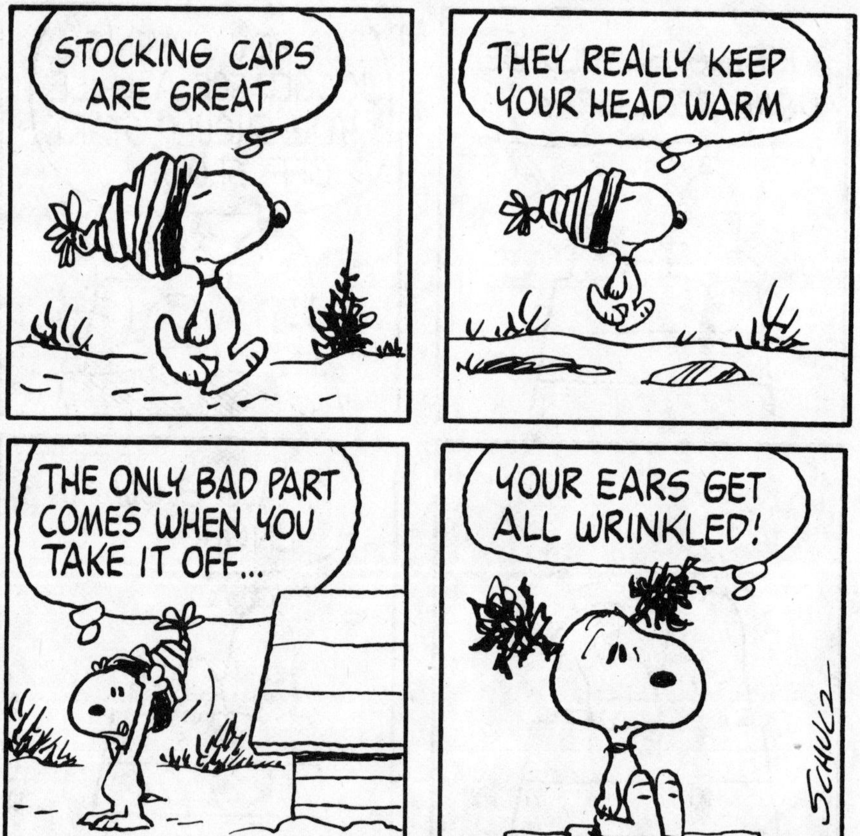
STOCKING CAPS ARE GREAT
THEY REALLY KEEP YOUR HEAD WARM
THE ONLY BAD PART COMES WHEN YOU TAKE IT OFF...
YOUR EARS GET ALL WRINKLED!

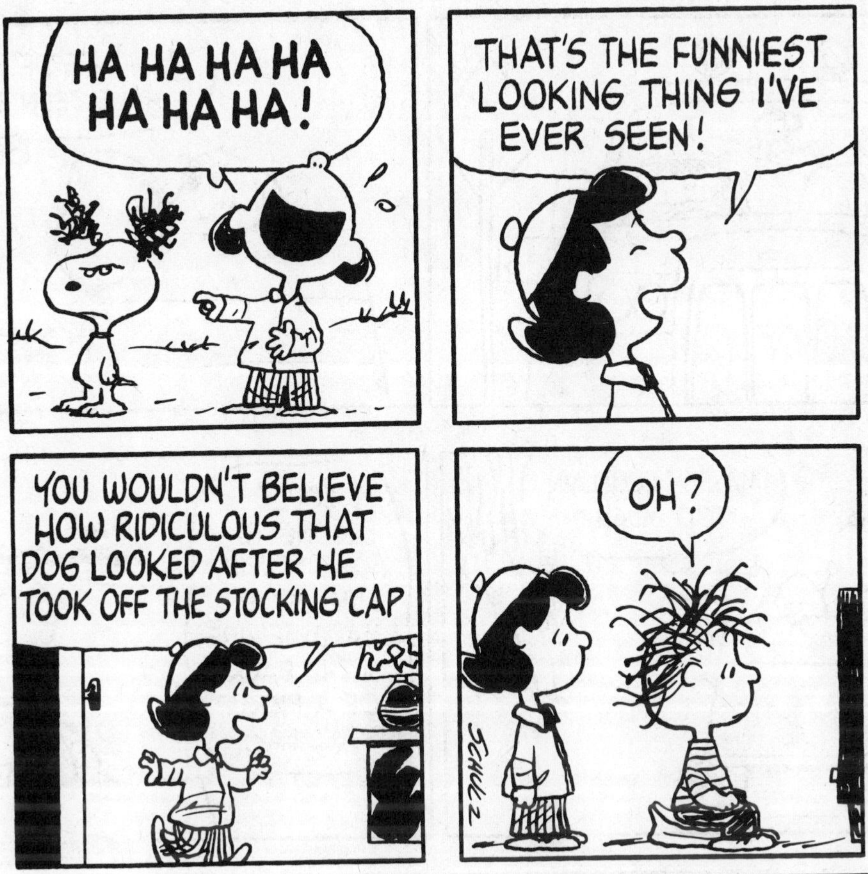
HA HA HA HA
HA HA HA!
THAT'S THE FUNNIEST LOOKING THING I'VE EVER SEEN!
YOU WOULDN'T BELIEVE HOW RIDICULOUS THAT DOG LOOKED AFTER HE TOOK OFF THE STOCKING CAP
OH?
SCHULZ

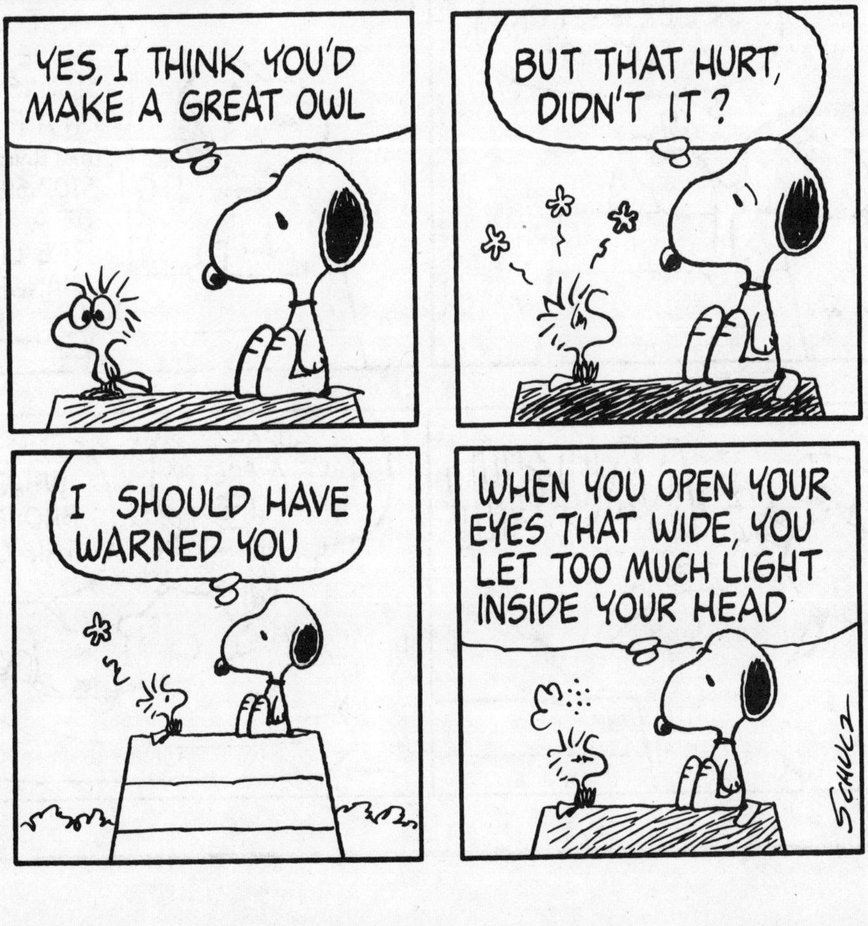
YES, I THINK YOU'D MAKE A GREAT OWL
BUT THAT HURT, DIDN'T IT?
I SHOULD HAVE WARNED YOU
WHEN YOU OPEN YOUR EYES THAT WIDE, YOU LET TOO MUCH LIGHT INSIDE YOUR HEAD
SCHULZ

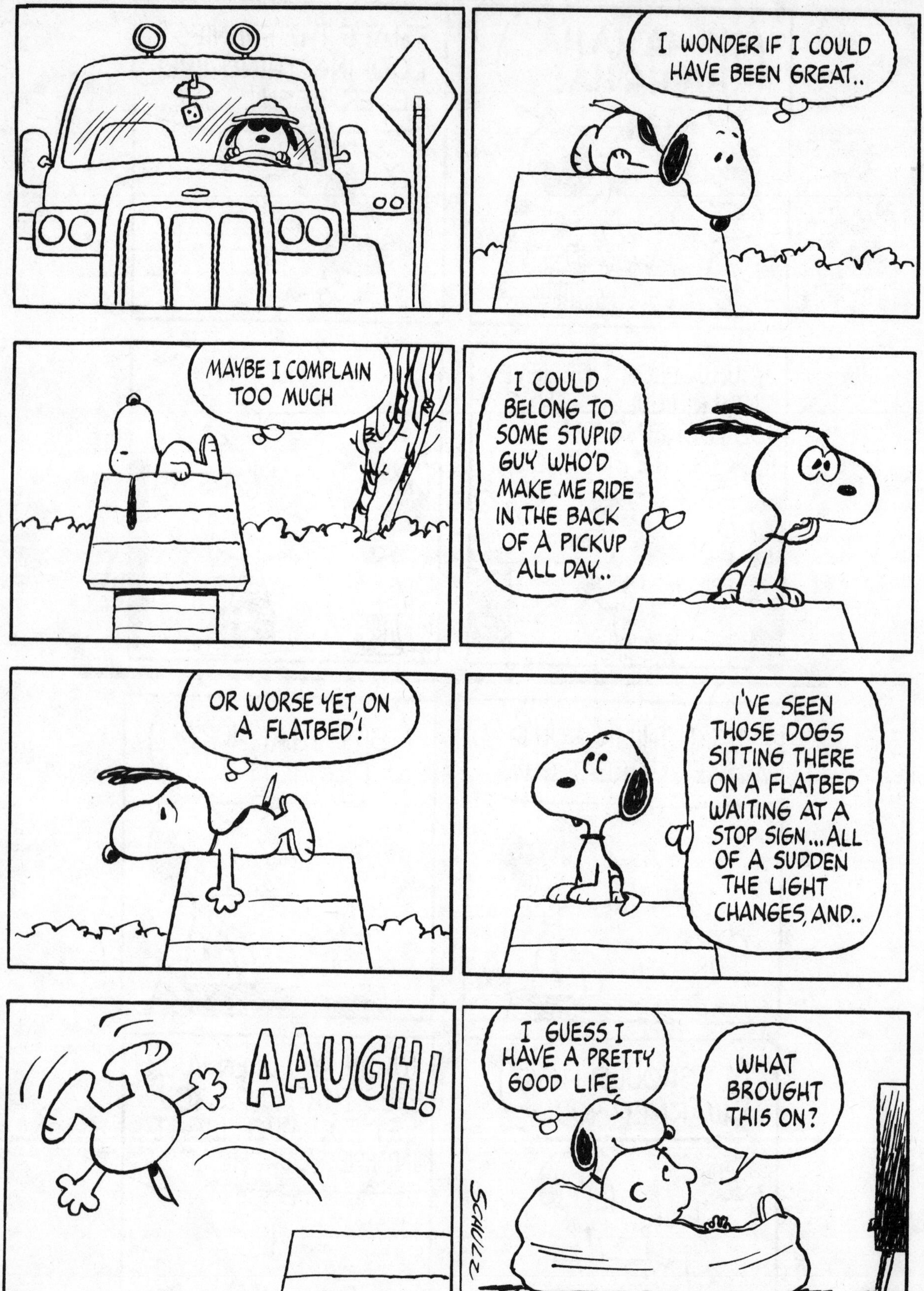
I WONDER IF I COULD HAVE BEEN GREAT..
MAYBE I COMPLAIN TOO MUCH
I COULD BELONG TO SOME STUPID GUY WHO'D MAKE ME RIDE IN THE BACK OF A PICKUP ALL DAY..
OR WORSE YET, ON A FLATBED!
I'VE SEEN THOSE DOGS SITTING THERE ON A FLATBED WAITING AT A STOP SIGN...ALL OF A SUDDEN THE LIGHT CHANGES, AND..
AAUGH!
I GUESS I HAVE A PRETTY GOOD LIFE
WHAT BROUGHT THIS ON?
SCHULZ

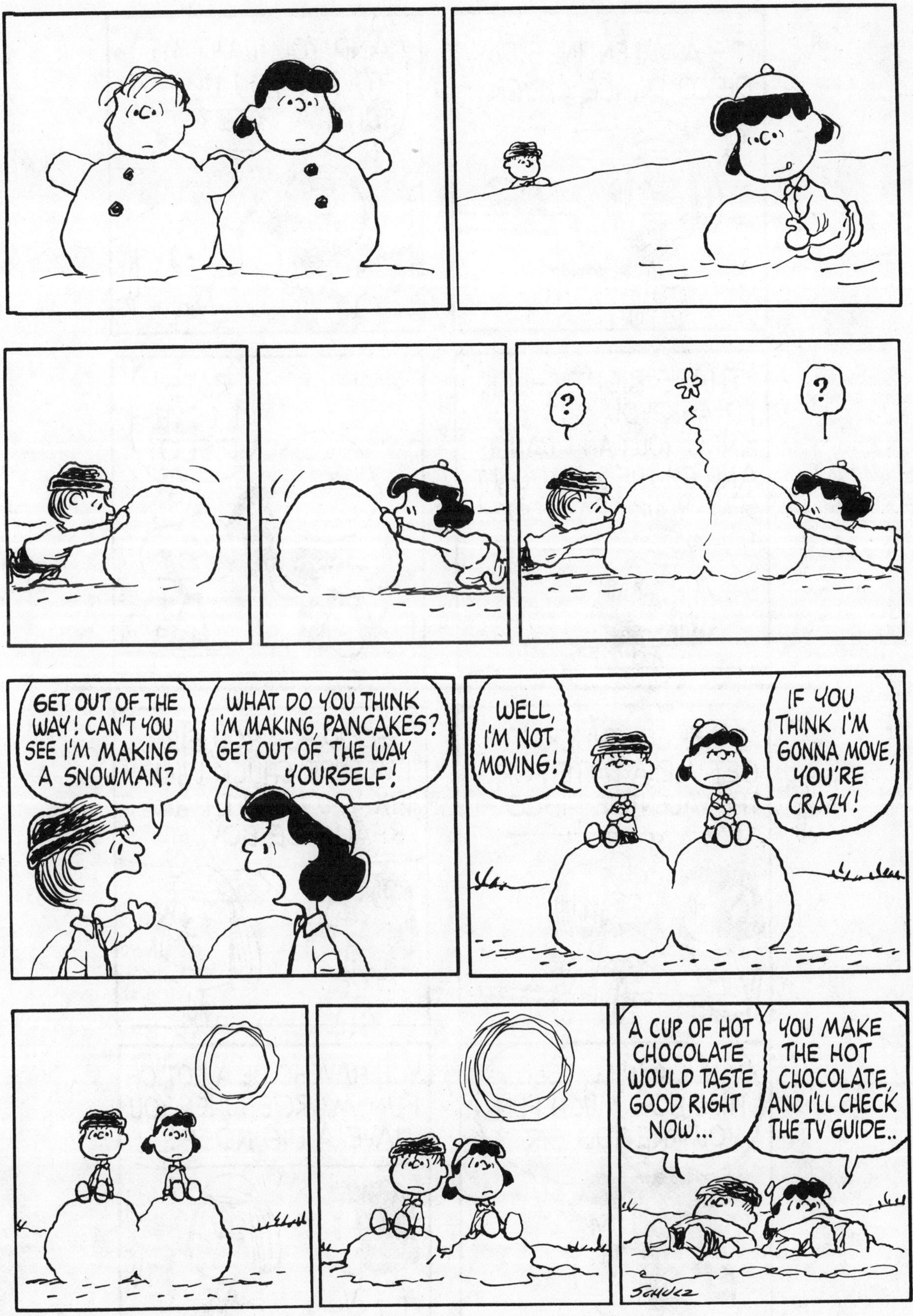
?
?
GET OUT OF THE WAY! CAN'T YOU SEE I'M MAKING A SNOWMAN?
WHAT DO YOU THINK I'M MAKING, PANCAKES? GET OUT OF THE WAY YOURSELF!
WELL, I'M NOT MOVING!
IF YOU THINK I'M GONNA MOVE, YOU'RE CRAZY!
A CUP OF HOT CHOCOLATE WOULD TASTE GOOD RIGHT NOW...
YOU MAKE THE HOT CHOCOLATE, AND I'LL CHECK THE TV GUIDE..
SCHULZ

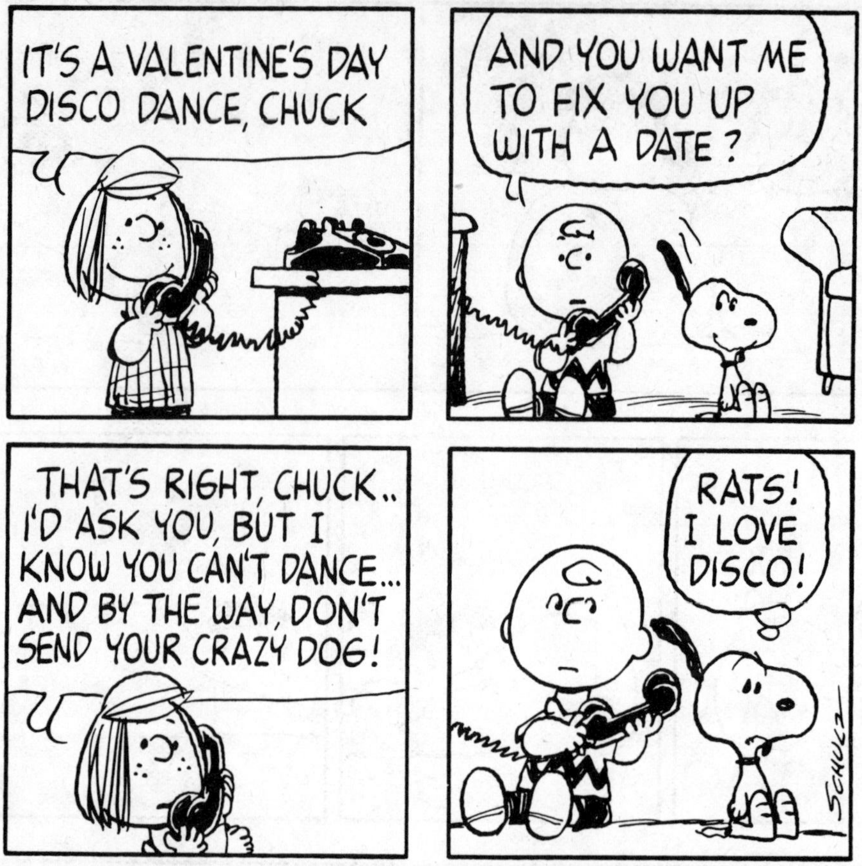
IT'S A VALENTINE'S DAY DISCO DANCE, CHUCK
AND YOU WANT ME TO FIX YOU UP WITH A DATE?
THAT'S RIGHT, CHUCK.. I'D ASK YOU, BUT I KNOW YOU CAN'T DANCE... AND BY THE WAY, DON'T SEND YOUR CRAZY DOG!
RATS! I LOVE DISCO!
SCHULZ

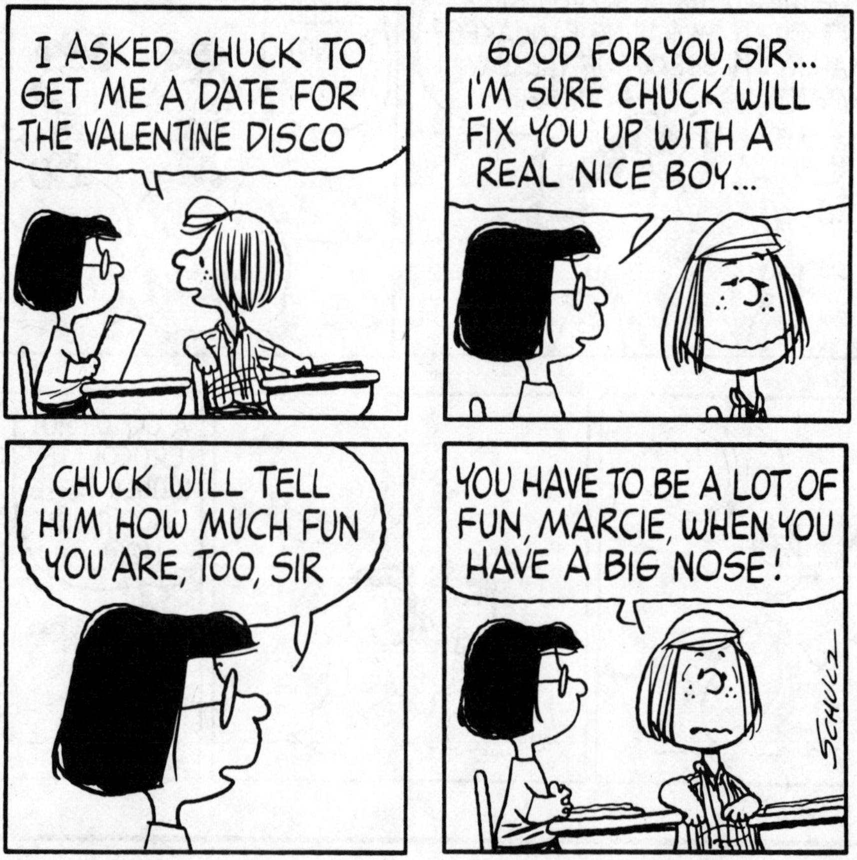
I ASKED CHUCK TO GET ME A DATE FOR THE VALENTINE DISCO
GOOD FOR YOU, SIR... I'M SURE CHUCK WILL FIX YOU UP WITH A REAL NICE BOY...
CHUCK WILL TELL HIM HOW MUCH FUN YOU ARE, TOO, SIR
YOU HAVE TO BE A LOT OF FUN, MARCIE, WHEN YOU HAVE A BIG NOSE!
SCHULZ

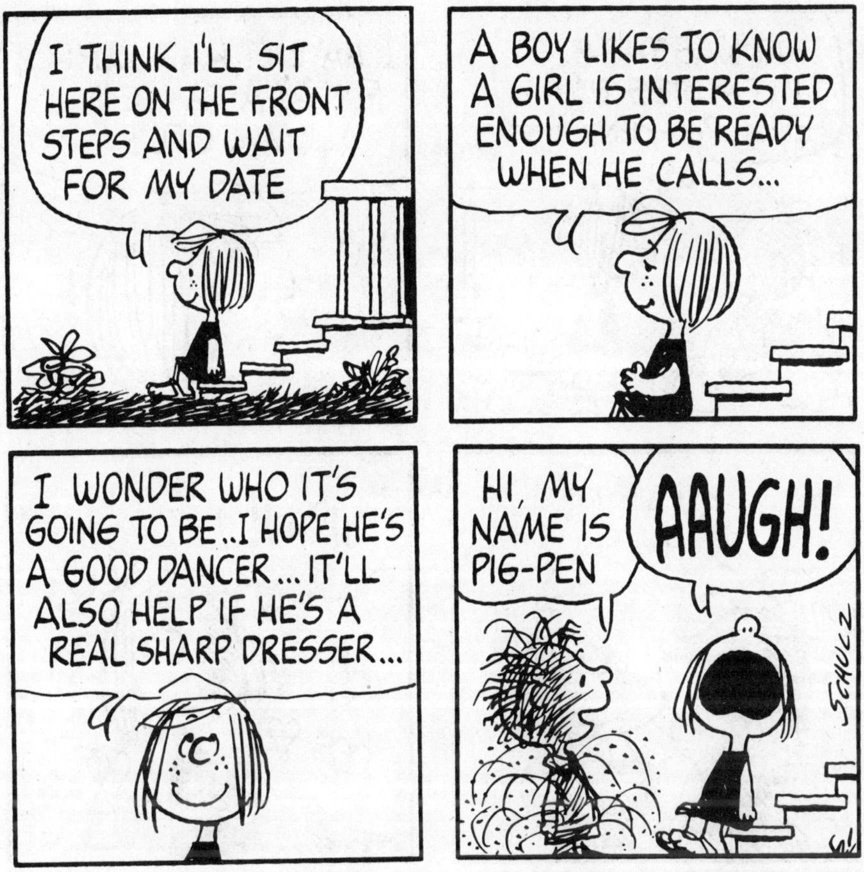
I THINK I'LL SIT HERE ON THE FRONT STEPS AND WAIT FOR MY DATE
A BOY LIKES TO KNOW A GIRL IS INTERESTED ENOUGH TO BE READY WHEN HE CALLS...
I WONDER WHO IT'S GOING TO BE..I HOPE HE'S A GOOD DANCER... IT'LL ALSO HELP IF HE'S A REAL SHARP DRESSER...
HI, MY NAME IS PIG-PEN
AAUGH!
SCHULZ

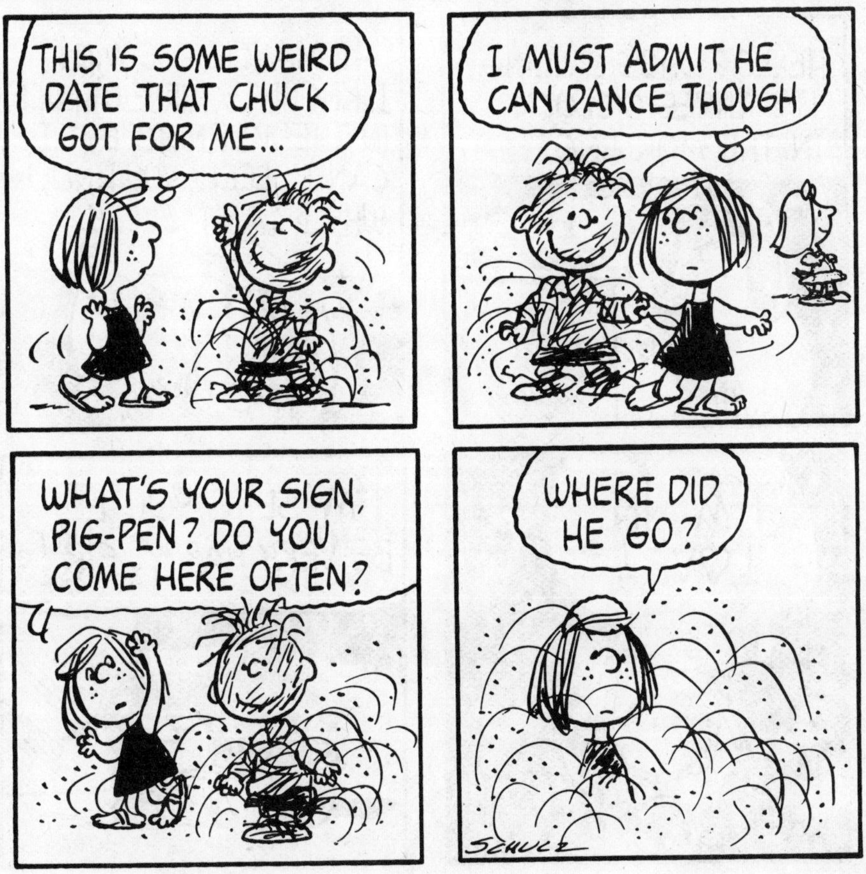
THIS IS SOME WEIRD DATE THAT CHUCK GOT FOR ME...
I MUST ADMIT HE CAN DANCE, THOUGH
WHAT'S YOUR SIGN, PIG-PEN? DO YOU COME HERE OFTEN?
WHERE DID HE GO?
SCHULZ

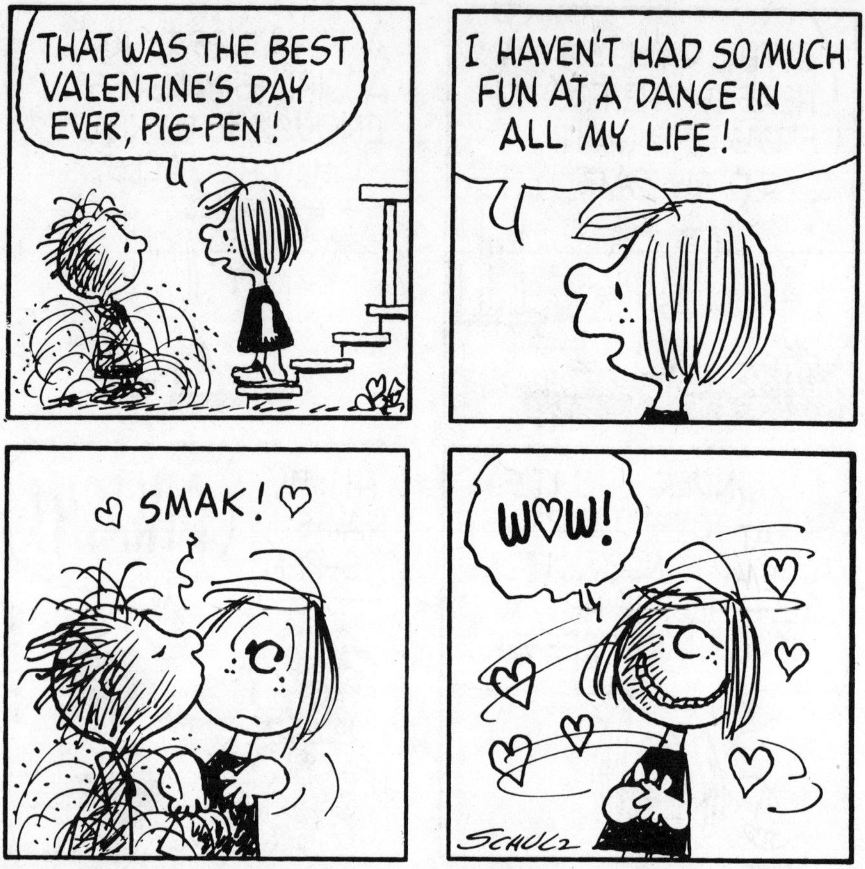
THAT WAS THE BEST VALENTINE'S DAY EVER, PIG-PEN!
I HAVEN'T HAD SO MUCH FUN AT A DANCE IN ALL MY LIFE!
SMAK!
WOW!
SCHULZ

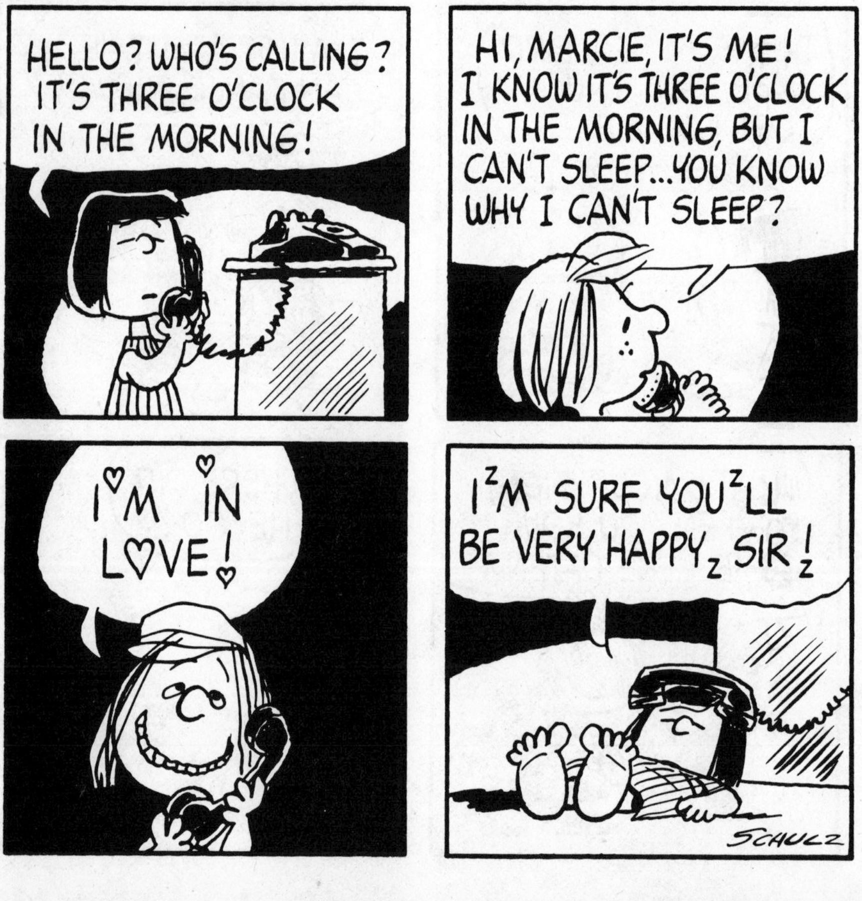
HELLO? WHO'S CALLING? IT'S THREE O'CLOCK IN THE MORNING!
HI, MARCIE, IT'S ME! I KNOW IT'S THREE O'CLOCK IN THE MORNING, BUT I CAN'T SLEEP...YOU KNOW WHY I CAN'T SLEEP?
I'M IN LOVE!
I'M SURE YOU'LL BE VERY HAPPY SIR!
SCHULZ

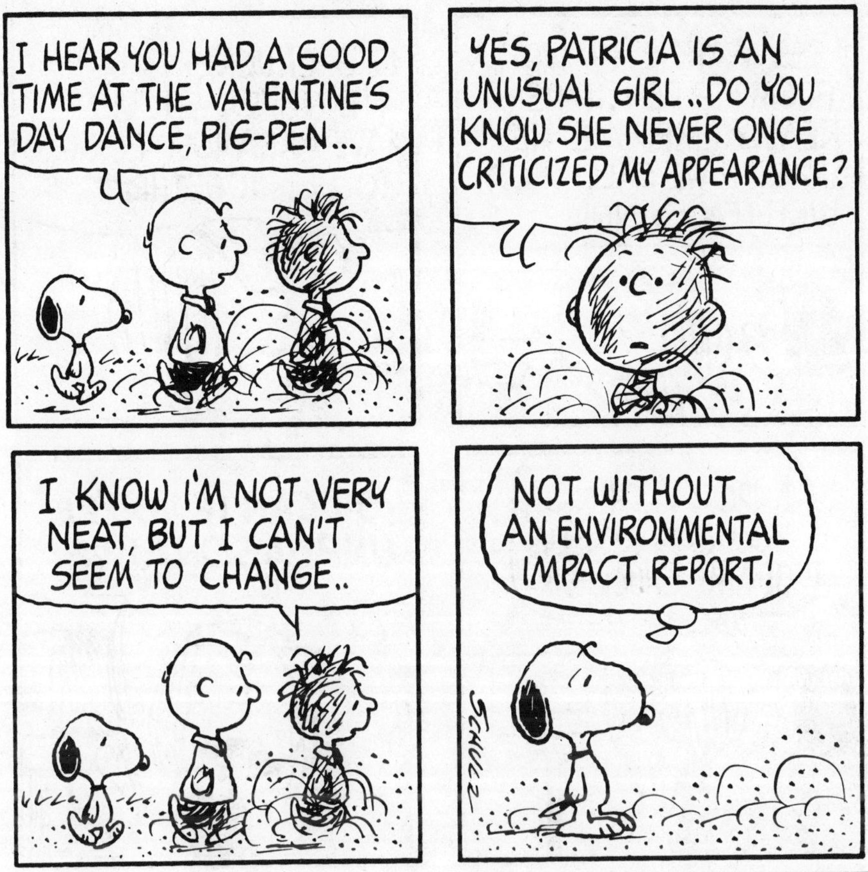
I HEAR YOU HAD A GOOD TIME AT THE VALENTINE'S DAY DANCE, PIG-PEN...
YES, PATRICIA IS AN UNUSUAL GIRL..DO YOU KNOW SHE NEVER ONCE CRITICIZED MY APPEARANCE?
I KNOW I'M NOT VERY NEAT, BUT I CAN'T SEEM TO CHANGE..
NOT WITHOUT AN ENVIRONMENTAL IMPACT REPORT!
SCHULZ

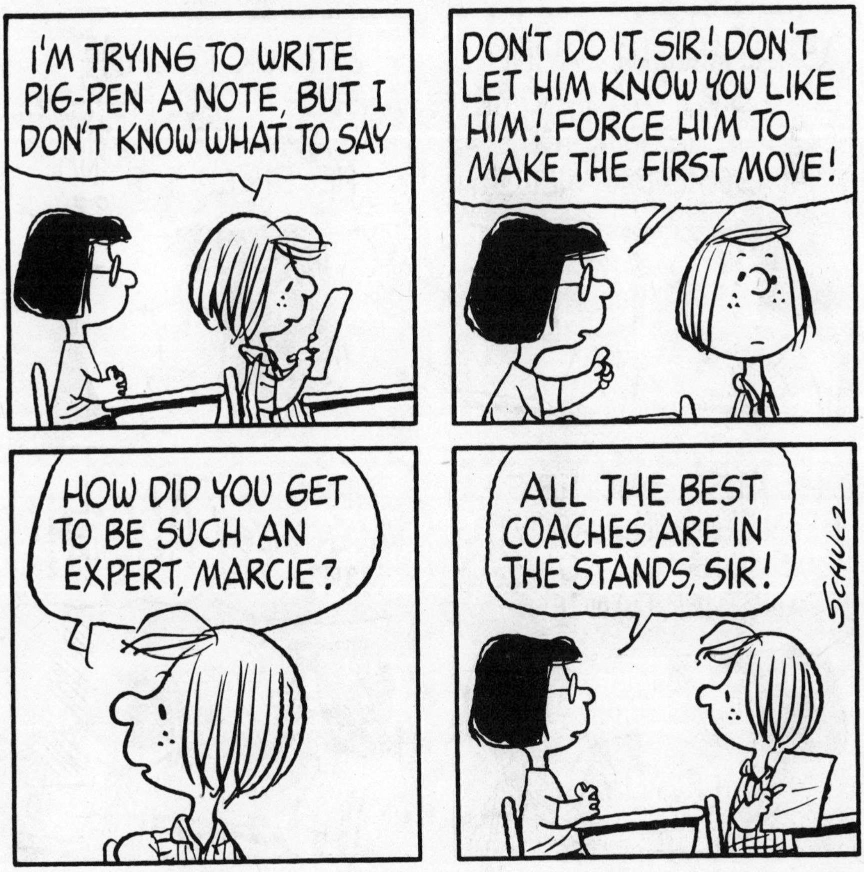
I'M TRYING TO WRITE PIG-PEN A NOTE, BUT I DON'T KNOW WHAT TO SAY
DON'T DO IT, SIR! DON'T LET HIM KNOW YOU LIKE HIM! FORCE HIM TO MAKE THE FIRST MOVE!
HOW DID YOU GET TO BE SUCH AN EXPERT, MARCIE?
ALL THE BEST COACHES ARE IN THE STANDS, SIR!
SCHULZ

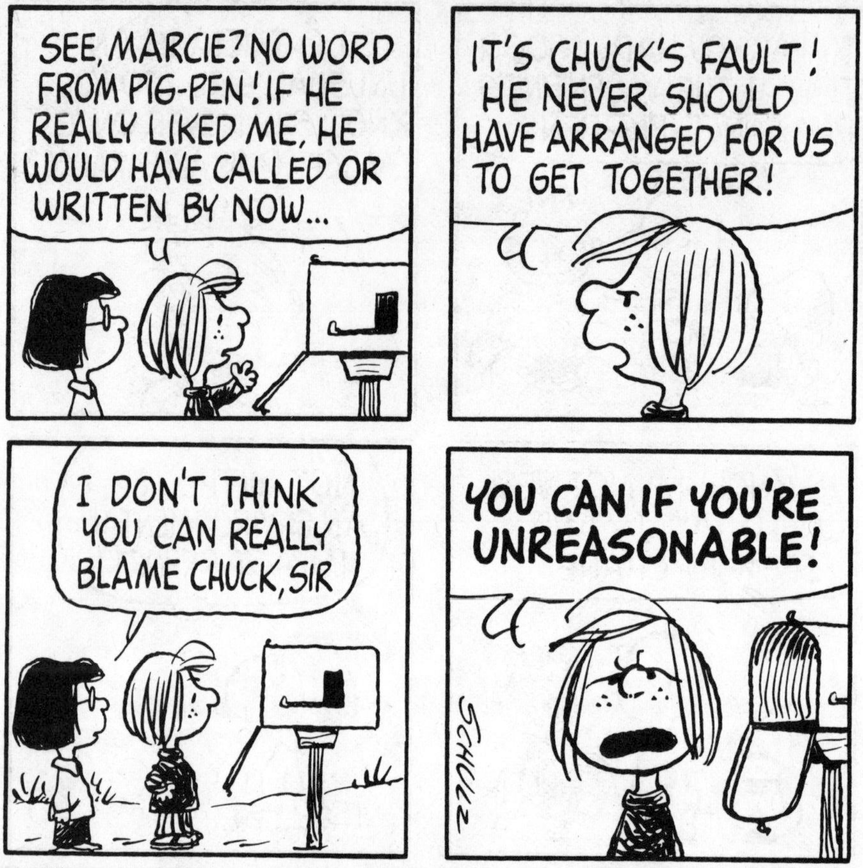
SEE, MARCIE? NO WORD FROM PIG-PEN! IF HE REALLY LIKED ME, HE WOULD HAVE CALLED OR WRITTEN BY NOW...
IT'S CHUCK'S FAULT! HE NEVER SHOULD HAVE ARRANGED FOR US TO GET TOGETHER!
I DON'T THINK YOU CAN REALLY BLAME CHUCK, SIR
YOU CAN IF YOU'RE UNREASONABLE!
SCHULZ

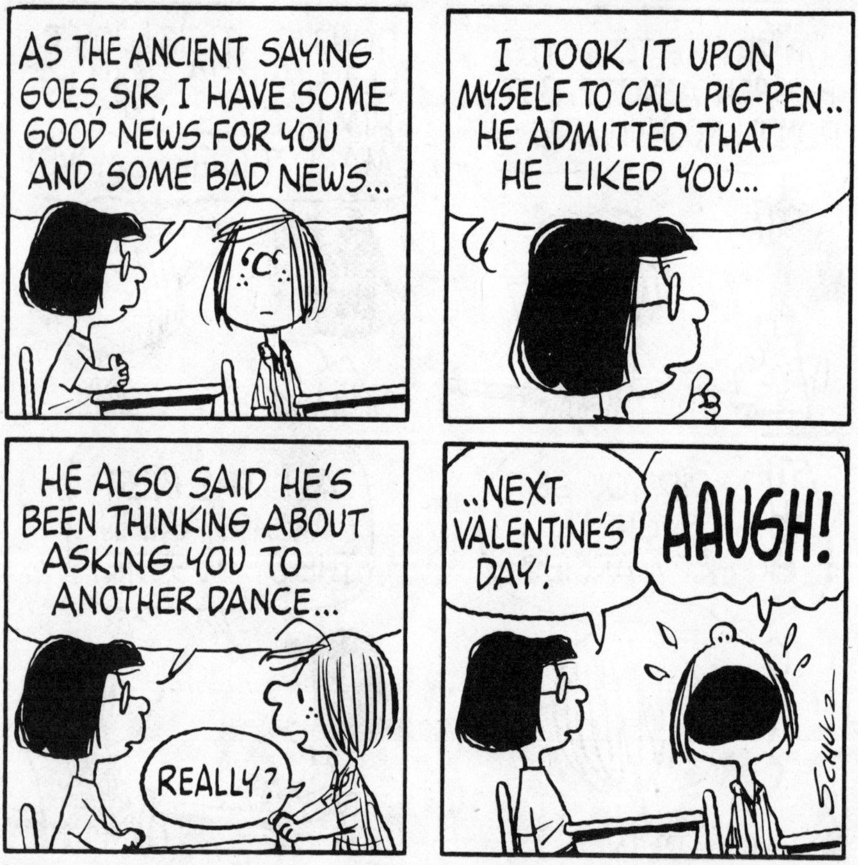
AS THE ANCIENT SAYING GOES, SIR, I HAVE SOME GOOD NEWS FOR YOU AND SOME BAD NEWS...
I TOOK IT UPON MYSELF TO CALL PIG-PEN.. HE ADMITTED THAT HE LIKED YOU...
HE ALSO SAID HE'S BEEN THINKING ABOUT ASKING YOU TO ANOTHER DANCE...
REALLY?
..NEXT VALENTINE'S DAY!
AAUGH!
SCHULZ

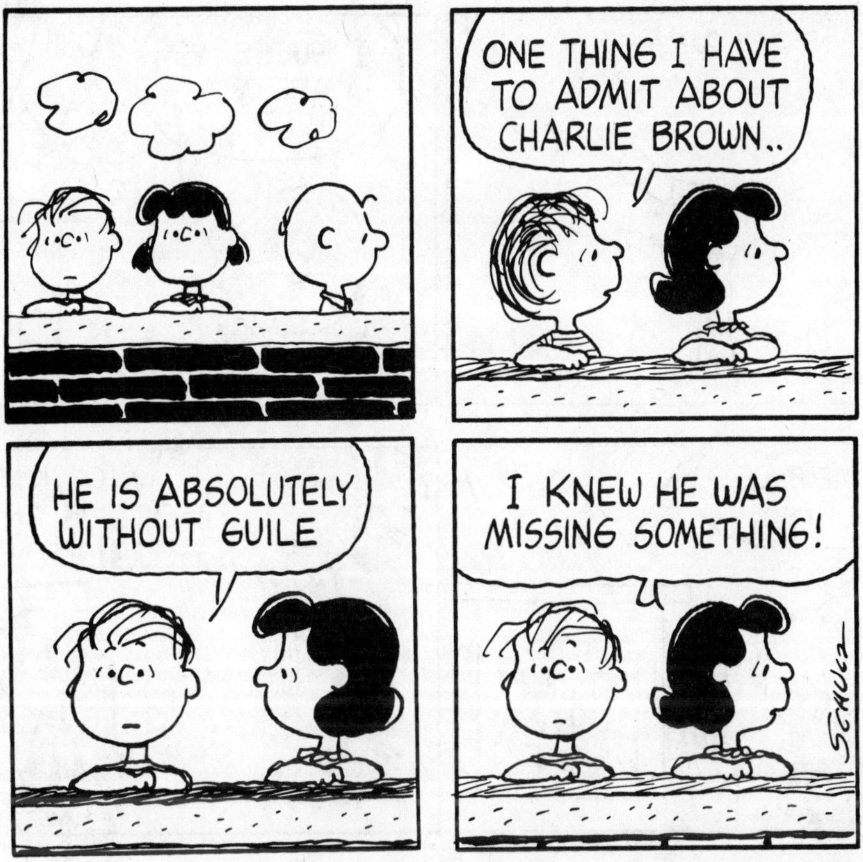
ONE THING I HAVE TO ADMIT ABOUT CHARLIE BROWN..
HE IS ABSOLUTELY WITHOUT GUILE
I KNEW HE WAS MISSING SOMETHING!
SCHULZ

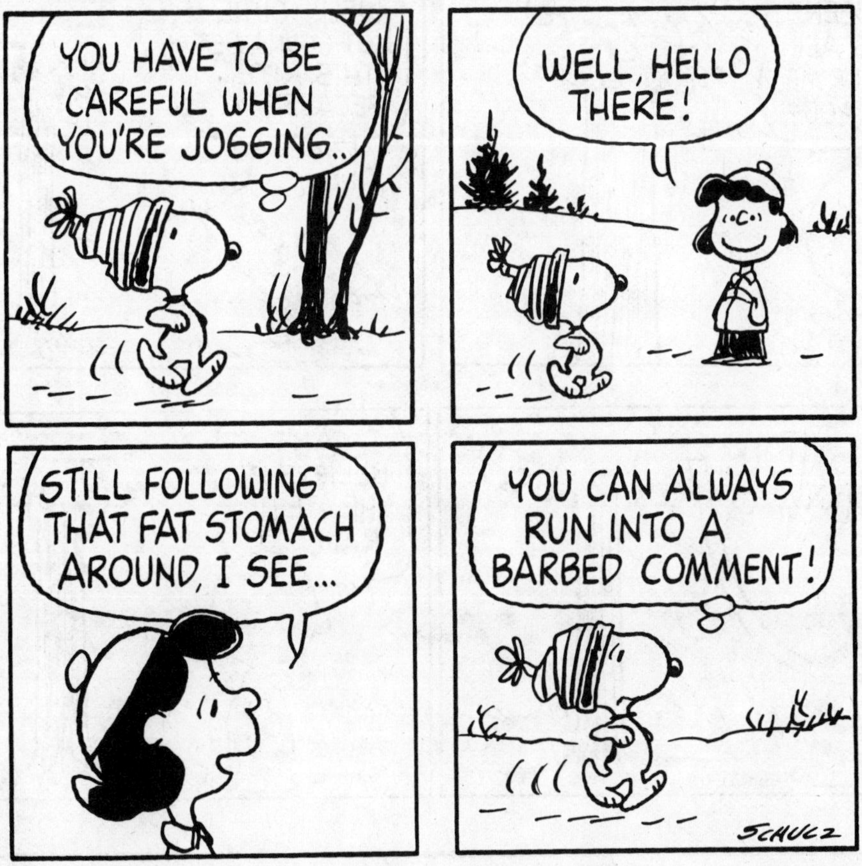
YOU HAVE TO BE CAREFUL WHEN YOU'RE JOGGING..
WELL, HELLO THERE!
STILL FOLLOWING THAT FAT STOMACH AROUND, I SEE...
YOU CAN ALWAYS RUN INTO A BARBED COMMENT!
SCHULZ

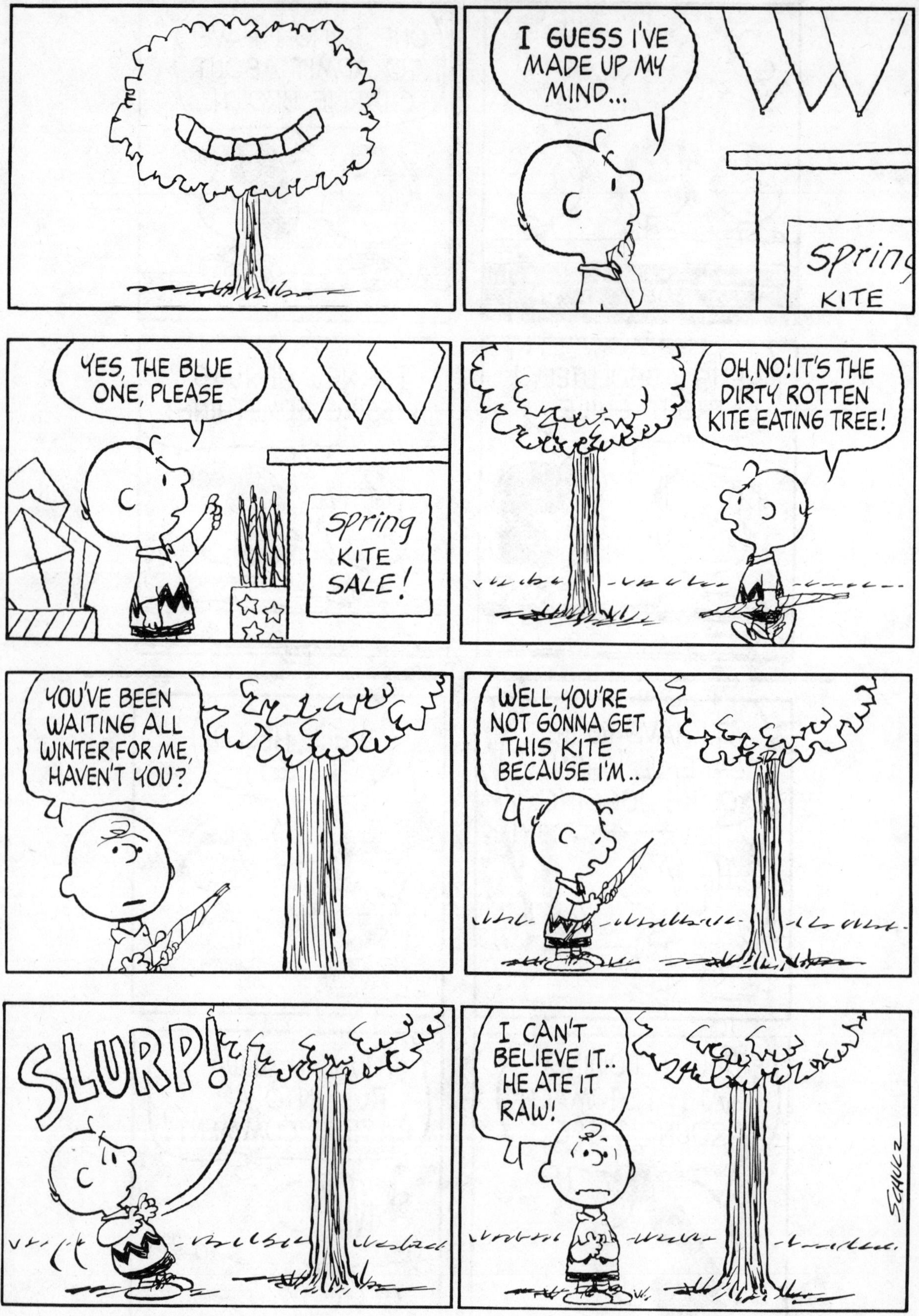
I GUESS I'VE MADE UP MY MIND...
Spring
KITE
YES, THE BLUE ONE, PLEASE
Spring KITE SALE!
OH, NO! IT'S THE DIRTY ROTTEN KITE EATING TREE!
YOU'VE BEEN WAITING ALL WINTER FOR ME, HAVEN'T YOU?
WELL, YOU'RE NOT GONNA GET THIS KITE BECAUSE I'M..
SLURP!
I CAN'T BELIEVE IT.. HE ATE IT RAW!
SCHULZ

I CAN'T DO IT!

HEY, BIG BROTHER, HOW ABOUT HELPING ME WITH MY HOMEWORK?

YOU MEAN DO IT FOR YOU, DON'T YOU?

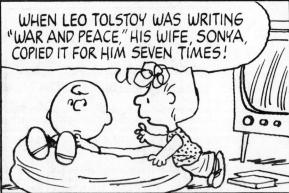

WHEN LEO TOLSTOY WAS WRITING "WAR AND PEACE," HIS WIFE, SONYA, COPIED IT FOR HIM SEVEN TIMES!

AND SHE DID IT BY CANDLELIGHT! AND WITH A DIP PEN!

AND SOMETIMES SHE HAD TO USE A MAGNIFYING GLASS TO MAKE OUT WHAT HE HAD WRITTEN...

AND SHE HAD TO DO IT AFTER THEIR CHILD HAD BEEN PUT TO BED, AND THE SERVANTS HAD GONE UP TO THEIR GARRETS AND IT WAS QUIET IN THE HOUSE

OKAY, I'LL HELP YOU WITH YOUR HOMEWORK

WORE YOU DOWN, DIDN'T I?

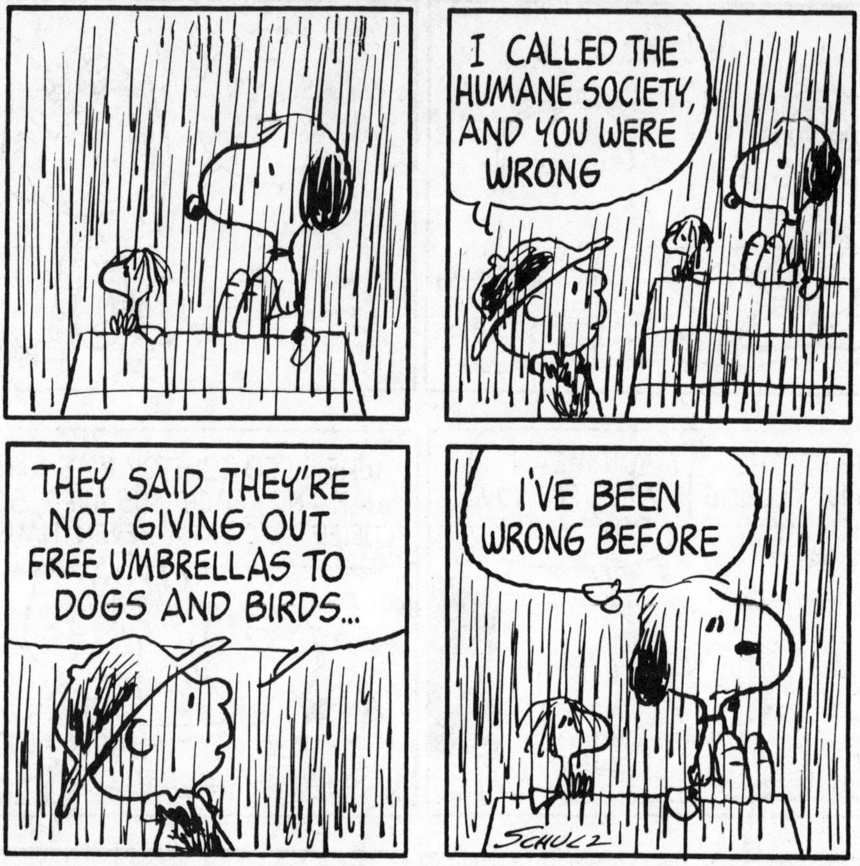
I CALLED THE HUMANE SOCIETY, AND YOU WERE WRONG
THEY SAID THEY'RE NOT GIVING OUT FREE UMBRELLAS TO DOGS AND BIRDS...
I'VE BEEN WRONG BEFORE
SCHULZ

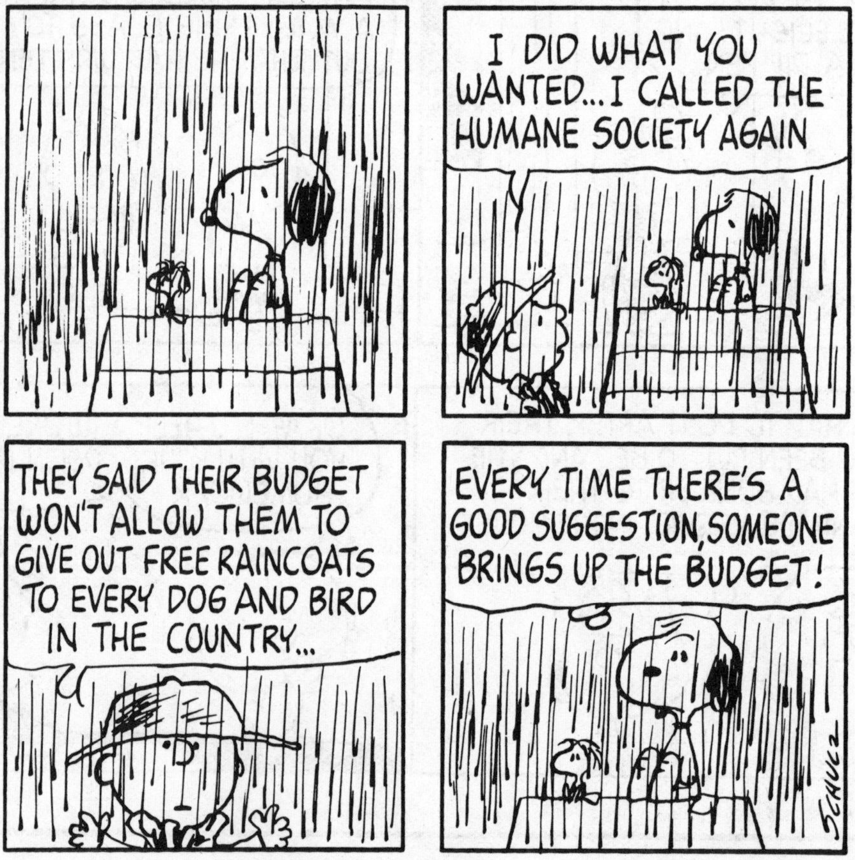
I DID WHAT YOU WANTED...I CALLED THE HUMANE SOCIETY AGAIN
THEY SAID THEIR BUDGET WON'T ALLOW THEM TO GIVE OUT FREE RAINCOATS TO EVERY DOG AND BIRD IN THE COUNTRY...
EVERY TIME THERE'S A GOOD SUGGESTION, SOMEONE BRINGS UP THE BUDGET!
SCHULZ

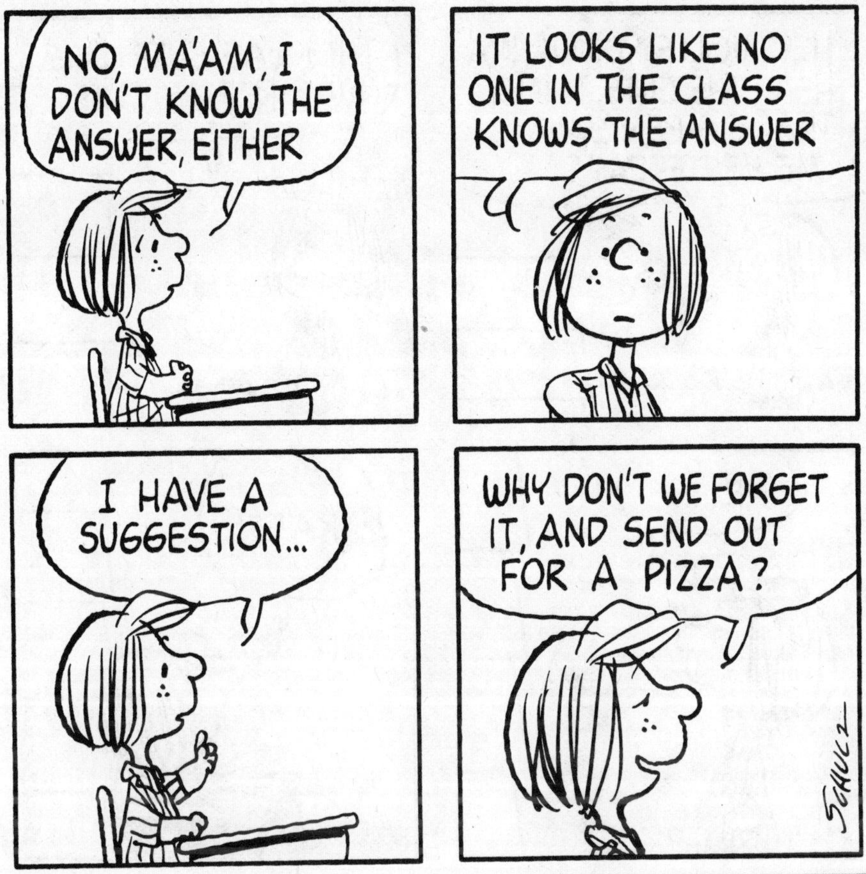
NO, MA'AM, I DON'T KNOW THE ANSWER, EITHER
IT LOOKS LIKE NO ONE IN THE CLASS KNOWS THE ANSWER
I HAVE A SUGGESTION...
WHY DON'T WE FORGET IT, AND SEND OUT FOR A PIZZA?
SCHULZ

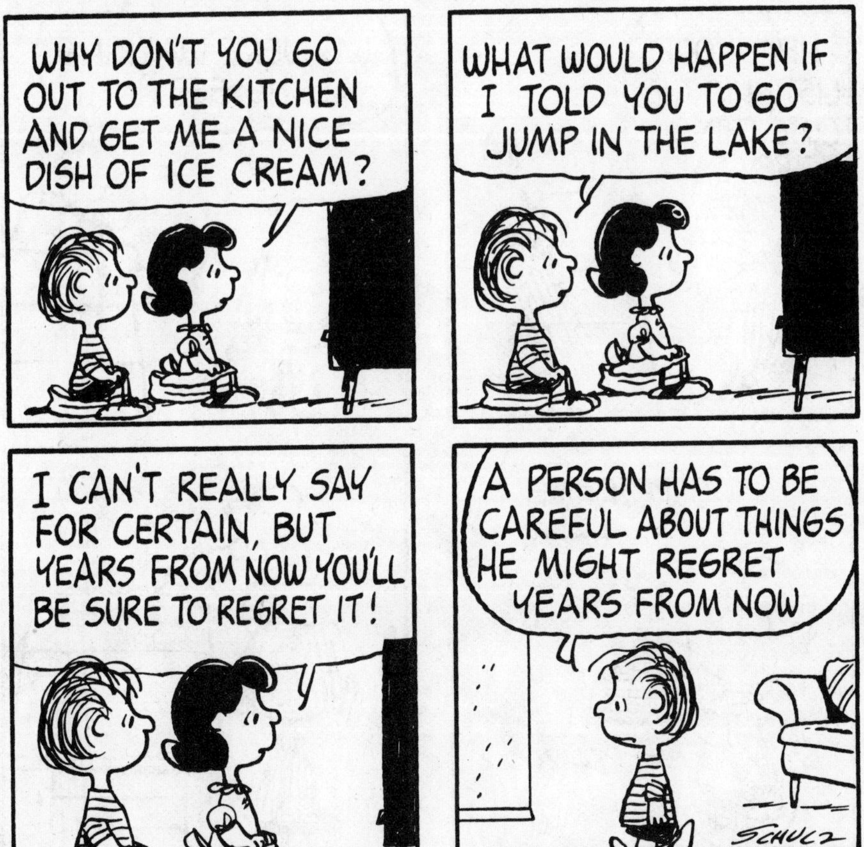
WHY DON'T YOU GO OUT TO THE KITCHEN AND GET ME A NICE DISH OF ICE CREAM?
WHAT WOULD HAPPEN IF I TOLD YOU TO GO JUMP IN THE LAKE?
I CAN'T REALLY SAY FOR CERTAIN, BUT YEARS FROM NOW YOU'LL BE SURE TO REGRET IT!
A PERSON HAS TO BE CAREFUL ABOUT THINGS HE MIGHT REGRET YEARS FROM NOW
SCHULZ

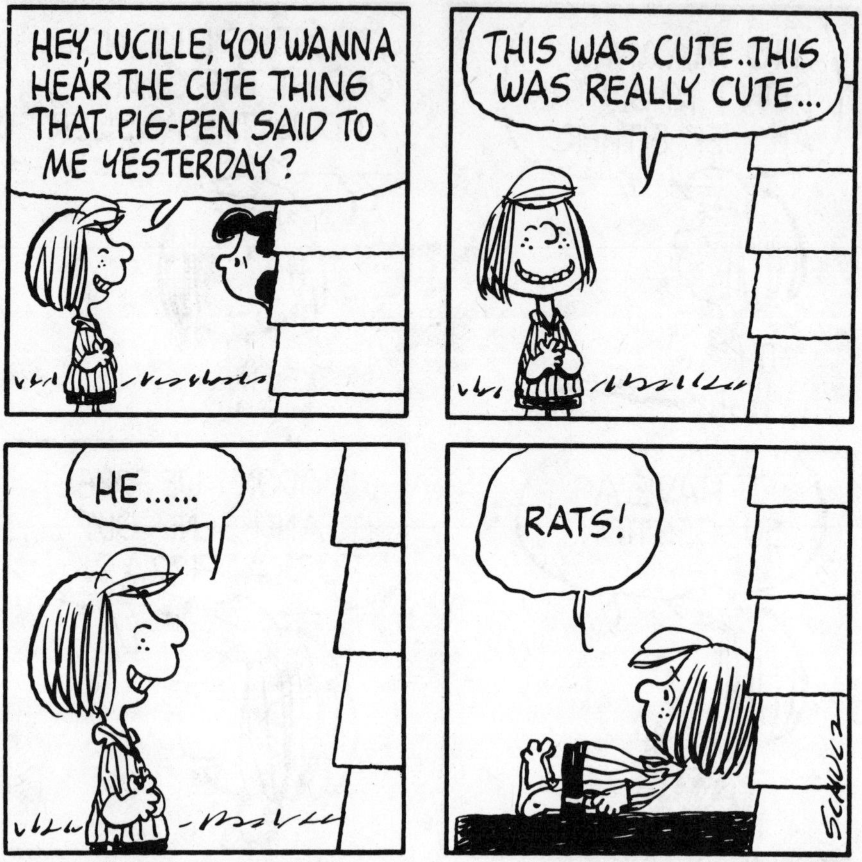
HEY, LUCILLE, YOU WANNA HEAR THE CUTE THING THAT PIG-PEN SAID TO ME YESTERDAY?
THIS WAS CUTE..THIS WAS REALLY CUTE...
HE......
RATS!
SCHULZ

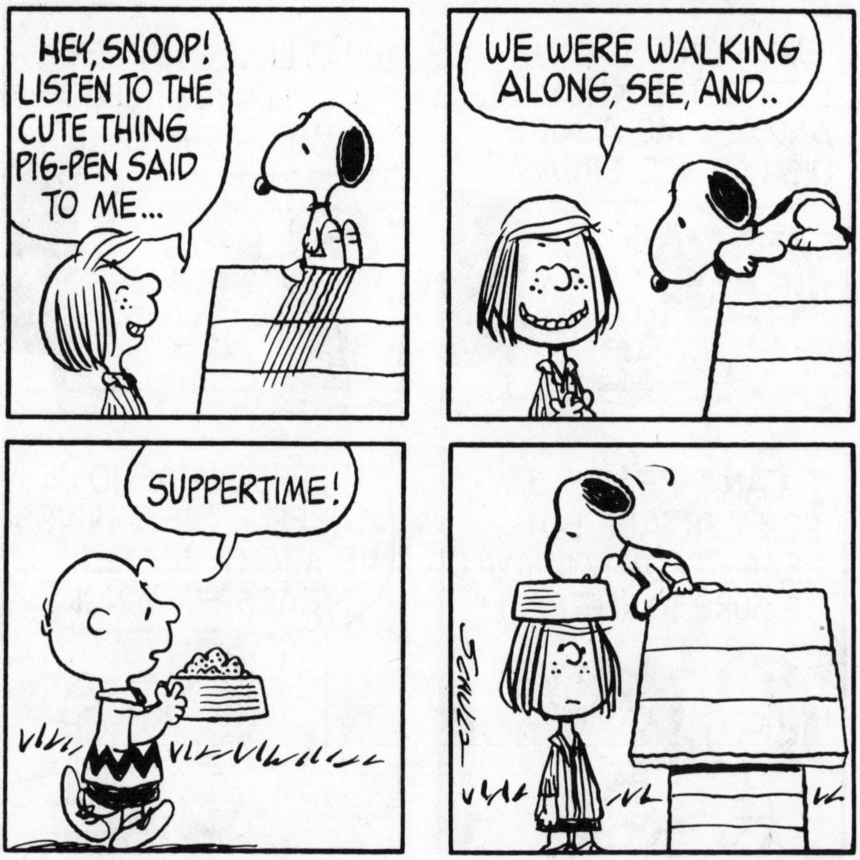
HEY, SNOOP! LISTEN TO THE CUTE THING PIG-PEN SAID TO ME...
WE WERE WALKING ALONG, SEE, AND..
SUPPERTIME!
SCHULZ

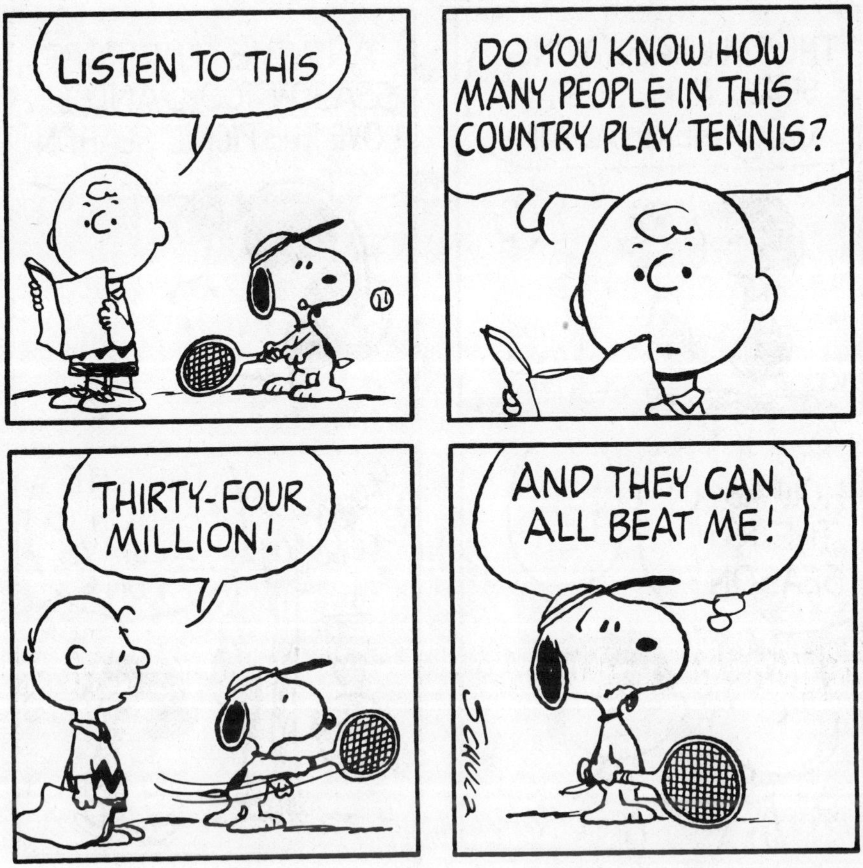
LISTEN TO THIS
DO YOU KNOW HOW MANY PEOPLE IN THIS COUNTRY PLAY TENNIS?
THIRTY-FOUR MILLION!
AND THEY CAN ALL BEAT ME!

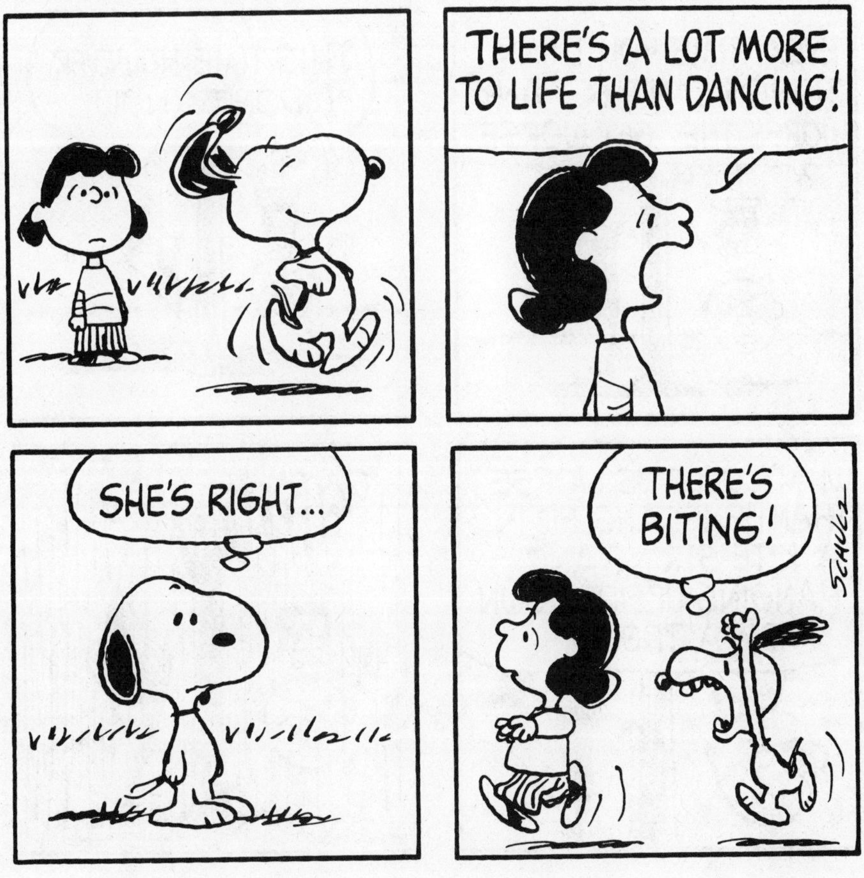
THERE'S A LOT MORE TO LIFE THAN DANCING!
SHE'S RIGHT...
THERE'S BITING!

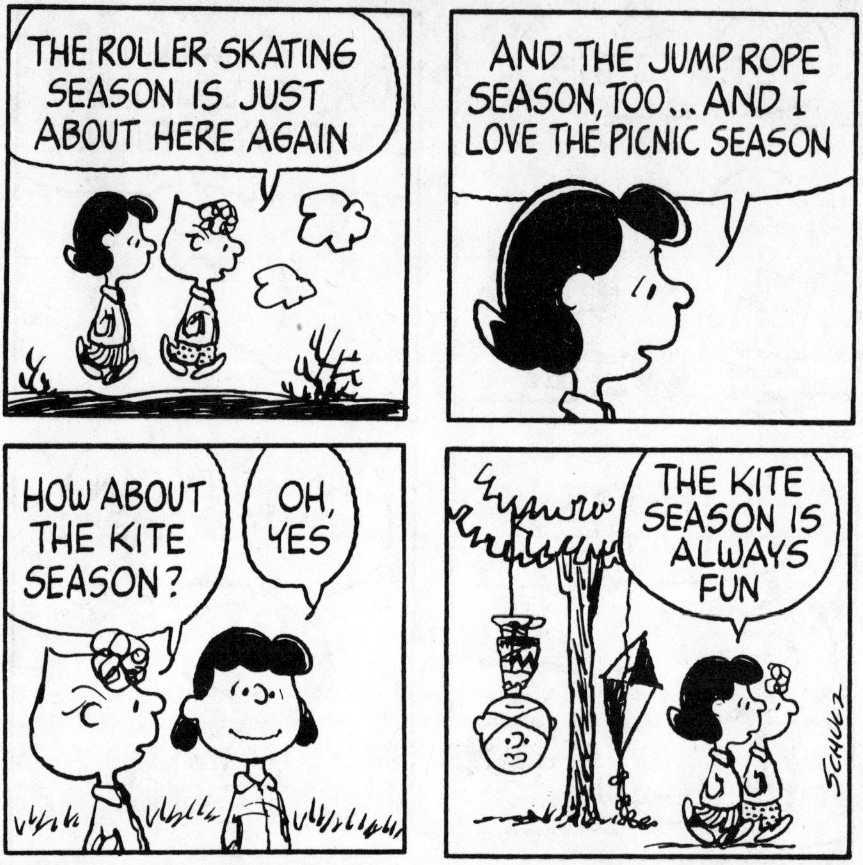
THE ROLLER SKATING SEASON IS JUST ABOUT HERE AGAIN
AND THE JUMP ROPE SEASON, TOO... AND I LOVE THE PICNIC SEASON
HOW ABOUT THE KITE SEASON?
OH, YES
THE KITE SEASON IS ALWAYS FUN
SCHULZ

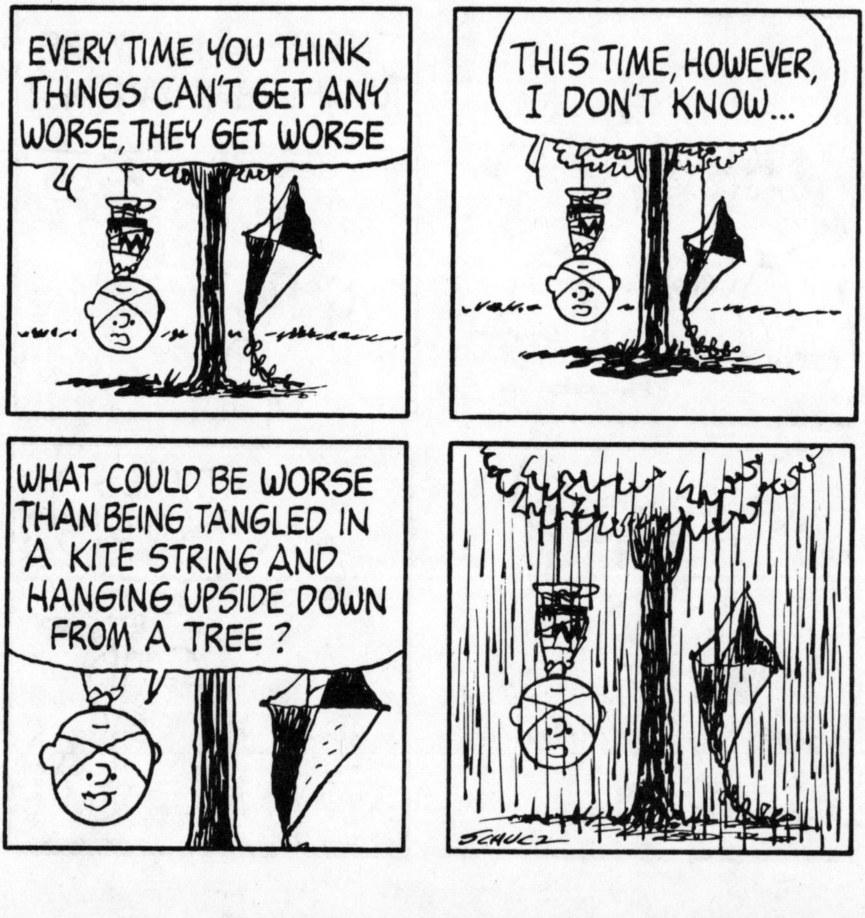
EVERY TIME YOU THINK THINGS CAN'T GET ANY WORSE, THEY GET WORSE
THIS TIME, HOWEVER, I DON'T KNOW...
WHAT COULD BE WORSE THAN BEING TANGLED IN A KITE STRING AND HANGING UPSIDE DOWN FROM A TREE?
SCHULZ

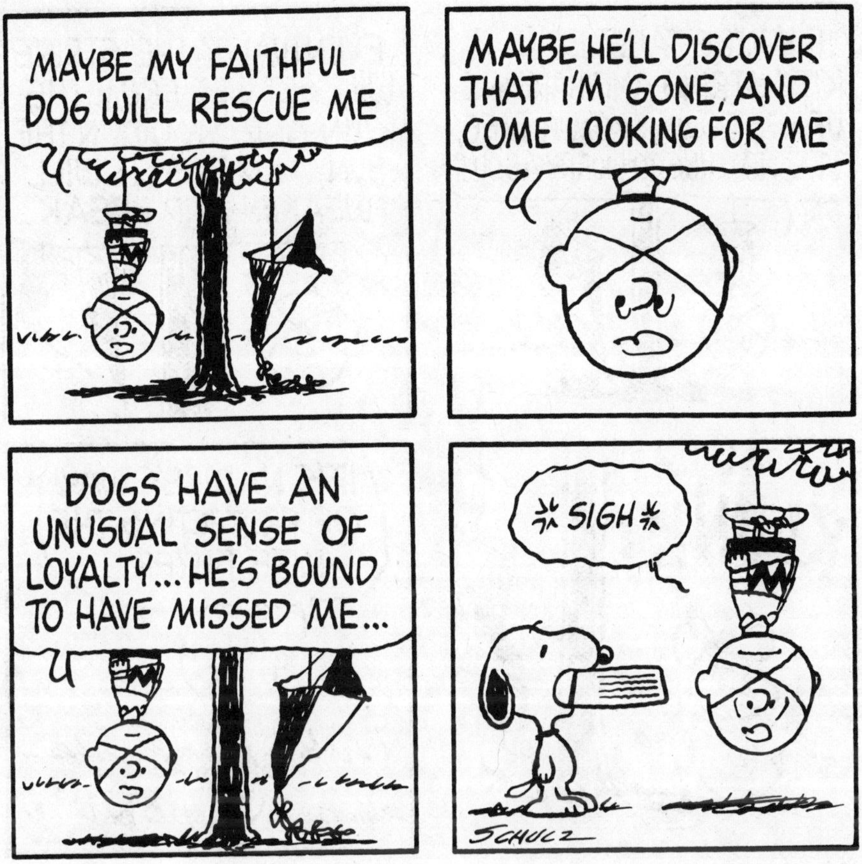
MAYBE MY FAITHFUL DOG WILL RESCUE ME
MAYBE HE'LL DISCOVER THAT I'M GONE, AND COME LOOKING FOR ME
DOGS HAVE AN UNUSUAL SENSE OF LOYALTY... HE'S BOUND TO HAVE MISSED ME...
SIGH
SCHULZ

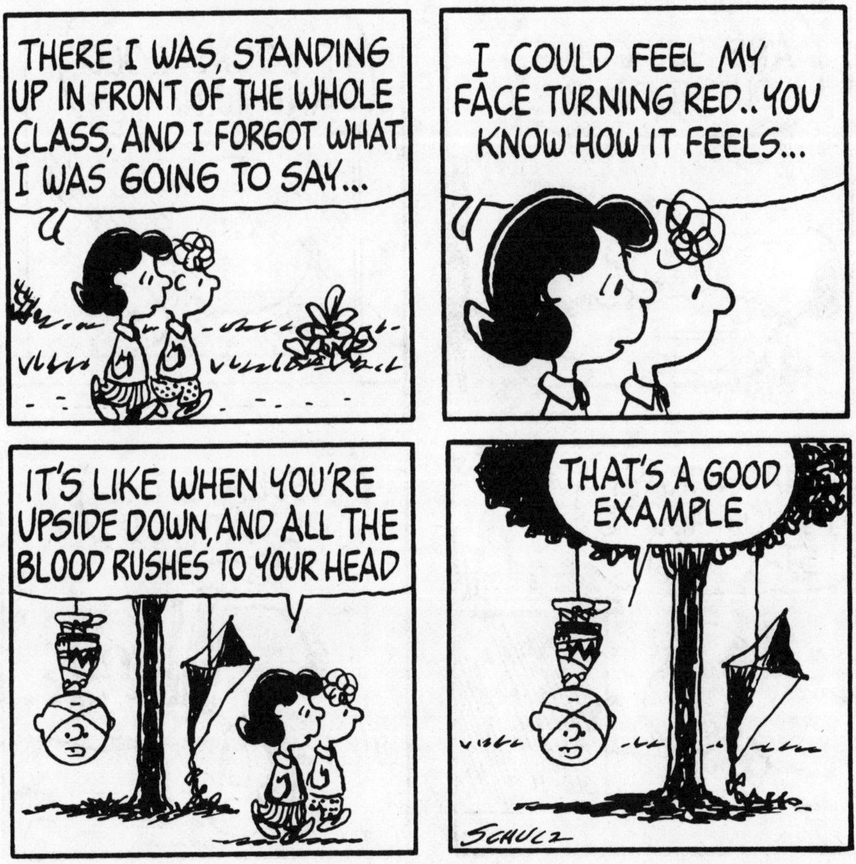
THERE I WAS, STANDING UP IN FRONT OF THE WHOLE CLASS, AND I FORGOT WHAT I WAS GOING TO SAY...
I COULD FEEL MY FACE TURNING RED.. YOU KNOW HOW IT FEELS...
IT'S LIKE WHEN YOU'RE UPSIDE DOWN, AND ALL THE BLOOD RUSHES TO YOUR HEAD
THAT'S A GOOD EXAMPLE
SCHULZ

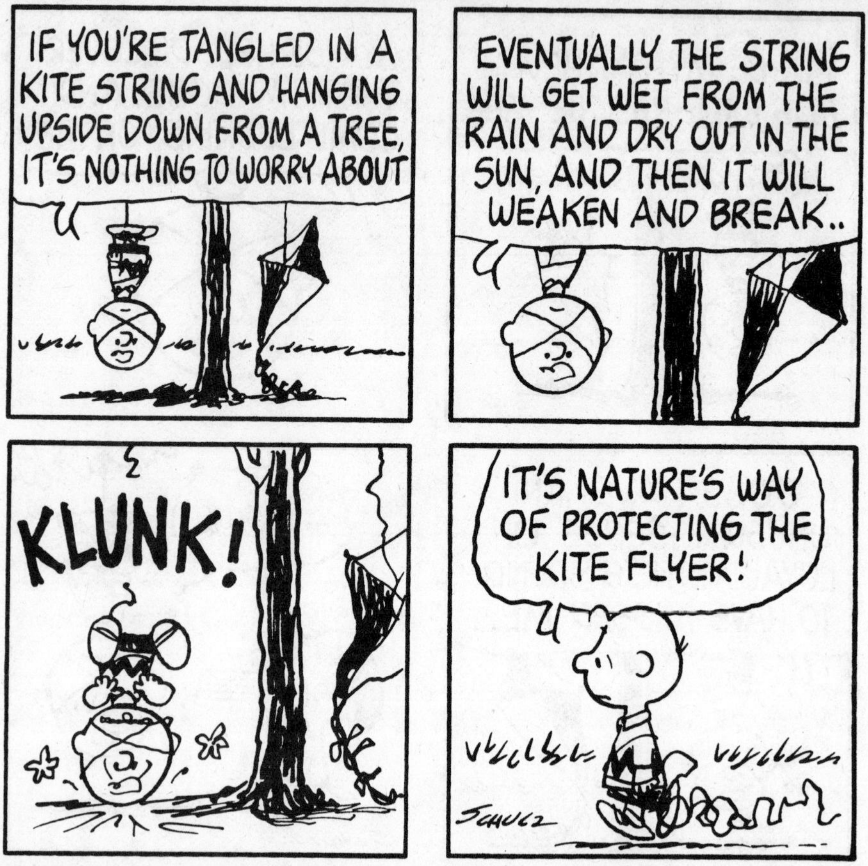
IF YOU'RE TANGLED IN A KITE STRING AND HANGING UPSIDE DOWN FROM A TREE, IT'S NOTHING TO WORRY ABOUT
EVENTUALLY THE STRING WILL GET WET FROM THE RAIN AND DRY OUT IN THE SUN, AND THEN IT WILL WEAKEN AND BREAK..
KLUNK!
IT'S NATURE'S WAY OF PROTECTING THE KITE FLYER!

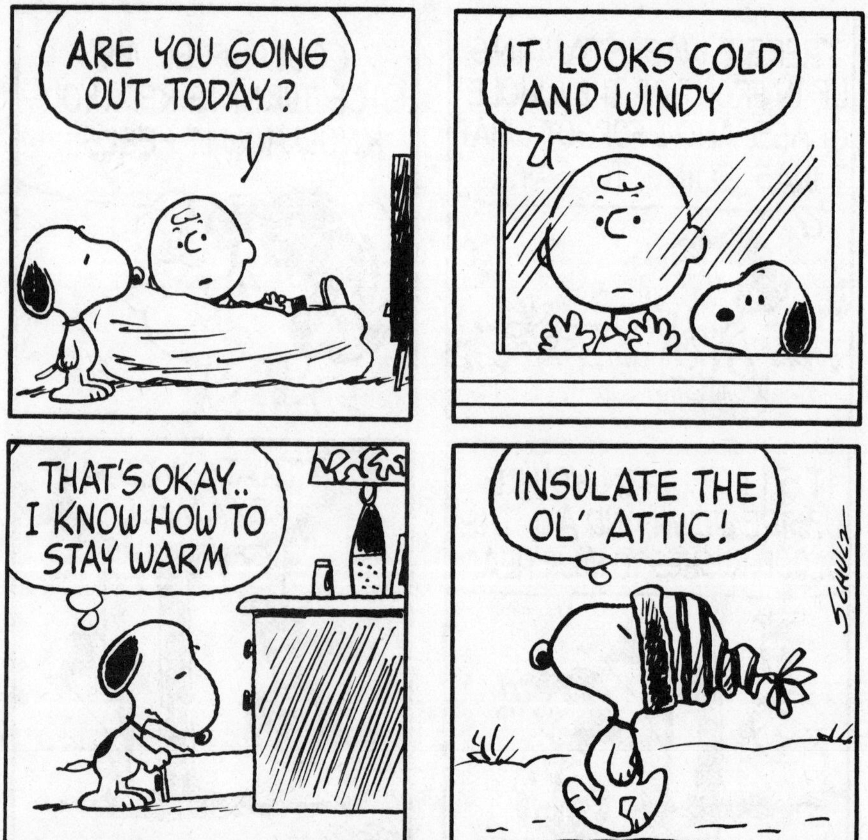
ARE YOU GOING OUT TODAY?
IT LOOKS COLD AND WINDY
THAT'S OKAY.. I KNOW HOW TO STAY WARM
INSULATE THE OL' ATTIC!

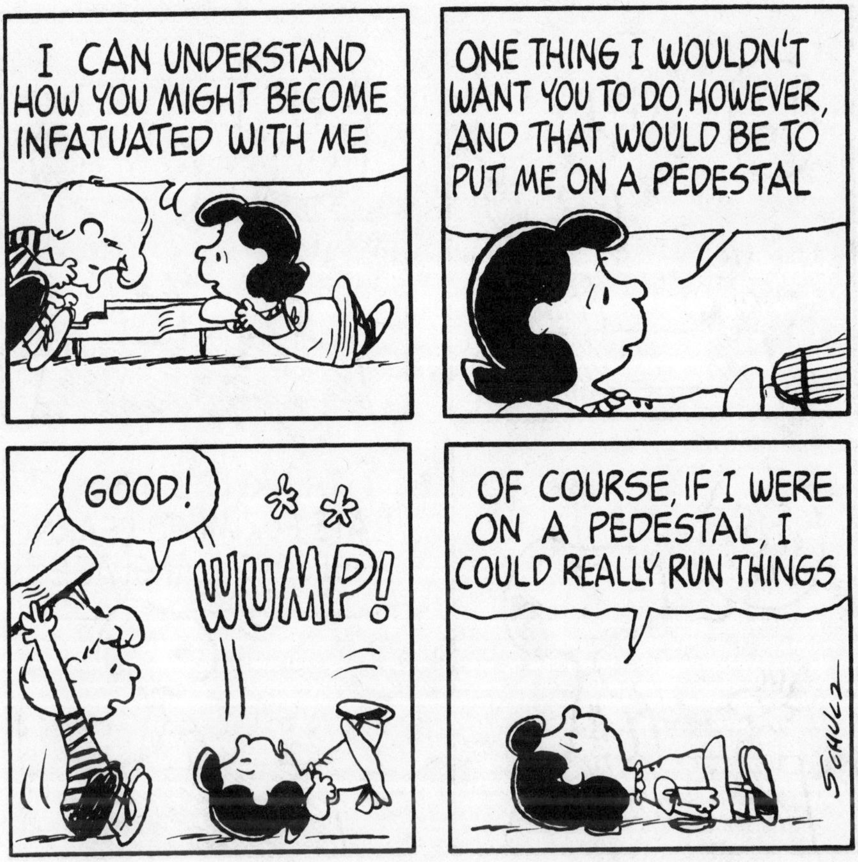
I CAN UNDERSTAND HOW YOU MIGHT BECOME INFATUATED WITH ME
ONE THING I WOULDN'T WANT YOU TO DO, HOWEVER, AND THAT WOULD BE TO PUT ME ON A PEDESTAL
GOOD!
WUMP!
OF COURSE, IF I WERE ON A PEDESTAL, I COULD REALLY RUN THINGS
SCHULZ

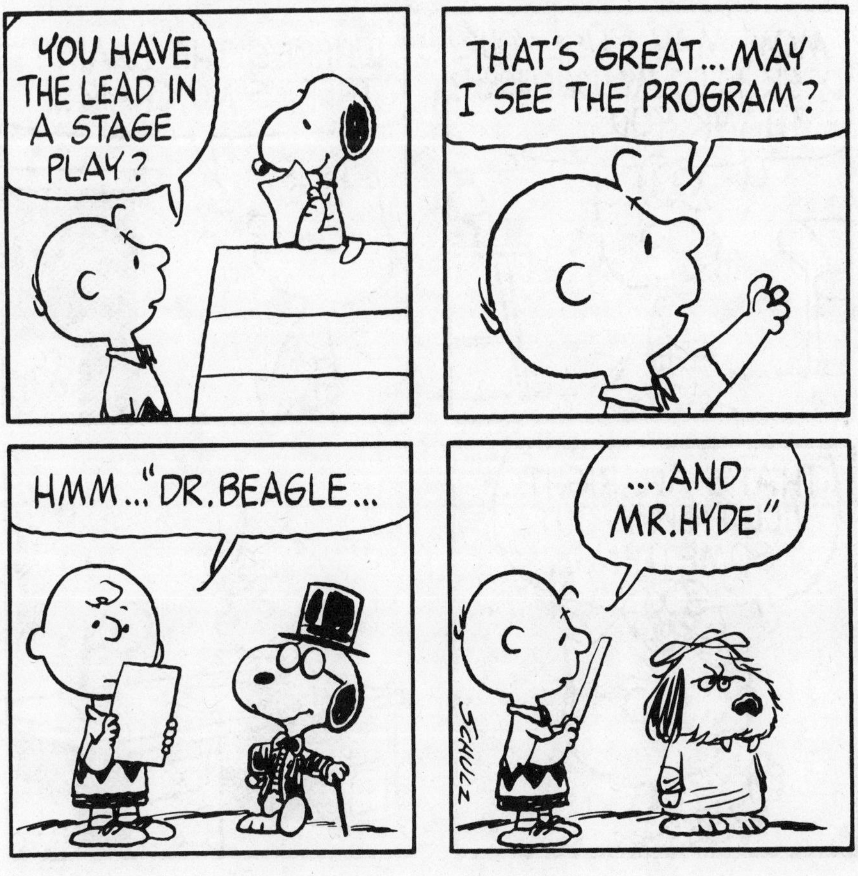
YOU HAVE THE LEAD IN A STAGE PLAY?
THAT'S GREAT... MAY I SEE THE PROGRAM?
HMM... "DR. BEAGLE...
... AND MR. HYDE"
SCHULZ

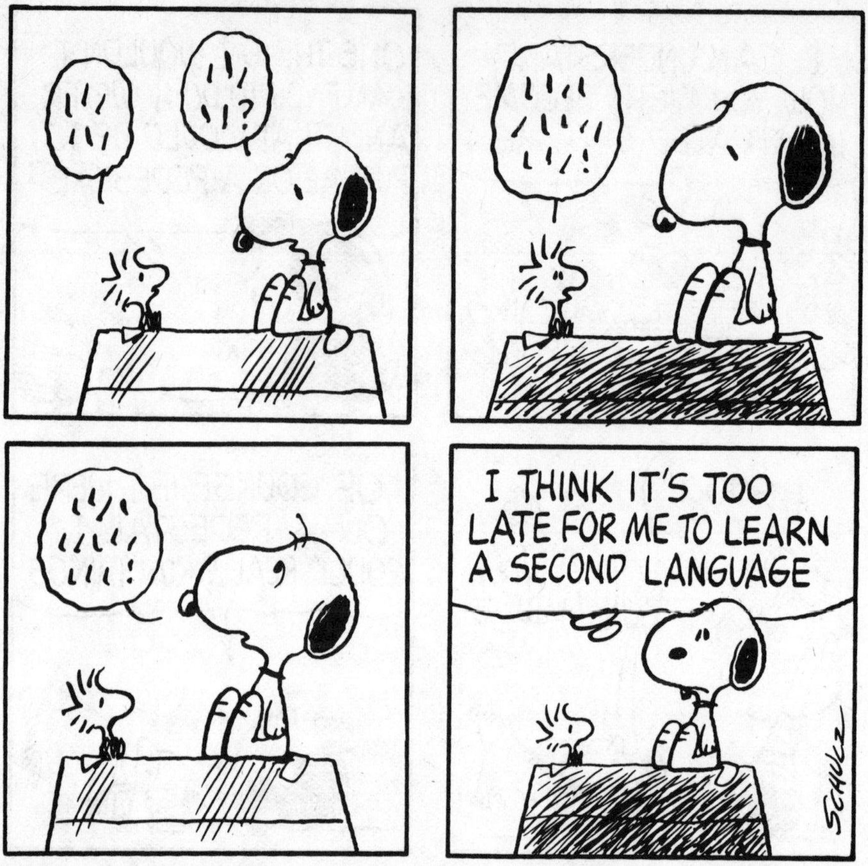
I THINK IT'S TOO LATE FOR ME TO LEARN A SECOND LANGUAGE
SCHULZ

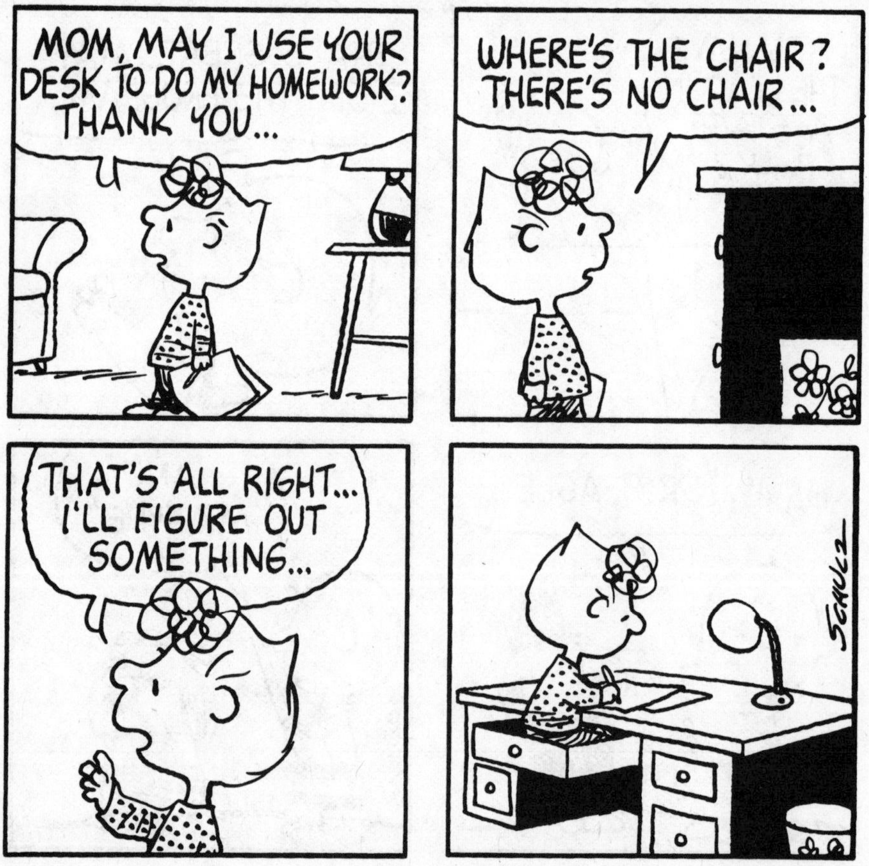
MOM, MAY I USE YOUR DESK TO DO MY HOMEWORK? THANK YOU...
WHERE'S THE CHAIR? THERE'S NO CHAIR...
THAT'S ALL RIGHT... I'LL FIGURE OUT SOMETHING...
SCHULZ

NO, NONE OF MY BROTHERS EVER WENT TO COLLEGE
I'VE OFTEN REGRETTED IT
OUR MOTHER WAS A GREAT BELIEVER IN EDUCATION
MOM ALWAYS WANTED ME TO GET A BEAGLE OF ARTS DEGREE
SCHULZ

SOMETIMES, WHEN YOU'RE DEPRESSED, ALL YOU WANT TO DO IS NOTHING
ALL YOU WANT TO DO IS LEAN YOUR HEAD ON YOUR ARM, AND STARE INTO SPACE
SOMETIMES THIS CAN GO ON FOR HOURS
IF YOU'RE UNUSUALLY DEPRESSED, YOU MAY HAVE TO CHANGE ARMS
SCHULZ

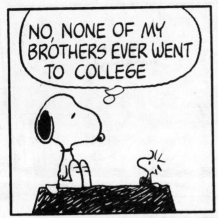

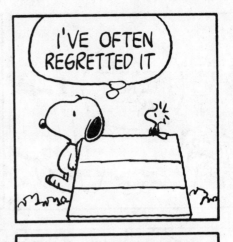

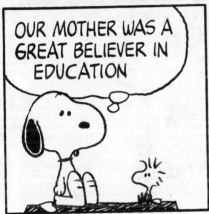

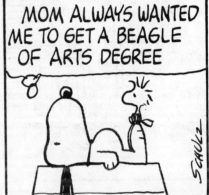

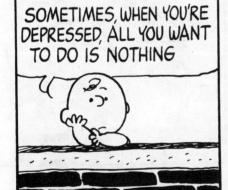

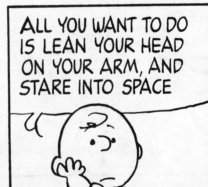

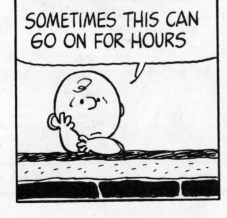

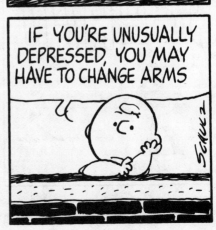

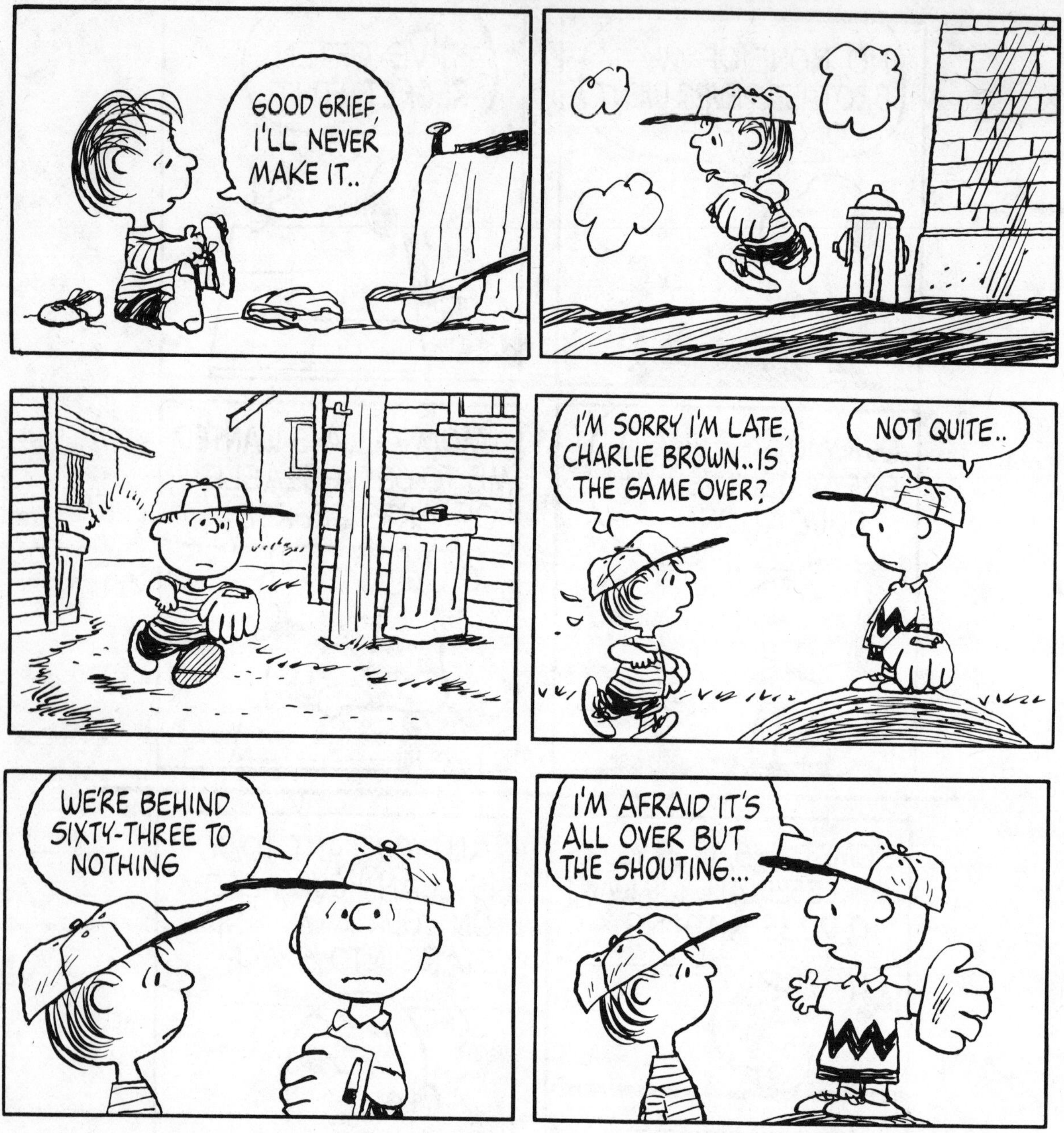
GOOD GRIEF, I'LL NEVER MAKE IT..
I'M SORRY I'M LATE, CHARLIE BROWN.. IS THE GAME OVER?
NOT QUITE..
WE'RE BEHIND SIXTY-THREE TO NOTHING
I'M AFRAID IT'S ALL OVER BUT THE SHOUTING...
AAUGHHH!
NOW, IT'S OVER
SCHULZ

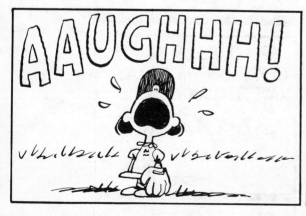

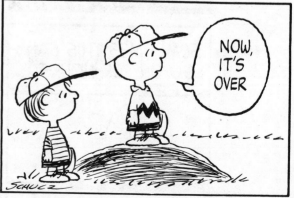

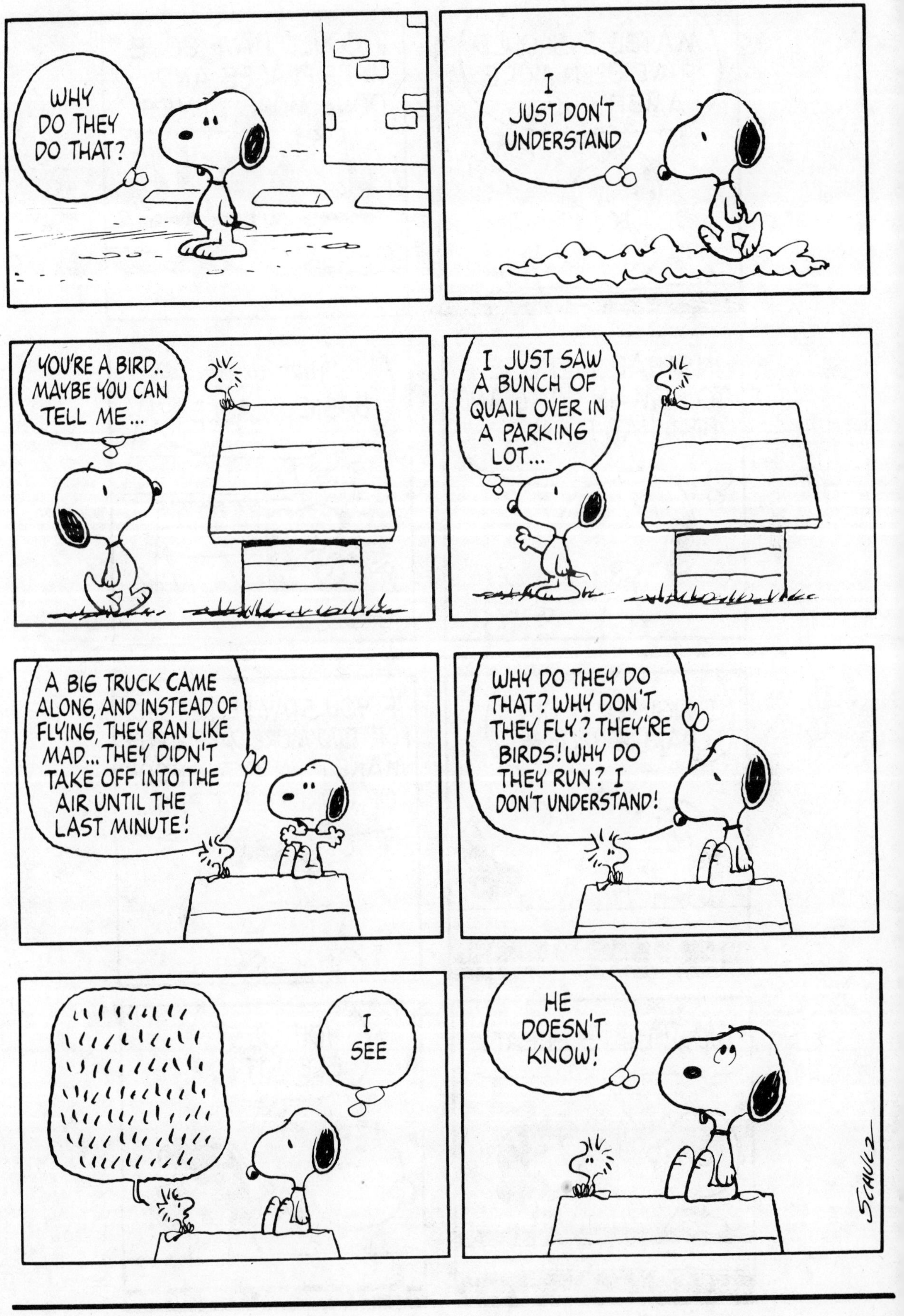
WHY DO THEY DO THAT?
I JUST DON'T UNDERSTAND
YOU'RE A BIRD.. MAYBE YOU CAN TELL ME...
I JUST SAW A BUNCH OF QUAIL OVER IN A PARKING LOT...
A BIG TRUCK CAME ALONG, AND INSTEAD OF FLYING, THEY RAN LIKE MAD... THEY DIDN'T TAKE OFF INTO THE AIR UNTIL THE LAST MINUTE!
WHY DO THEY DO THAT? WHY DON'T THEY FLY? THEY'RE BIRDS! WHY DO THEY RUN? I DON'T UNDERSTAND!
I SEE
HE DOESN'T KNOW!
SCHULZ

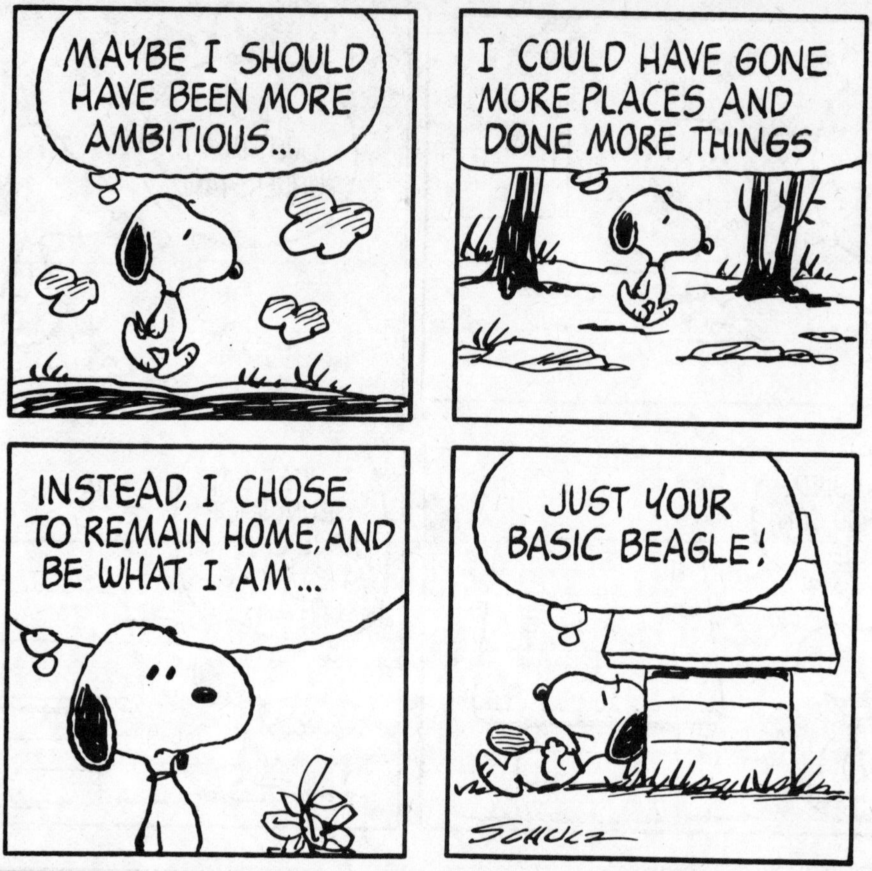
MAYBE I SHOULD HAVE BEEN MORE AMBITIOUS...
I COULD HAVE GONE MORE PLACES AND DONE MORE THINGS
INSTEAD, I CHOSE TO REMAIN HOME, AND BE WHAT I AM...
JUST YOUR BASIC BEAGLE!

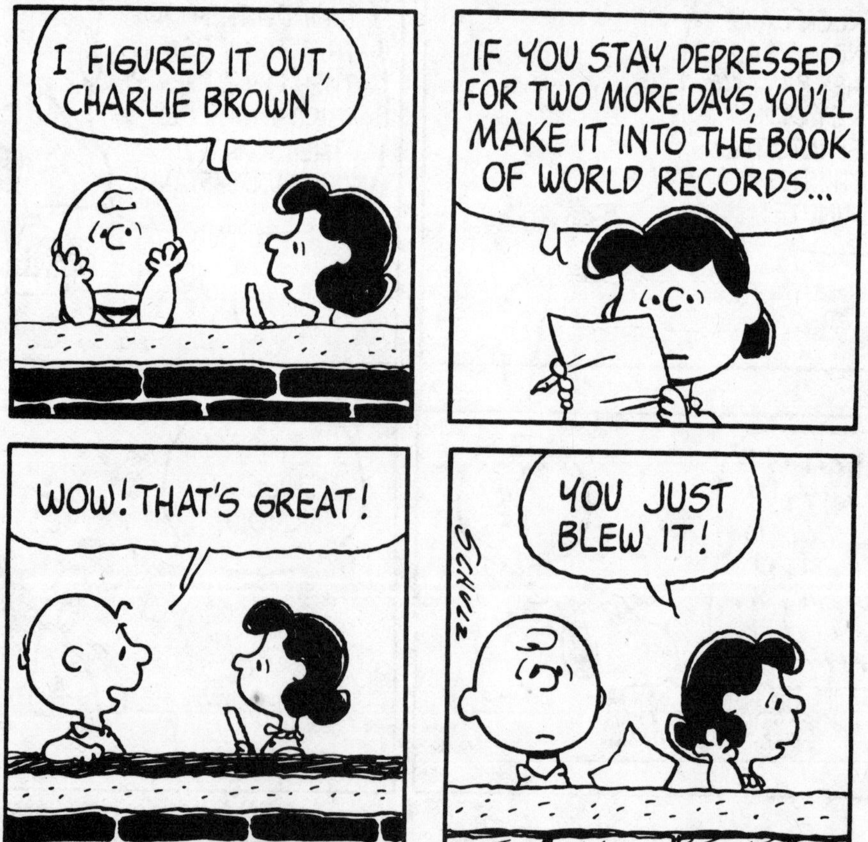
I FIGURED IT OUT, CHARLIE BROWN
IF YOU STAY DEPRESSED FOR TWO MORE DAYS, YOU'LL MAKE IT INTO THE BOOK OF WORLD RECORDS...
WOW! THAT'S GREAT!
YOU JUST BLEW IT!

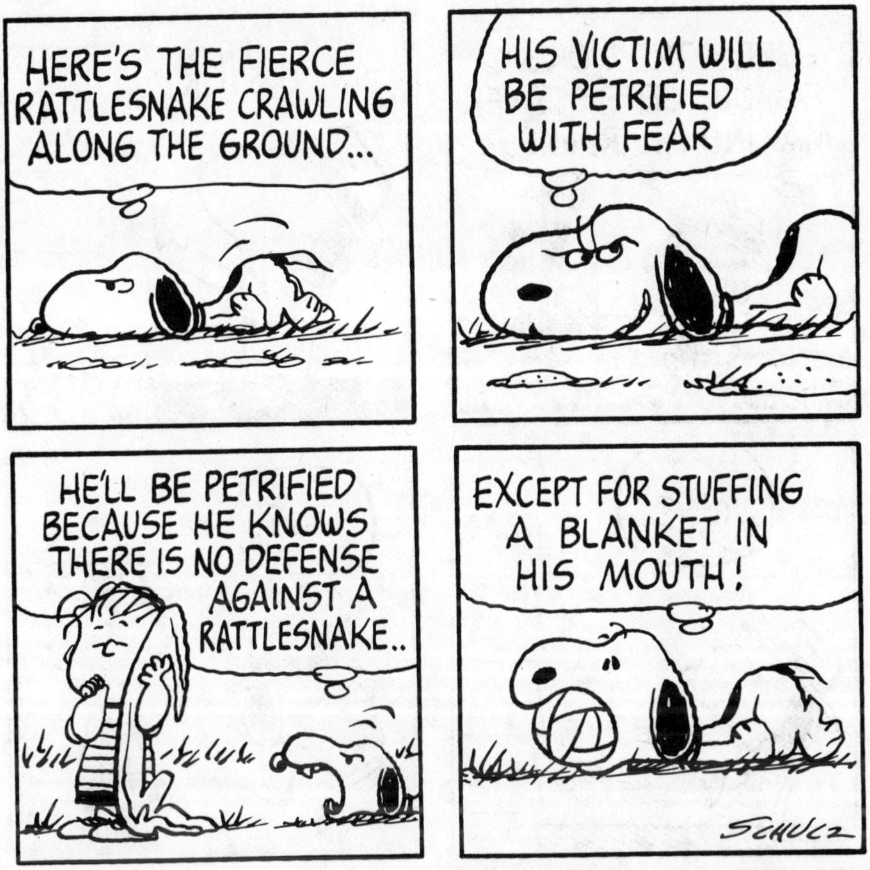
HERE'S THE FIERCE RATTLESNAKE CRAWLING ALONG THE GROUND...
HIS VICTIM WILL BE PETRIFIED WITH FEAR
HE'LL BE PETRIFIED BECAUSE HE KNOWS THERE IS NO DEFENSE AGAINST A RATTLESNAKE..
EXCEPT FOR STUFFING A BLANKET IN HIS MOUTH!
SCHULZ

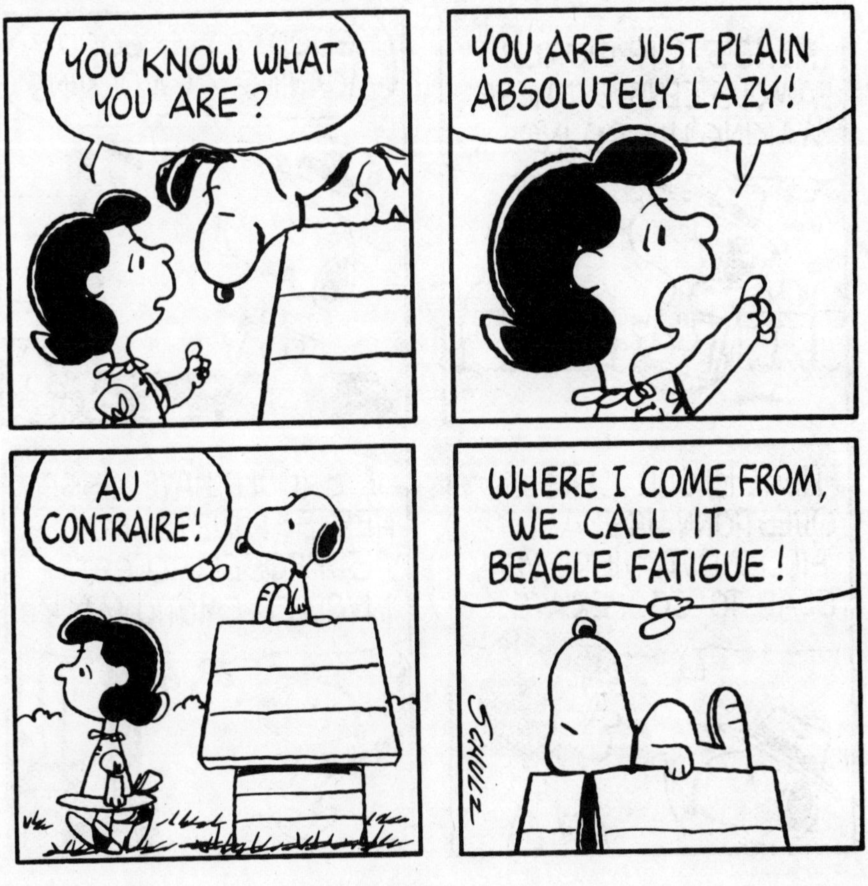
YOU KNOW WHAT YOU ARE?
YOU ARE JUST PLAIN ABSOLUTELY LAZY!
AU CONTRAIRE!
WHERE I COME FROM, WE CALL IT BEAGLE FATIGUE!
SCHULZ

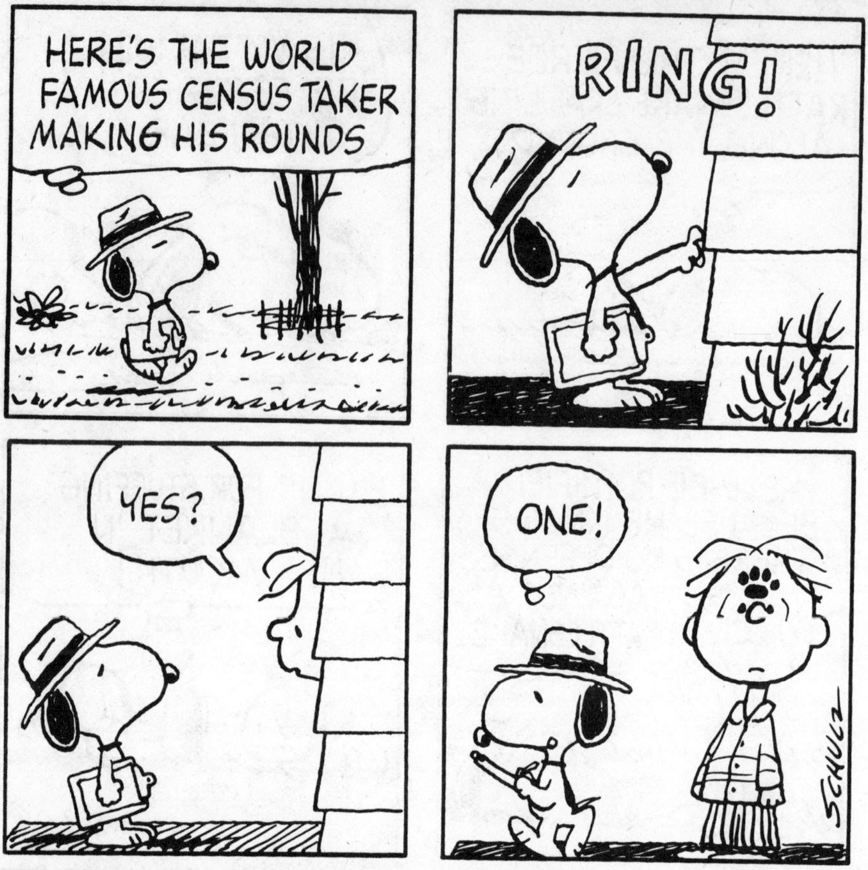
HERE'S THE WORLD FAMOUS CENSUS TAKER MAKING HIS ROUNDS
RING!
YES?
ONE!
SCHULZ

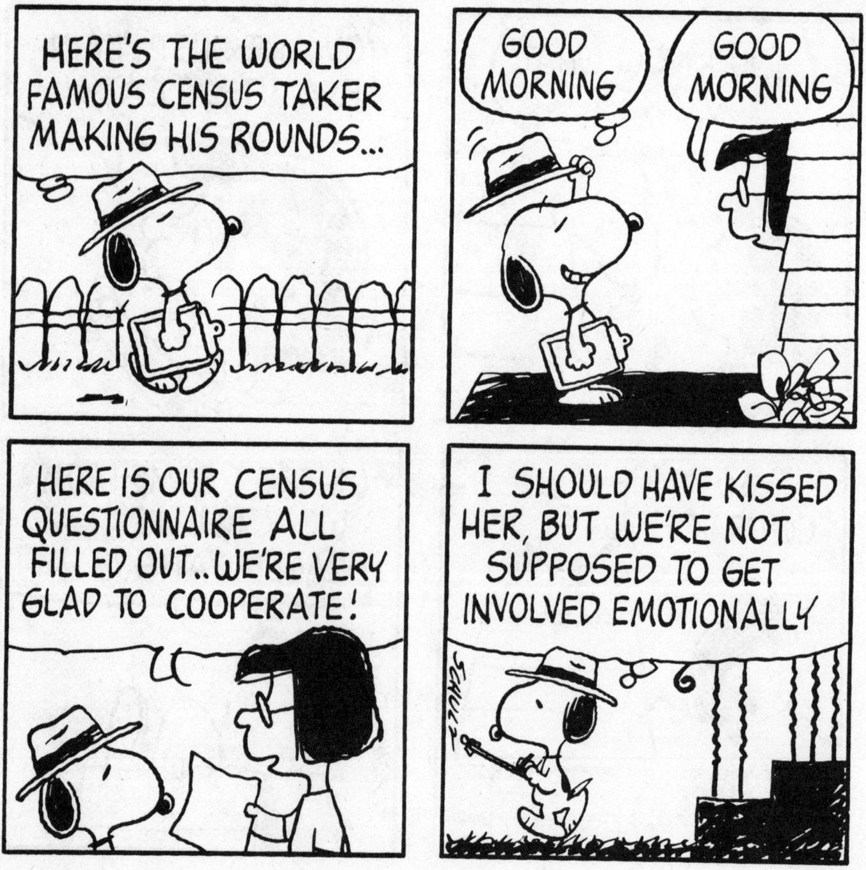
HERE'S THE WORLD FAMOUS CENSUS TAKER MAKING HIS ROUNDS...
GOOD MORNING
GOOD MORNING
HERE IS OUR CENSUS QUESTIONNAIRE ALL FILLED OUT..WE'RE VERY GLAD TO COOPERATE!
I SHOULD HAVE KISSED HER, BUT WE'RE NOT SUPPOSED TO GET INVOLVED EMOTIONALLY
SCHULZ

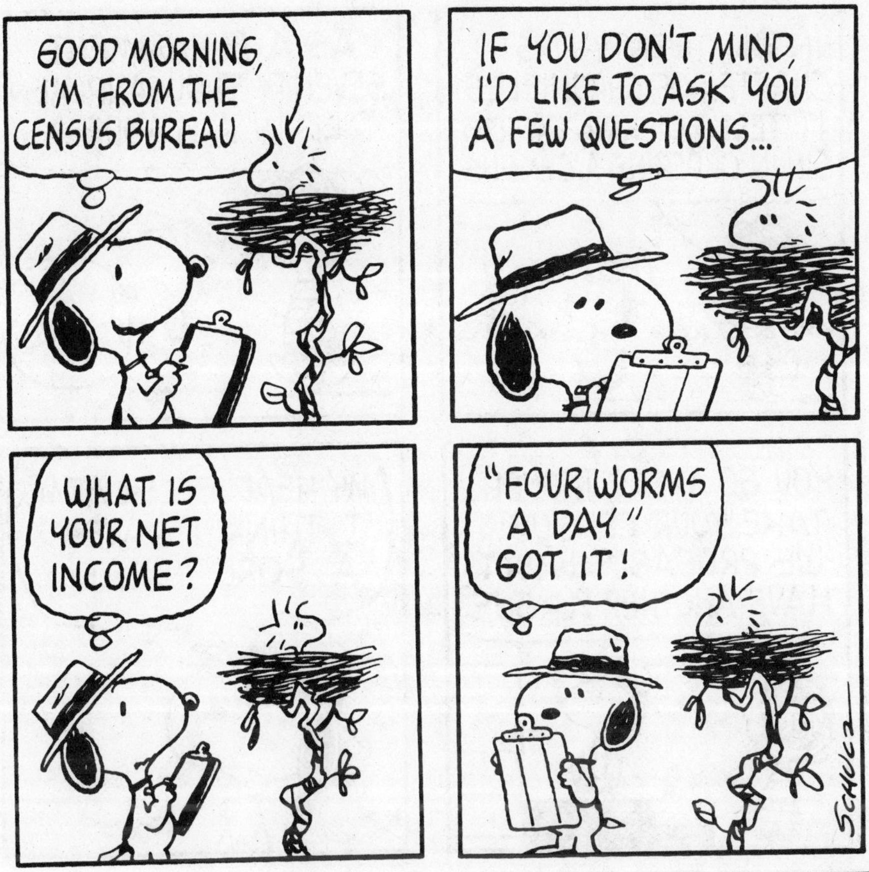
GOOD MORNING, I'M FROM THE CENSUS BUREAU
IF YOU DON'T MIND, I'D LIKE TO ASK YOU A FEW QUESTIONS...
WHAT IS YOUR NET INCOME?
"FOUR WORMS A DAY" GOT IT!
SCHULZ

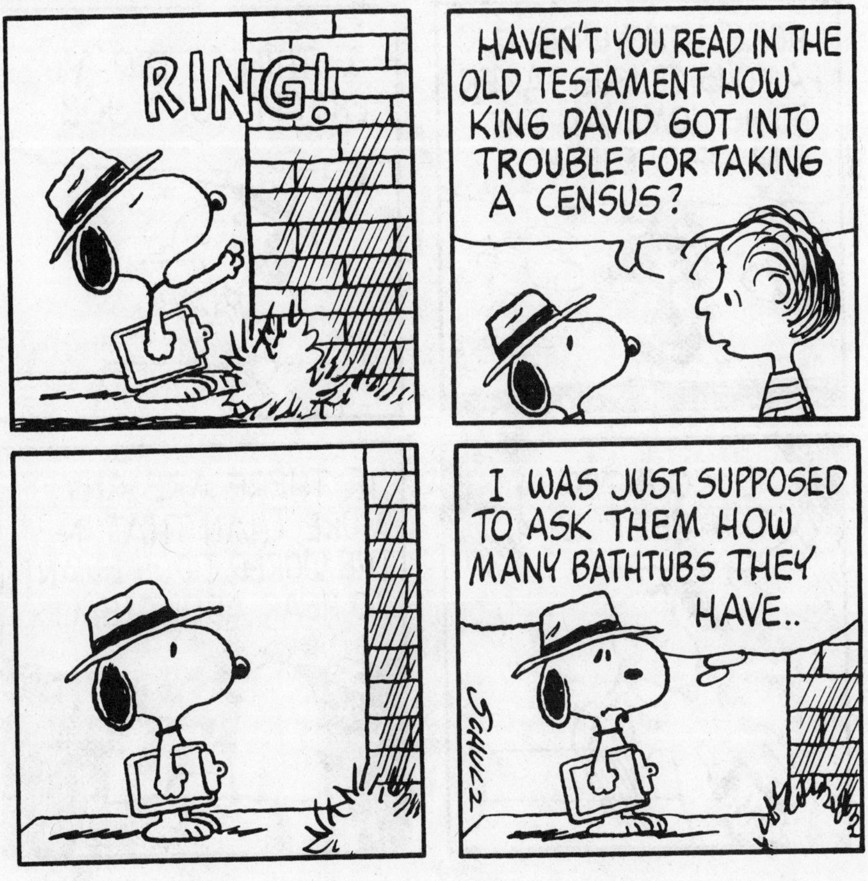
RING!
HAVEN'T YOU READ IN THE OLD TESTAMENT HOW KING DAVID GOT INTO TROUBLE FOR TAKING A CENSUS?
I WAS JUST SUPPOSED TO ASK THEM HOW MANY BATHTUBS THEY HAVE..
SCHULZ

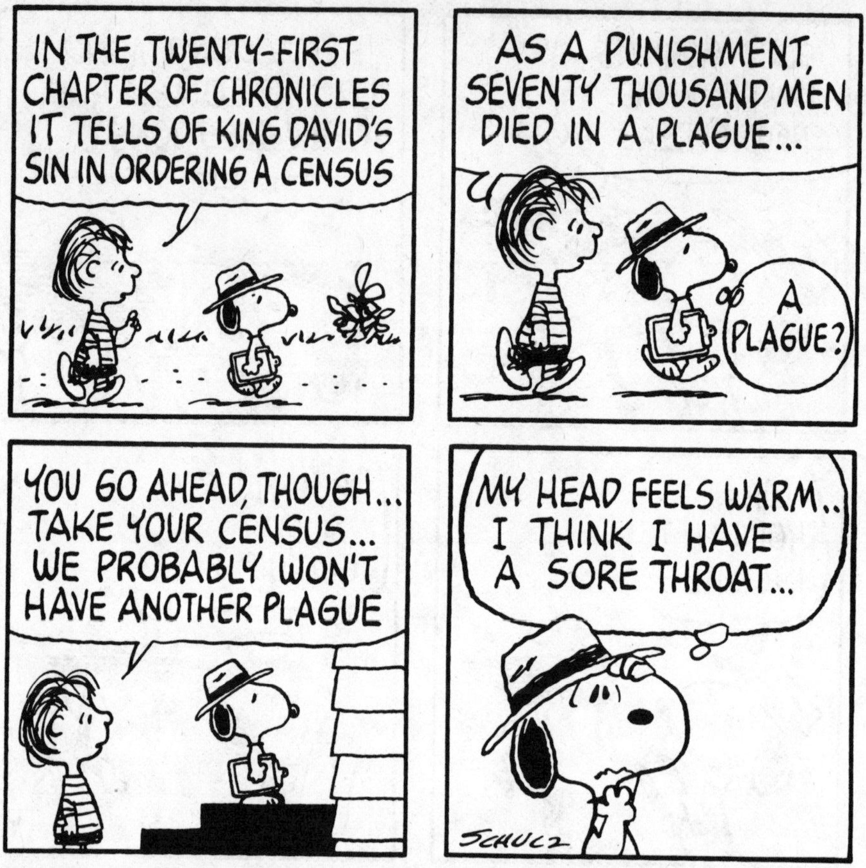
IN THE TWENTY-FIRST CHAPTER OF CHRONICLES IT TELLS OF KING DAVID'S SIN IN ORDERING A CENSUS
AS A PUNISHMENT, SEVENTY THOUSAND MEN DIED IN A PLAGUE...
A PLAGUE?
YOU GO AHEAD, THOUGH... TAKE YOUR CENSUS... WE PROBABLY WON'T HAVE ANOTHER PLAGUE
MY HEAD FEELS WARM.. I THINK I HAVE A SORE THROAT...
SCHULZ

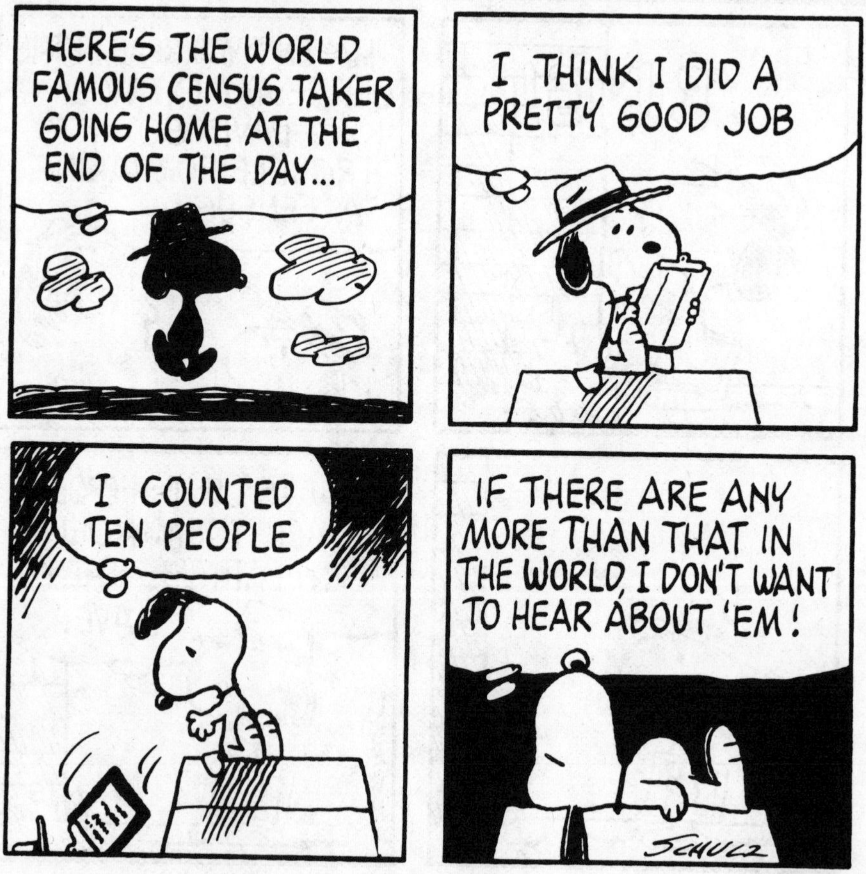
HERE'S THE WORLD FAMOUS CENSUS TAKER GOING HOME AT THE END OF THE DAY...
I THINK I DID A PRETTY GOOD JOB
I COUNTED TEN PEOPLE
IF THERE ARE ANY MORE THAN THAT IN THE WORLD, I DON'T WANT TO HEAR ABOUT 'EM!
SCHULZ

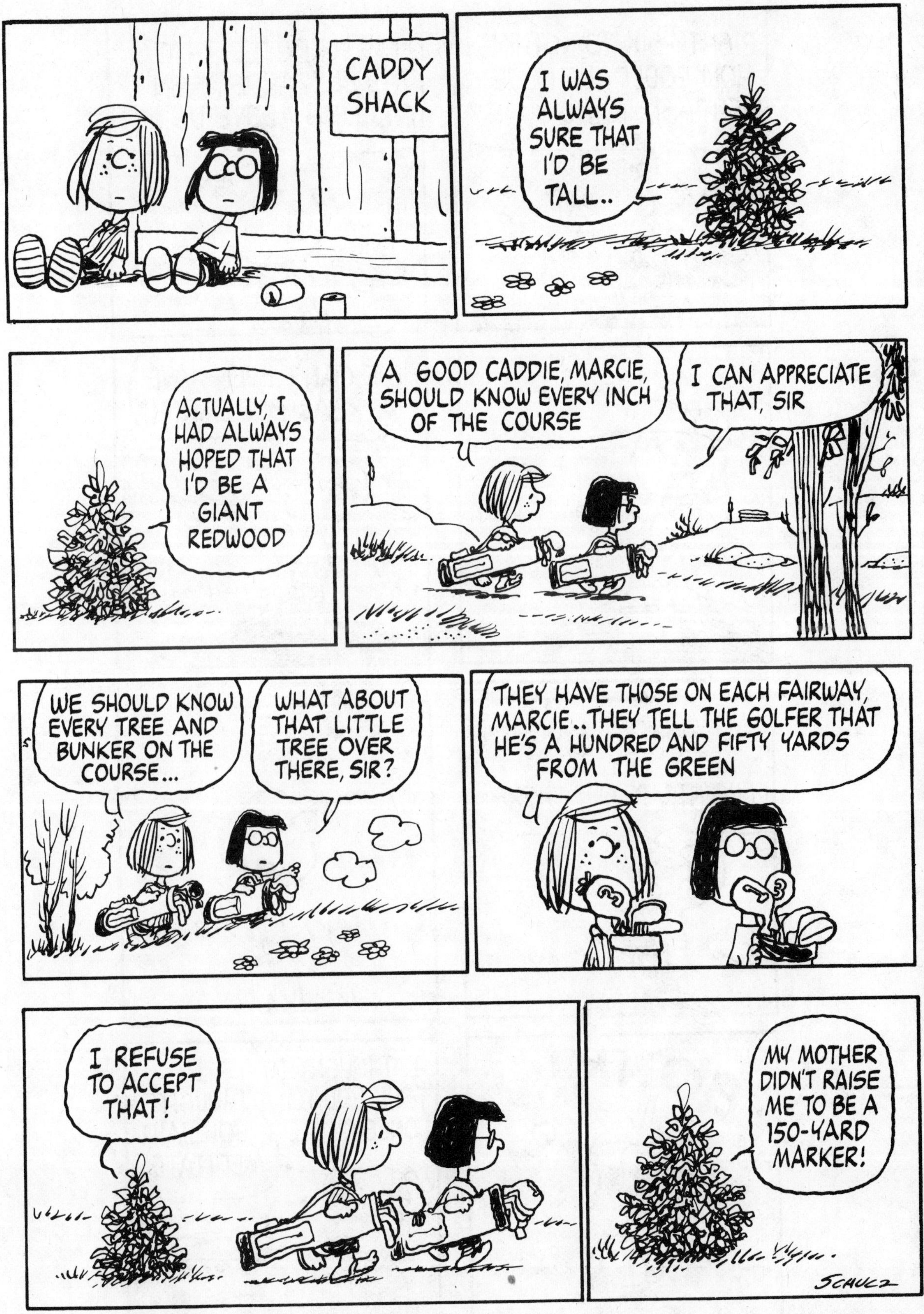
CADDY SHACK
I WAS ALWAYS SURE THAT I'D BE TALL..
ACTUALLY, I HAD ALWAYS HOPED THAT I'D BE A GIANT REDWOOD
A GOOD CADDIE, MARCIE, SHOULD KNOW EVERY INCH OF THE COURSE
I CAN APPRECIATE THAT, SIR
WE SHOULD KNOW EVERY TREE AND BUNKER ON THE COURSE...
WHAT ABOUT THAT LITTLE TREE OVER THERE, SIR?
THEY HAVE THOSE ON EACH FAIRWAY, MARCIE..THEY TELL THE GOLFER THAT HE'S A HUNDRED AND FIFTY YARDS FROM THE GREEN
I REFUSE TO ACCEPT THAT!
MY MOTHER DIDN'T RAISE ME TO BE A 150-YARD MARKER!
SCHULZ

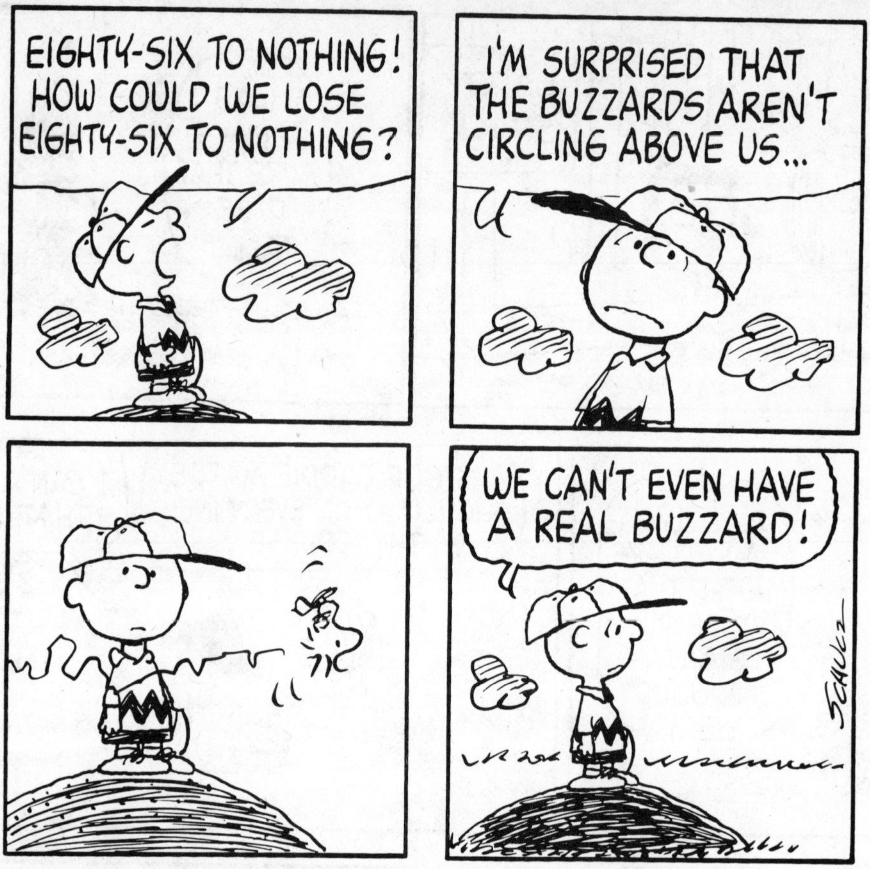
EIGHTY-SIX TO NOTHING! HOW COULD WE LOSE EIGHTY-SIX TO NOTHING?
I'M SURPRISED THAT THE BUZZARDS AREN'T CIRCLING ABOVE US...
WE CAN'T EVEN HAVE A REAL BUZZARD!
SCHULZ

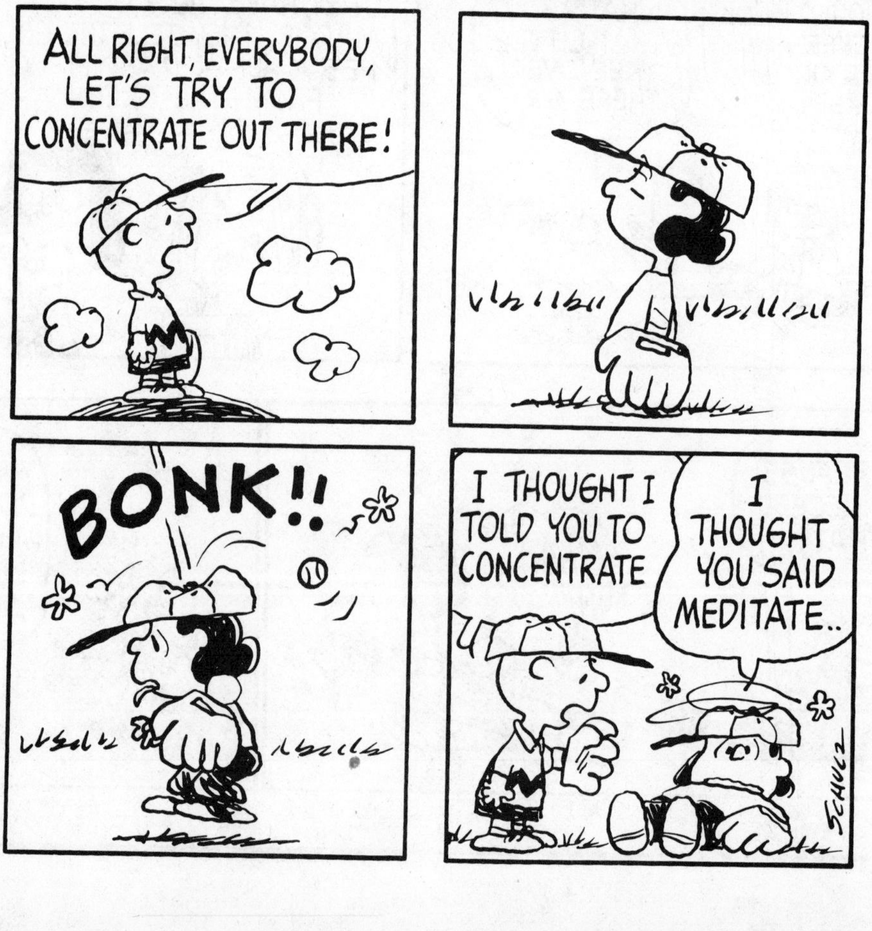
ALL RIGHT, EVERYBODY, LET'S TRY TO CONCENTRATE OUT THERE!
BONK!!
I THOUGHT I TOLD YOU TO CONCENTRATE
I THOUGHT YOU SAID MEDITATE..
SCHULZ

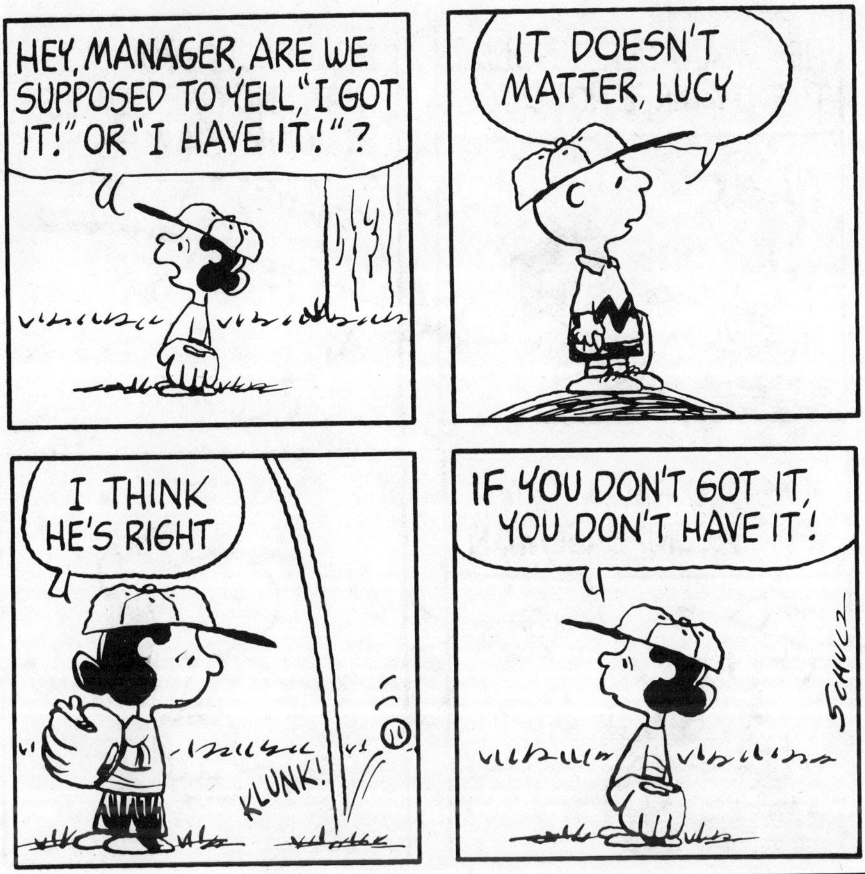
HEY, MANAGER, ARE WE SUPPOSED TO YELL, "I GOT IT!" OR "I HAVE IT!"?
IT DOESN'T MATTER, LUCY
I THINK HE'S RIGHT
KLUNK!
IF YOU DON'T GOT IT, YOU DON'T HAVE IT!
SCHULZ

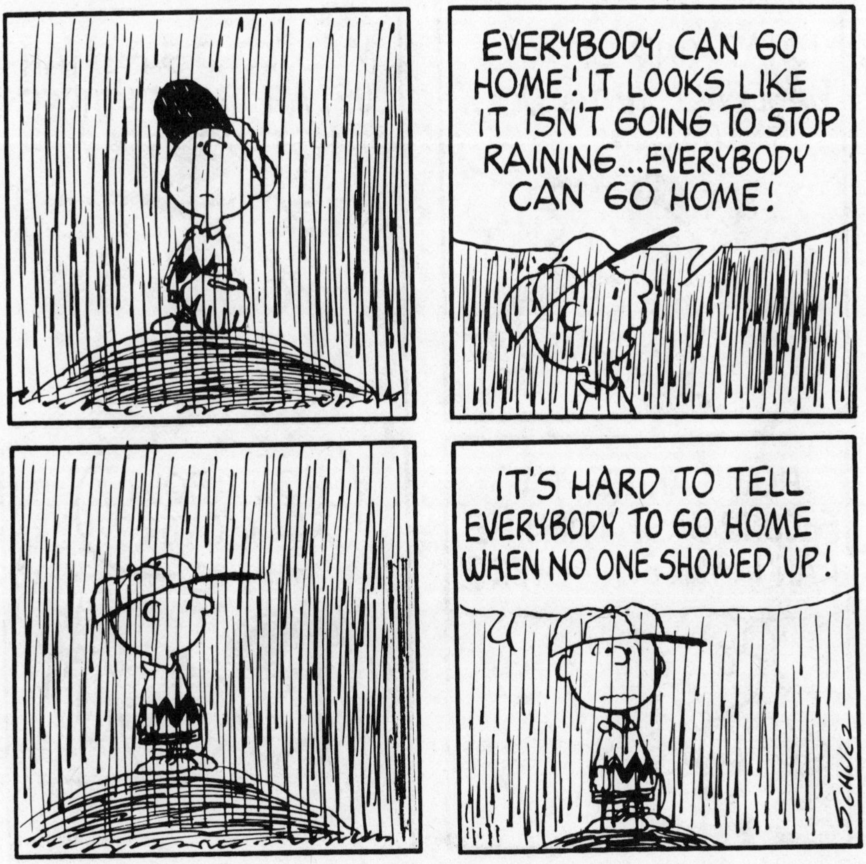
EVERYBODY CAN GO HOME! IT LOOKS LIKE IT ISN'T GOING TO STOP RAINING...EVERYBODY CAN GO HOME!
IT'S HARD TO TELL EVERYBODY TO GO HOME WHEN NO ONE SHOWED UP!
SCHULZ

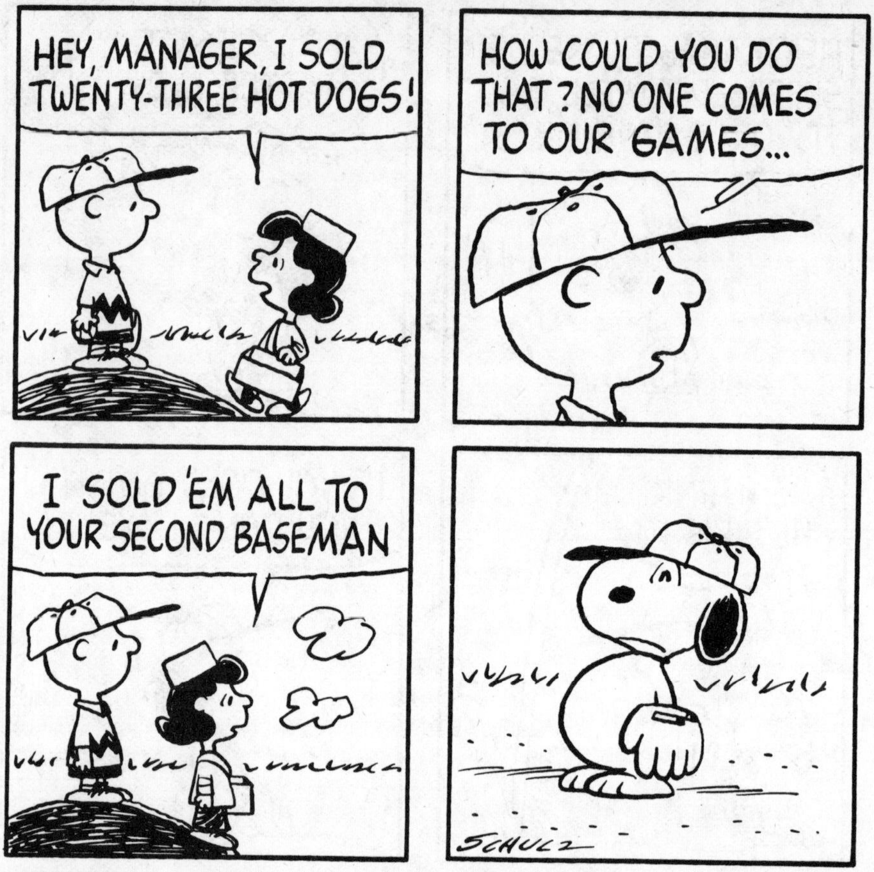
HEY, MANAGER, I SOLD TWENTY-THREE HOT DOGS!
HOW COULD YOU DO THAT? NO ONE COMES TO OUR GAMES...
I SOLD 'EM ALL TO YOUR SECOND BASEMAN
SCHULZ

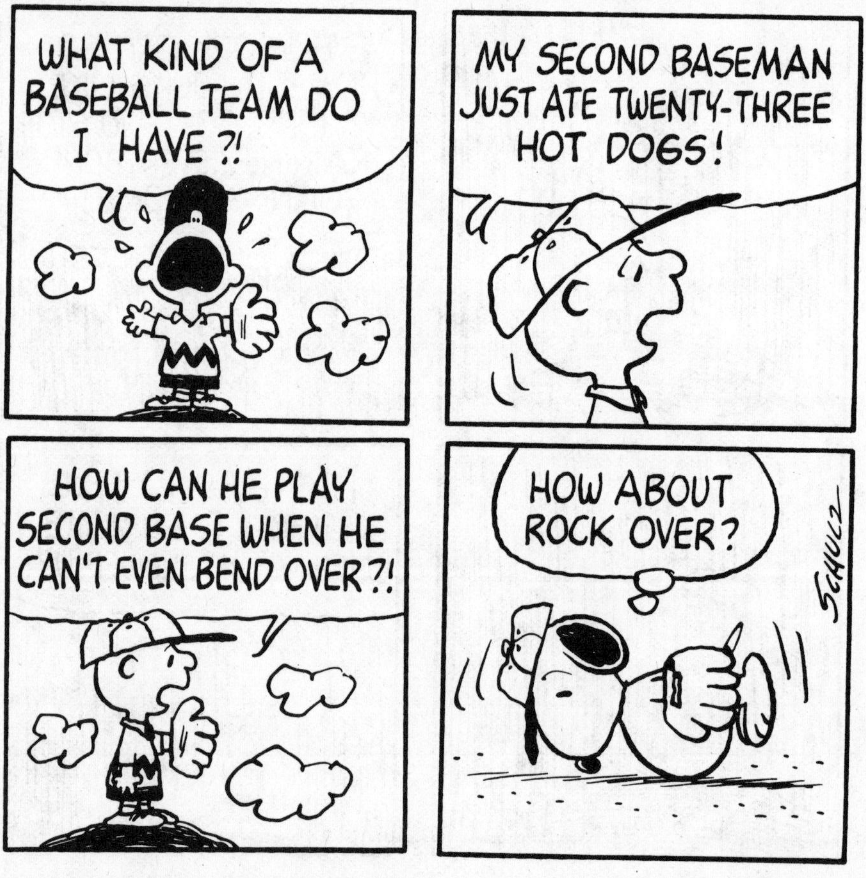
WHAT KIND OF A BASEBALL TEAM DO I HAVE ?!
MY SECOND BASEMAN JUST ATE TWENTY-THREE HOT DOGS!
HOW CAN HE PLAY SECOND BASE WHEN HE CAN'T EVEN BEND OVER ?!
HOW ABOUT ROCK OVER?
SCHULZ

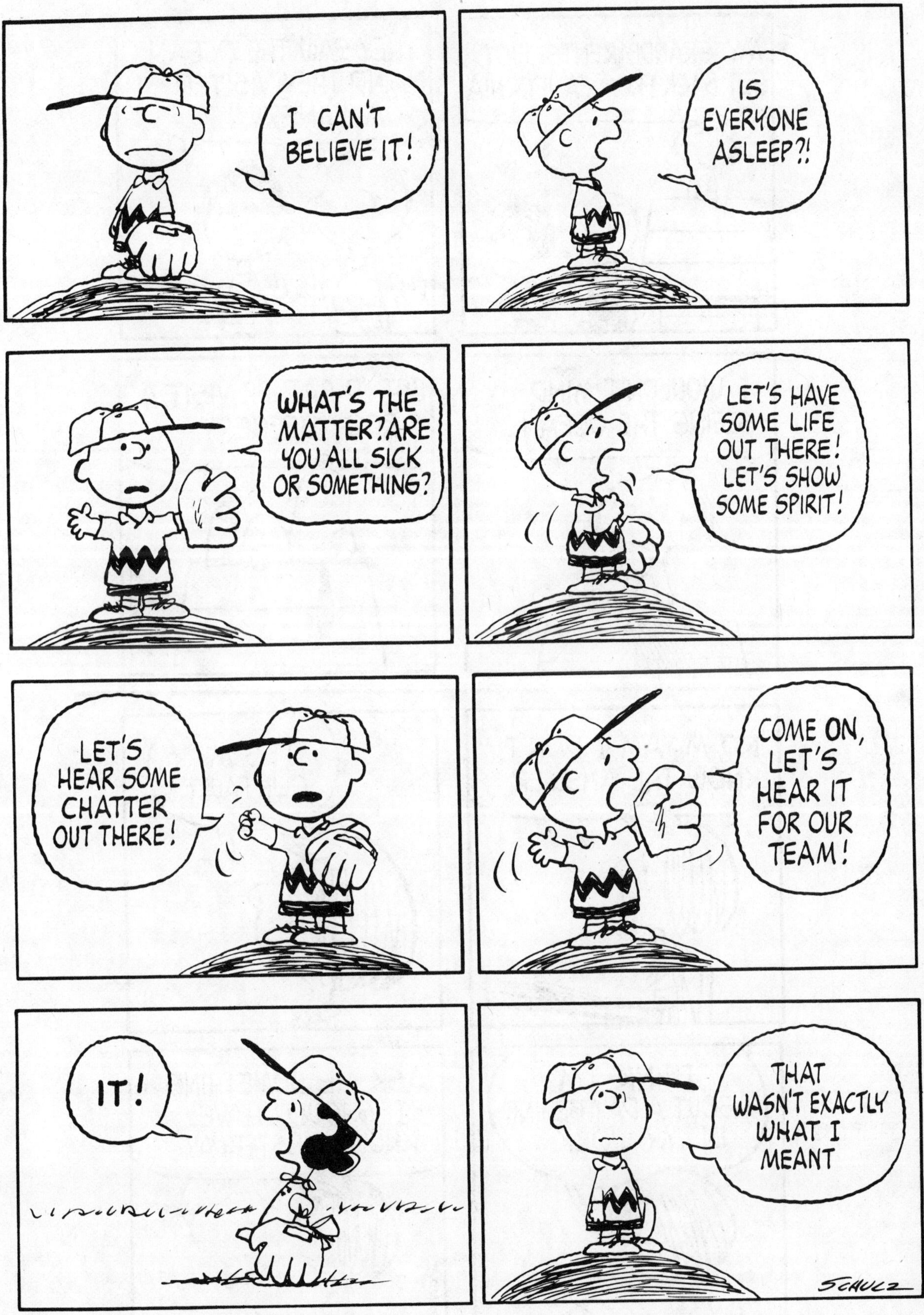
I CAN'T BELIEVE IT!
IS EVERYONE ASLEEP?!
WHAT'S THE MATTER? ARE YOU ALL SICK OR SOMETHING?
LET'S HAVE SOME LIFE OUT THERE! LET'S SHOW SOME SPIRIT!
LET'S HEAR SOME CHATTER OUT THERE!
COME ON, LET'S HEAR IT FOR OUR TEAM!
IT!
THAT WASN'T EXACTLY WHAT I MEANT
SCHULZ

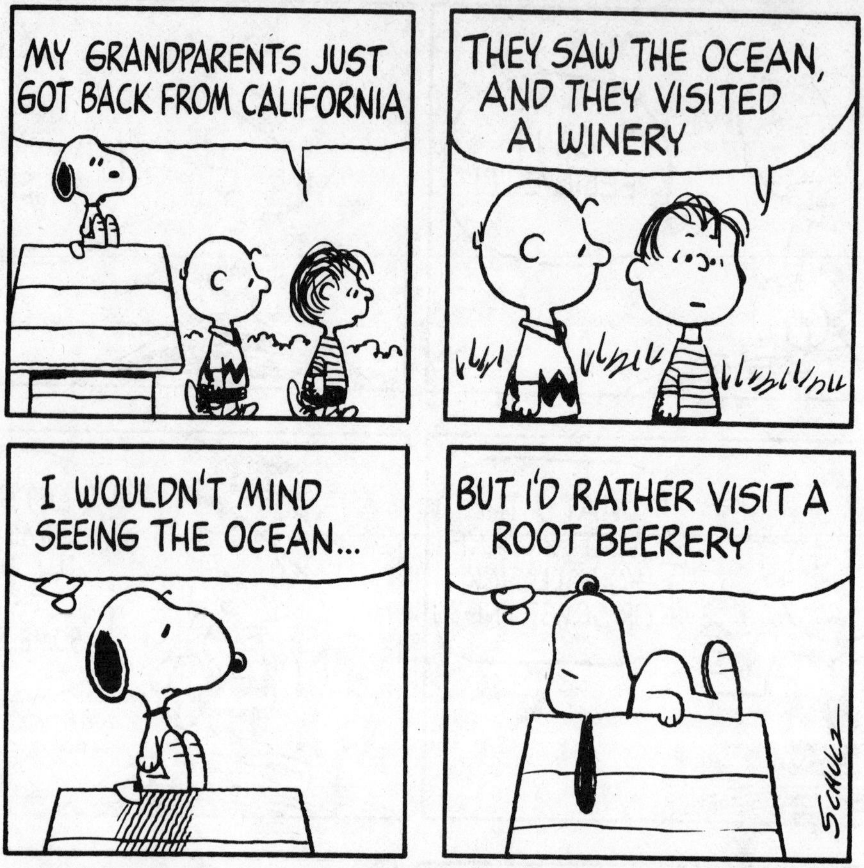
MY GRANDPARENTS JUST GOT BACK FROM CALIFORNIA
THEY SAW THE OCEAN, AND THEY VISITED A WINERY
I WOULDN'T MIND SEEING THE OCEAN...
BUT I'D RATHER VISIT A ROOT BEERERY
SCHULZ

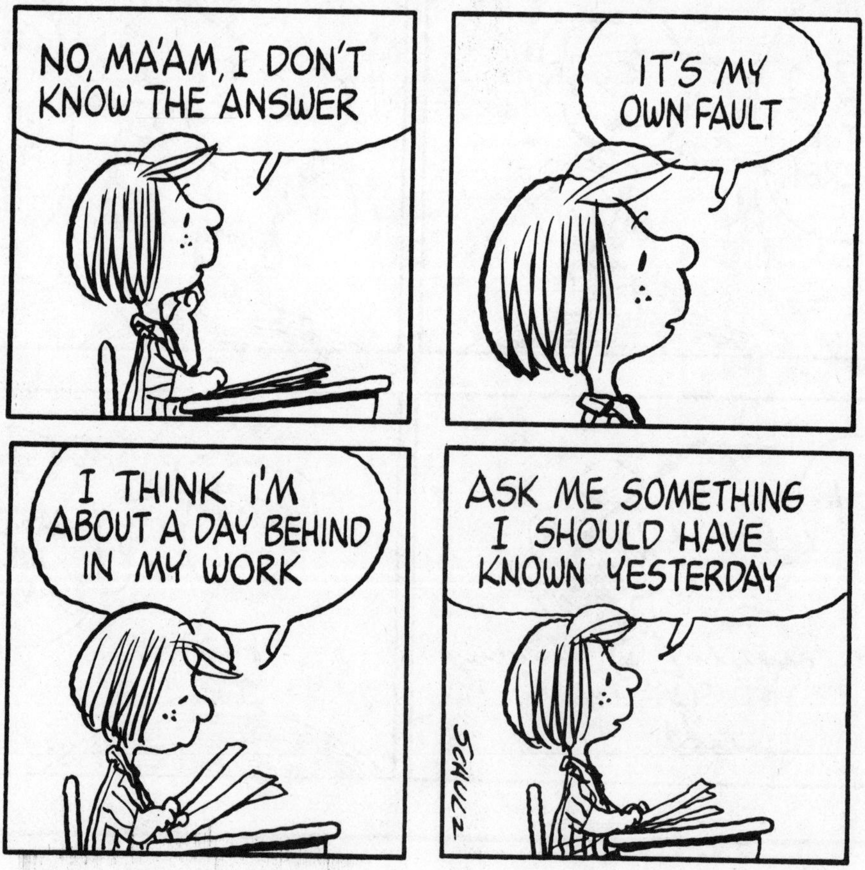
NO, MA'AM, I DON'T KNOW THE ANSWER
IT'S MY OWN FAULT
I THINK I'M ABOUT A DAY BEHIND IN MY WORK
ASK ME SOMETHING I SHOULD HAVE KNOWN YESTERDAY
SCHULZ

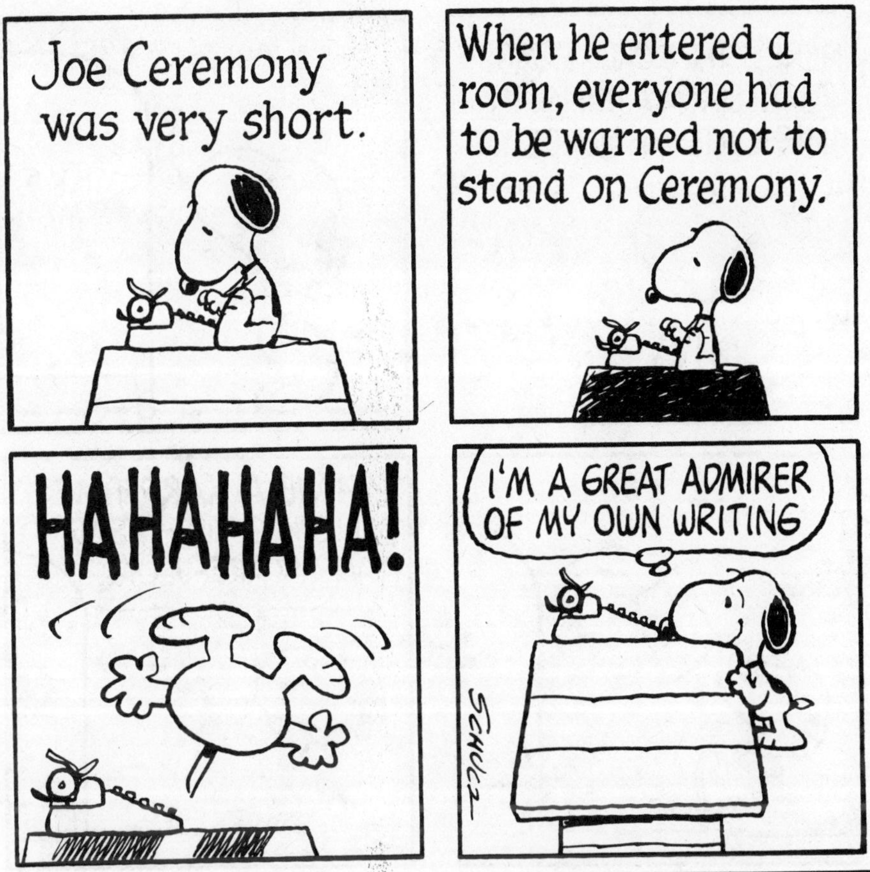
Joe Ceremony was very short.
When he entered a room, everyone had to be warned not to stand on Ceremony.
HAHAHAHA!
I'M A GREAT ADMIRER OF MY OWN WRITING
SCHULZ

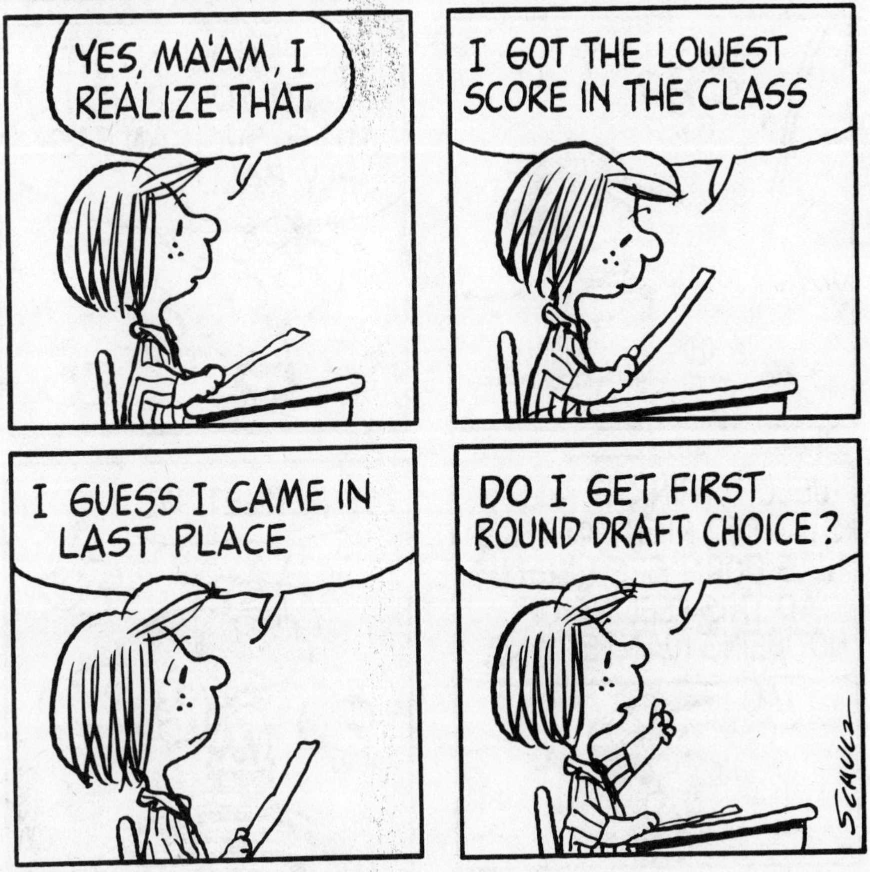
YES, MA'AM, I REALIZE THAT
I GOT THE LOWEST SCORE IN THE CLASS
I GUESS I CAME IN LAST PLACE
DO I GET FIRST ROUND DRAFT CHOICE?
SCHULZ

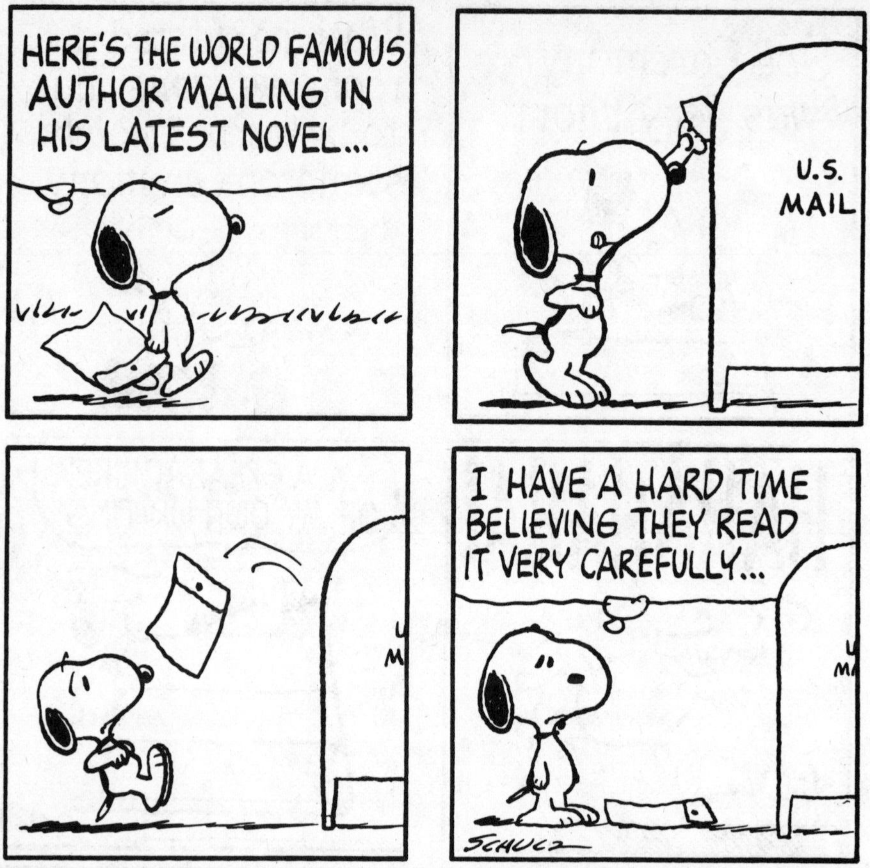
HERE'S THE WORLD FAMOUS AUTHOR MAILING IN HIS LATEST NOVEL...
U.S. MAIL
I HAVE A HARD TIME BELIEVING THEY READ IT VERY CAREFULLY...
SCHULZ

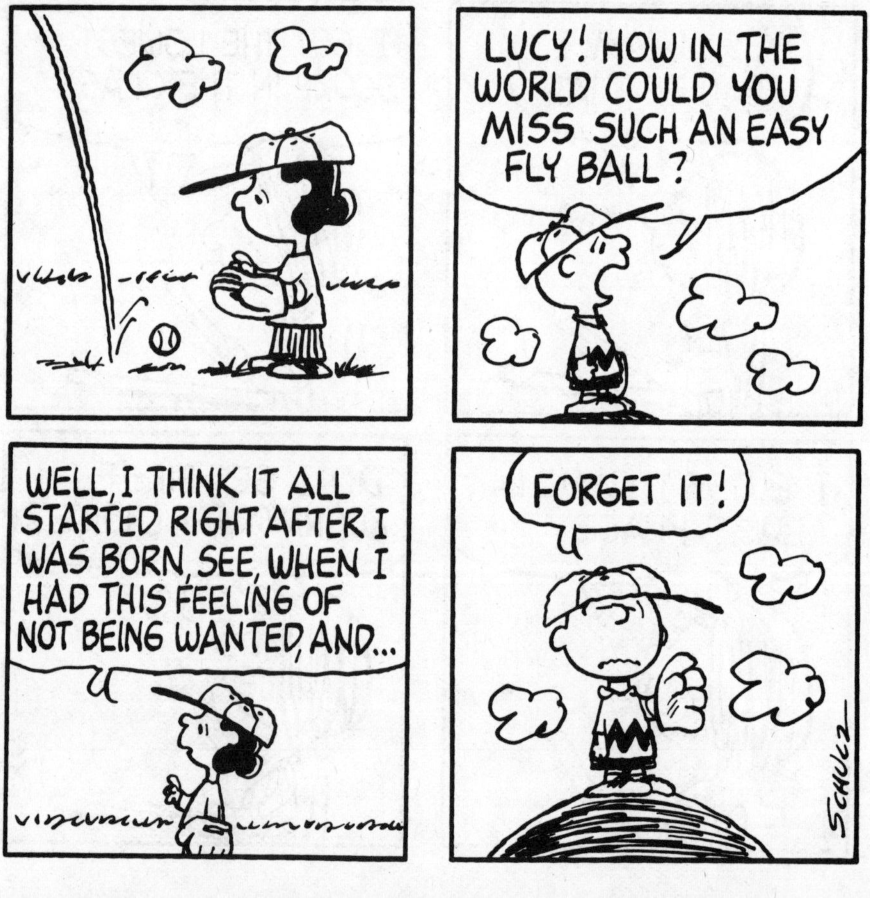
LUCY! HOW IN THE WORLD COULD YOU MISS SUCH AN EASY FLY BALL?
WELL, I THINK IT ALL STARTED RIGHT AFTER I WAS BORN, SEE, WHEN I HAD THIS FEELING OF NOT BEING WANTED, AND...
FORGET IT!
SCHULZ

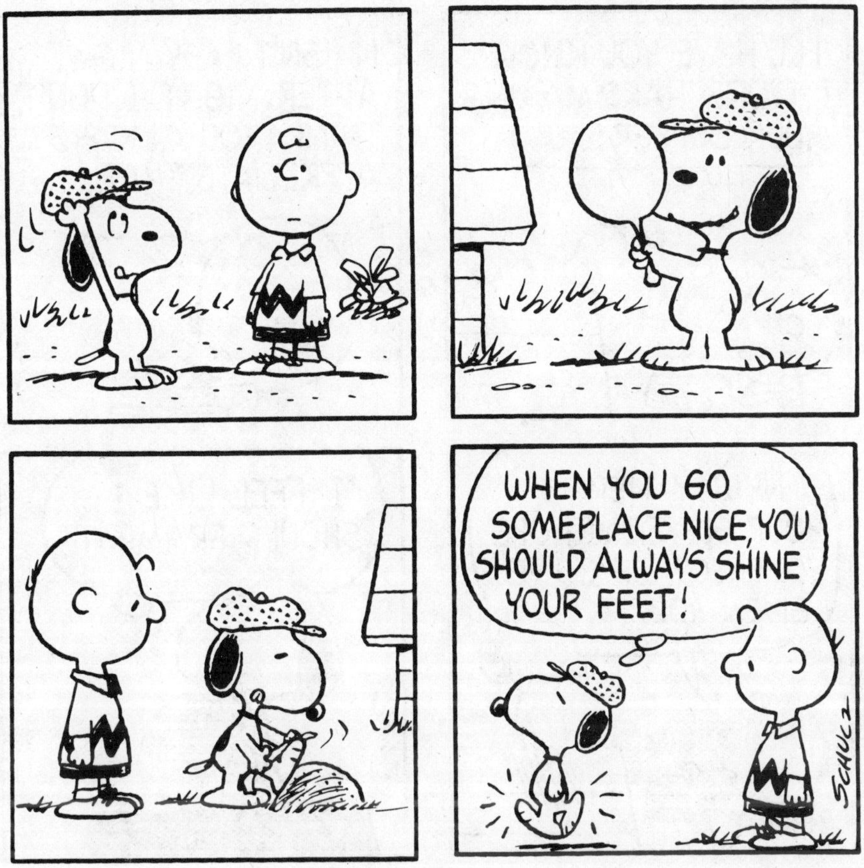
WHEN YOU GO SOMEPLACE NICE, YOU SHOULD ALWAYS SHINE YOUR FEET!
SCHULZ

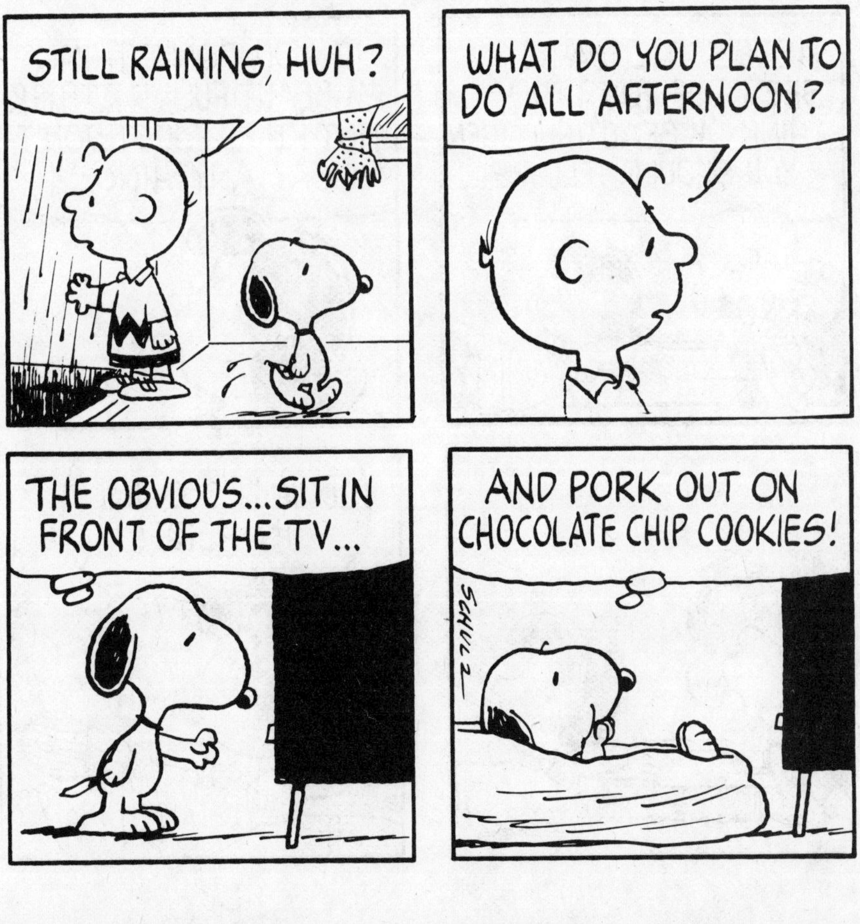
STILL RAINING, HUH?
WHAT DO YOU PLAN TO DO ALL AFTERNOON?
THE OBVIOUS...SIT IN FRONT OF THE TV...
AND PORK OUT ON CHOCOLATE CHIP COOKIES!
SCHULZ

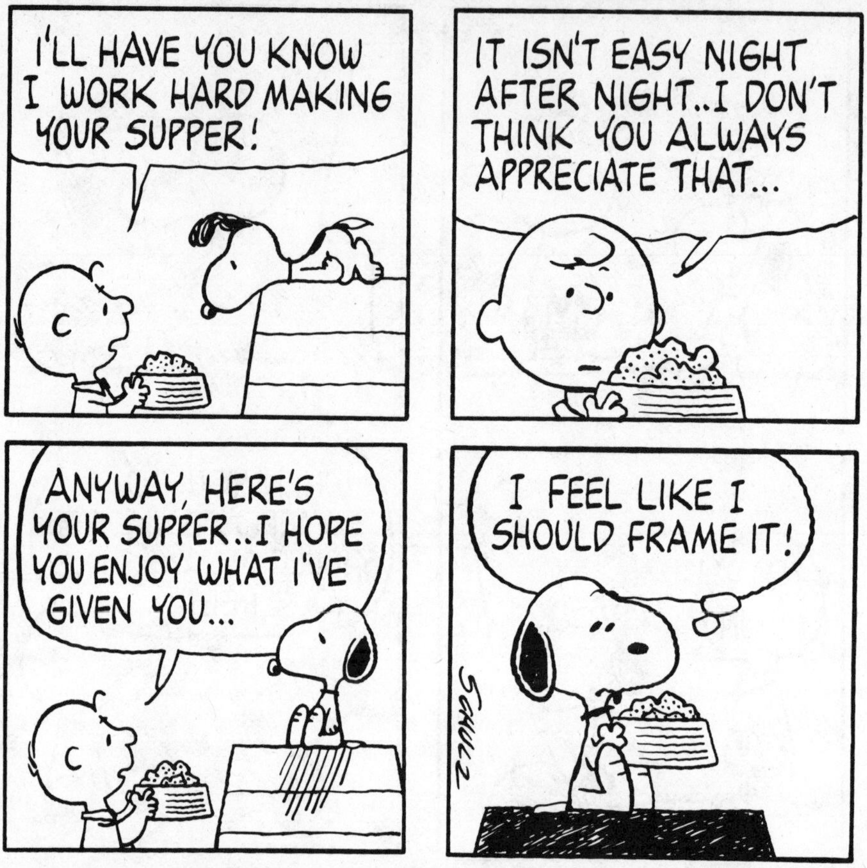
I'LL HAVE YOU KNOW I WORK HARD MAKING YOUR SUPPER!
IT ISN'T EASY NIGHT AFTER NIGHT..I DON'T THINK YOU ALWAYS APPRECIATE THAT...
ANYWAY, HERE'S YOUR SUPPER..I HOPE YOU ENJOY WHAT I'VE GIVEN YOU...
I FEEL LIKE I SHOULD FRAME IT!
SCHULZ

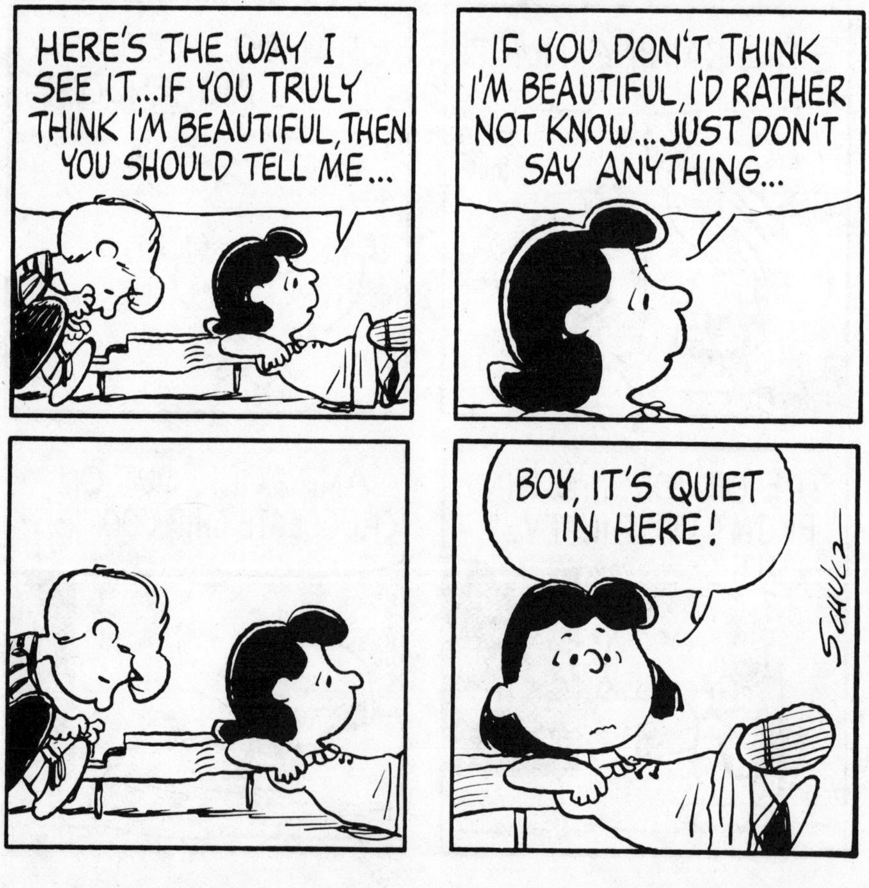
HERE'S THE WAY I SEE IT...IF YOU TRULY THINK I'M BEAUTIFUL, THEN YOU SHOULD TELL ME...
IF YOU DON'T THINK I'M BEAUTIFUL, I'D RATHER NOT KNOW...JUST DON'T SAY ANYTHING...
BOY, IT'S QUIET IN HERE!
SCHULZ

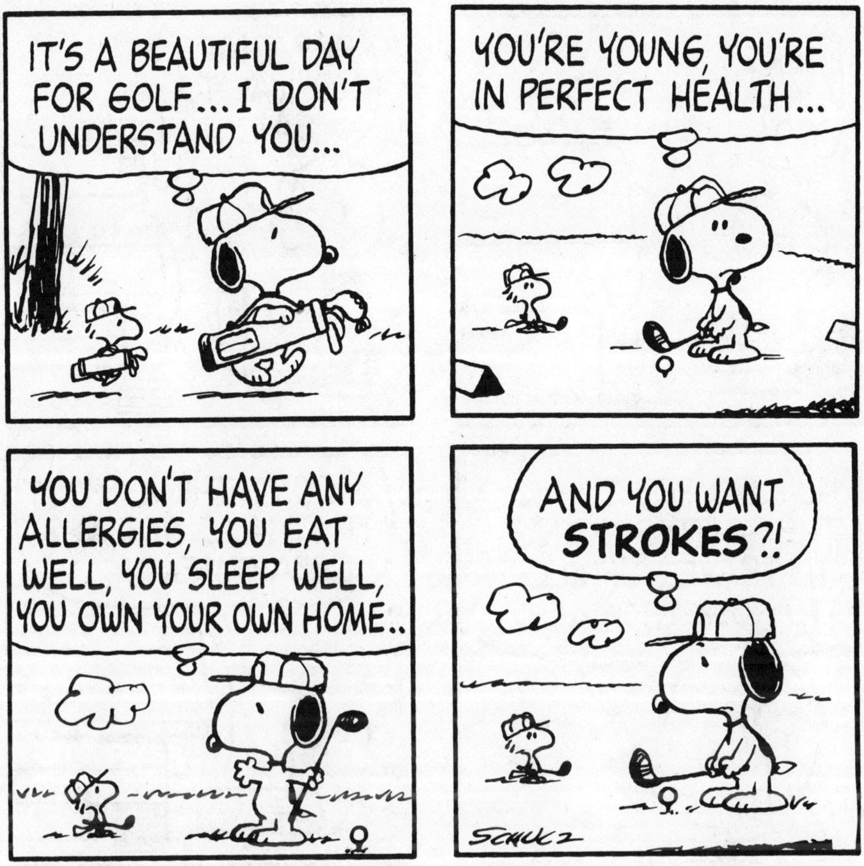
IT'S A BEAUTIFUL DAY FOR GOLF... I DON'T UNDERSTAND YOU...
YOU'RE YOUNG, YOU'RE IN PERFECT HEALTH...
YOU DON'T HAVE ANY ALLERGIES, YOU EAT WELL, YOU SLEEP WELL, YOU OWN YOUR OWN HOME..
AND YOU WANT **STROKES**?!

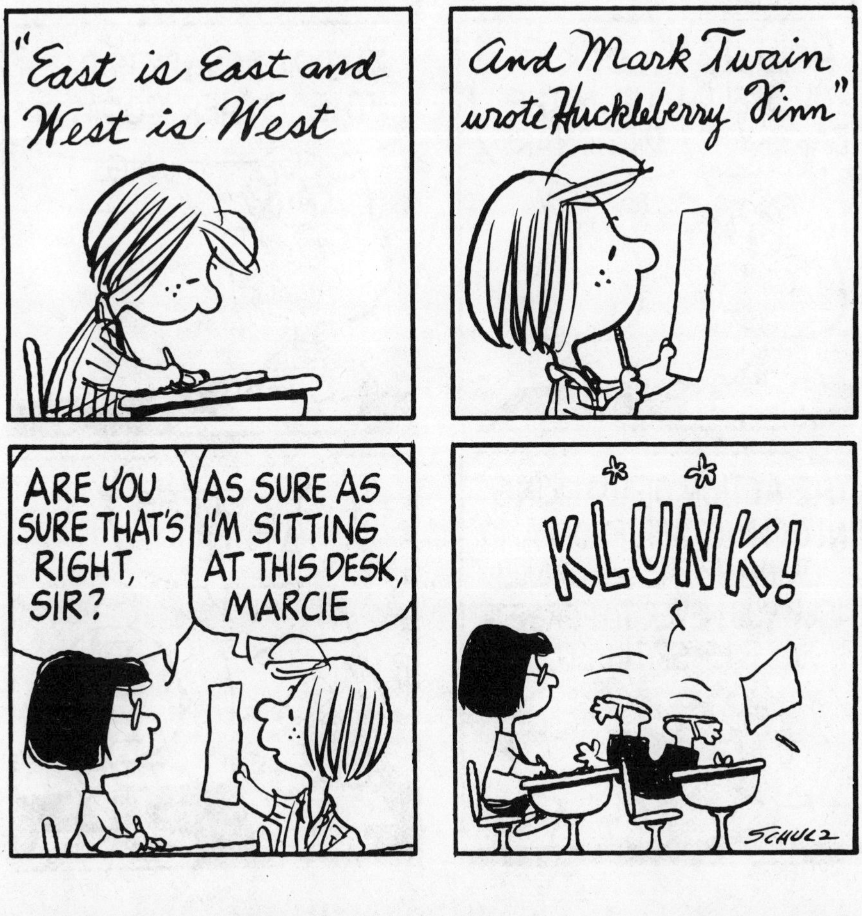
"East is East and West is West
And Mark Twain wrote Huckleberry Finn"
ARE YOU SURE THAT'S RIGHT, SIR?
AS SURE AS I'M SITTING AT THIS DESK, MARCIE
KLUNK!

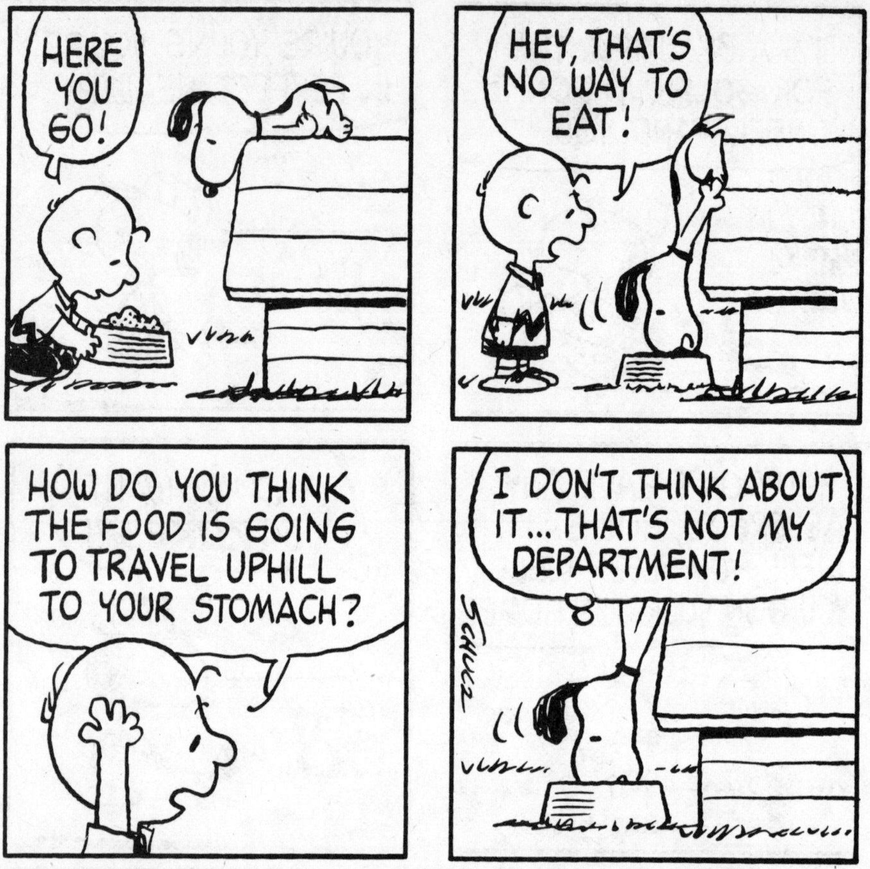
HERE YOU GO!
HEY, THAT'S NO WAY TO EAT!
HOW DO YOU THINK THE FOOD IS GOING TO TRAVEL UPHILL TO YOUR STOMACH?
I DON'T THINK ABOUT IT... THAT'S NOT MY DEPARTMENT!
SCHULZ

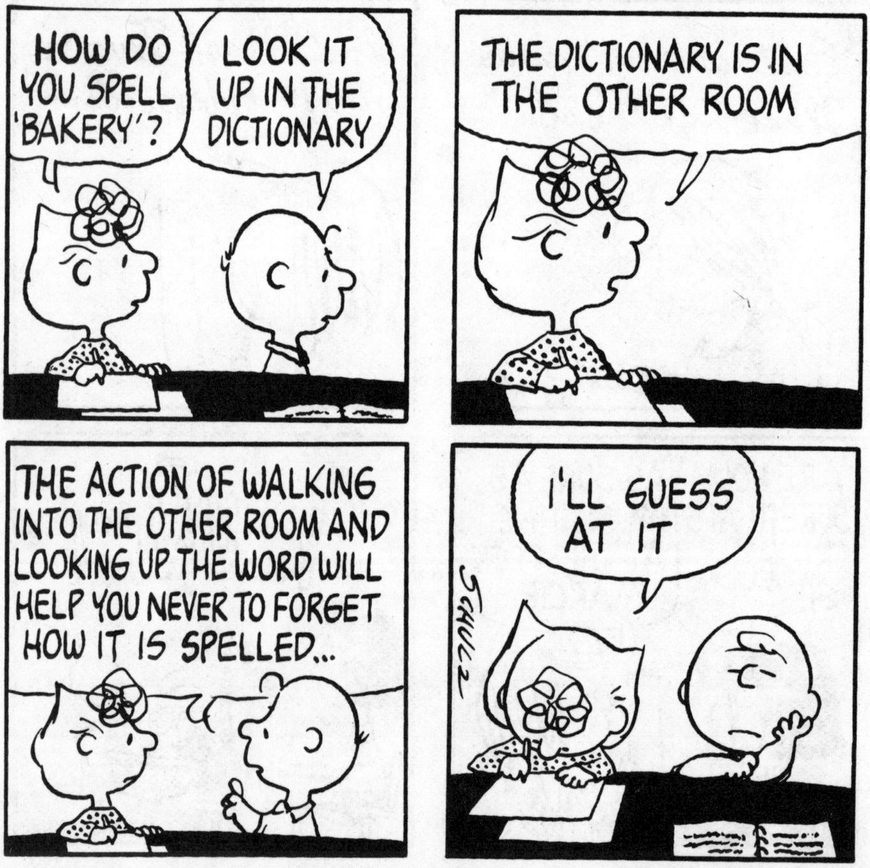
HOW DO YOU SPELL 'BAKERY'?
LOOK IT UP IN THE DICTIONARY
THE DICTIONARY IS IN THE OTHER ROOM
THE ACTION OF WALKING INTO THE OTHER ROOM AND LOOKING UP THE WORD WILL HELP YOU NEVER TO FORGET HOW IT IS SPELLED...
I'LL GUESS AT IT
SCHULZ

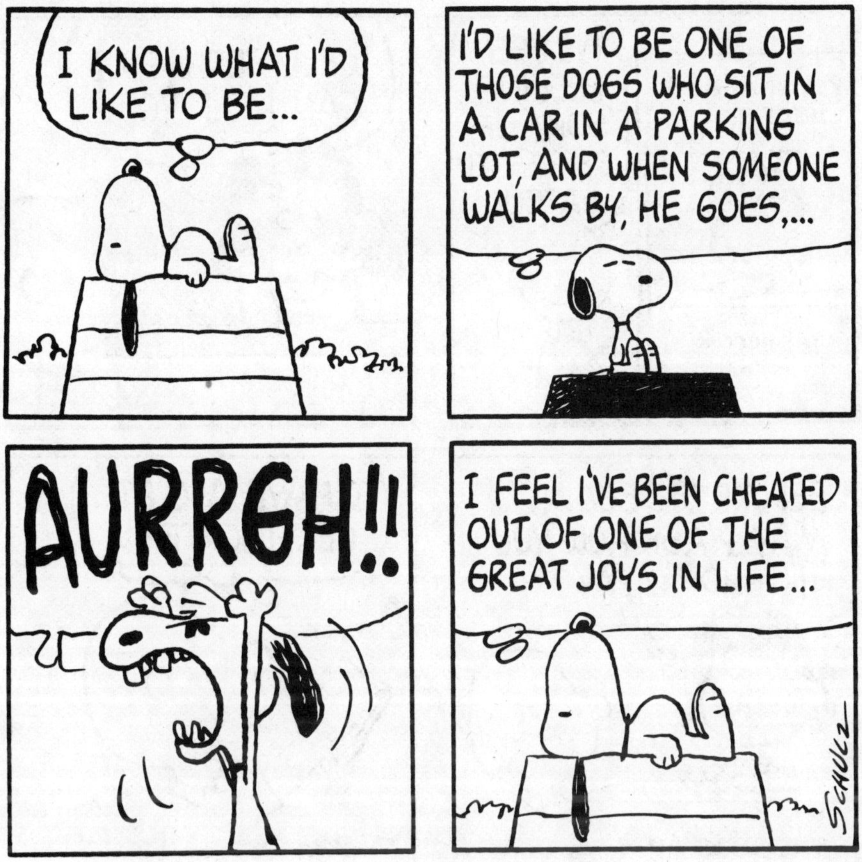
I KNOW WHAT I'D LIKE TO BE...
I'D LIKE TO BE ONE OF THOSE DOGS WHO SIT IN A CAR IN A PARKING LOT, AND WHEN SOMEONE WALKS BY, HE GOES,...
AURRGH!!
I FEEL I'VE BEEN CHEATED OUT OF ONE OF THE GREAT JOYS IN LIFE...
SCHULZ

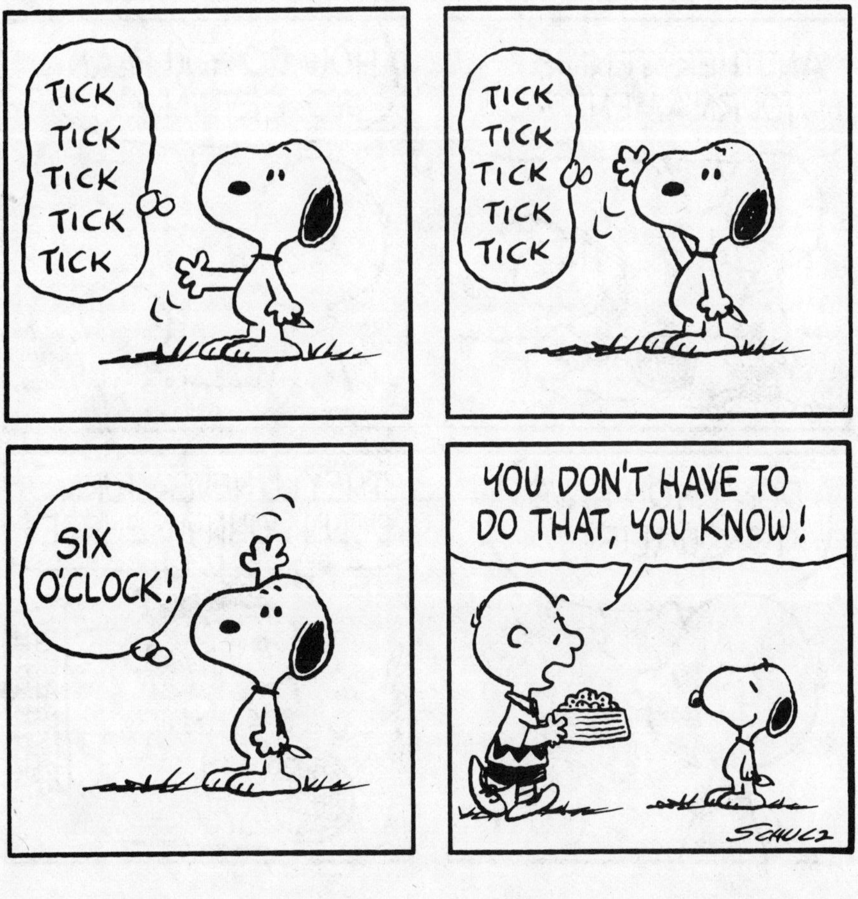
TICK TICK TICK TICK TICK
TICK TICK TICK TICK TICK
SIX O'CLOCK!
YOU DON'T HAVE TO DO THAT, YOU KNOW!
SCHULZ

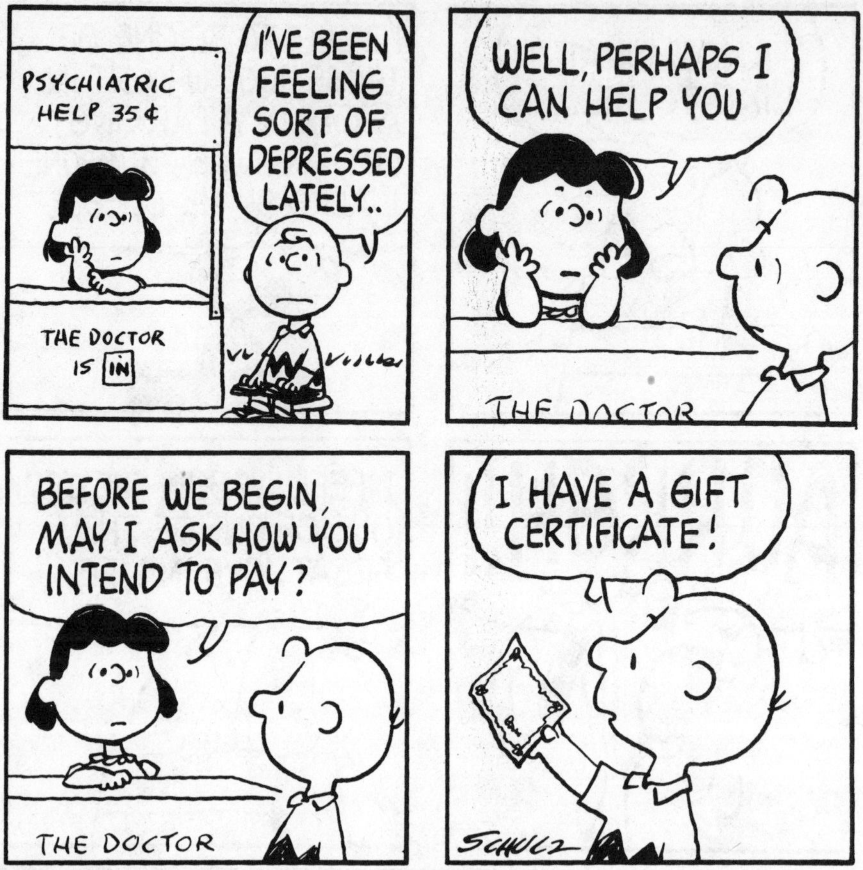
PSYCHIATRIC HELP 35¢
THE DOCTOR IS IN
I'VE BEEN FEELING SORT OF DEPRESSED LATELY..
WELL, PERHAPS I CAN HELP YOU
THE DOCTOR
BEFORE WE BEGIN, MAY I ASK HOW YOU INTEND TO PAY?
THE DOCTOR
I HAVE A GIFT CERTIFICATE!
SCHULZ

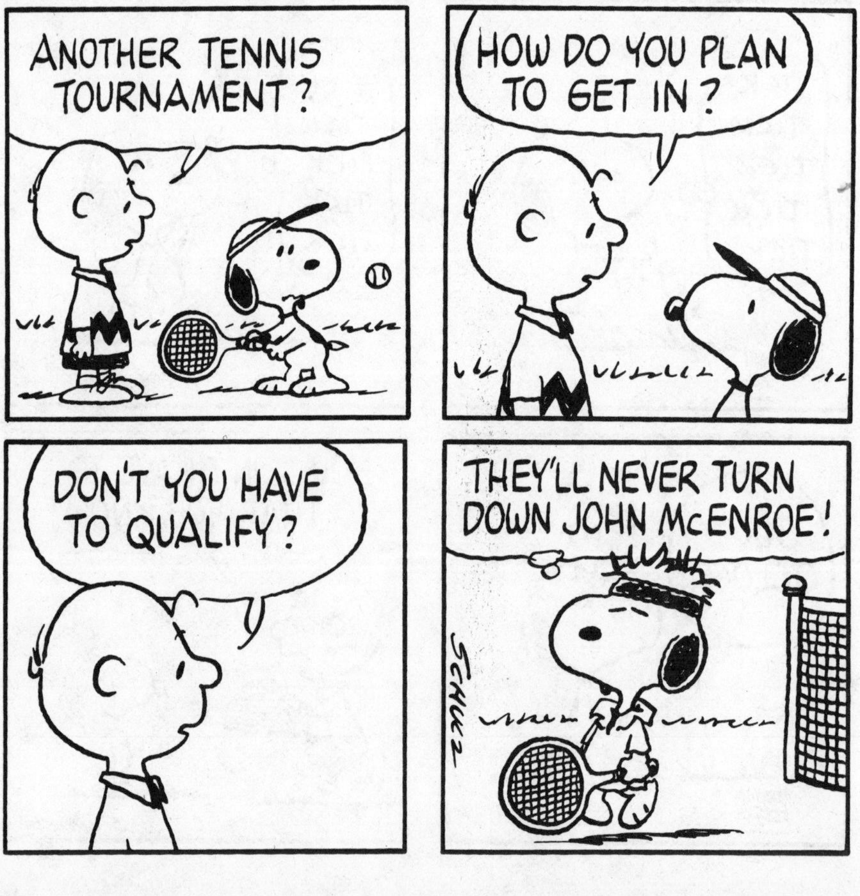
ANOTHER TENNIS TOURNAMENT?
HOW DO YOU PLAN TO GET IN?
DON'T YOU HAVE TO QUALIFY?
THEY'LL NEVER TURN DOWN JOHN McENROE!
SCHULZ

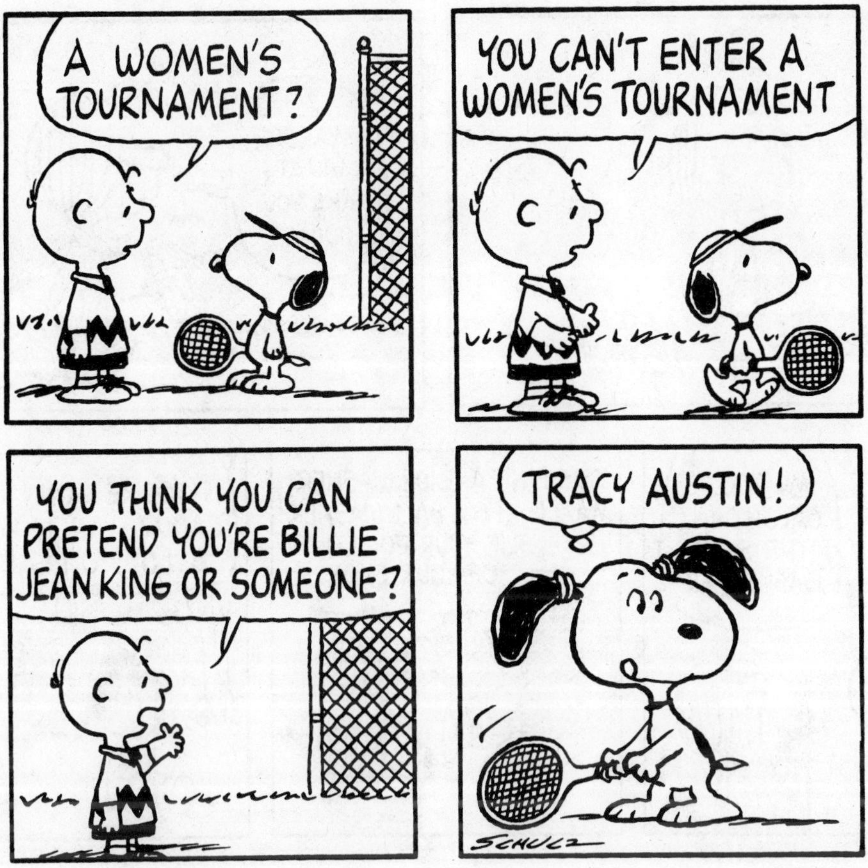
A WOMEN'S TOURNAMENT?
YOU CAN'T ENTER A WOMEN'S TOURNAMENT
YOU THINK YOU CAN PRETEND YOU'RE BILLIE JEAN KING OR SOMEONE?
TRACY AUSTIN!
SCHULZ

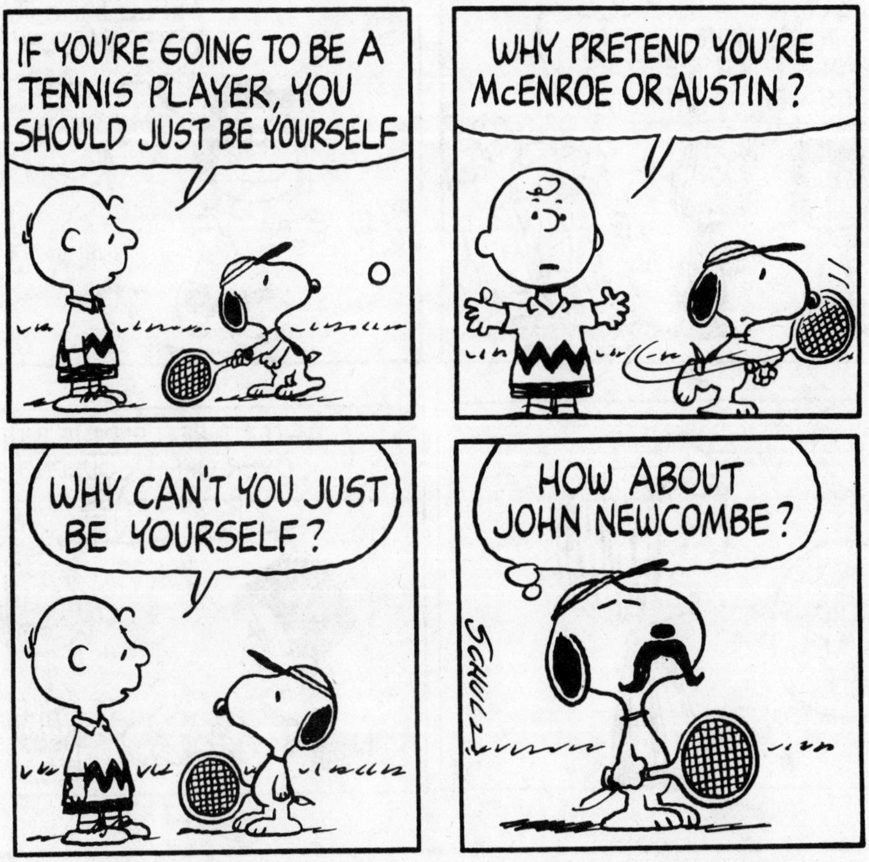
IF YOU'RE GOING TO BE A TENNIS PLAYER, YOU SHOULD JUST BE YOURSELF
WHY PRETEND YOU'RE McENROE OR AUSTIN?
WHY CAN'T YOU JUST BE YOURSELF?
HOW ABOUT JOHN NEWCOMBE?
SCHULZ

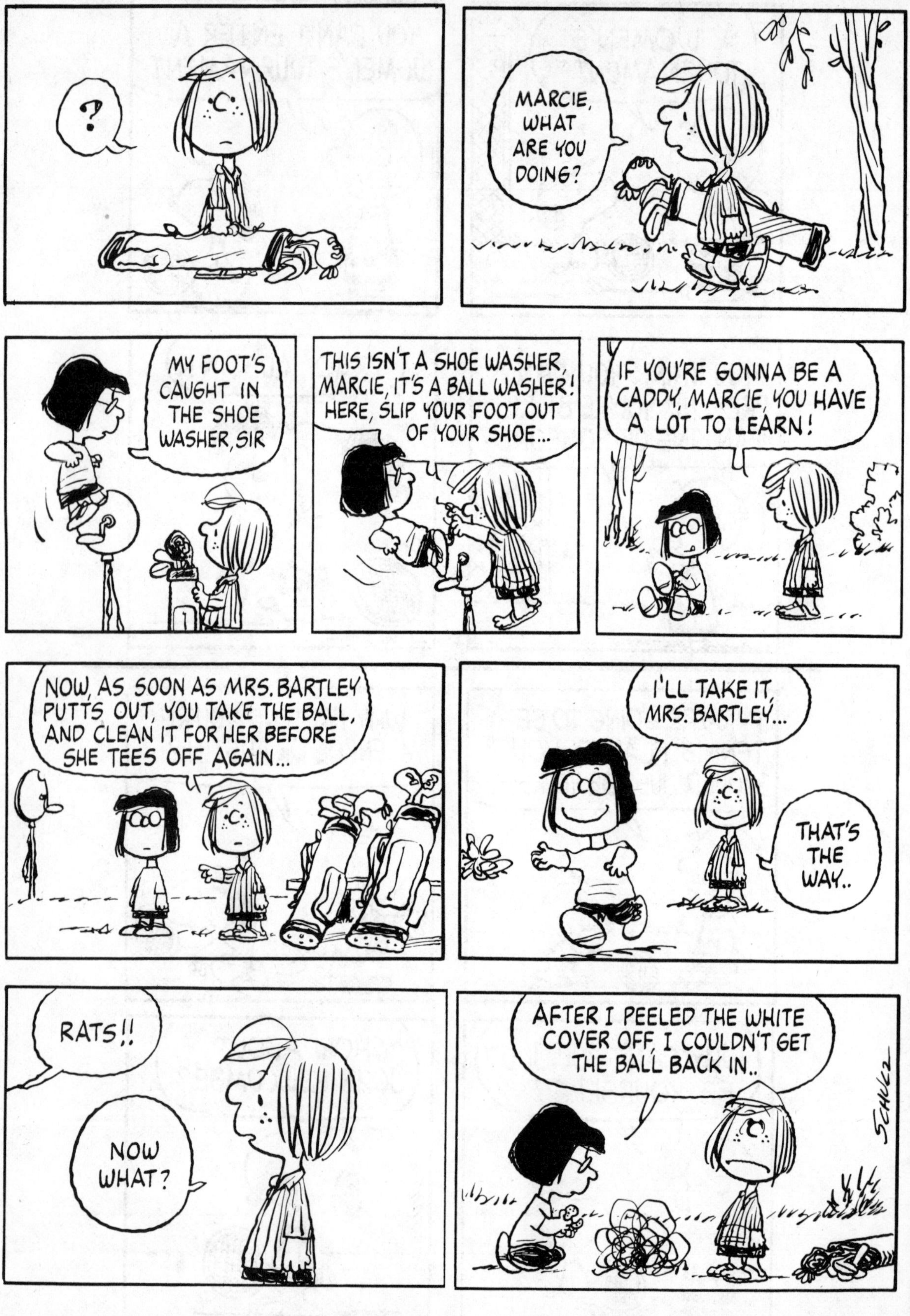
?
MARCIE, WHAT ARE YOU DOING?
MY FOOT'S CAUGHT IN THE SHOE WASHER, SIR
THIS ISN'T A SHOE WASHER, MARCIE, IT'S A BALL WASHER! HERE, SLIP YOUR FOOT OUT OF YOUR SHOE...
IF YOU'RE GONNA BE A CADDY, MARCIE, YOU HAVE A LOT TO LEARN!
NOW, AS SOON AS MRS. BARTLEY PUTTS OUT, YOU TAKE THE BALL, AND CLEAN IT FOR HER BEFORE SHE TEES OFF AGAIN...
I'LL TAKE IT, MRS. BARTLEY...
THAT'S THE WAY..
RATS!!
NOW WHAT?
AFTER I PEELED THE WHITE COVER OFF, I COULDN'T GET THE BALL BACK IN..
SCHULZ

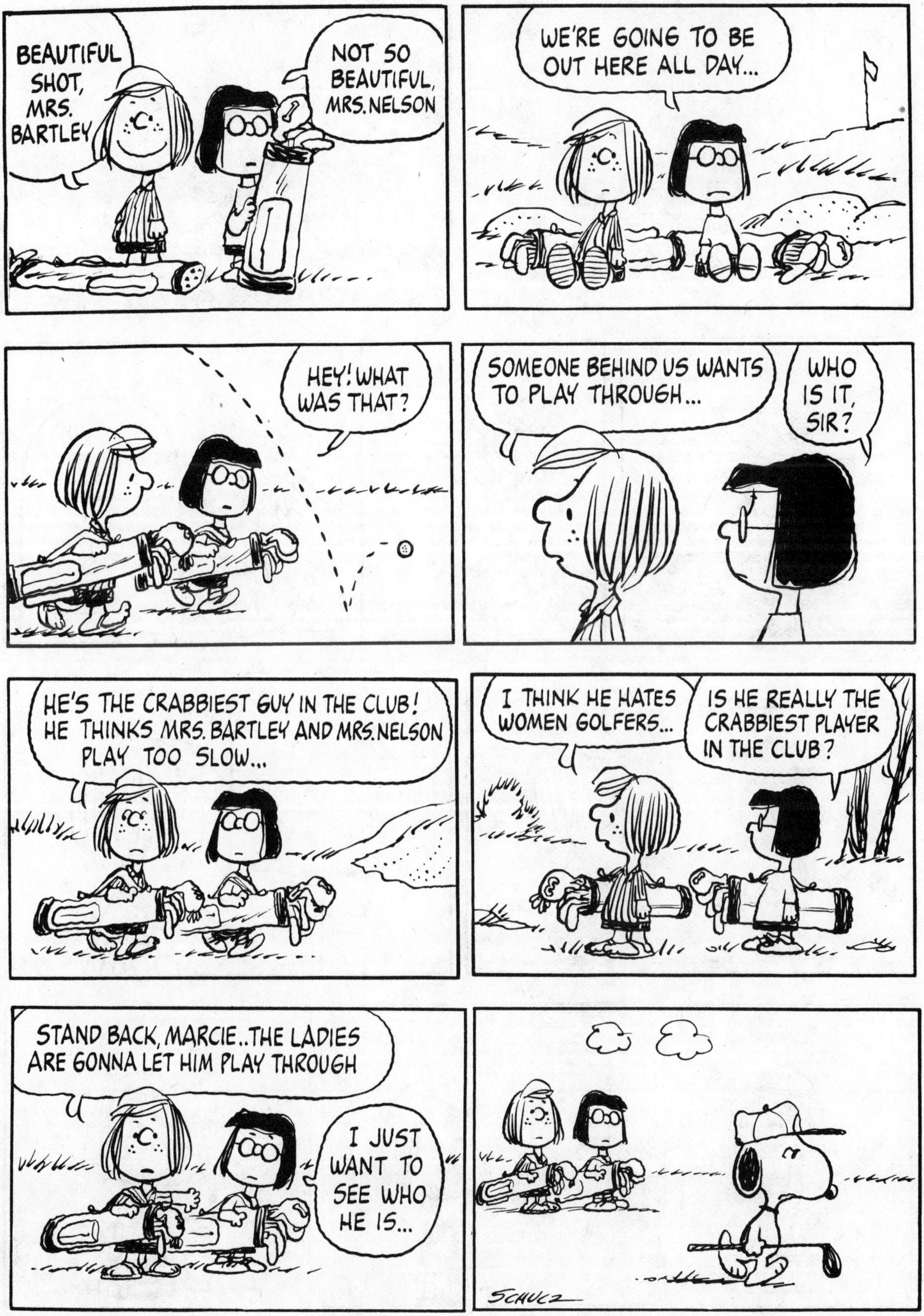
BEAUTIFUL SHOT, MRS. BARTLEY
NOT SO BEAUTIFUL, MRS. NELSON
WE'RE GOING TO BE OUT HERE ALL DAY...
HEY! WHAT WAS THAT?
SOMEONE BEHIND US WANTS TO PLAY THROUGH...
WHO IS IT, SIR?
HE'S THE CRABBIEST GUY IN THE CLUB! HE THINKS MRS. BARTLEY AND MRS. NELSON PLAY TOO SLOW...
I THINK HE HATES WOMEN GOLFERS...
IS HE REALLY THE CRABBIEST PLAYER IN THE CLUB?
STAND BACK, MARCIE..THE LADIES ARE GONNA LET HIM PLAY THROUGH
I JUST WANT TO SEE WHO HE IS...
SCHULZ

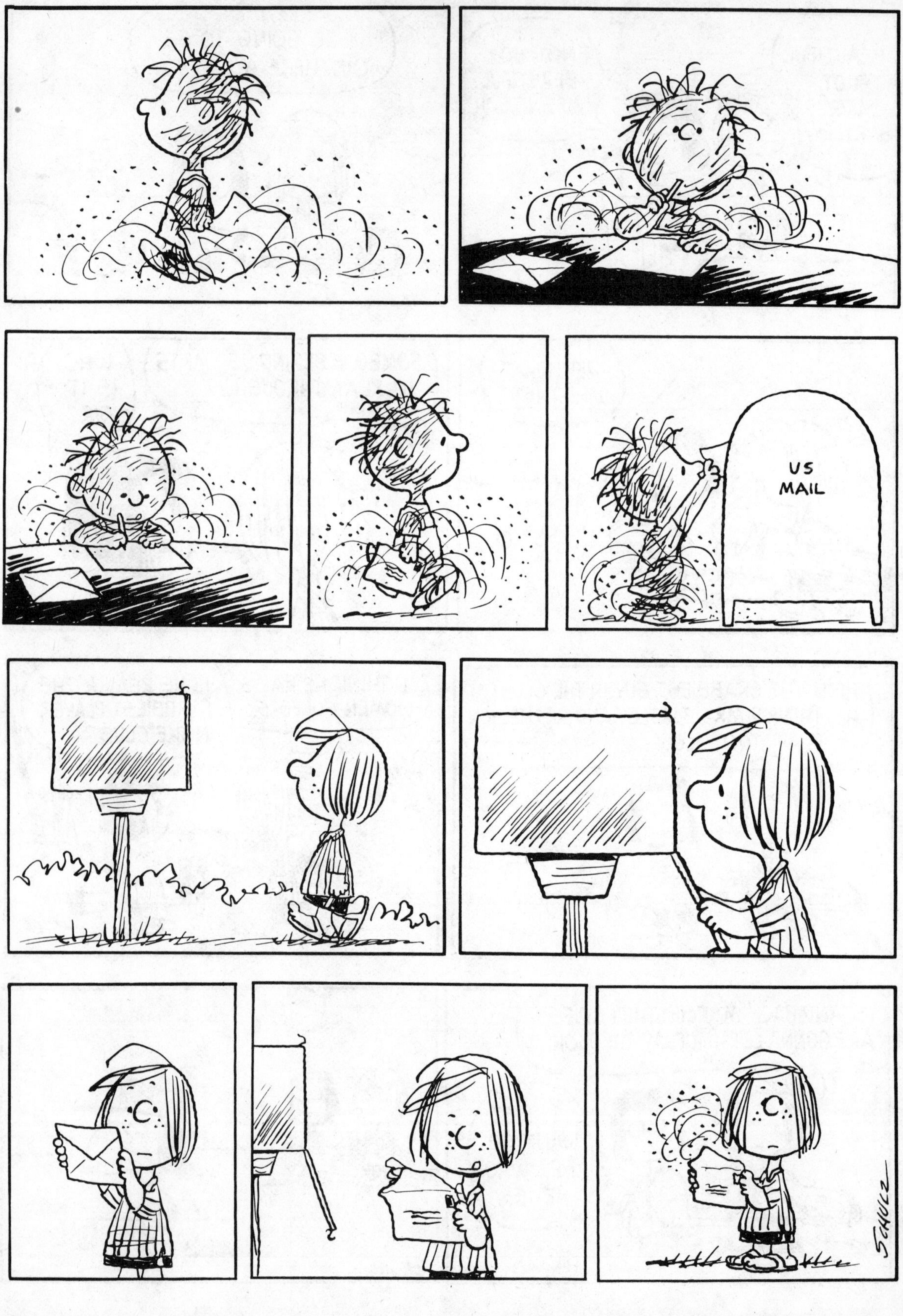
US
MAIL
SCHULZ

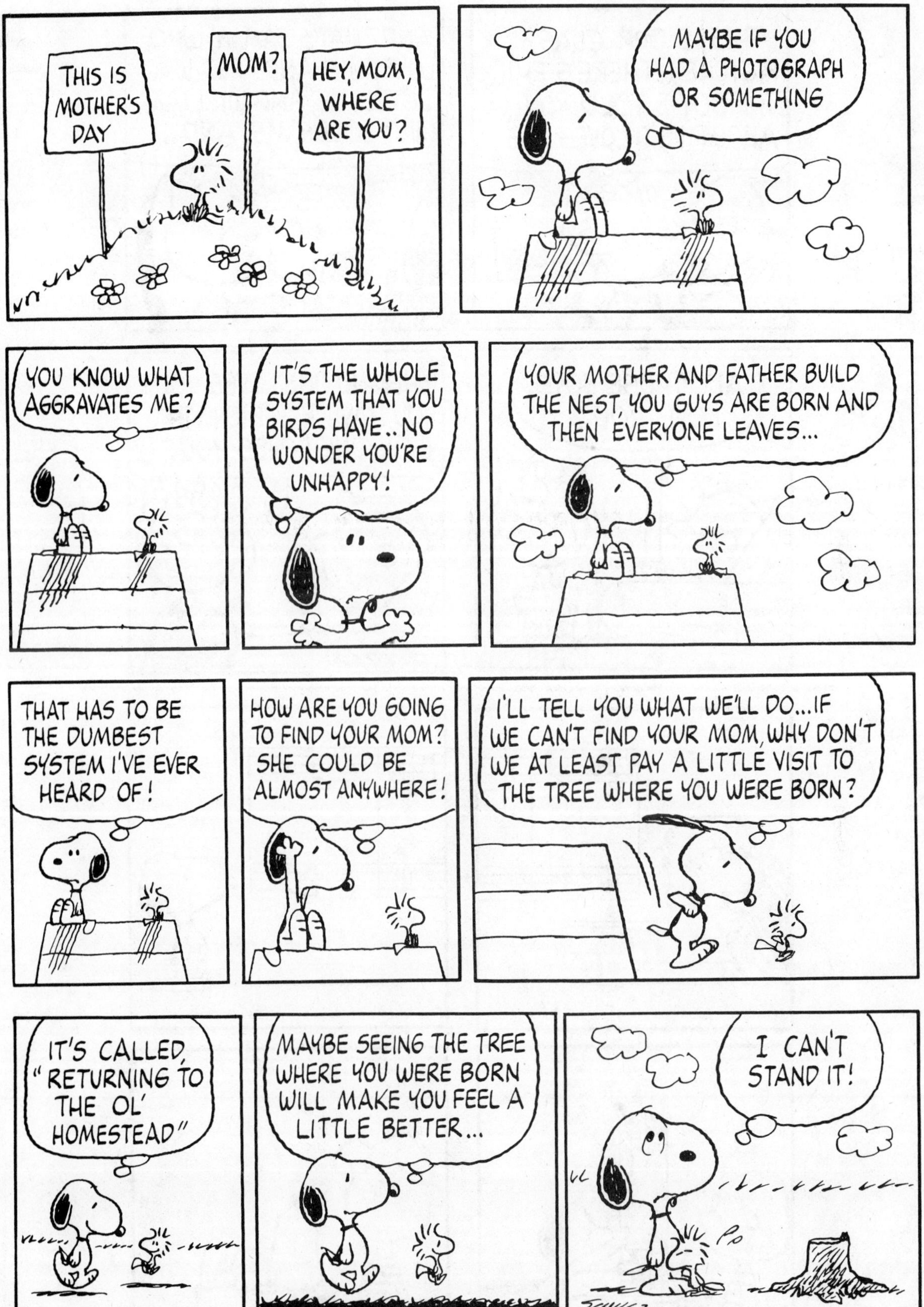
THIS IS MOTHER'S DAY
MOM?
HEY, MOM, WHERE ARE YOU?
MAYBE IF YOU HAD A PHOTOGRAPH OR SOMETHING
YOU KNOW WHAT AGGRAVATES ME?
IT'S THE WHOLE SYSTEM THAT YOU BIRDS HAVE..NO WONDER YOU'RE UNHAPPY!
YOUR MOTHER AND FATHER BUILD THE NEST, YOU GUYS ARE BORN AND THEN EVERYONE LEAVES...
THAT HAS TO BE THE DUMBEST SYSTEM I'VE EVER HEARD OF!
HOW ARE YOU GOING TO FIND YOUR MOM? SHE COULD BE ALMOST ANYWHERE!
I'LL TELL YOU WHAT WE'LL DO...IF WE CAN'T FIND YOUR MOM, WHY DON'T WE AT LEAST PAY A LITTLE VISIT TO THE TREE WHERE YOU WERE BORN?
IT'S CALLED, "RETURNING TO THE OL' HOMESTEAD"
MAYBE SEEING THE TREE WHERE YOU WERE BORN WILL MAKE YOU FEEL A LITTLE BETTER...
I CAN'T STAND IT!
SCHULZ

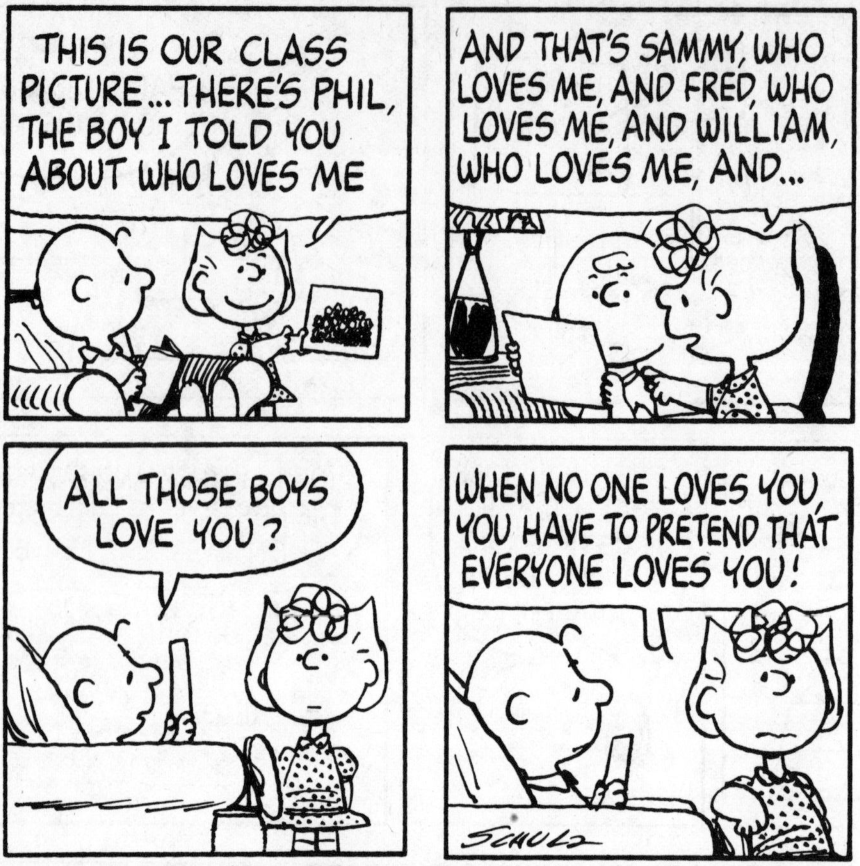
THIS IS OUR CLASS PICTURE... THERE'S PHIL, THE BOY I TOLD YOU ABOUT WHO LOVES ME
AND THAT'S SAMMY, WHO LOVES ME, AND FRED, WHO LOVES ME, AND WILLIAM, WHO LOVES ME, AND...
ALL THOSE BOYS LOVE YOU?
WHEN NO ONE LOVES YOU, YOU HAVE TO PRETEND THAT EVERYONE LOVES YOU!
SCHULZ

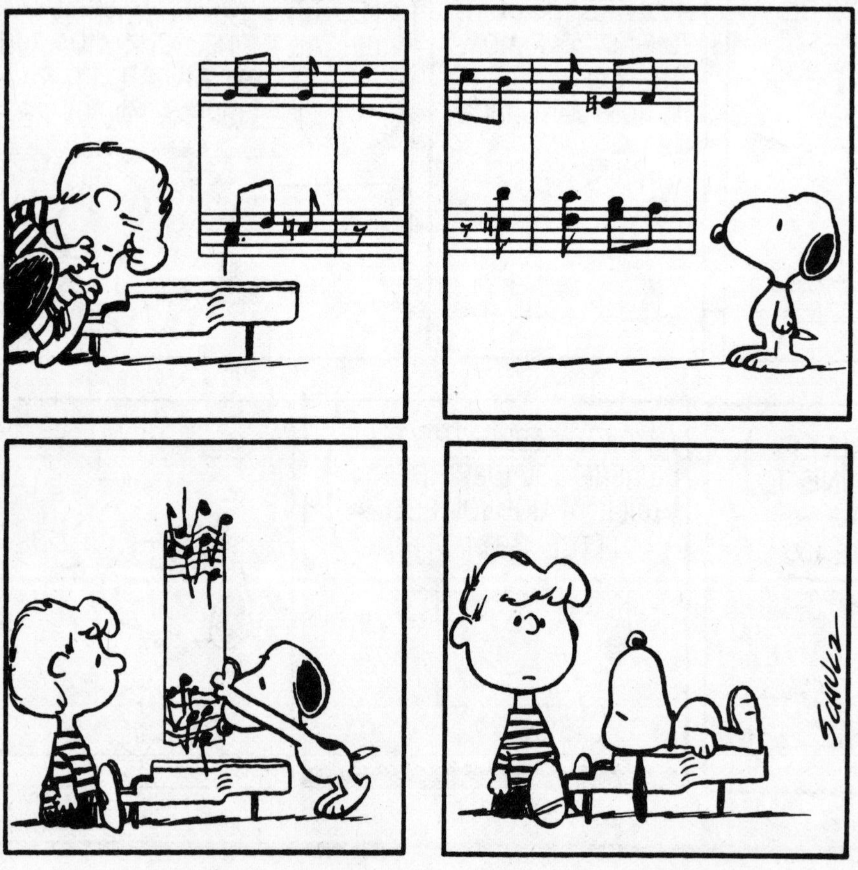
SCHULZ

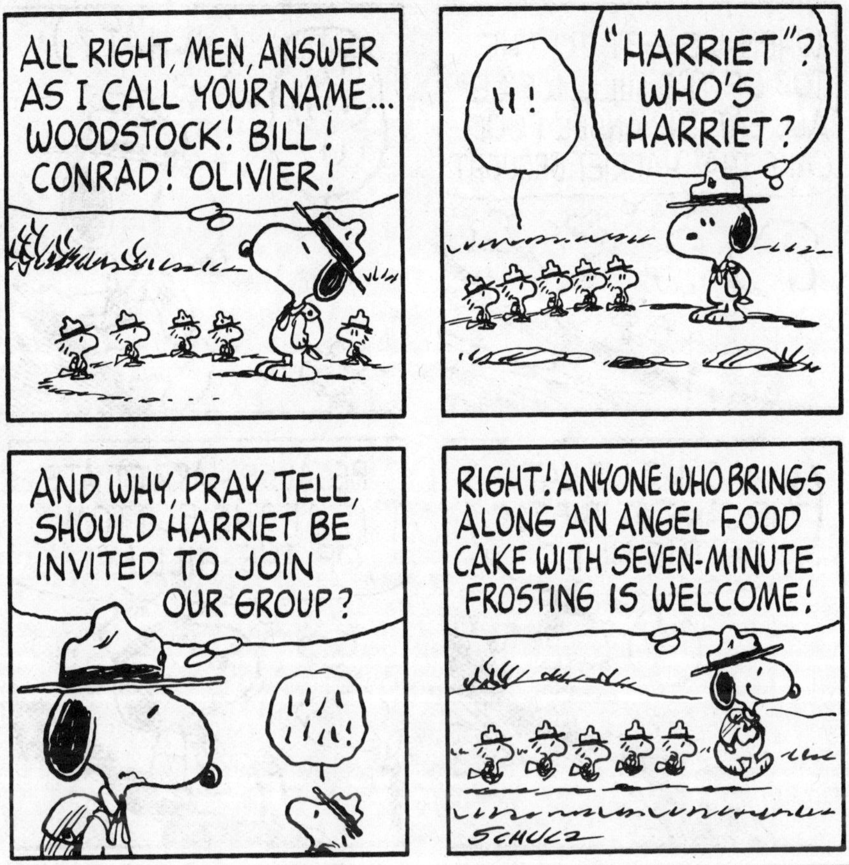
ALL RIGHT, MEN, ANSWER AS I CALL YOUR NAME... WOODSTOCK! BILL! CONRAD! OLIVIER!
"HARRIET"? WHO'S HARRIET?
AND WHY, PRAY TELL, SHOULD HARRIET BE INVITED TO JOIN OUR GROUP?
RIGHT! ANYONE WHO BRINGS ALONG AN ANGEL FOOD CAKE WITH SEVEN-MINUTE FROSTING IS WELCOME!
SCHULZ

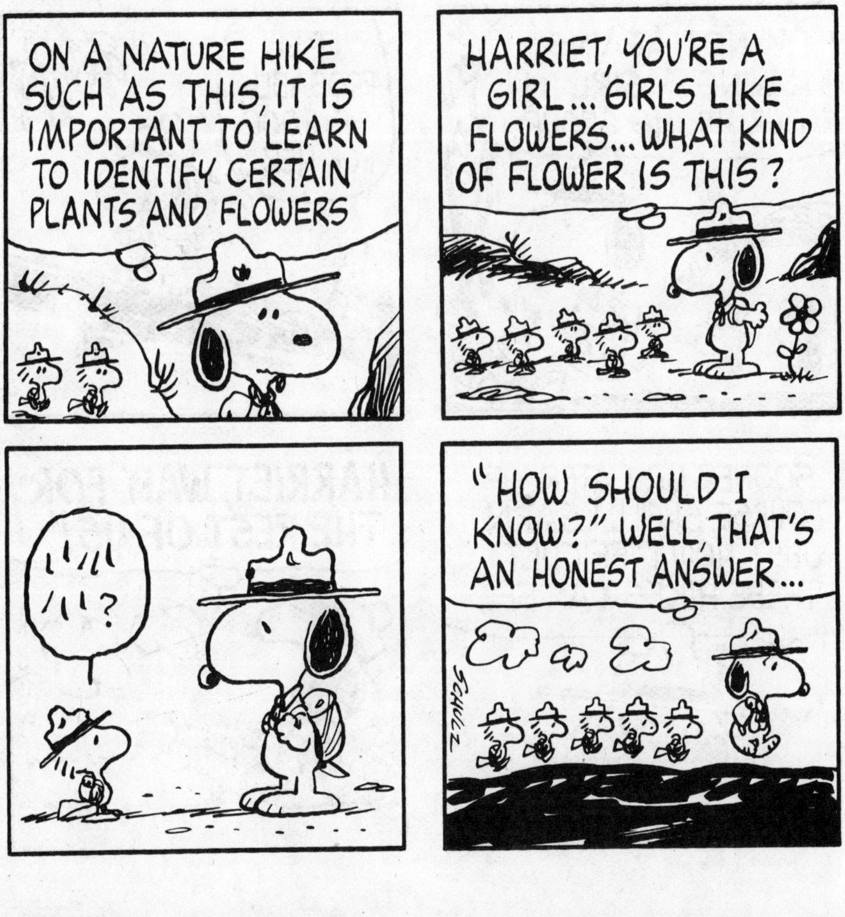
ON A NATURE HIKE SUCH AS THIS, IT IS IMPORTANT TO LEARN TO IDENTIFY CERTAIN PLANTS AND FLOWERS
HARRIET, YOU'RE A GIRL... GIRLS LIKE FLOWERS... WHAT KIND OF FLOWER IS THIS?
"HOW SHOULD I KNOW?" WELL, THAT'S AN HONEST ANSWER...
SCHULZ

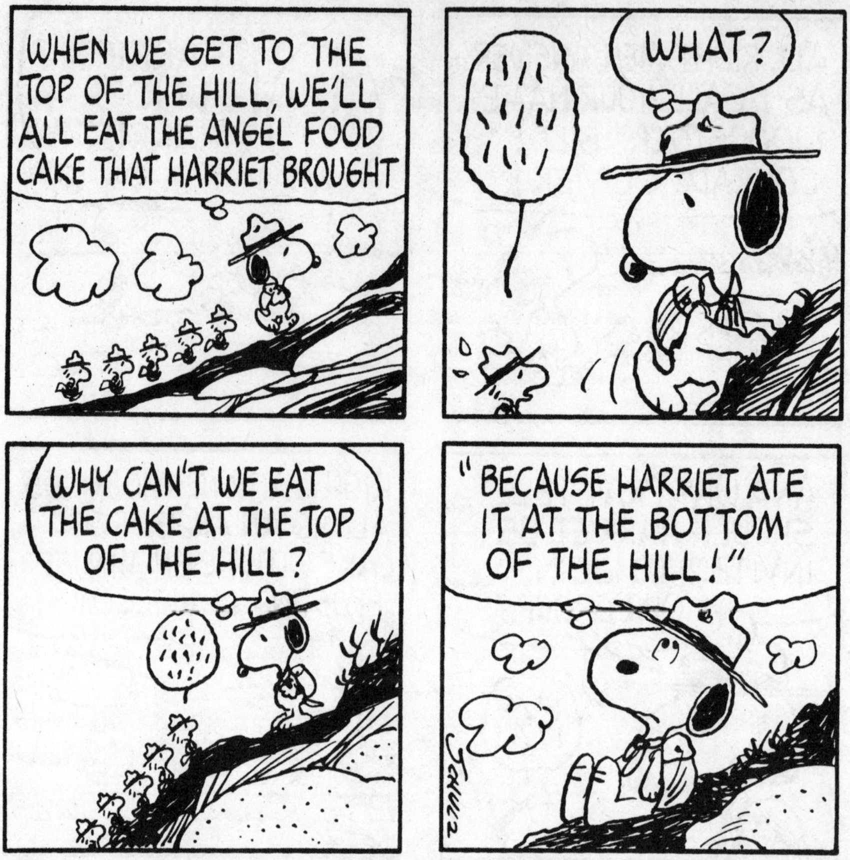
WHEN WE GET TO THE TOP OF THE HILL, WE'LL ALL EAT THE ANGEL FOOD CAKE THAT HARRIET BROUGHT
WHAT?
WHY CAN'T WE EAT THE CAKE AT THE TOP OF THE HILL?
"BECAUSE HARRIET ATE IT AT THE BOTTOM OF THE HILL!"

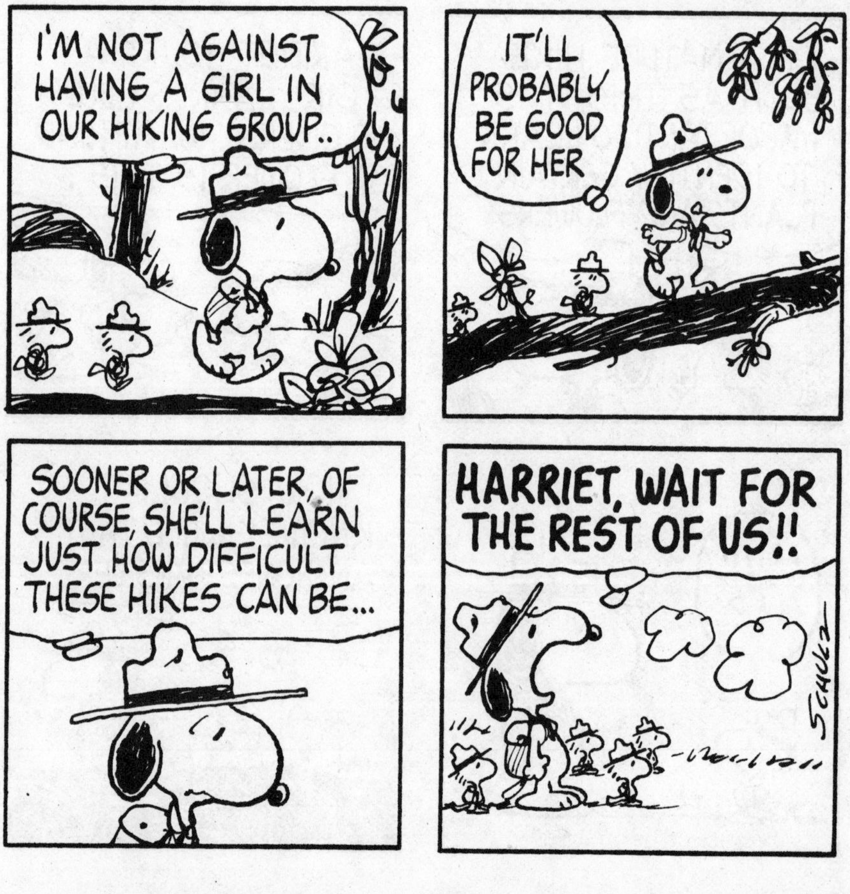
I'M NOT AGAINST HAVING A GIRL IN OUR HIKING GROUP..
IT'LL PROBABLY BE GOOD FOR HER
SOONER OR LATER, OF COURSE, SHE'LL LEARN JUST HOW DIFFICULT THESE HIKES CAN BE...
HARRIET, WAIT FOR THE REST OF US!!

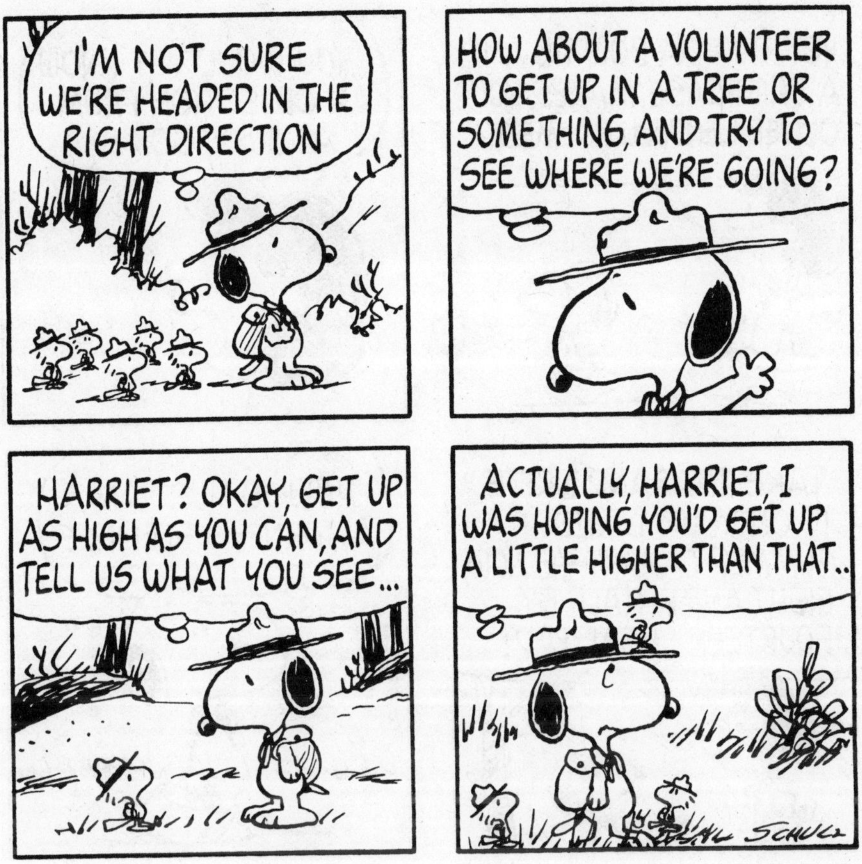
I'M NOT SURE WE'RE HEADED IN THE RIGHT DIRECTION
HOW ABOUT A VOLUNTEER TO GET UP IN A TREE OR SOMETHING, AND TRY TO SEE WHERE WE'RE GOING?
HARRIET? OKAY, GET UP AS HIGH AS YOU CAN, AND TELL US WHAT YOU SEE...
ACTUALLY, HARRIET, I WAS HOPING YOU'D GET UP A LITTLE HIGHER THAN THAT..
SCHULZ

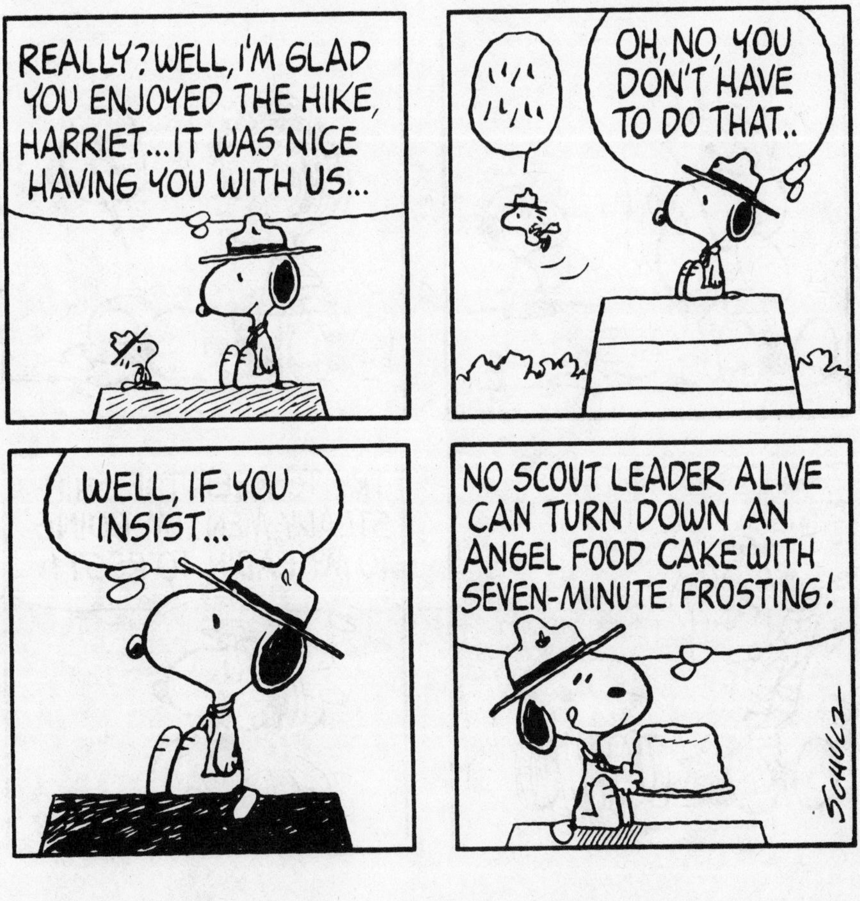
REALLY? WELL, I'M GLAD YOU ENJOYED THE HIKE, HARRIET...IT WAS NICE HAVING YOU WITH US...
OH, NO, YOU DON'T HAVE TO DO THAT..
WELL, IF YOU INSIST...
NO SCOUT LEADER ALIVE CAN TURN DOWN AN ANGEL FOOD CAKE WITH SEVEN-MINUTE FROSTING!
SCHULZ

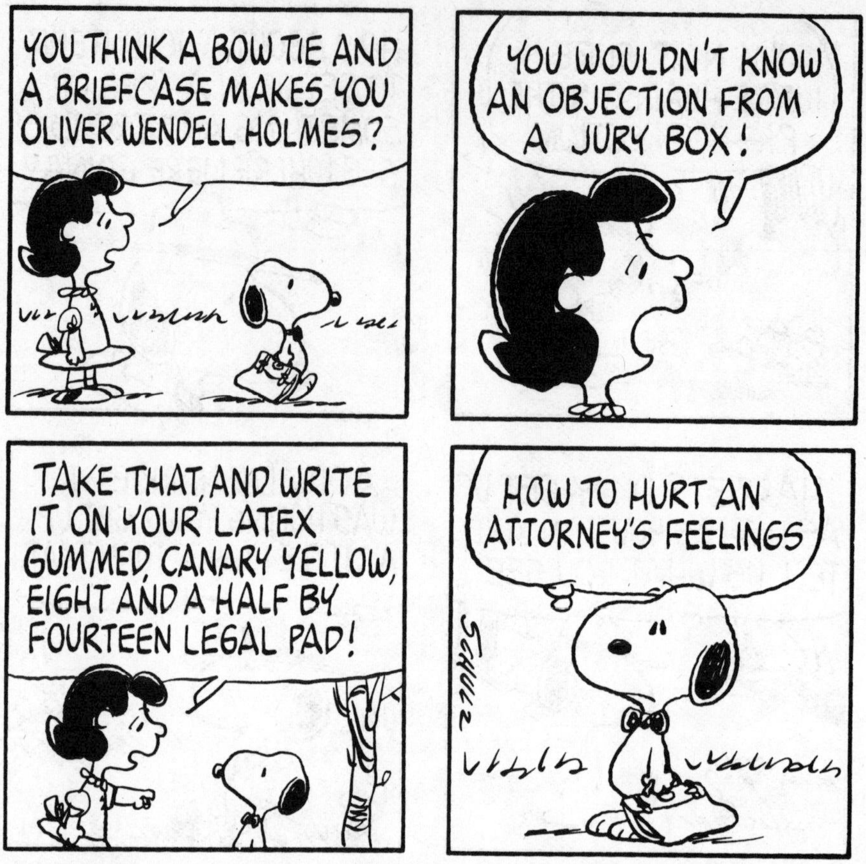
YOU THINK A BOW TIE AND A BRIEFCASE MAKES YOU OLIVER WENDELL HOLMES?
YOU WOULDN'T KNOW AN OBJECTION FROM A JURY BOX!
TAKE THAT, AND WRITE IT ON YOUR LATEX GUMMED, CANARY YELLOW, EIGHT AND A HALF BY FOURTEEN LEGAL PAD!
HOW TO HURT AN ATTORNEY'S FEELINGS
SCHULZ

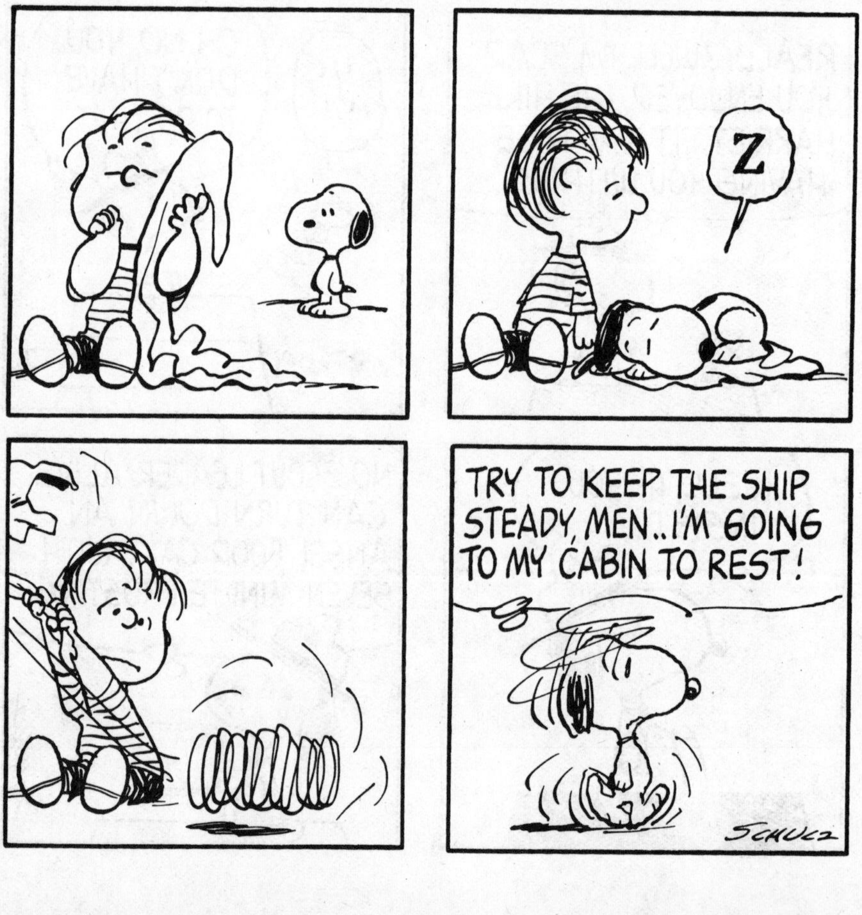
Z
TRY TO KEEP THE SHIP STEADY, MEN..I'M GOING TO MY CABIN TO REST!
SCHULZ

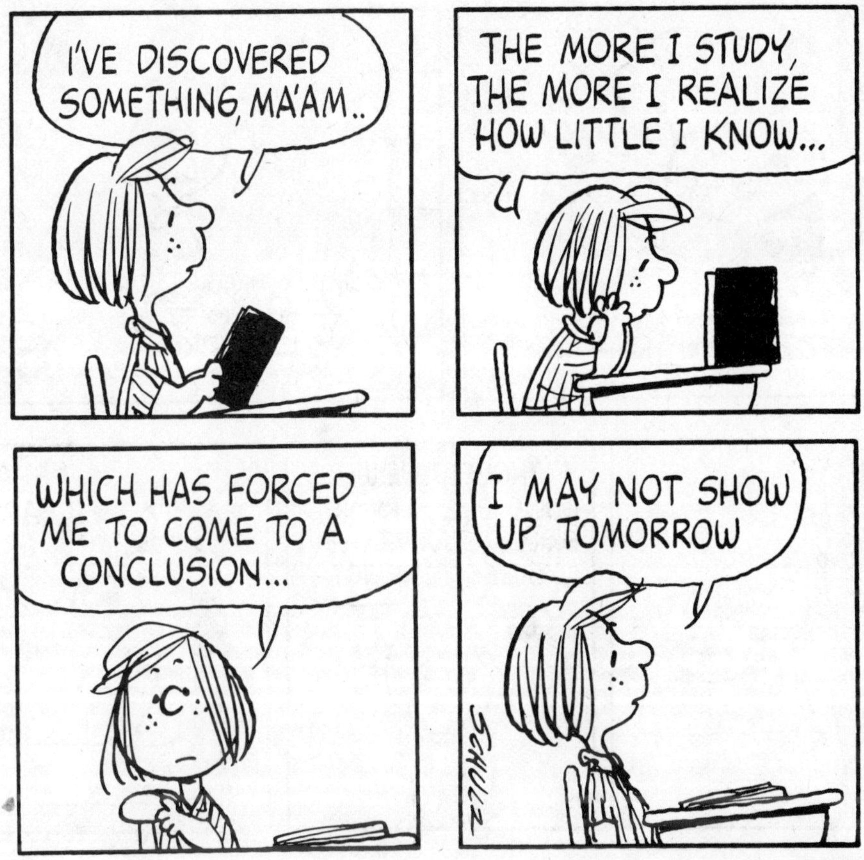
I'VE DISCOVERED SOMETHING, MA'AM..
THE MORE I STUDY, THE MORE I REALIZE HOW LITTLE I KNOW...
WHICH HAS FORCED ME TO COME TO A CONCLUSION...
I MAY NOT SHOW UP TOMORROW
SCHULZ

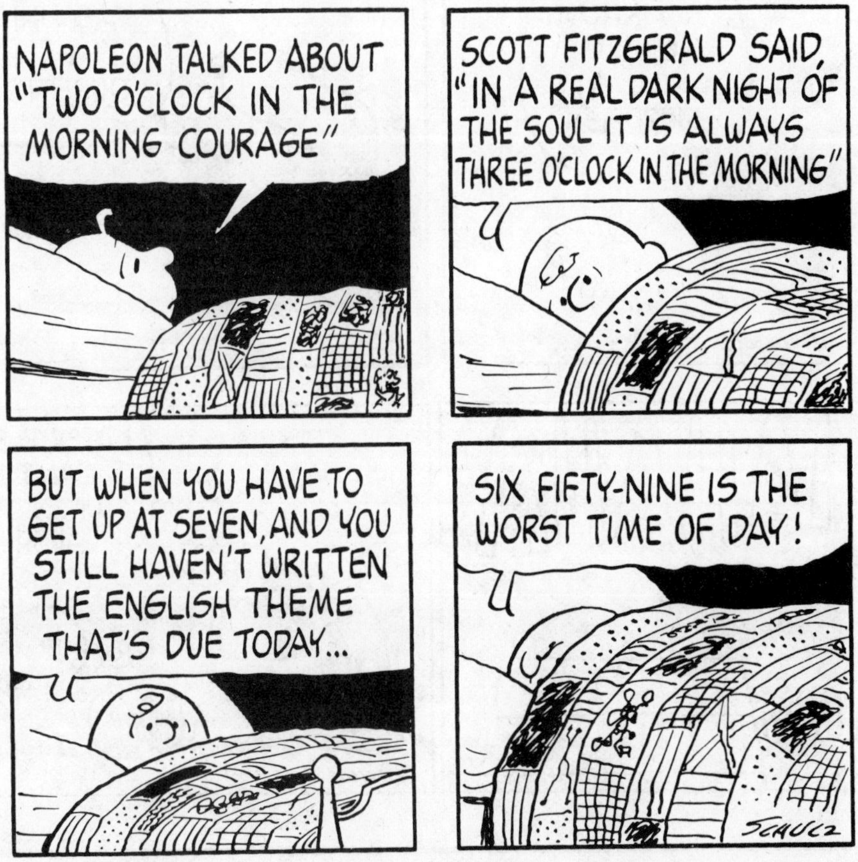
NAPOLEON TALKED ABOUT "TWO O'CLOCK IN THE MORNING COURAGE"
SCOTT FITZGERALD SAID, "IN A REAL DARK NIGHT OF THE SOUL IT IS ALWAYS THREE O'CLOCK IN THE MORNING"
BUT WHEN YOU HAVE TO GET UP AT SEVEN, AND YOU STILL HAVEN'T WRITTEN THE ENGLISH THEME THAT'S DUE TODAY...
SIX FIFTY-NINE IS THE WORST TIME OF DAY!
SCHULZ

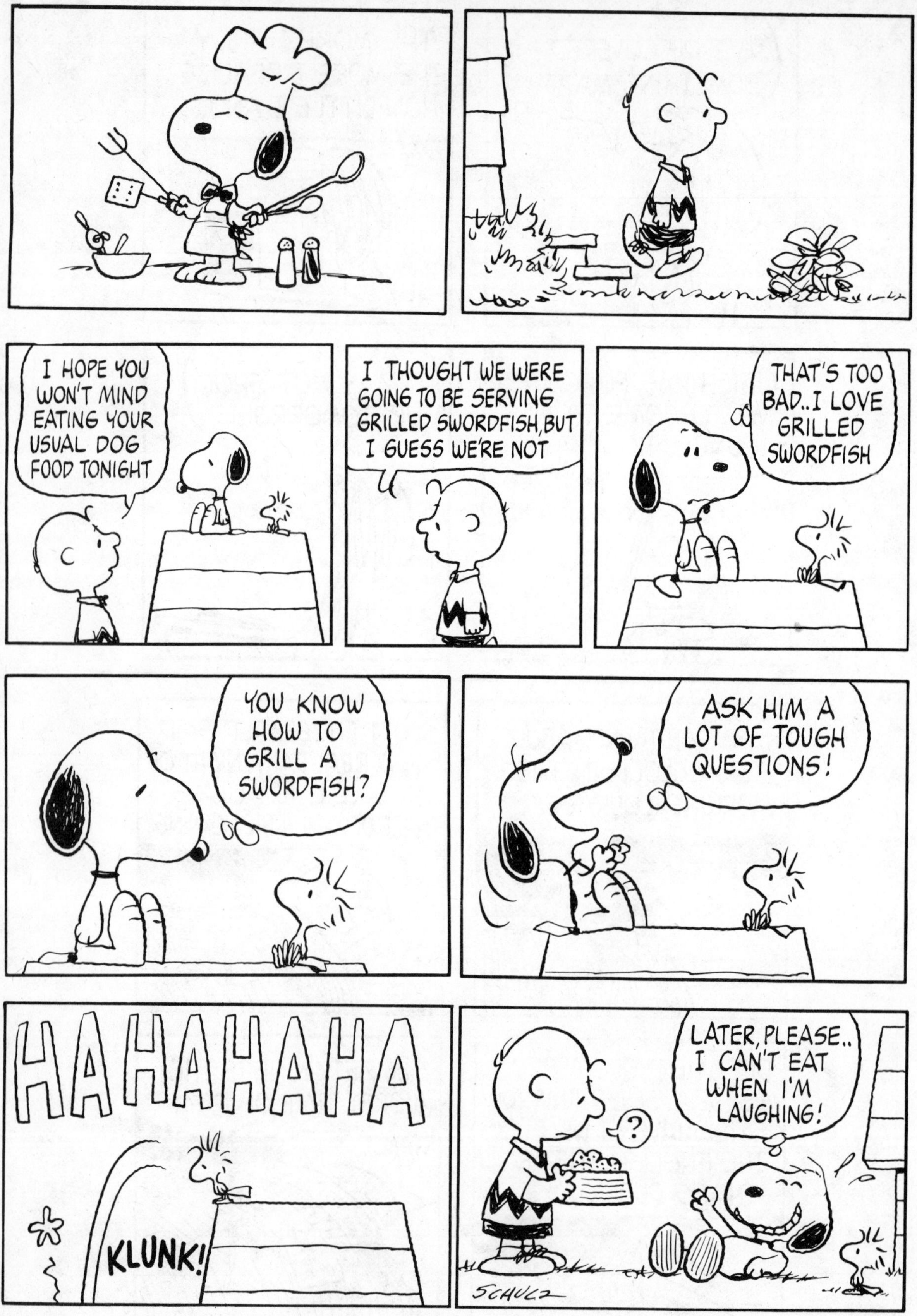
I HOPE YOU WON'T MIND EATING YOUR USUAL DOG FOOD TONIGHT
I THOUGHT WE WERE GOING TO BE SERVING GRILLED SWORDFISH, BUT I GUESS WE'RE NOT
THAT'S TOO BAD..I LOVE GRILLED SWORDFISH
YOU KNOW HOW TO GRILL A SWORDFISH?
ASK HIM A LOT OF TOUGH QUESTIONS!
HAHAHAHA
KLUNK!
?
LATER, PLEASE.. I CAN'T EAT WHEN I'M LAUGHING!
SCHULZ

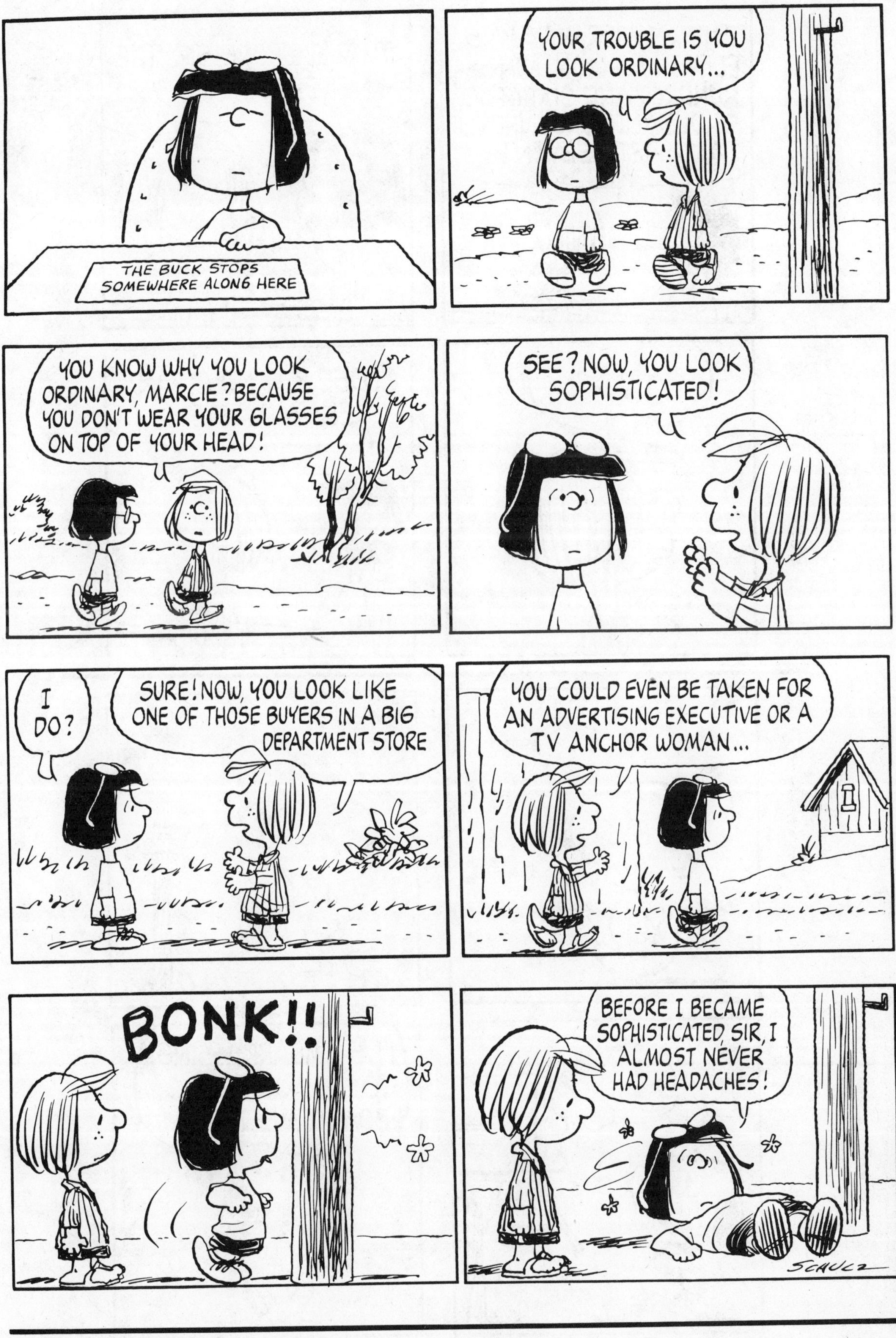
THE BUCK STOPS SOMEWHERE ALONG HERE
YOUR TROUBLE IS YOU LOOK ORDINARY...
YOU KNOW WHY YOU LOOK ORDINARY, MARCIE? BECAUSE YOU DON'T WEAR YOUR GLASSES ON TOP OF YOUR HEAD!
SEE? NOW, YOU LOOK SOPHISTICATED!
I DO?
SURE! NOW, YOU LOOK LIKE ONE OF THOSE BUYERS IN A BIG DEPARTMENT STORE
YOU COULD EVEN BE TAKEN FOR AN ADVERTISING EXECUTIVE OR A TV ANCHOR WOMAN...
BONK!!
BEFORE I BECAME SOPHISTICATED, SIR, I ALMOST NEVER HAD HEADACHES!
SCHULZ

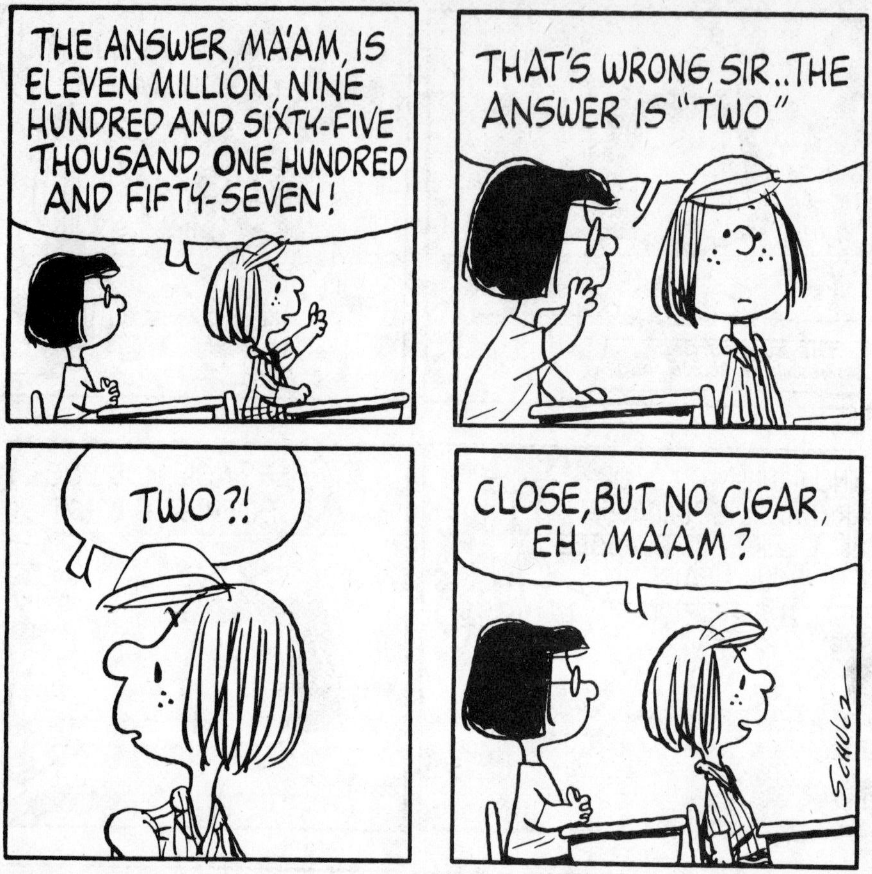
THE ANSWER, MA'AM, IS ELEVEN MILLION, NINE HUNDRED AND SIXTY-FIVE THOUSAND, ONE HUNDRED AND FIFTY-SEVEN!
THAT'S WRONG, SIR..THE ANSWER IS "TWO"
TWO?!
CLOSE, BUT NO CIGAR, EH, MA'AM?
SCHULZ

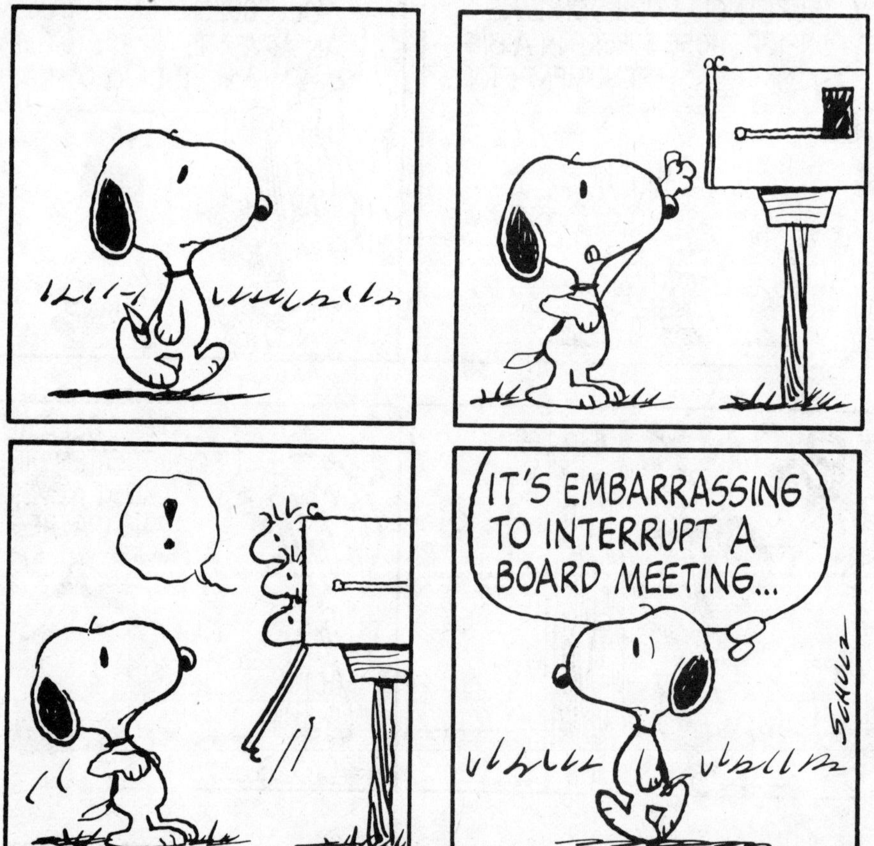
!
IT'S EMBARRASSING TO INTERRUPT A BOARD MEETING...
SCHULZ

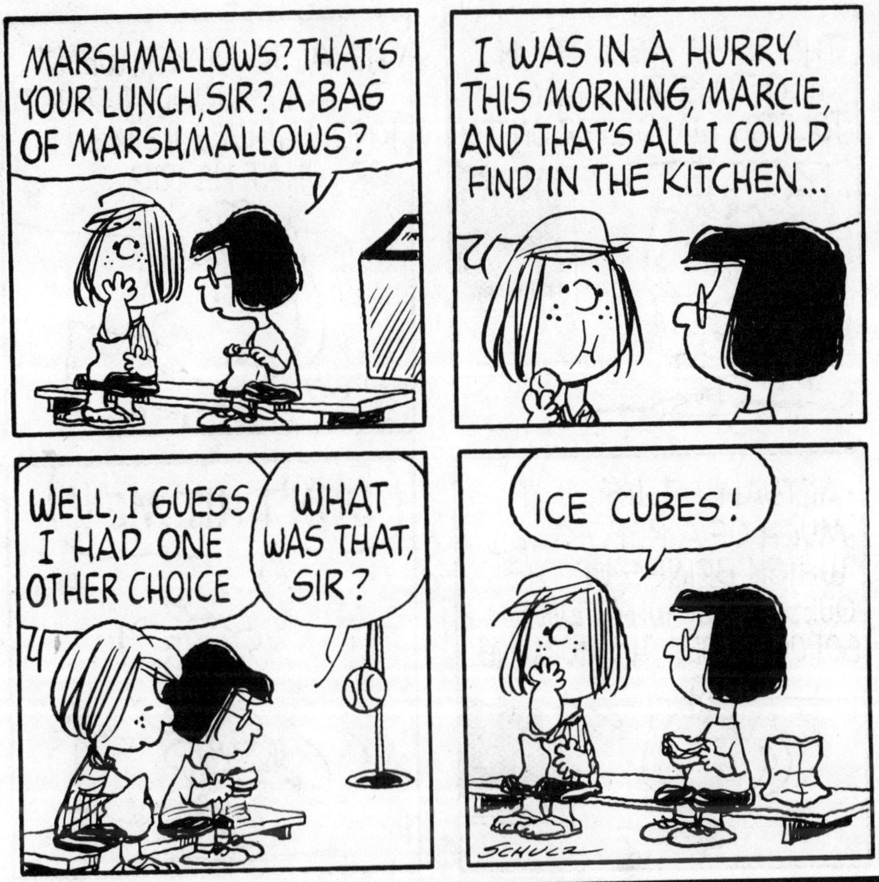
MARSHMALLOWS? THAT'S YOUR LUNCH, SIR? A BAG OF MARSHMALLOWS?
I WAS IN A HURRY THIS MORNING, MARCIE, AND THAT'S ALL I COULD FIND IN THE KITCHEN...
WELL, I GUESS I HAD ONE OTHER CHOICE
WHAT WAS THAT, SIR?
ICE CUBES!
SCHULZ

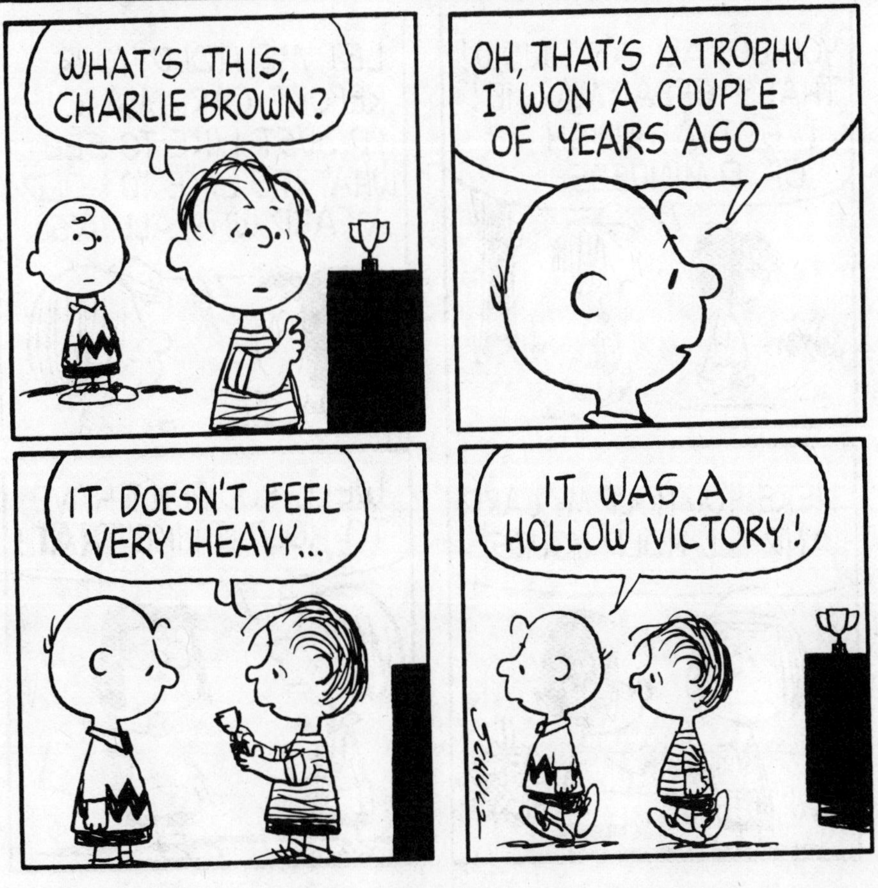
WHAT'S THIS, CHARLIE BROWN?
OH, THAT'S A TROPHY I WON A COUPLE OF YEARS AGO
IT DOESN'T FEEL VERY HEAVY...
IT WAS A HOLLOW VICTORY!
SCHULZ

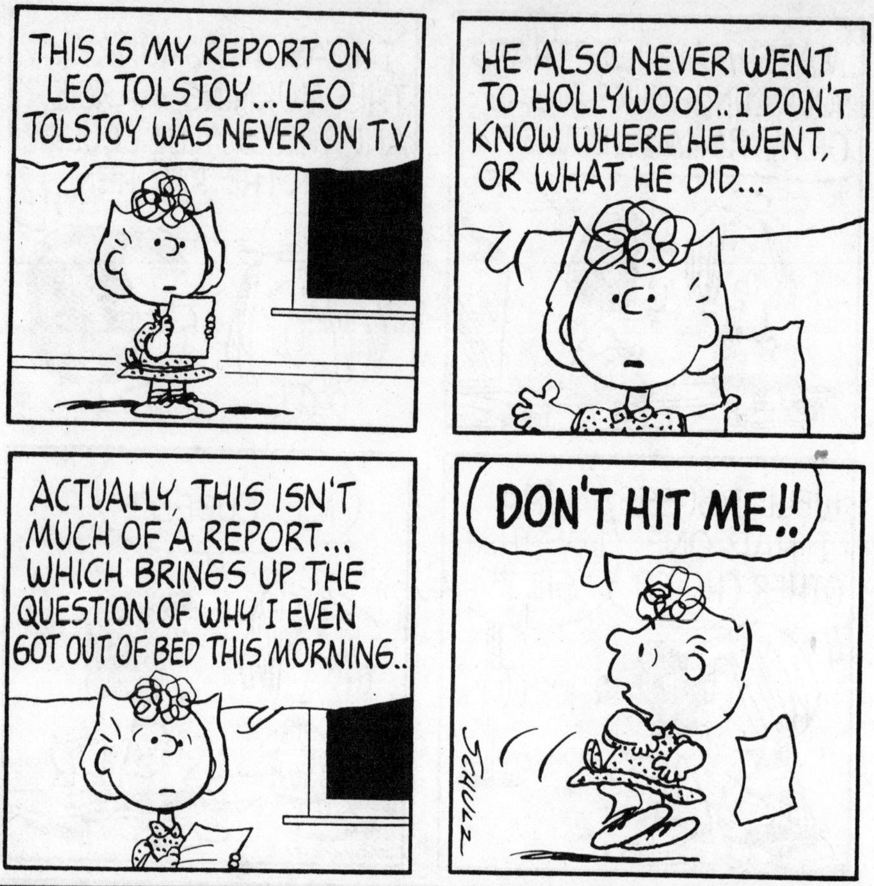
THIS IS MY REPORT ON LEO TOLSTOY... LEO TOLSTOY WAS NEVER ON TV
HE ALSO NEVER WENT TO HOLLYWOOD.. I DON'T KNOW WHERE HE WENT, OR WHAT HE DID...
ACTUALLY, THIS ISN'T MUCH OF A REPORT... WHICH BRINGS UP THE QUESTION OF WHY I EVEN GOT OUT OF BED THIS MORNING..
DON'T HIT ME!!
SCHULZ

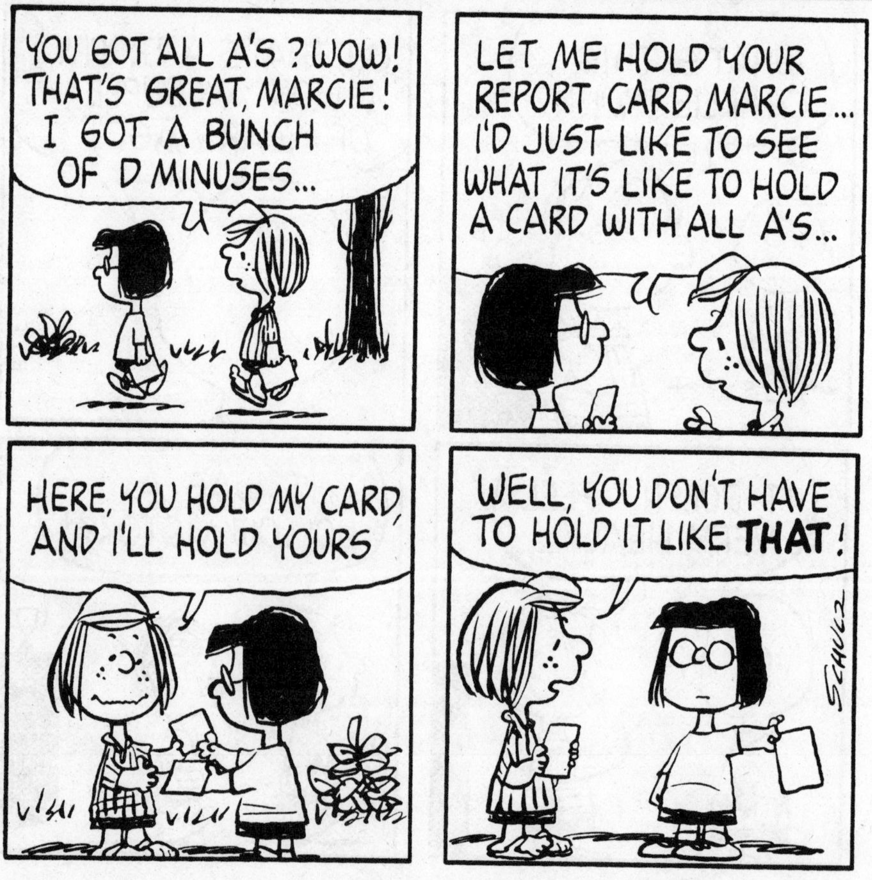
YOU GOT ALL A'S ? WOW! THAT'S GREAT, MARCIE! I GOT A BUNCH OF D MINUSES...
LET ME HOLD YOUR REPORT CARD, MARCIE... I'D JUST LIKE TO SEE WHAT IT'S LIKE TO HOLD A CARD WITH ALL A'S...
HERE, YOU HOLD MY CARD, AND I'LL HOLD YOURS
WELL, YOU DON'T HAVE TO HOLD IT LIKE THAT!
SCHULZ

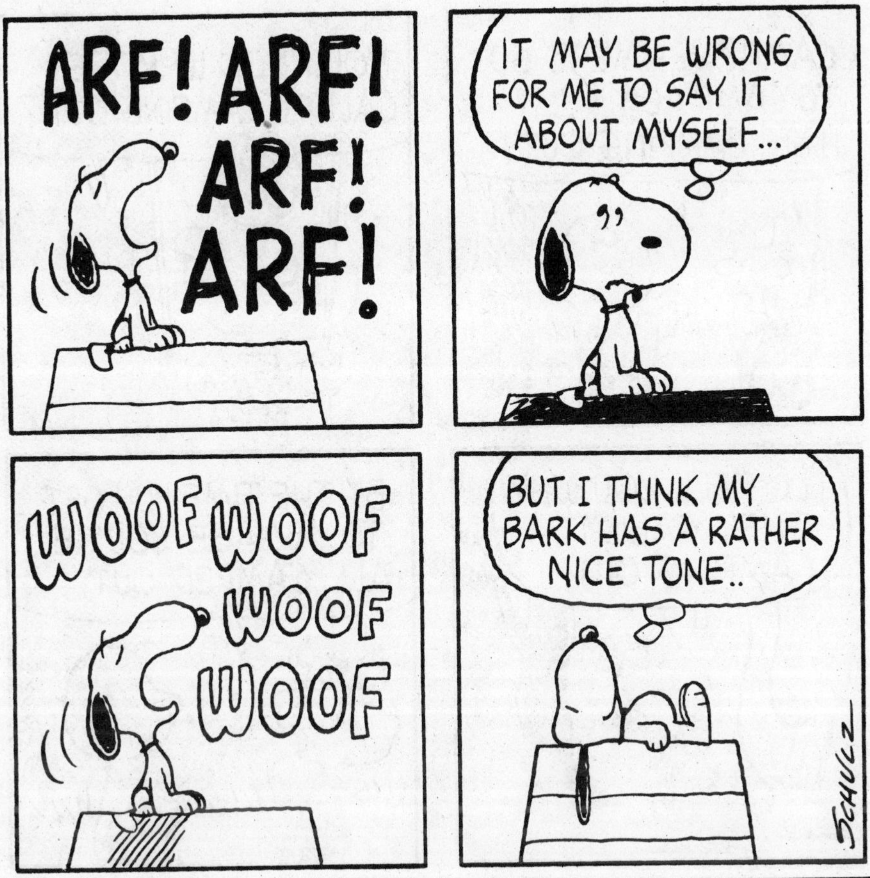
ARF! ARF!
ARF!
ARF!
IT MAY BE WRONG FOR ME TO SAY IT ABOUT MYSELF...
WOOF WOOF
WOOF
WOOF
BUT I THINK MY BARK HAS A RATHER NICE TONE..
SCHULZ

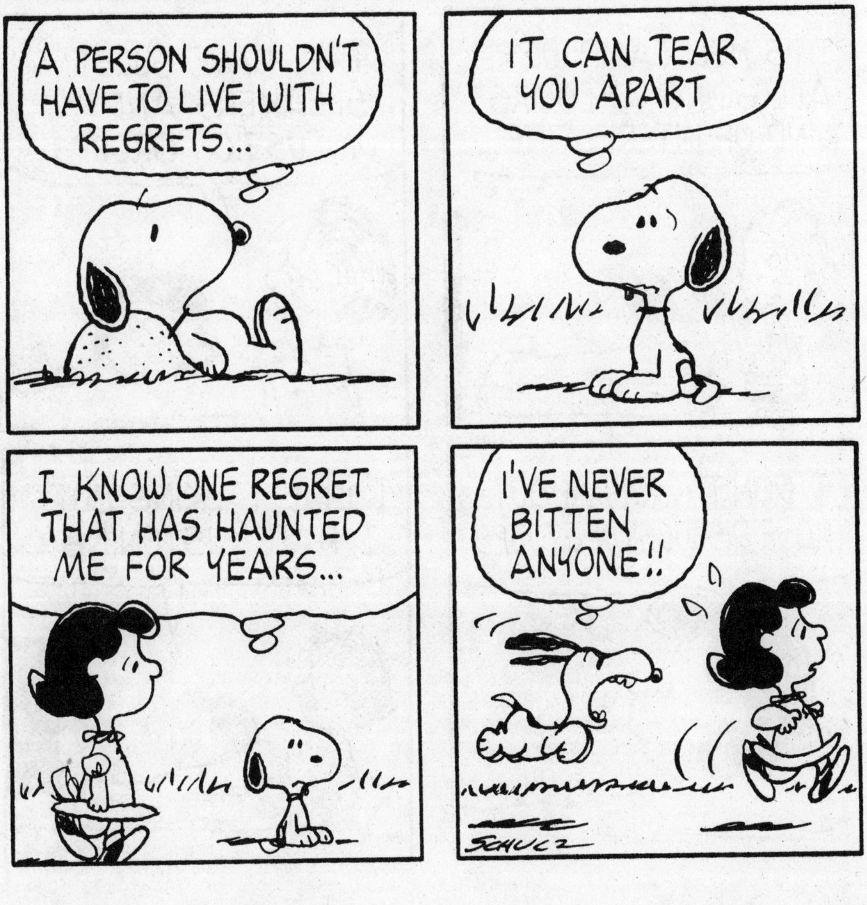
A PERSON SHOULDN'T HAVE TO LIVE WITH REGRETS...
IT CAN TEAR YOU APART
I KNOW ONE REGRET THAT HAS HAUNTED ME FOR YEARS...
I'VE NEVER BITTEN ANYONE!!
SCHULZ

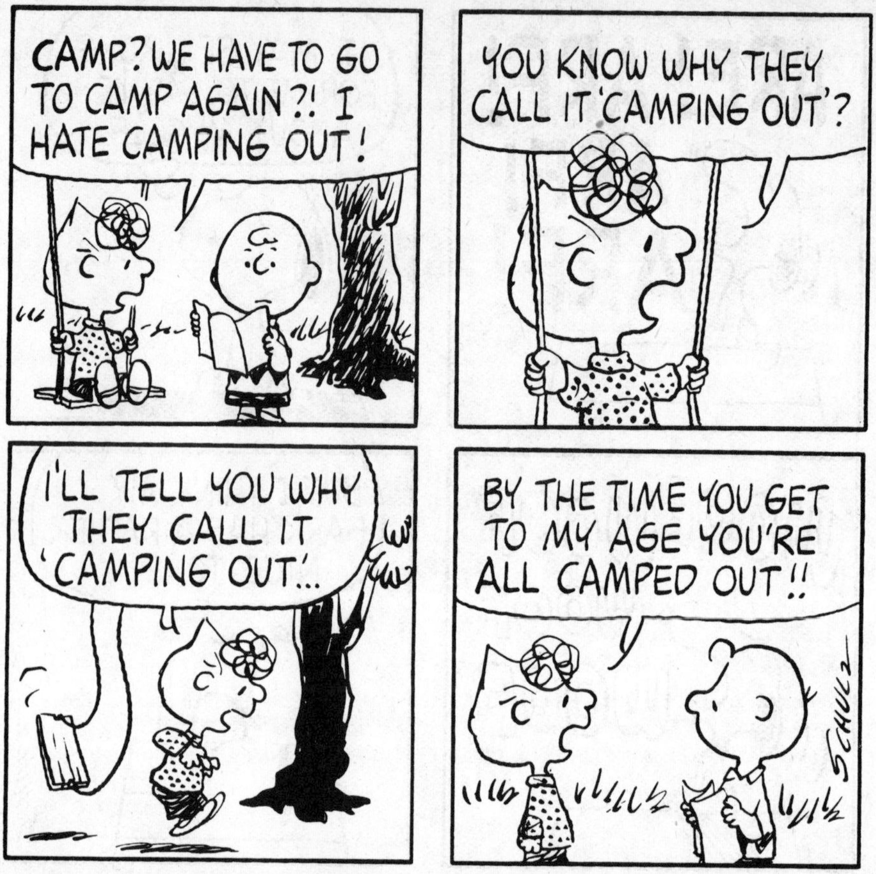
CAMP? WE HAVE TO GO TO CAMP AGAIN?! I HATE CAMPING OUT!
YOU KNOW WHY THEY CALL IT 'CAMPING OUT'?
I'LL TELL YOU WHY THEY CALL IT 'CAMPING OUT'...
BY THE TIME YOU GET TO MY AGE YOU'RE ALL CAMPED OUT!!
SCHULZ

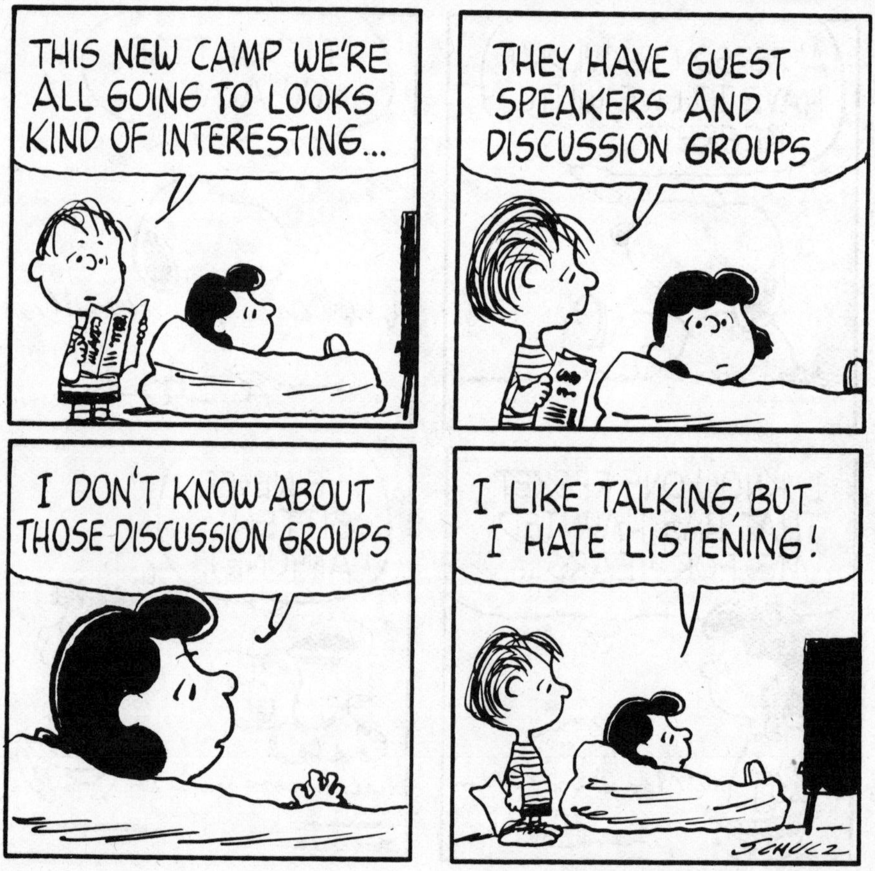
THIS NEW CAMP WE'RE ALL GOING TO LOOKS KIND OF INTERESTING...
THEY HAVE GUEST SPEAKERS AND DISCUSSION GROUPS
I DON'T KNOW ABOUT THOSE DISCUSSION GROUPS
I LIKE TALKING, BUT I HATE LISTENING!
SCHULZ

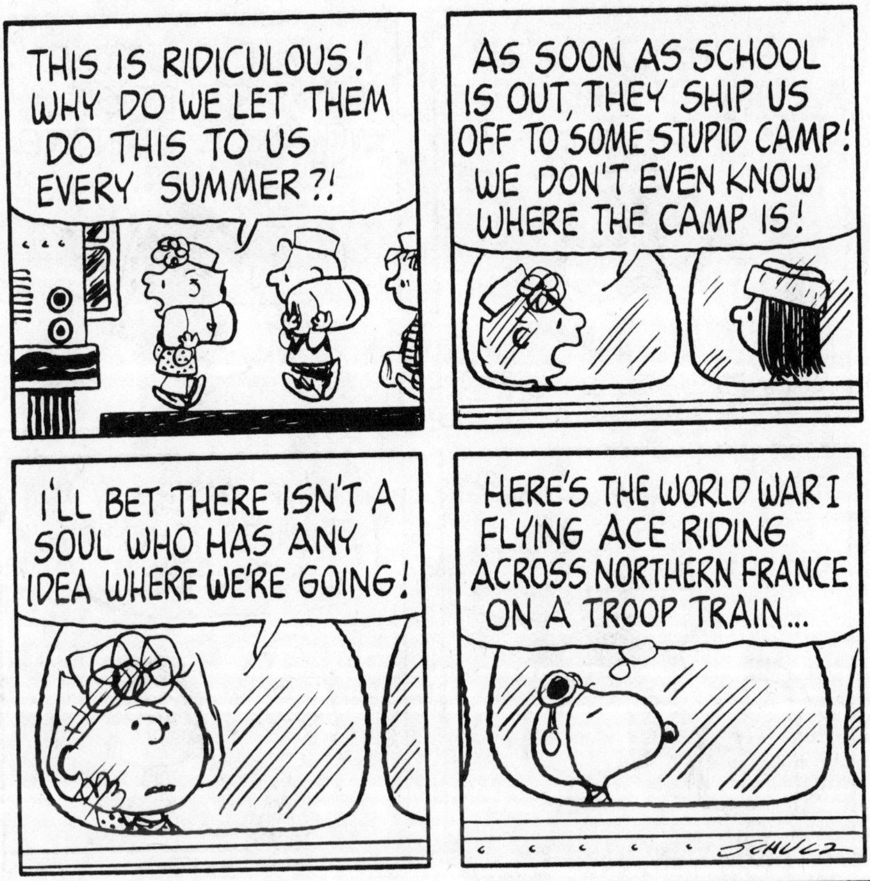
THIS IS RIDICULOUS! WHY DO WE LET THEM DO THIS TO US EVERY SUMMER?!
AS SOON AS SCHOOL IS OUT, THEY SHIP US OFF TO SOME STUPID CAMP! WE DON'T EVEN KNOW WHERE THE CAMP IS!
I'LL BET THERE ISN'T A SOUL WHO HAS ANY IDEA WHERE WE'RE GOING!
HERE'S THE WORLD WAR I FLYING ACE RIDING ACROSS NORTHERN FRANCE ON A TROOP TRAIN...
SCHULZ

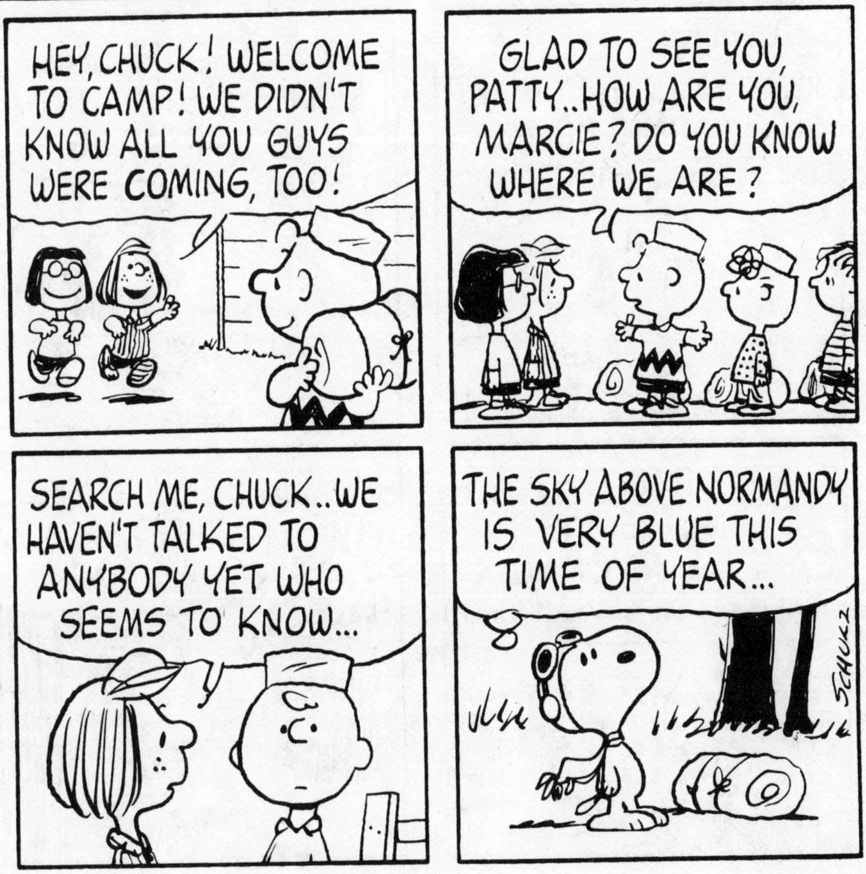
HEY, CHUCK! WELCOME TO CAMP! WE DIDN'T KNOW ALL YOU GUYS WERE COMING, TOO!
GLAD TO SEE YOU, PATTY..HOW ARE YOU, MARCIE? DO YOU KNOW WHERE WE ARE?
SEARCH ME, CHUCK..WE HAVEN'T TALKED TO ANYBODY YET WHO SEEMS TO KNOW...
THE SKY ABOVE NORMANDY IS VERY BLUE THIS TIME OF YEAR...
SCHULZ

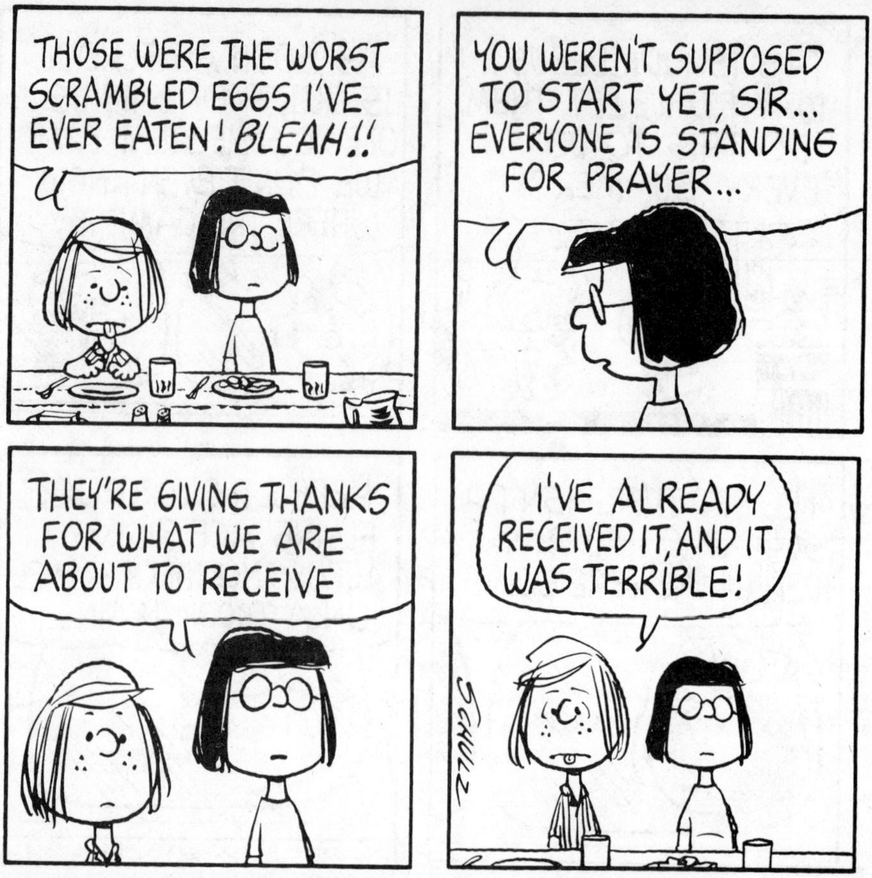
THOSE WERE THE WORST SCRAMBLED EGGS I'VE EVER EATEN! *BLEAH!!*
YOU WEREN'T SUPPOSED TO START YET, SIR... EVERYONE IS STANDING FOR PRAYER...
THEY'RE GIVING THANKS FOR WHAT WE ARE ABOUT TO RECEIVE
I'VE ALREADY RECEIVED IT, AND IT WAS TERRIBLE!

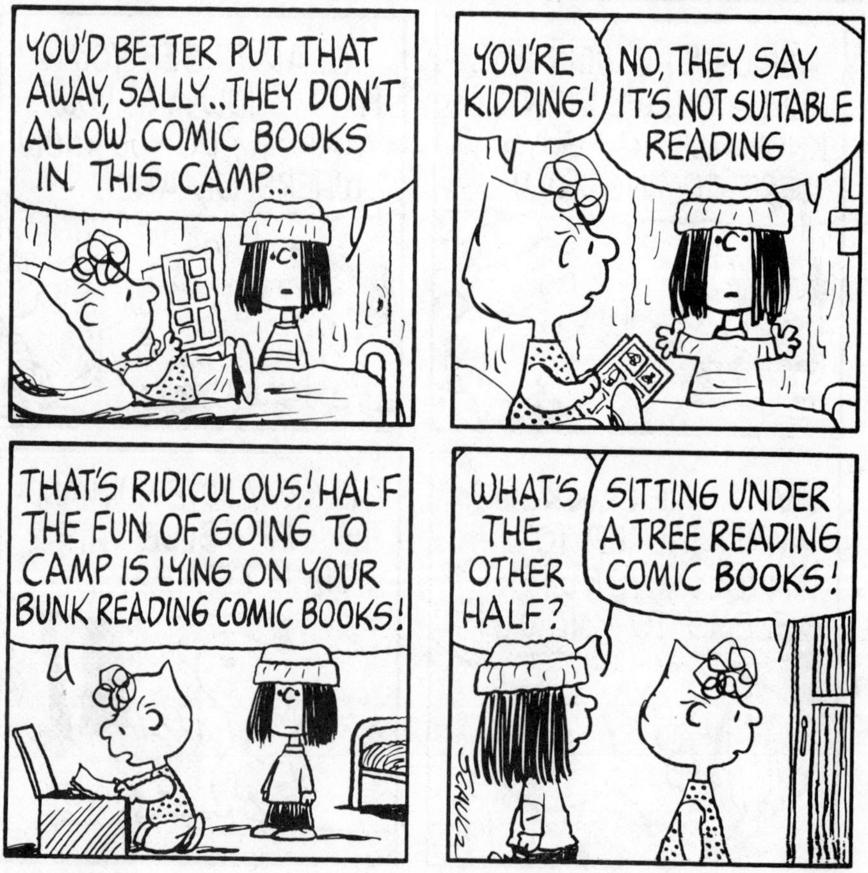
YOU'D BETTER PUT THAT AWAY, SALLY..THEY DON'T ALLOW COMIC BOOKS IN THIS CAMP...
YOU'RE KIDDING!
NO, THEY SAY IT'S NOT SUITABLE READING
THAT'S RIDICULOUS! HALF THE FUN OF GOING TO CAMP IS LYING ON YOUR BUNK READING COMIC BOOKS!
WHAT'S THE OTHER HALF?
SITTING UNDER A TREE READING COMIC BOOKS!

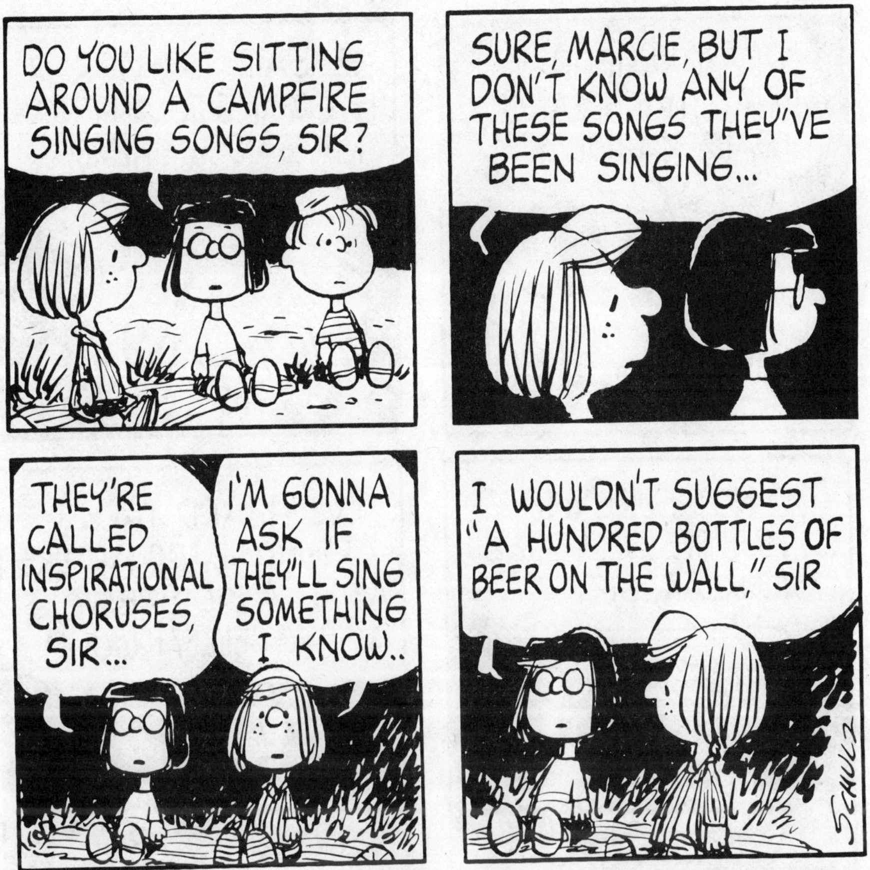
DO YOU LIKE SITTING AROUND A CAMPFIRE SINGING SONGS, SIR?
SURE, MARCIE, BUT I DON'T KNOW ANY OF THESE SONGS THEY'VE BEEN SINGING...
THEY'RE CALLED INSPIRATIONAL CHORUSES, SIR...
I'M GONNA ASK IF THEY'LL SING SOMETHING I KNOW..
I WOULDN'T SUGGEST "A HUNDRED BOTTLES OF BEER ON THE WALL," SIR
SCHULZ

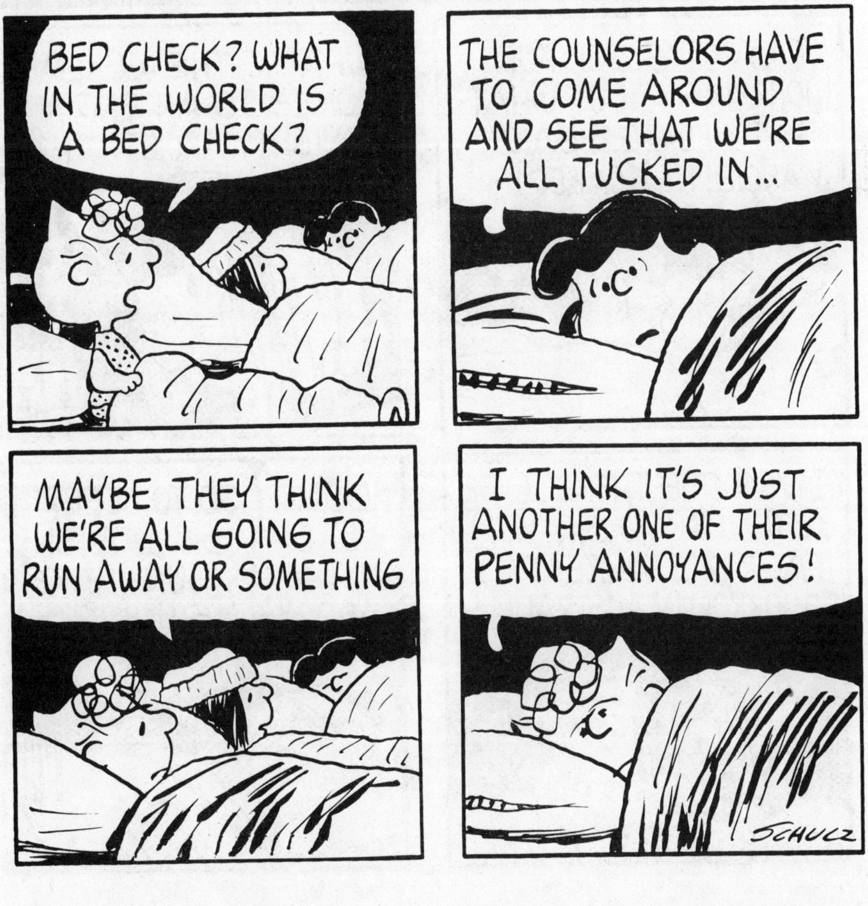
BED CHECK? WHAT IN THE WORLD IS A BED CHECK?
THE COUNSELORS HAVE TO COME AROUND AND SEE THAT WE'RE ALL TUCKED IN...
MAYBE THEY THINK WE'RE ALL GOING TO RUN AWAY OR SOMETHING
I THINK IT'S JUST ANOTHER ONE OF THEIR PENNY ANNOYANCES!
SCHULZ

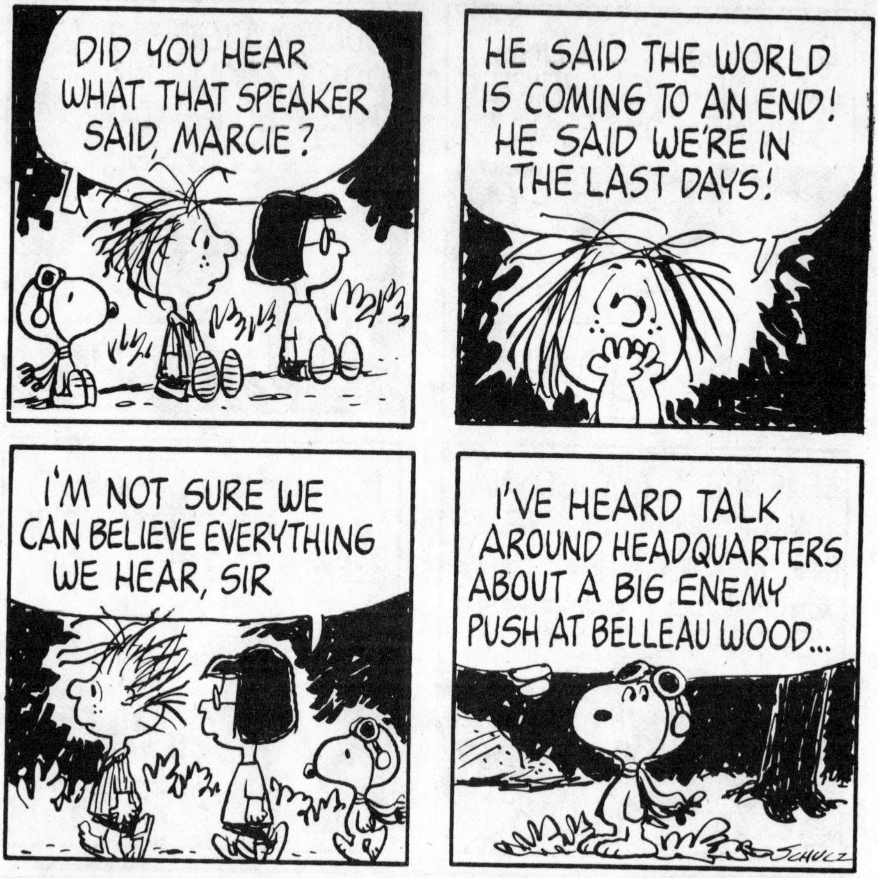
DID YOU HEAR WHAT THAT SPEAKER SAID, MARCIE?
HE SAID THE WORLD IS COMING TO AN END! HE SAID WE'RE IN THE LAST DAYS!
I'M NOT SURE WE CAN BELIEVE EVERYTHING WE HEAR, SIR
I'VE HEARD TALK AROUND HEADQUARTERS ABOUT A BIG ENEMY PUSH AT BELLEAU WOOD...
SCHULZ

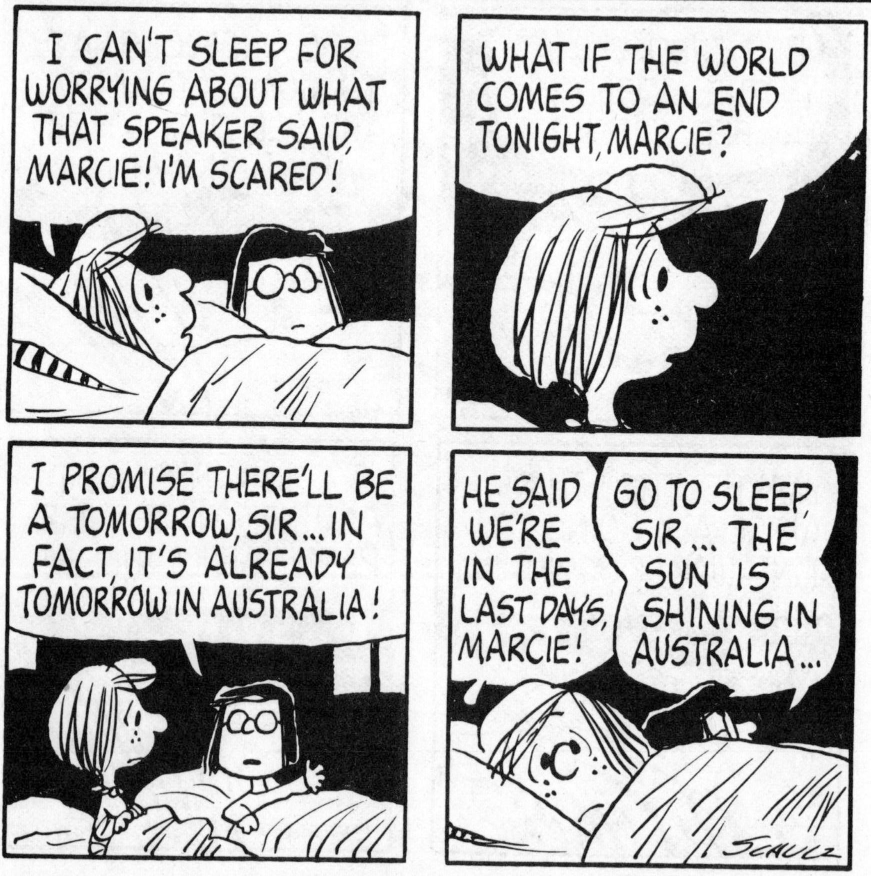
I CAN'T SLEEP FOR WORRYING ABOUT WHAT THAT SPEAKER SAID, MARCIE! I'M SCARED!
WHAT IF THE WORLD COMES TO AN END TONIGHT, MARCIE?
I PROMISE THERE'LL BE A TOMORROW, SIR... IN FACT, IT'S ALREADY TOMORROW IN AUSTRALIA!
HE SAID WE'RE IN THE LAST DAYS, MARCIE!
GO TO SLEEP, SIR... THE SUN IS SHINING IN AUSTRALIA...
SCHULZ

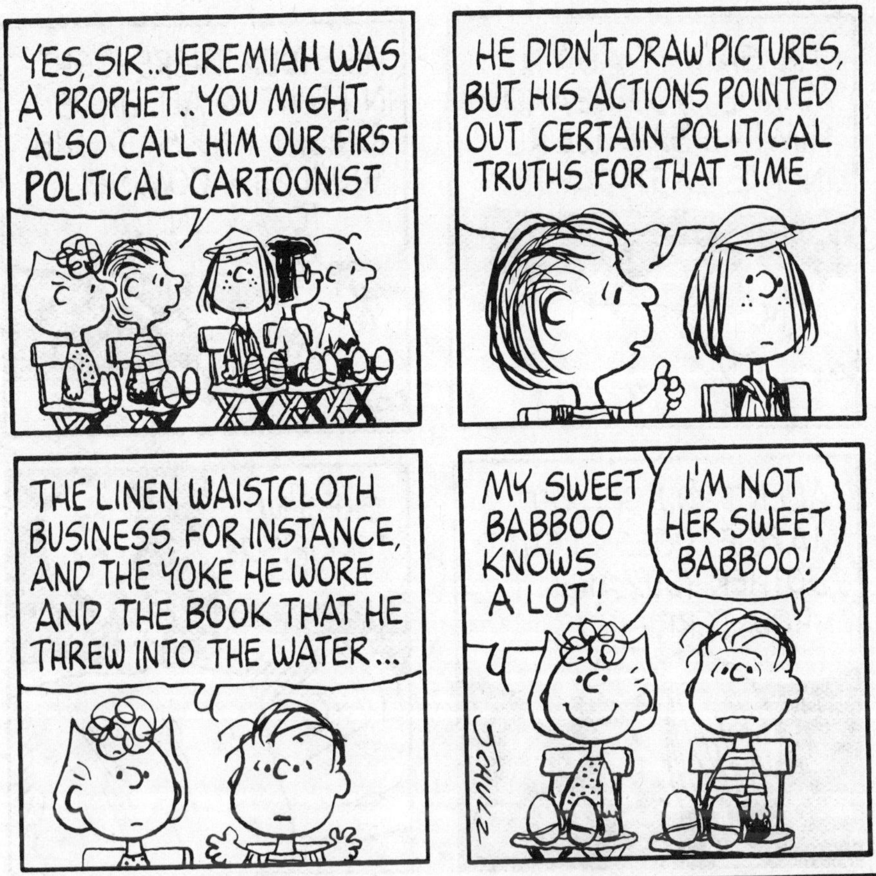
YES, SIR..JEREMIAH WAS A PROPHET..YOU MIGHT ALSO CALL HIM OUR FIRST POLITICAL CARTOONIST
HE DIDN'T DRAW PICTURES, BUT HIS ACTIONS POINTED OUT CERTAIN POLITICAL TRUTHS FOR THAT TIME
THE LINEN WAISTCLOTH BUSINESS, FOR INSTANCE, AND THE YOKE HE WORE AND THE BOOK THAT HE THREW INTO THE WATER...
MY SWEET BABBOO KNOWS A LOT!
I'M NOT HER SWEET BABBOO!
SCHULZ

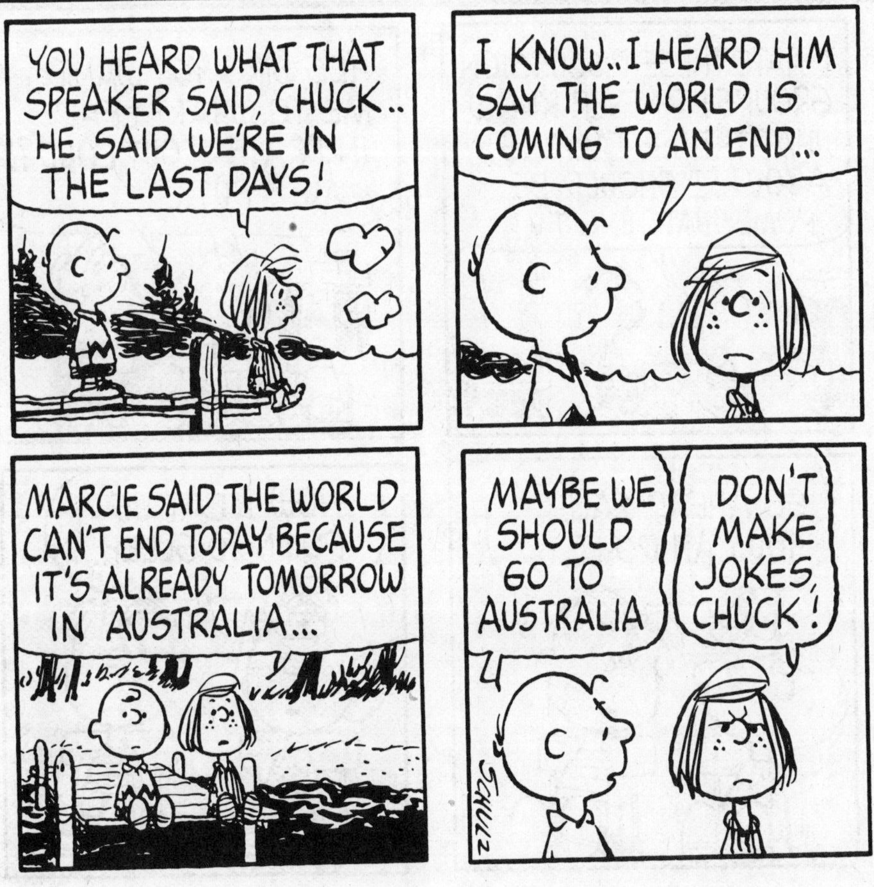
YOU HEARD WHAT THAT SPEAKER SAID, CHUCK.. HE SAID WE'RE IN THE LAST DAYS!
I KNOW..I HEARD HIM SAY THE WORLD IS COMING TO AN END...
MARCIE SAID THE WORLD CAN'T END TODAY BECAUSE IT'S ALREADY TOMORROW IN AUSTRALIA...
MAYBE WE SHOULD GO TO AUSTRALIA
DON'T MAKE JOKES, CHUCK!
SCHULZ

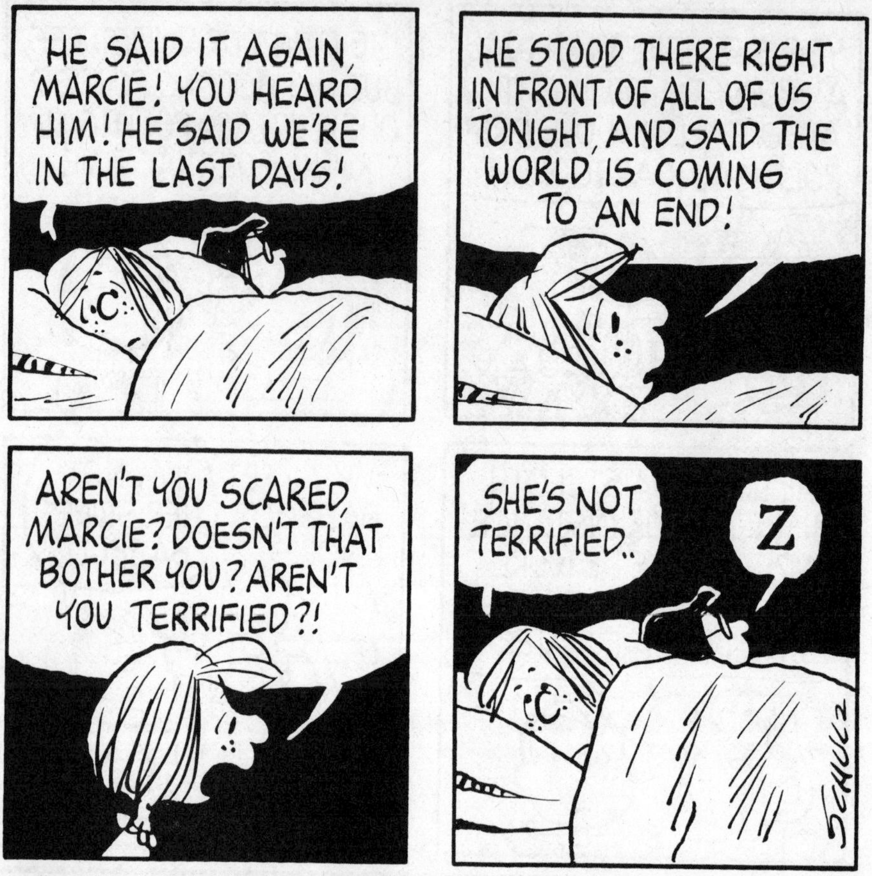
HE SAID IT AGAIN, MARCIE! YOU HEARD HIM! HE SAID WE'RE IN THE LAST DAYS!
HE STOOD THERE RIGHT IN FRONT OF ALL OF US TONIGHT, AND SAID THE WORLD IS COMING TO AN END!
AREN'T YOU SCARED, MARCIE? DOESN'T THAT BOTHER YOU? AREN'T YOU TERRIFIED?!
SHE'S NOT TERRIFIED..
Z
SCHULZ

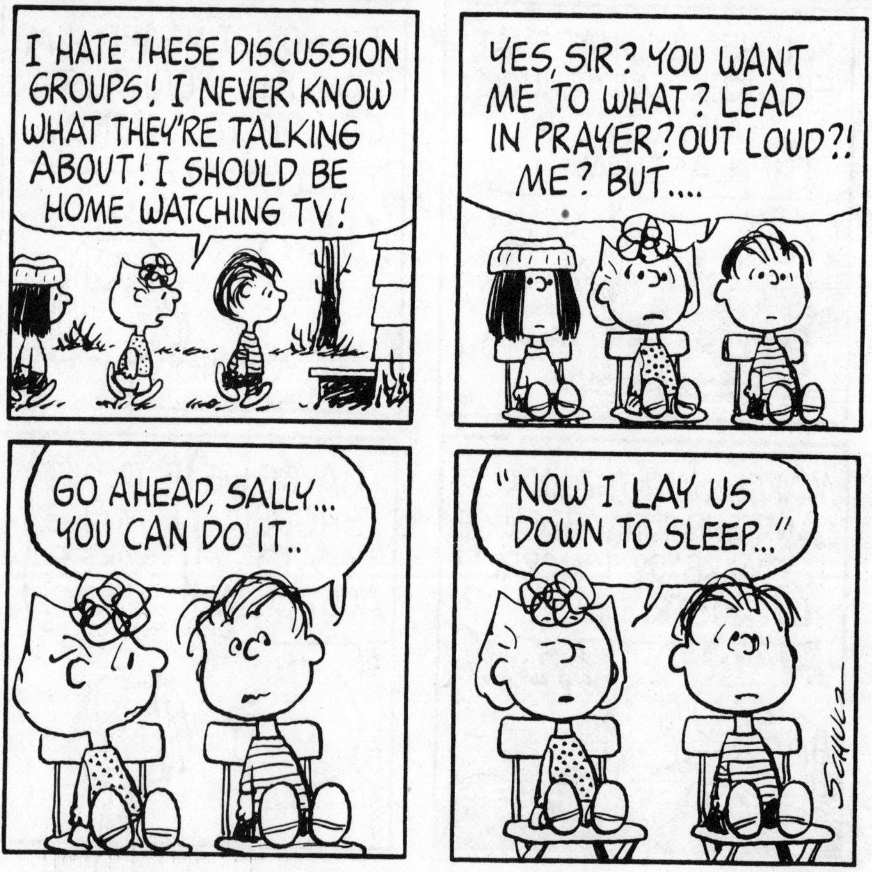
I HATE THESE DISCUSSION GROUPS! I NEVER KNOW WHAT THEY'RE TALKING ABOUT! I SHOULD BE HOME WATCHING TV!
YES, SIR? YOU WANT ME TO WHAT? LEAD IN PRAYER? OUT LOUD?! ME? BUT....
GO AHEAD, SALLY... YOU CAN DO IT..
"NOW I LAY US DOWN TO SLEEP..."
SCHULZ

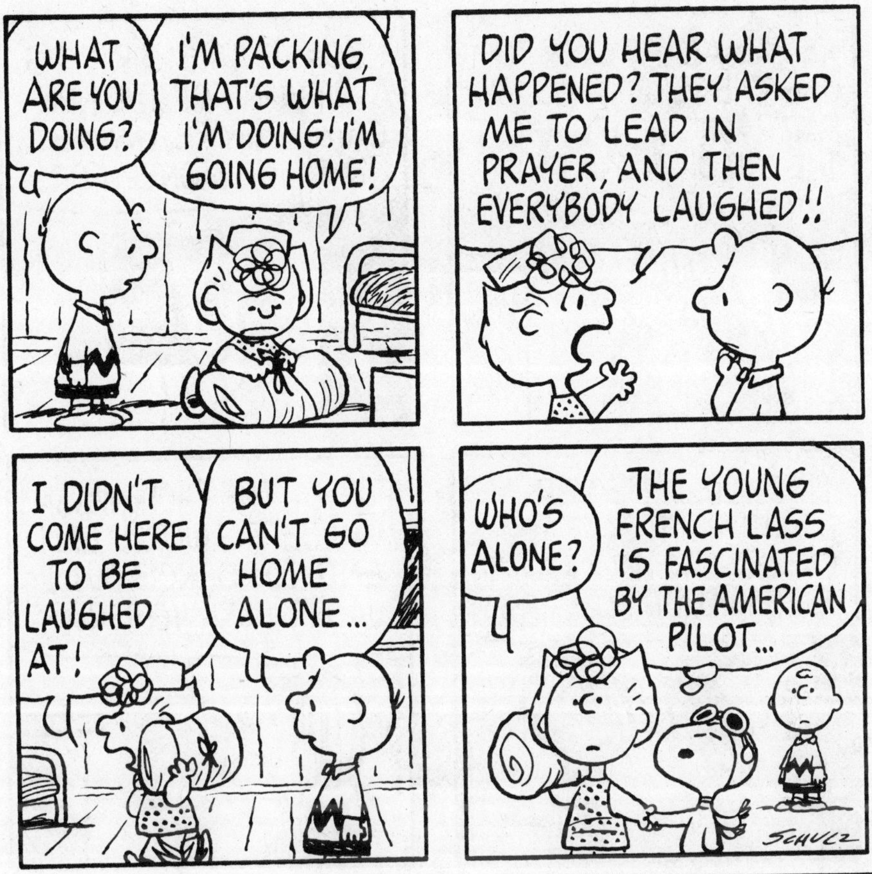
WHAT ARE YOU DOING?
I'M PACKING, THAT'S WHAT I'M DOING! I'M GOING HOME!
DID YOU HEAR WHAT HAPPENED? THEY ASKED ME TO LEAD IN PRAYER, AND THEN EVERYBODY LAUGHED!!
I DIDN'T COME HERE TO BE LAUGHED AT!
BUT YOU CAN'T GO HOME ALONE...
WHO'S ALONE?
THE YOUNG FRENCH LASS IS FASCINATED BY THE AMERICAN PILOT...
SCHULZ

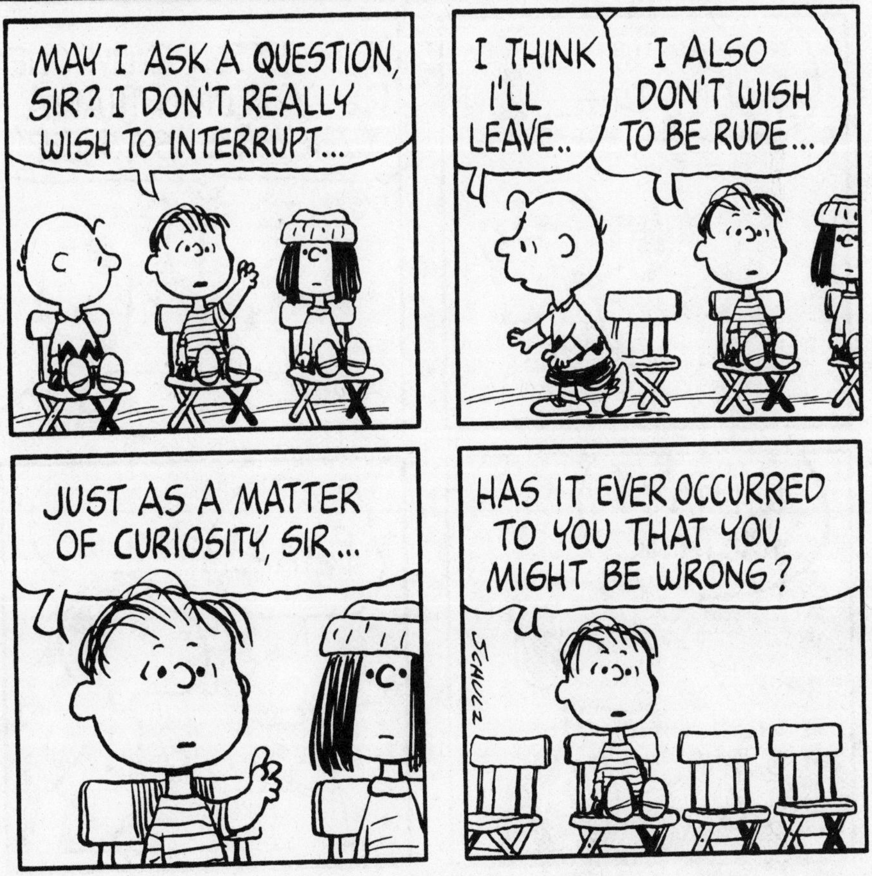
MAY I ASK A QUESTION, SIR? I DON'T REALLY WISH TO INTERRUPT...
I THINK I'LL LEAVE..
I ALSO DON'T WISH TO BE RUDE...
JUST AS A MATTER OF CURIOSITY, SIR...
HAS IT EVER OCCURRED TO YOU THAT YOU MIGHT BE WRONG?
SCHULZ

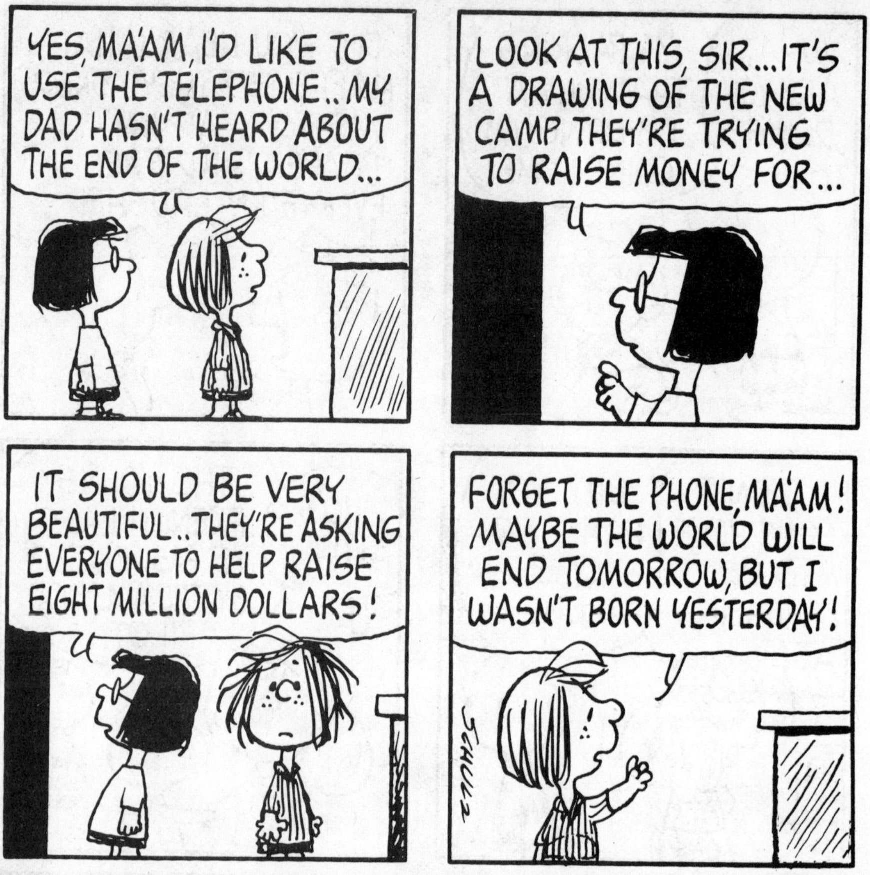
YES, MA'AM, I'D LIKE TO USE THE TELEPHONE.. MY DAD HASN'T HEARD ABOUT THE END OF THE WORLD...
LOOK AT THIS, SIR...IT'S A DRAWING OF THE NEW CAMP THEY'RE TRYING TO RAISE MONEY FOR...
IT SHOULD BE VERY BEAUTIFUL..THEY'RE ASKING EVERYONE TO HELP RAISE EIGHT MILLION DOLLARS!
FORGET THE PHONE, MA'AM! MAYBE THE WORLD WILL END TOMORROW, BUT I WASN'T BORN YESTERDAY!
SCHULZ

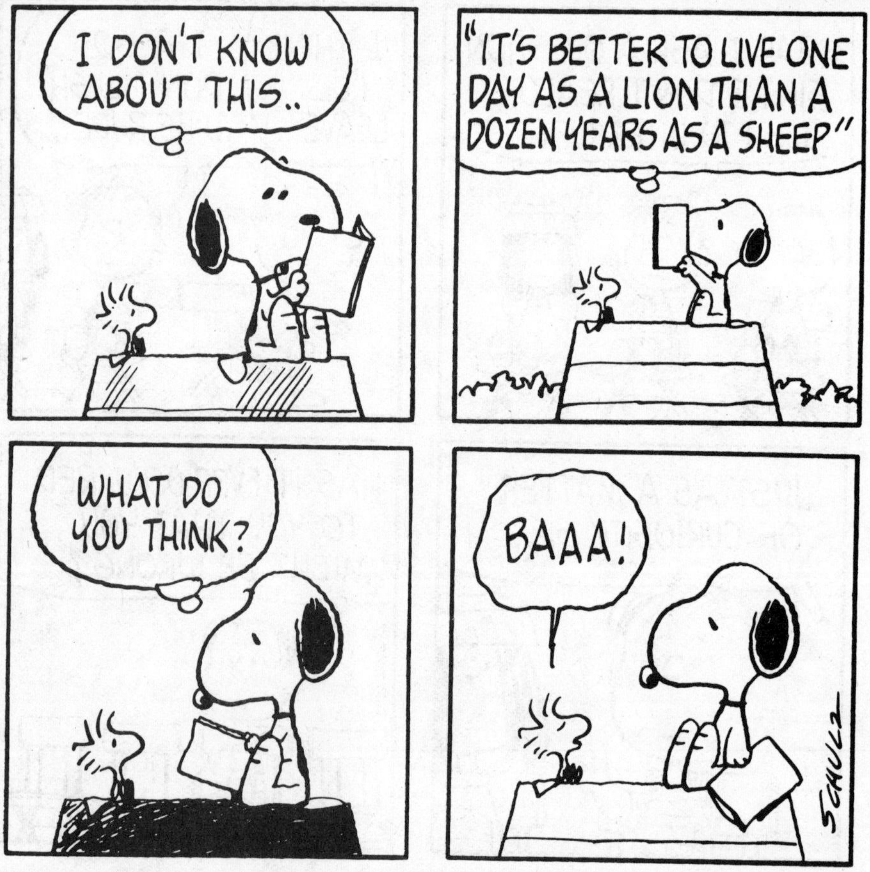
I DON'T KNOW ABOUT THIS..
"IT'S BETTER TO LIVE ONE DAY AS A LION THAN A DOZEN YEARS AS A SHEEP"
WHAT DO YOU THINK?
BAAA!
SCHULZ

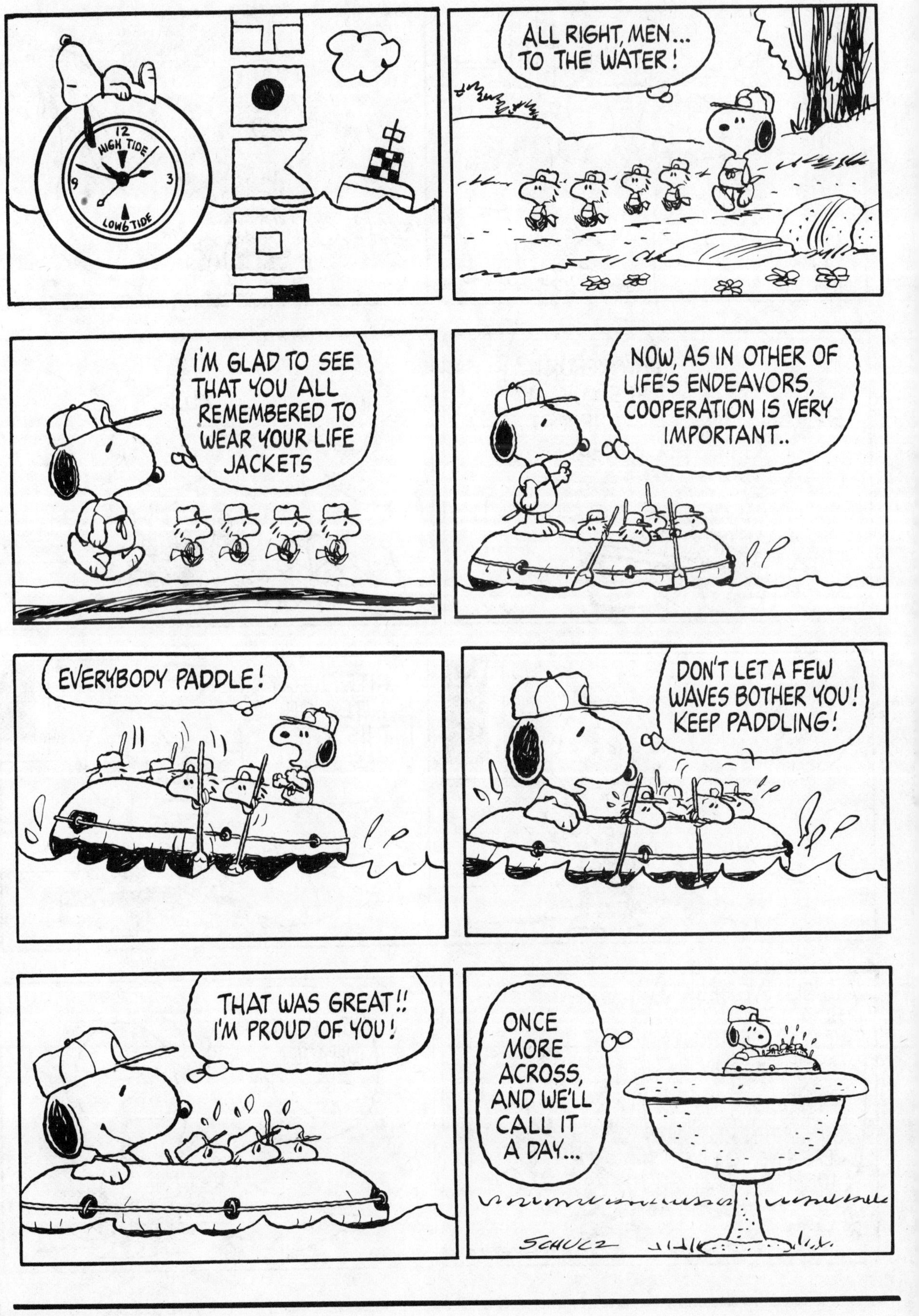
HIGH TIDE
LOW TIDE
ALL RIGHT, MEN... TO THE WATER!
I'M GLAD TO SEE THAT YOU ALL REMEMBERED TO WEAR YOUR LIFE JACKETS
NOW, AS IN OTHER OF LIFE'S ENDEAVORS, COOPERATION IS VERY IMPORTANT..
EVERYBODY PADDLE!
DON'T LET A FEW WAVES BOTHER YOU! KEEP PADDLING!
THAT WAS GREAT!! I'M PROUD OF YOU!
ONCE MORE ACROSS, AND WE'LL CALL IT A DAY...
SCHULZ

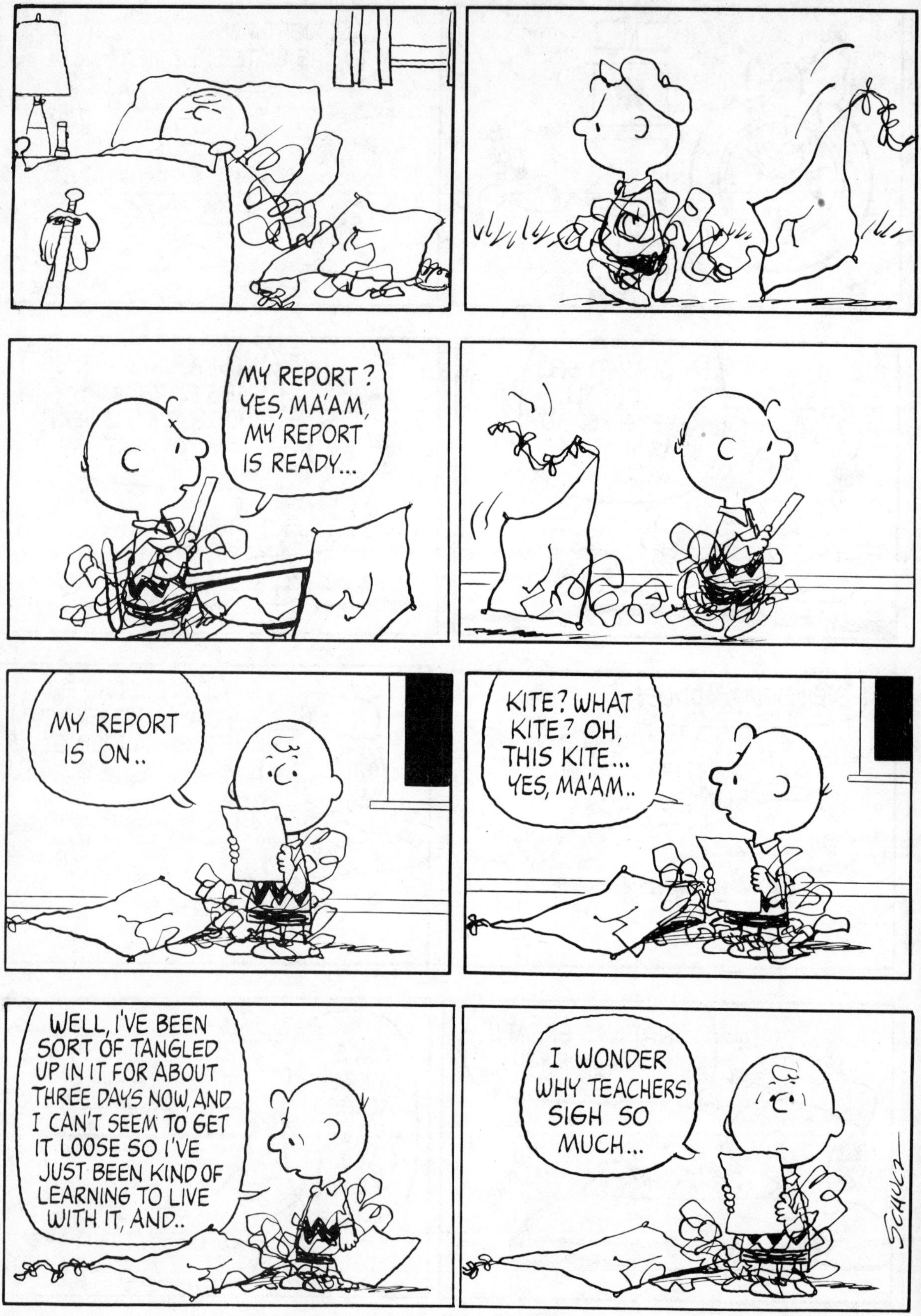
MY REPORT? YES, MA'AM, MY REPORT IS READY...
MY REPORT IS ON..
KITE? WHAT KITE? OH, THIS KITE... YES, MA'AM..
WELL, I'VE BEEN SORT OF TANGLED UP IN IT FOR ABOUT THREE DAYS NOW, AND I CAN'T SEEM TO GET IT LOOSE SO I'VE JUST BEEN KIND OF LEARNING TO LIVE WITH IT, AND..
I WONDER WHY TEACHERS SIGH SO MUCH...
SCHULZ

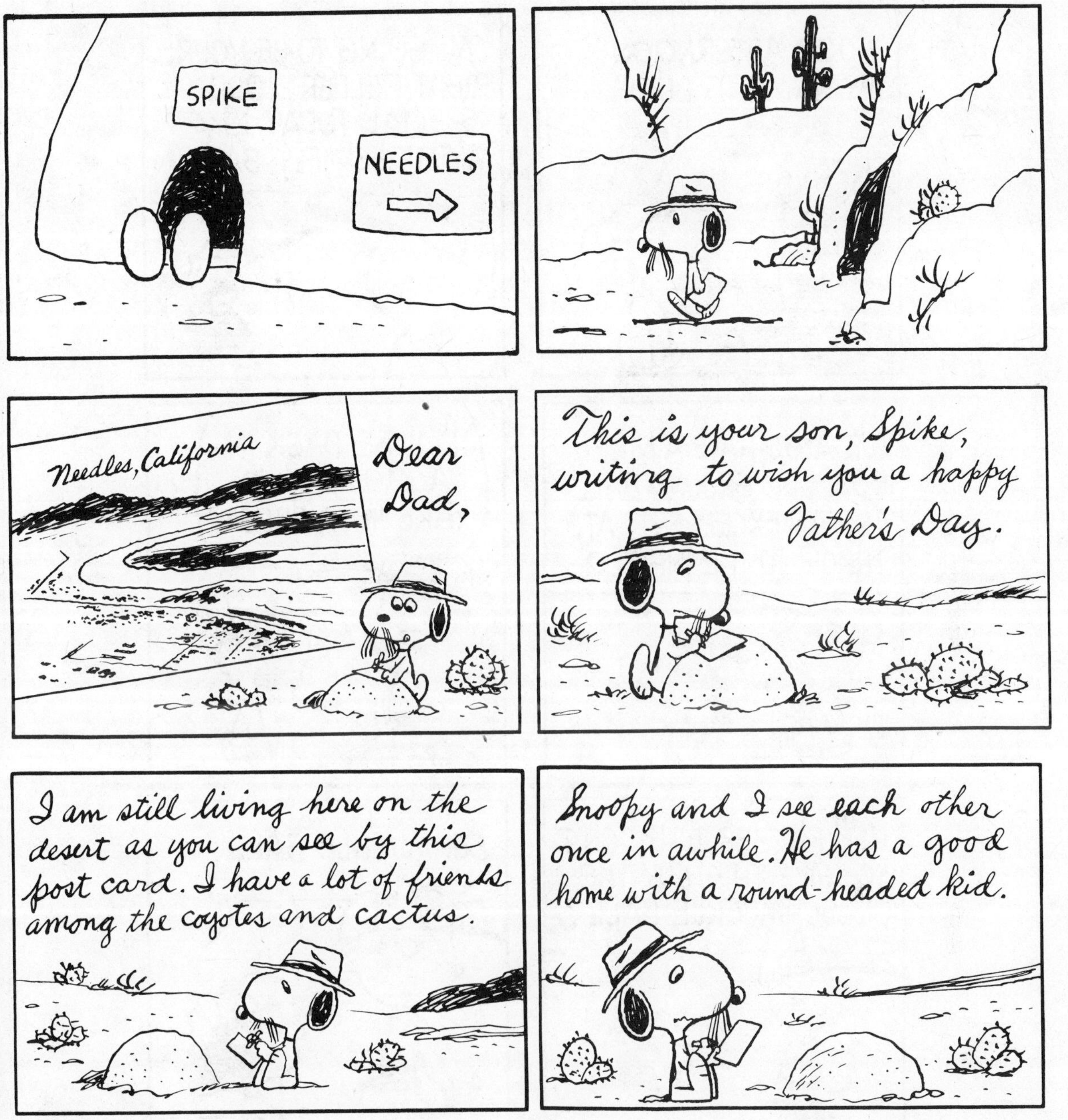
SPIKE
NEEDLES
Needles, California
Dear Dad,
This is your son, Spike, writing to wish you a happy Father's Day.
I am still living here on the desert as you can see by this post card. I have a lot of friends among the coyotes and cactus.
Snoopy and I see each other once in awhile. He has a good home with a round-headed kid.
I could never be a house dog. I like being independent.
Say "Hi" to Mom, and have a happy Father's Day.
Love, Spike
P.S. Please send me ten dollars.
SCHULZ

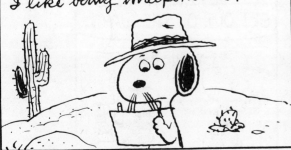

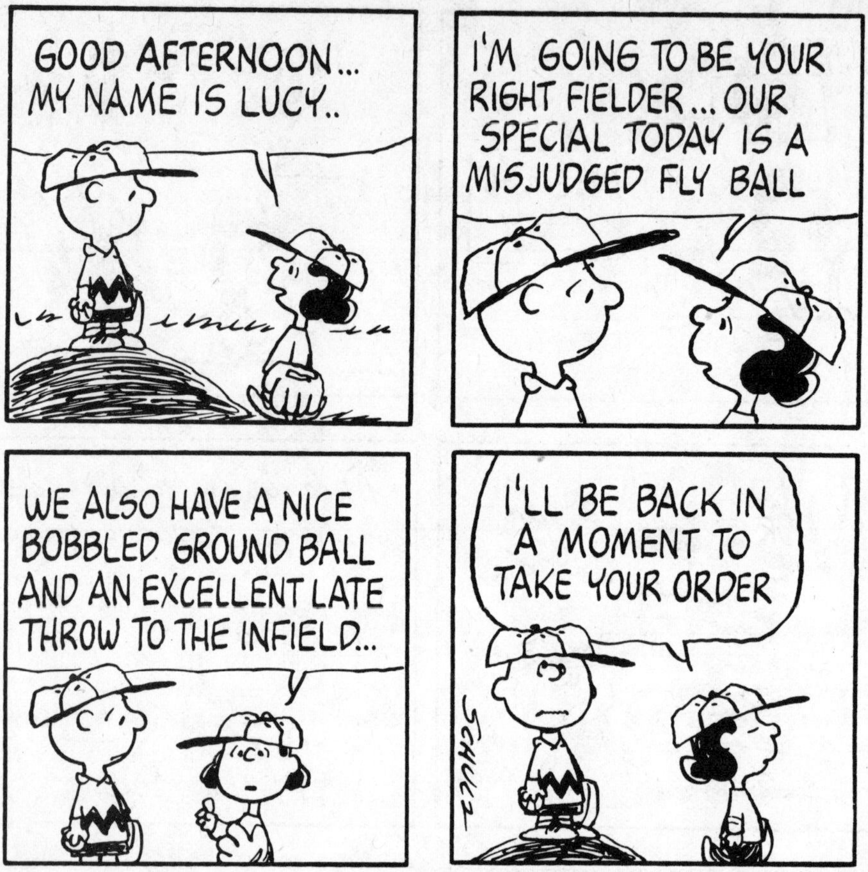
GOOD AFTERNOON... MY NAME IS LUCY..
I'M GOING TO BE YOUR RIGHT FIELDER... OUR SPECIAL TODAY IS A MISJUDGED FLY BALL
WE ALSO HAVE A NICE BOBBLED GROUND BALL AND AN EXCELLENT LATE THROW TO THE INFIELD...
I'LL BE BACK IN A MOMENT TO TAKE YOUR ORDER
SCHULZ

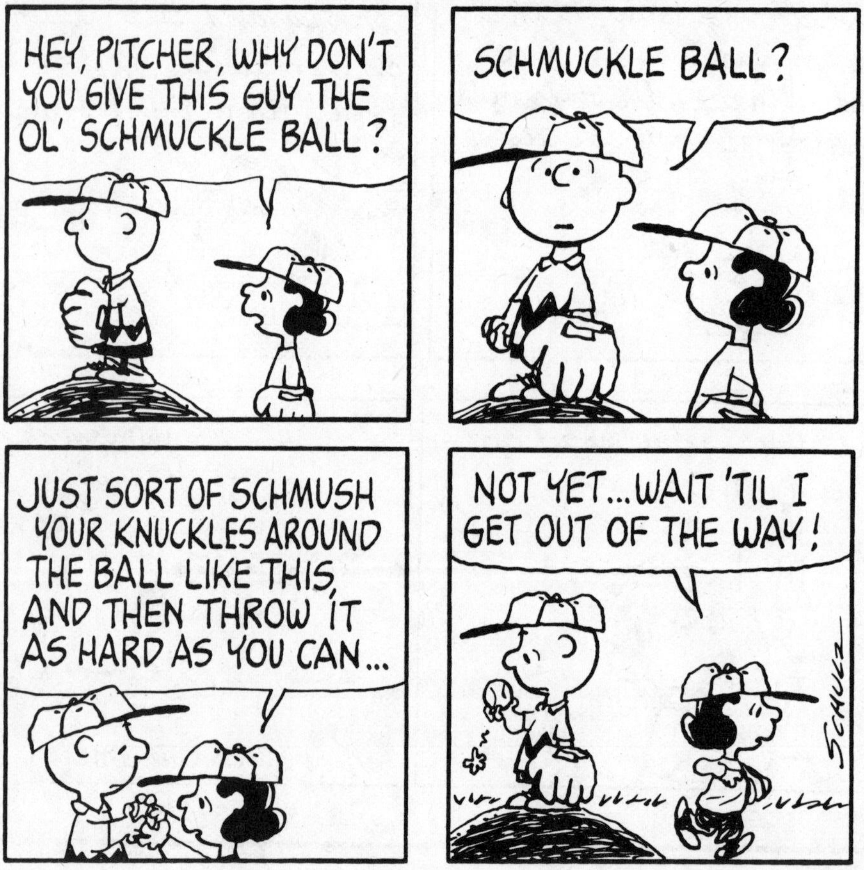
HEY, PITCHER, WHY DON'T YOU GIVE THIS GUY THE OL' SCHMUCKLE BALL?
SCHMUCKLE BALL?
JUST SORT OF SCHMUSH YOUR KNUCKLES AROUND THE BALL LIKE THIS, AND THEN THROW IT AS HARD AS YOU CAN...
NOT YET... WAIT 'TIL I GET OUT OF THE WAY!
SCHULZ

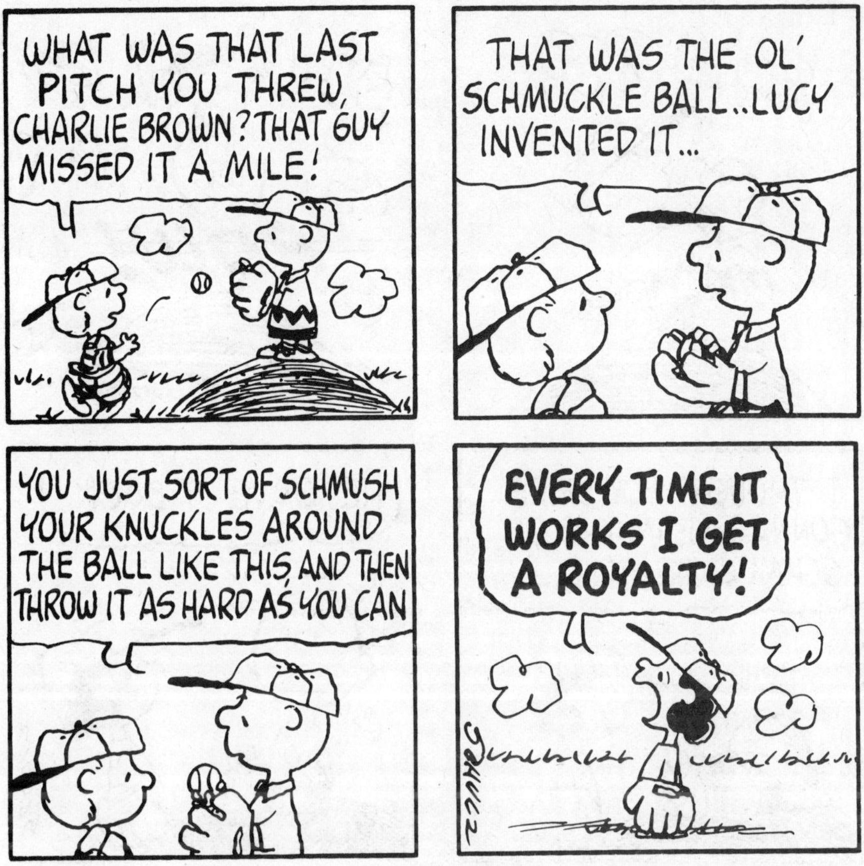
WHAT WAS THAT LAST PITCH YOU THREW, CHARLIE BROWN? THAT GUY MISSED IT A MILE!
THAT WAS THE OL' SCHMUCKLE BALL..LUCY INVENTED IT...
YOU JUST SORT OF SCHMUSH YOUR KNUCKLES AROUND THE BALL LIKE THIS, AND THEN THROW IT AS HARD AS YOU CAN
EVERY TIME IT WORKS I GET A ROYALTY!
SCHULZ

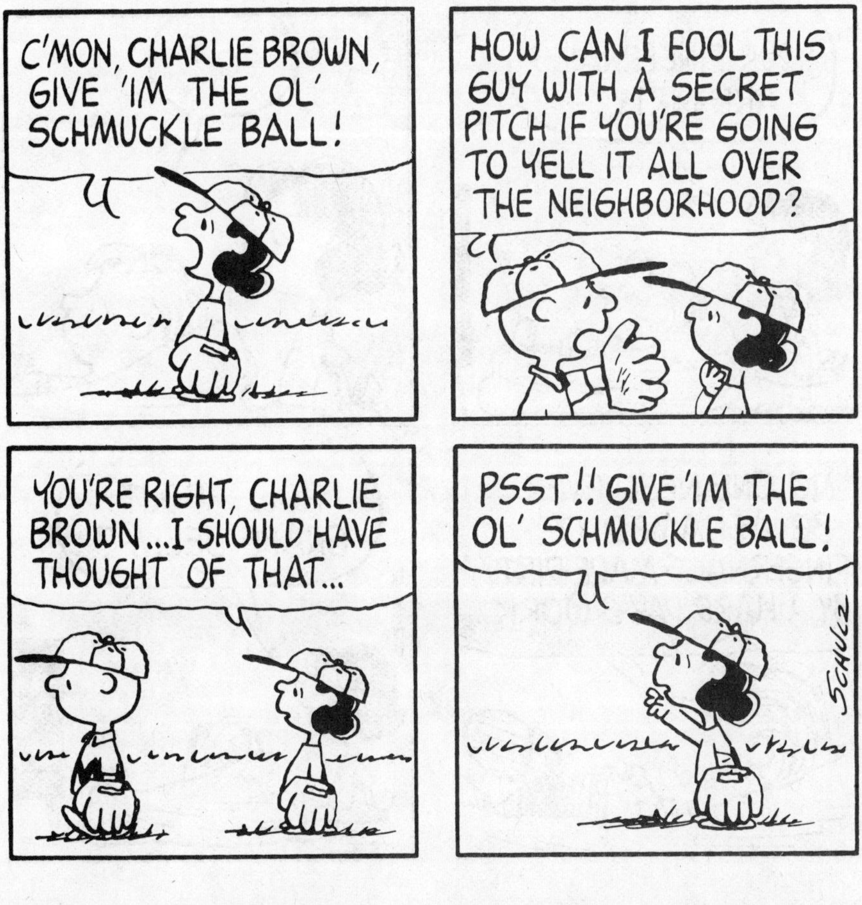
C'MON, CHARLIE BROWN, GIVE 'IM THE OL' SCHMUCKLE BALL!
HOW CAN I FOOL THIS GUY WITH A SECRET PITCH IF YOU'RE GOING TO YELL IT ALL OVER THE NEIGHBORHOOD?
YOU'RE RIGHT, CHARLIE BROWN...I SHOULD HAVE THOUGHT OF THAT...
PSST!! GIVE 'IM THE OL' SCHMUCKLE BALL!
SCHULZ

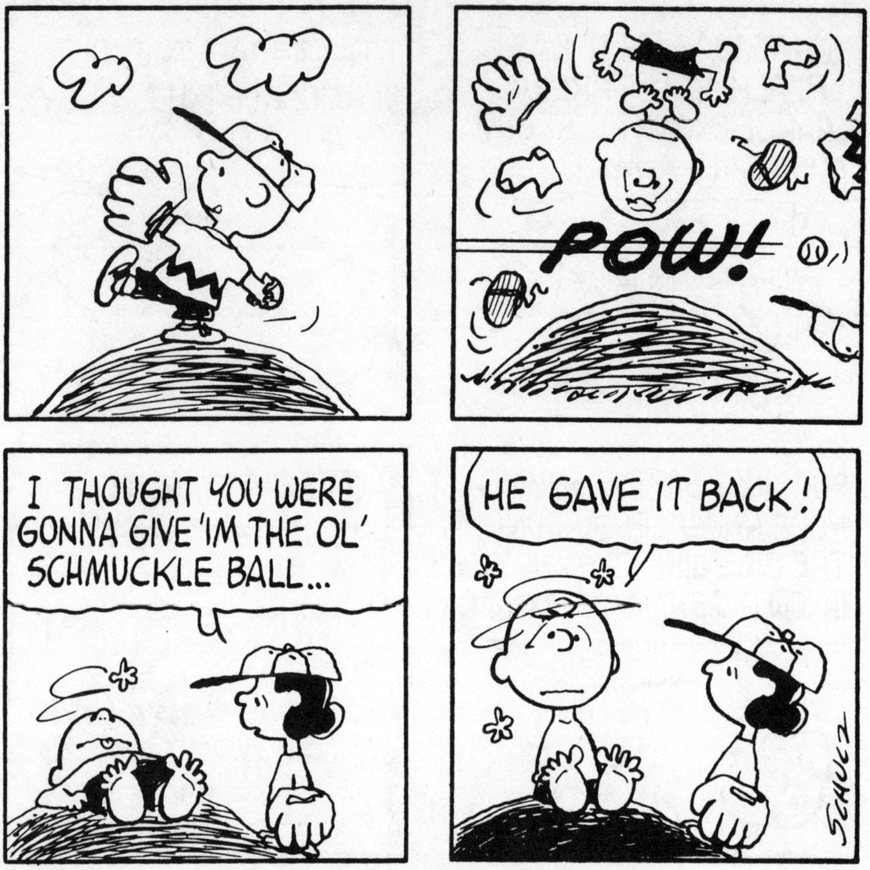
POW!
I THOUGHT YOU WERE GONNA GIVE 'IM THE OL' SCHMUCKLE BALL...
HE GAVE IT BACK!
SCHULZ

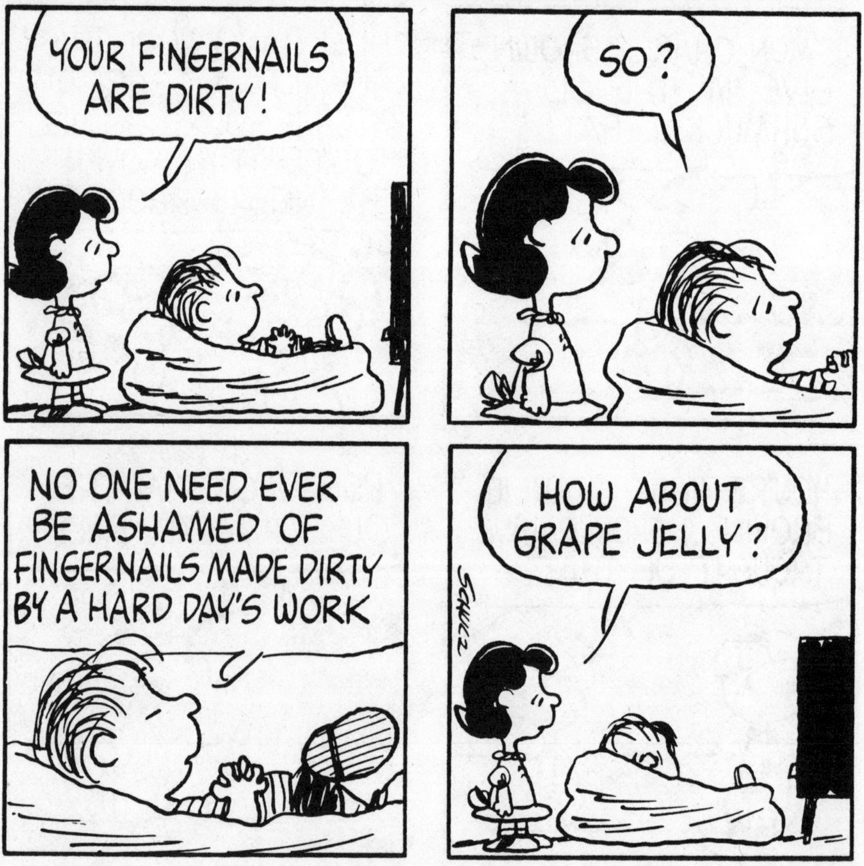
YOUR FINGERNAILS ARE DIRTY!
SO?
NO ONE NEED EVER BE ASHAMED OF FINGERNAILS MADE DIRTY BY A HARD DAY'S WORK
HOW ABOUT GRAPE JELLY?
SCHULZ

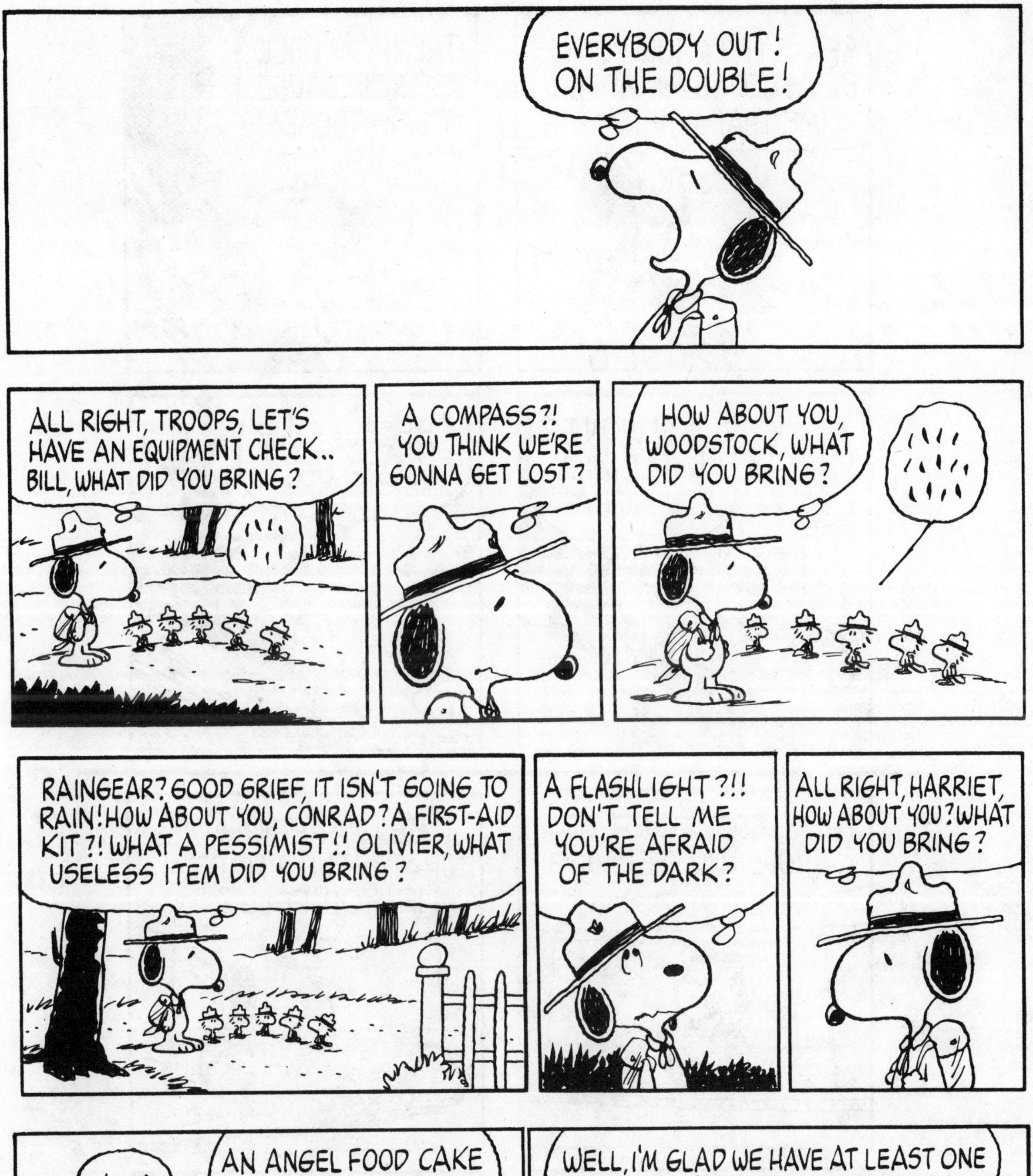

EVERYBODY OUT! ON THE DOUBLE!
ALL RIGHT, TROOPS, LET'S HAVE AN EQUIPMENT CHECK.. BILL, WHAT DID YOU BRING?
A COMPASS?! YOU THINK WE'RE GONNA GET LOST?
HOW ABOUT YOU, WOODSTOCK, WHAT DID YOU BRING?
RAINGEAR? GOOD GRIEF, IT ISN'T GOING TO RAIN! HOW ABOUT YOU, CONRAD? A FIRST-AID KIT?! WHAT A PESSIMIST!! OLIVIER, WHAT USELESS ITEM DID YOU BRING?
A FLASHLIGHT?!! DON'T TELL ME YOU'RE AFRAID OF THE DARK?
ALL RIGHT, HARRIET, HOW ABOUT YOU? WHAT DID YOU BRING?
AN ANGEL FOOD CAKE WITH SEVEN-MINUTE FROSTING?!!!
WELL, I'M GLAD WE HAVE AT LEAST ONE SENSIBLE HIKER IN OUR GROUP!
SCHULZ

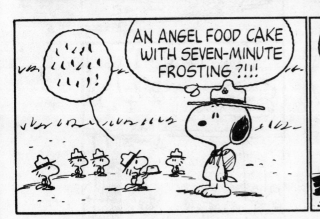

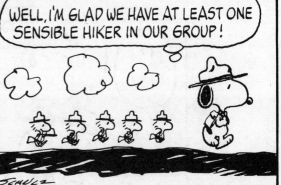

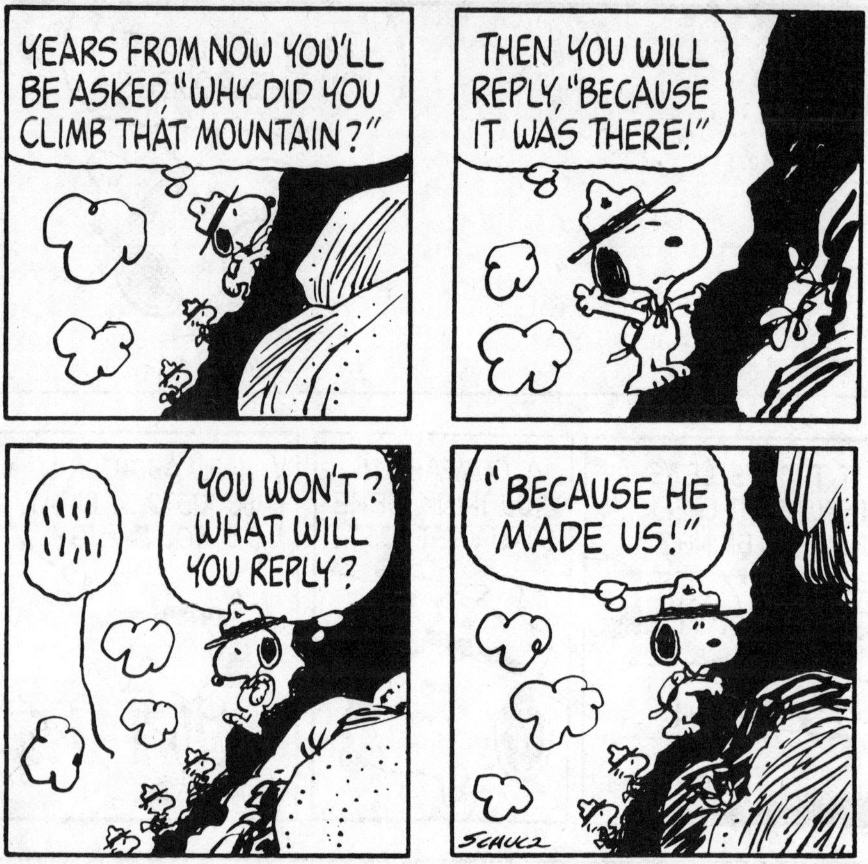
YEARS FROM NOW YOU'LL BE ASKED, "WHY DID YOU CLIMB THAT MOUNTAIN?"
THEN YOU WILL REPLY, "BECAUSE IT WAS THERE!"
YOU WON'T? WHAT WILL YOU REPLY?
"BECAUSE HE MADE US!"

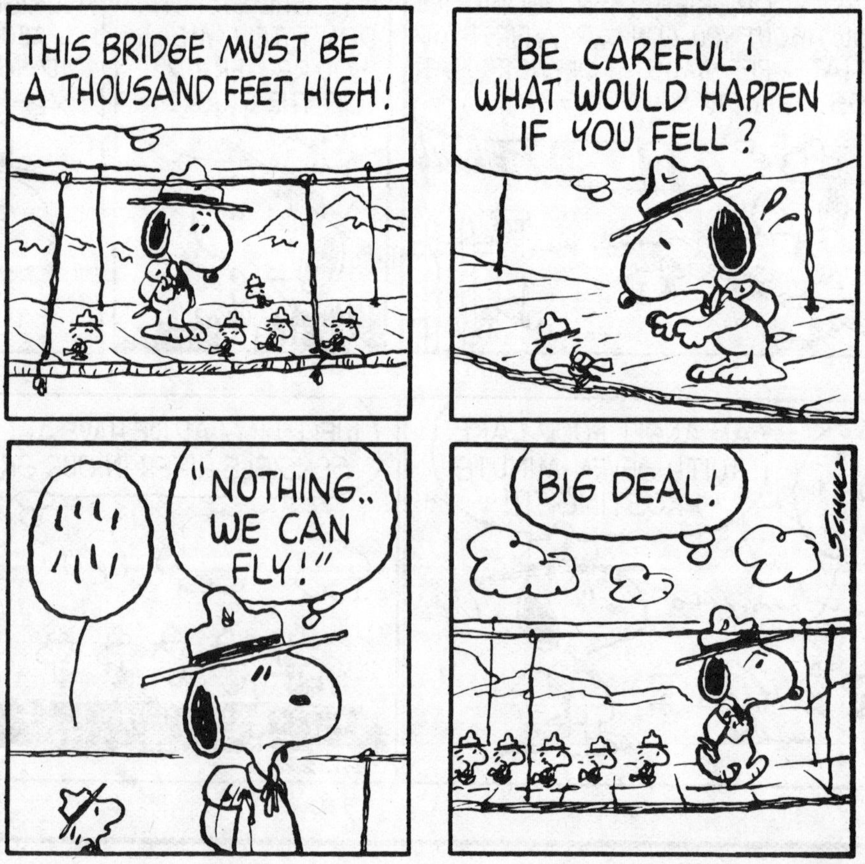
THIS BRIDGE MUST BE A THOUSAND FEET HIGH!
BE CAREFUL! WHAT WOULD HAPPEN IF YOU FELL?
"NOTHING.. WE CAN FLY!"
BIG DEAL!

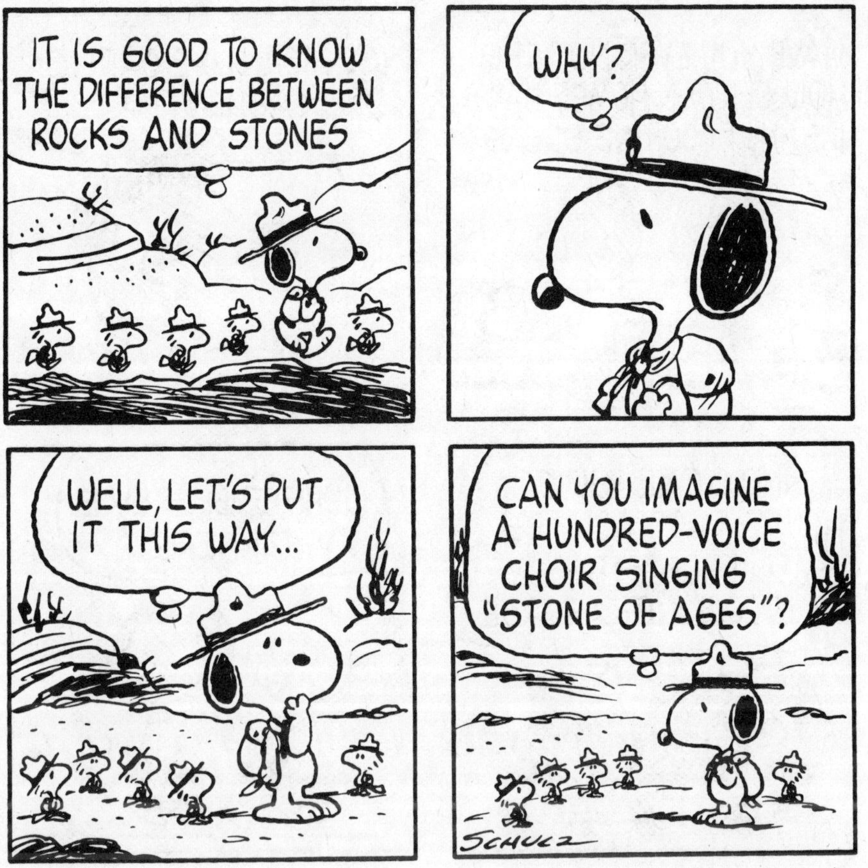
IT IS GOOD TO KNOW THE DIFFERENCE BETWEEN ROCKS AND STONES
WHY?
WELL, LET'S PUT IT THIS WAY...
CAN YOU IMAGINE A HUNDRED-VOICE CHOIR SINGING "STONE OF AGES"?
SCHULZ

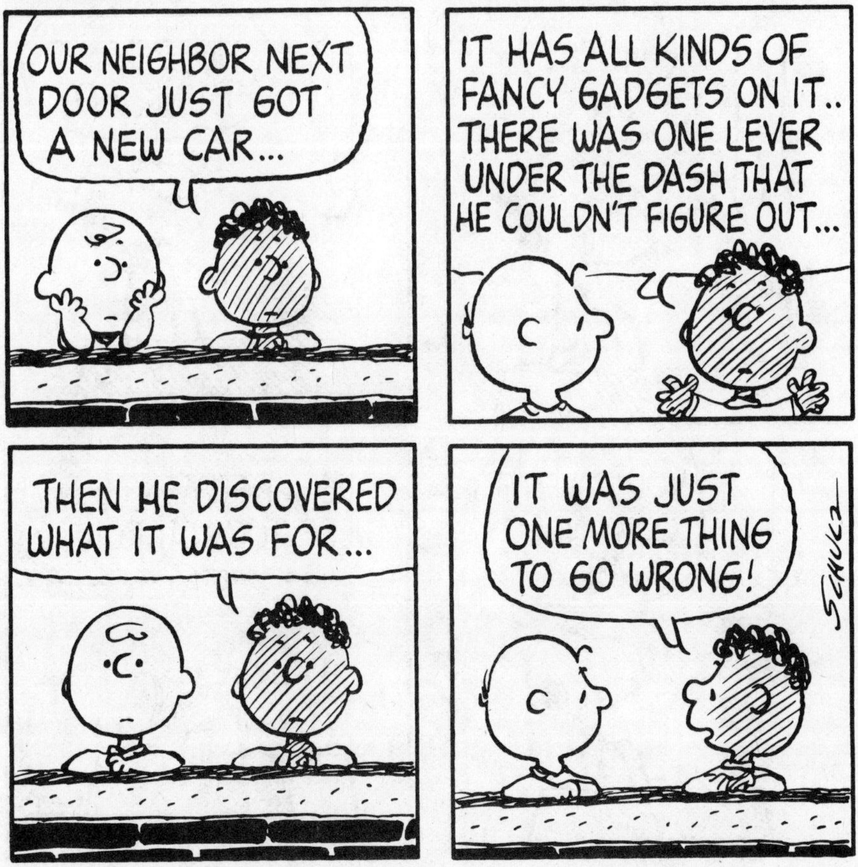
OUR NEIGHBOR NEXT DOOR JUST GOT A NEW CAR...
IT HAS ALL KINDS OF FANCY GADGETS ON IT.. THERE WAS ONE LEVER UNDER THE DASH THAT HE COULDN'T FIGURE OUT...
THEN HE DISCOVERED WHAT IT WAS FOR...
IT WAS JUST ONE MORE THING TO GO WRONG!
SCHULZ

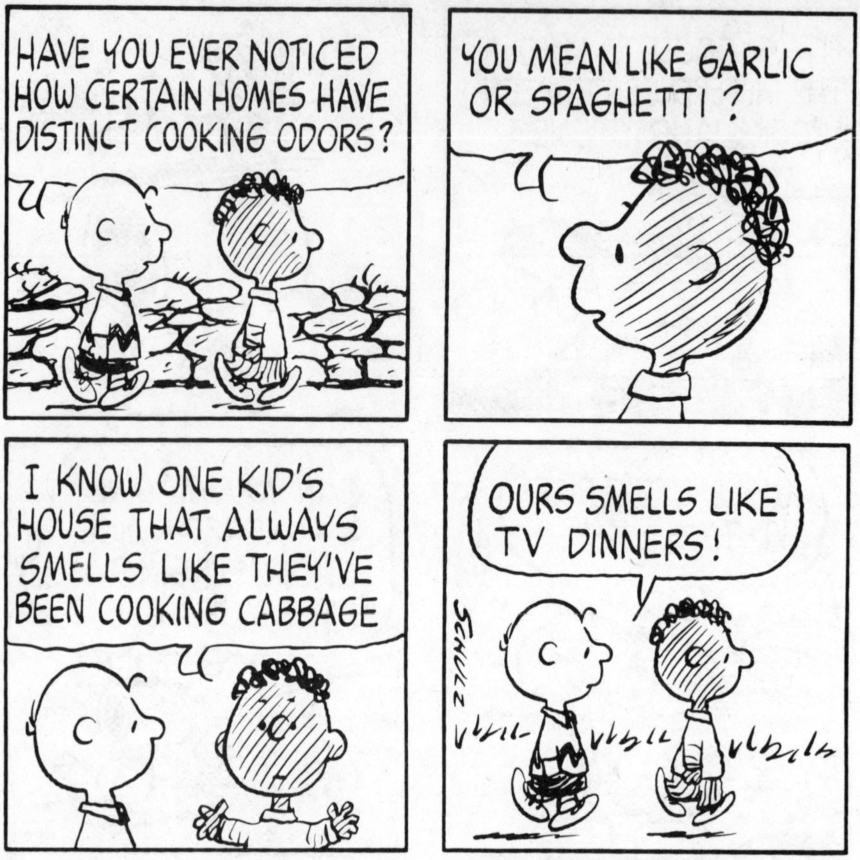
HAVE YOU EVER NOTICED HOW CERTAIN HOMES HAVE DISTINCT COOKING ODORS?
YOU MEAN LIKE GARLIC OR SPAGHETTI ?
I KNOW ONE KID'S HOUSE THAT ALWAYS SMELLS LIKE THEY'VE BEEN COOKING CABBAGE
OURS SMELLS LIKE TV DINNERS!
SCHULZ

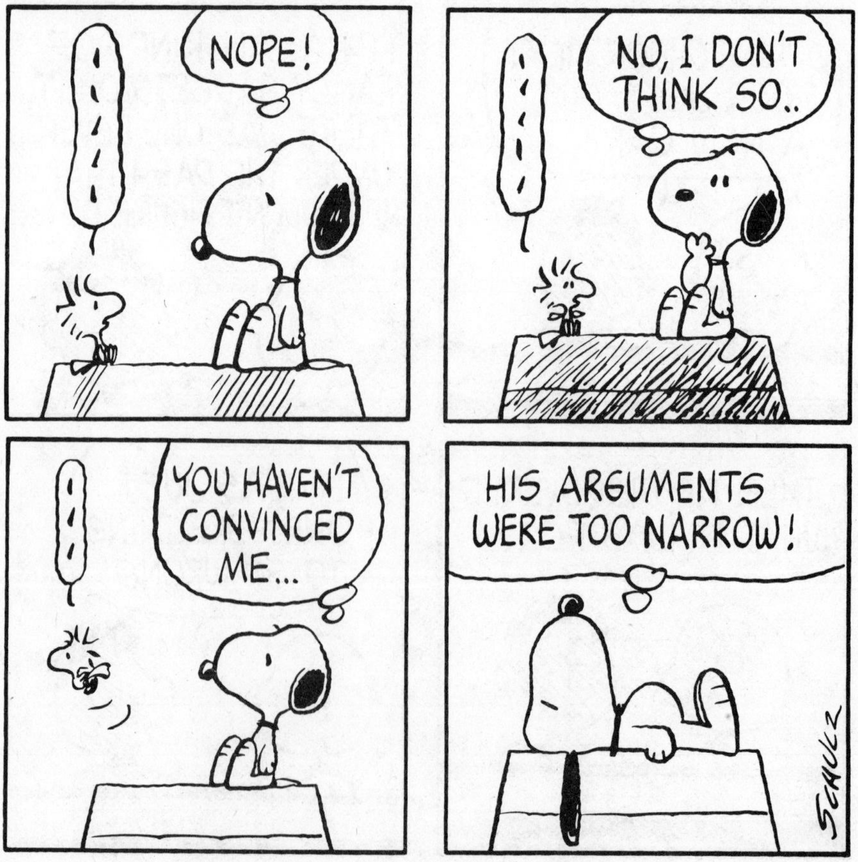
NOPE!
NO, I DON'T THINK SO..
YOU HAVEN'T CONVINCED ME...
HIS ARGUMENTS WERE TOO NARROW!
SCHULZ

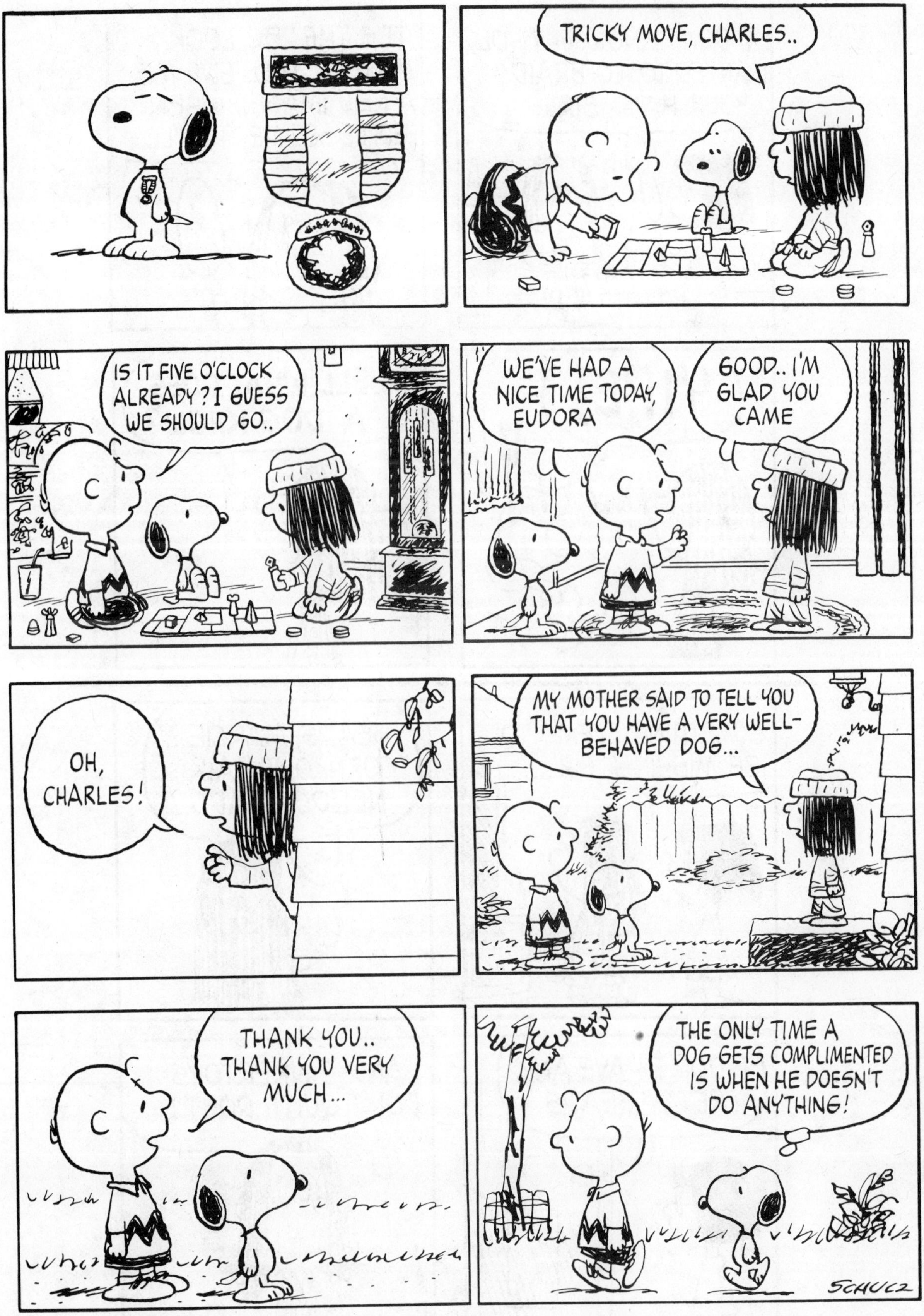
TRICKY MOVE, CHARLES..
IS IT FIVE O'CLOCK ALREADY? I GUESS WE SHOULD GO..
WE'VE HAD A NICE TIME TODAY, EUDORA
GOOD.. I'M GLAD YOU CAME
OH, CHARLES!
MY MOTHER SAID TO TELL YOU THAT YOU HAVE A VERY WELL-BEHAVED DOG...
THANK YOU.. THANK YOU VERY MUCH...
THE ONLY TIME A DOG GETS COMPLIMENTED IS WHEN HE DOESN'T DO ANYTHING!
SCHULZ

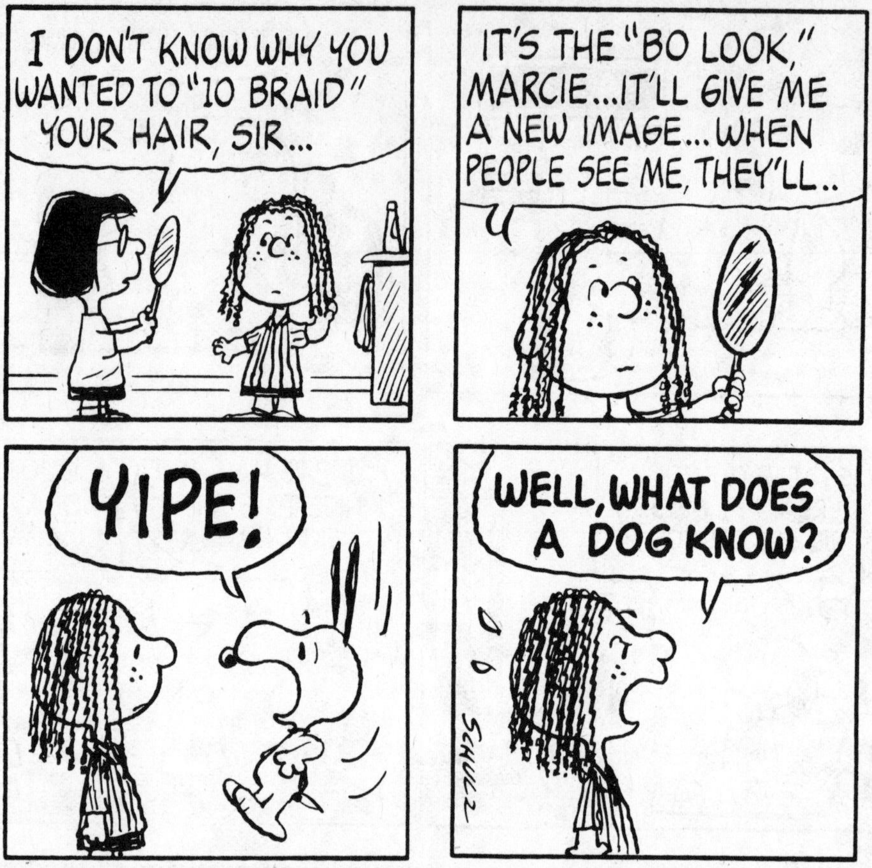
I DON'T KNOW WHY YOU WANTED TO "10 BRAID" YOUR HAIR, SIR...
IT'S THE "BO LOOK," MARCIE...IT'LL GIVE ME A NEW IMAGE...WHEN PEOPLE SEE ME, THEY'LL..
YIPE!
WELL, WHAT DOES A DOG KNOW?
SCHULZ

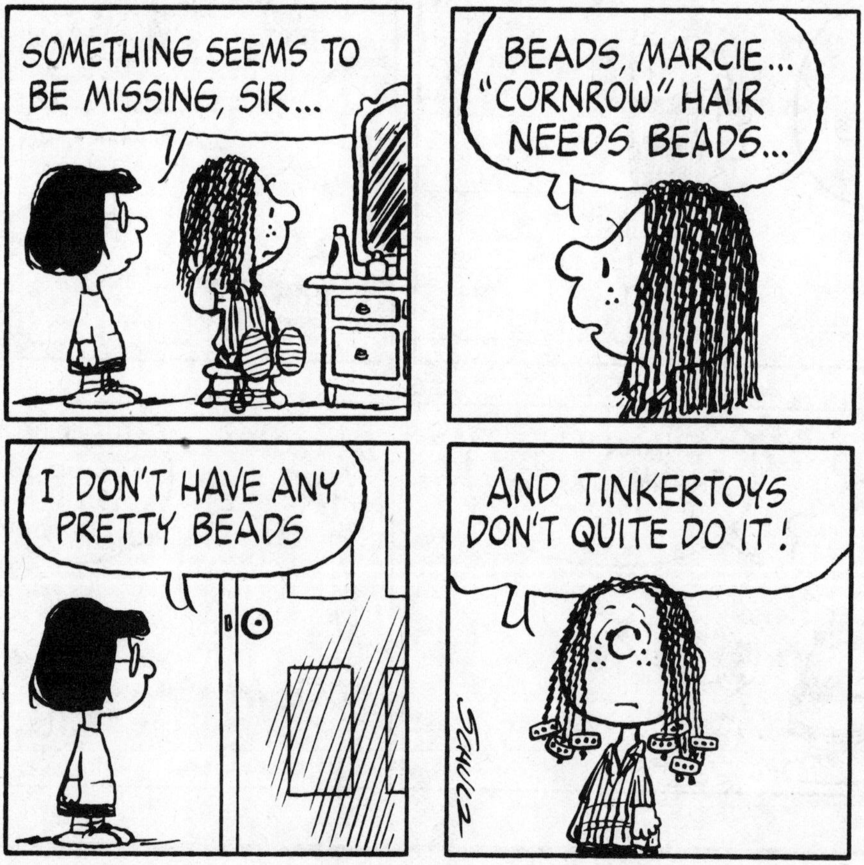
SOMETHING SEEMS TO BE MISSING, SIR...
BEADS, MARCIE... "CORNROW" HAIR NEEDS BEADS...
I DON'T HAVE ANY PRETTY BEADS
AND TINKERTOYS DON'T QUITE DO IT!
SCHULZ

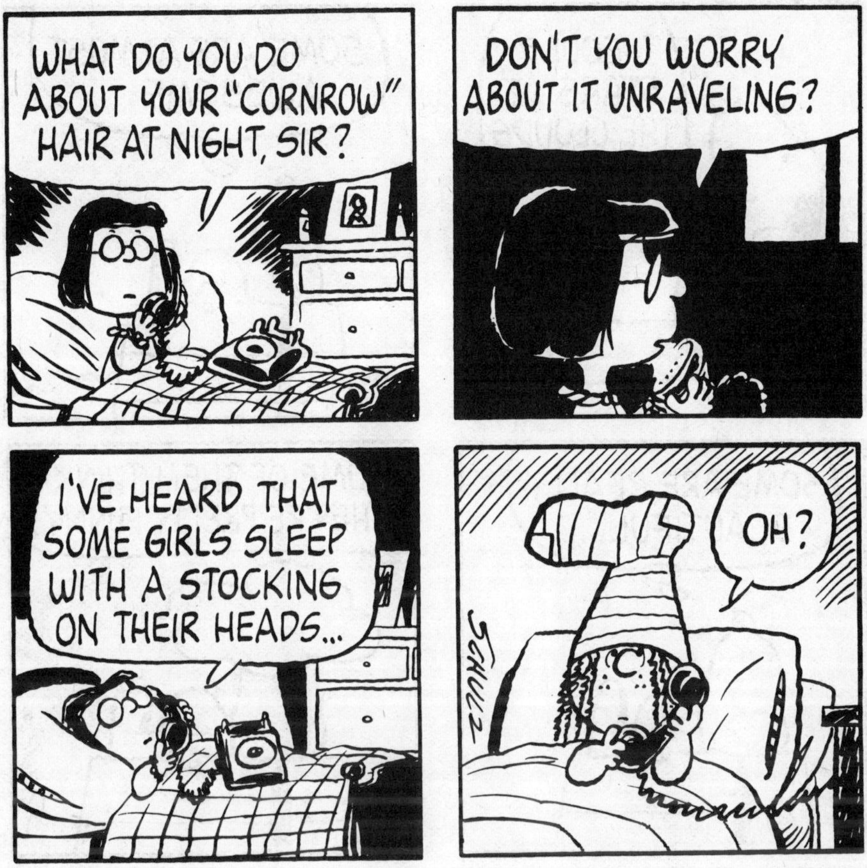
WHAT DO YOU DO ABOUT YOUR "CORNROW" HAIR AT NIGHT, SIR?
DON'T YOU WORRY ABOUT IT UNRAVELING?
I'VE HEARD THAT SOME GIRLS SLEEP WITH A STOCKING ON THEIR HEADS...
OH?
SCHULZ

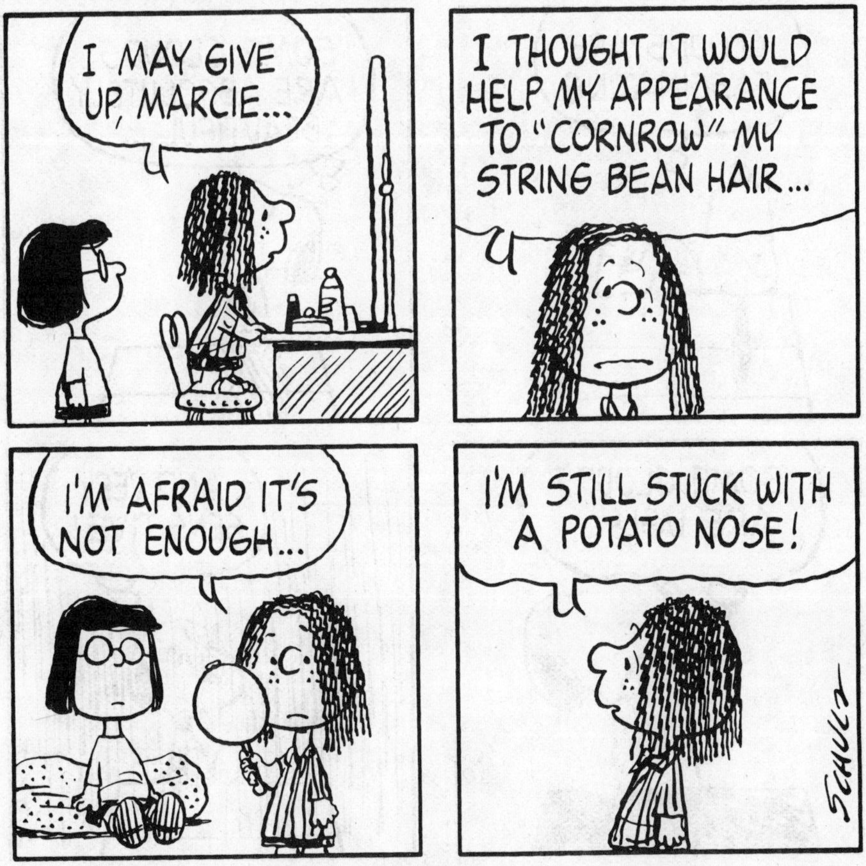
I MAY GIVE UP, MARCIE...
I THOUGHT IT WOULD HELP MY APPEARANCE TO "CORNROW" MY STRING BEAN HAIR...
I'M AFRAID IT'S NOT ENOUGH...
I'M STILL STUCK WITH A POTATO NOSE!
SCHULZ

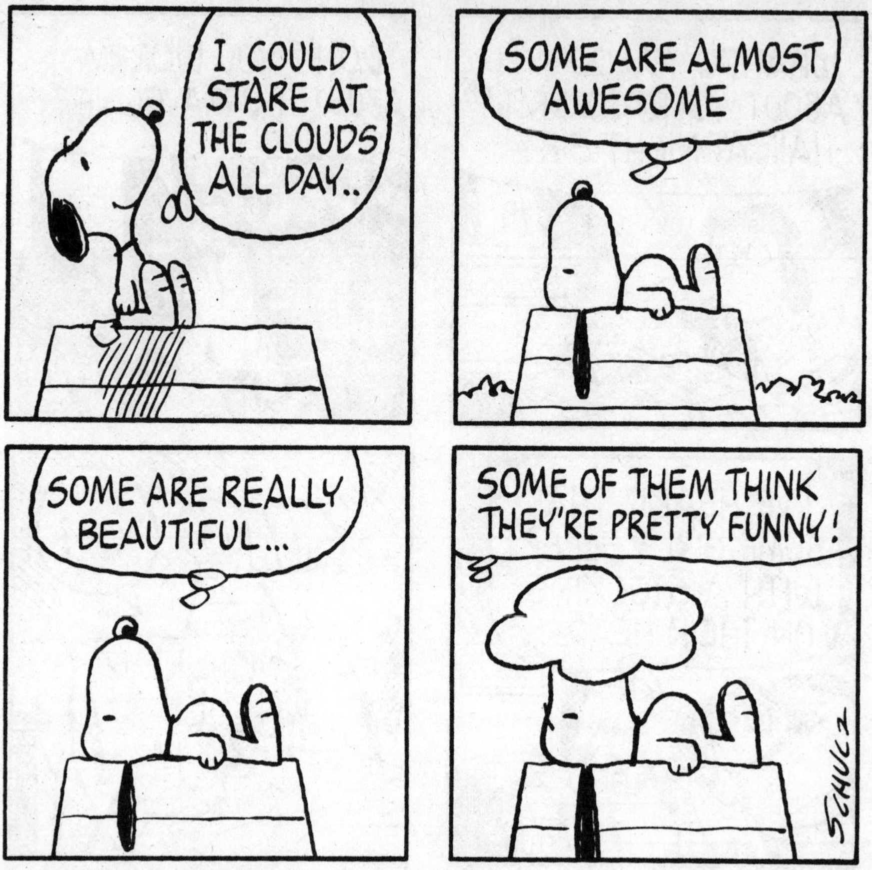
I COULD STARE AT THE CLOUDS ALL DAY..
SOME ARE ALMOST AWESOME
SOME ARE REALLY BEAUTIFUL...
SOME OF THEM THINK THEY'RE PRETTY FUNNY!
SCHULZ

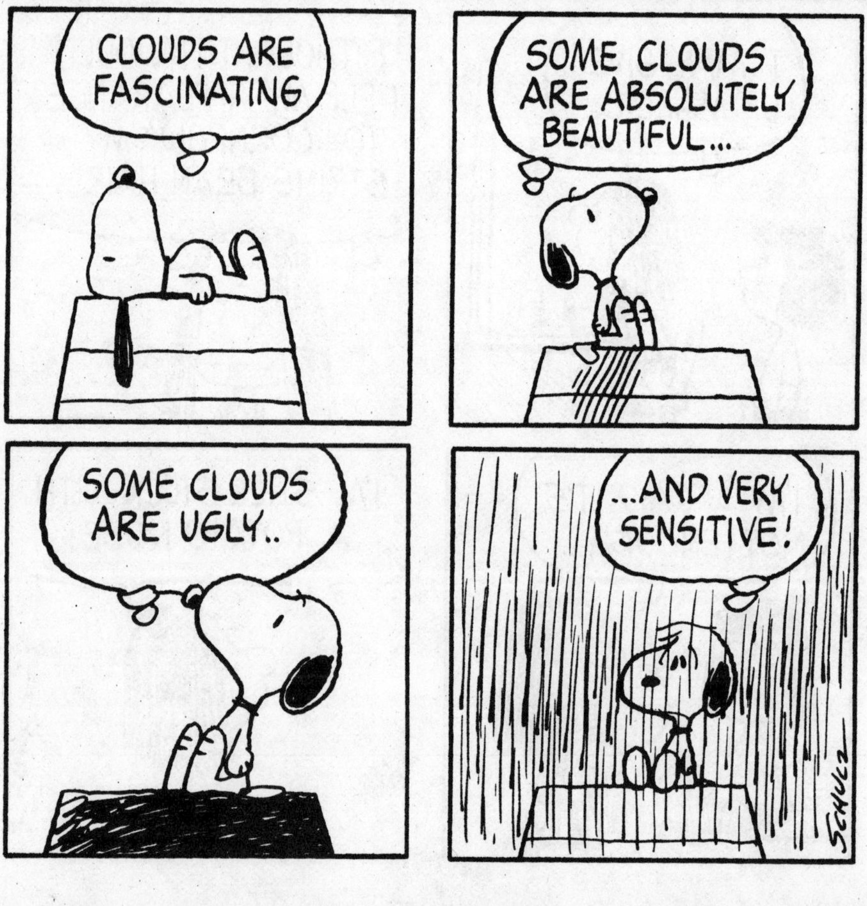
CLOUDS ARE FASCINATING
SOME CLOUDS ARE ABSOLUTELY BEAUTIFUL...
SOME CLOUDS ARE UGLY..
...AND VERY SENSITIVE!
SCHULZ

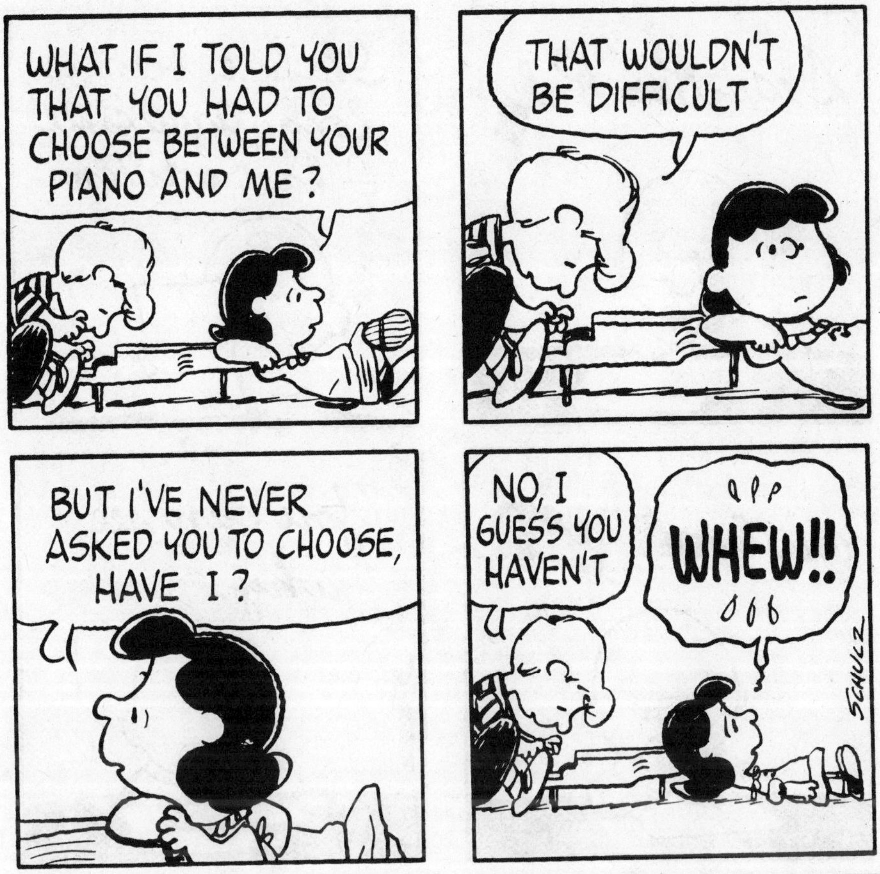
WHAT IF I TOLD YOU THAT YOU HAD TO CHOOSE BETWEEN YOUR PIANO AND ME?
THAT WOULDN'T BE DIFFICULT
BUT I'VE NEVER ASKED YOU TO CHOOSE, HAVE I?
NO, I GUESS YOU HAVEN'T
WHEW!!
SCHULZ

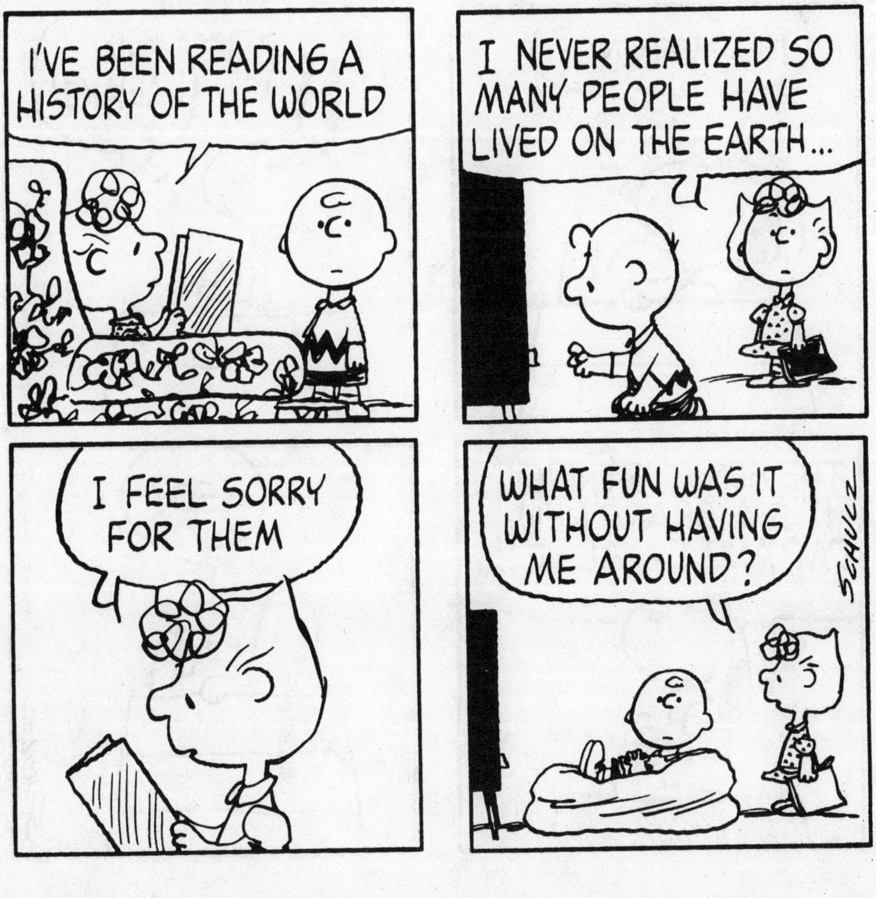
I'VE BEEN READING A HISTORY OF THE WORLD
I NEVER REALIZED SO MANY PEOPLE HAVE LIVED ON THE EARTH...
I FEEL SORRY FOR THEM
WHAT FUN WAS IT WITHOUT HAVING ME AROUND?
SCHULZ

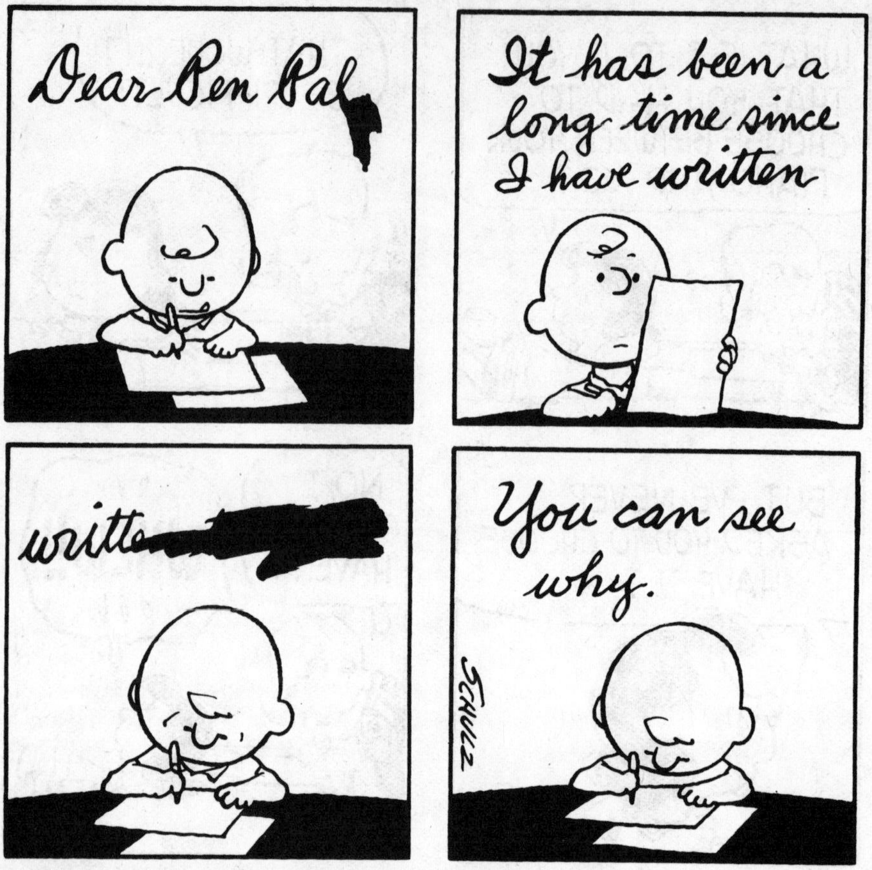
Dear Pen Pal
It has been a long time since I have written
writte
You can see why.
SCHULZ

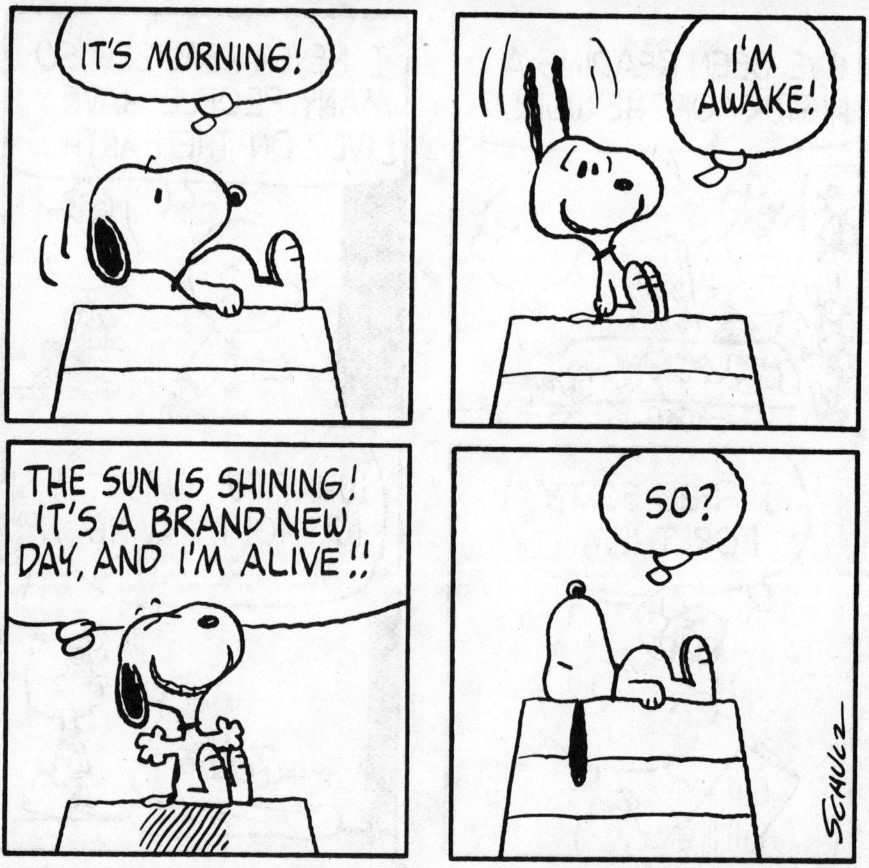
IT'S MORNING!
I'M AWAKE!
THE SUN IS SHINING! IT'S A BRAND NEW DAY, AND I'M ALIVE!!
SO?
SCHULZ

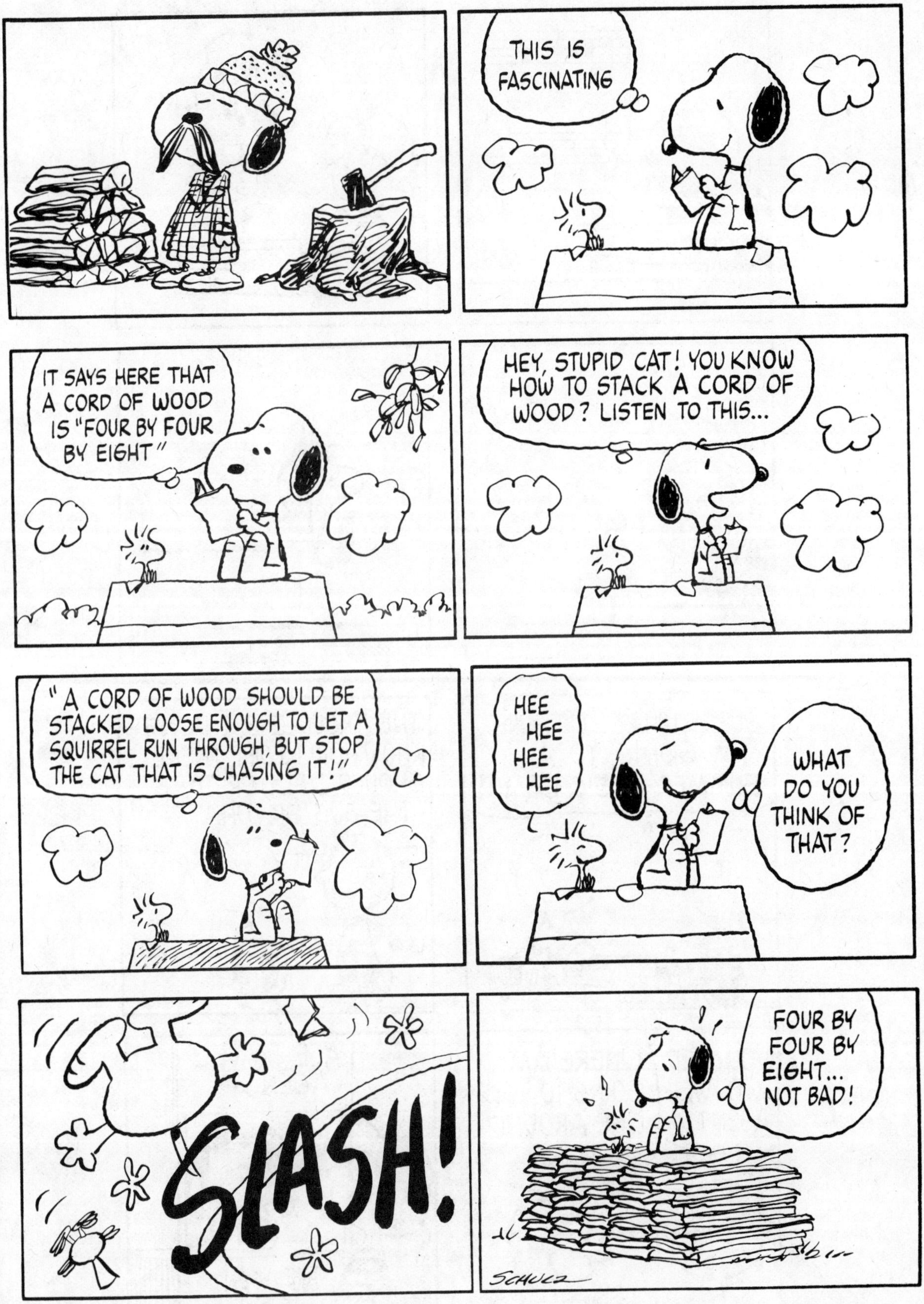
THIS IS FASCINATING
IT SAYS HERE THAT A CORD OF WOOD IS "FOUR BY FOUR BY EIGHT"
HEY, STUPID CAT! YOU KNOW HOW TO STACK A CORD OF WOOD? LISTEN TO THIS...
"A CORD OF WOOD SHOULD BE STACKED LOOSE ENOUGH TO LET A SQUIRREL RUN THROUGH, BUT STOP THE CAT THAT IS CHASING IT!"
HEE HEE HEE HEE
WHAT DO YOU THINK OF THAT?
SLASH!
FOUR BY FOUR BY EIGHT... NOT BAD!
SCHULZ

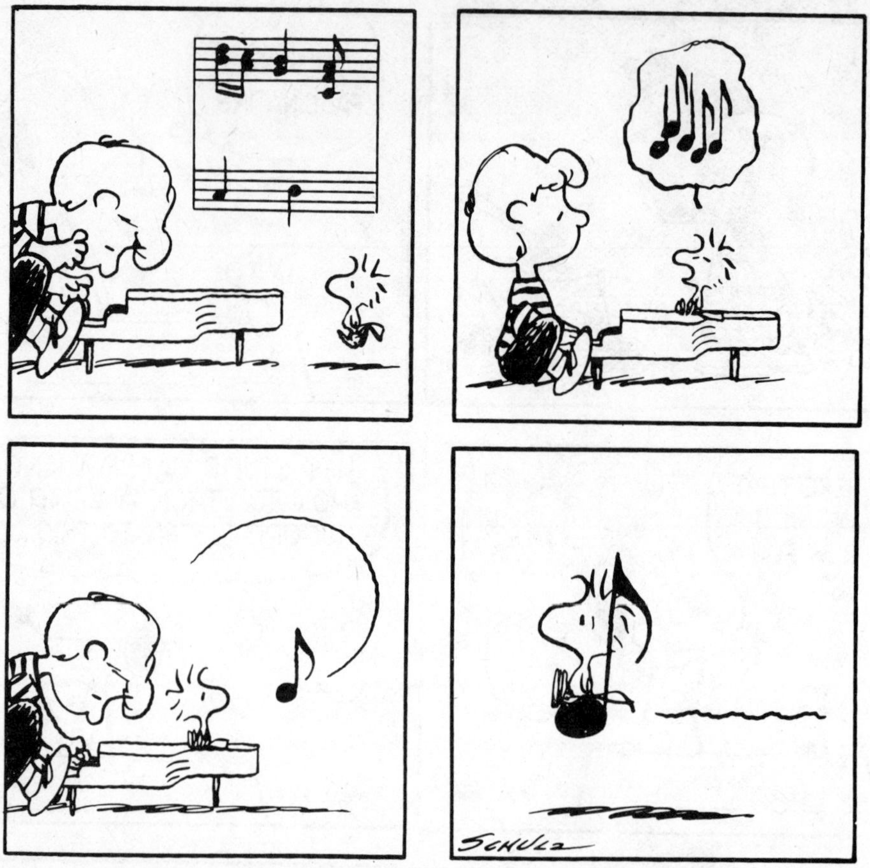
SCHULZ

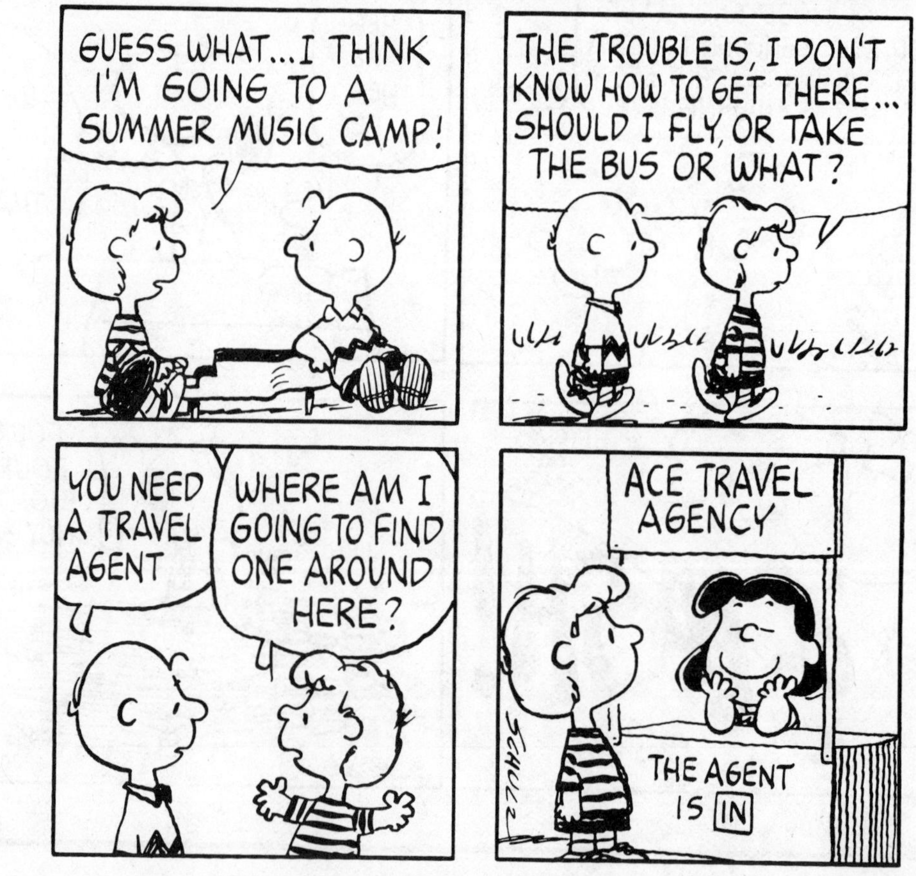
GUESS WHAT...I THINK I'M GOING TO A SUMMER MUSIC CAMP!
THE TROUBLE IS, I DON'T KNOW HOW TO GET THERE... SHOULD I FLY, OR TAKE THE BUS OR WHAT?
YOU NEED A TRAVEL AGENT
WHERE AM I GOING TO FIND ONE AROUND HERE?
ACE TRAVEL AGENCY
THE AGENT IS IN
SCHULZ

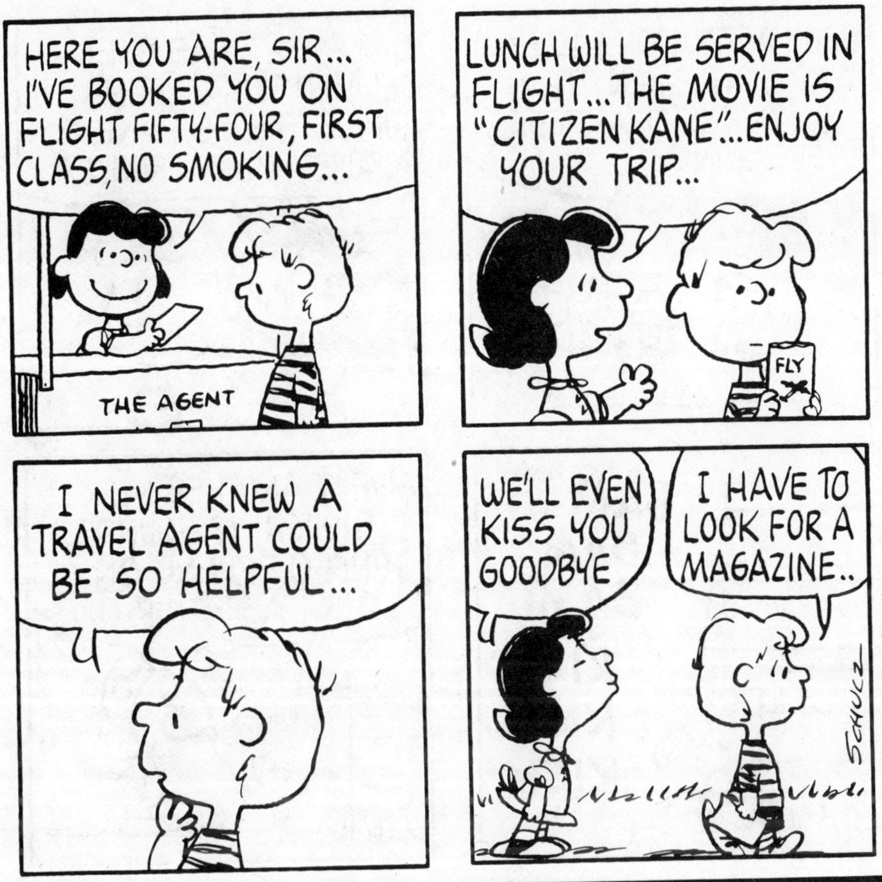
HERE YOU ARE, SIR... I'VE BOOKED YOU ON FLIGHT FIFTY-FOUR, FIRST CLASS, NO SMOKING...
THE AGENT
LUNCH WILL BE SERVED IN FLIGHT...THE MOVIE IS "CITIZEN KANE"...ENJOY YOUR TRIP...
FLY
I NEVER KNEW A TRAVEL AGENT COULD BE SO HELPFUL...
WE'LL EVEN KISS YOU GOODBYE
I HAVE TO LOOK FOR A MAGAZINE..
SCHULZ

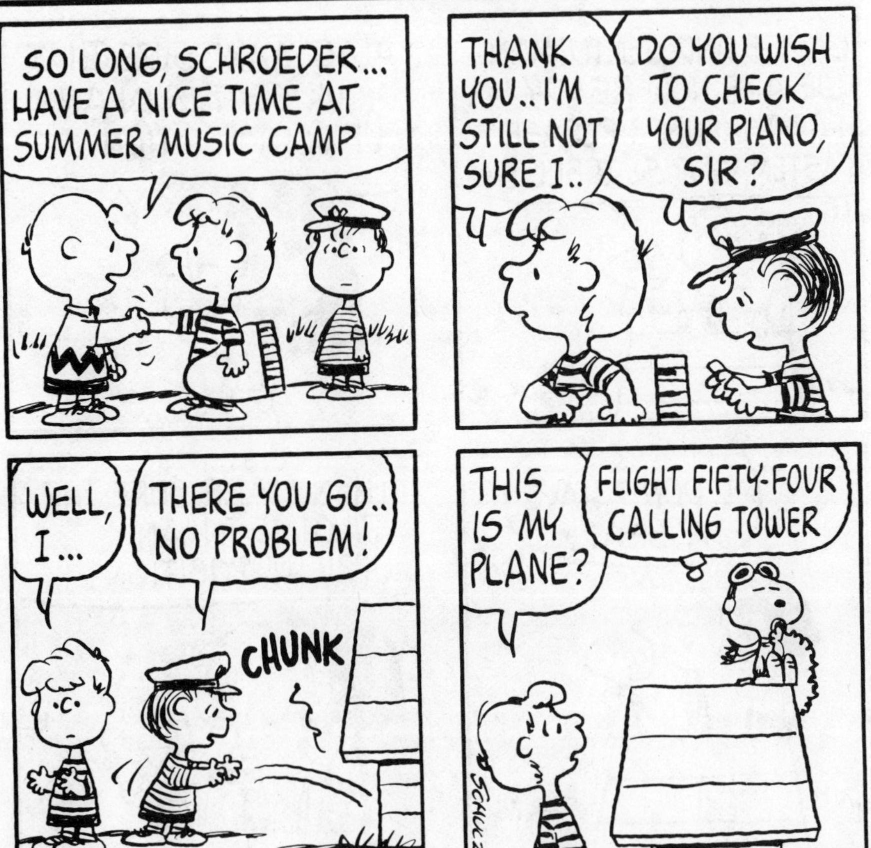
SO LONG, SCHROEDER... HAVE A NICE TIME AT SUMMER MUSIC CAMP
THANK YOU.. I'M STILL NOT SURE I..
DO YOU WISH TO CHECK YOUR PIANO, SIR?
WELL, I...
THERE YOU GO.. NO PROBLEM!
CHUNK
THIS IS MY PLANE?
FLIGHT FIFTY-FOUR CALLING TOWER
SCHULZ

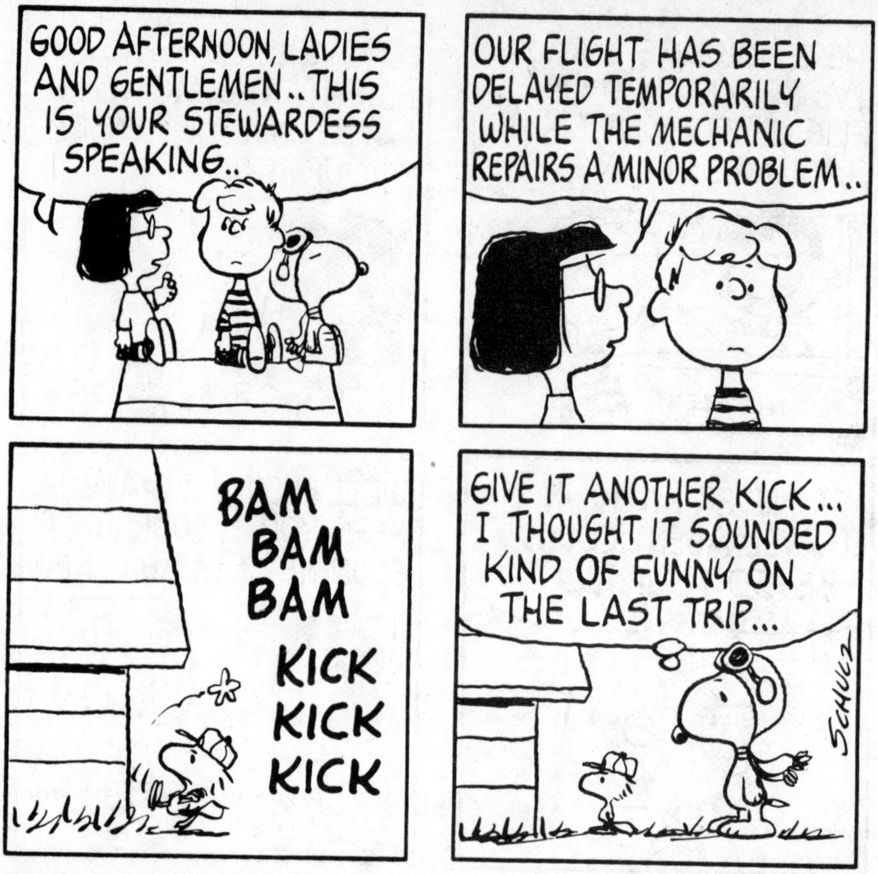
GOOD AFTERNOON, LADIES AND GENTLEMEN.. THIS IS YOUR STEWARDESS SPEAKING..
OUR FLIGHT HAS BEEN DELAYED TEMPORARILY WHILE THE MECHANIC REPAIRS A MINOR PROBLEM..
BAM BAM BAM
KICK KICK KICK
GIVE IT ANOTHER KICK... I THOUGHT IT SOUNDED KIND OF FUNNY ON THE LAST TRIP...
SCHULZ

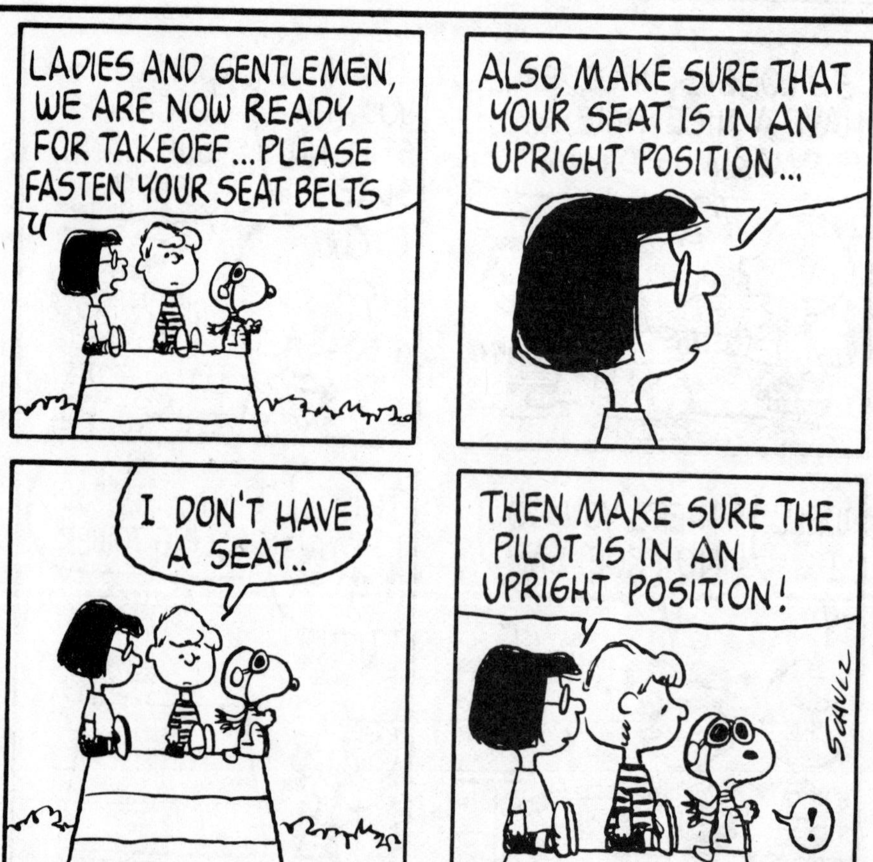
LADIES AND GENTLEMEN, WE ARE NOW READY FOR TAKEOFF... PLEASE FASTEN YOUR SEAT BELTS
ALSO, MAKE SURE THAT YOUR SEAT IS IN AN UPRIGHT POSITION...
I DON'T HAVE A SEAT..
THEN MAKE SURE THE PILOT IS IN AN UPRIGHT POSITION!
!
SCHULZ

I'VE NEVER TAKEN A LONG TRIP ON AN AIRLINER BEFORE... IS IT SAFE?
OH, YES, THIS PLANE HAS ALL THE LATEST BACKUP SYSTEMS...
WHAT ARE THEY?
IF WE HAVE ANY TROUBLE, WE JUST BACK UP!

I'VE HEARD THAT OUR CAPTAIN WAS A FIGHTER PILOT DURING THE WAR...
I DON'T SUPPOSE THOSE EXPERIENCES ARE EASILY FORGOTTEN...
CURSE YOU, RED BARON!
NO, I GUESS NOT

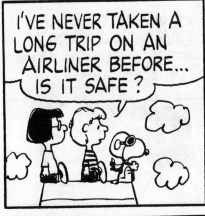

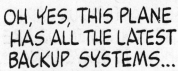

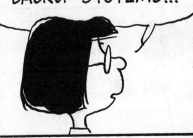

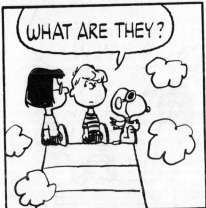

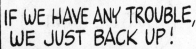

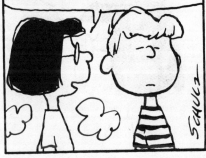

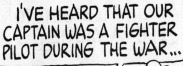

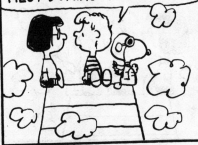

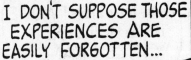

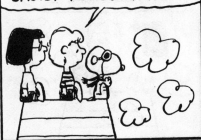

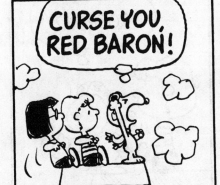

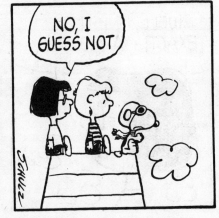

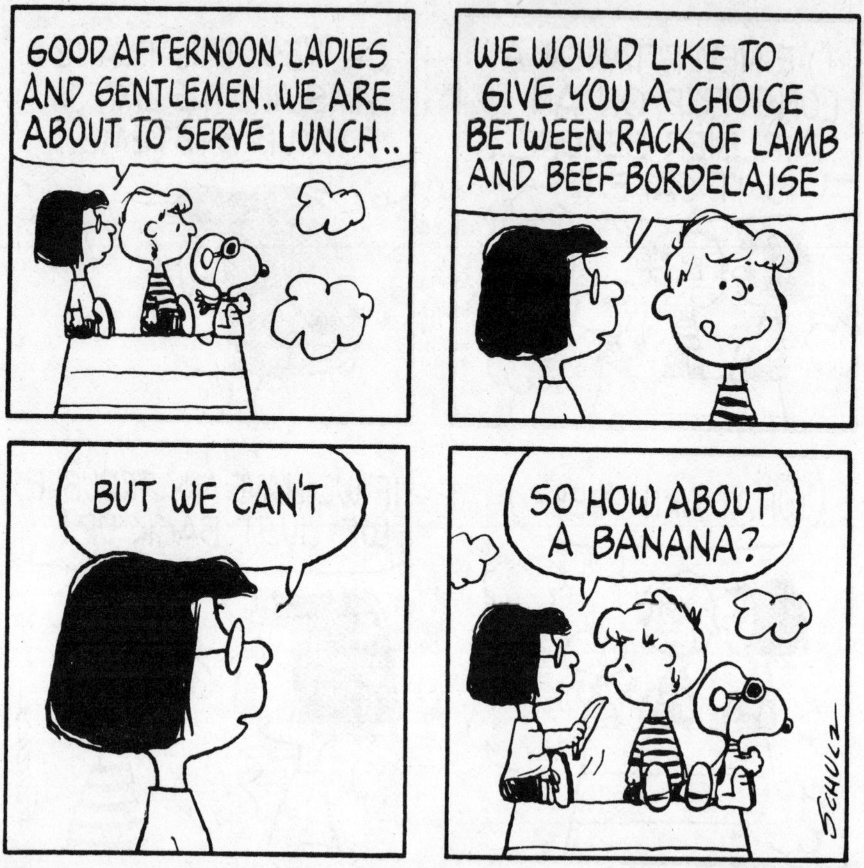
GOOD AFTERNOON, LADIES AND GENTLEMEN.. WE ARE ABOUT TO SERVE LUNCH..
WE WOULD LIKE TO GIVE YOU A CHOICE BETWEEN RACK OF LAMB AND BEEF BORDELAISE
BUT WE CAN'T
SO HOW ABOUT A BANANA?
SCHULZ

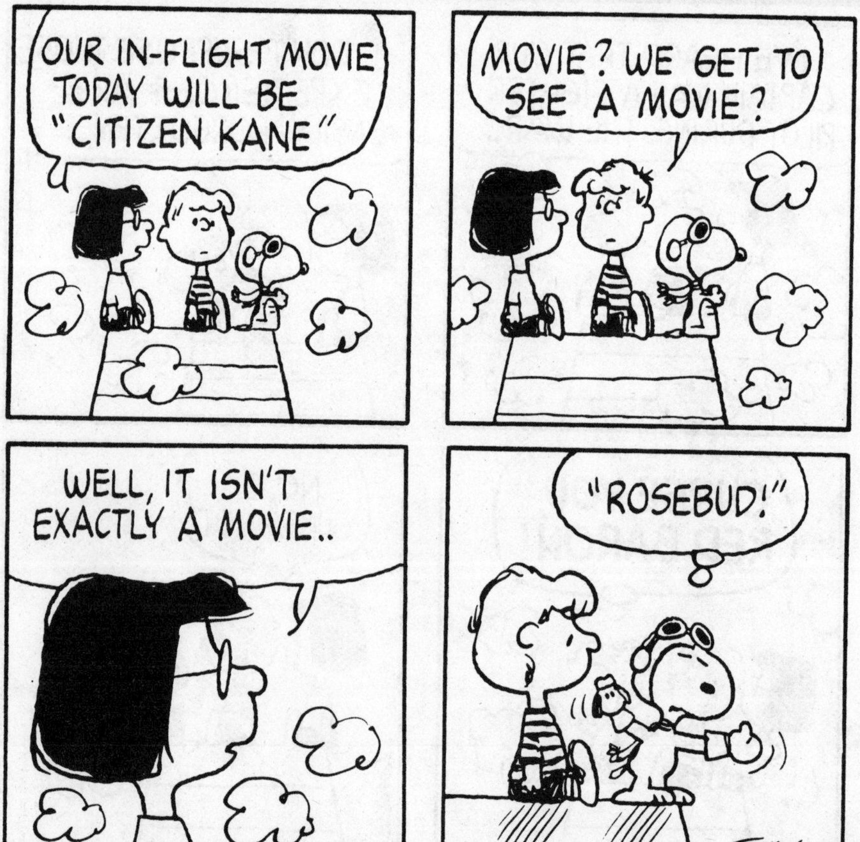
OUR IN-FLIGHT MOVIE TODAY WILL BE "CITIZEN KANE"
MOVIE? WE GET TO SEE A MOVIE?
WELL, IT ISN'T EXACTLY A MOVIE..
"ROSEBUD!"
SCHULZ

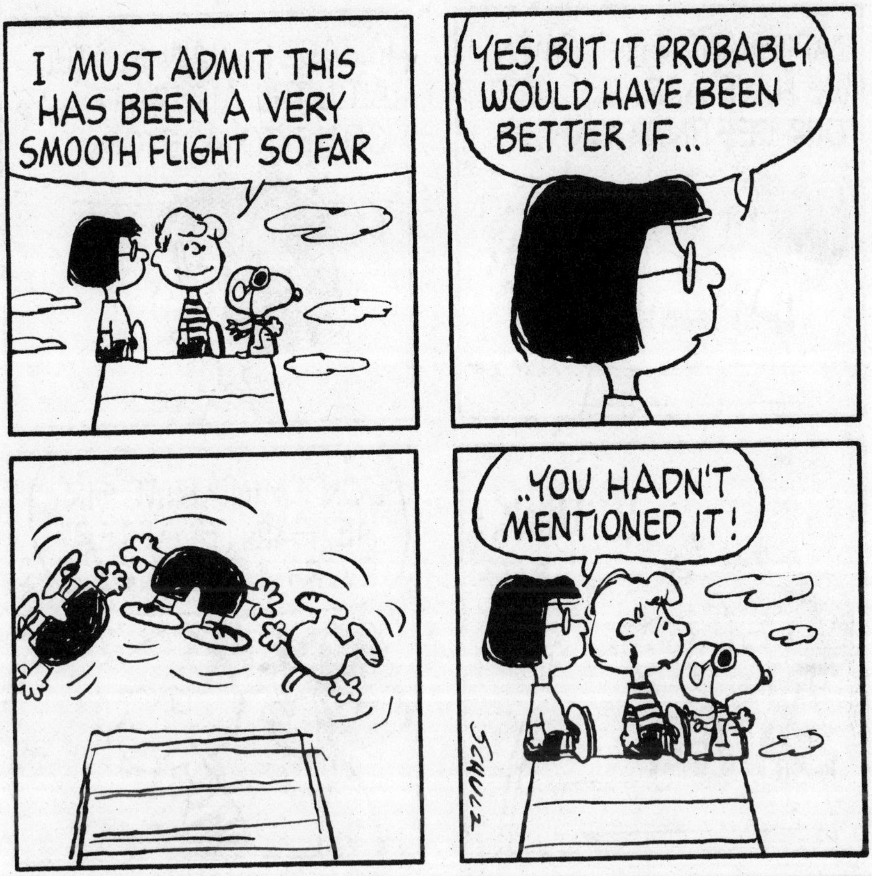
I MUST ADMIT THIS HAS BEEN A VERY SMOOTH FLIGHT SO FAR
YES, BUT IT PROBABLY WOULD HAVE BEEN BETTER IF...
..YOU HADN'T MENTIONED IT!
SCHULZ

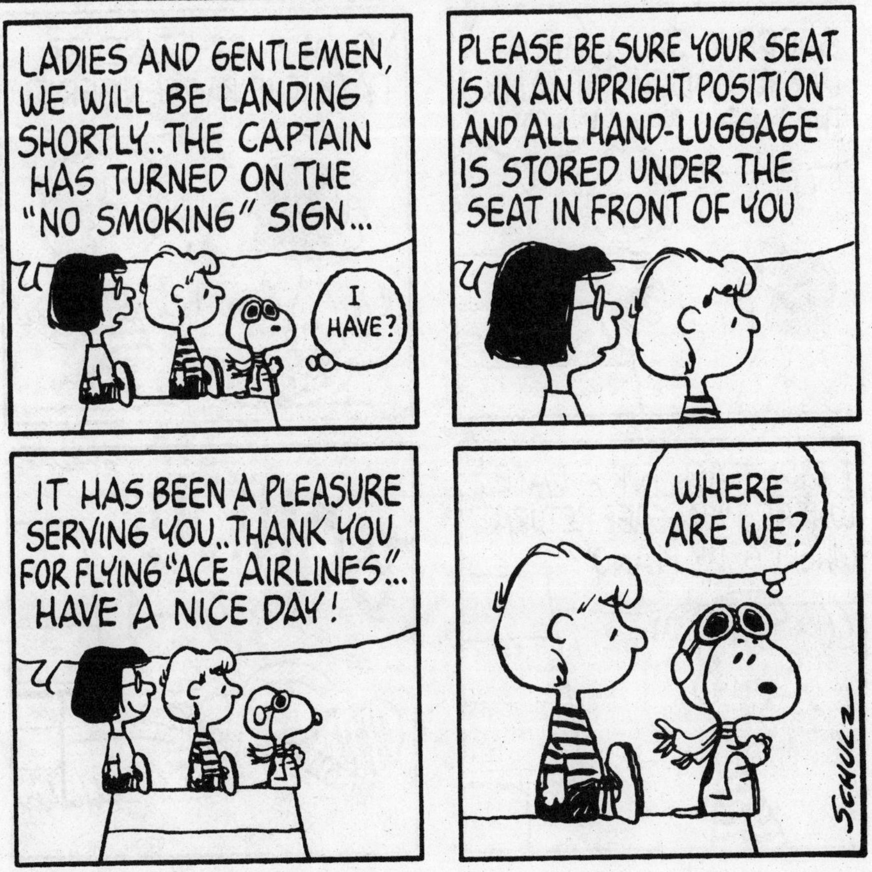
LADIES AND GENTLEMEN, WE WILL BE LANDING SHORTLY..THE CAPTAIN HAS TURNED ON THE "NO SMOKING" SIGN...
I HAVE?
PLEASE BE SURE YOUR SEAT IS IN AN UPRIGHT POSITION AND ALL HAND-LUGGAGE IS STORED UNDER THE SEAT IN FRONT OF YOU
IT HAS BEEN A PLEASURE SERVING YOU..THANK YOU FOR FLYING "ACE AIRLINES"... HAVE A NICE DAY!
WHERE ARE WE?
SCHULZ

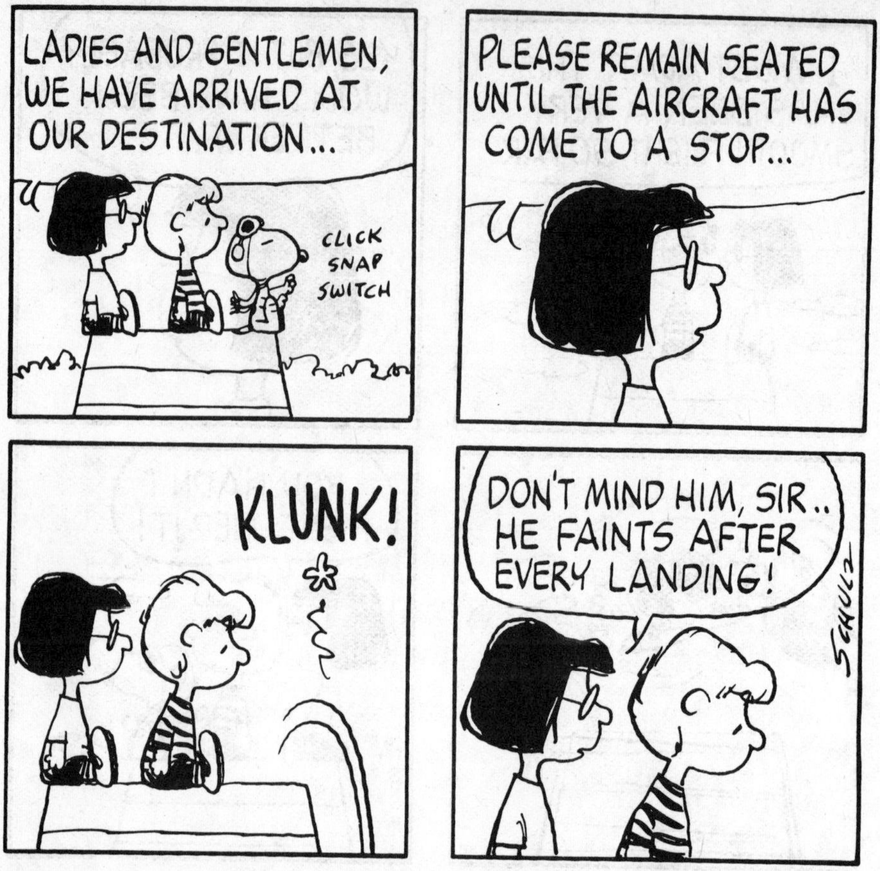
LADIES AND GENTLEMEN, WE HAVE ARRIVED AT OUR DESTINATION...
CLICK
SNAP
SWITCH
PLEASE REMAIN SEATED UNTIL THE AIRCRAFT HAS COME TO A STOP...
KLUNK!
DON'T MIND HIM, SIR.. HE FAINTS AFTER EVERY LANDING!
SCHULZ

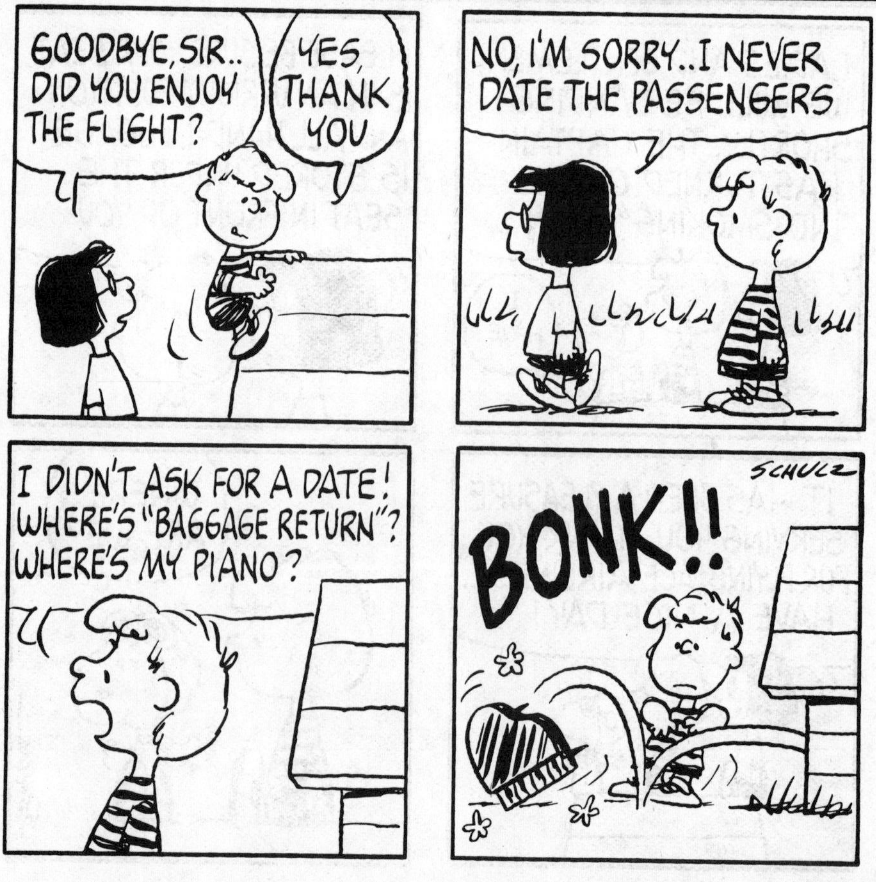
GOODBYE, SIR.. DID YOU ENJOY THE FLIGHT?
YES, THANK YOU
NO, I'M SORRY..I NEVER DATE THE PASSENGERS
I DIDN'T ASK FOR A DATE! WHERE'S "BAGGAGE RETURN"? WHERE'S MY PIANO?
SCHULZ
BONK!!

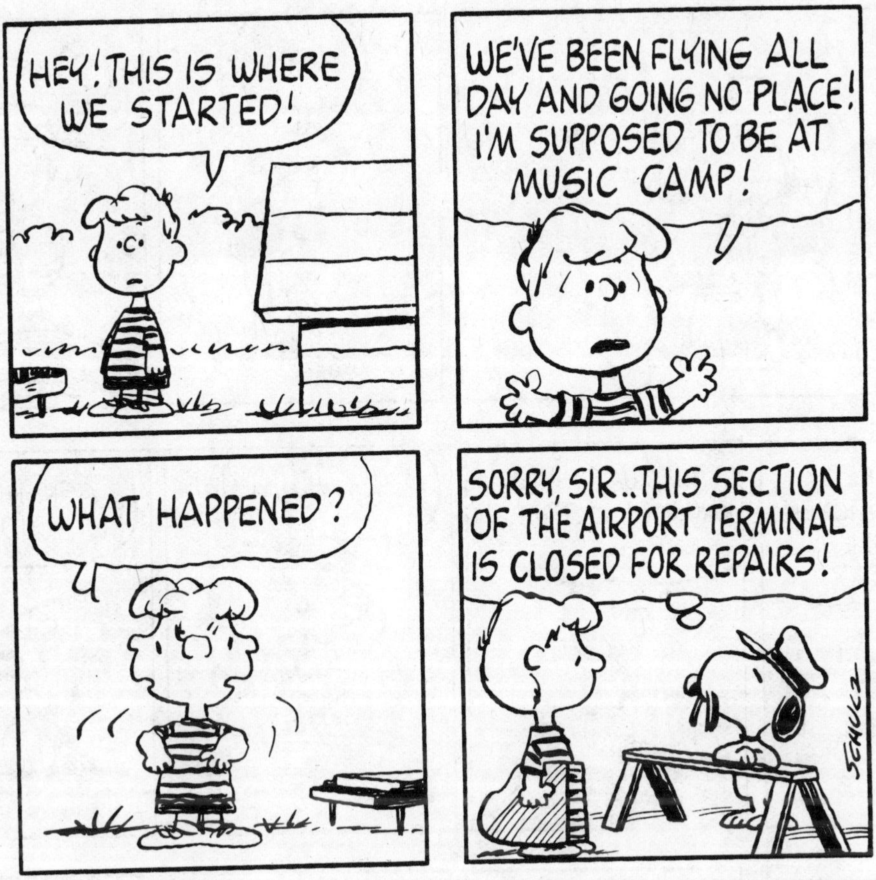
HEY! THIS IS WHERE WE STARTED!
WE'VE BEEN FLYING ALL DAY AND GOING NO PLACE! I'M SUPPOSED TO BE AT MUSIC CAMP!
WHAT HAPPENED?
SORRY, SIR..THIS SECTION OF THE AIRPORT TERMINAL IS CLOSED FOR REPAIRS!
SCHULZ

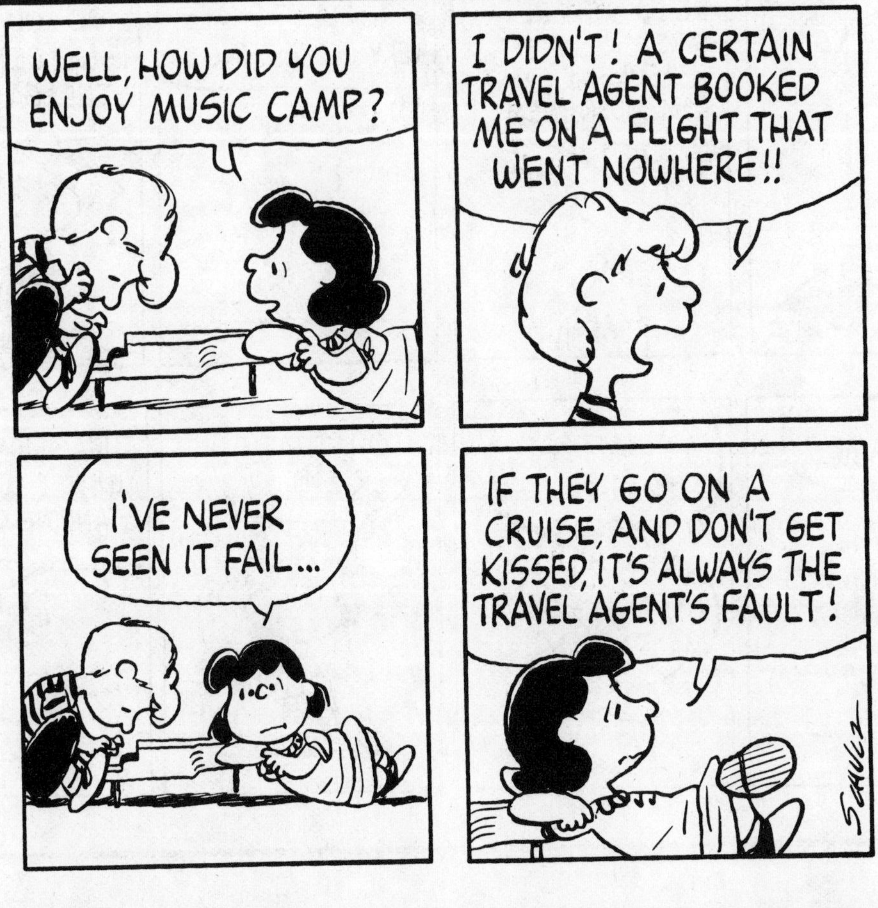
WELL, HOW DID YOU ENJOY MUSIC CAMP?
I DIDN'T! A CERTAIN TRAVEL AGENT BOOKED ME ON A FLIGHT THAT WENT NOWHERE!!
I'VE NEVER SEEN IT FAIL...
IF THEY GO ON A CRUISE, AND DON'T GET KISSED, IT'S ALWAYS THE TRAVEL AGENT'S FAULT!
SCHULZ

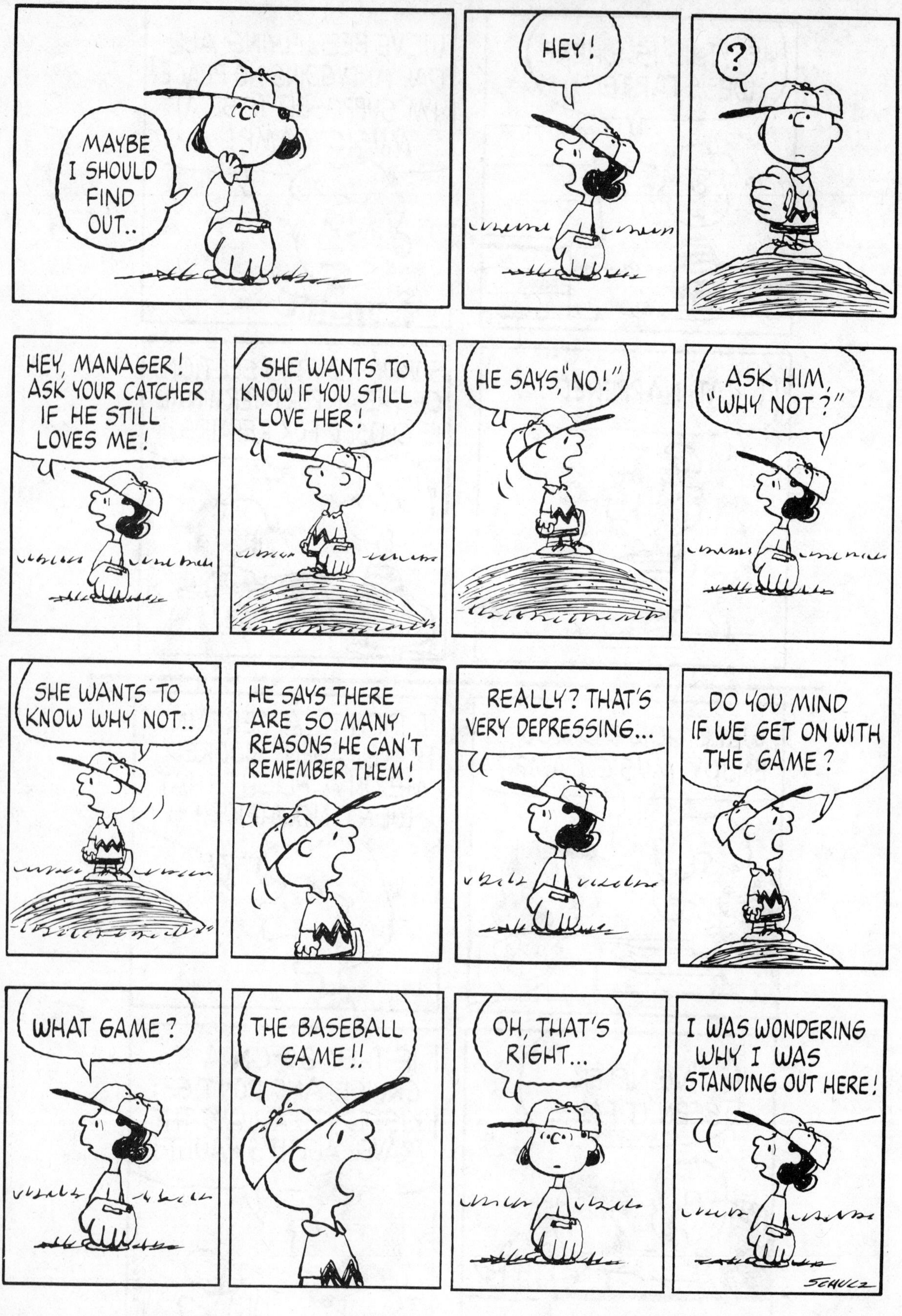
MAYBE I SHOULD FIND OUT..
HEY!
?
HEY, MANAGER! ASK YOUR CATCHER IF HE STILL LOVES ME!
SHE WANTS TO KNOW IF YOU STILL LOVE HER!
HE SAYS, "NO!"
ASK HIM, "WHY NOT?"
SHE WANTS TO KNOW WHY NOT..
HE SAYS THERE ARE SO MANY REASONS HE CAN'T REMEMBER THEM!
REALLY? THAT'S VERY DEPRESSING...
DO YOU MIND IF WE GET ON WITH THE GAME?
WHAT GAME?
THE BASEBALL GAME!!
OH, THAT'S RIGHT...
I WAS WONDERING WHY I WAS STANDING OUT HERE!
SCHULZ

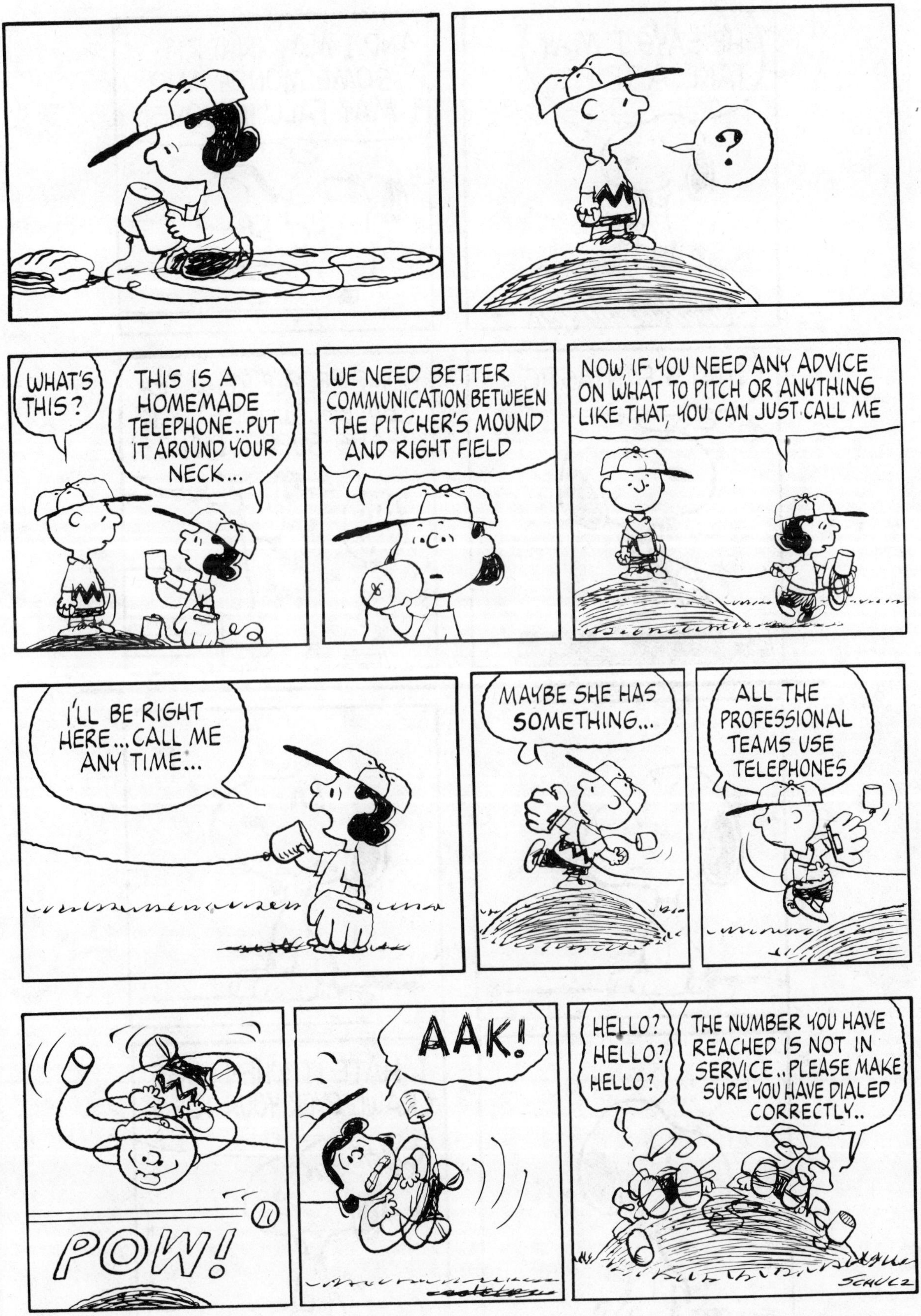
?
WHAT'S THIS?
THIS IS A HOMEMADE TELEPHONE..PUT IT AROUND YOUR NECK...
WE NEED BETTER COMMUNICATION BETWEEN THE PITCHER'S MOUND AND RIGHT FIELD
NOW, IF YOU NEED ANY ADVICE ON WHAT TO PITCH OR ANYTHING LIKE THAT, YOU CAN JUST CALL ME
I'LL BE RIGHT HERE...CALL ME ANY TIME...
MAYBE SHE HAS SOMETHING...
ALL THE PROFESSIONAL TEAMS USE TELEPHONES
POW!
AAK!
HELLO? HELLO? HELLO?
THE NUMBER YOU HAVE REACHED IS NOT IN SERVICE..PLEASE MAKE SURE YOU HAVE DIALED CORRECTLY..
SCHULZ

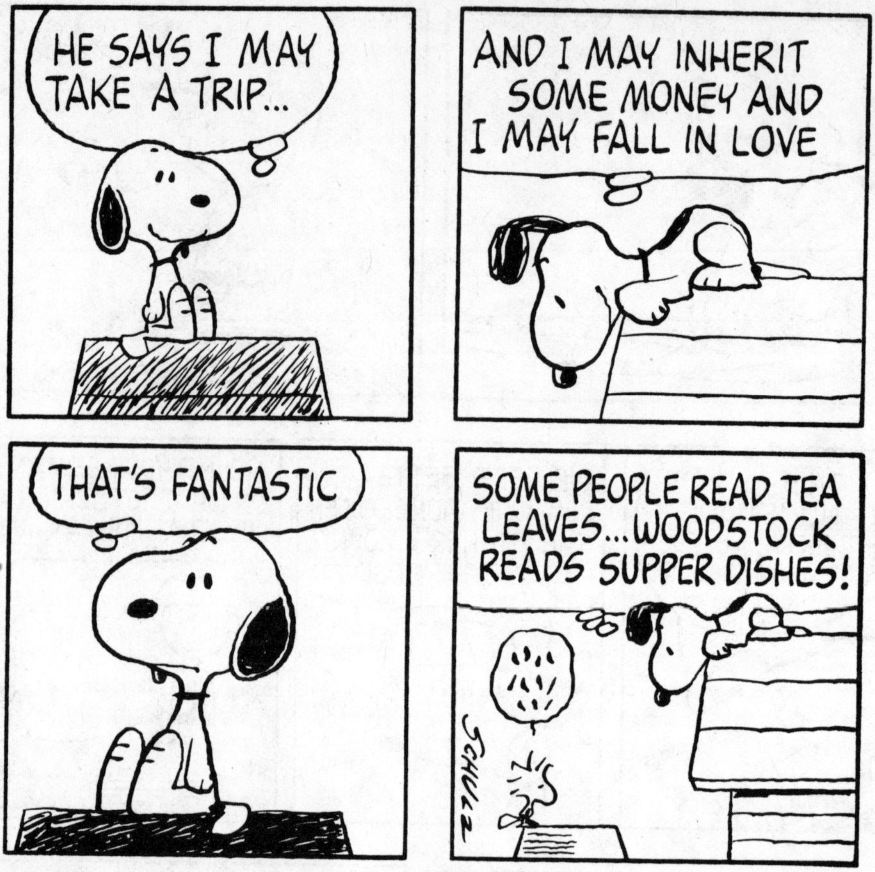
HE SAYS I MAY TAKE A TRIP...
AND I MAY INHERIT SOME MONEY AND I MAY FALL IN LOVE
THAT'S FANTASTIC
SOME PEOPLE READ TEA LEAVES...WOODSTOCK READS SUPPER DISHES!
SCHULZ

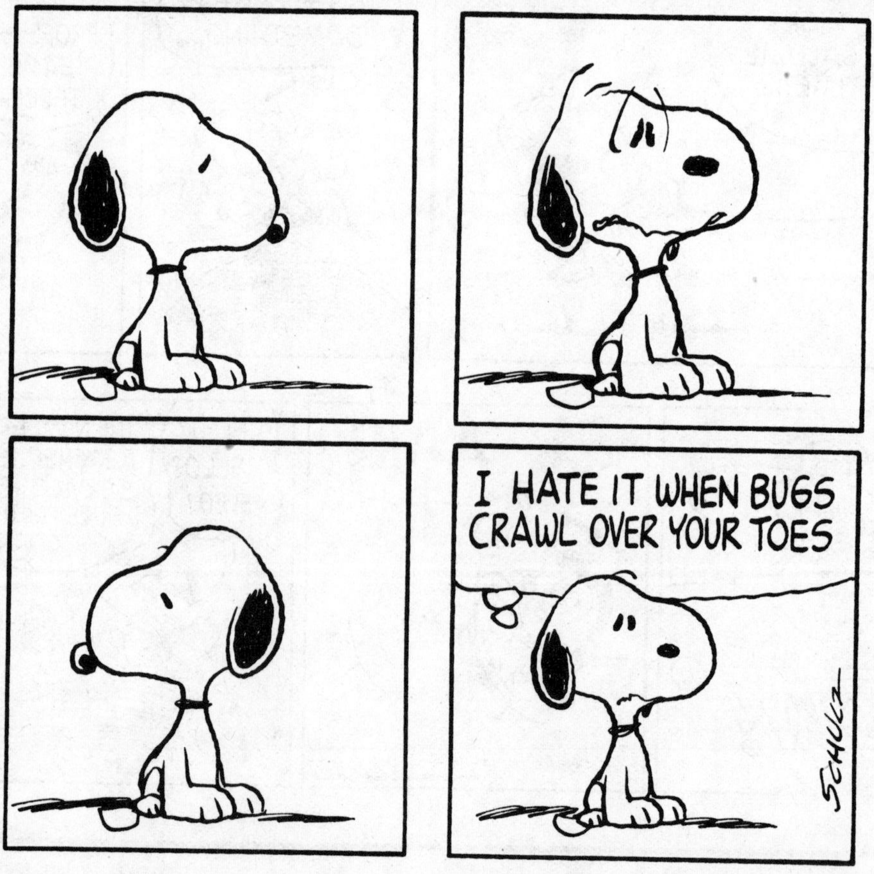
I HATE IT WHEN BUGS CRAWL OVER YOUR TOES
SCHULZ

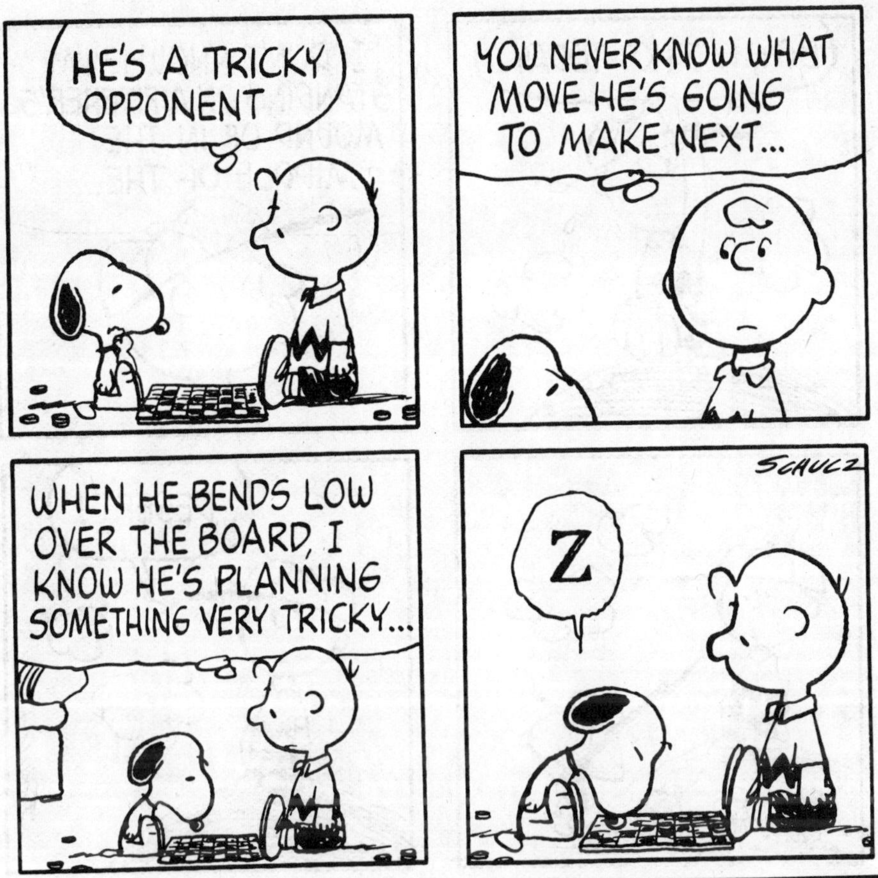
HE'S A TRICKY OPPONENT
YOU NEVER KNOW WHAT MOVE HE'S GOING TO MAKE NEXT...
WHEN HE BENDS LOW OVER THE BOARD, I KNOW HE'S PLANNING SOMETHING VERY TRICKY...
Z
SCHULZ

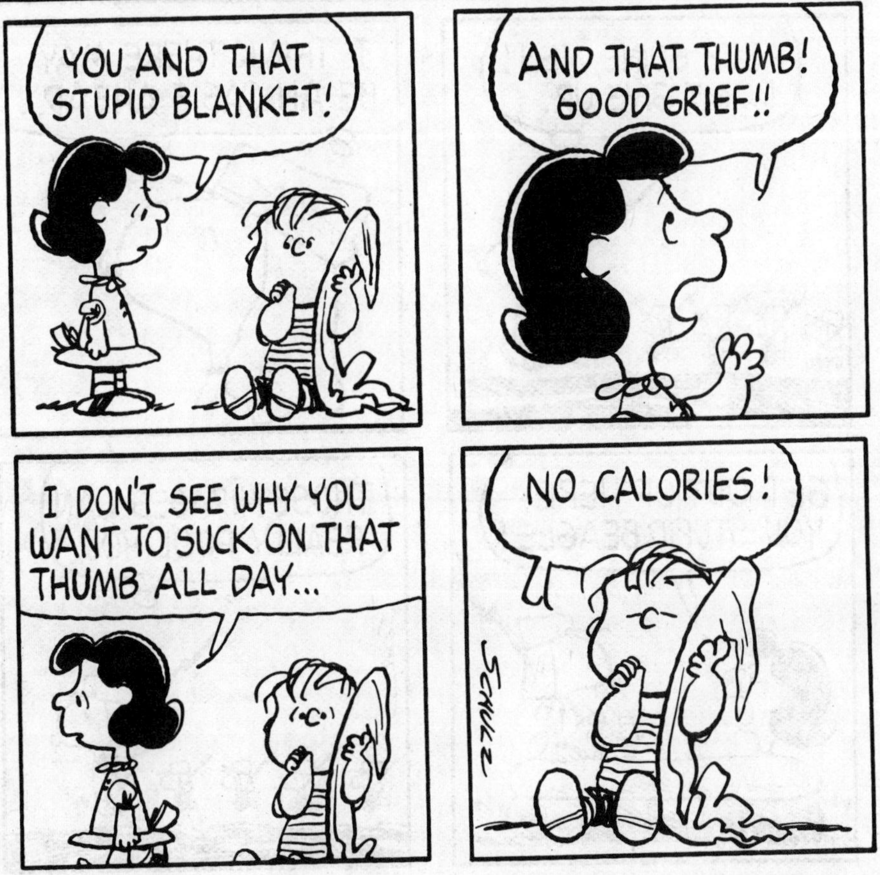
YOU AND THAT STUPID BLANKET!
AND THAT THUMB! GOOD GRIEF!!
I DON'T SEE WHY YOU WANT TO SUCK ON THAT THUMB ALL DAY...
NO CALORIES!
SCHULZ

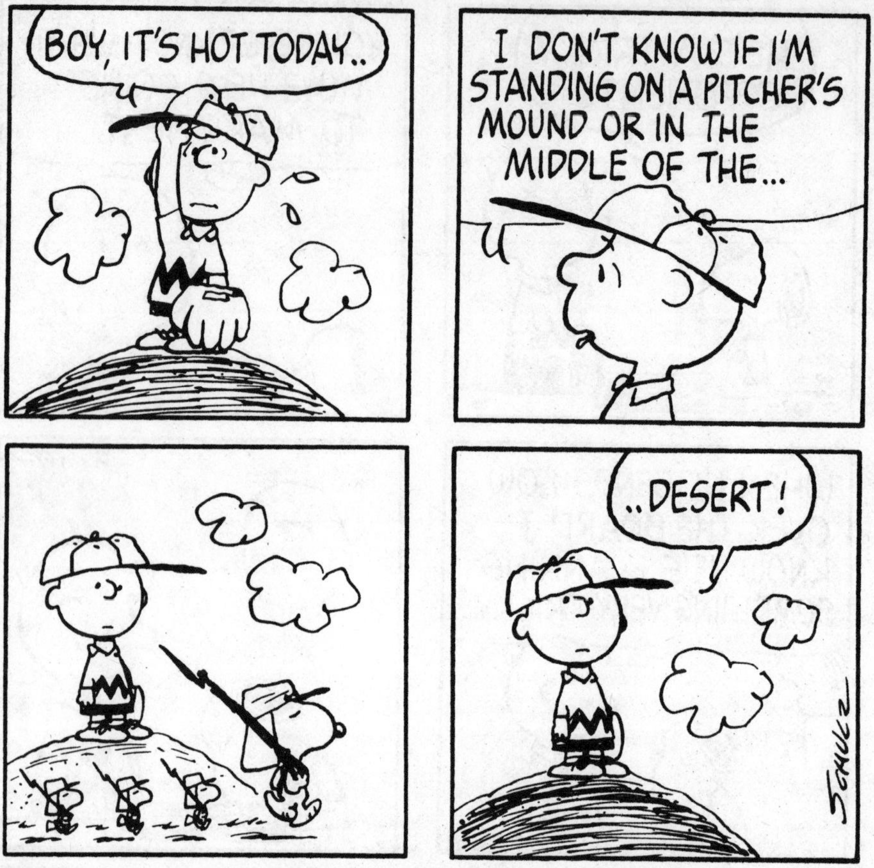
BOY, IT'S HOT TODAY..
I DON'T KNOW IF I'M STANDING ON A PITCHER'S MOUND OR IN THE MIDDLE OF THE...
..DESERT!
SCHULZ

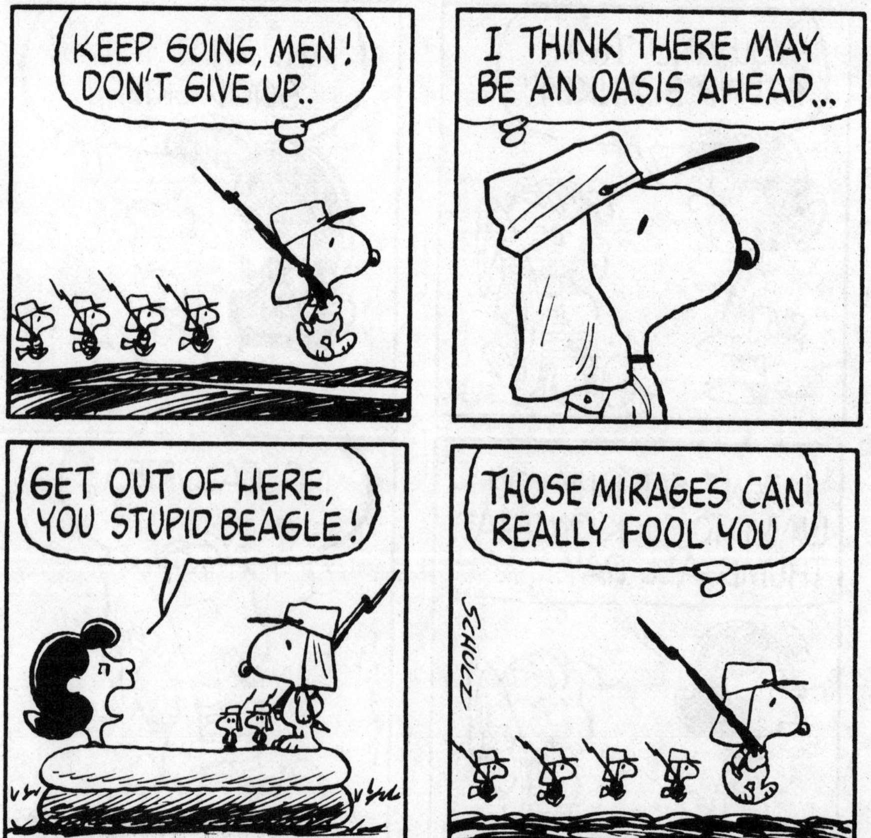
KEEP GOING, MEN! DON'T GIVE UP..
I THINK THERE MAY BE AN OASIS AHEAD...
GET OUT OF HERE, YOU STUPID BEAGLE!
THOSE MIRAGES CAN REALLY FOOL YOU
SCHULZ

A MIRAGE IN THE DESERT CAN REALLY FOOL YOU...YOU MAY THINK YOU SEE AN OASIS OFF IN THE DISTANCE, BUT...

WHEN YOU FINALLY GET THERE, YOU'LL FIND YOURSELF WALKING RIGHT THROUGH IT...

I HATE TO SAY IT, BUT I'LL BE GLAD WHEN WINTER COMES

LIFE IS A LOT LIKE A BASEBALL GAME

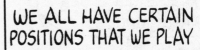

WE ALL HAVE CERTAIN POSITIONS THAT WE PLAY

WE ALL MAKE A FEW HITS AND WE ALL MAKE A FEW ERRORS

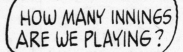

HOW MANY INNINGS ARE WE PLAYING?

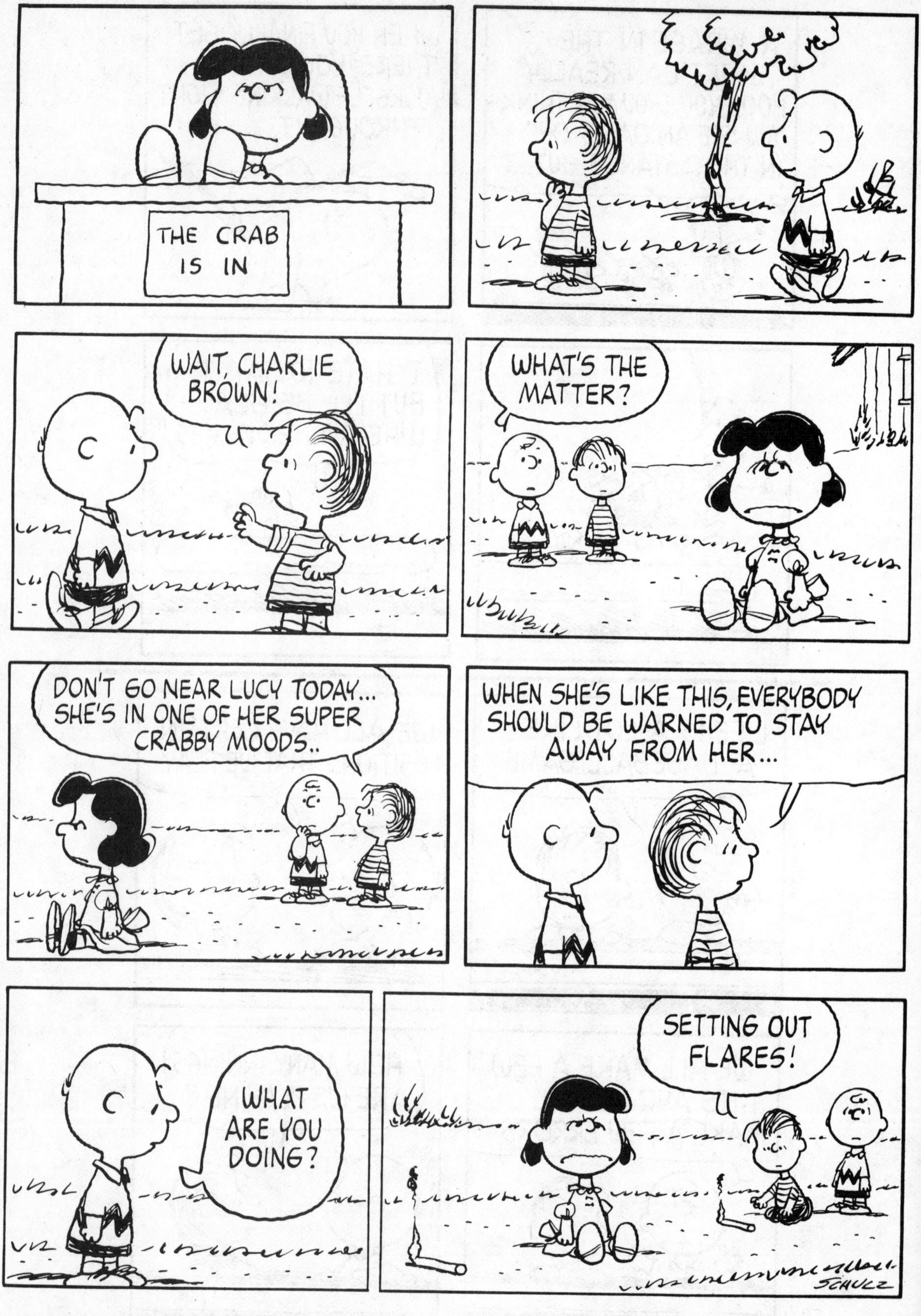
THE CRAB IS IN
WAIT, CHARLIE BROWN!
WHAT'S THE MATTER?
DON'T GO NEAR LUCY TODAY... SHE'S IN ONE OF HER SUPER CRABBY MOODS..
WHEN SHE'S LIKE THIS, EVERYBODY SHOULD BE WARNED TO STAY AWAY FROM HER...
WHAT ARE YOU DOING?
SETTING OUT FLARES!
SCHULZ

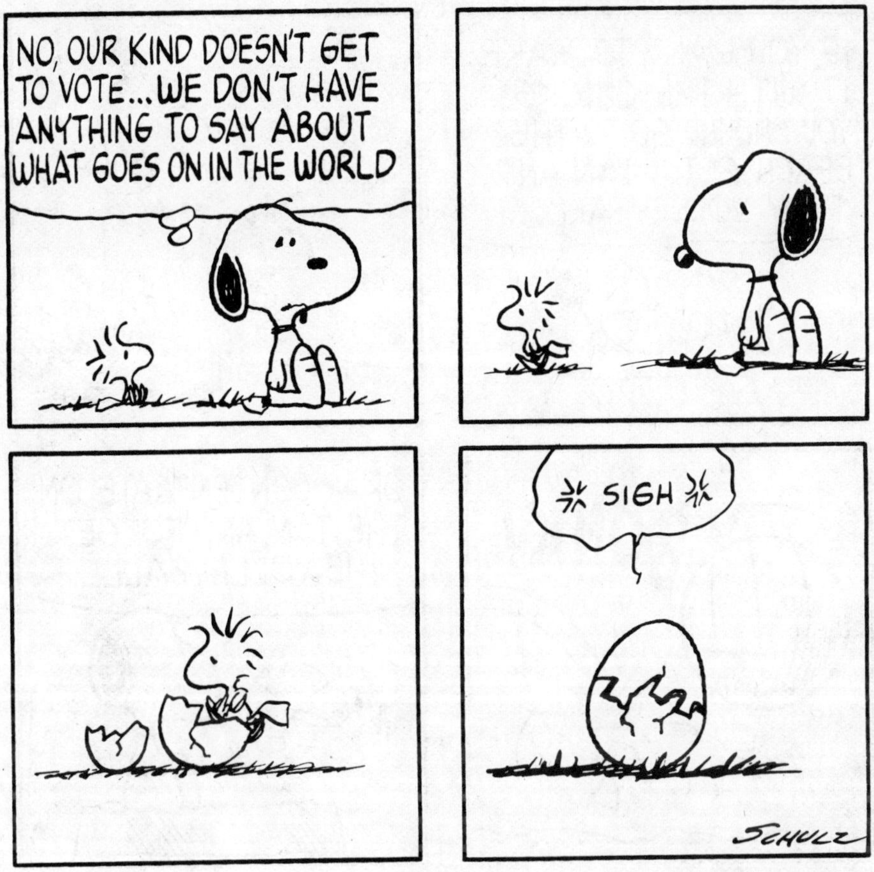
NO, OUR KIND DOESN'T GET TO VOTE...WE DON'T HAVE ANYTHING TO SAY ABOUT WHAT GOES ON IN THE WORLD
SIGH
SCHULZ

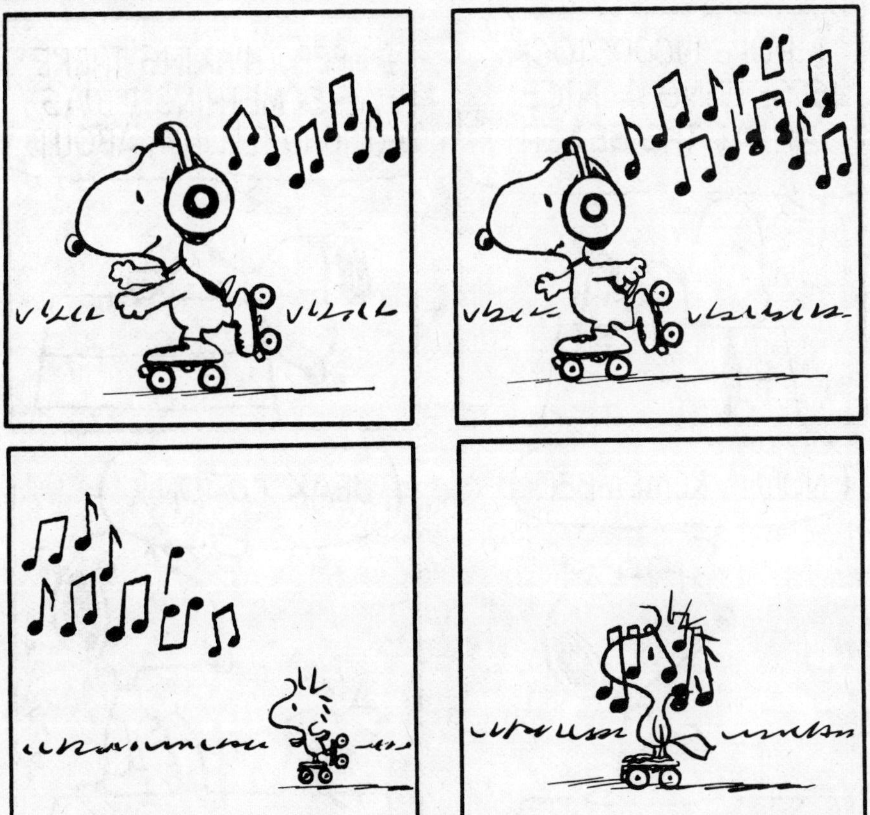
SCHULZ

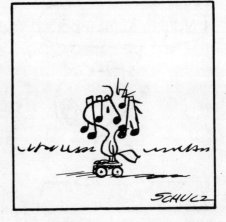

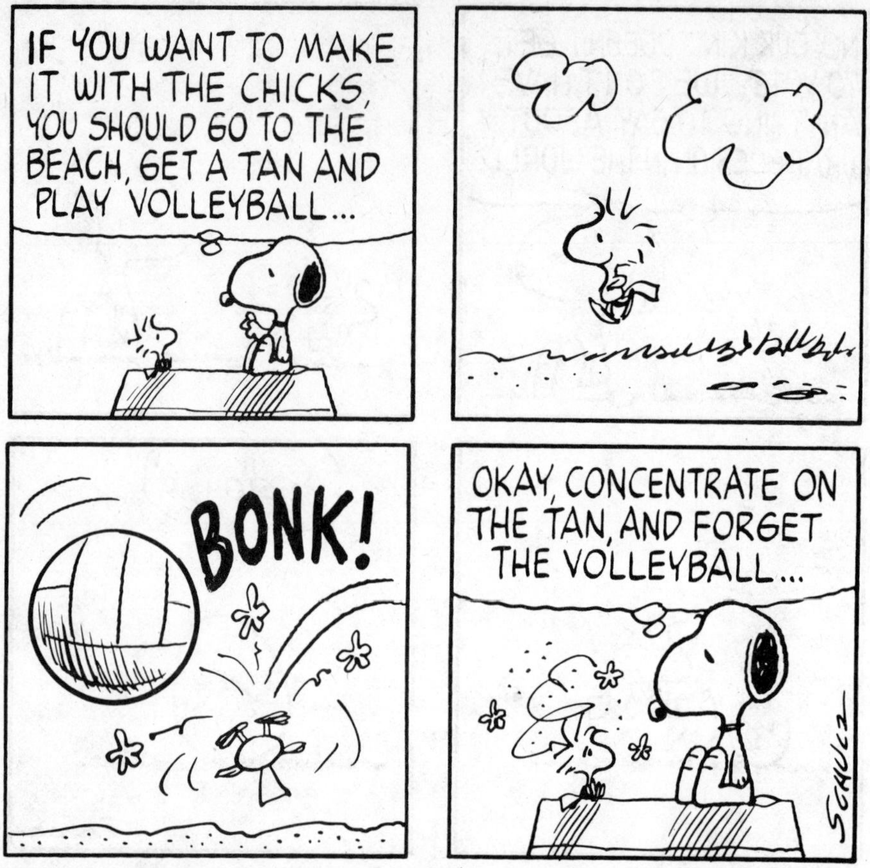
IF YOU WANT TO MAKE IT WITH THE CHICKS, YOU SHOULD GO TO THE BEACH, GET A TAN AND PLAY VOLLEYBALL...
BONK!
OKAY, CONCENTRATE ON THE TAN, AND FORGET THE VOLLEYBALL...
SCHULZ

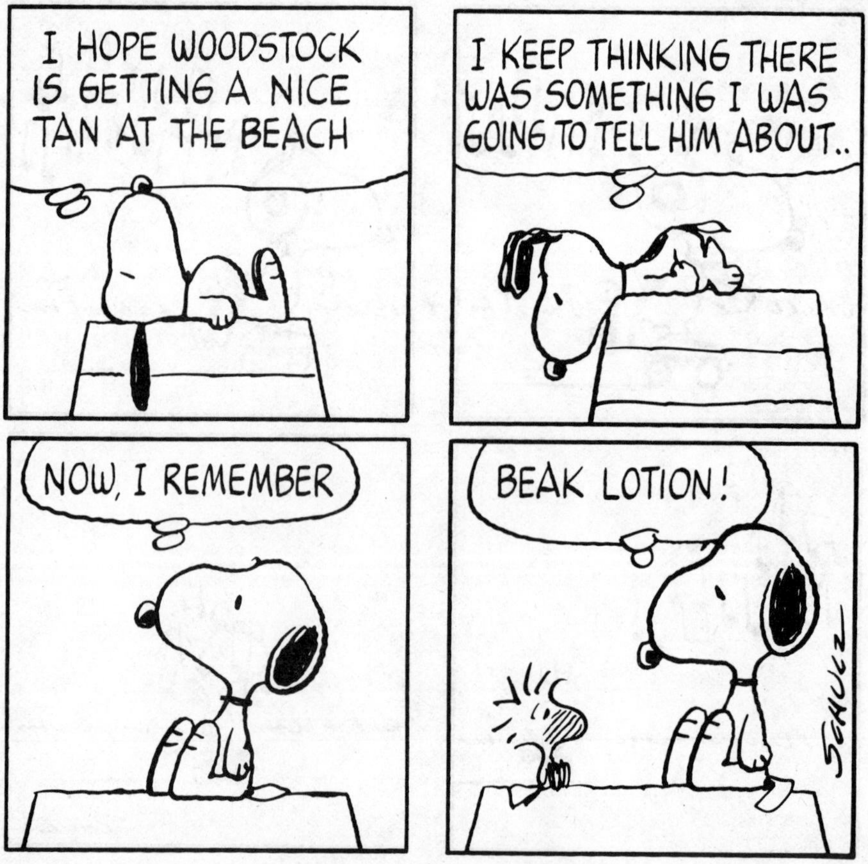
I HOPE WOODSTOCK IS GETTING A NICE TAN AT THE BEACH
I KEEP THINKING THERE WAS SOMETHING I WAS GOING TO TELL HIM ABOUT..
NOW, I REMEMBER
BEAK LOTION!
SCHULZ

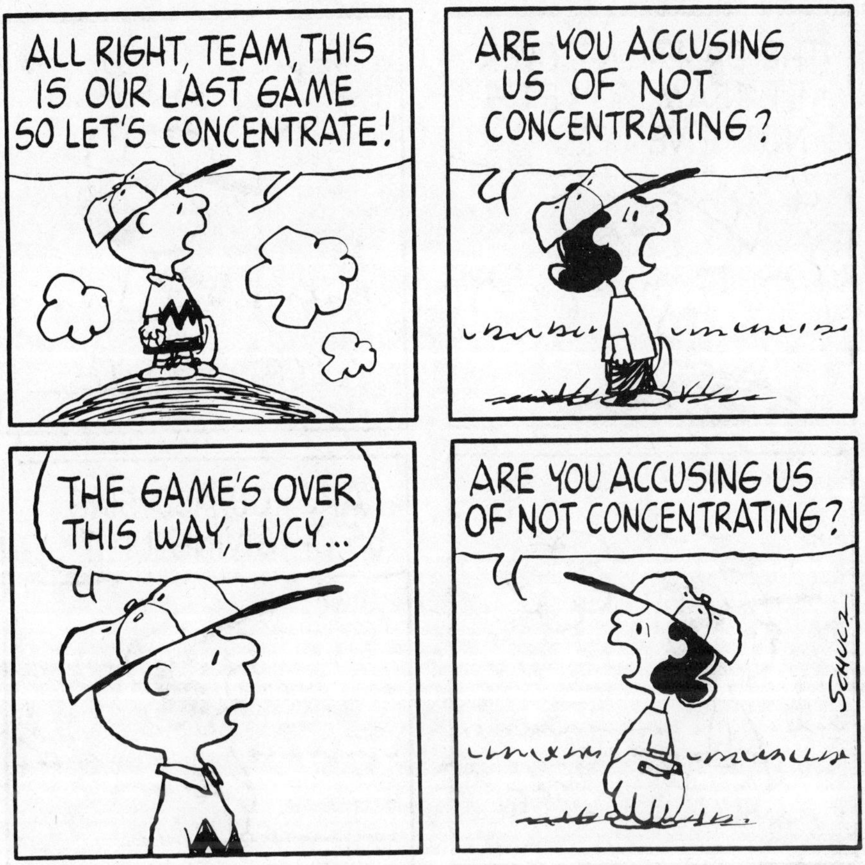
ALL RIGHT, TEAM, THIS IS OUR LAST GAME SO LET'S CONCENTRATE!
ARE YOU ACCUSING US OF NOT CONCENTRATING?
THE GAME'S OVER THIS WAY, LUCY...
ARE YOU ACCUSING US OF NOT CONCENTRATING?
SCHULZ

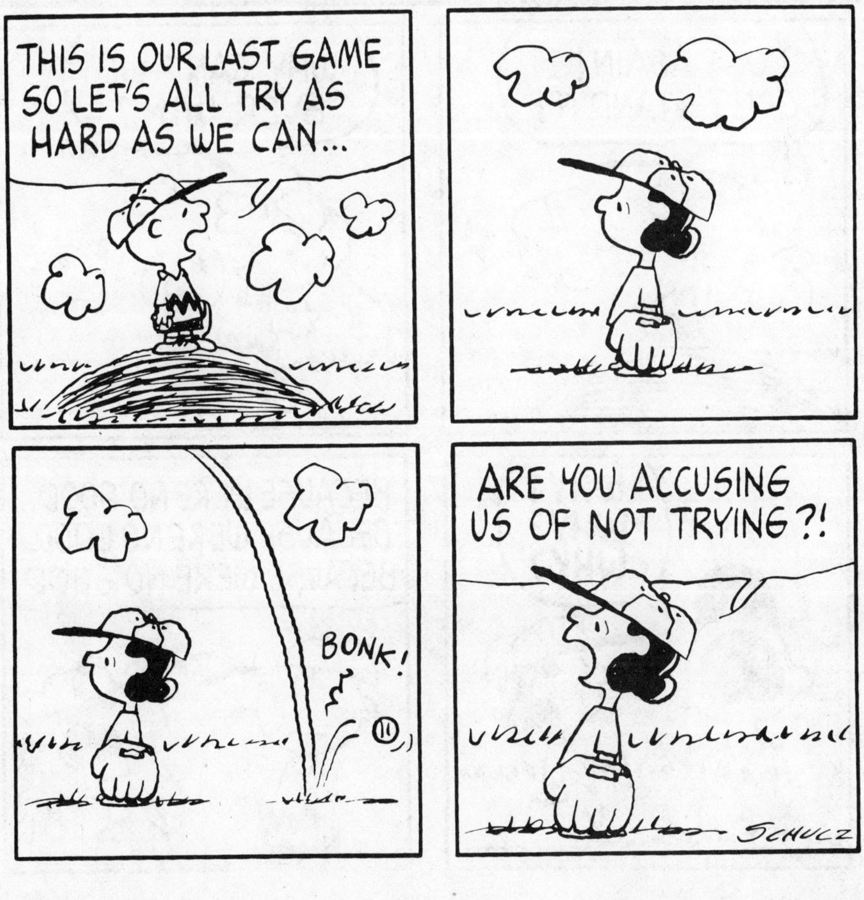
THIS IS OUR LAST GAME SO LET'S ALL TRY AS HARD AS WE CAN...
BONK!
ARE YOU ACCUSING US OF NOT TRYING?!
SCHULZ

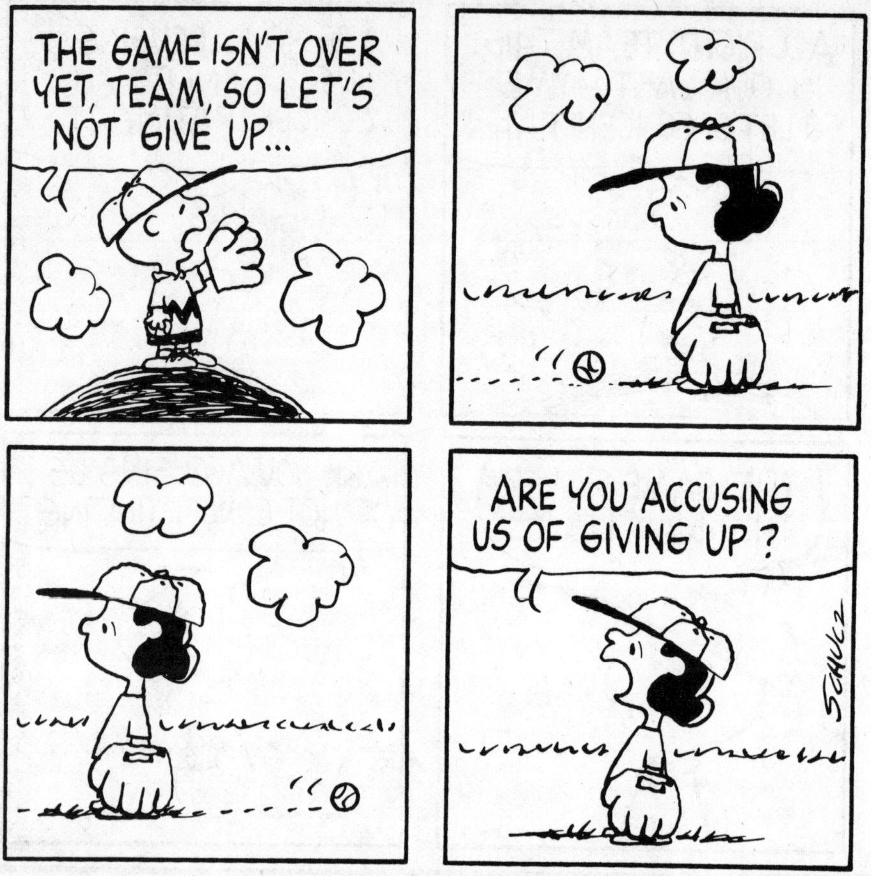
THE GAME ISN'T OVER YET, TEAM, SO LET'S NOT GIVE UP...
ARE YOU ACCUSING US OF GIVING UP ?
SCHULZ

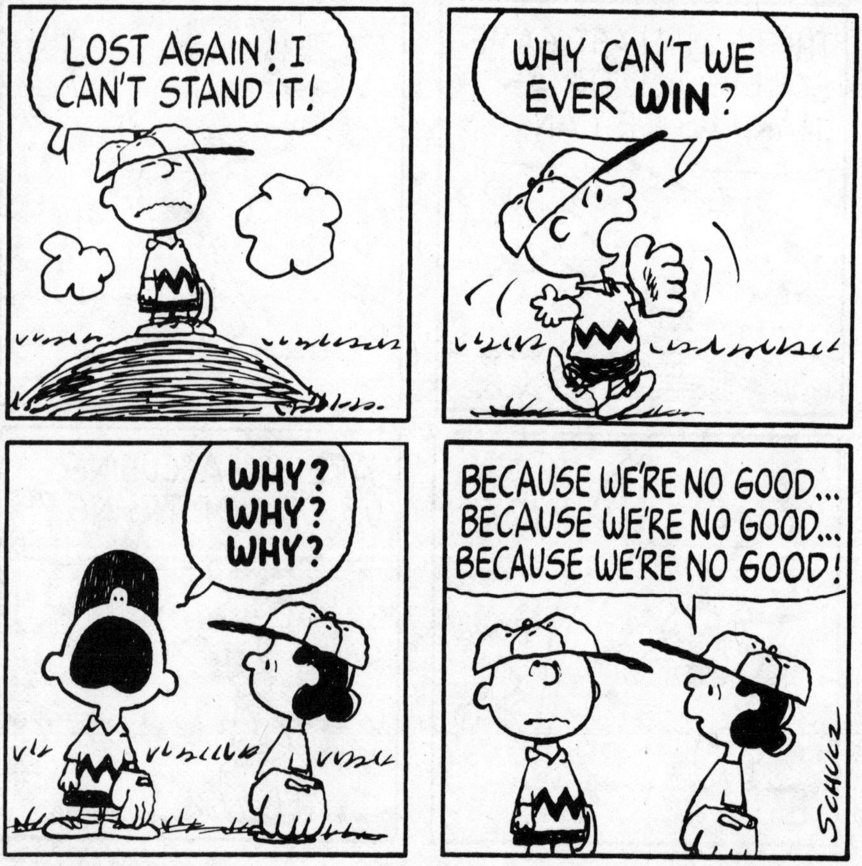
LOST AGAIN! I CAN'T STAND IT!
WHY CAN'T WE EVER **WIN**?
WHY? WHY? WHY?
BECAUSE WE'RE NO GOOD... BECAUSE WE'RE NO GOOD... BECAUSE WE'RE NO GOOD!
SCHULZ

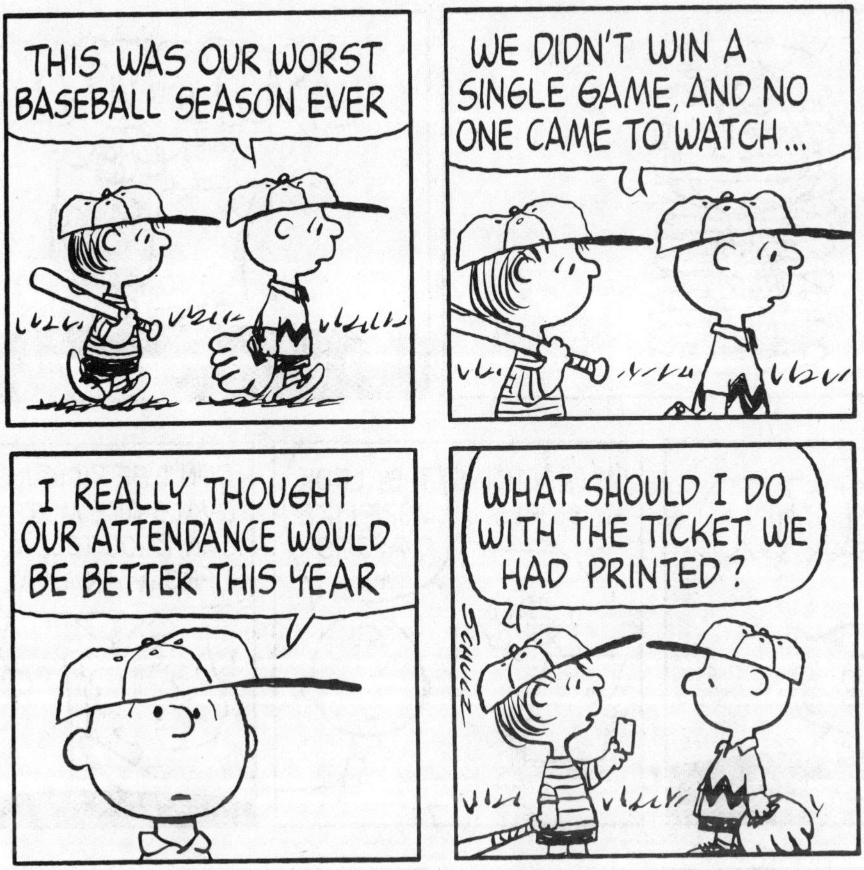
THIS WAS OUR WORST BASEBALL SEASON EVER
WE DIDN'T WIN A SINGLE GAME, AND NO ONE CAME TO WATCH...
I REALLY THOUGHT OUR ATTENDANCE WOULD BE BETTER THIS YEAR
WHAT SHOULD I DO WITH THE TICKET WE HAD PRINTED?
SCHULZ

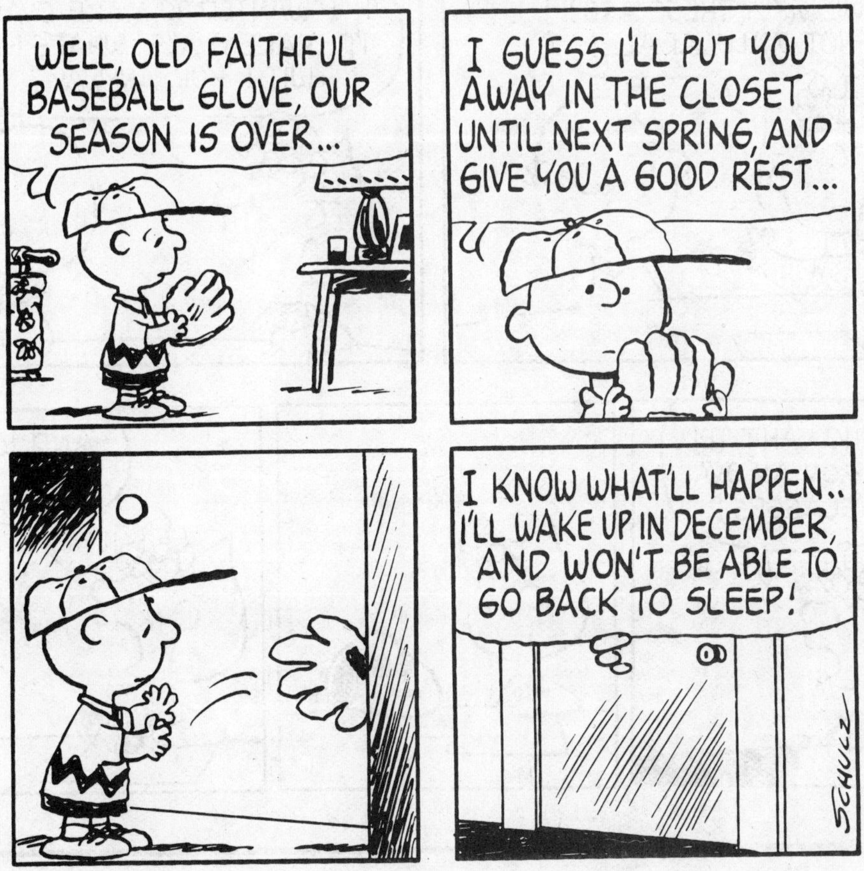
WELL, OLD FAITHFUL BASEBALL GLOVE, OUR SEASON IS OVER...
I GUESS I'LL PUT YOU AWAY IN THE CLOSET UNTIL NEXT SPRING, AND GIVE YOU A GOOD REST...
I KNOW WHAT'LL HAPPEN.. I'LL WAKE UP IN DECEMBER, AND WON'T BE ABLE TO GO BACK TO SLEEP!
SCHULZ

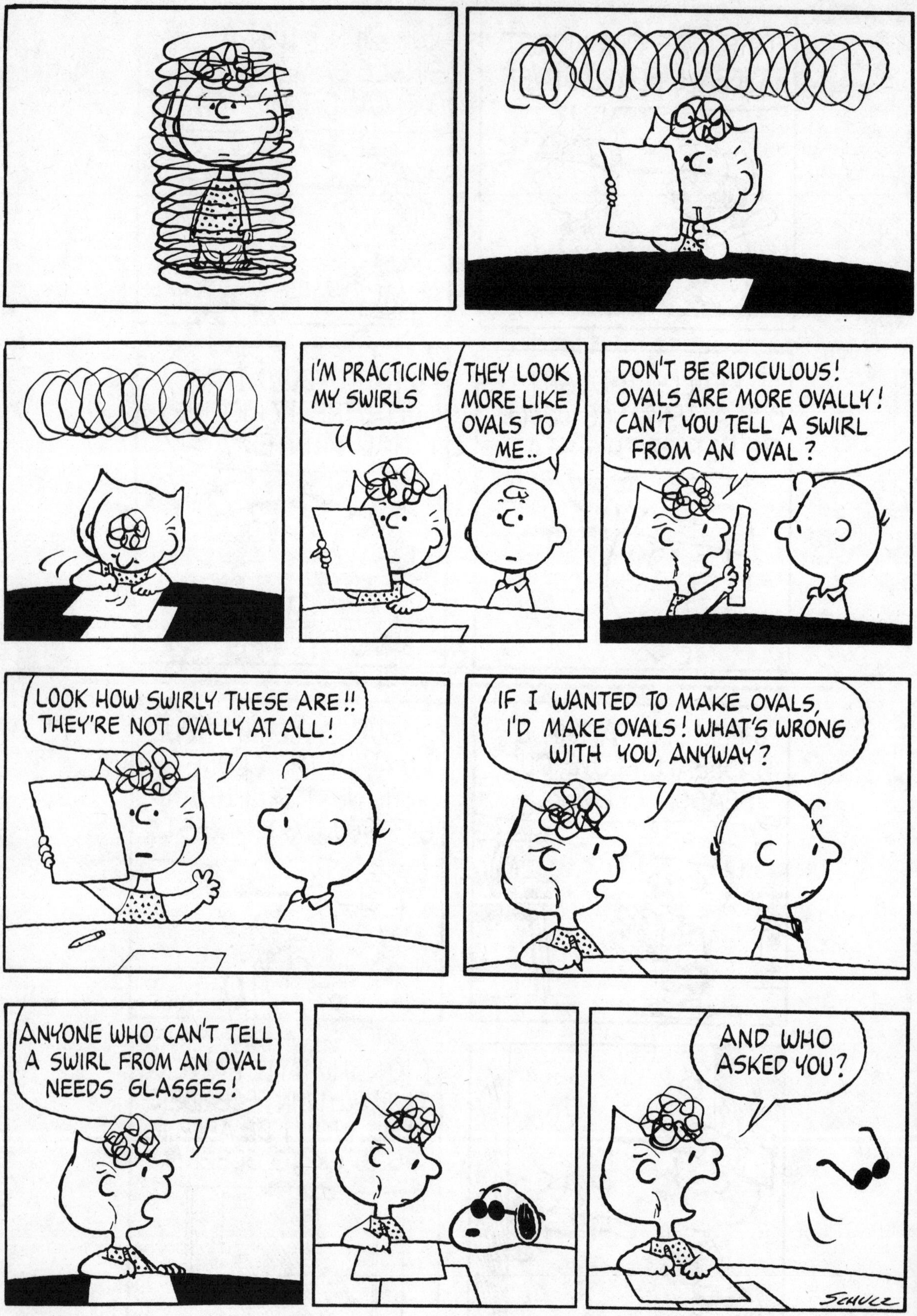

I'M PRACTICING MY SWIRLS
THEY LOOK MORE LIKE OVALS TO ME..
DON'T BE RIDICULOUS! OVALS ARE MORE OVALLY! CAN'T YOU TELL A SWIRL FROM AN OVAL?
LOOK HOW SWIRLY THESE ARE!! THEY'RE NOT OVALLY AT ALL!
IF I WANTED TO MAKE OVALS, I'D MAKE OVALS! WHAT'S WRONG WITH YOU, ANYWAY?
ANYONE WHO CAN'T TELL A SWIRL FROM AN OVAL NEEDS GLASSES!
AND WHO ASKED YOU?
SCHULZ

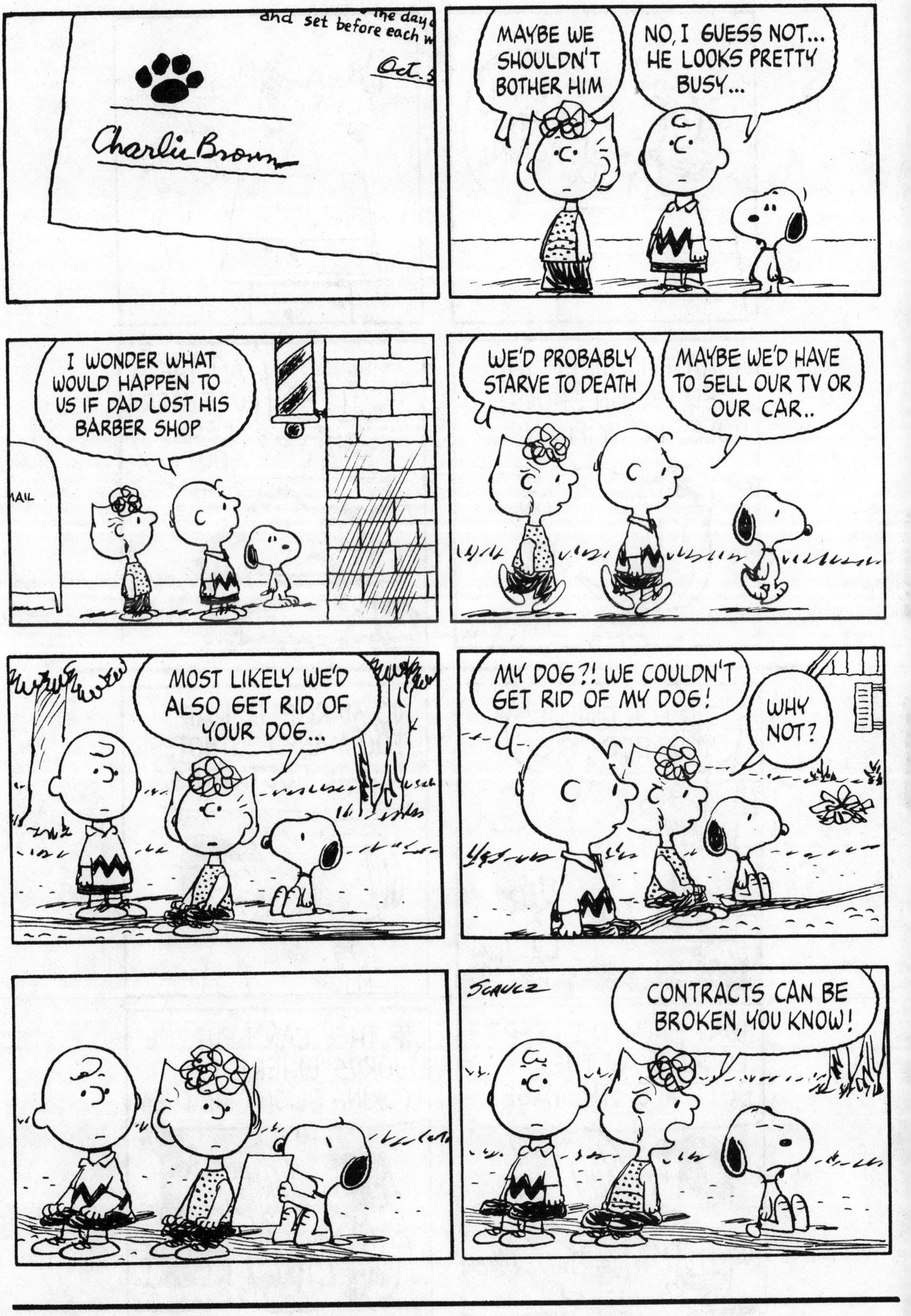

the day
and set before each
Oct. 5
Charlie Brown
MAYBE WE SHOULDN'T BOTHER HIM
NO, I GUESS NOT... HE LOOKS PRETTY BUSY...
I WONDER WHAT WOULD HAPPEN TO US IF DAD LOST HIS BARBER SHOP
MAIL
WE'D PROBABLY STARVE TO DEATH
MAYBE WE'D HAVE TO SELL OUR TV OR OUR CAR..
MOST LIKELY WE'D ALSO GET RID OF YOUR DOG...
MY DOG?! WE COULDN'T GET RID OF MY DOG!
WHY NOT?
SCHULZ
CONTRACTS CAN BE BROKEN, YOU KNOW!

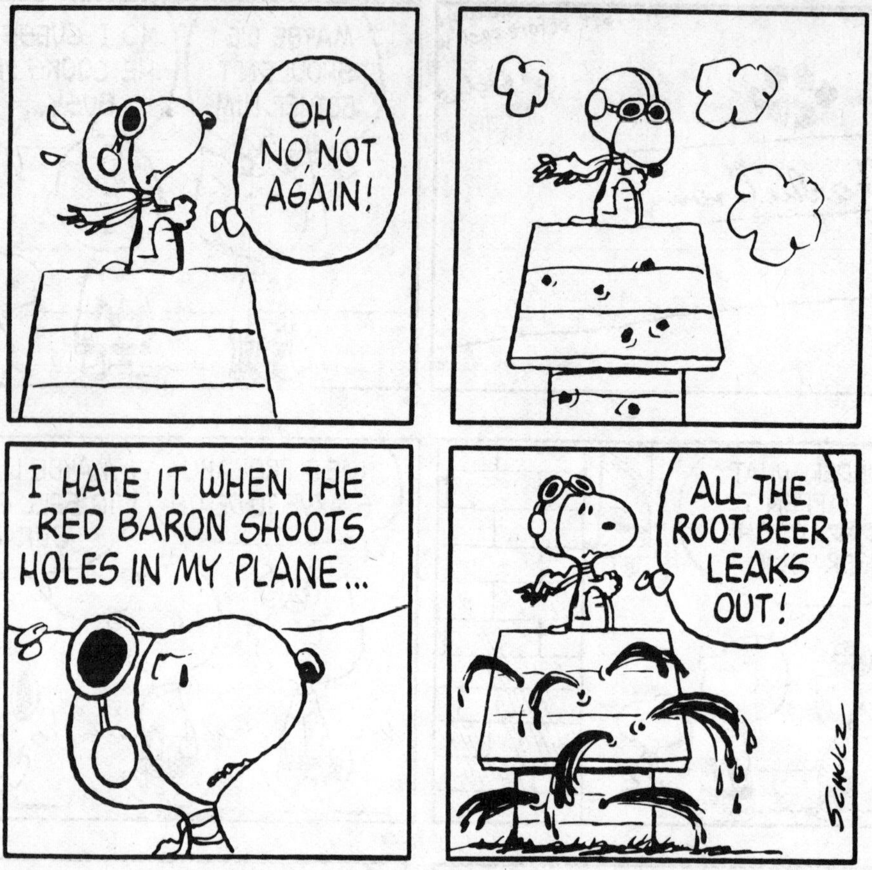
OH, NO, NOT AGAIN!
I HATE IT WHEN THE RED BARON SHOOTS HOLES IN MY PLANE...
ALL THE ROOT BEER LEAKS OUT!
SCHULZ

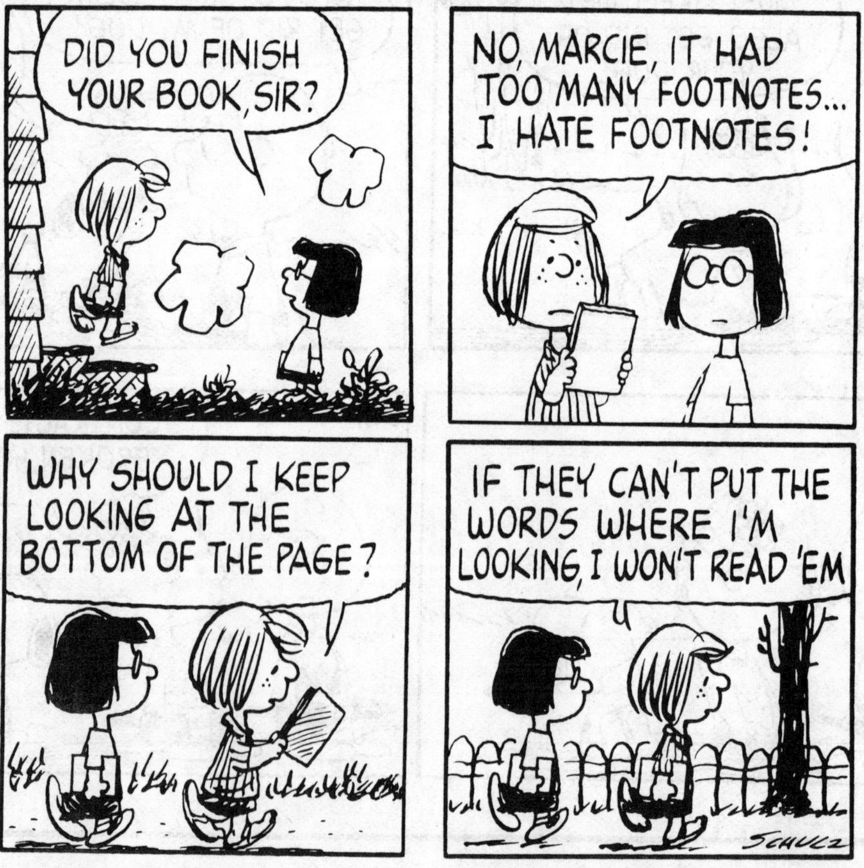
DID YOU FINISH YOUR BOOK, SIR?
NO, MARCIE, IT HAD TOO MANY FOOTNOTES... I HATE FOOTNOTES!
WHY SHOULD I KEEP LOOKING AT THE BOTTOM OF THE PAGE?
IF THEY CAN'T PUT THE WORDS WHERE I'M LOOKING, I WON'T READ 'EM
SCHULZ

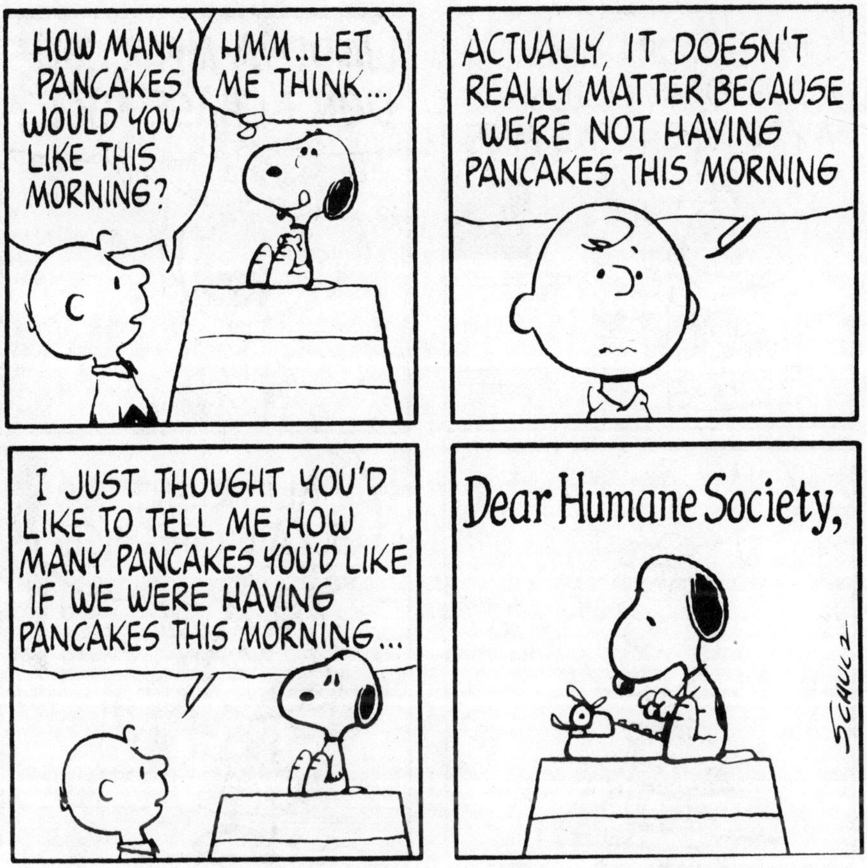
HOW MANY PANCAKES WOULD YOU LIKE THIS MORNING?
HMM..LET ME THINK...
ACTUALLY, IT DOESN'T REALLY MATTER BECAUSE WE'RE NOT HAVING PANCAKES THIS MORNING
I JUST THOUGHT YOU'D LIKE TO TELL ME HOW MANY PANCAKES YOU'D LIKE IF WE WERE HAVING PANCAKES THIS MORNING...
Dear Humane Society,
SCHULZ

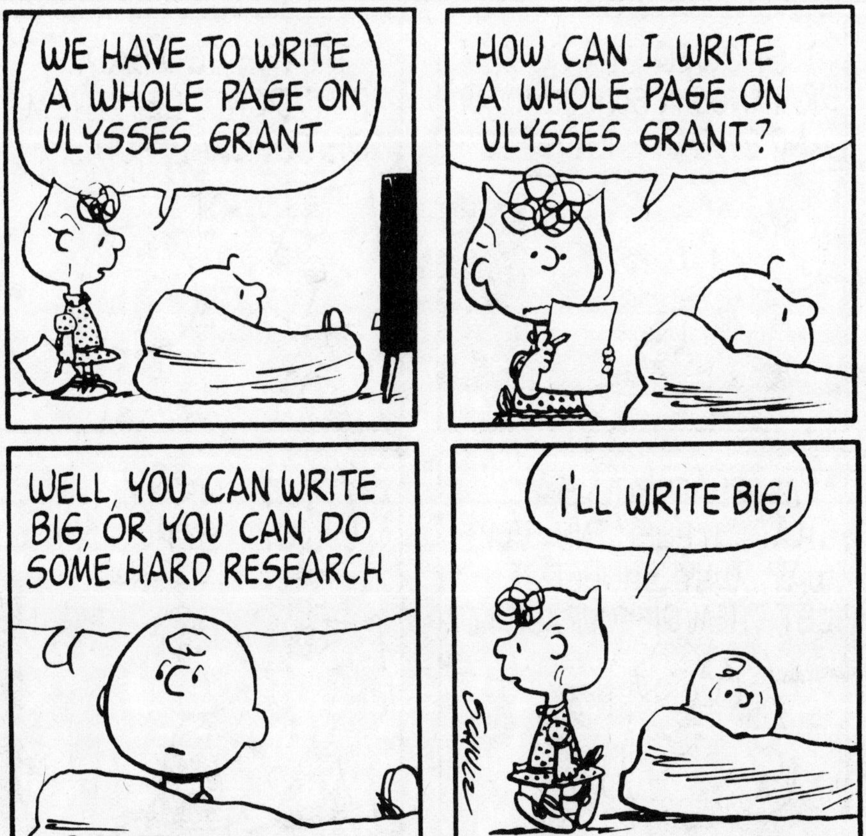
WE HAVE TO WRITE A WHOLE PAGE ON ULYSSES GRANT
HOW CAN I WRITE A WHOLE PAGE ON ULYSSES GRANT?
WELL, YOU CAN WRITE BIG, OR YOU CAN DO SOME HARD RESEARCH
I'LL WRITE BIG!
SCHULZ

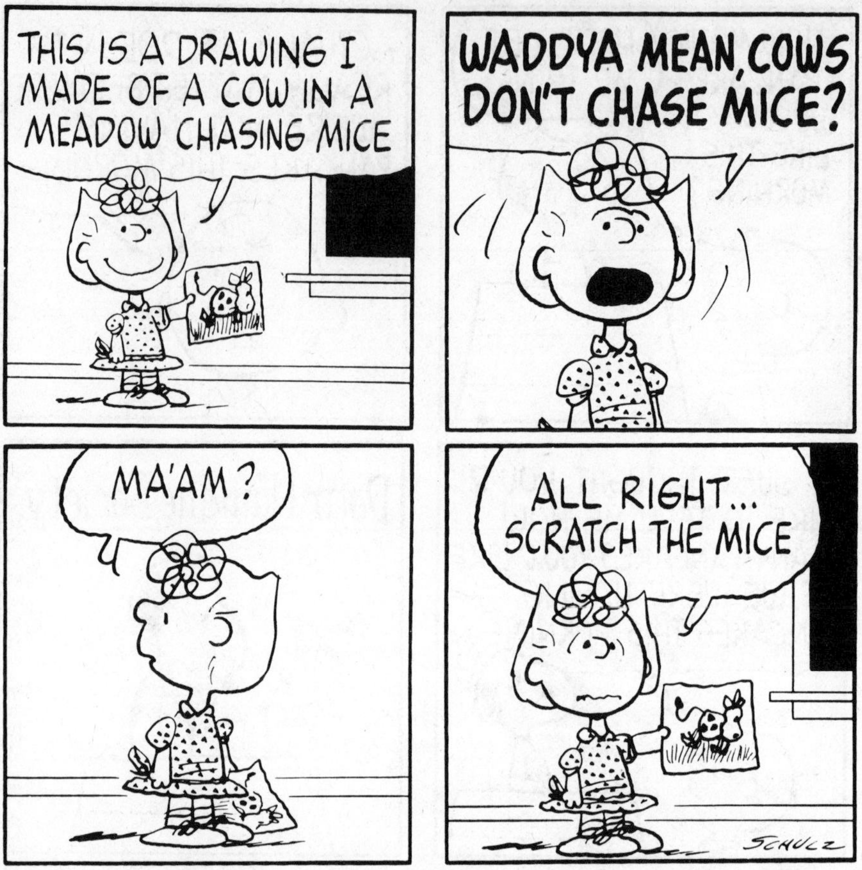
THIS IS A DRAWING I MADE OF A COW IN A MEADOW CHASING MICE
WADDYA MEAN, COWS DON'T CHASE MICE?
MA'AM?
ALL RIGHT... SCRATCH THE MICE
SCHULZ

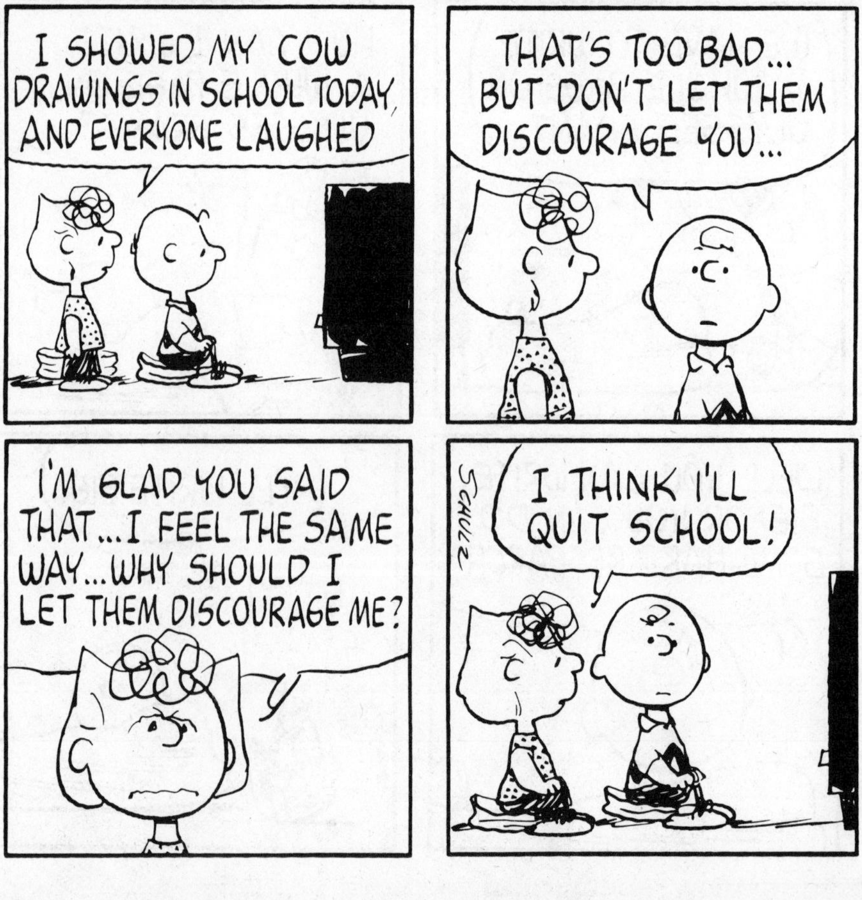
I SHOWED MY COW DRAWINGS IN SCHOOL TODAY, AND EVERYONE LAUGHED
THAT'S TOO BAD... BUT DON'T LET THEM DISCOURAGE YOU...
I'M GLAD YOU SAID THAT...I FEEL THE SAME WAY...WHY SHOULD I LET THEM DISCOURAGE ME?
SCHULZ
I THINK I'LL QUIT SCHOOL!

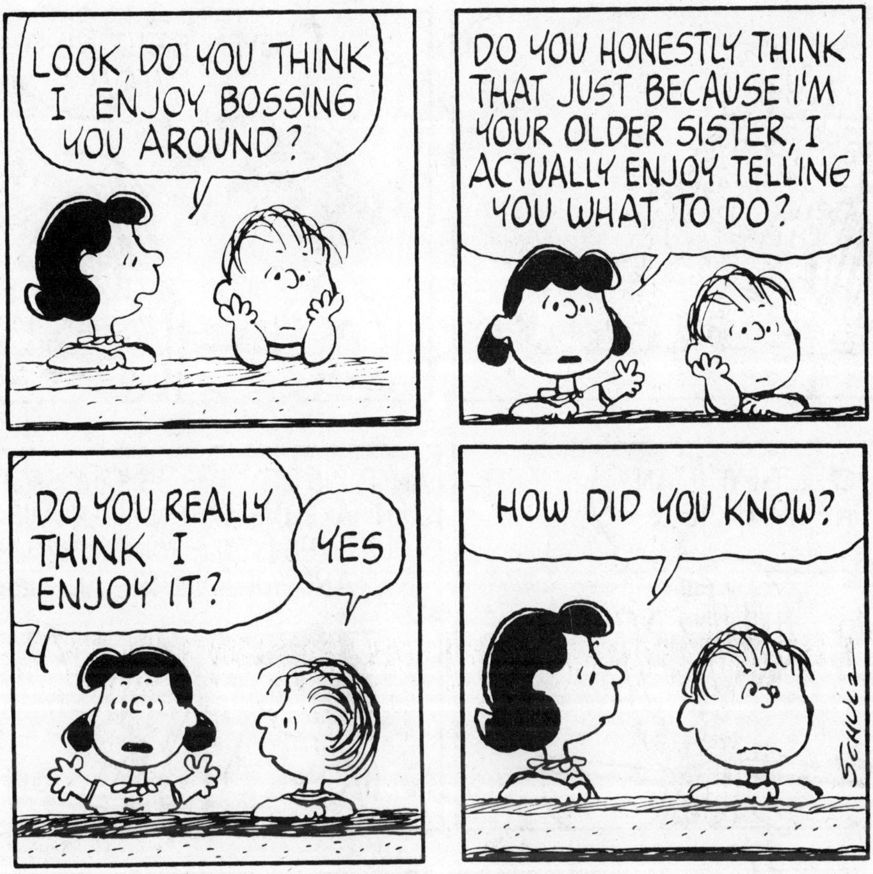
LOOK, DO YOU THINK I ENJOY BOSSING YOU AROUND?
DO YOU HONESTLY THINK THAT JUST BECAUSE I'M YOUR OLDER SISTER, I ACTUALLY ENJOY TELLING YOU WHAT TO DO?
DO YOU REALLY THINK I ENJOY IT?
YES
HOW DID YOU KNOW?
SCHULZ

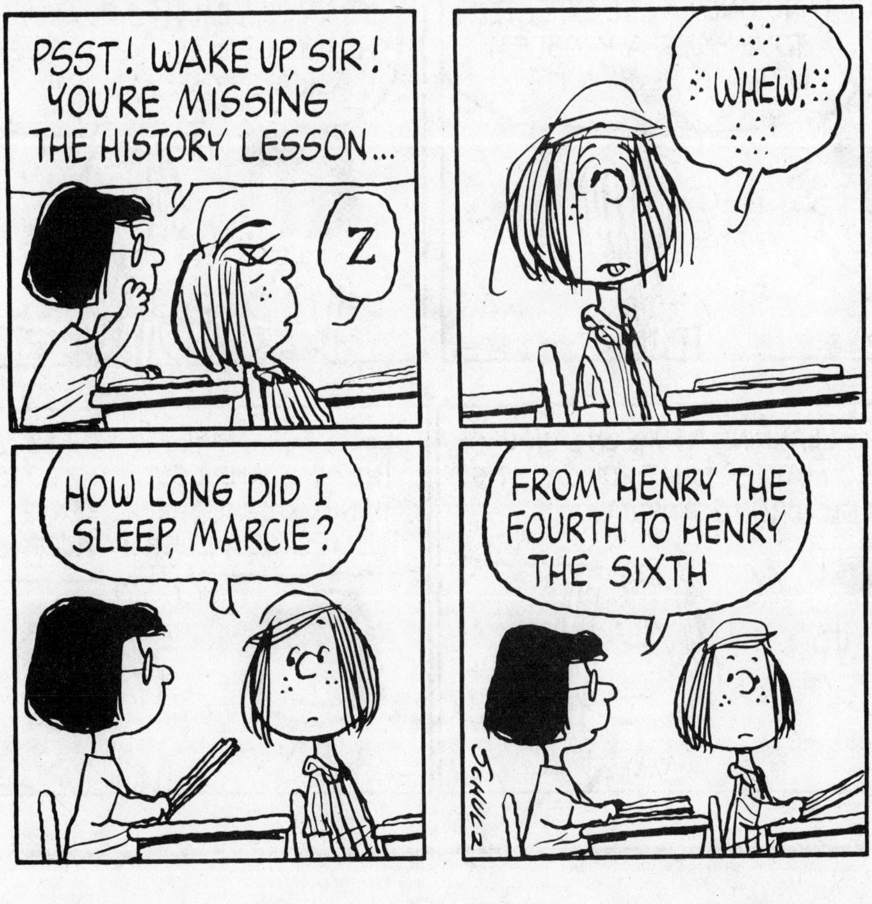
PSST! WAKE UP, SIR! YOU'RE MISSING THE HISTORY LESSON...
Z
WHEW!
HOW LONG DID I SLEEP, MARCIE?
FROM HENRY THE FOURTH TO HENRY THE SIXTH
SCHULZ

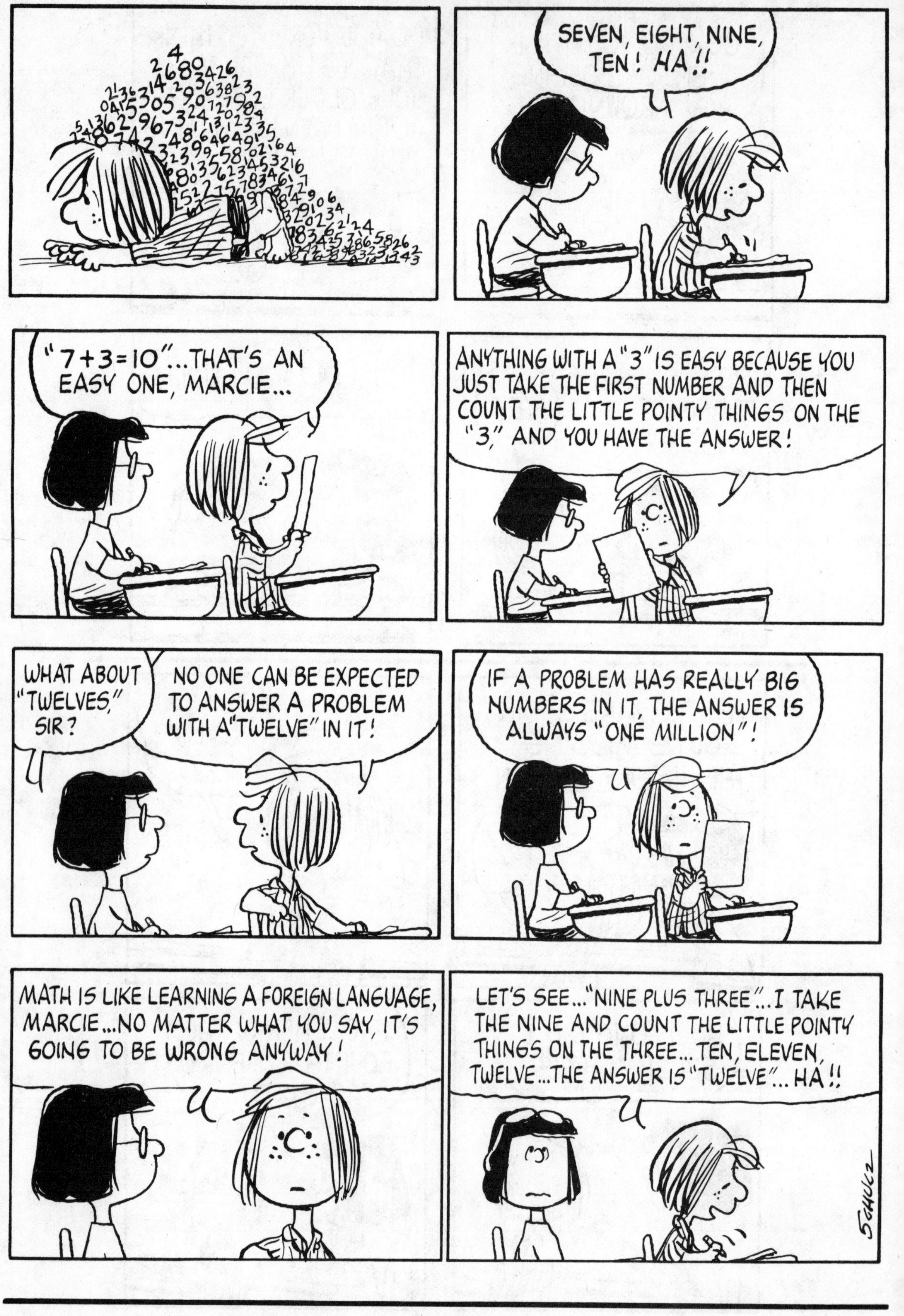
SEVEN, EIGHT, NINE, TEN! HA!!
"7+3=10"...THAT'S AN EASY ONE, MARCIE...
ANYTHING WITH A "3" IS EASY BECAUSE YOU JUST TAKE THE FIRST NUMBER AND THEN COUNT THE LITTLE POINTY THINGS ON THE "3," AND YOU HAVE THE ANSWER!
WHAT ABOUT "TWELVES," SIR?
NO ONE CAN BE EXPECTED TO ANSWER A PROBLEM WITH A "TWELVE" IN IT!
IF A PROBLEM HAS REALLY BIG NUMBERS IN IT, THE ANSWER IS ALWAYS "ONE MILLION"!
MATH IS LIKE LEARNING A FOREIGN LANGUAGE, MARCIE...NO MATTER WHAT YOU SAY, IT'S GOING TO BE WRONG ANYWAY!
LET'S SEE..."NINE PLUS THREE"...I TAKE THE NINE AND COUNT THE LITTLE POINTY THINGS ON THE THREE... TEN, ELEVEN, TWELVE...THE ANSWER IS "TWELVE"... HA!!
SCHULZ

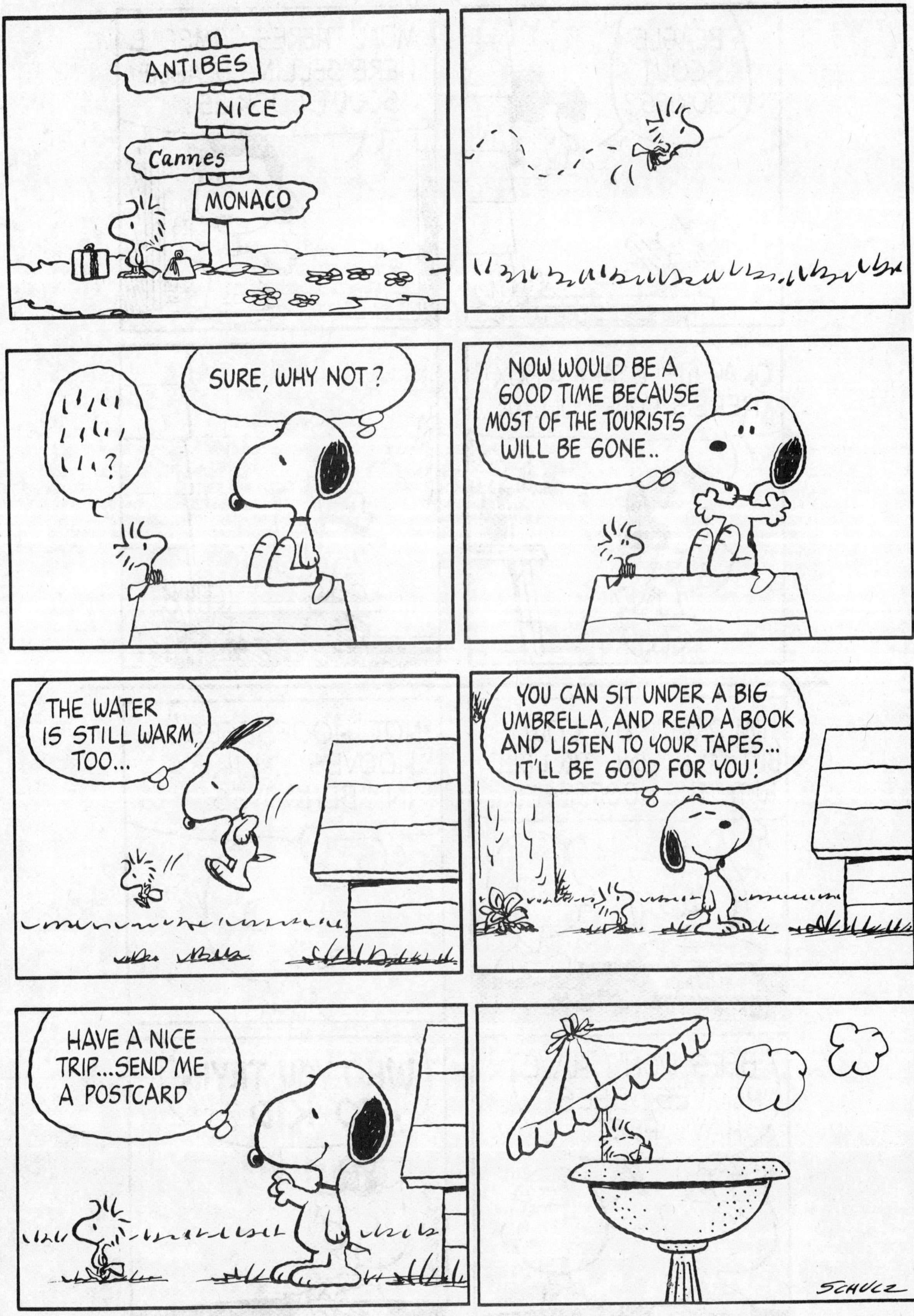
ANTIBES
NICE
Cannes
MONACO
SURE, WHY NOT?
NOW WOULD BE A GOOD TIME BECAUSE MOST OF THE TOURISTS WILL BE GONE..
THE WATER IS STILL WARM, TOO...
YOU CAN SIT UNDER A BIG UMBRELLA, AND READ A BOOK AND LISTEN TO YOUR TAPES... IT'LL BE GOOD FOR YOU!
HAVE A NICE TRIP...SEND ME A POSTCARD
SCHULZ

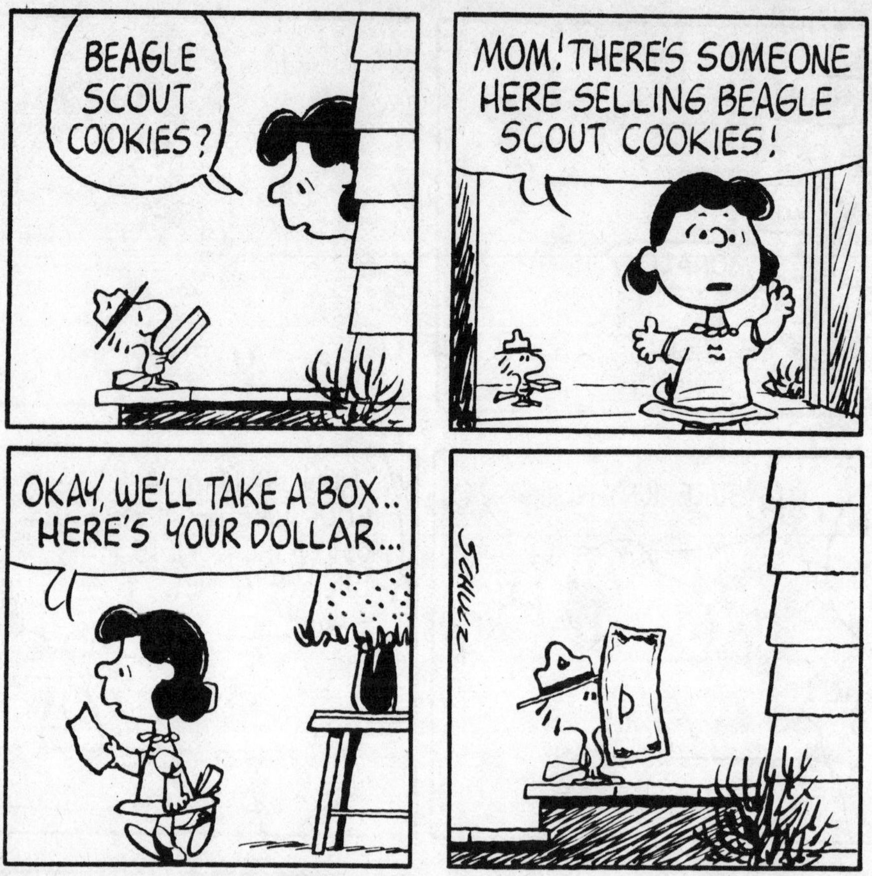
BEAGLE SCOUT COOKIES?
MOM! THERE'S SOMEONE HERE SELLING BEAGLE SCOUT COOKIES!
OKAY, WE'LL TAKE A BOX.. HERE'S YOUR DOLLAR...
SCHULZ

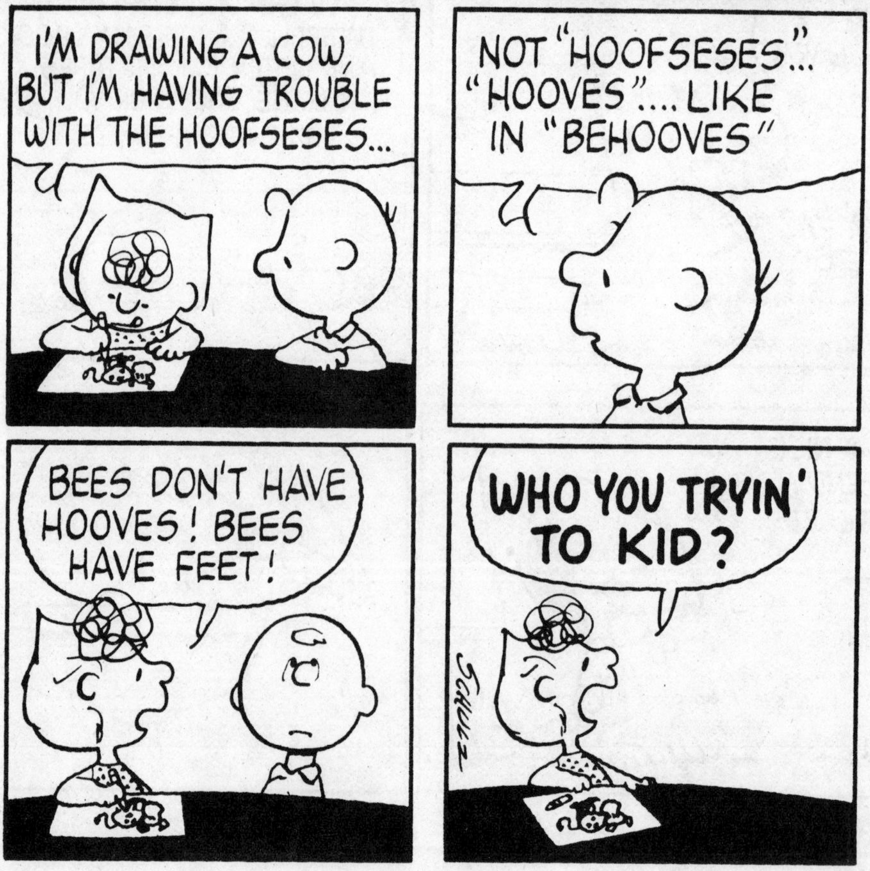
I'M DRAWING A COW, BUT I'M HAVING TROUBLE WITH THE HOOFSESES...
NOT "HOOFSESES"... "HOOVES".... LIKE IN "BEHOOVES"
BEES DON'T HAVE HOOVES! BEES HAVE FEET!
WHO YOU TRYIN' TO KID?
SCHULZ

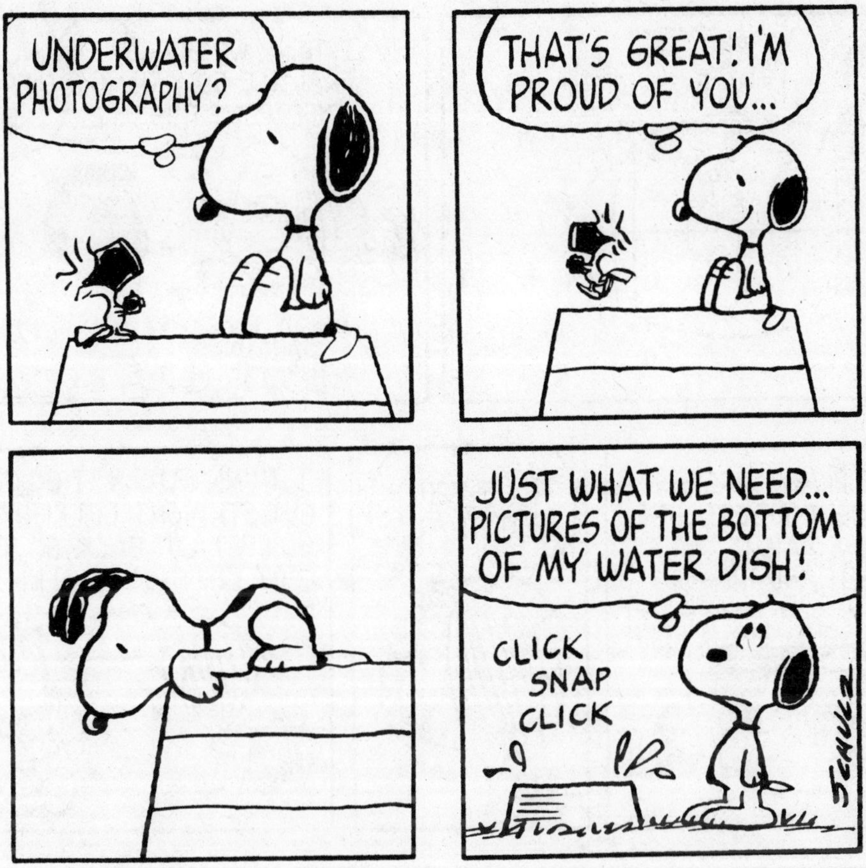
UNDERWATER PHOTOGRAPHY?
THAT'S GREAT! I'M PROUD OF YOU...
JUST WHAT WE NEED... PICTURES OF THE BOTTOM OF MY WATER DISH!
CLICK
SNAP
CLICK
SCHULZ

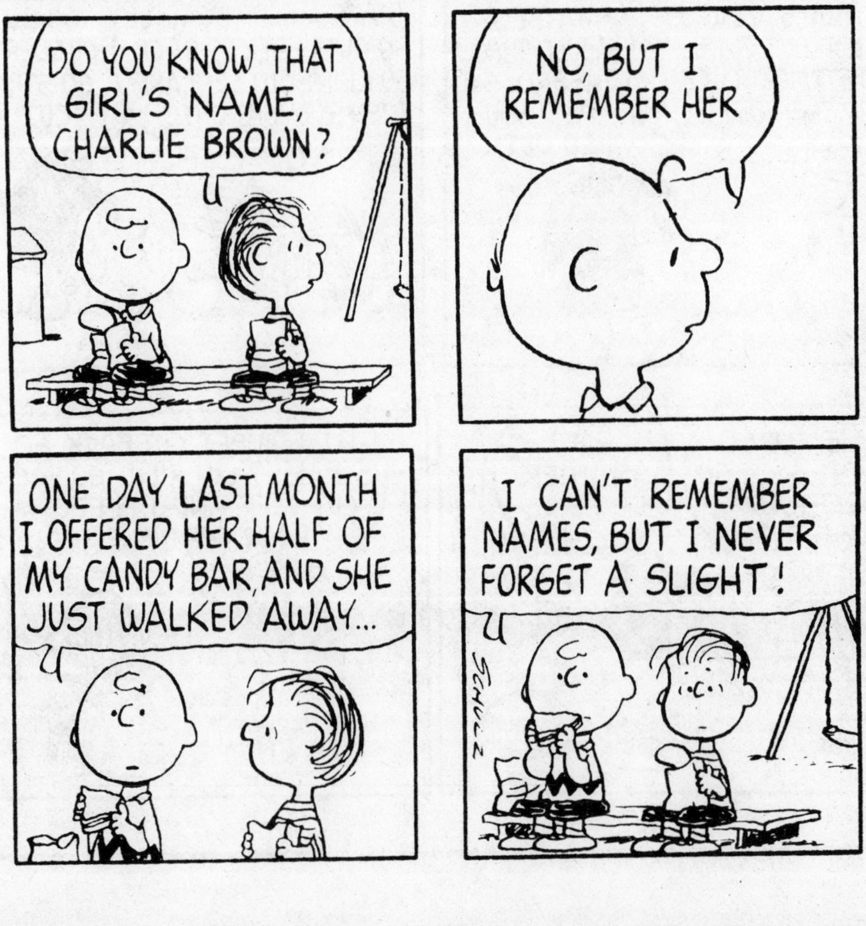
DO YOU KNOW THAT GIRL'S NAME, CHARLIE BROWN?
NO, BUT I REMEMBER HER
ONE DAY LAST MONTH I OFFERED HER HALF OF MY CANDY BAR, AND SHE JUST WALKED AWAY...
I CAN'T REMEMBER NAMES, BUT I NEVER FORGET A SLIGHT!
SCHULZ

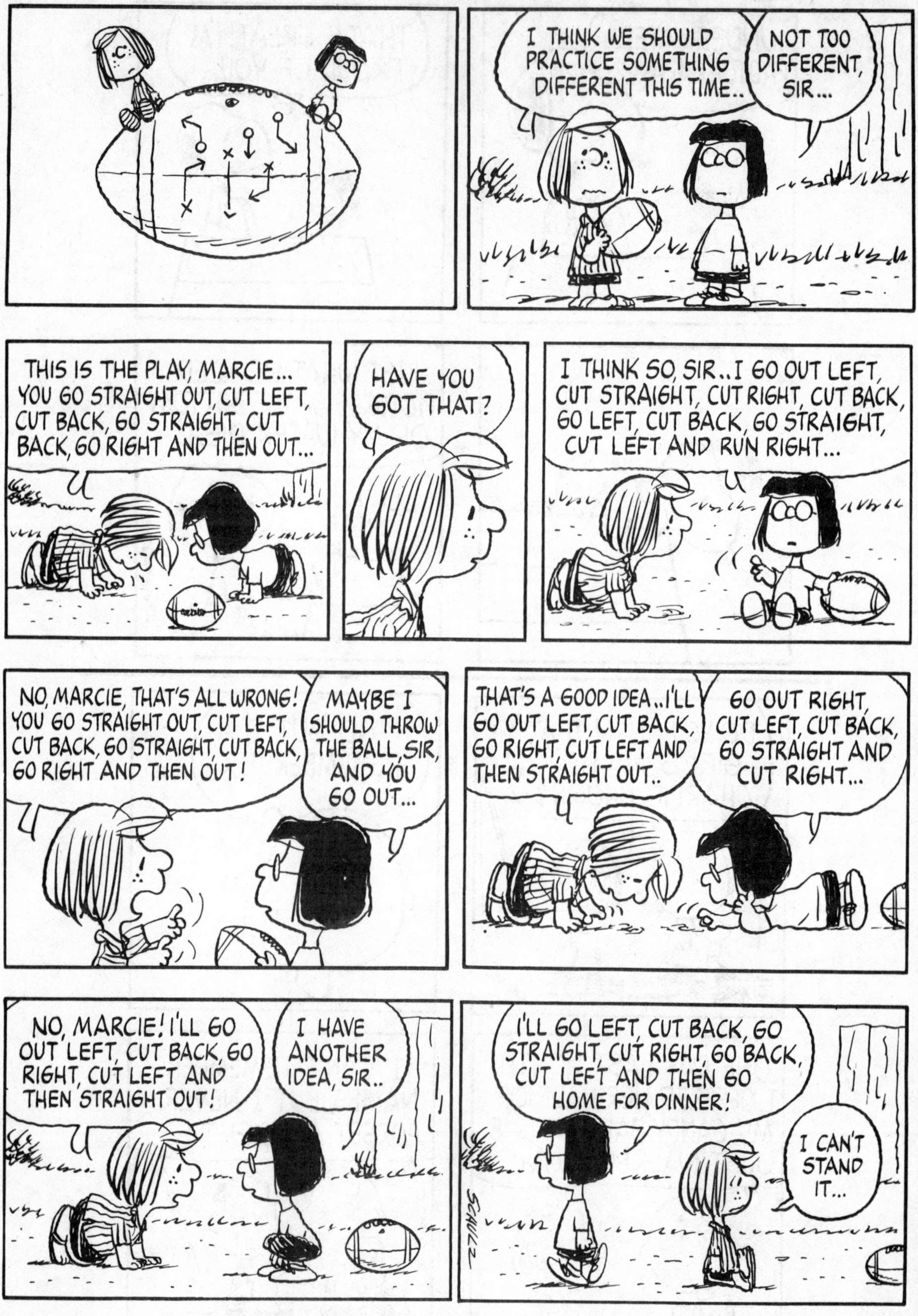
I THINK WE SHOULD PRACTICE SOMETHING DIFFERENT THIS TIME..
NOT TOO DIFFERENT, SIR...
THIS IS THE PLAY, MARCIE... YOU GO STRAIGHT OUT, CUT LEFT, CUT BACK, GO STRAIGHT, CUT BACK, GO RIGHT AND THEN OUT...
HAVE YOU GOT THAT?
I THINK SO, SIR..I GO OUT LEFT, CUT STRAIGHT, CUT RIGHT, CUT BACK, GO LEFT, CUT BACK, GO STRAIGHT, CUT LEFT AND RUN RIGHT...
NO, MARCIE, THAT'S ALL WRONG! YOU GO STRAIGHT OUT, CUT LEFT, CUT BACK, GO STRAIGHT, CUT BACK, GO RIGHT AND THEN OUT!
MAYBE I SHOULD THROW THE BALL, SIR, AND YOU GO OUT...
THAT'S A GOOD IDEA..I'LL GO OUT LEFT, CUT BACK, GO RIGHT, CUT LEFT AND THEN STRAIGHT OUT..
GO OUT RIGHT, CUT LEFT, CUT BACK, GO STRAIGHT AND CUT RIGHT...
NO, MARCIE! I'LL GO OUT LEFT, CUT BACK, GO RIGHT, CUT LEFT AND THEN STRAIGHT OUT!
I HAVE ANOTHER IDEA, SIR..
SCHULZ
I'LL GO LEFT, CUT BACK, GO STRAIGHT, CUT RIGHT, GO BACK, CUT LEFT AND THEN GO HOME FOR DINNER!
I CAN'T STAND IT...

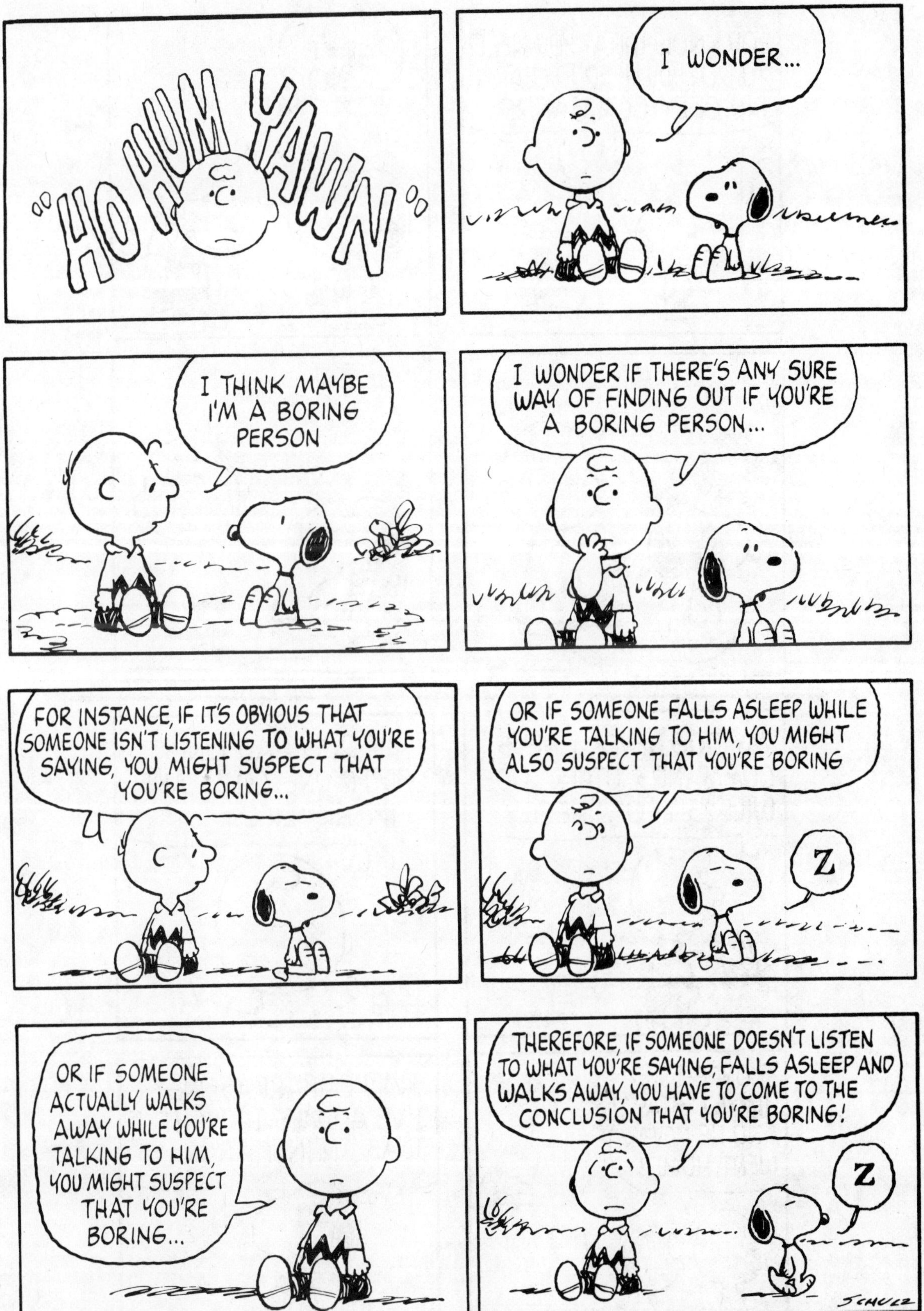
HO HUM YAWN
I WONDER...
I THINK MAYBE I'M A BORING PERSON
I WONDER IF THERE'S ANY SURE WAY OF FINDING OUT IF YOU'RE A BORING PERSON...
FOR INSTANCE, IF IT'S OBVIOUS THAT SOMEONE ISN'T LISTENING TO WHAT YOU'RE SAYING, YOU MIGHT SUSPECT THAT YOU'RE BORING...
OR IF SOMEONE FALLS ASLEEP WHILE YOU'RE TALKING TO HIM, YOU MIGHT ALSO SUSPECT THAT YOU'RE BORING
Z
OR IF SOMEONE ACTUALLY WALKS AWAY WHILE YOU'RE TALKING TO HIM, YOU MIGHT SUSPECT THAT YOU'RE BORING...
THEREFORE, IF SOMEONE DOESN'T LISTEN TO WHAT YOU'RE SAYING, FALLS ASLEEP AND WALKS AWAY, YOU HAVE TO COME TO THE CONCLUSION THAT YOU'RE BORING!
Z
SCHULZ

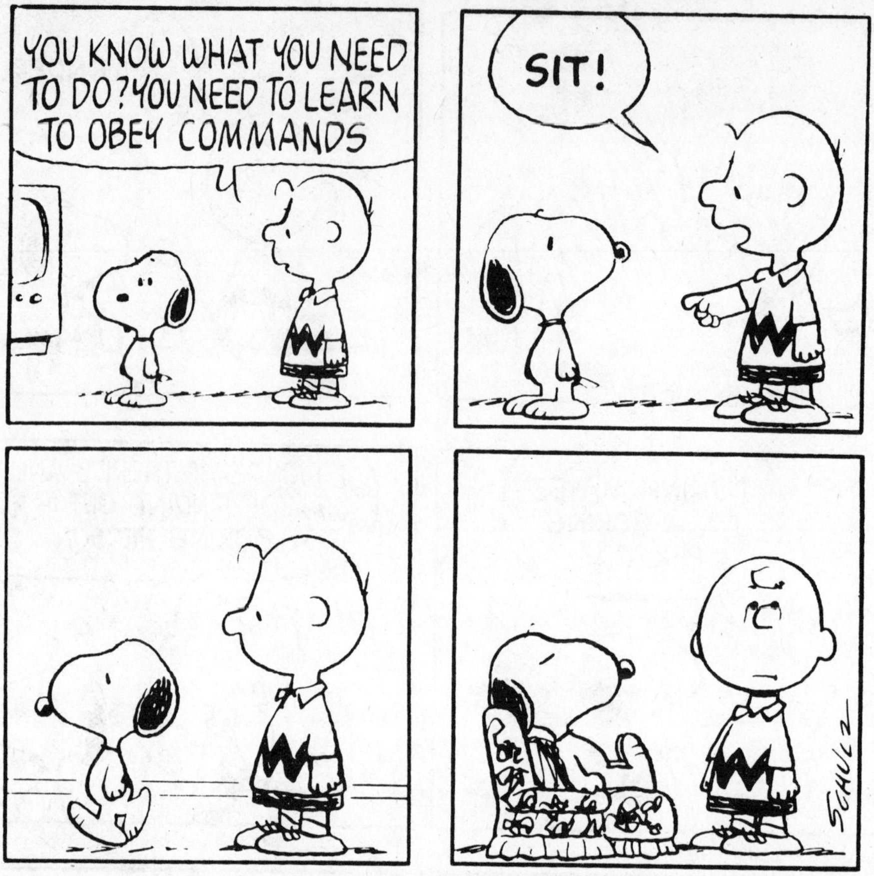
YOU KNOW WHAT YOU NEED TO DO? YOU NEED TO LEARN TO OBEY COMMANDS
SIT!
SCHULZ

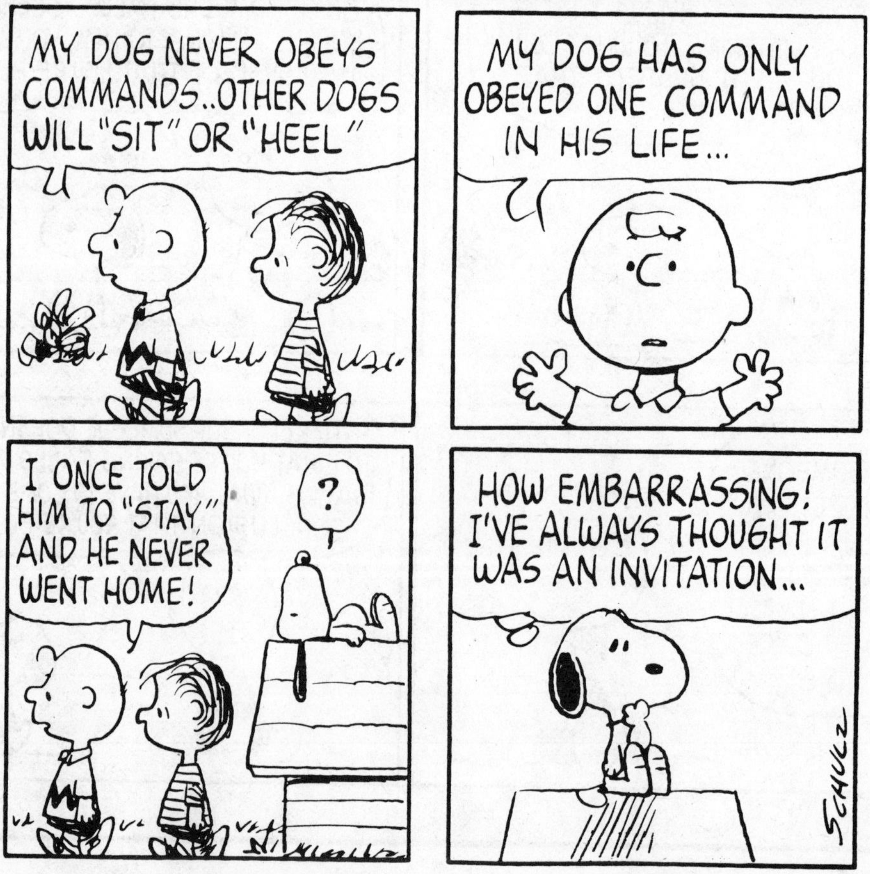
MY DOG NEVER OBEYS COMMANDS..OTHER DOGS WILL "SIT" OR "HEEL"
MY DOG HAS ONLY OBEYED ONE COMMAND IN HIS LIFE...
I ONCE TOLD HIM TO "STAY," AND HE NEVER WENT HOME!
?
HOW EMBARRASSING! I'VE ALWAYS THOUGHT IT WAS AN INVITATION...
SCHULZ

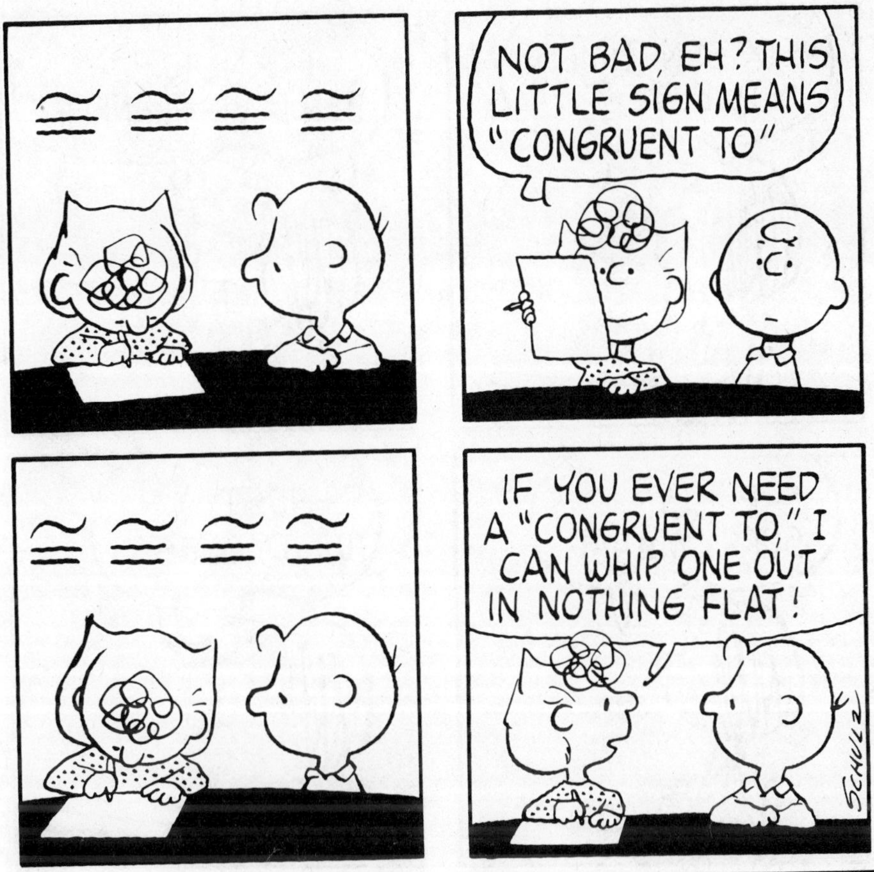
NOT BAD, EH? THIS LITTLE SIGN MEANS "CONGRUENT TO"
IF YOU EVER NEED A "CONGRUENT TO," I CAN WHIP ONE OUT IN NOTHING FLAT!
SCHULZ

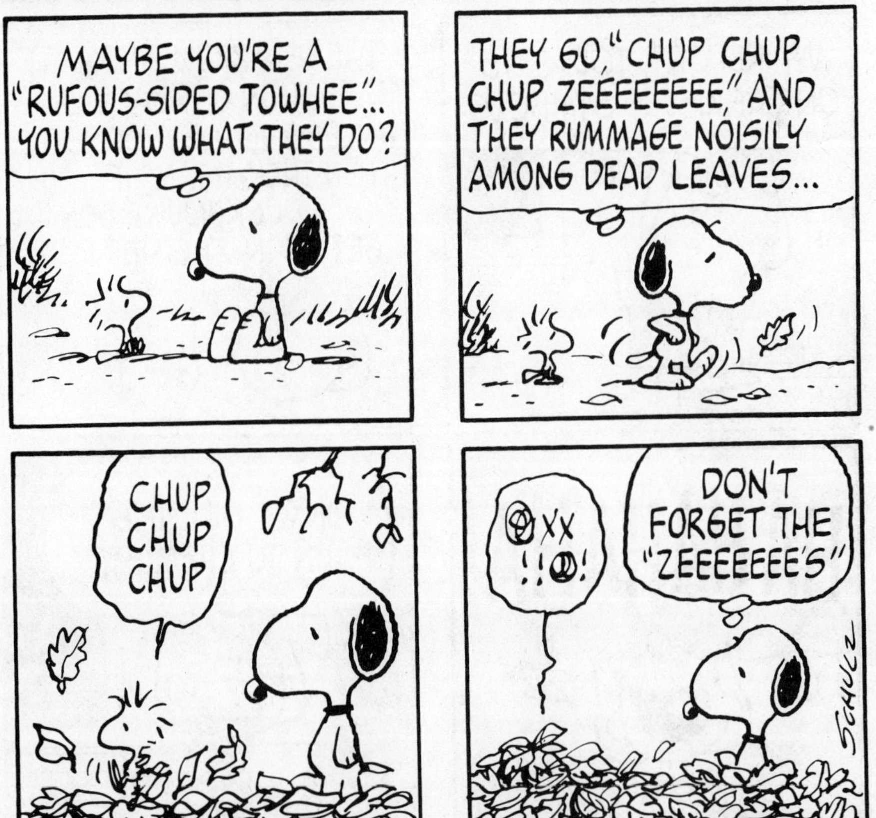
MAYBE YOU'RE A "RUFOUS-SIDED TOWHEE"... YOU KNOW WHAT THEY DO?
THEY GO, "CHUP CHUP CHUP ZEEEEEEEE," AND THEY RUMMAGE NOISILY AMONG DEAD LEAVES...
CHUP CHUP CHUP
DON'T FORGET THE "ZEEEEEEE'S"
SCHULZ

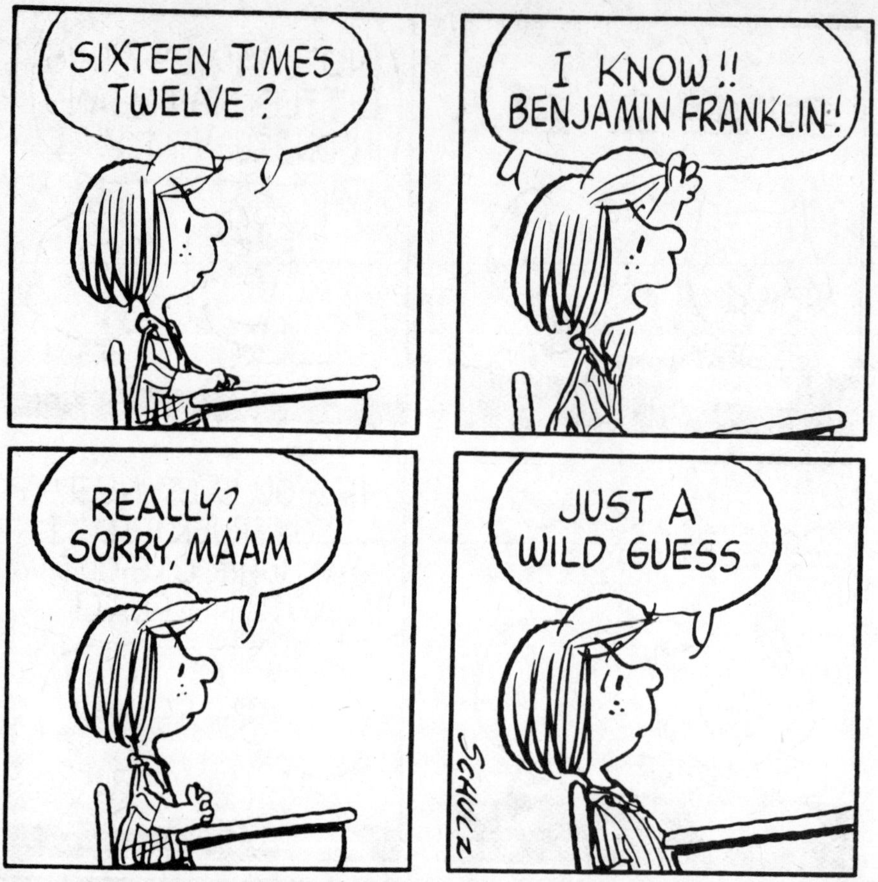
SIXTEEN TIMES TWELVE?
I KNOW!! BENJAMIN FRANKLIN!
REALLY? SORRY, MA'AM
JUST A WILD GUESS
SCHULZ

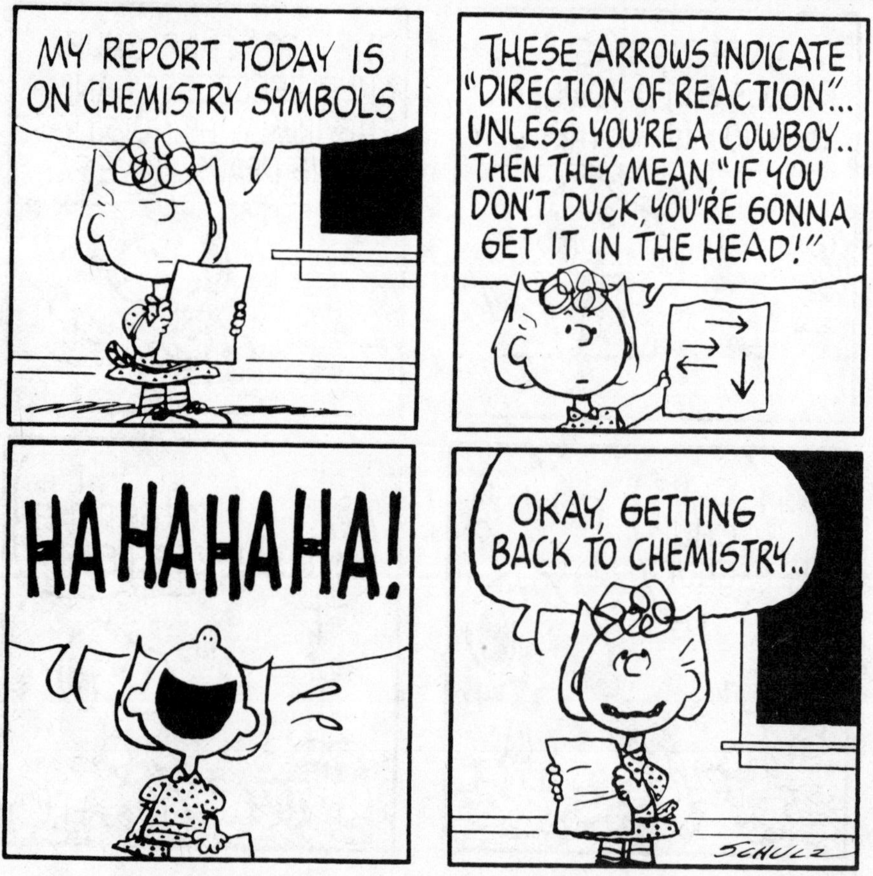
MY REPORT TODAY IS ON CHEMISTRY SYMBOLS
THESE ARROWS INDICATE "DIRECTION OF REACTION"... UNLESS YOU'RE A COWBOY.. THEN THEY MEAN, "IF YOU DON'T DUCK, YOU'RE GONNA GET IT IN THE HEAD!"
HAHAHAHA!
OKAY, GETTING BACK TO CHEMISTRY..
SCHULZ

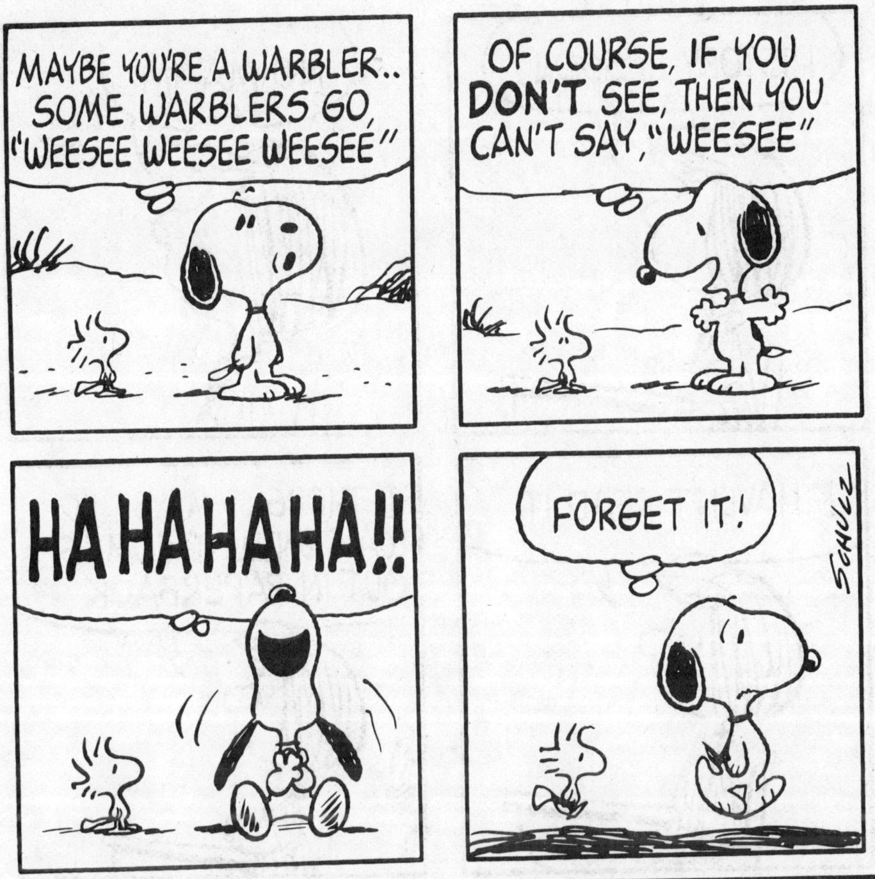
MAYBE YOU'RE A WARBLER.. SOME WARBLERS GO, "WEESEE WEESEE WEESEE"
OF COURSE, IF YOU DON'T SEE, THEN YOU CAN'T SAY, "WEESEE"
HA HA HA HA!!
FORGET IT!
SCHULZ

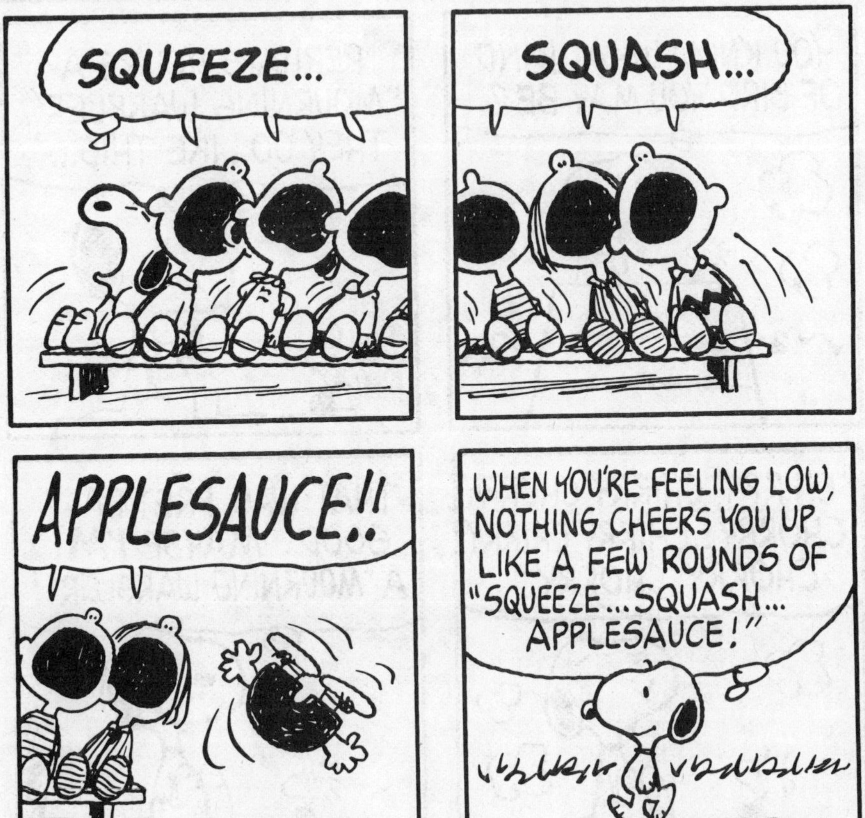
SQUEEZE...
SQUASH...
APPLESAUCE!!
WHEN YOU'RE FEELING LOW, NOTHING CHEERS YOU UP LIKE A FEW ROUNDS OF "SQUEEZE...SQUASH... APPLESAUCE!"
SCHULZ

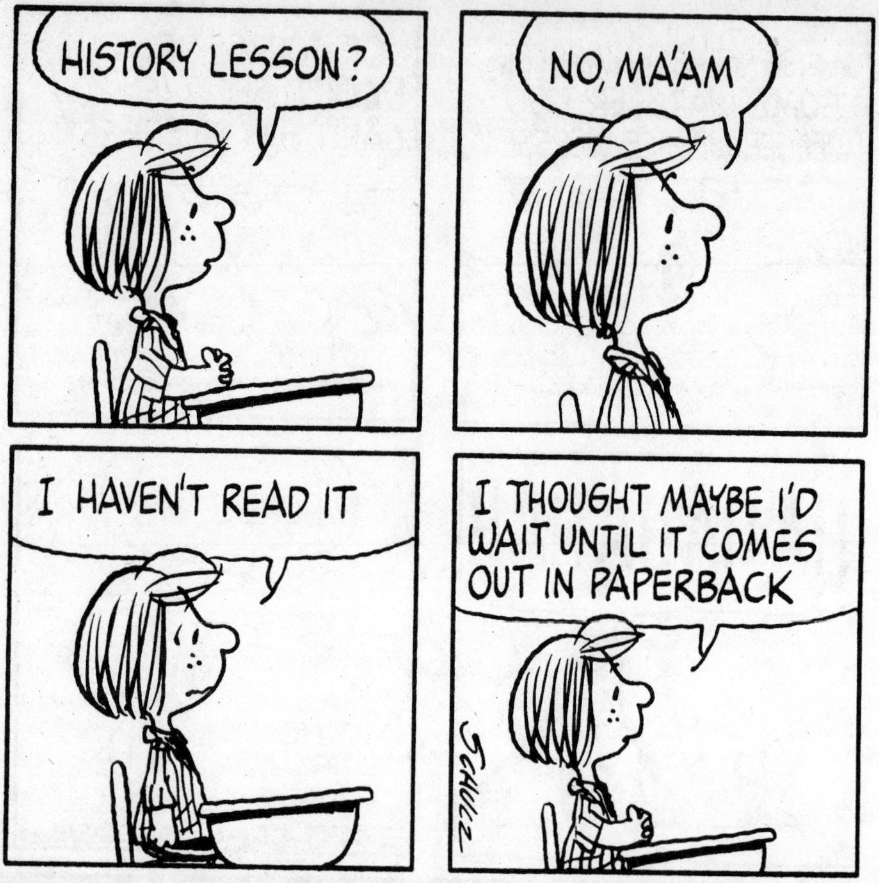
HISTORY LESSON?
NO, MA'AM
I HAVEN'T READ IT
I THOUGHT MAYBE I'D WAIT UNTIL IT COMES OUT IN PAPERBACK
SCHULZ

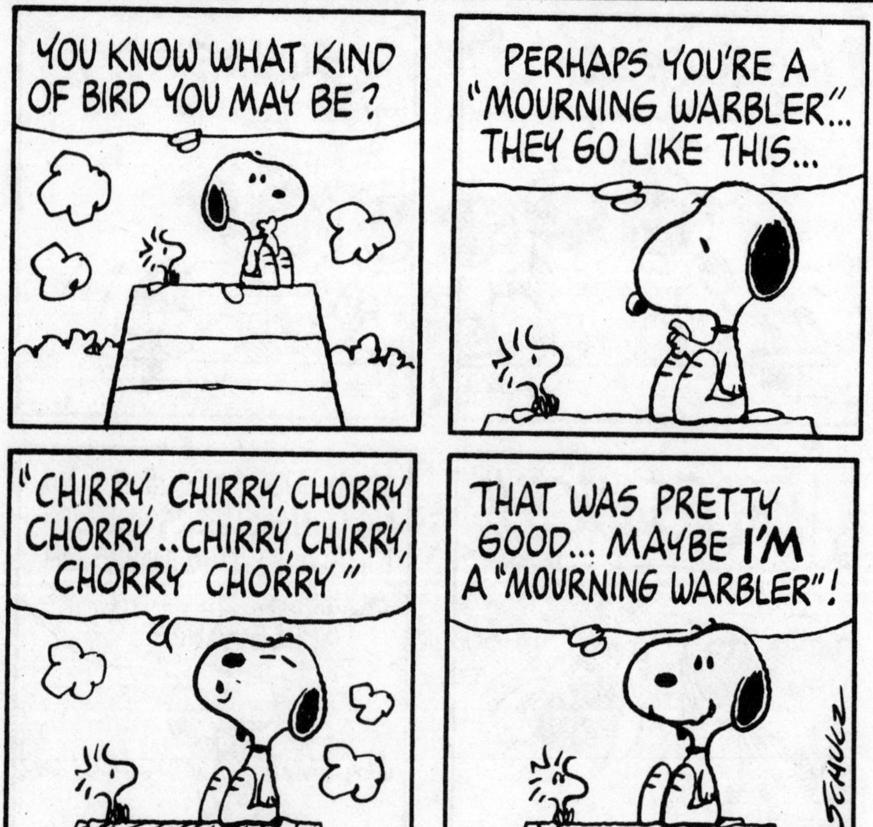
YOU KNOW WHAT KIND OF BIRD YOU MAY BE?
PERHAPS YOU'RE A "MOURNING WARBLER"... THEY GO LIKE THIS...
"CHIRRY, CHIRRY, CHORRY CHORRY..CHIRRY, CHIRRY, CHORRY CHORRY"
THAT WAS PRETTY GOOD... MAYBE I'M A "MOURNING WARBLER"!
SCHULZ

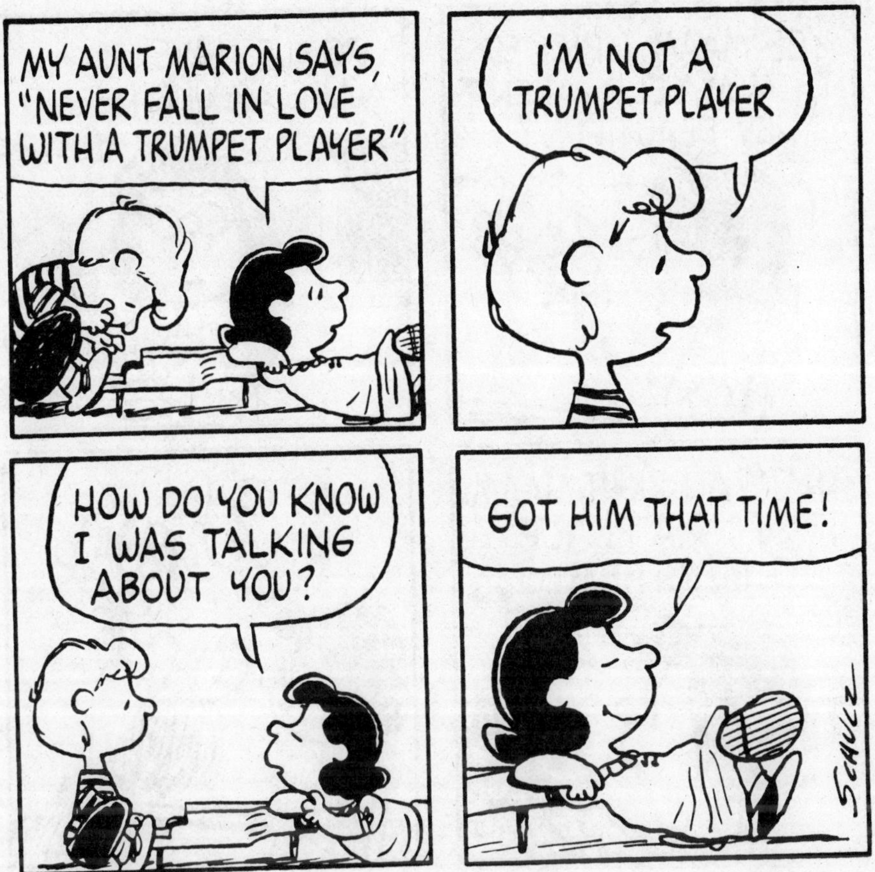
MY AUNT MARION SAYS, "NEVER FALL IN LOVE WITH A TRUMPET PLAYER"
I'M NOT A TRUMPET PLAYER
HOW DO YOU KNOW I WAS TALKING ABOUT YOU?
GOT HIM THAT TIME!
SCHULZ

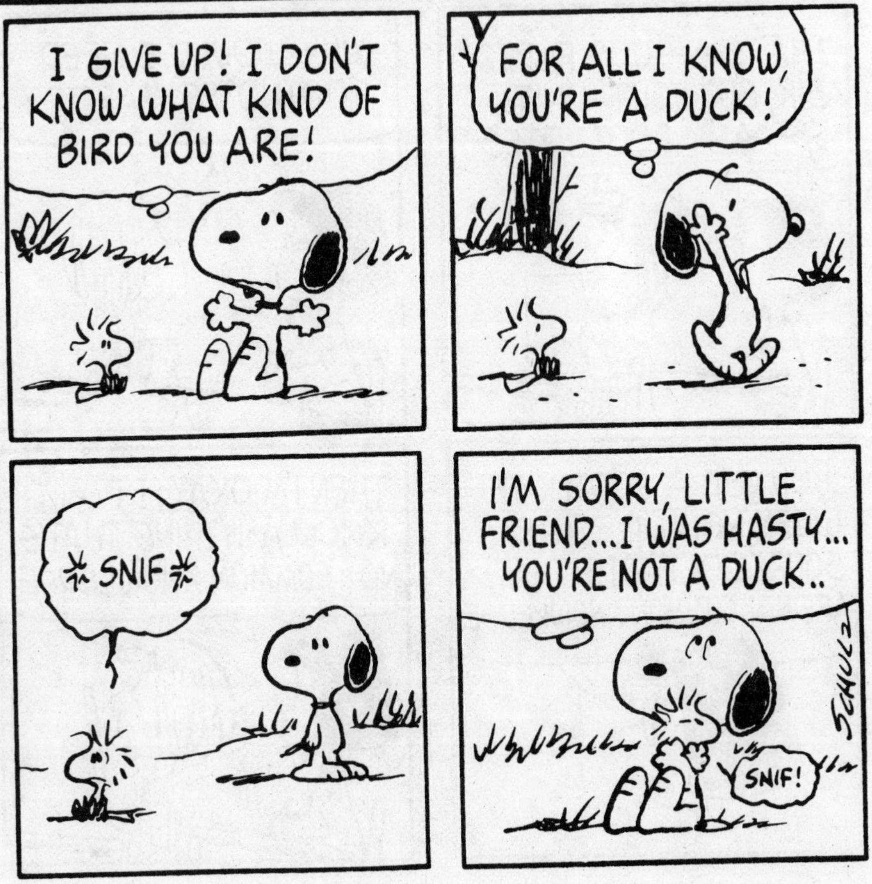
I GIVE UP! I DON'T KNOW WHAT KIND OF BIRD YOU ARE!
FOR ALL I KNOW, YOU'RE A DUCK!
SNIF
I'M SORRY, LITTLE FRIEND...I WAS HASTY... YOU'RE NOT A DUCK..
SNIF!
SCHULZ

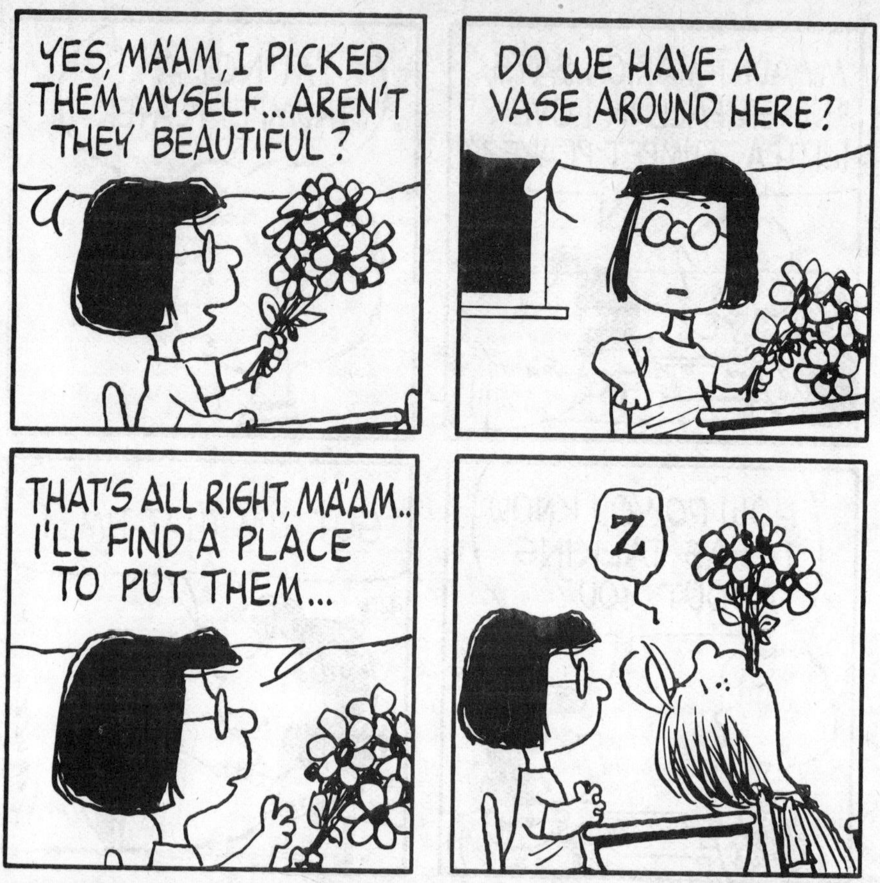
YES, MA'AM, I PICKED THEM MYSELF...AREN'T THEY BEAUTIFUL?
DO WE HAVE A VASE AROUND HERE?
THAT'S ALL RIGHT, MA'AM.. I'LL FIND A PLACE TO PUT THEM...
Z

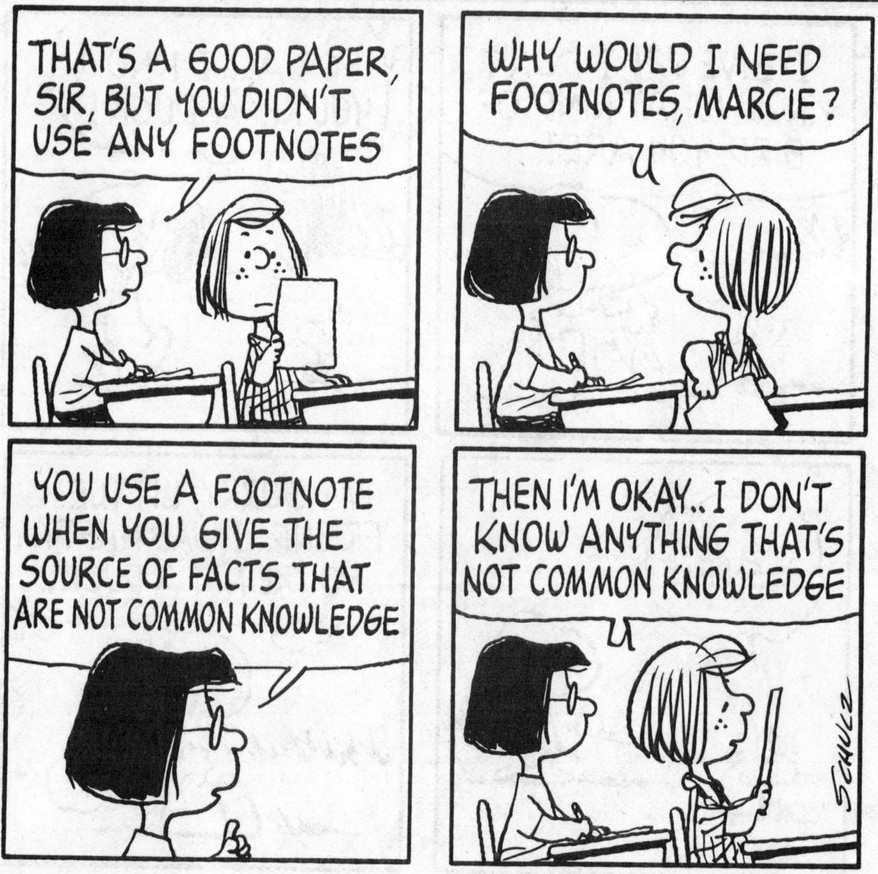
THAT'S A GOOD PAPER, SIR, BUT YOU DIDN'T USE ANY FOOTNOTES
WHY WOULD I NEED FOOTNOTES, MARCIE?
YOU USE A FOOTNOTE WHEN YOU GIVE THE SOURCE OF FACTS THAT ARE NOT COMMON KNOWLEDGE
THEN I'M OKAY.. I DON'T KNOW ANYTHING THAT'S NOT COMMON KNOWLEDGE
SCHULZ

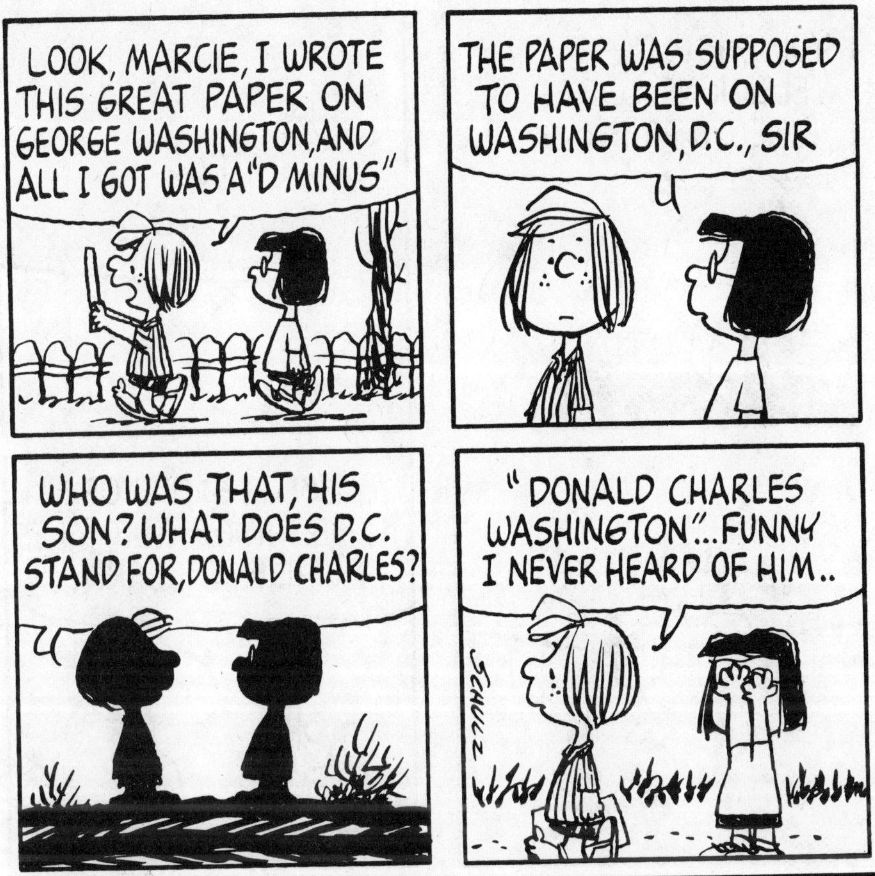
LOOK, MARCIE, I WROTE THIS GREAT PAPER ON GEORGE WASHINGTON, AND ALL I GOT WAS A "D MINUS"
THE PAPER WAS SUPPOSED TO HAVE BEEN ON WASHINGTON, D.C., SIR
WHO WAS THAT, HIS SON? WHAT DOES D.C. STAND FOR, DONALD CHARLES?
"DONALD CHARLES WASHINGTON"... FUNNY I NEVER HEARD OF HIM..
SCHULZ

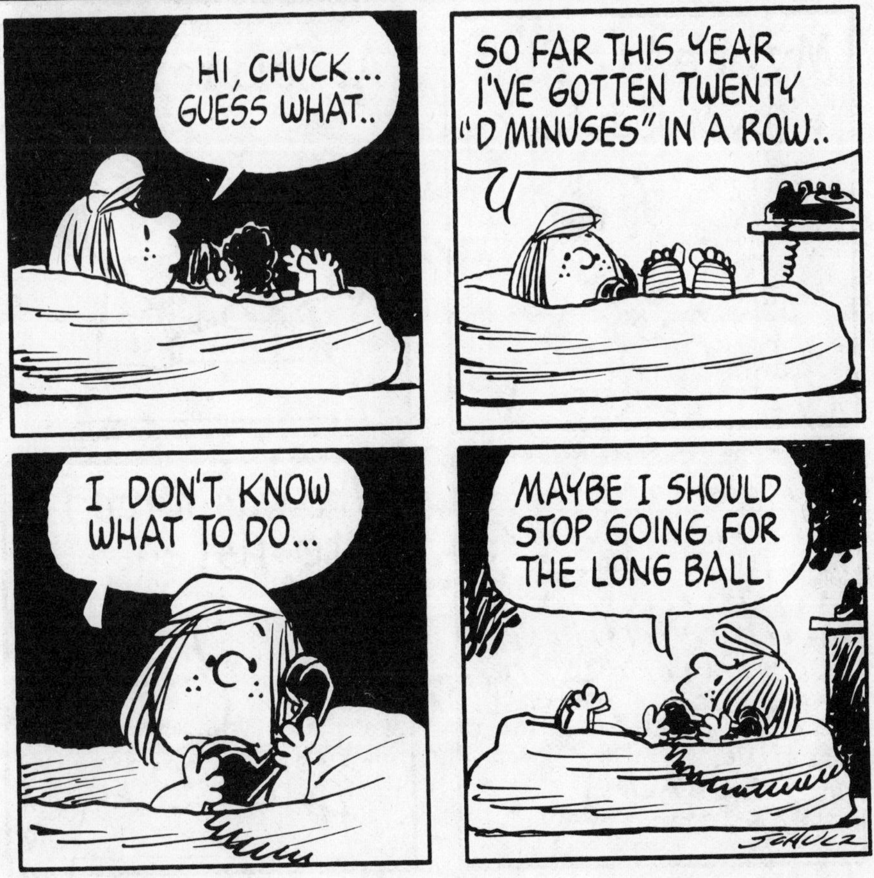
HI, CHUCK... GUESS WHAT..
SO FAR THIS YEAR I'VE GOTTEN TWENTY "D MINUSES" IN A ROW..
I DON'T KNOW WHAT TO DO...
MAYBE I SHOULD STOP GOING FOR THE LONG BALL
SCHULZ

YOU SHOULD SIT ON TELEPHONE WIRES LIKE OTHER BIRDS...
MAYBE IT'S ONE OF THOSE THINGS THAT TAKES A WHILE TO LEARN...
SCHULZ

My Life As a Bird by Woodstock
As Told to Snoopy
Who was forced to listen.
SCHULZ

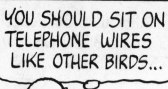

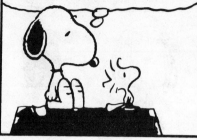

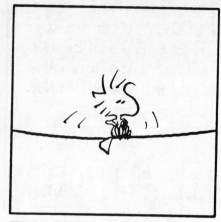

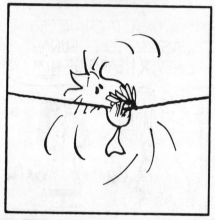

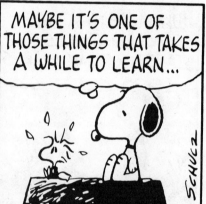

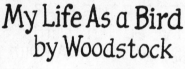

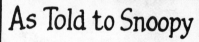

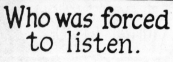

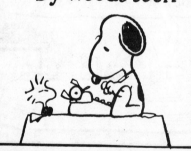

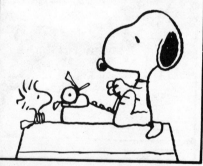

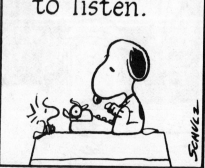

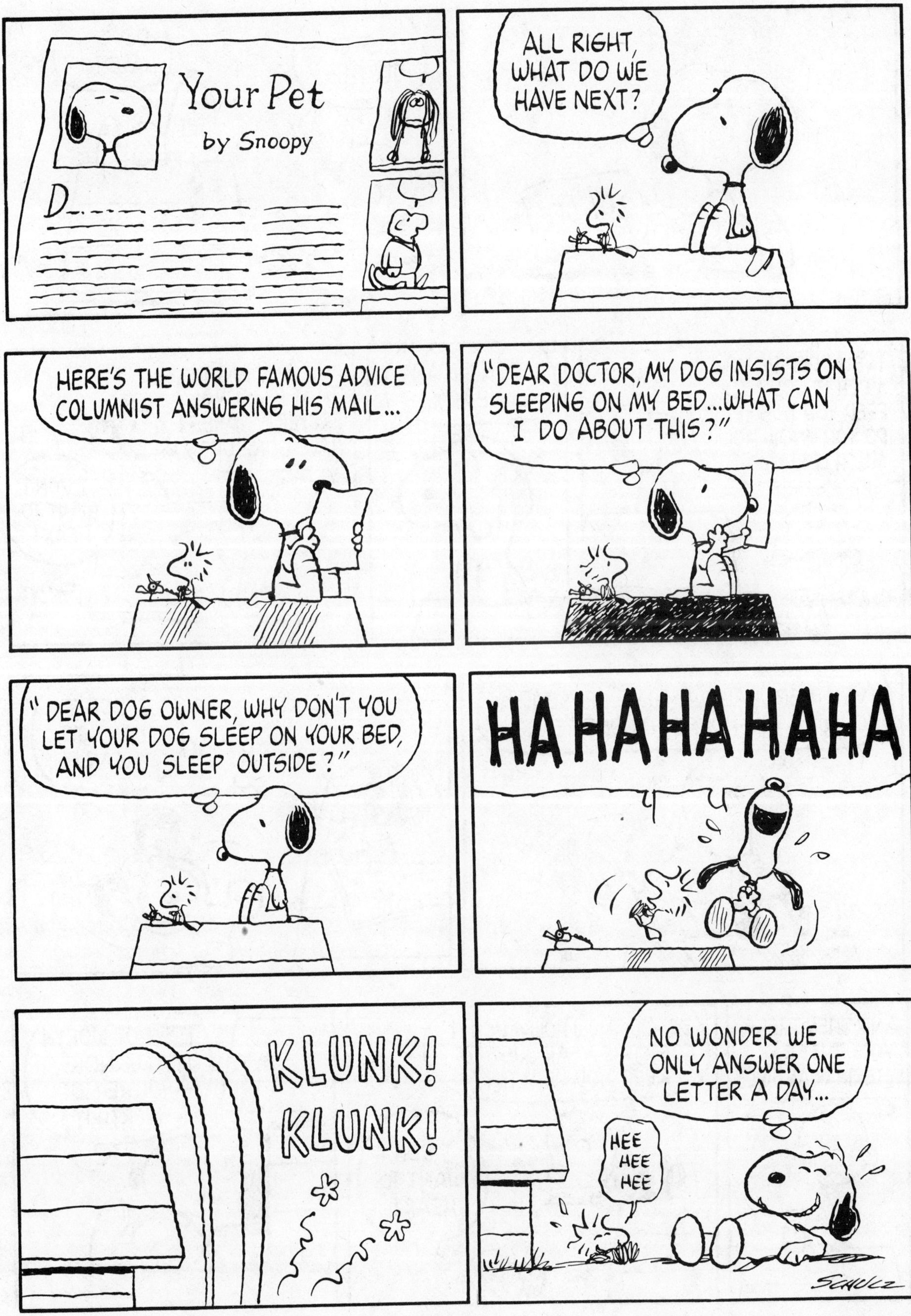
Your Pet
by Snoopy
ALL RIGHT, WHAT DO WE HAVE NEXT?
HERE'S THE WORLD FAMOUS ADVICE COLUMNIST ANSWERING HIS MAIL...
"DEAR DOCTOR, MY DOG INSISTS ON SLEEPING ON MY BED...WHAT CAN I DO ABOUT THIS?"
"DEAR DOG OWNER, WHY DON'T YOU LET YOUR DOG SLEEP ON YOUR BED, AND YOU SLEEP OUTSIDE?"
HAHAHAHAHA
KLUNK! KLUNK!
NO WONDER WE ONLY ANSWER ONE LETTER A DAY...
HEE HEE HEE
SCHULZ

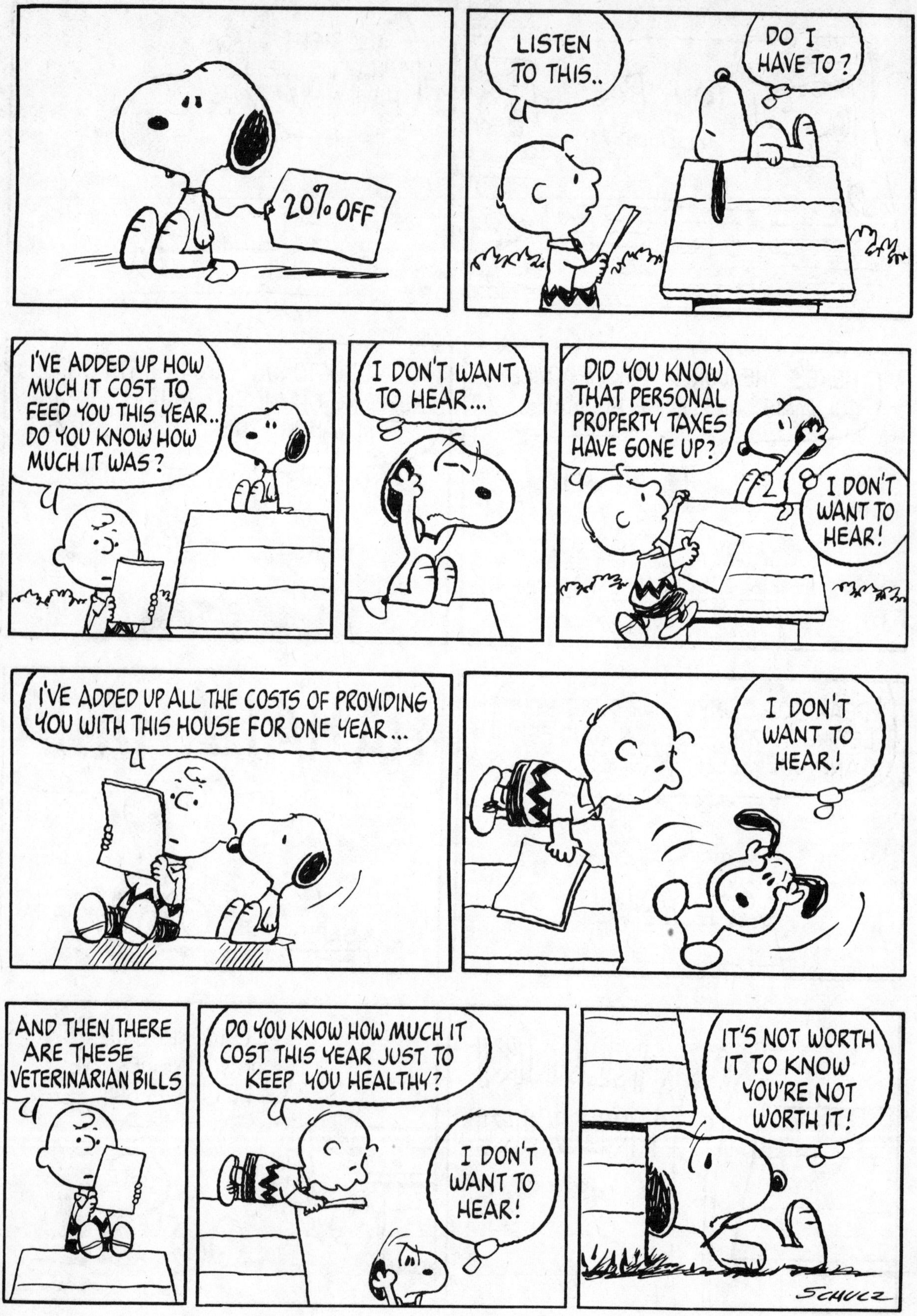
20% OFF
LISTEN TO THIS..
DO I HAVE TO?
I'VE ADDED UP HOW MUCH IT COST TO FEED YOU THIS YEAR.. DO YOU KNOW HOW MUCH IT WAS?
I DON'T WANT TO HEAR...
DID YOU KNOW THAT PERSONAL PROPERTY TAXES HAVE GONE UP?
I DON'T WANT TO HEAR!
I'VE ADDED UP ALL THE COSTS OF PROVIDING YOU WITH THIS HOUSE FOR ONE YEAR...
I DON'T WANT TO HEAR!
AND THEN THERE ARE THESE VETERINARIAN BILLS
DO YOU KNOW HOW MUCH IT COST THIS YEAR JUST TO KEEP YOU HEALTHY?
I DON'T WANT TO HEAR!
IT'S NOT WORTH IT TO KNOW YOU'RE NOT WORTH IT!
SCHULZ

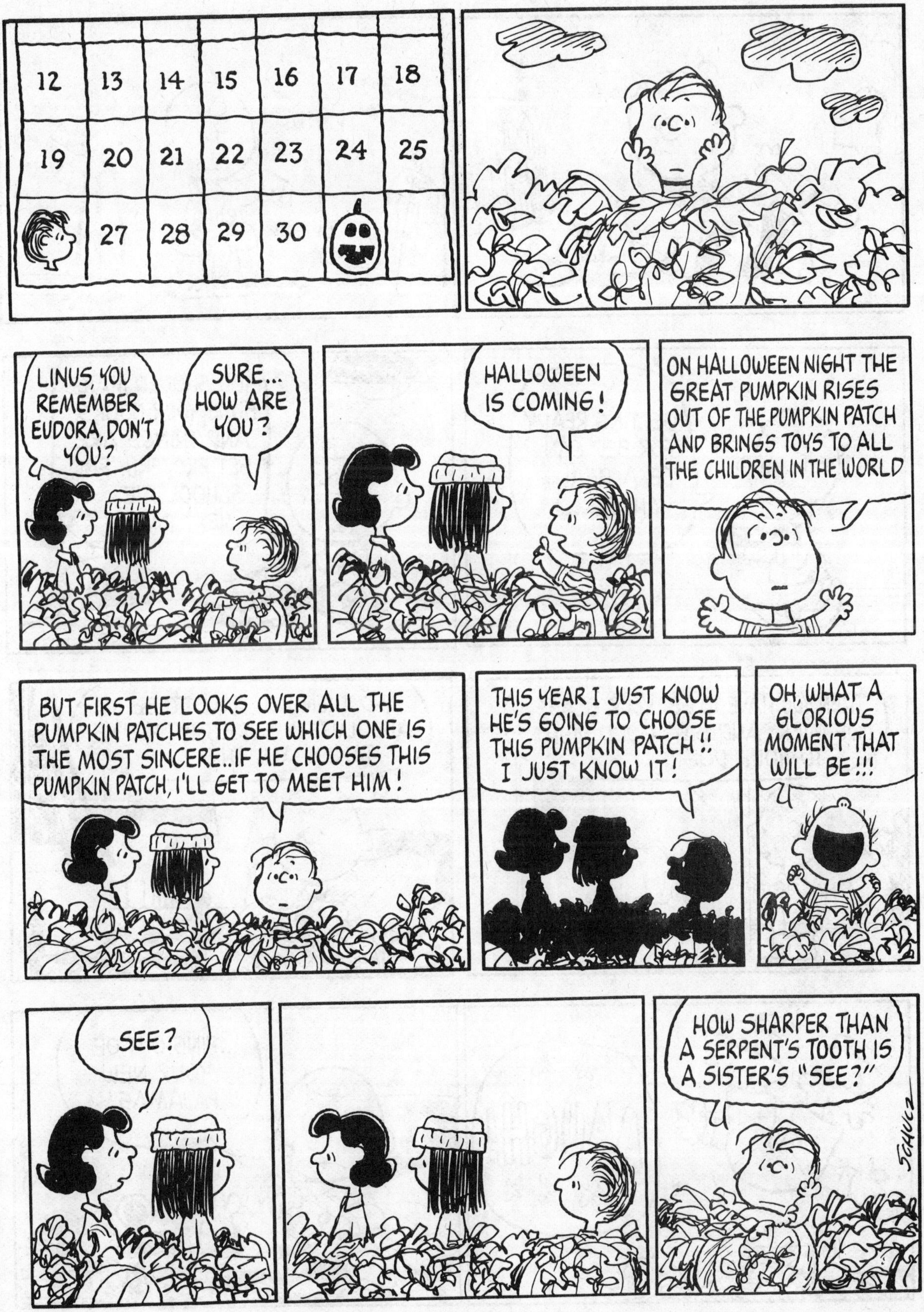
12 13 14 15 16 17 18
19 20 21 22 23 24 25
27 28 29 30
LINUS, YOU REMEMBER EUDORA, DON'T YOU?
SURE... HOW ARE YOU?
HALLOWEEN IS COMING!
ON HALLOWEEN NIGHT THE GREAT PUMPKIN RISES OUT OF THE PUMPKIN PATCH AND BRINGS TOYS TO ALL THE CHILDREN IN THE WORLD
BUT FIRST HE LOOKS OVER ALL THE PUMPKIN PATCHES TO SEE WHICH ONE IS THE MOST SINCERE..IF HE CHOOSES THIS PUMPKIN PATCH, I'LL GET TO MEET HIM!
THIS YEAR I JUST KNOW HE'S GOING TO CHOOSE THIS PUMPKIN PATCH!! I JUST KNOW IT!
OH, WHAT A GLORIOUS MOMENT THAT WILL BE!!!
SEE?
HOW SHARPER THAN A SERPENT'S TOOTH IS A SISTER'S "SEE?"
SCHULZ

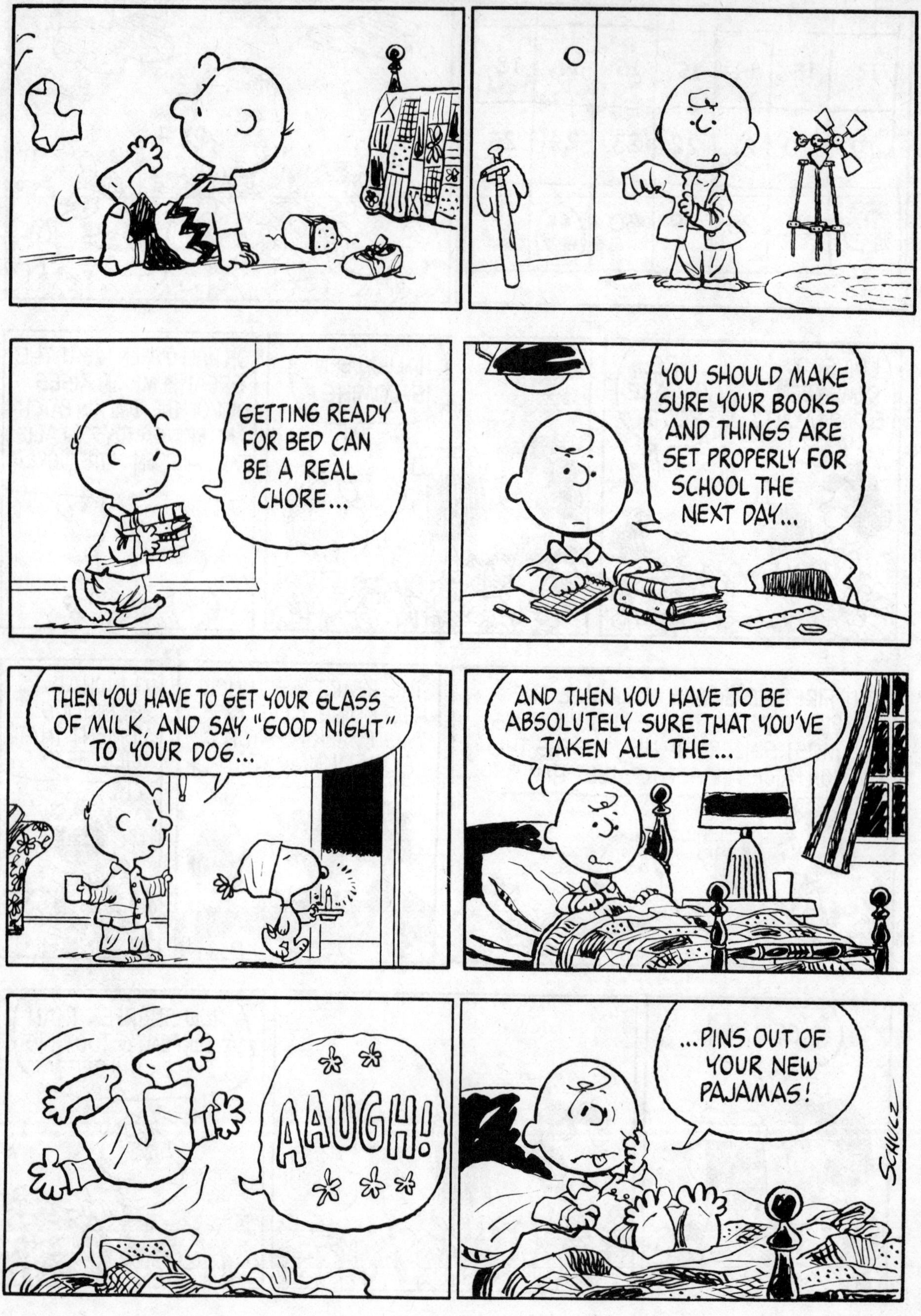
GETTING READY FOR BED CAN BE A REAL CHORE...
YOU SHOULD MAKE SURE YOUR BOOKS AND THINGS ARE SET PROPERLY FOR SCHOOL THE NEXT DAY...
THEN YOU HAVE TO GET YOUR GLASS OF MILK, AND SAY, "GOOD NIGHT" TO YOUR DOG...
AND THEN YOU HAVE TO BE ABSOLUTELY SURE THAT YOU'VE TAKEN ALL THE...
AAUGH!
...PINS OUT OF YOUR NEW PAJAMAS!
SCHULZ

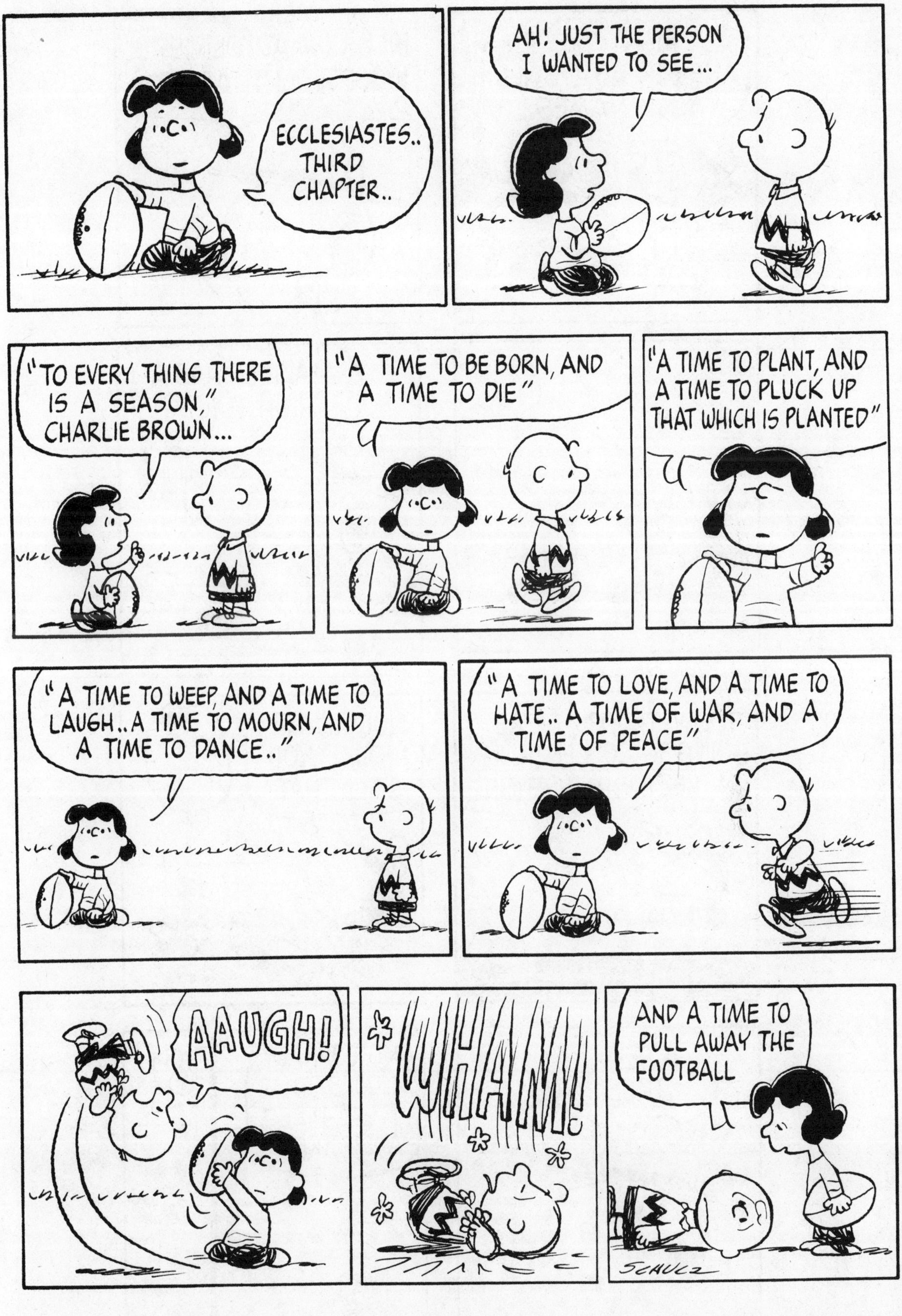
ECCLESIASTES.. THIRD CHAPTER..
AH! JUST THE PERSON I WANTED TO SEE...
"TO EVERY THING THERE IS A SEASON," CHARLIE BROWN...
"A TIME TO BE BORN, AND A TIME TO DIE"
"A TIME TO PLANT, AND A TIME TO PLUCK UP THAT WHICH IS PLANTED"
"A TIME TO WEEP, AND A TIME TO LAUGH.. A TIME TO MOURN, AND A TIME TO DANCE.."
"A TIME TO LOVE, AND A TIME TO HATE.. A TIME OF WAR, AND A TIME OF PEACE"
AAUGH!
WHAM!
AND A TIME TO PULL AWAY THE FOOTBALL
SCHULZ

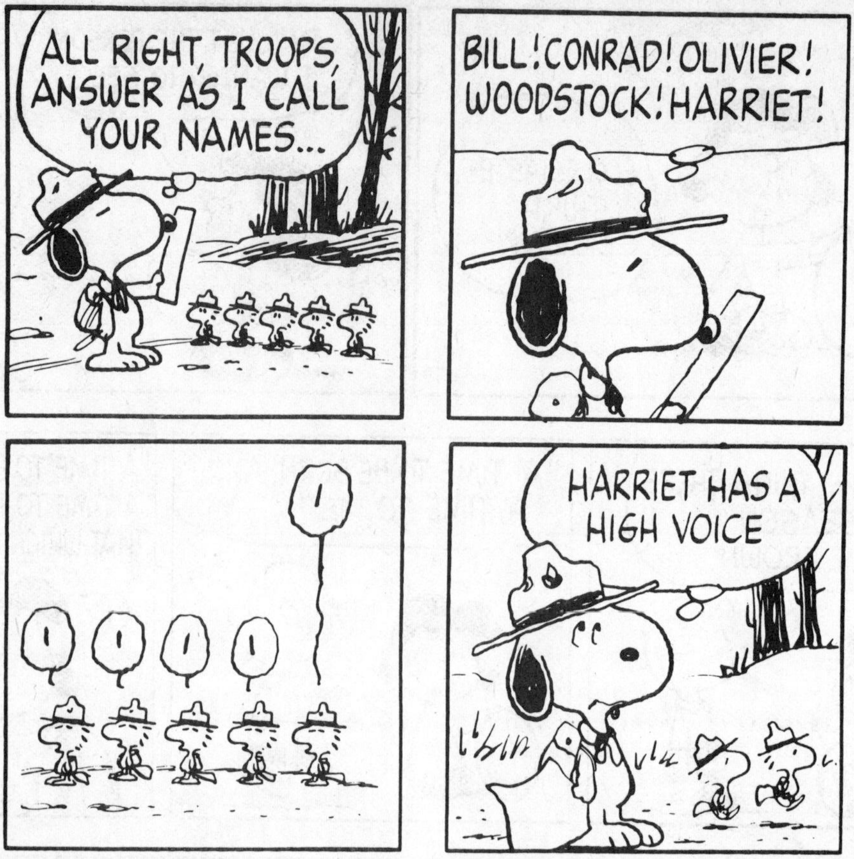
ALL RIGHT, TROOPS, ANSWER AS I CALL YOUR NAMES...
BILL! CONRAD! OLIVIER! WOODSTOCK! HARRIET!
HARRIET HAS A HIGH VOICE

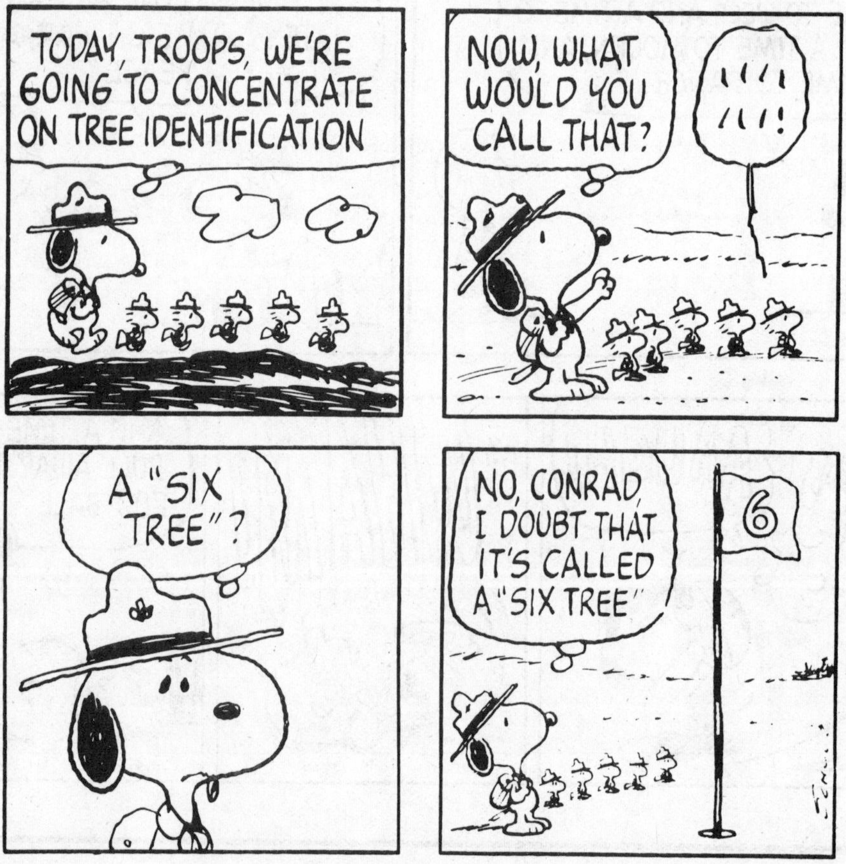
TODAY, TROOPS, WE'RE GOING TO CONCENTRATE ON TREE IDENTIFICATION
NOW, WHAT WOULD YOU CALL THAT?
A "SIX TREE"?
NO, CONRAD, I DOUBT THAT IT'S CALLED A "SIX TREE"
6

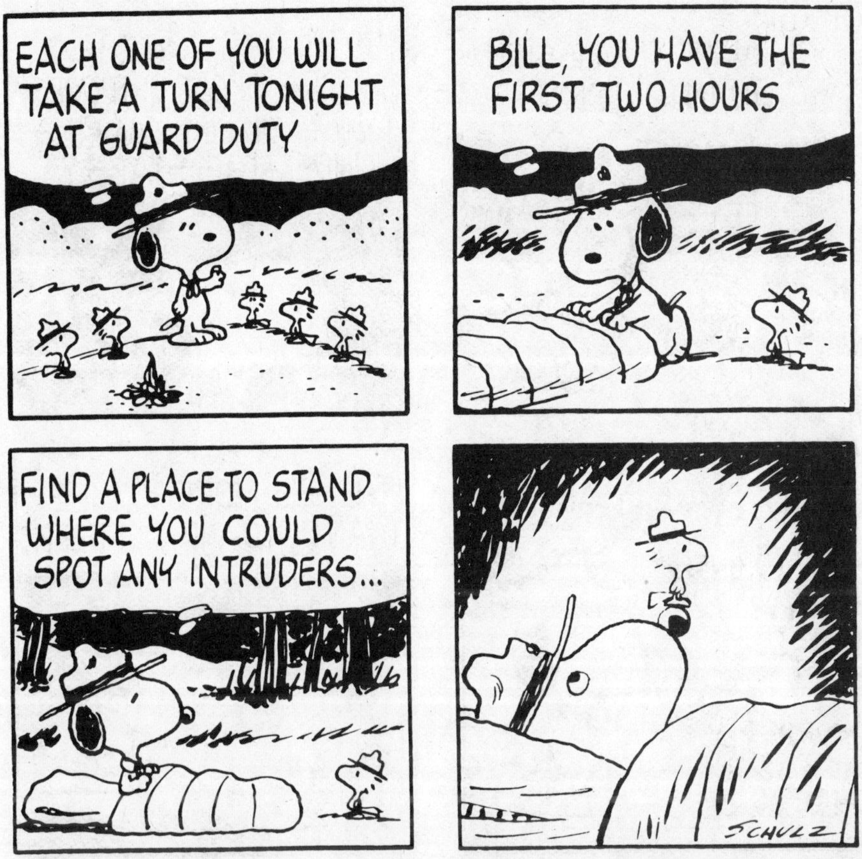
EACH ONE OF YOU WILL TAKE A TURN TONIGHT AT GUARD DUTY
BILL, YOU HAVE THE FIRST TWO HOURS
FIND A PLACE TO STAND WHERE YOU COULD SPOT ANY INTRUDERS...
SCHULZ

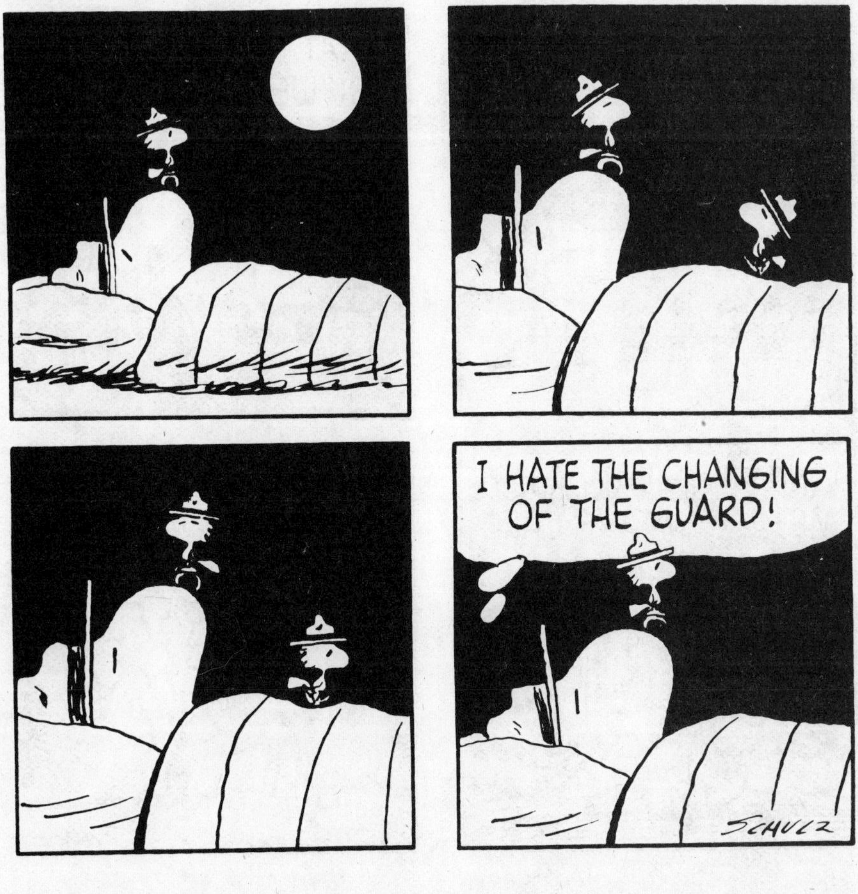
I HATE THE CHANGING OF THE GUARD!
SCHULZ

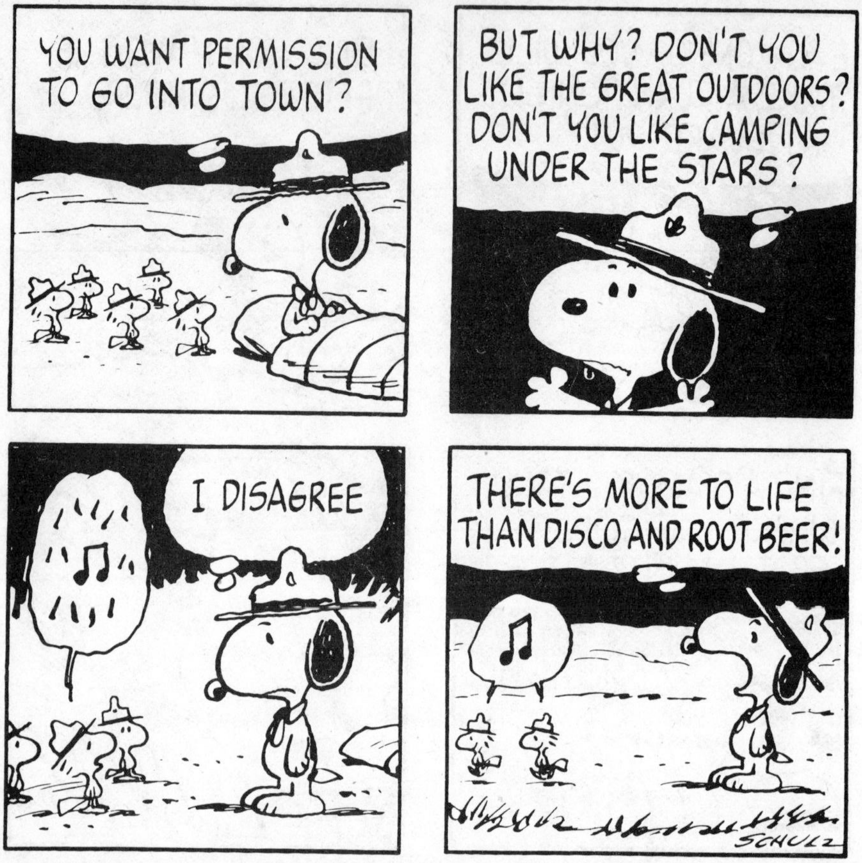
YOU WANT PERMISSION TO GO INTO TOWN?
BUT WHY? DON'T YOU LIKE THE GREAT OUTDOORS? DON'T YOU LIKE CAMPING UNDER THE STARS?
I DISAGREE
THERE'S MORE TO LIFE THAN DISCO AND ROOT BEER!
SCHULZ

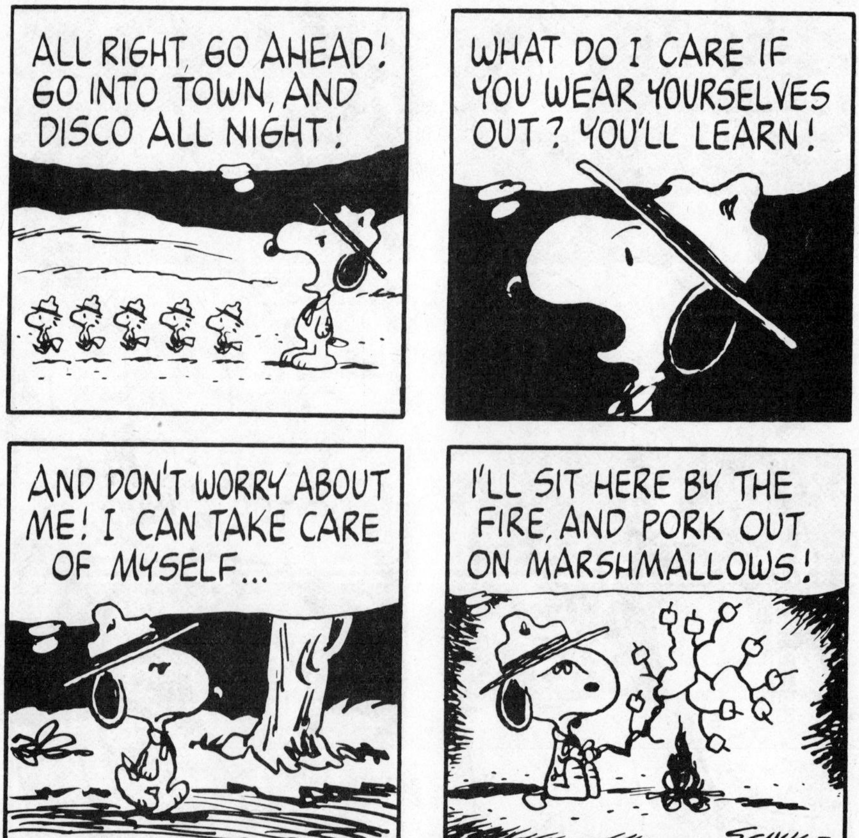
ALL RIGHT, GO AHEAD! GO INTO TOWN, AND DISCO ALL NIGHT!
WHAT DO I CARE IF YOU WEAR YOURSELVES OUT? YOU'LL LEARN!
AND DON'T WORRY ABOUT ME! I CAN TAKE CARE OF MYSELF...
I'LL SIT HERE BY THE FIRE, AND PORK OUT ON MARSHMALLOWS!
SCHULZ

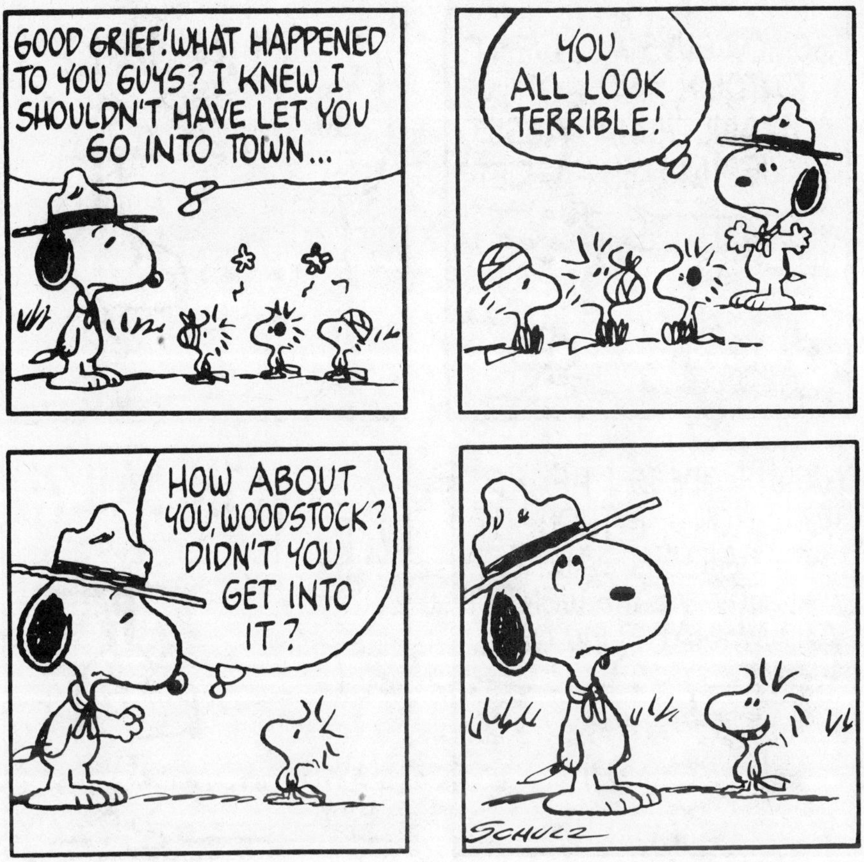
GOOD GRIEF! WHAT HAPPENED TO YOU GUYS? I KNEW I SHOULDN'T HAVE LET YOU GO INTO TOWN...
YOU ALL LOOK TERRIBLE!
HOW ABOUT YOU, WOODSTOCK? DIDN'T YOU GET INTO IT?
SCHULZ

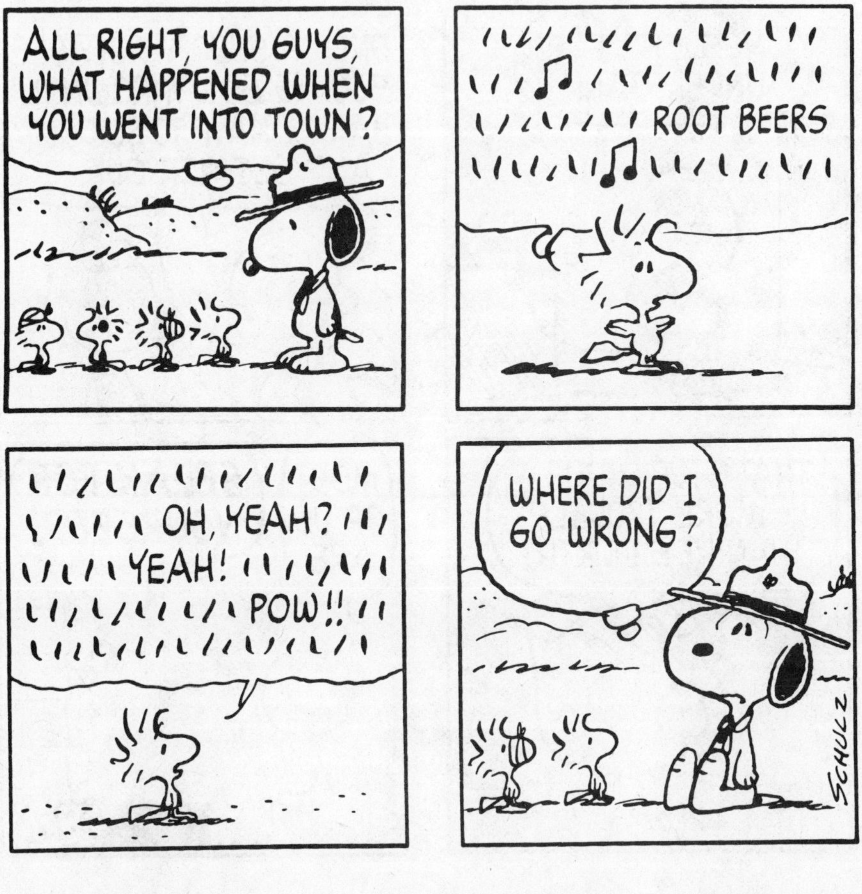
ALL RIGHT, YOU GUYS, WHAT HAPPENED WHEN YOU WENT INTO TOWN?
ROOT BEERS
OH, YEAH?
YEAH!
POW!!
WHERE DID I GO WRONG?
SCHULZ

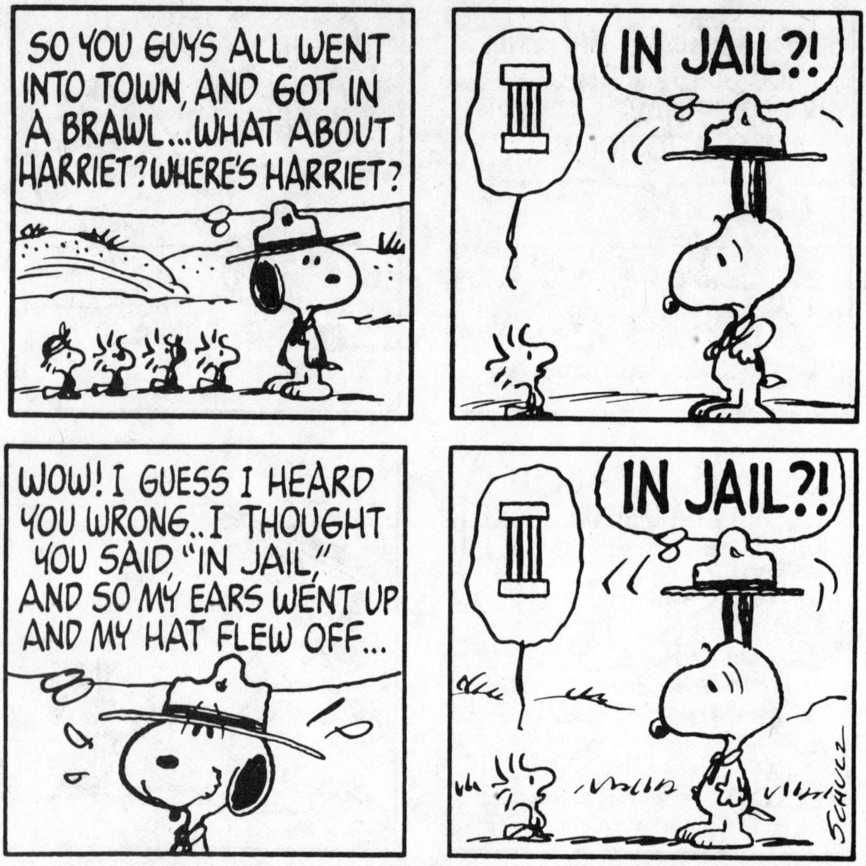
SO YOU GUYS ALL WENT INTO TOWN, AND GOT IN A BRAWL...WHAT ABOUT HARRIET? WHERE'S HARRIET?
IN JAIL?!
WOW! I GUESS I HEARD YOU WRONG..I THOUGHT YOU SAID, "IN JAIL," AND SO MY EARS WENT UP AND MY HAT FLEW OFF...
IN JAIL?!
SCHULZ

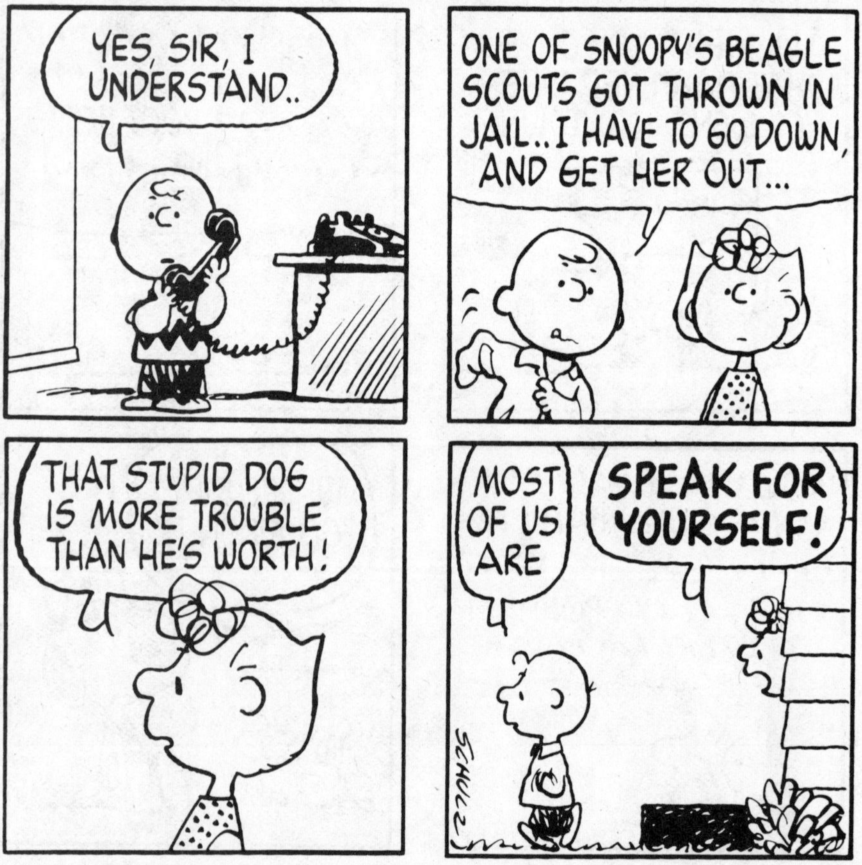
YES, SIR, I UNDERSTAND..
ONE OF SNOOPY'S BEAGLE SCOUTS GOT THROWN IN JAIL..I HAVE TO GO DOWN, AND GET HER OUT...
THAT STUPID DOG IS MORE TROUBLE THAN HE'S WORTH!
MOST OF US ARE
SPEAK FOR YOURSELF!
SCHULZ

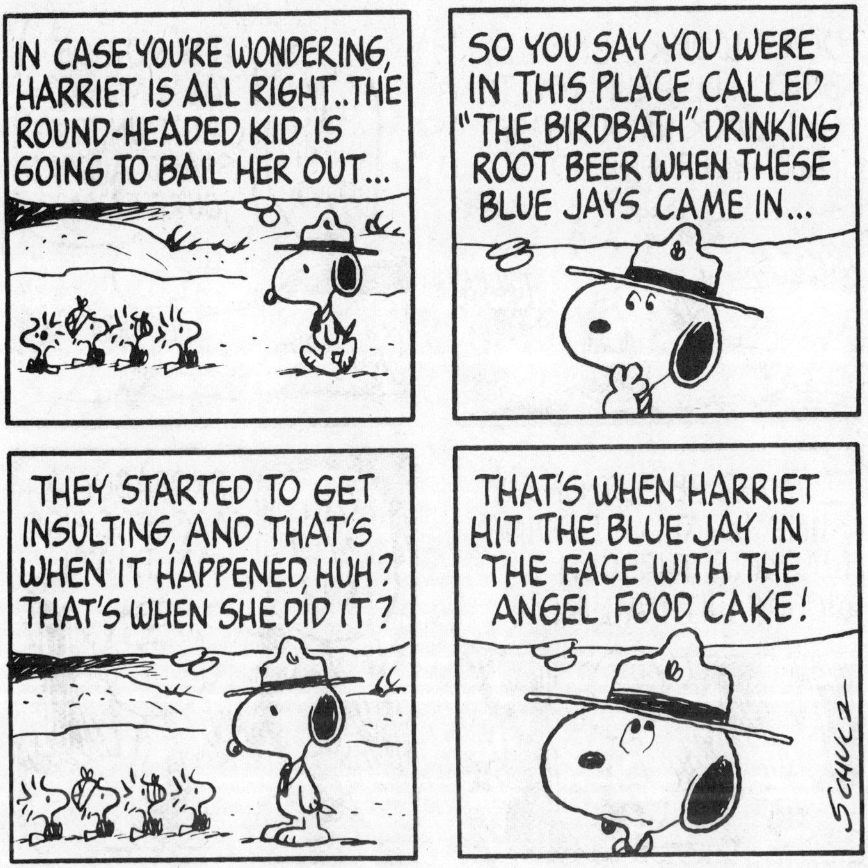
IN CASE YOU'RE WONDERING, HARRIET IS ALL RIGHT..THE ROUND-HEADED KID IS GOING TO BAIL HER OUT...
SO YOU SAY YOU WERE IN THIS PLACE CALLED "THE BIRDBATH" DRINKING ROOT BEER WHEN THESE BLUE JAYS CAME IN...
THEY STARTED TO GET INSULTING, AND THAT'S WHEN IT HAPPENED, HUH? THAT'S WHEN SHE DID IT?
THAT'S WHEN HARRIET HIT THE BLUE JAY IN THE FACE WITH THE ANGEL FOOD CAKE!
SCHULZ

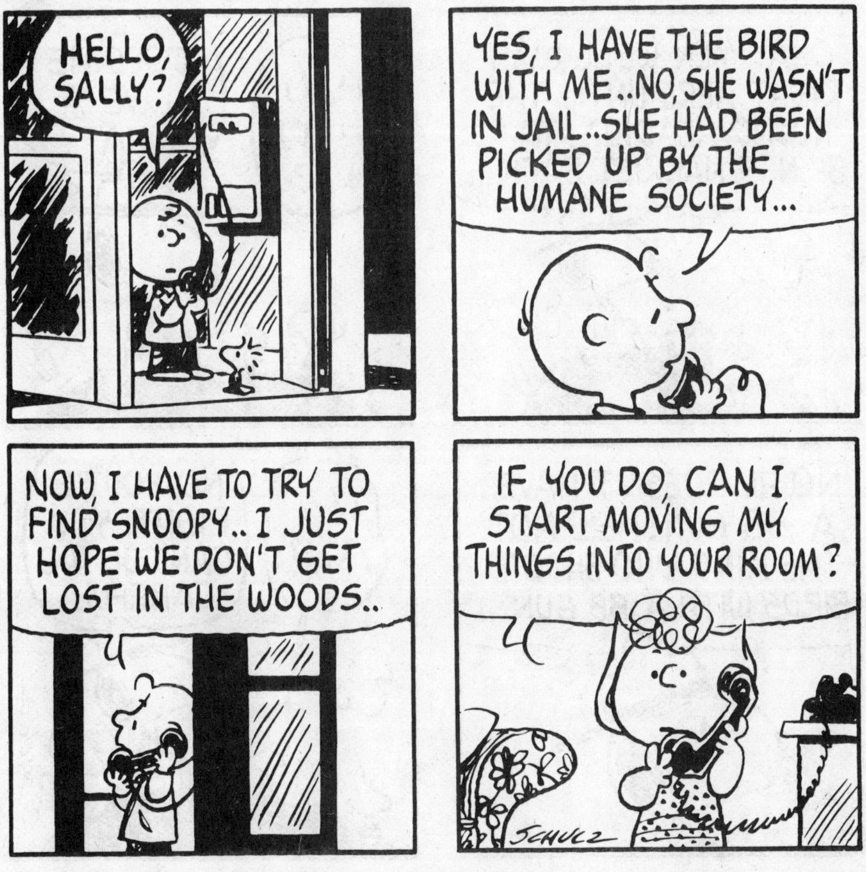
HELLO, SALLY?
YES, I HAVE THE BIRD WITH ME..NO, SHE WASN'T IN JAIL..SHE HAD BEEN PICKED UP BY THE HUMANE SOCIETY...
NOW, I HAVE TO TRY TO FIND SNOOPY.. I JUST HOPE WE DON'T GET LOST IN THE WOODS..
IF YOU DO, CAN I START MOVING MY THINGS INTO YOUR ROOM?
SCHULZ

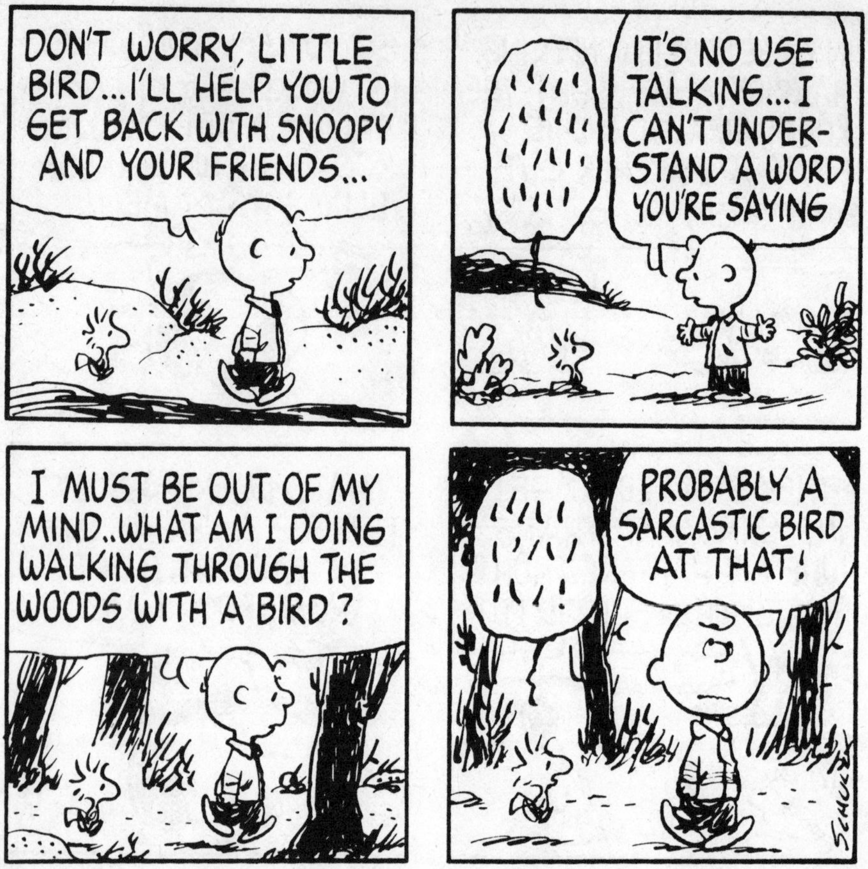
DON'T WORRY, LITTLE BIRD...I'LL HELP YOU TO GET BACK WITH SNOOPY AND YOUR FRIENDS...
IT'S NO USE TALKING...I CAN'T UNDER-STAND A WORD YOU'RE SAYING
I MUST BE OUT OF MY MIND..WHAT AM I DOING WALKING THROUGH THE WOODS WITH A BIRD?
PROBABLY A SARCASTIC BIRD AT THAT!
SCHULZ

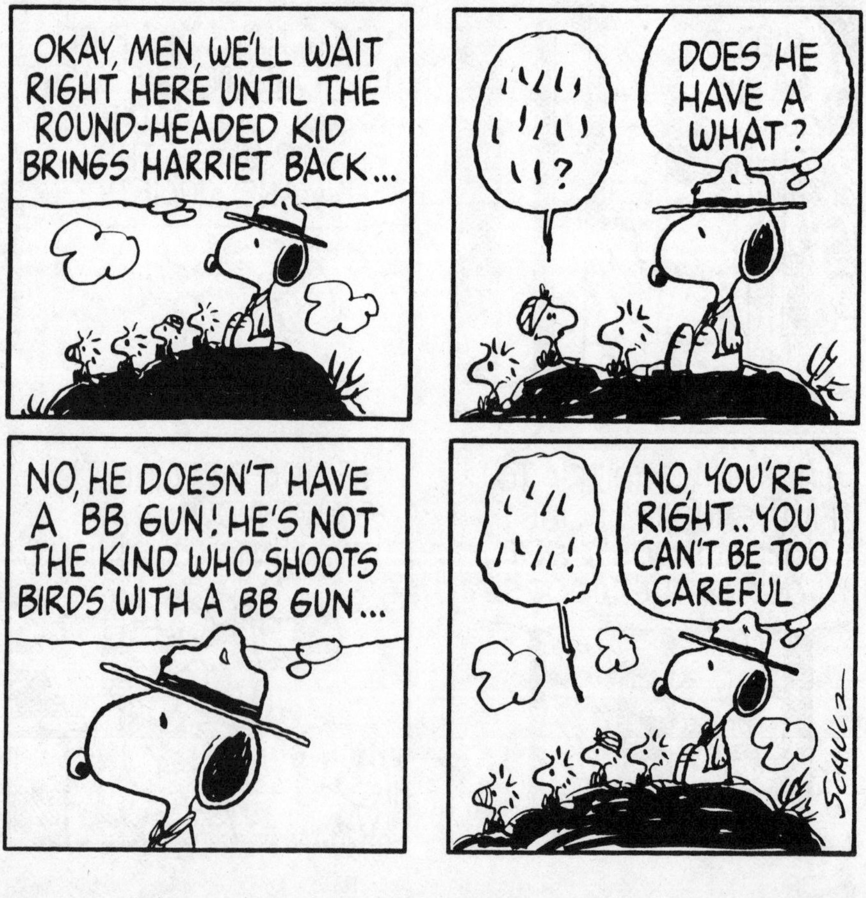
OKAY, MEN, WE'LL WAIT RIGHT HERE UNTIL THE ROUND-HEADED KID BRINGS HARRIET BACK...
DOES HE HAVE A WHAT?
NO, HE DOESN'T HAVE A BB GUN! HE'S NOT THE KIND WHO SHOOTS BIRDS WITH A BB GUN...
NO, YOU'RE RIGHT..YOU CAN'T BE TOO CAREFUL
SCHULZ

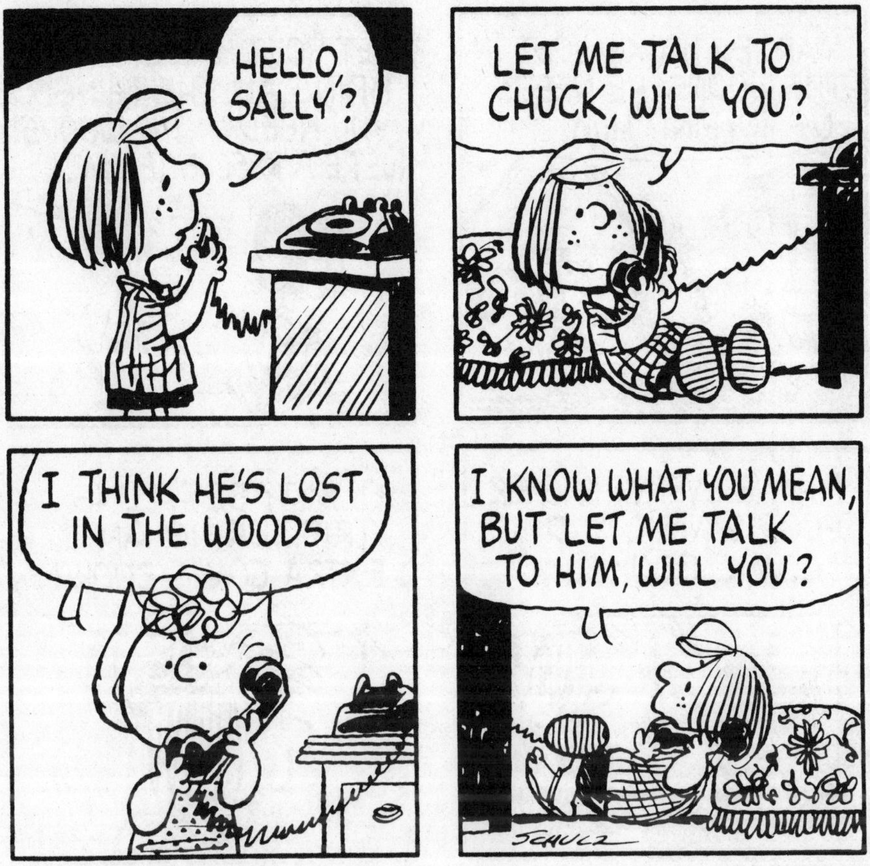
HELLO, SALLY?
LET ME TALK TO CHUCK, WILL YOU?
I THINK HE'S LOST IN THE WOODS
I KNOW WHAT YOU MEAN, BUT LET ME TALK TO HIM, WILL YOU?
SCHULZ

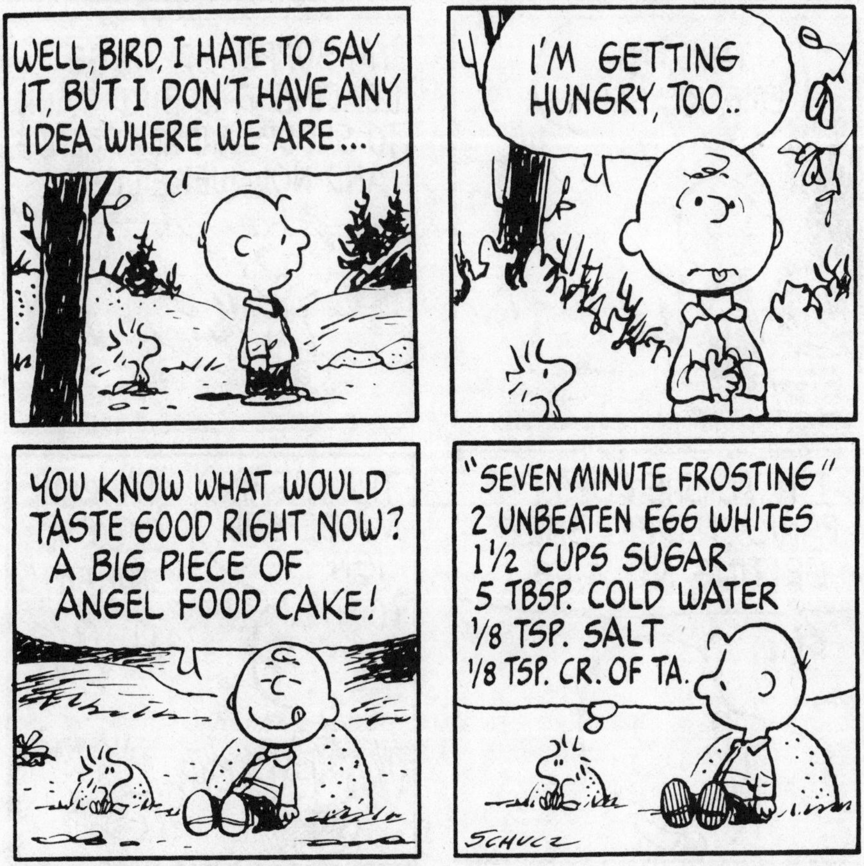
WELL, BIRD, I HATE TO SAY IT, BUT I DON'T HAVE ANY IDEA WHERE WE ARE...
I'M GETTING HUNGRY, TOO..
YOU KNOW WHAT WOULD TASTE GOOD RIGHT NOW? A BIG PIECE OF ANGEL FOOD CAKE!
"SEVEN MINUTE FROSTING"
2 UNBEATEN EGG WHITES
1½ CUPS SUGAR
5 TBSP. COLD WATER
1/8 TSP. SALT
1/8 TSP. CR. OF TA.
SCHULZ

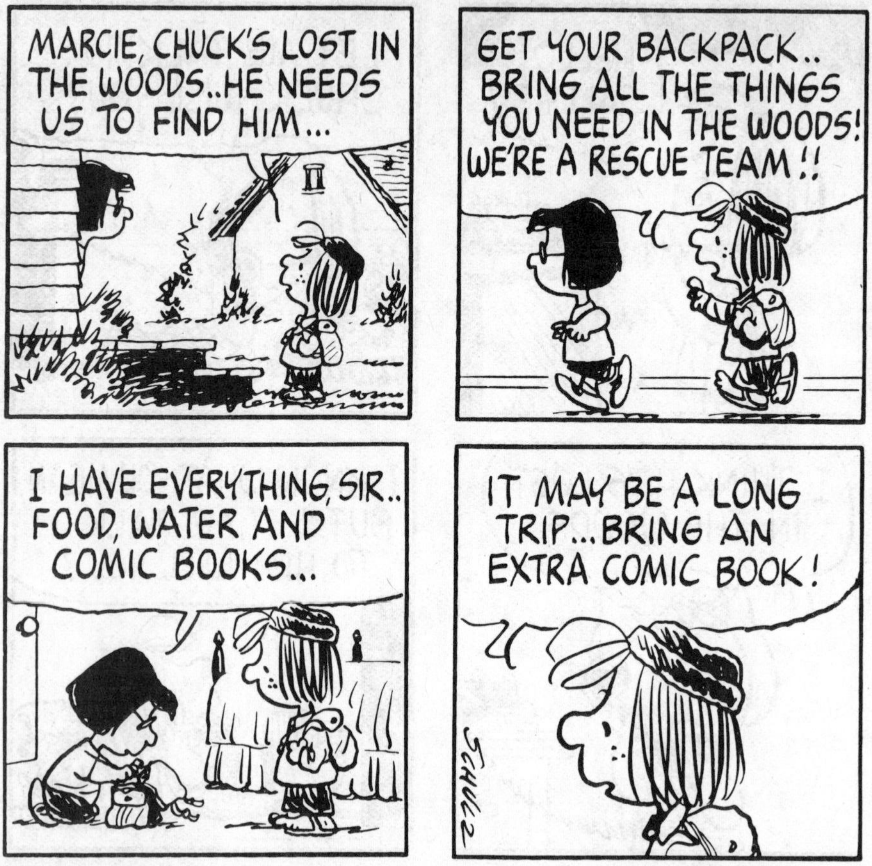
MARCIE, CHUCK'S LOST IN THE WOODS..HE NEEDS US TO FIND HIM...
GET YOUR BACKPACK.. BRING ALL THE THINGS YOU NEED IN THE WOODS! WE'RE A RESCUE TEAM!!
I HAVE EVERYTHING, SIR.. FOOD, WATER AND COMIC BOOKS...
IT MAY BE A LONG TRIP... BRING AN EXTRA COMIC BOOK!
SCHULZ

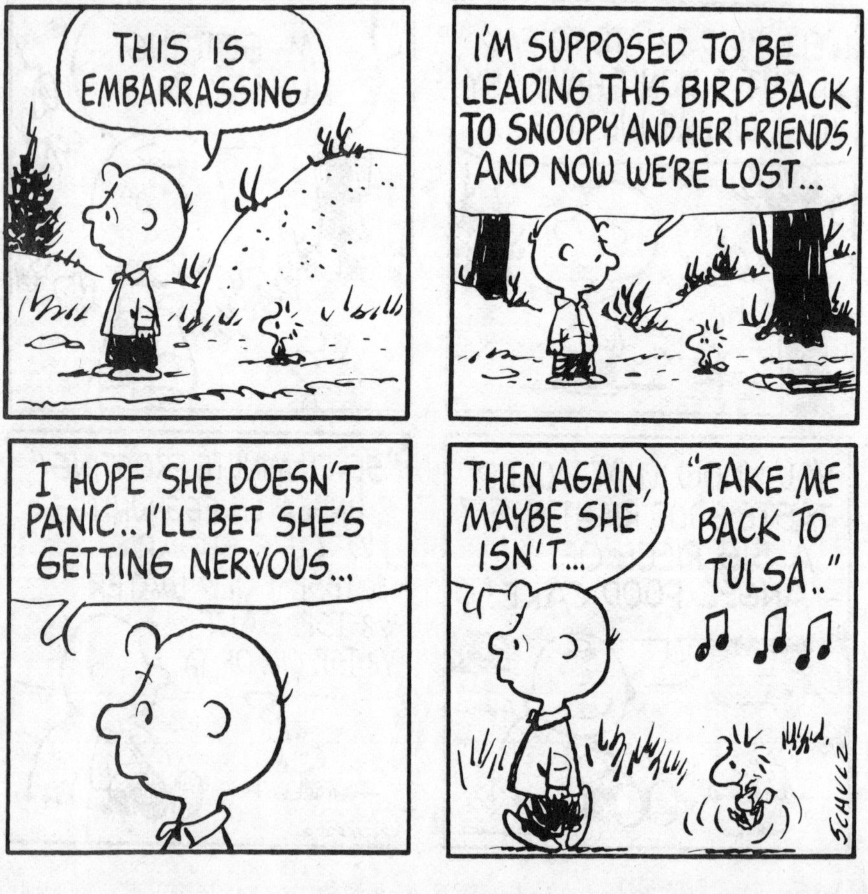
THIS IS EMBARRASSING
I'M SUPPOSED TO BE LEADING THIS BIRD BACK TO SNOOPY AND HER FRIENDS, AND NOW WE'RE LOST...
I HOPE SHE DOESN'T PANIC.. I'LL BET SHE'S GETTING NERVOUS...
THEN AGAIN, MAYBE SHE ISN'T...
"TAKE ME BACK TO TULSA.."
SCHULZ

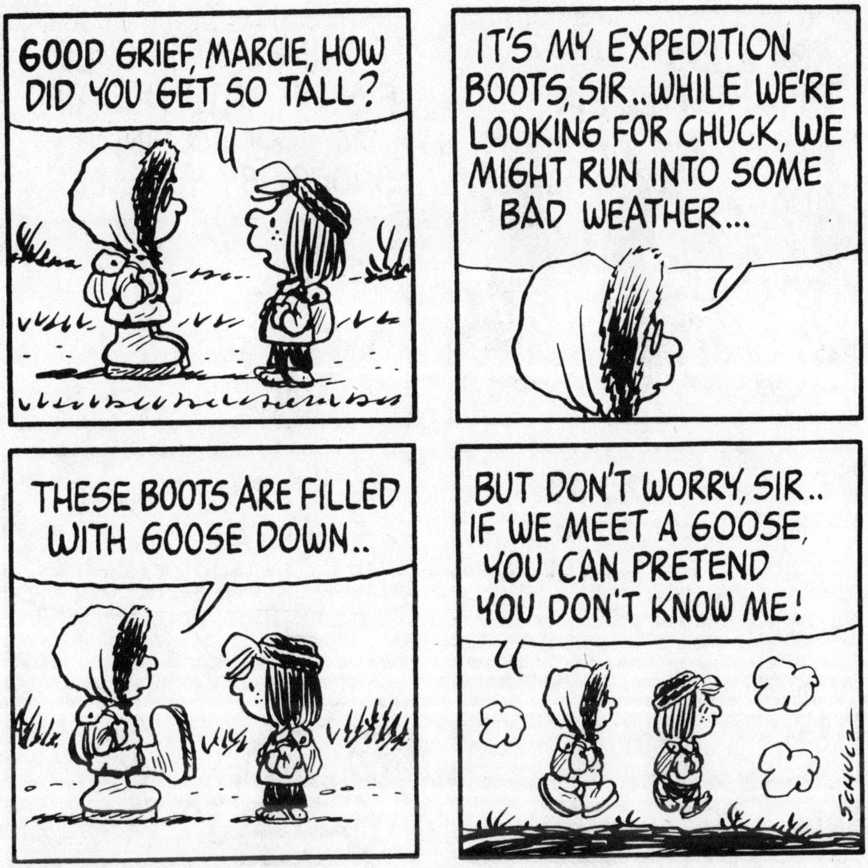
GOOD GRIEF, MARCIE, HOW DID YOU GET SO TALL?
IT'S MY EXPEDITION BOOTS, SIR.. WHILE WE'RE LOOKING FOR CHUCK, WE MIGHT RUN INTO SOME BAD WEATHER...
THESE BOOTS ARE FILLED WITH GOOSE DOWN..
BUT DON'T WORRY, SIR.. IF WE MEET A GOOSE, YOU CAN PRETEND YOU DON'T KNOW ME!
SCHULZ

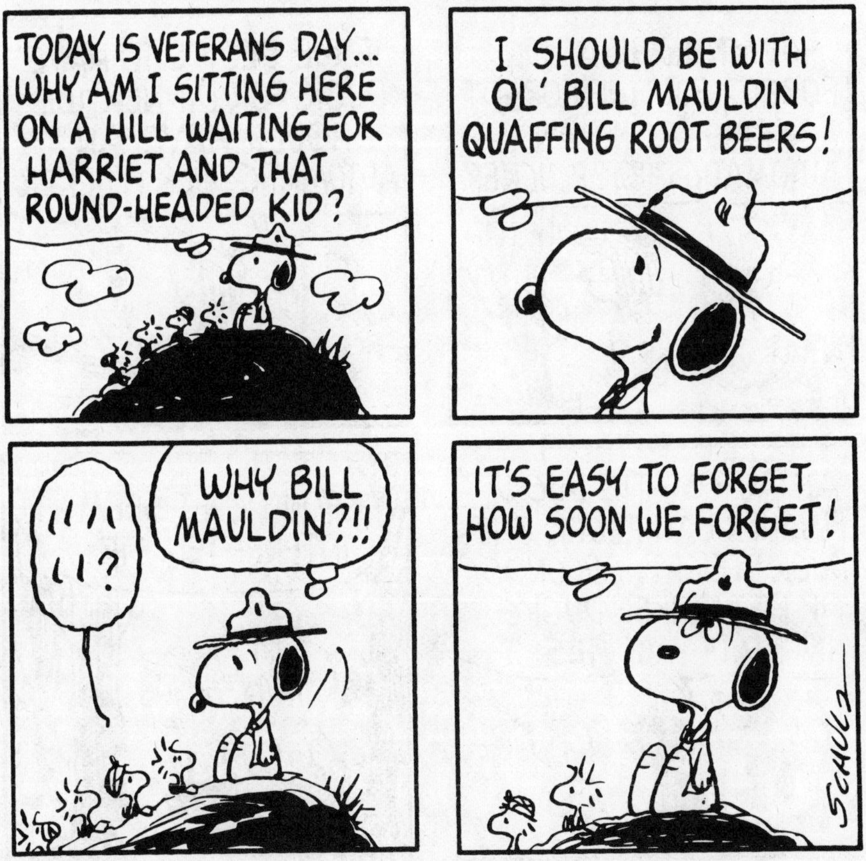
TODAY IS VETERANS DAY... WHY AM I SITTING HERE ON A HILL WAITING FOR HARRIET AND THAT ROUND-HEADED KID?
I SHOULD BE WITH OL' BILL MAULDIN QUAFFING ROOT BEERS!
WHY BILL MAULDIN?!!
IT'S EASY TO FORGET HOW SOON WE FORGET!
SCHULZ

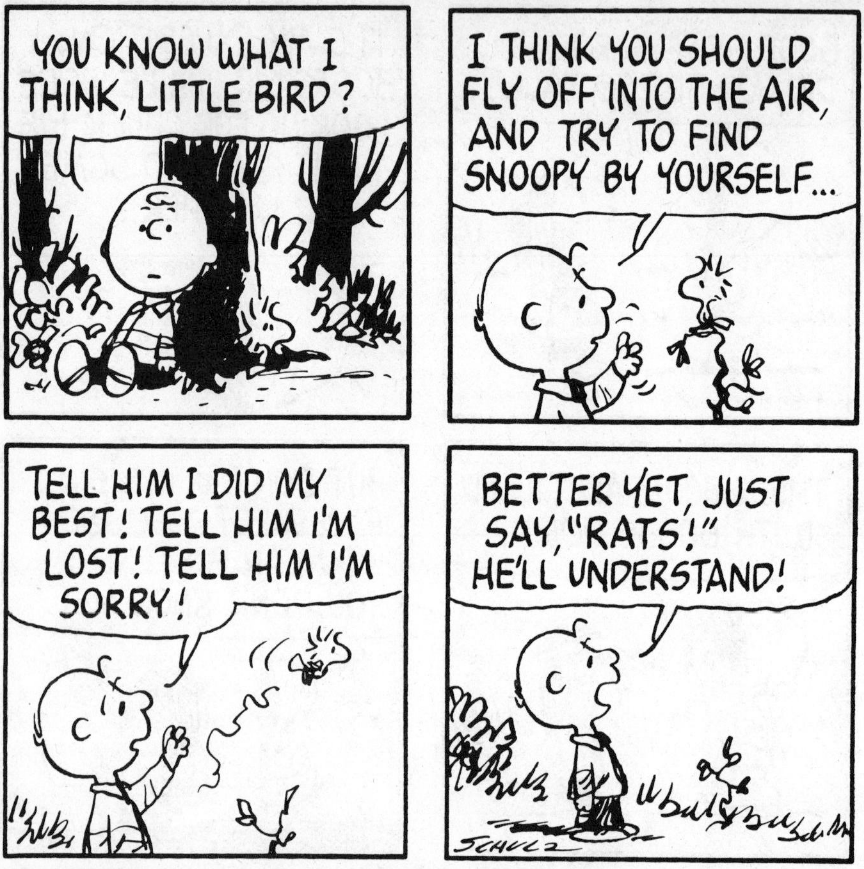
YOU KNOW WHAT I THINK, LITTLE BIRD?
I THINK YOU SHOULD FLY OFF INTO THE AIR, AND TRY TO FIND SNOOPY BY YOURSELF...
TELL HIM I DID MY BEST! TELL HIM I'M LOST! TELL HIM I'M SORRY!
BETTER YET, JUST SAY, "RATS!" HE'LL UNDERSTAND!

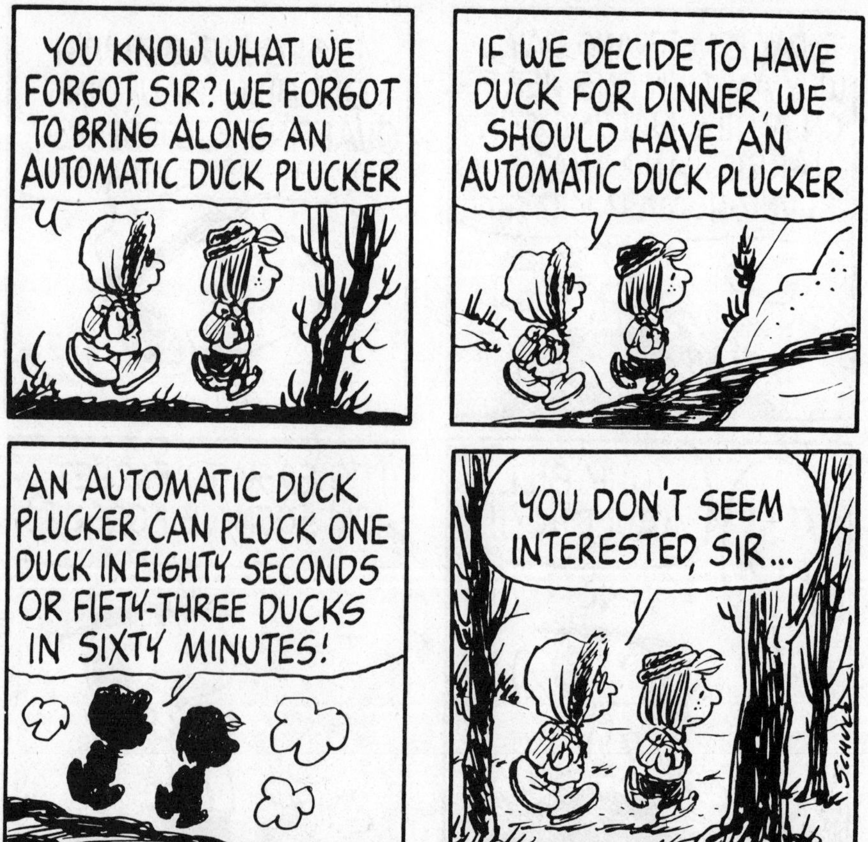
YOU KNOW WHAT WE FORGOT, SIR? WE FORGOT TO BRING ALONG AN AUTOMATIC DUCK PLUCKER
IF WE DECIDE TO HAVE DUCK FOR DINNER, WE SHOULD HAVE AN AUTOMATIC DUCK PLUCKER
AN AUTOMATIC DUCK PLUCKER CAN PLUCK ONE DUCK IN EIGHTY SECONDS OR FIFTY-THREE DUCKS IN SIXTY MINUTES!
YOU DON'T SEEM INTERESTED, SIR...

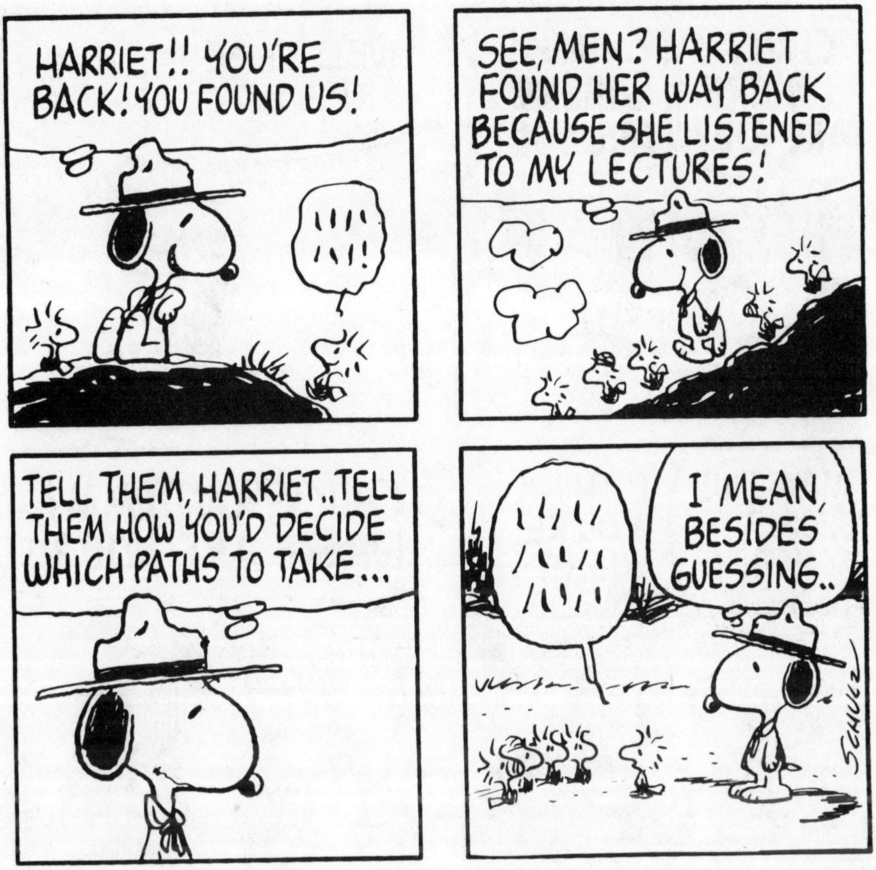
HARRIET!! YOU'RE BACK! YOU FOUND US!
SEE, MEN? HARRIET FOUND HER WAY BACK BECAUSE SHE LISTENED TO MY LECTURES!
TELL THEM, HARRIET.. TELL THEM HOW YOU'D DECIDE WHICH PATHS TO TAKE...
I MEAN, BESIDES GUESSING..
SCHULZ

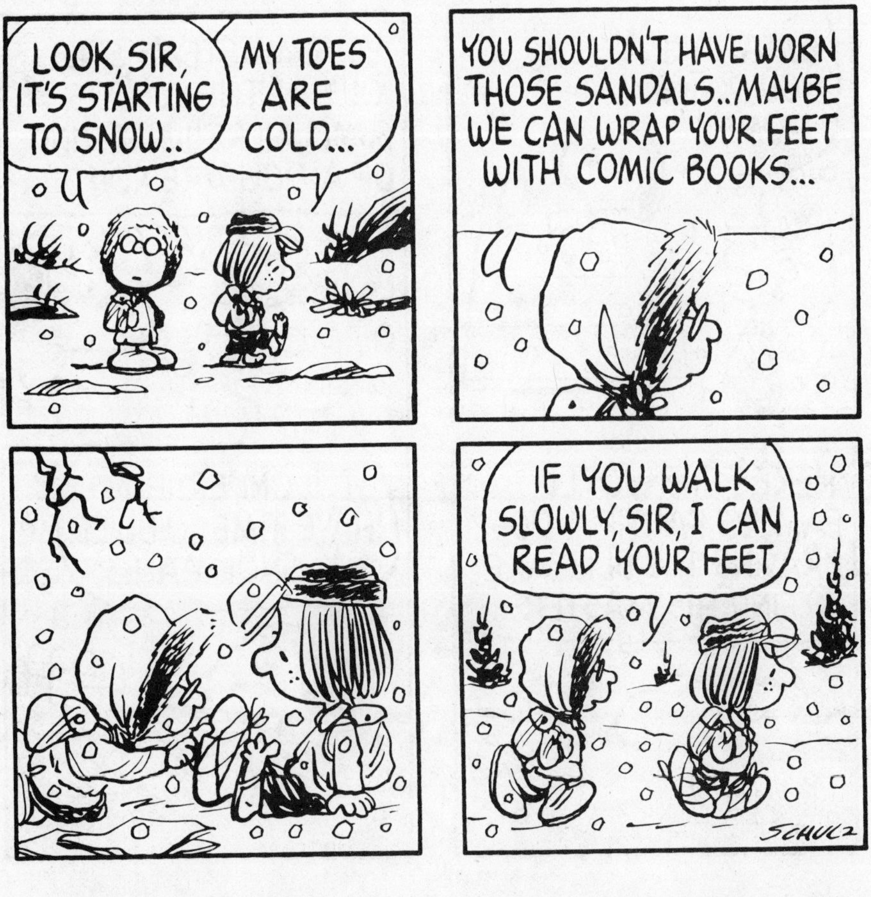
LOOK, SIR, IT'S STARTING TO SNOW..
MY TOES ARE COLD...
YOU SHOULDN'T HAVE WORN THOSE SANDALS.. MAYBE WE CAN WRAP YOUR FEET WITH COMIC BOOKS...
IF YOU WALK SLOWLY, SIR, I CAN READ YOUR FEET
SCHULZ

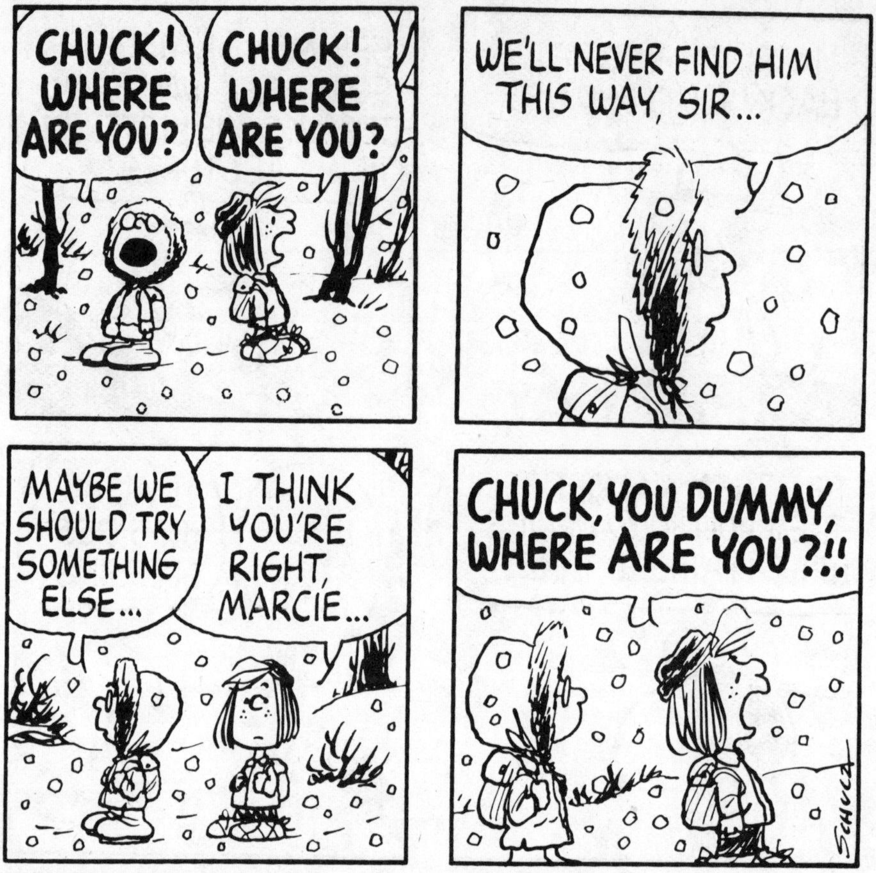
CHUCK! WHERE ARE YOU?
CHUCK! WHERE ARE YOU?
WE'LL NEVER FIND HIM THIS WAY, SIR...
MAYBE WE SHOULD TRY SOMETHING ELSE...
I THINK YOU'RE RIGHT, MARCIE...
CHUCK, YOU DUMMY, WHERE ARE YOU?!!
SCHULZ

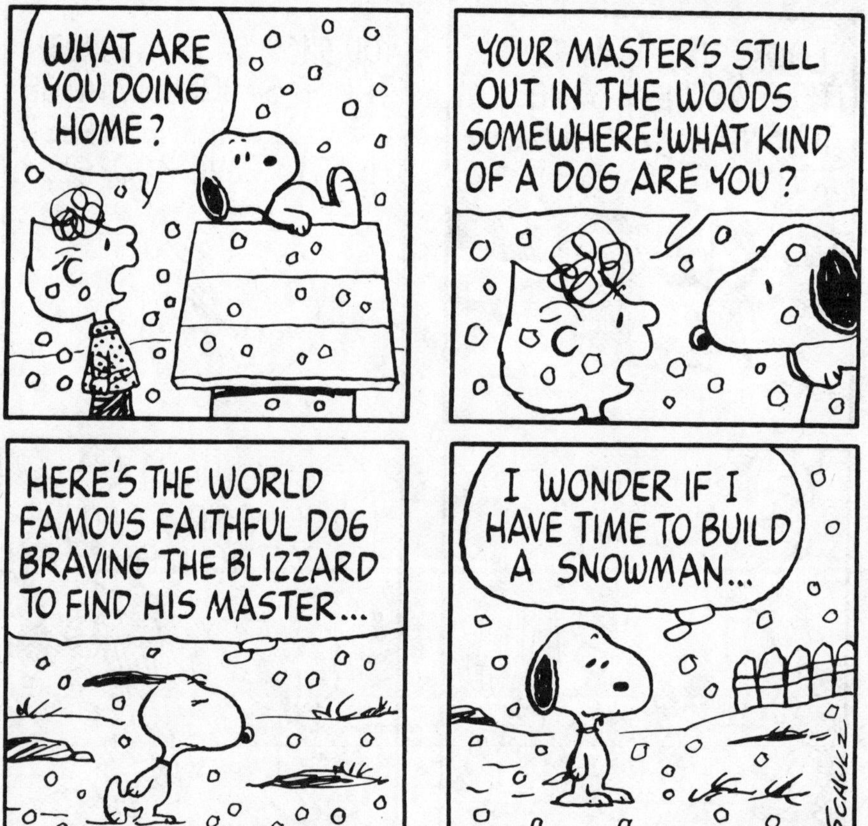
WHAT ARE YOU DOING HOME?
YOUR MASTER'S STILL OUT IN THE WOODS SOMEWHERE! WHAT KIND OF A DOG ARE YOU?
HERE'S THE WORLD FAMOUS FAITHFUL DOG BRAVING THE BLIZZARD TO FIND HIS MASTER...
I WONDER IF I HAVE TIME TO BUILD A SNOWMAN...
SCHULZ

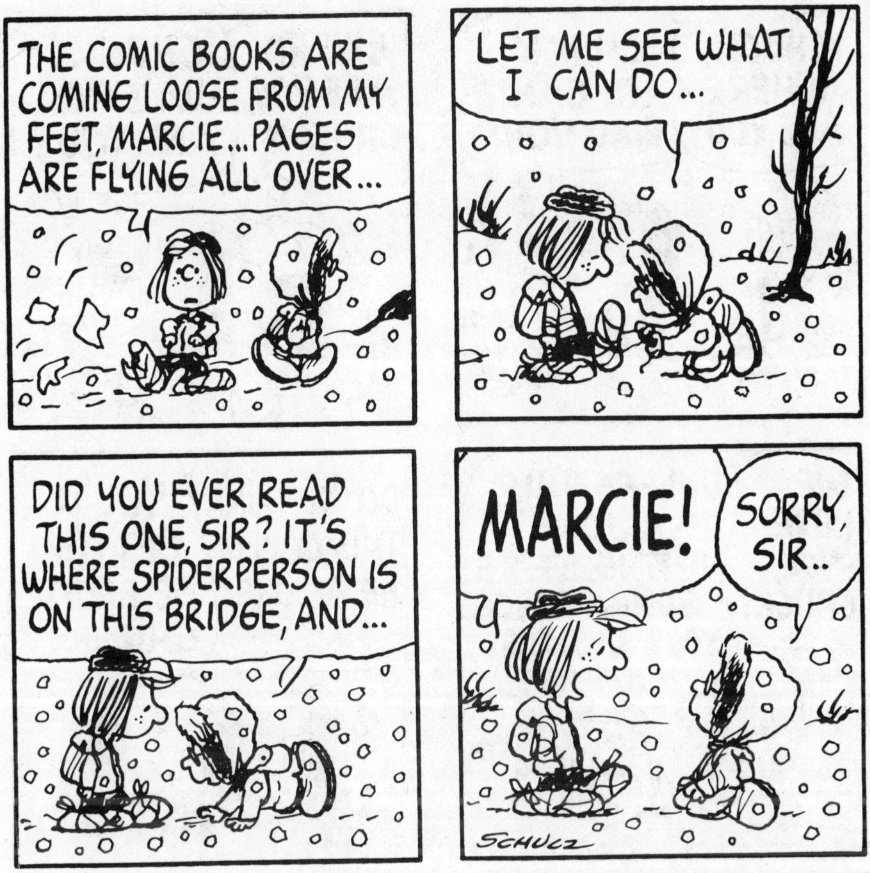
THE COMIC BOOKS ARE COMING LOOSE FROM MY FEET, MARCIE...PAGES ARE FLYING ALL OVER...
LET ME SEE WHAT I CAN DO...
DID YOU EVER READ THIS ONE, SIR? IT'S WHERE SPIDERPERSON IS ON THIS BRIDGE, AND...
MARCIE!
SORRY, SIR..
SCHULZ

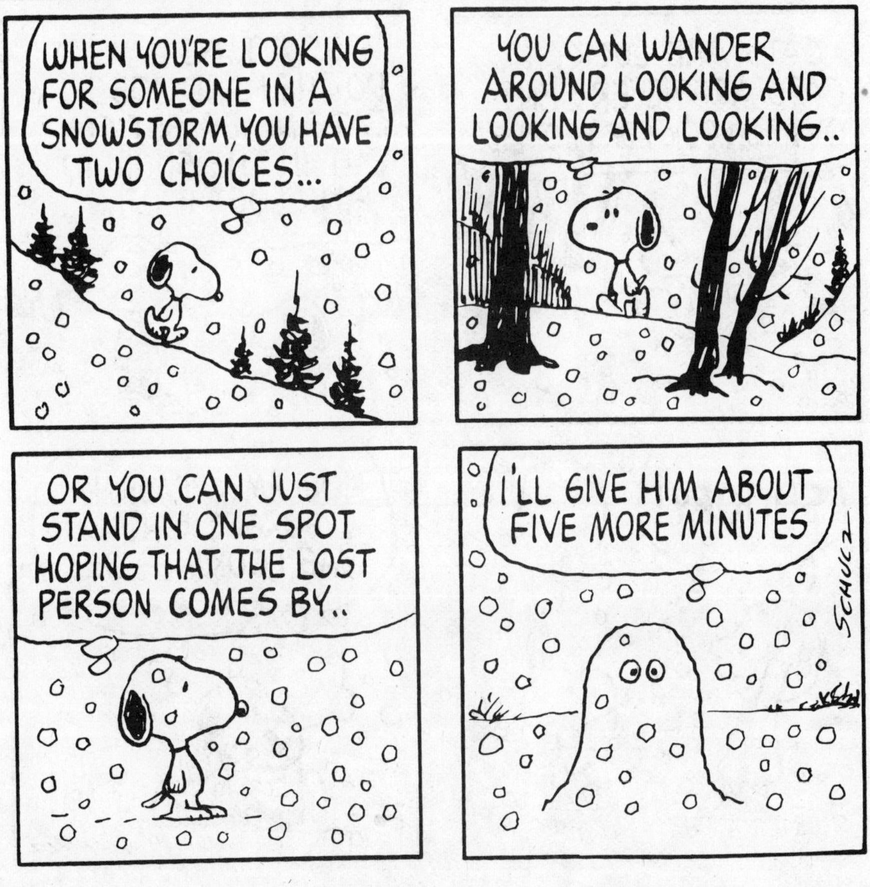
WHEN YOU'RE LOOKING FOR SOMEONE IN A SNOWSTORM, YOU HAVE TWO CHOICES...
YOU CAN WANDER AROUND LOOKING AND LOOKING AND LOOKING..
OR YOU CAN JUST STAND IN ONE SPOT HOPING THAT THE LOST PERSON COMES BY..
I'LL GIVE HIM ABOUT FIVE MORE MINUTES
SCHULZ

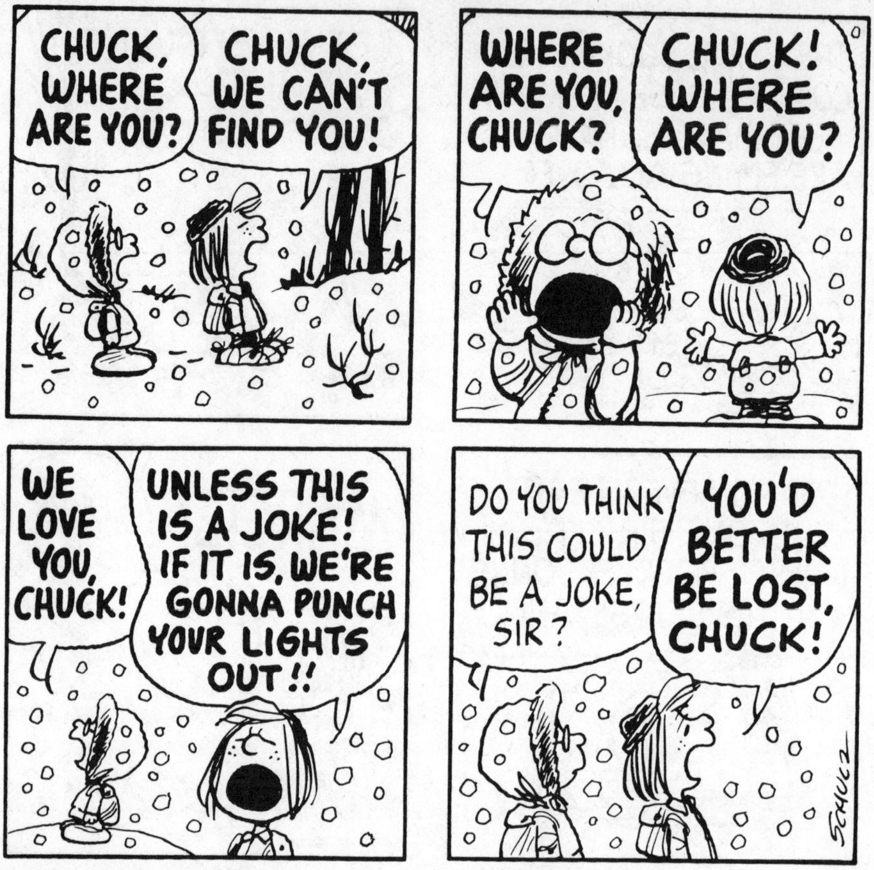
CHUCK, WHERE ARE YOU?
CHUCK, WE CAN'T FIND YOU!
WHERE ARE YOU, CHUCK?
CHUCK! WHERE ARE YOU?
WE LOVE YOU, CHUCK!
UNLESS THIS IS A JOKE! IF IT IS, WE'RE GONNA PUNCH YOUR LIGHTS OUT!!
DO YOU THINK THIS COULD BE A JOKE, SIR?
YOU'D BETTER BE LOST, CHUCK!
SCHULZ

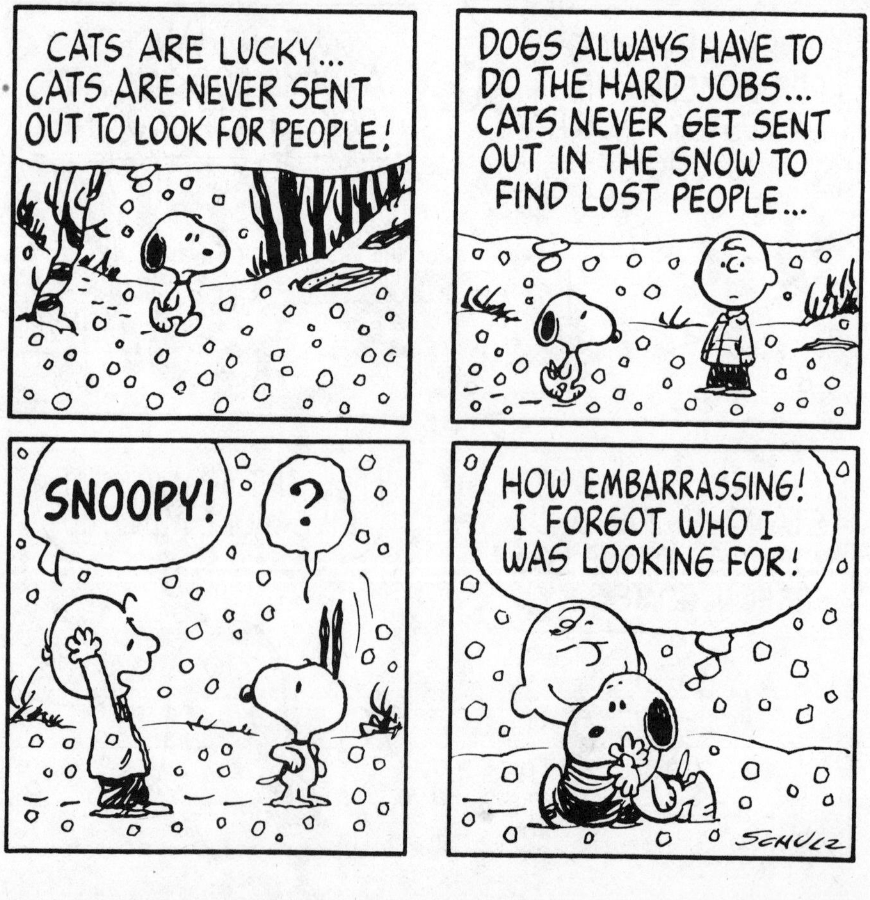
CATS ARE LUCKY... CATS ARE NEVER SENT OUT TO LOOK FOR PEOPLE!
DOGS ALWAYS HAVE TO DO THE HARD JOBS... CATS NEVER GET SENT OUT IN THE SNOW TO FIND LOST PEOPLE...
SNOOPY!
?
HOW EMBARRASSING! I FORGOT WHO I WAS LOOKING FOR!
SCHULZ

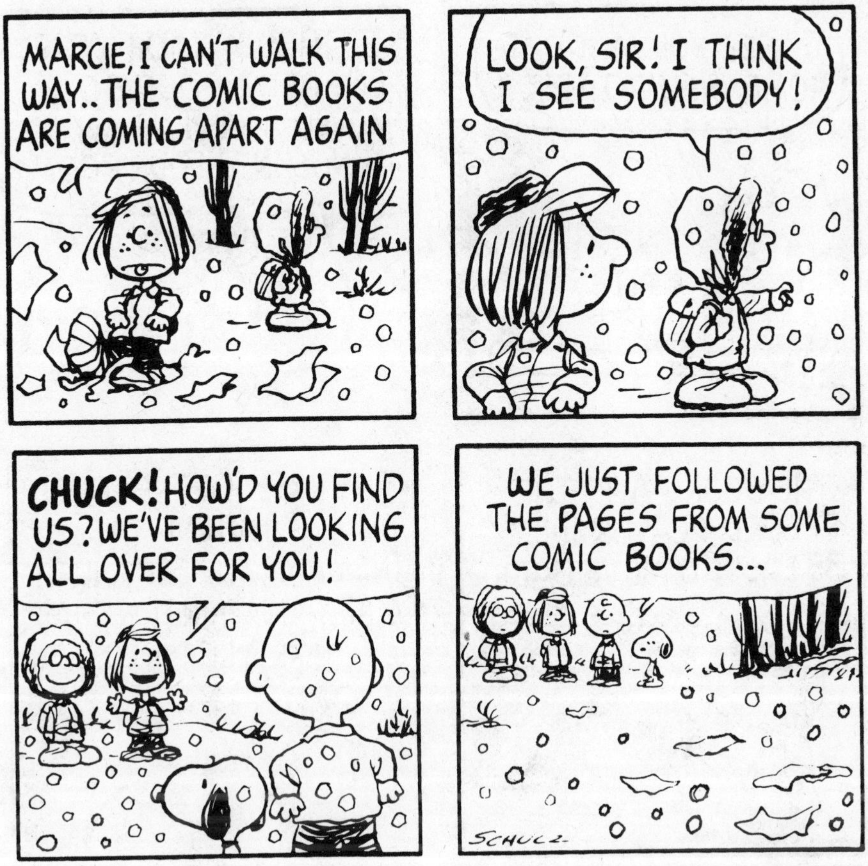
MARCIE, I CAN'T WALK THIS WAY.. THE COMIC BOOKS ARE COMING APART AGAIN
LOOK, SIR! I THINK I SEE SOMEBODY!
CHUCK! HOW'D YOU FIND US? WE'VE BEEN LOOKING ALL OVER FOR YOU!
WE JUST FOLLOWED THE PAGES FROM SOME COMIC BOOKS...
SCHULZ

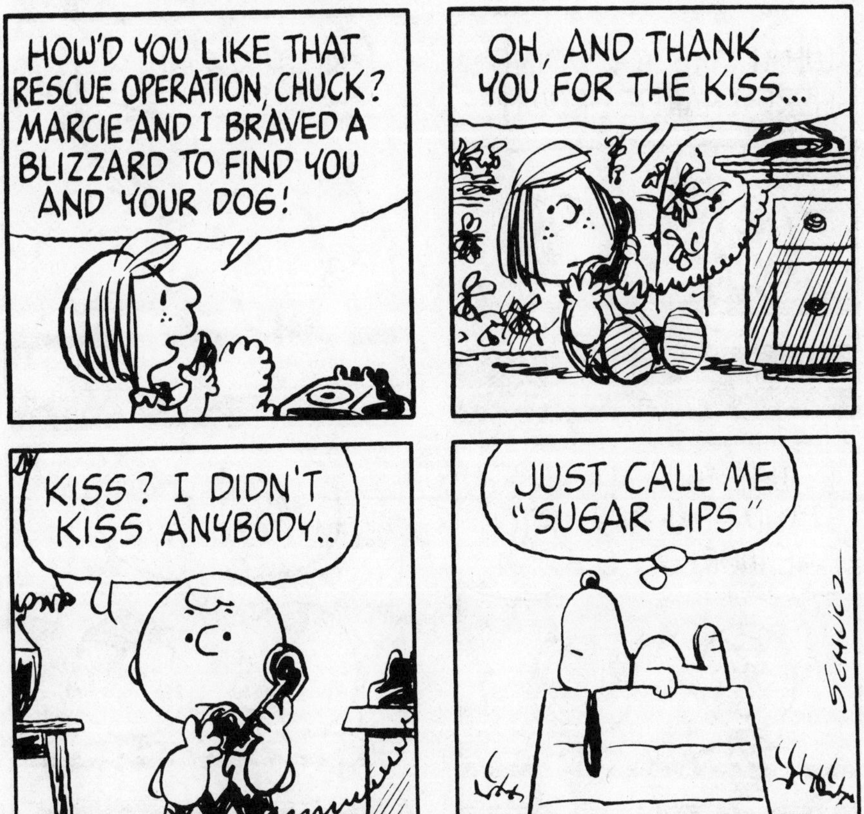
HOW'D YOU LIKE THAT RESCUE OPERATION, CHUCK? MARCIE AND I BRAVED A BLIZZARD TO FIND YOU AND YOUR DOG!
OH, AND THANK YOU FOR THE KISS...
KISS? I DIDN'T KISS ANYBODY..
JUST CALL ME "SUGAR LIPS"
SCHULZ

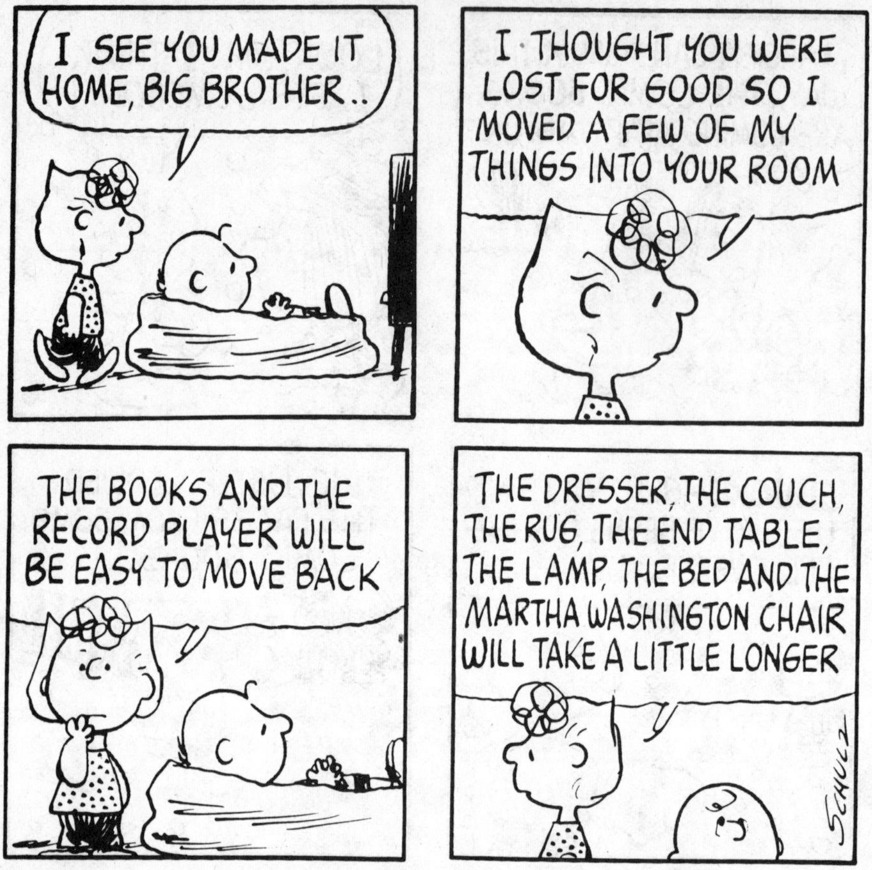
I SEE YOU MADE IT HOME, BIG BROTHER..
I THOUGHT YOU WERE LOST FOR GOOD SO I MOVED A FEW OF MY THINGS INTO YOUR ROOM
THE BOOKS AND THE RECORD PLAYER WILL BE EASY TO MOVE BACK
THE DRESSER, THE COUCH, THE RUG, THE END TABLE, THE LAMP, THE BED AND THE MARTHA WASHINGTON CHAIR WILL TAKE A LITTLE LONGER
SCHULZ

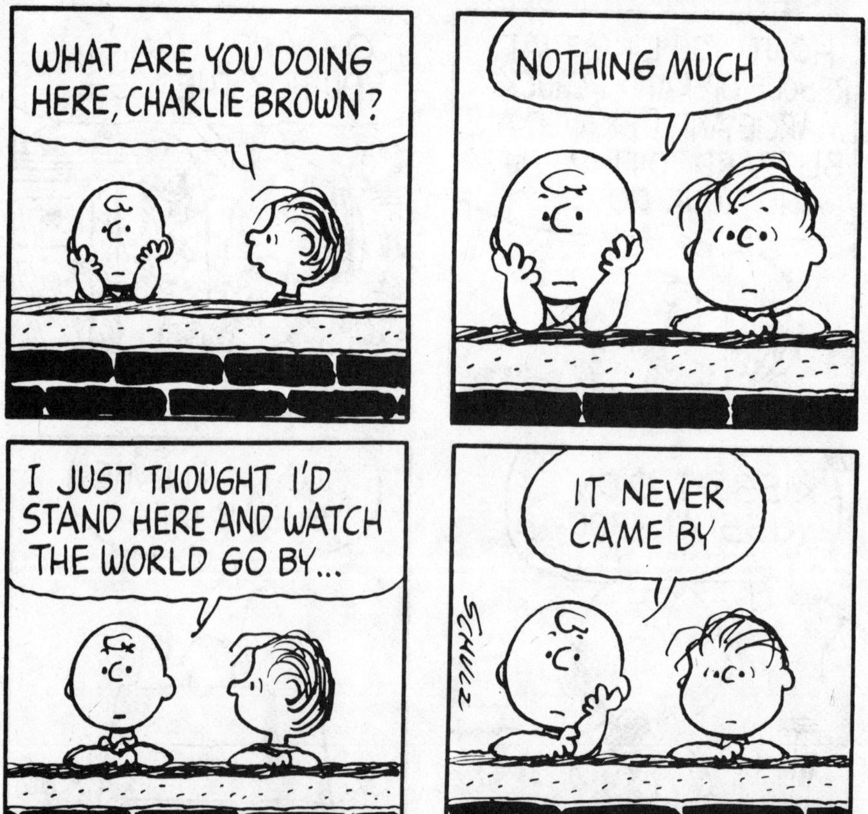
WHAT ARE YOU DOING HERE, CHARLIE BROWN?
NOTHING MUCH
I JUST THOUGHT I'D STAND HERE AND WATCH THE WORLD GO BY...
IT NEVER CAME BY
SCHULZ

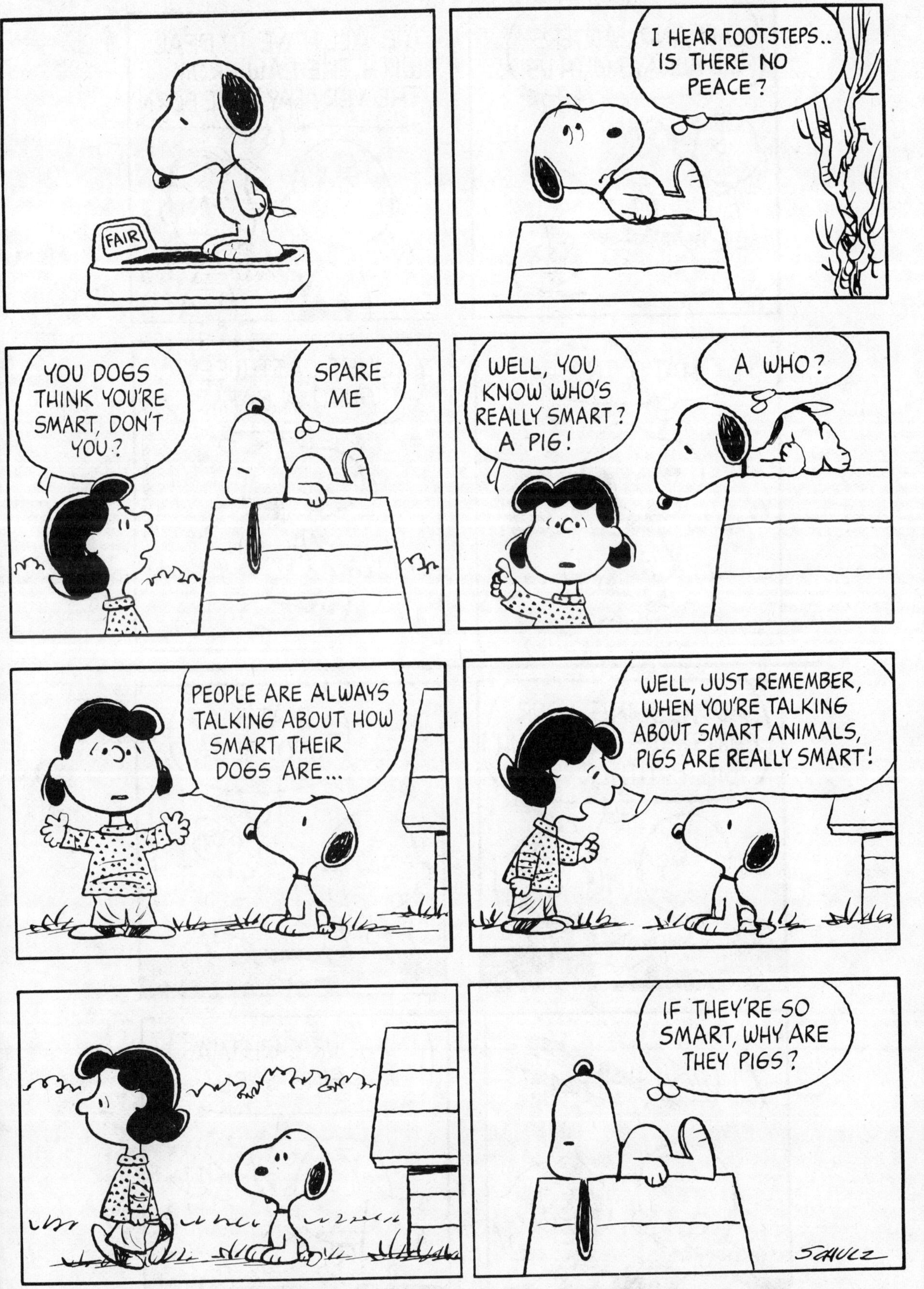
FAIR
I HEAR FOOTSTEPS.. IS THERE NO PEACE?
YOU DOGS THINK YOU'RE SMART, DON'T YOU?
SPARE ME
WELL, YOU KNOW WHO'S REALLY SMART? A PIG!
A WHO?
PEOPLE ARE ALWAYS TALKING ABOUT HOW SMART THEIR DOGS ARE...
WELL, JUST REMEMBER, WHEN YOU'RE TALKING ABOUT SMART ANIMALS, PIGS ARE REALLY SMART!
IF THEY'RE SO SMART, WHY ARE THEY PIGS?
SCHULZ

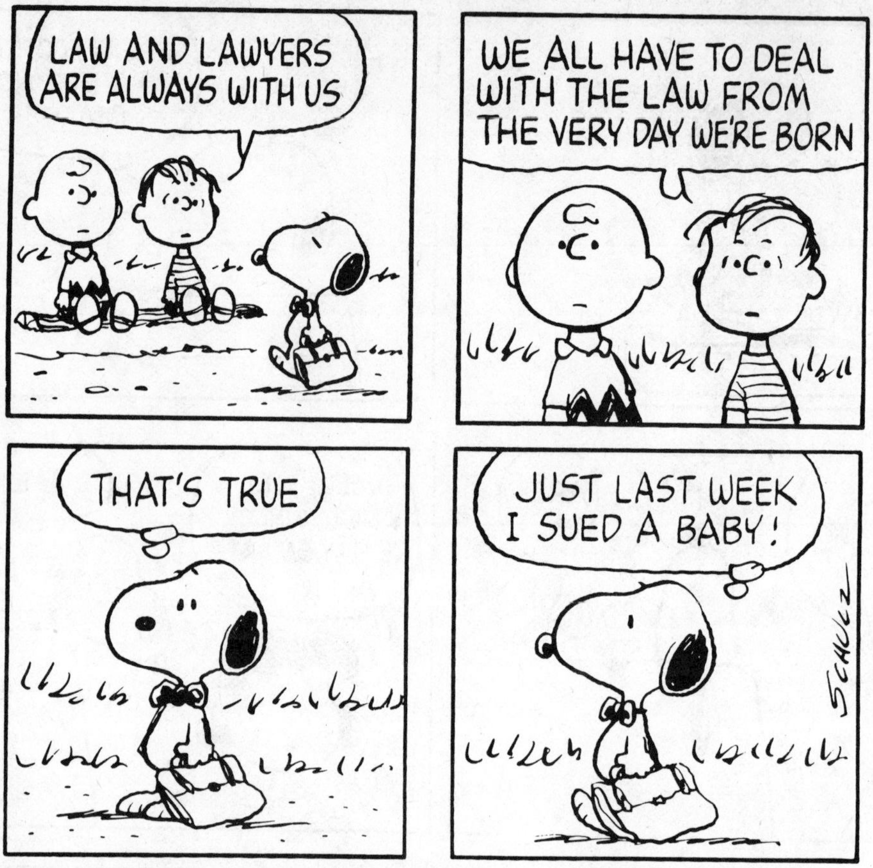
LAW AND LAWYERS ARE ALWAYS WITH US
WE ALL HAVE TO DEAL WITH THE LAW FROM THE VERY DAY WE'RE BORN
THAT'S TRUE
JUST LAST WEEK I SUED A BABY!

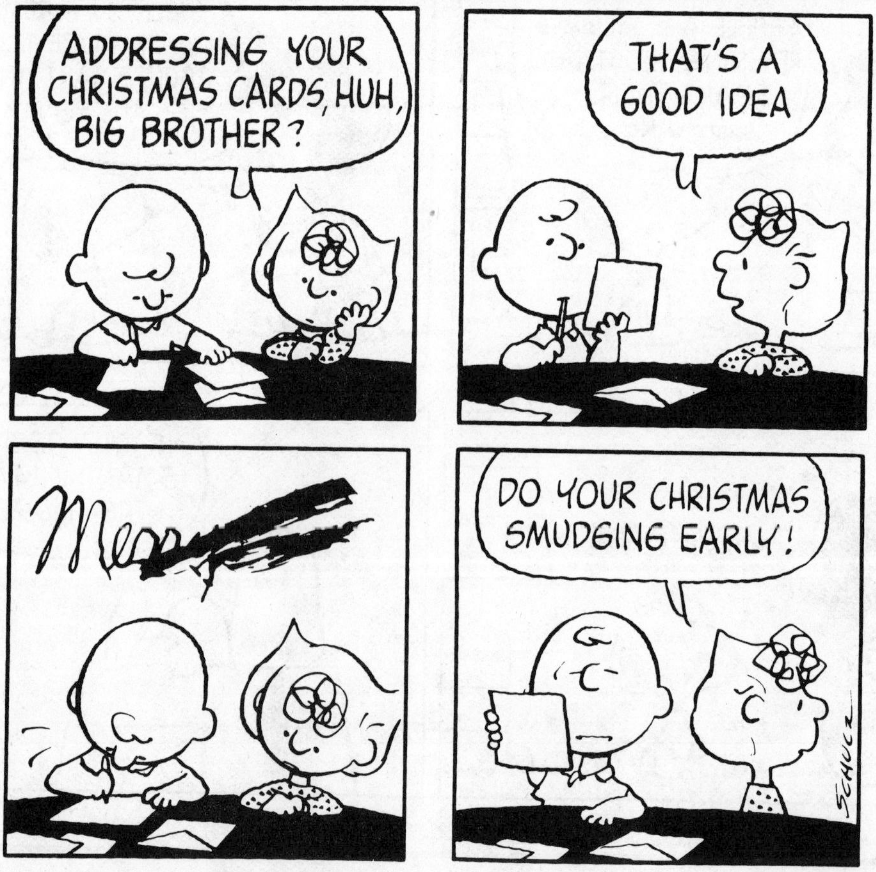
ADDRESSING YOUR CHRISTMAS CARDS, HUH, BIG BROTHER?
THAT'S A GOOD IDEA
DO YOUR CHRISTMAS SMUDGING EARLY!

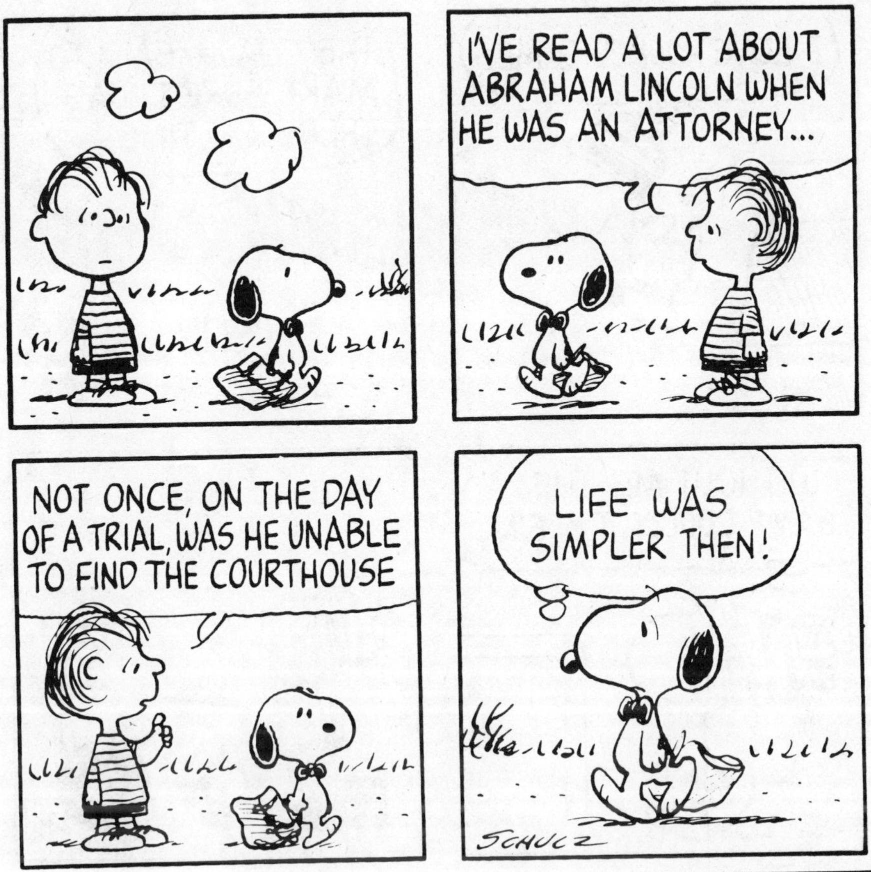
I'VE READ A LOT ABOUT ABRAHAM LINCOLN WHEN HE WAS AN ATTORNEY...
NOT ONCE, ON THE DAY OF A TRIAL, WAS HE UNABLE TO FIND THE COURTHOUSE
LIFE WAS SIMPLER THEN!

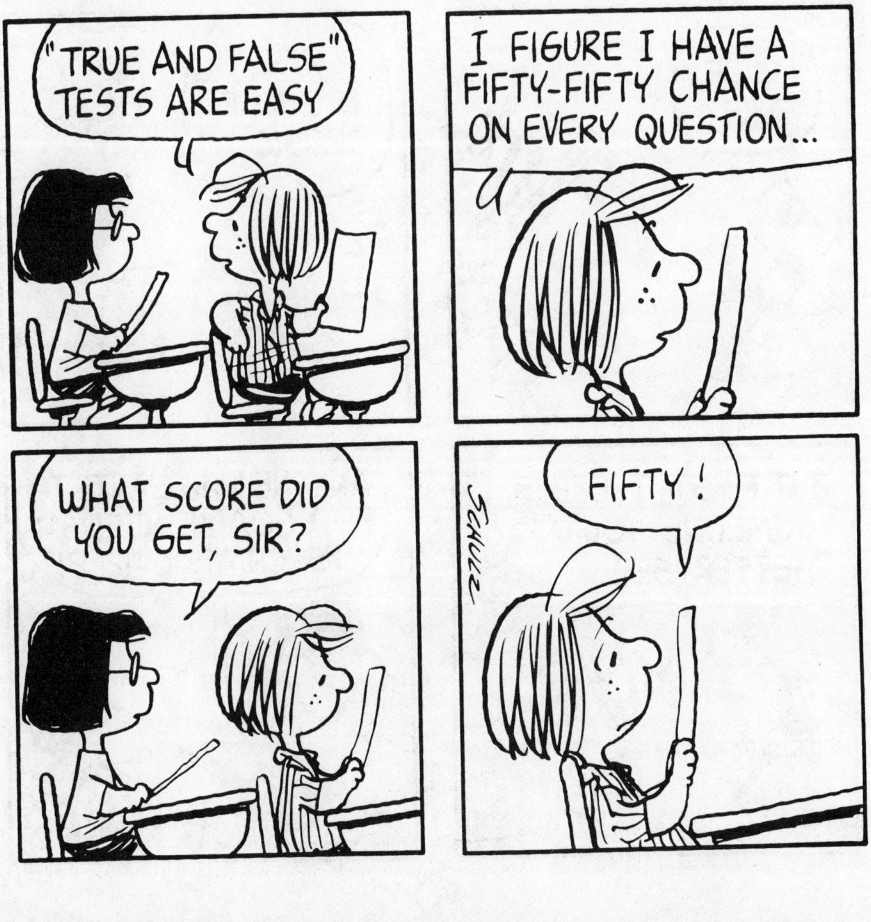
"TRUE AND FALSE" TESTS ARE EASY
I FIGURE I HAVE A FIFTY-FIFTY CHANCE ON EVERY QUESTION...
WHAT SCORE DID YOU GET, SIR?
FIFTY!

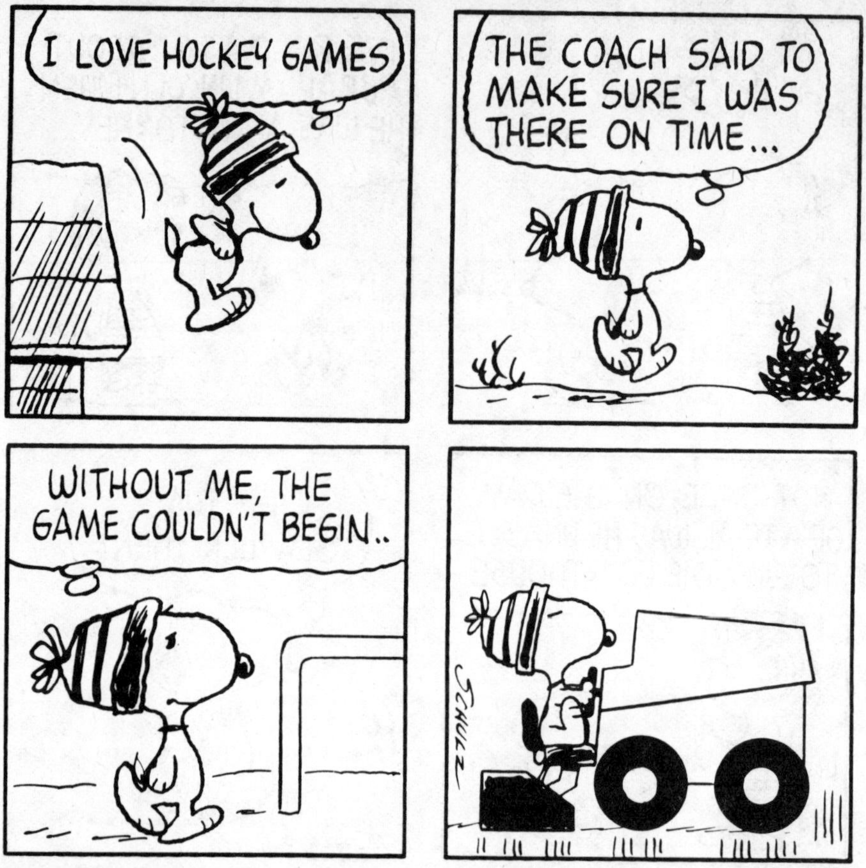
I LOVE HOCKEY GAMES
THE COACH SAID TO MAKE SURE I WAS THERE ON TIME...
WITHOUT ME, THE GAME COULDN'T BEGIN..
SCHULZ

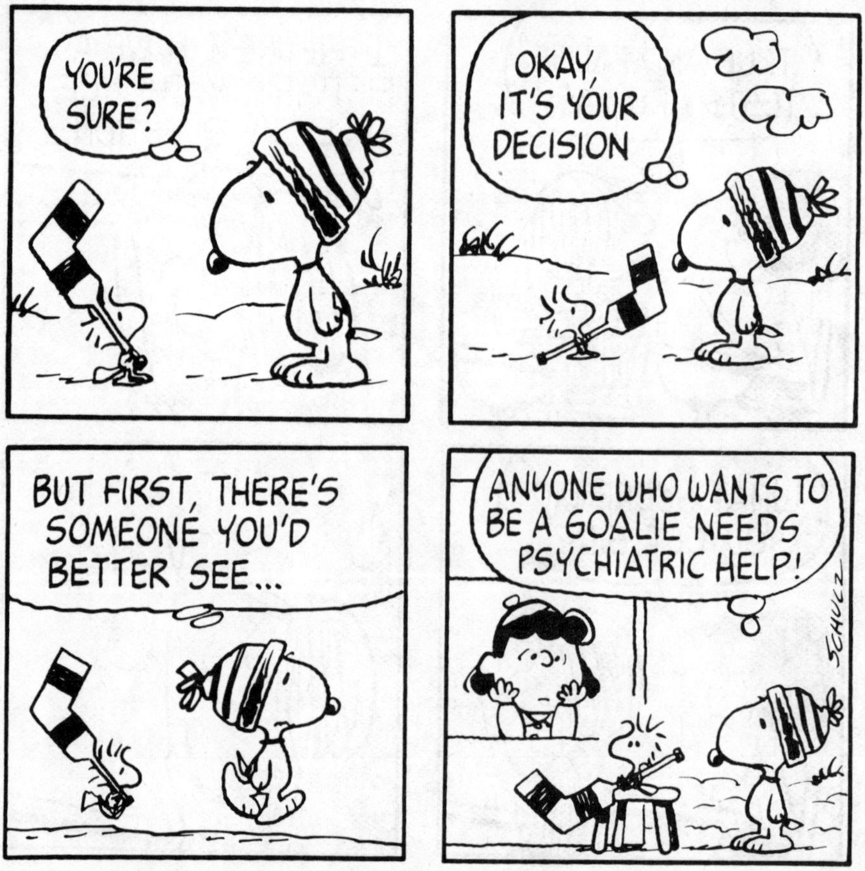
YOU'RE SURE?
OKAY, IT'S YOUR DECISION
BUT FIRST, THERE'S SOMEONE YOU'D BETTER SEE...
ANYONE WHO WANTS TO BE A GOALIE NEEDS PSYCHIATRIC HELP!
SCHULZ

WELL, GO AHEAD, AND EAT.. WHAT ARE YOU WAITING FOR?

I WAS HOPING THERE WAS A SALAD BAR

I HAVE A SUGGESTION, MA'AM..YOU KNOW WHAT WOULD MAKE A PERFECT GIFT TO YOUR CLASS?

DON'T ASSIGN US A BOOK TO READ DURING CHRISTMAS VACATION!

WHAT DO YOU SAY, MA'AM?

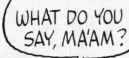

EVEN MY SUGGESTIONS GET A "D MINUS"!

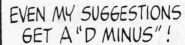

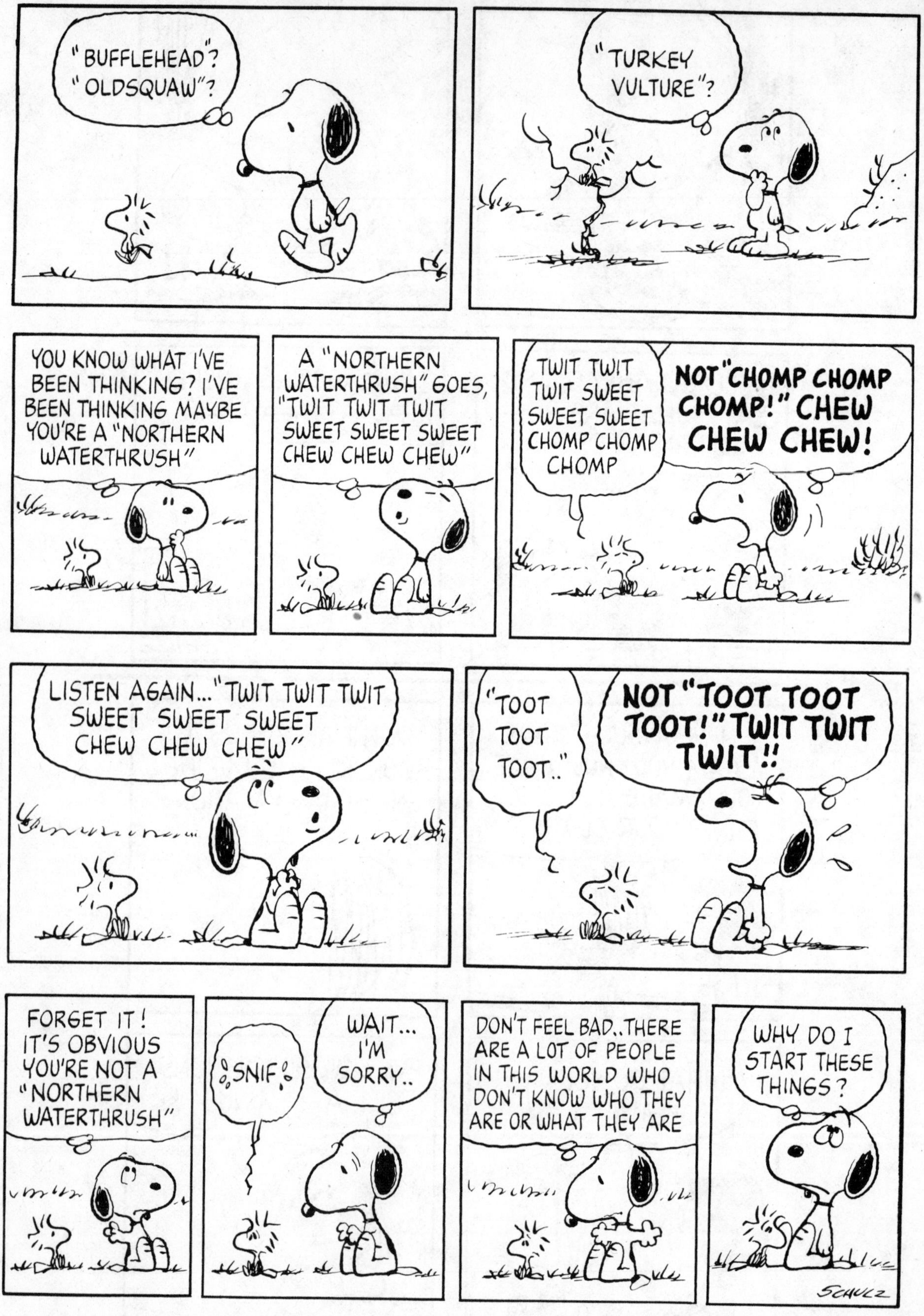
"BUFFLEHEAD"? "OLDSQUAW"?
"TURKEY VULTURE"?
YOU KNOW WHAT I'VE BEEN THINKING? I'VE BEEN THINKING MAYBE YOU'RE A "NORTHERN WATERTHRUSH"
A "NORTHERN WATERTHRUSH" GOES, "TWIT TWIT TWIT SWEET SWEET SWEET CHEW CHEW CHEW"
TWIT TWIT TWIT SWEET SWEET SWEET CHOMP CHOMP CHOMP
NOT "CHOMP CHOMP CHOMP!" CHEW CHEW CHEW!
LISTEN AGAIN..."TWIT TWIT TWIT SWEET SWEET SWEET CHEW CHEW CHEW"
"TOOT TOOT TOOT.."
NOT "TOOT TOOT TOOT!" TWIT TWIT TWIT!!
FORGET IT! IT'S OBVIOUS YOU'RE NOT A "NORTHERN WATERTHRUSH"
SNIF
WAIT... I'M SORRY..
DON'T FEEL BAD..THERE ARE A LOT OF PEOPLE IN THIS WORLD WHO DON'T KNOW WHO THEY ARE OR WHAT THEY ARE
WHY DO I START THESE THINGS?
SCHULZ

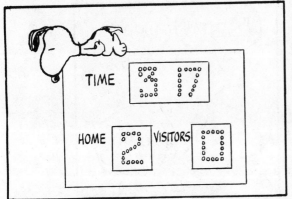

TIME 17

HOME 2 VISITORS 0

HE SHOULD LIKE THIS..

LOOK WHAT I FOUND FOR YOU.. A SHOE!

A WHAT?

I SAW A DOG DOWN THE STREET PLAYING WITH AN OLD SHOE SO I THOUGHT YOU MIGHT LIKE ONE, TOO...

A SHOE? HOW DO YOU PLAY WITH A SHOE?

WELL, IF WE MUST, WE MUST...

OKAY, SHOE, FIRST WE NEED TO GET ORGANIZED...

YOU CAN BE THE HOME TEAM..GAMES WILL BE SIXTY MINUTES..NO OVERTIME.. BODY CHECKING IS OUT..

HEARTS ARE HIGH... CLUBS ARE LOW..TWO MINUTES FOR TRIPPING... WE'LL CHANGE ENDS AT THE HALF...

HERE WE GO...

DOGS LOVE TO PLAY WITH OLD SHOES...

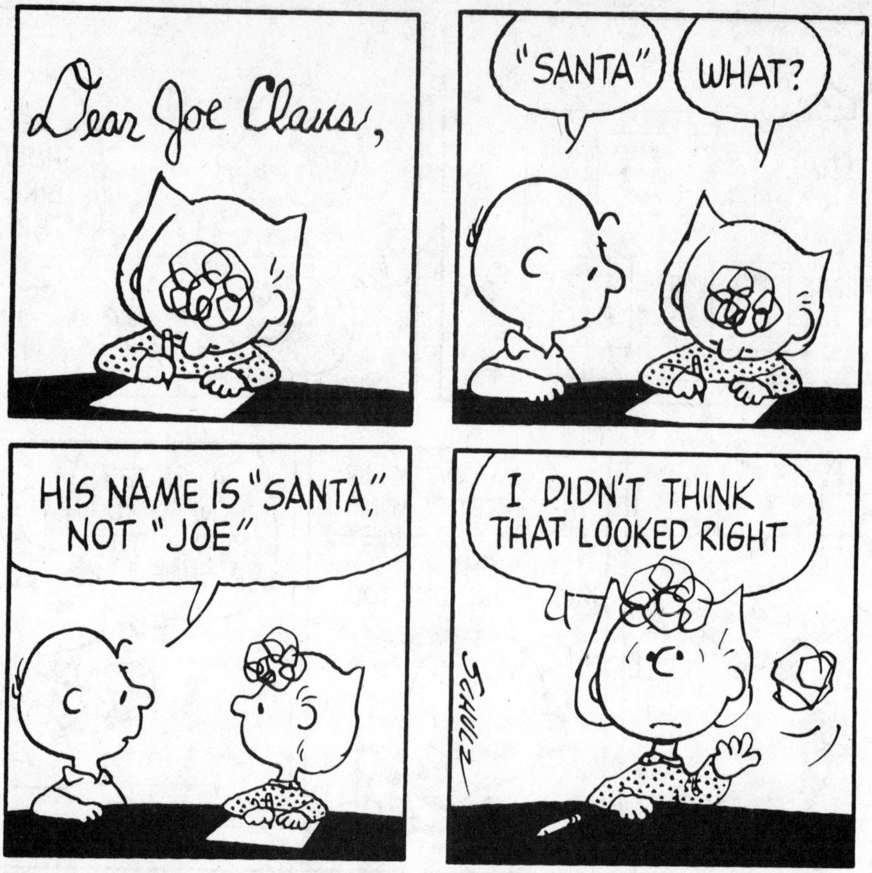
Dear Joe Claus,
"SANTA"
WHAT?
HIS NAME IS "SANTA," NOT "JOE"
I DIDN'T THINK THAT LOOKED RIGHT
SCHULZ

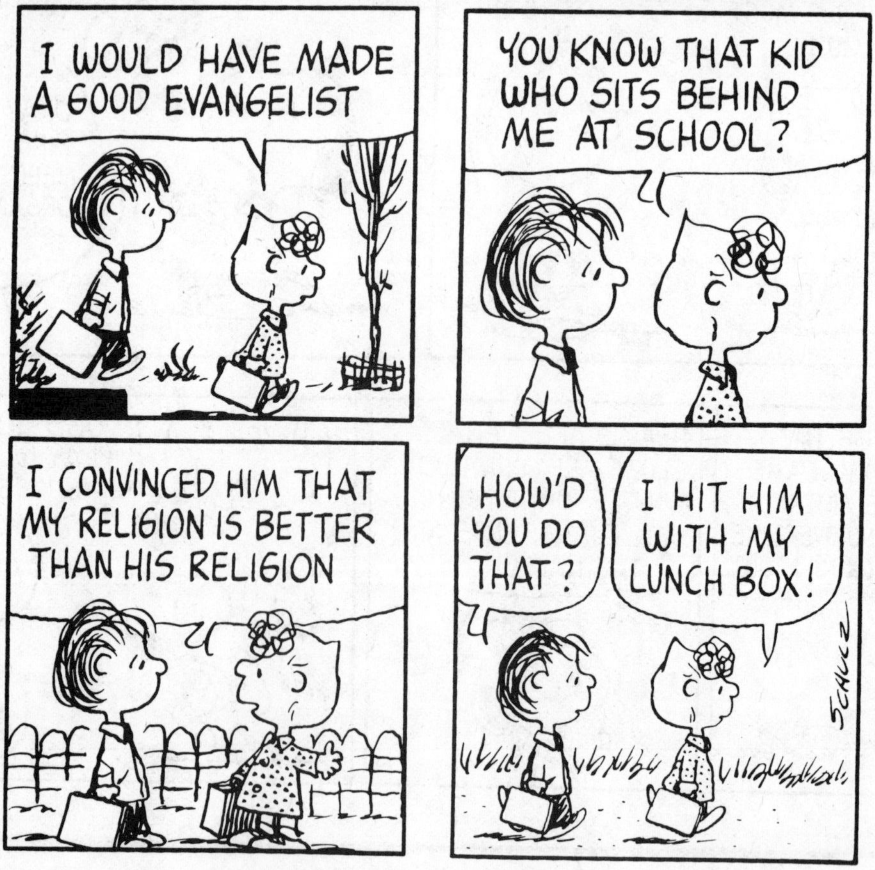
I WOULD HAVE MADE A GOOD EVANGELIST
YOU KNOW THAT KID WHO SITS BEHIND ME AT SCHOOL?
I CONVINCED HIM THAT MY RELIGION IS BETTER THAN HIS RELIGION
HOW'D YOU DO THAT?
I HIT HIM WITH MY LUNCH BOX!
SCHULZ

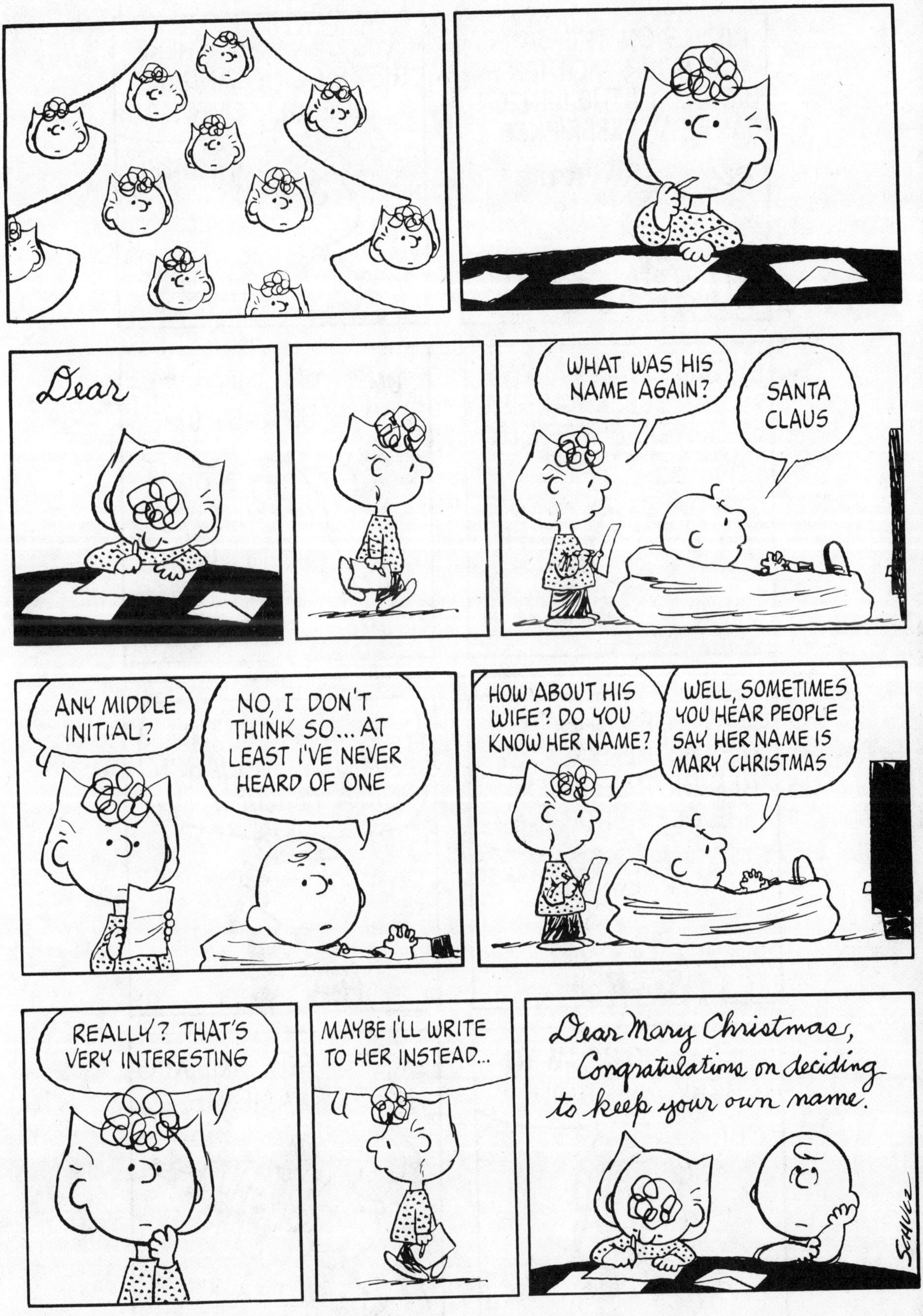
Dear
WHAT WAS HIS NAME AGAIN?
SANTA CLAUS
ANY MIDDLE INITIAL?
NO, I DON'T THINK SO... AT LEAST I'VE NEVER HEARD OF ONE
HOW ABOUT HIS WIFE? DO YOU KNOW HER NAME?
WELL, SOMETIMES YOU HEAR PEOPLE SAY HER NAME IS MARY CHRISTMAS
REALLY? THAT'S VERY INTERESTING
MAYBE I'LL WRITE TO HER INSTEAD...
Dear Mary Christmas,
Congratulations on deciding to keep your own name.
SCHULZ

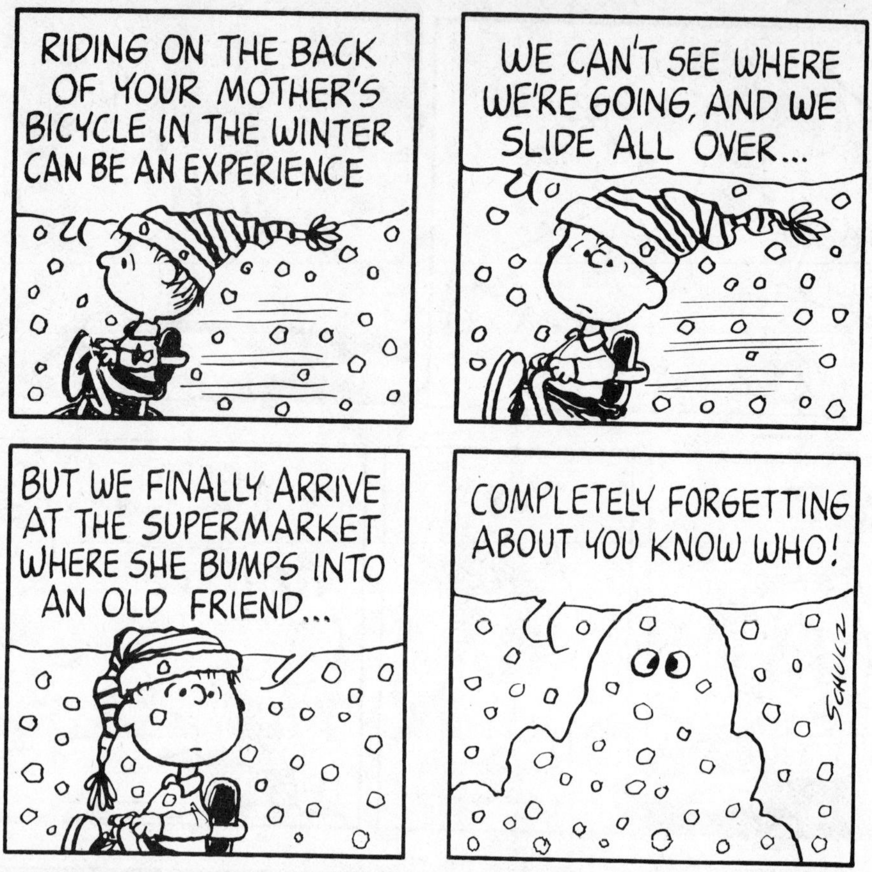
RIDING ON THE BACK OF YOUR MOTHER'S BICYCLE IN THE WINTER CAN BE AN EXPERIENCE
WE CAN'T SEE WHERE WE'RE GOING, AND WE SLIDE ALL OVER...
BUT WE FINALLY ARRIVE AT THE SUPERMARKET WHERE SHE BUMPS INTO AN OLD FRIEND...
COMPLETELY FORGETTING ABOUT YOU KNOW WHO!
SCHULZ

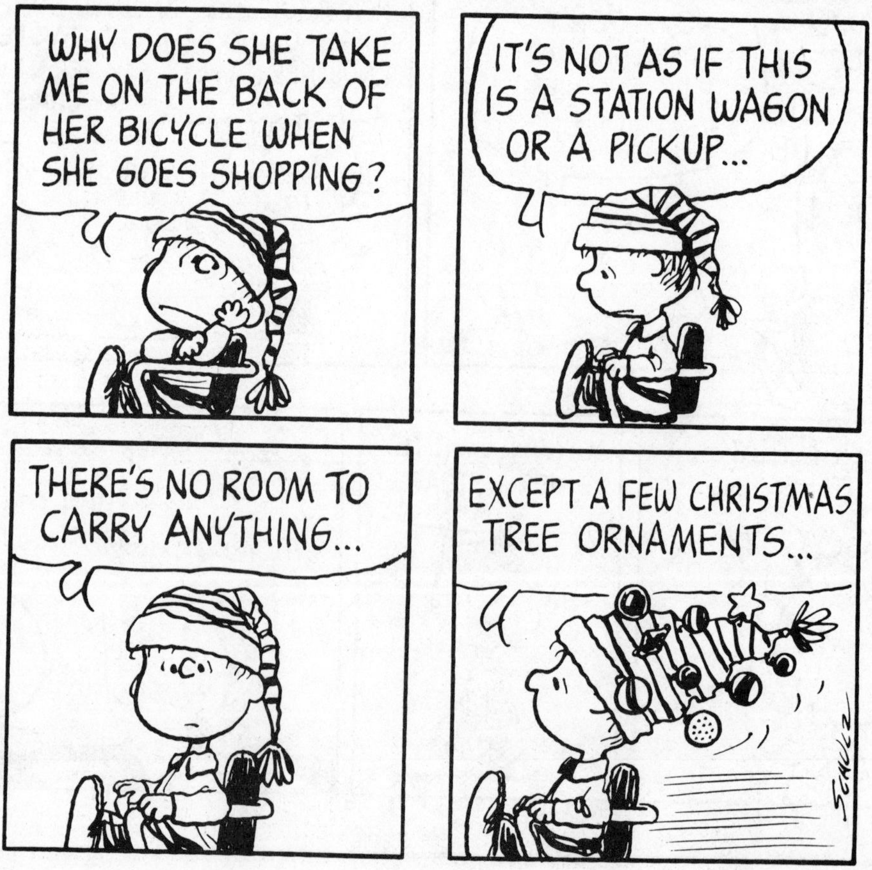
WHY DOES SHE TAKE ME ON THE BACK OF HER BICYCLE WHEN SHE GOES SHOPPING?
IT'S NOT AS IF THIS IS A STATION WAGON OR A PICKUP...
THERE'S NO ROOM TO CARRY ANYTHING...
EXCEPT A FEW CHRISTMAS TREE ORNAMENTS...
SCHULZ

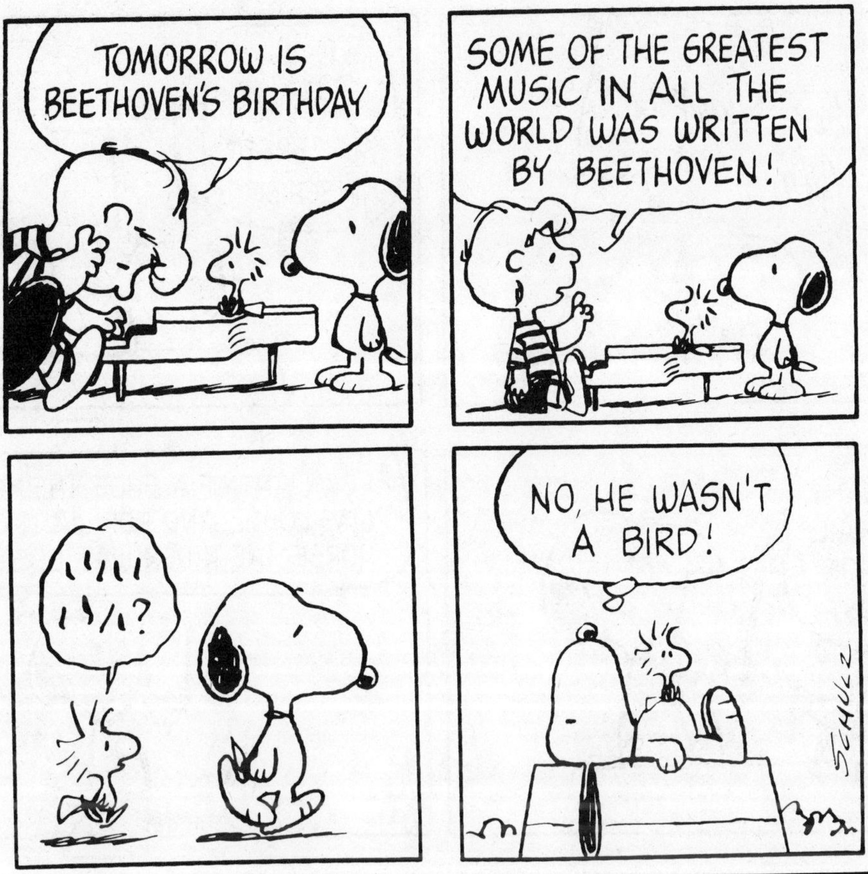
TOMORROW IS BEETHOVEN'S BIRTHDAY
SOME OF THE GREATEST MUSIC IN ALL THE WORLD WAS WRITTEN BY BEETHOVEN!
NO, HE WASN'T A BIRD!
SCHULZ

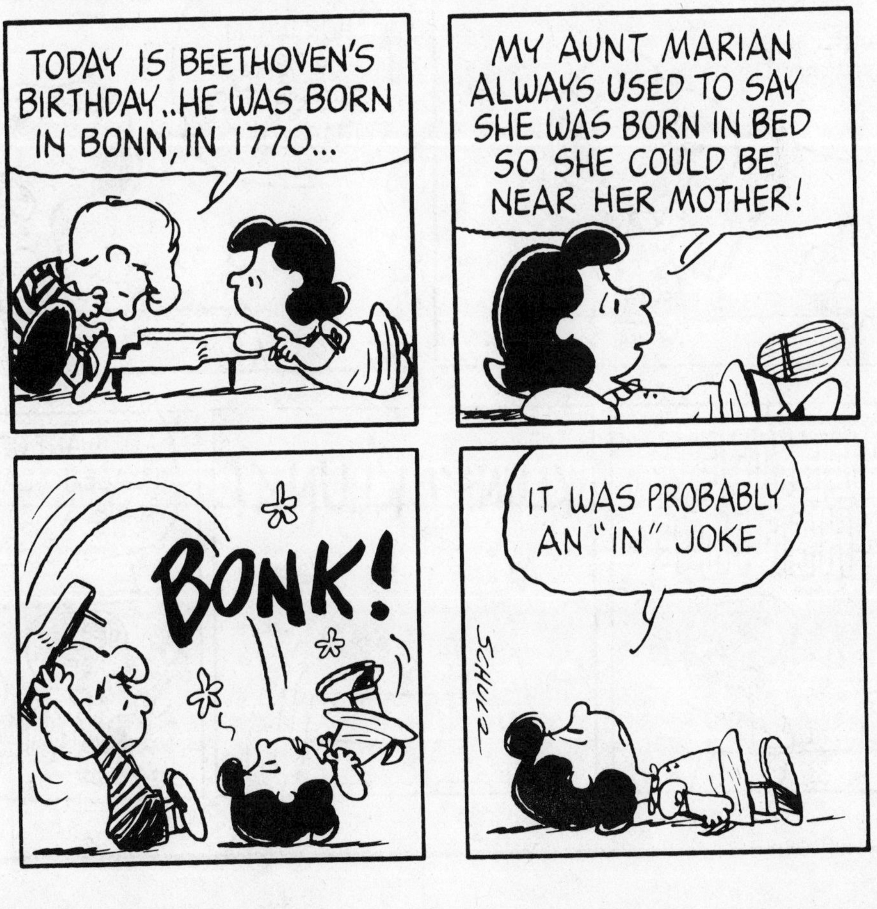
TODAY IS BEETHOVEN'S BIRTHDAY..HE WAS BORN IN BONN, IN 1770...
MY AUNT MARIAN ALWAYS USED TO SAY SHE WAS BORN IN BED SO SHE COULD BE NEAR HER MOTHER!
BONK!
SCHULZ
IT WAS PROBABLY AN "IN" JOKE

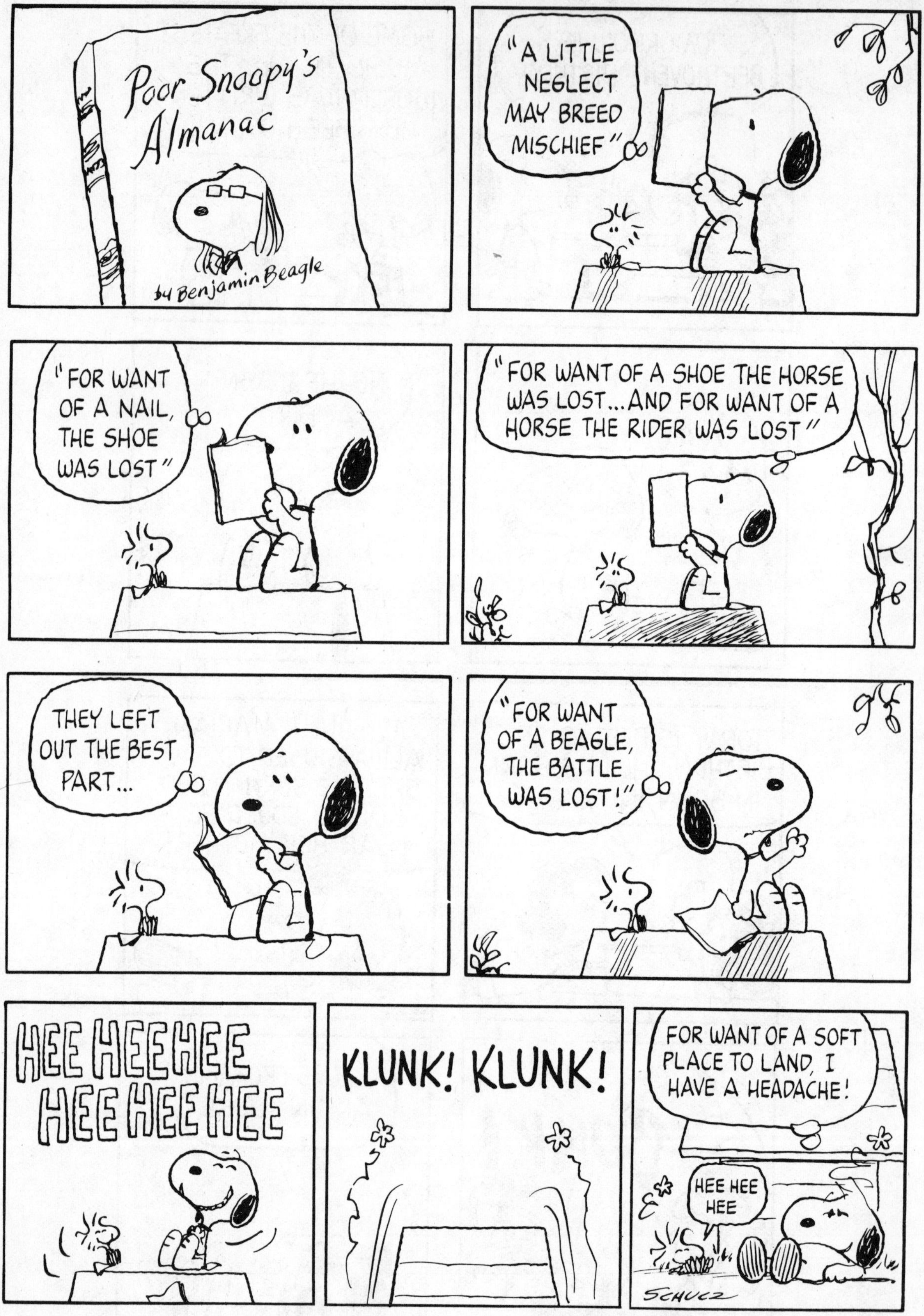
Poor Snoopy's Almanac
by Benjamin Beagle
"A LITTLE NEGLECT MAY BREED MISCHIEF"
"FOR WANT OF A NAIL, THE SHOE WAS LOST"
"FOR WANT OF A SHOE THE HORSE WAS LOST... AND FOR WANT OF A HORSE THE RIDER WAS LOST"
THEY LEFT OUT THE BEST PART...
"FOR WANT OF A BEAGLE, THE BATTLE WAS LOST!"
HEE HEEHEE HEE HEE HEE
KLUNK! KLUNK!
FOR WANT OF A SOFT PLACE TO LAND, I HAVE A HEADACHE!
HEE HEE HEE
SCHULZ

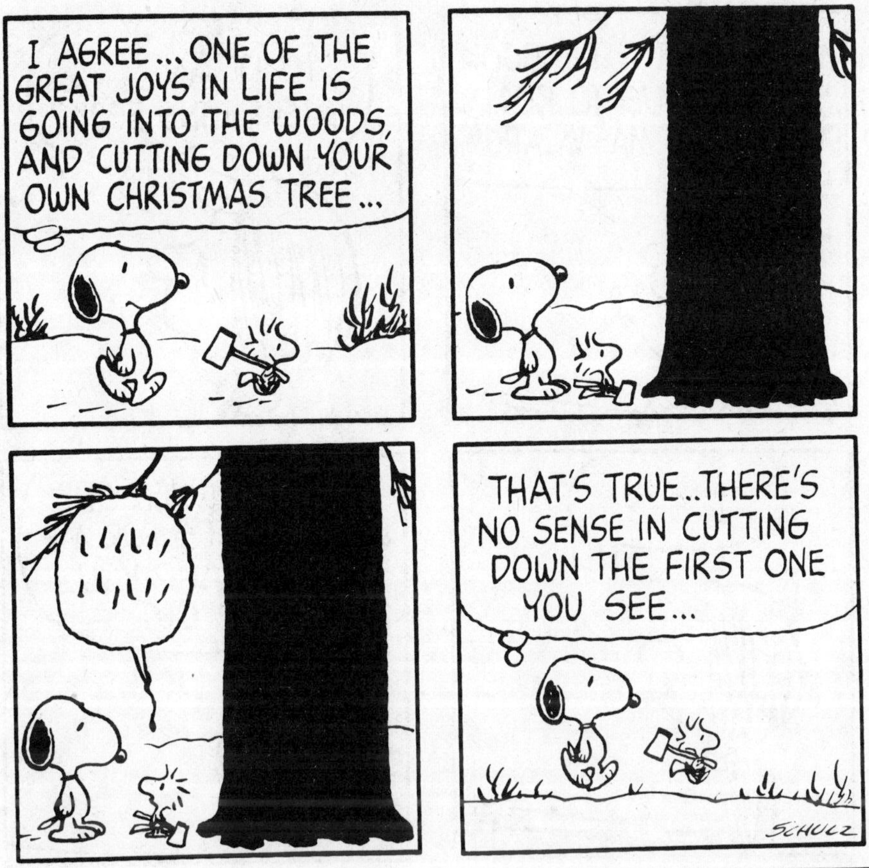
I AGREE... ONE OF THE GREAT JOYS IN LIFE IS GOING INTO THE WOODS, AND CUTTING DOWN YOUR OWN CHRISTMAS TREE...
THAT'S TRUE..THERE'S NO SENSE IN CUTTING DOWN THE FIRST ONE YOU SEE...
SCHULZ

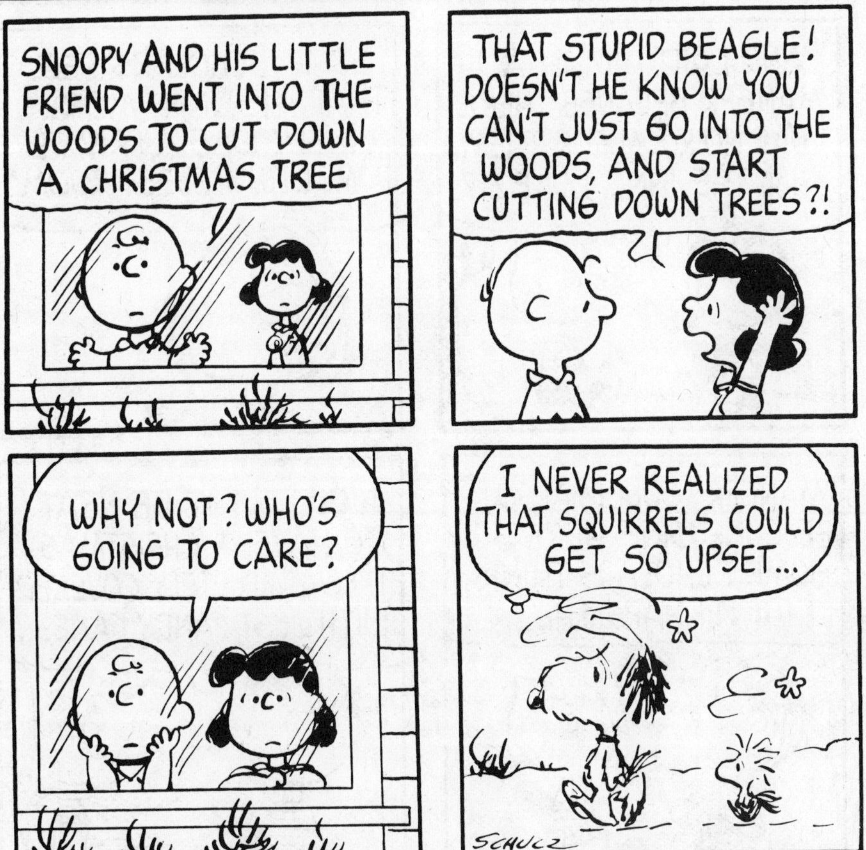
SNOOPY AND HIS LITTLE FRIEND WENT INTO THE WOODS TO CUT DOWN A CHRISTMAS TREE
THAT STUPID BEAGLE! DOESN'T HE KNOW YOU CAN'T JUST GO INTO THE WOODS, AND START CUTTING DOWN TREES?!
WHY NOT? WHO'S GOING TO CARE?
I NEVER REALIZED THAT SQUIRRELS COULD GET SO UPSET...
SCHULZ

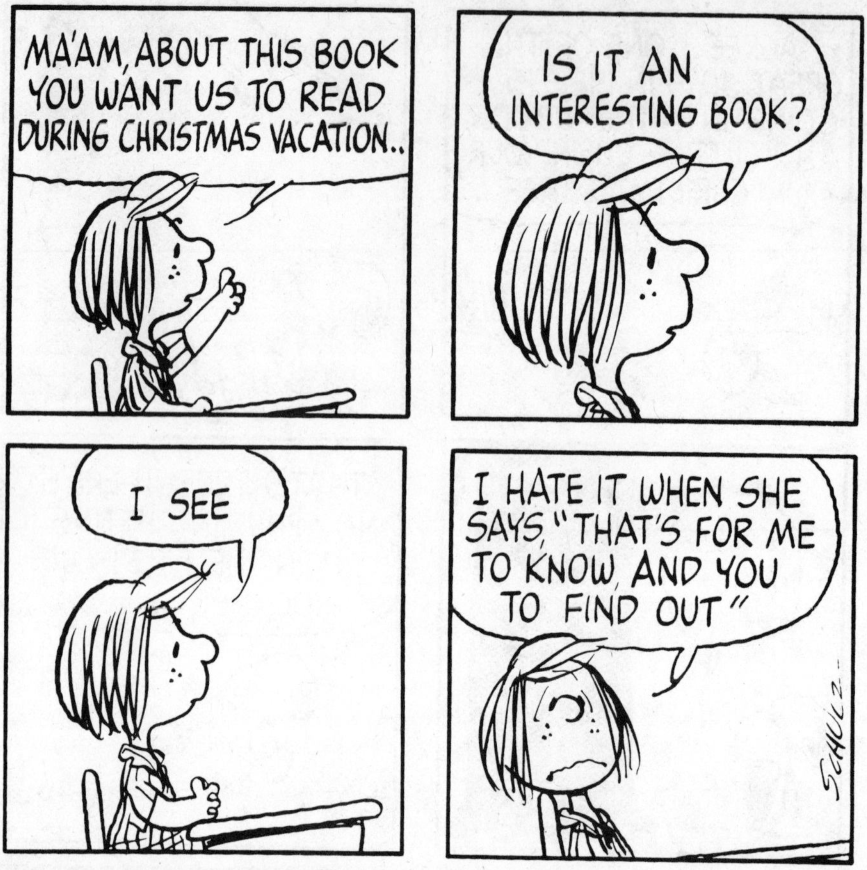
MA'AM, ABOUT THIS BOOK YOU WANT US TO READ DURING CHRISTMAS VACATION..
IS IT AN INTERESTING BOOK?
I SEE
I HATE IT WHEN SHE SAYS, "THAT'S FOR ME TO KNOW, AND YOU TO FIND OUT"
SCHULZ

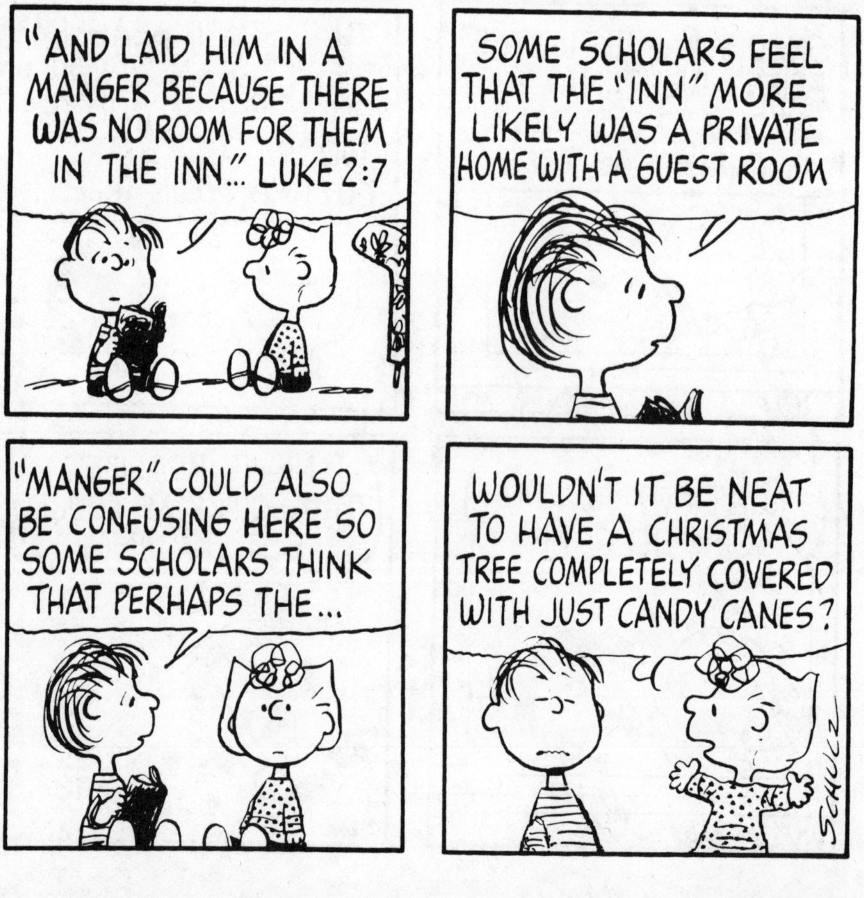
"AND LAID HIM IN A MANGER BECAUSE THERE WAS NO ROOM FOR THEM IN THE INN." LUKE 2:7
SOME SCHOLARS FEEL THAT THE "INN" MORE LIKELY WAS A PRIVATE HOME WITH A GUEST ROOM
"MANGER" COULD ALSO BE CONFUSING HERE SO SOME SCHOLARS THINK THAT PERHAPS THE...
WOULDN'T IT BE NEAT TO HAVE A CHRISTMAS TREE COMPLETELY COVERED WITH JUST CANDY CANES?
SCHULZ

HEY! ANYBODY HOME?
I THREW A CHRISTMAS STOCKING UP TO YOU... DID YOU GET IT?
SCHULZ

THERE WERE THREE WISE MEN, SEE...
THEY CAME FROM THE EAST, AND THEY WERE LOOKING FOR BETHLEHEM
YOU KNOW HOW THEY FOUND IT? THEY FOLLOWED A STAR!
WHO WAS THE STAR?
SCHULZ

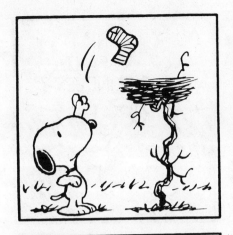

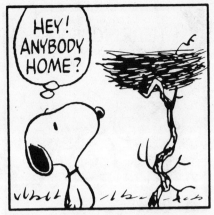

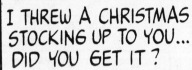

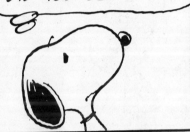

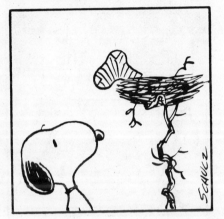

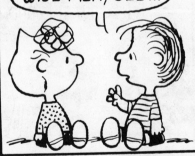

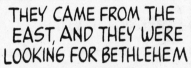

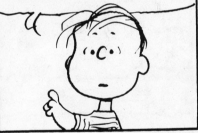

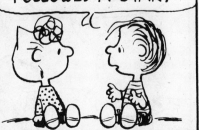

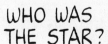

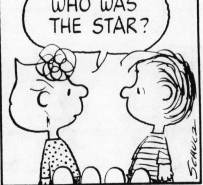

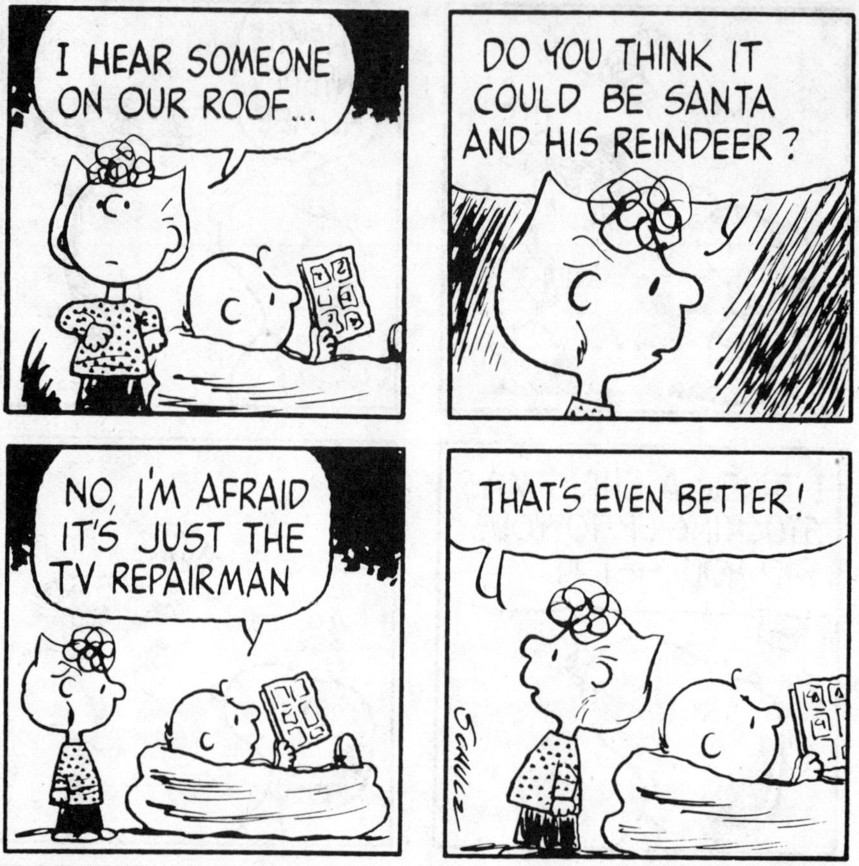
I HEAR SOMEONE ON OUR ROOF...
DO YOU THINK IT COULD BE SANTA AND HIS REINDEER?
NO, I'M AFRAID IT'S JUST THE TV REPAIRMAN
THAT'S EVEN BETTER!
SCHULZ

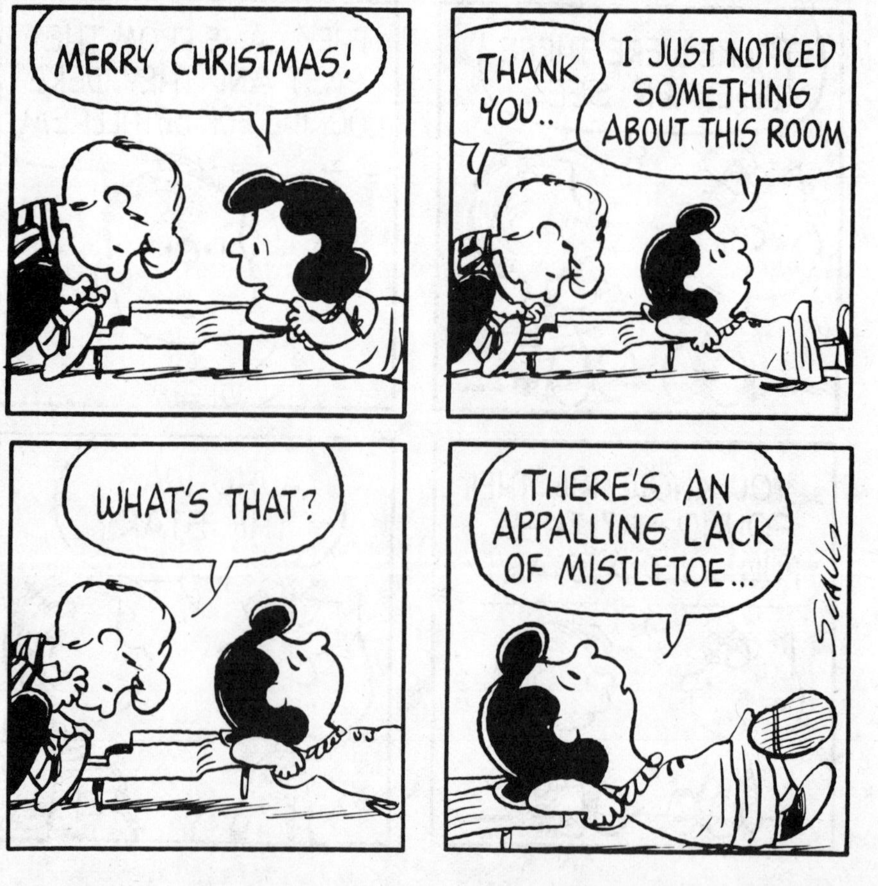
MERRY CHRISTMAS!
THANK YOU..
I JUST NOTICED SOMETHING ABOUT THIS ROOM
WHAT'S THAT?
THERE'S AN APPALLING LACK OF MISTLETOE...
SCHULZ

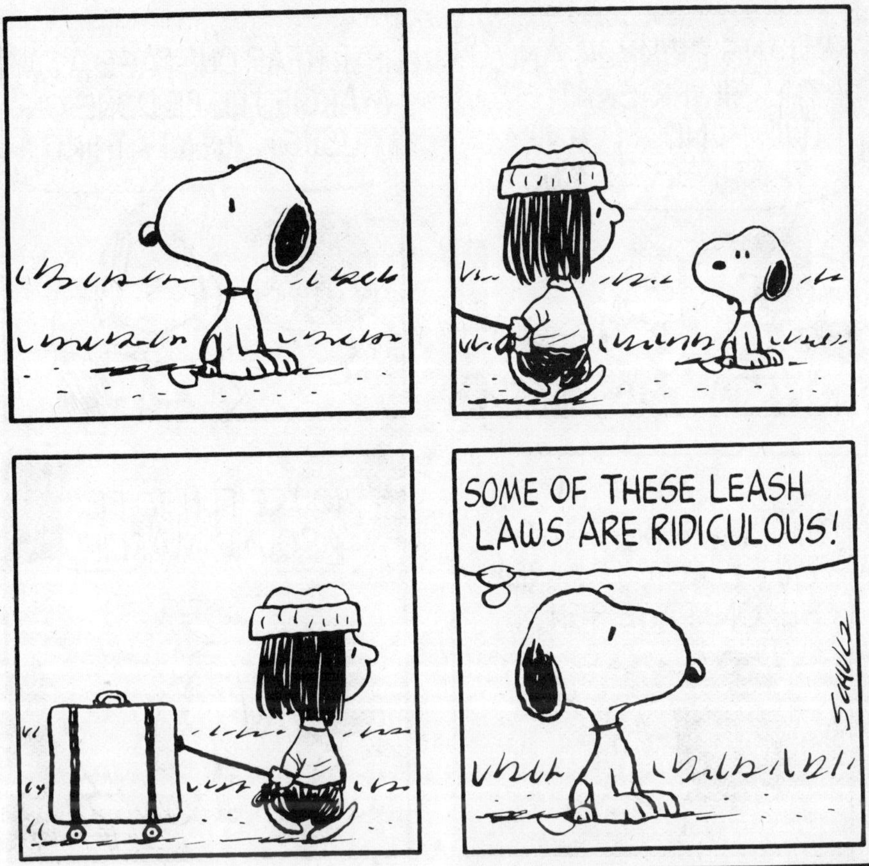
SOME OF THESE LEASH LAWS ARE RIDICULOUS!
SCHULZ

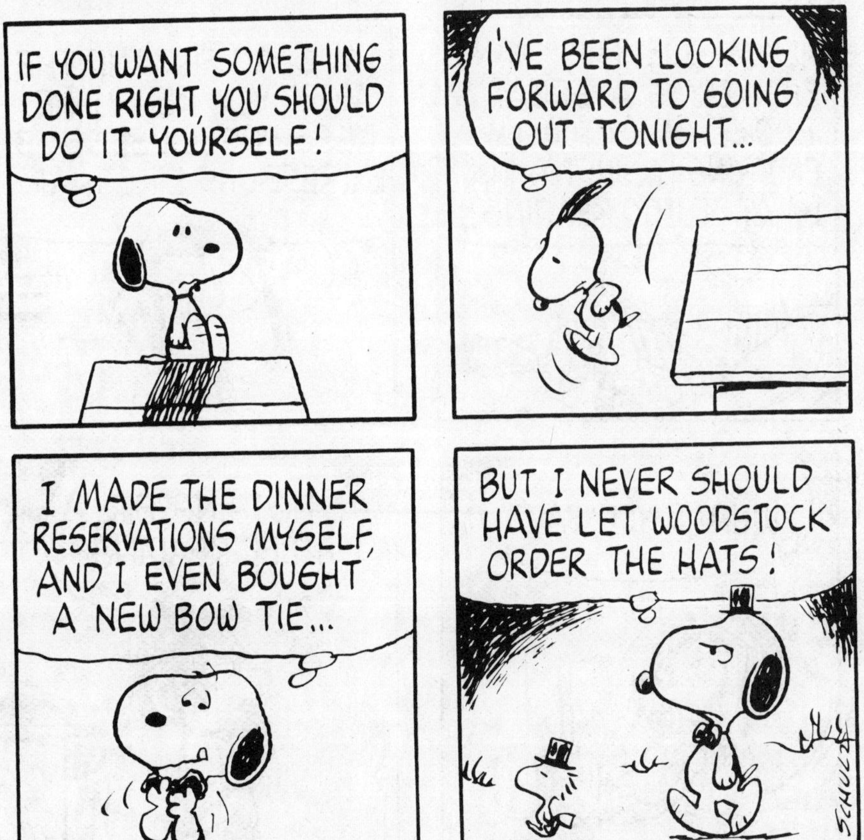
IF YOU WANT SOMETHING DONE RIGHT, YOU SHOULD DO IT YOURSELF!
I'VE BEEN LOOKING FORWARD TO GOING OUT TONIGHT...
I MADE THE DINNER RESERVATIONS MYSELF, AND I EVEN BOUGHT A NEW BOW TIE...
BUT I NEVER SHOULD HAVE LET WOODSTOCK ORDER THE HATS!
SCHULZ

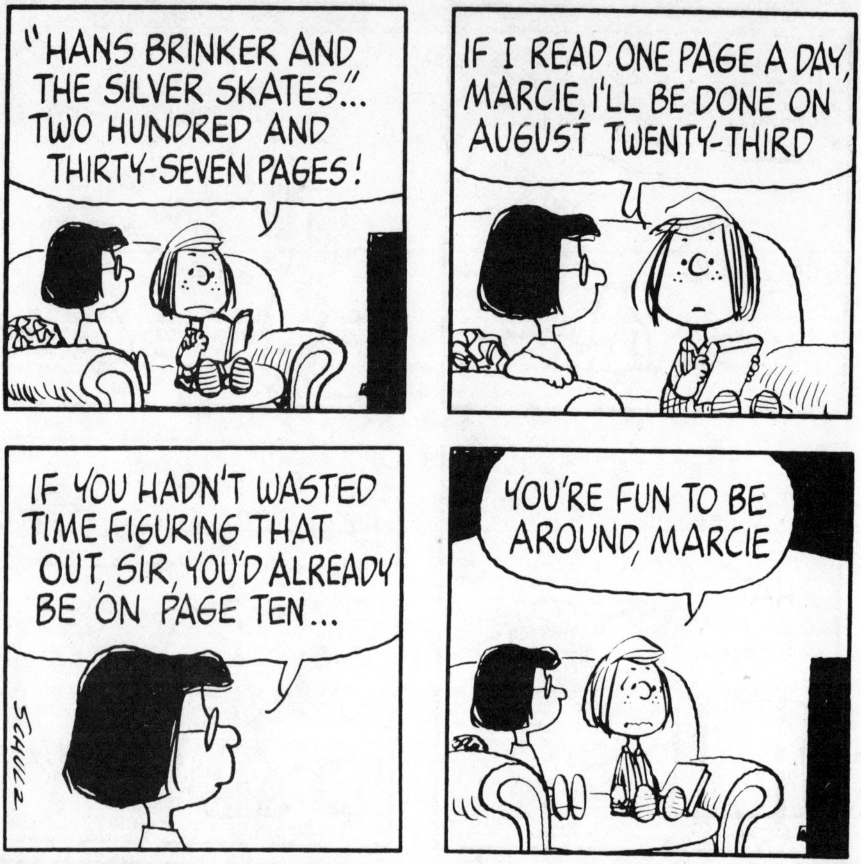
"HANS BRINKER AND THE SILVER SKATES"... TWO HUNDRED AND THIRTY-SEVEN PAGES!
IF I READ ONE PAGE A DAY, MARCIE, I'LL BE DONE ON AUGUST TWENTY-THIRD
IF YOU HADN'T WASTED TIME FIGURING THAT OUT, SIR, YOU'D ALREADY BE ON PAGE TEN...
SCHULZ
YOU'RE FUN TO BE AROUND, MARCIE

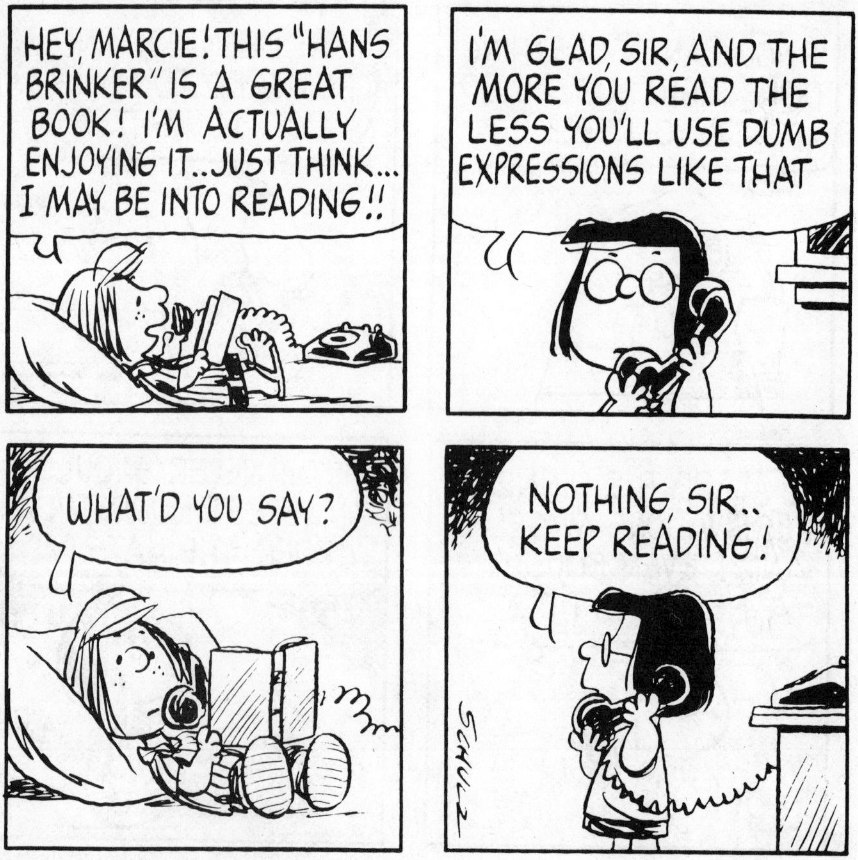
HEY, MARCIE! THIS "HANS BRINKER" IS A GREAT BOOK! I'M ACTUALLY ENJOYING IT...JUST THINK... I MAY BE INTO READING!!
I'M GLAD, SIR, AND THE MORE YOU READ THE LESS YOU'LL USE DUMB EXPRESSIONS LIKE THAT
WHAT'D YOU SAY?
NOTHING, SIR.. KEEP READING!
SCHULZ

FIRST YOU COUNT THE RISING OF THE MOONS

ADD THE FALLING OF THE TIDES AND THE SHOOTING OF THE STARS

DIVIDE THAT BY THE COST OF LIVING, AND WHAT DO YOU GET?

1981

PRETTY CLEVER, HUH?

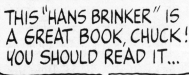

THIS "HANS BRINKER" IS A GREAT BOOK, CHUCK! YOU SHOULD READ IT...

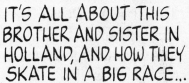

IT'S ALL ABOUT THIS BROTHER AND SISTER IN HOLLAND, AND HOW THEY SKATE IN A BIG RACE...

I'M SURPRISED.. I MUST ADMIT THAT I NEVER THOUGHT I'D SEE YOU ENJOYING A BOOK...

I'M INTO READING, CHUCK!

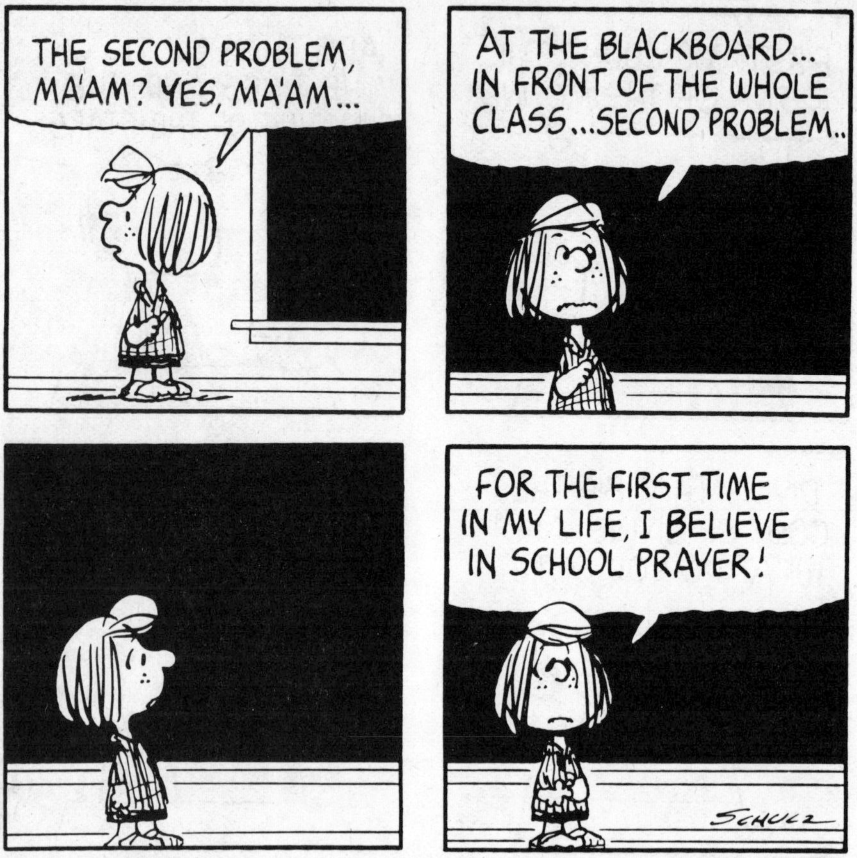
THE SECOND PROBLEM, MA'AM? YES, MA'AM...
AT THE BLACKBOARD... IN FRONT OF THE WHOLE CLASS...SECOND PROBLEM..
FOR THE FIRST TIME IN MY LIFE, I BELIEVE IN SCHOOL PRAYER!
SCHULZ

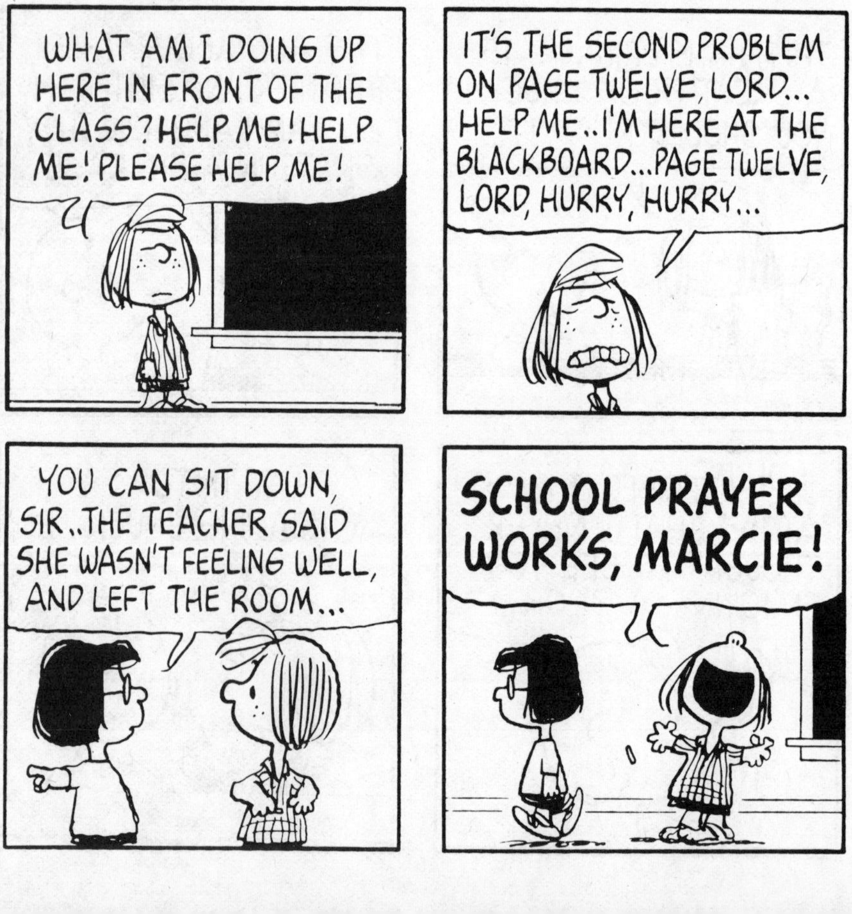
WHAT AM I DOING UP HERE IN FRONT OF THE CLASS? HELP ME! HELP ME! PLEASE HELP ME!
IT'S THE SECOND PROBLEM ON PAGE TWELVE, LORD... HELP ME..I'M HERE AT THE BLACKBOARD...PAGE TWELVE, LORD, HURRY, HURRY...
YOU CAN SIT DOWN, SIR..THE TEACHER SAID SHE WASN'T FEELING WELL, AND LEFT THE ROOM...
SCHOOL PRAYER WORKS, MARCIE!

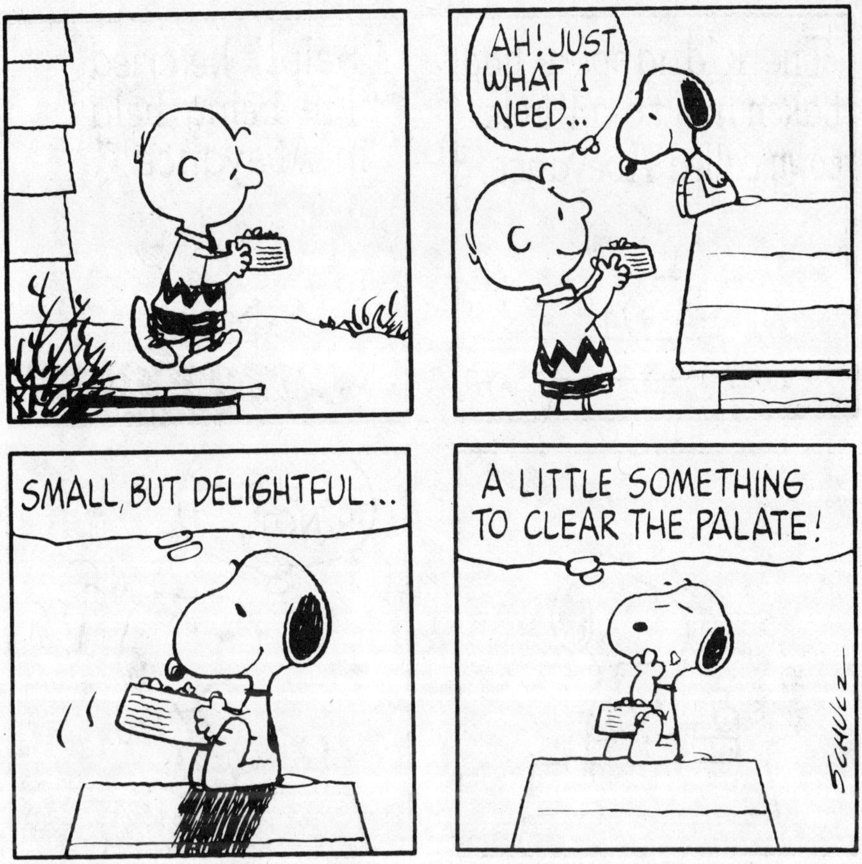
AH! JUST WHAT I NEED...
SMALL, BUT DELIGHTFUL...
A LITTLE SOMETHING TO CLEAR THE PALATE!
SCHULZ

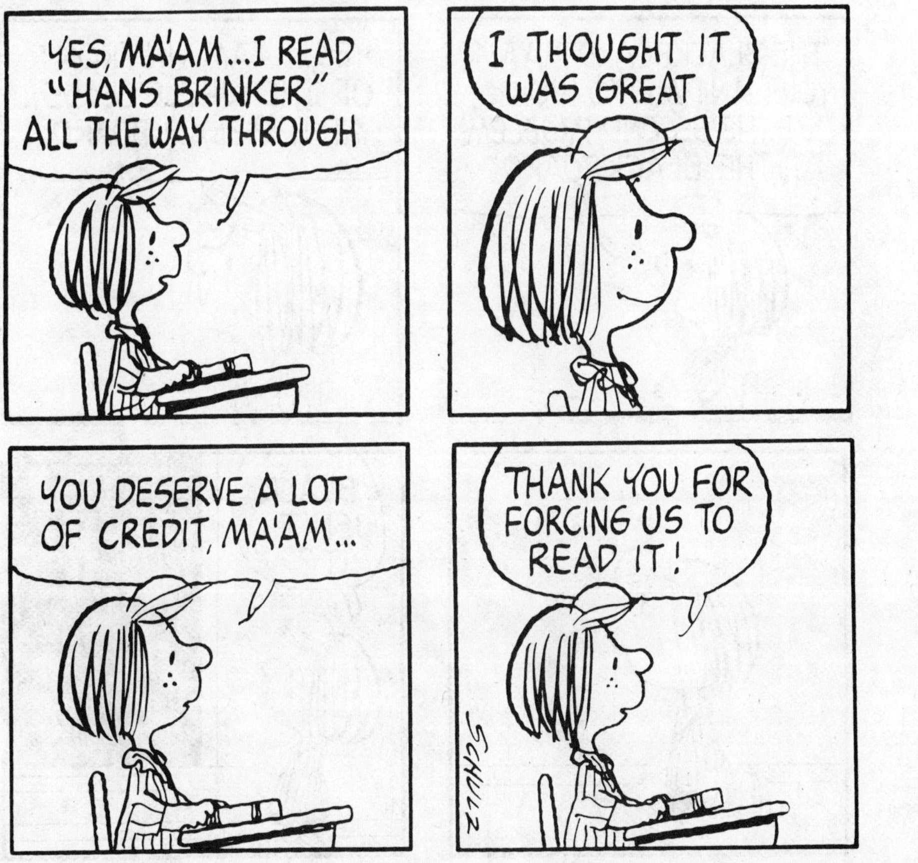
YES, MA'AM...I READ "HANS BRINKER" ALL THE WAY THROUGH
I THOUGHT IT WAS GREAT
YOU DESERVE A LOT OF CREDIT, MA'AM...
THANK YOU FOR FORCING US TO READ IT!
SCHULZ

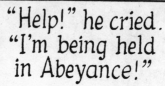

The kidnappers had taken him to a little town called Abeyance.

"Help!" he cried. "I'm being held in Abeyance!"

I GUESS NOT..

THE BLACKBOARD, MA'AM? YOU WANT ME TO WORK OUT THE SECOND PROBLEM AT THE BLACKBOARD?

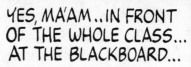

YES, MA'AM..IN FRONT OF THE WHOLE CLASS... AT THE BLACKBOARD...

BLACK, ISN'T IT?

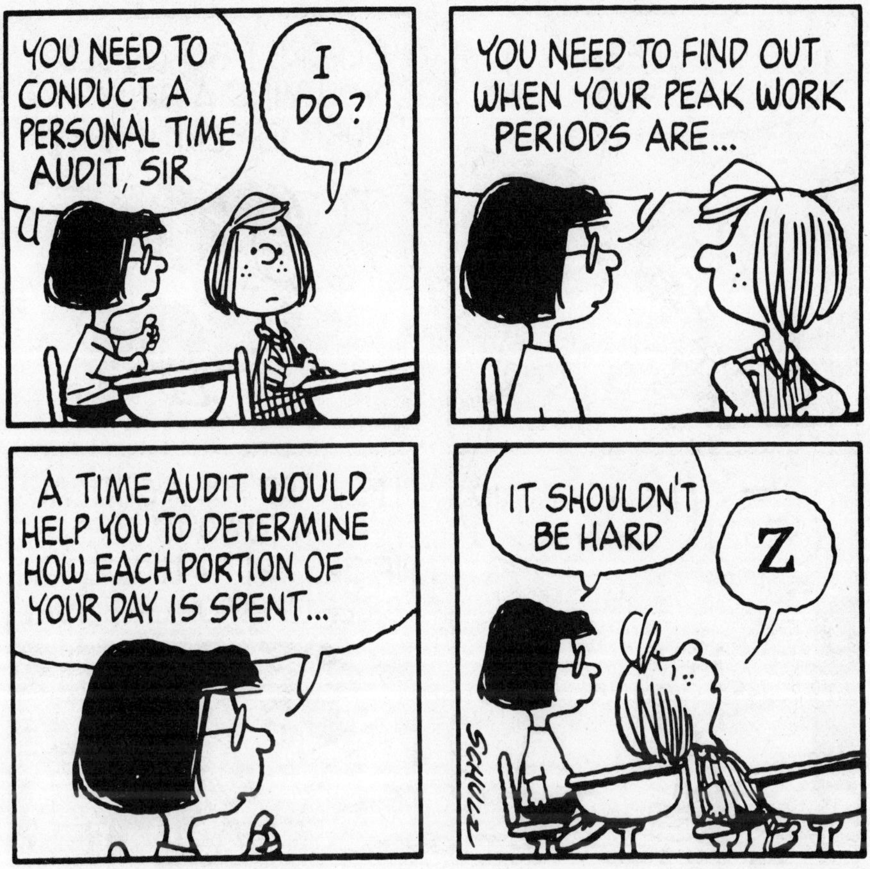
YOU NEED TO CONDUCT A PERSONAL TIME AUDIT, SIR
I DO?
YOU NEED TO FIND OUT WHEN YOUR PEAK WORK PERIODS ARE...
A TIME AUDIT WOULD HELP YOU TO DETERMINE HOW EACH PORTION OF YOUR DAY IS SPENT...
IT SHOULDN'T BE HARD
Z
SCHULZ

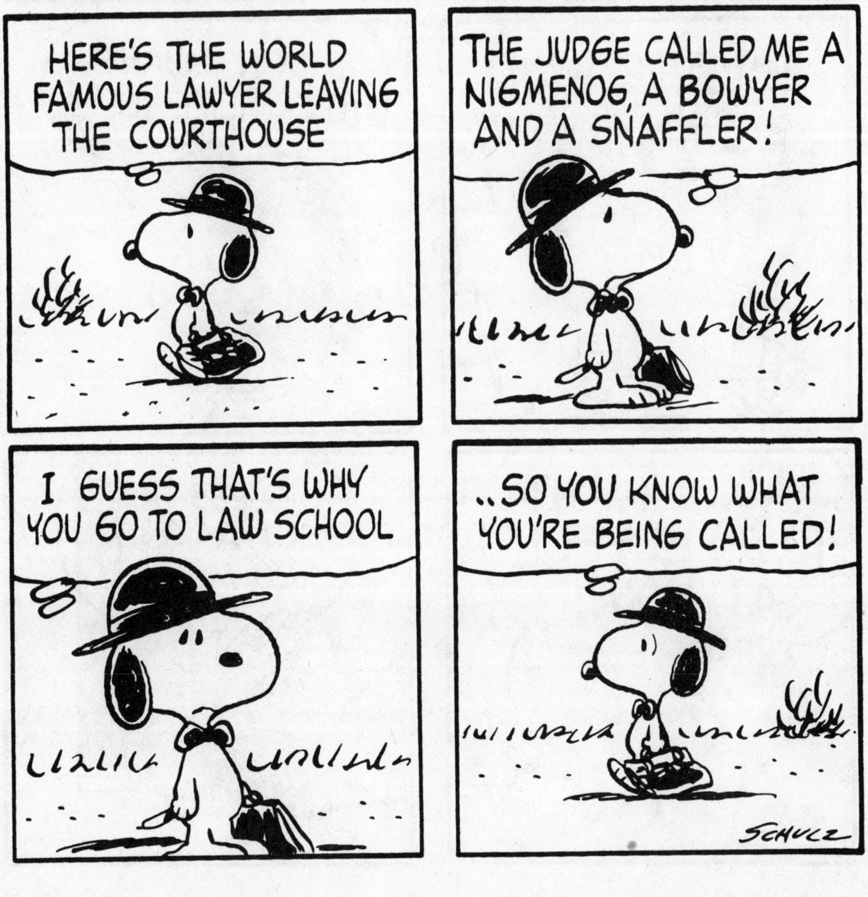
HERE'S THE WORLD FAMOUS LAWYER LEAVING THE COURTHOUSE
THE JUDGE CALLED ME A NIGMENOG, A BOWYER AND A SNAFFLER!
I GUESS THAT'S WHY YOU GO TO LAW SCHOOL
..SO YOU KNOW WHAT YOU'RE BEING CALLED!
SCHULZ

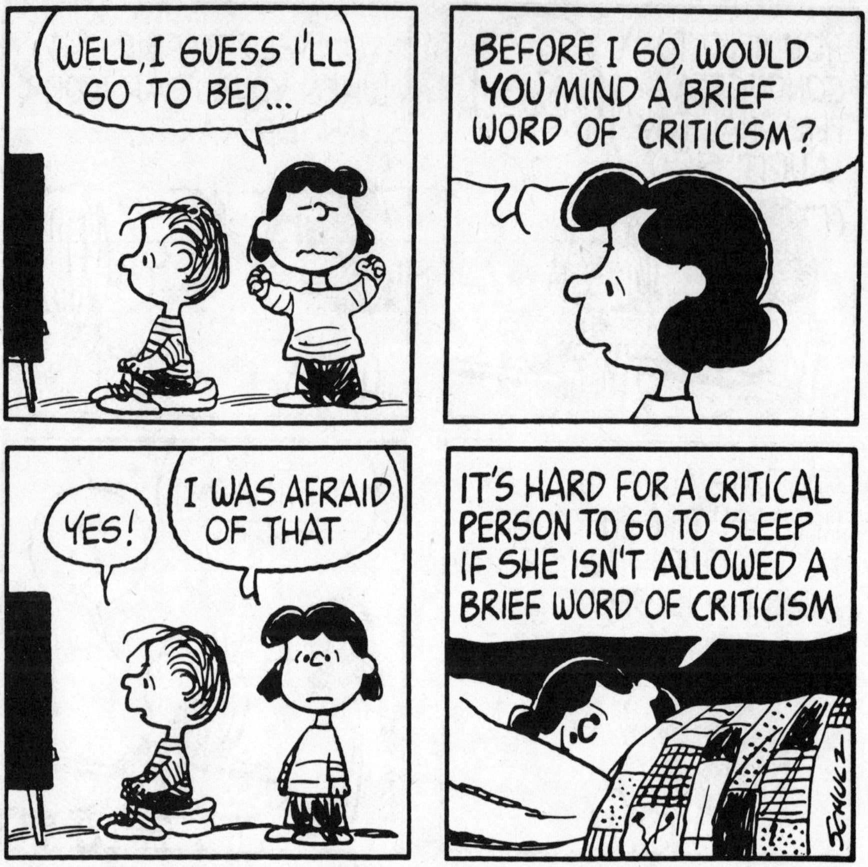
WELL, I GUESS I'LL GO TO BED...
BEFORE I GO, WOULD YOU MIND A BRIEF WORD OF CRITICISM?
YES!
I WAS AFRAID OF THAT
IT'S HARD FOR A CRITICAL PERSON TO GO TO SLEEP IF SHE ISN'T ALLOWED A BRIEF WORD OF CRITICISM
SCHULZ

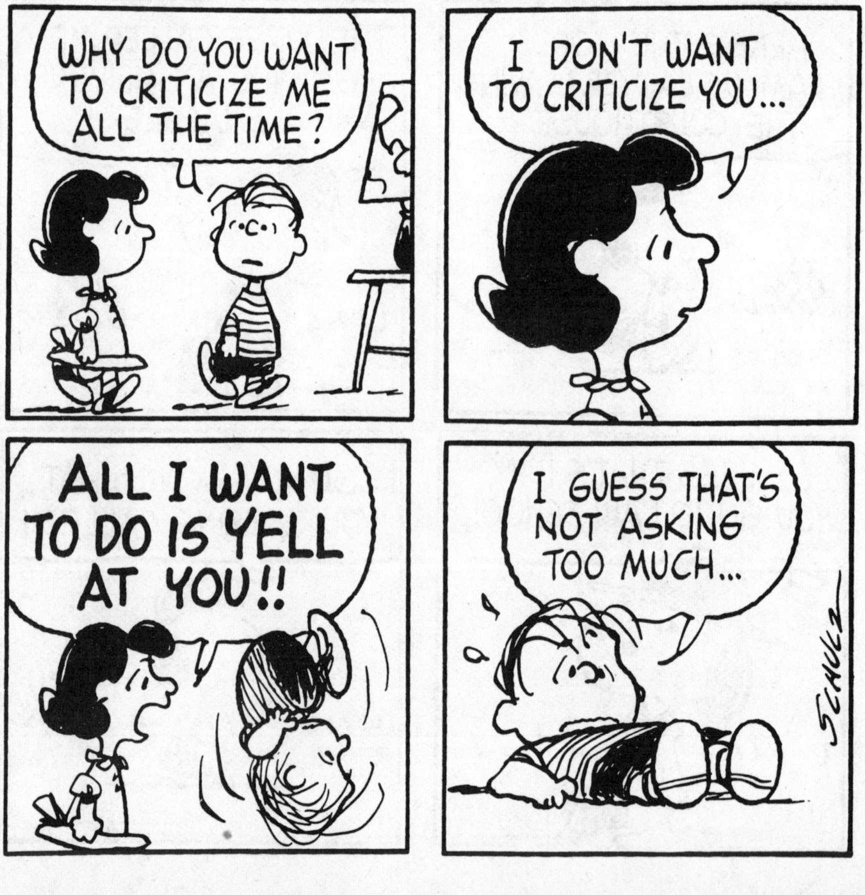
WHY DO YOU WANT TO CRITICIZE ME ALL THE TIME?
I DON'T WANT TO CRITICIZE YOU...
ALL I WANT TO DO IS YELL AT YOU!!
I GUESS THAT'S NOT ASKING TOO MUCH...
SCHULZ

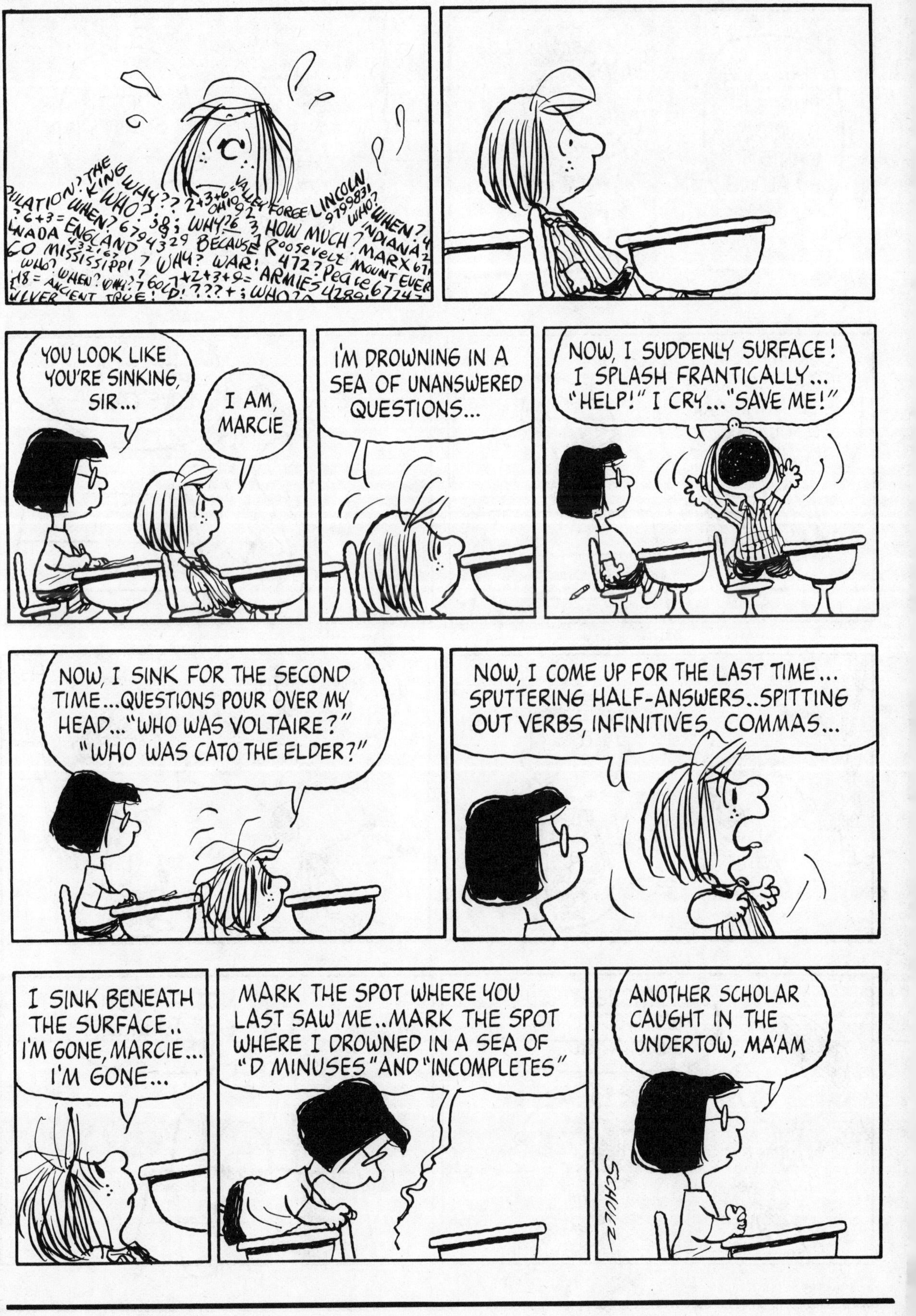
YOU LOOK LIKE YOU'RE SINKING, SIR...
I AM, MARCIE
I'M DROWNING IN A SEA OF UNANSWERED QUESTIONS...
NOW, I SUDDENLY SURFACE! I SPLASH FRANTICALLY... "HELP!" I CRY... "SAVE ME!"
NOW, I SINK FOR THE SECOND TIME...QUESTIONS POUR OVER MY HEAD..."WHO WAS VOLTAIRE?" "WHO WAS CATO THE ELDER?"
NOW, I COME UP FOR THE LAST TIME... SPUTTERING HALF-ANSWERS..SPITTING OUT VERBS, INFINITIVES, COMMAS...
I SINK BENEATH THE SURFACE.. I'M GONE, MARCIE... I'M GONE...
MARK THE SPOT WHERE YOU LAST SAW ME..MARK THE SPOT WHERE I DROWNED IN A SEA OF "D MINUSES" AND "INCOMPLETES"
ANOTHER SCHOLAR CAUGHT IN THE UNDERTOW, MA'AM
SCHULZ

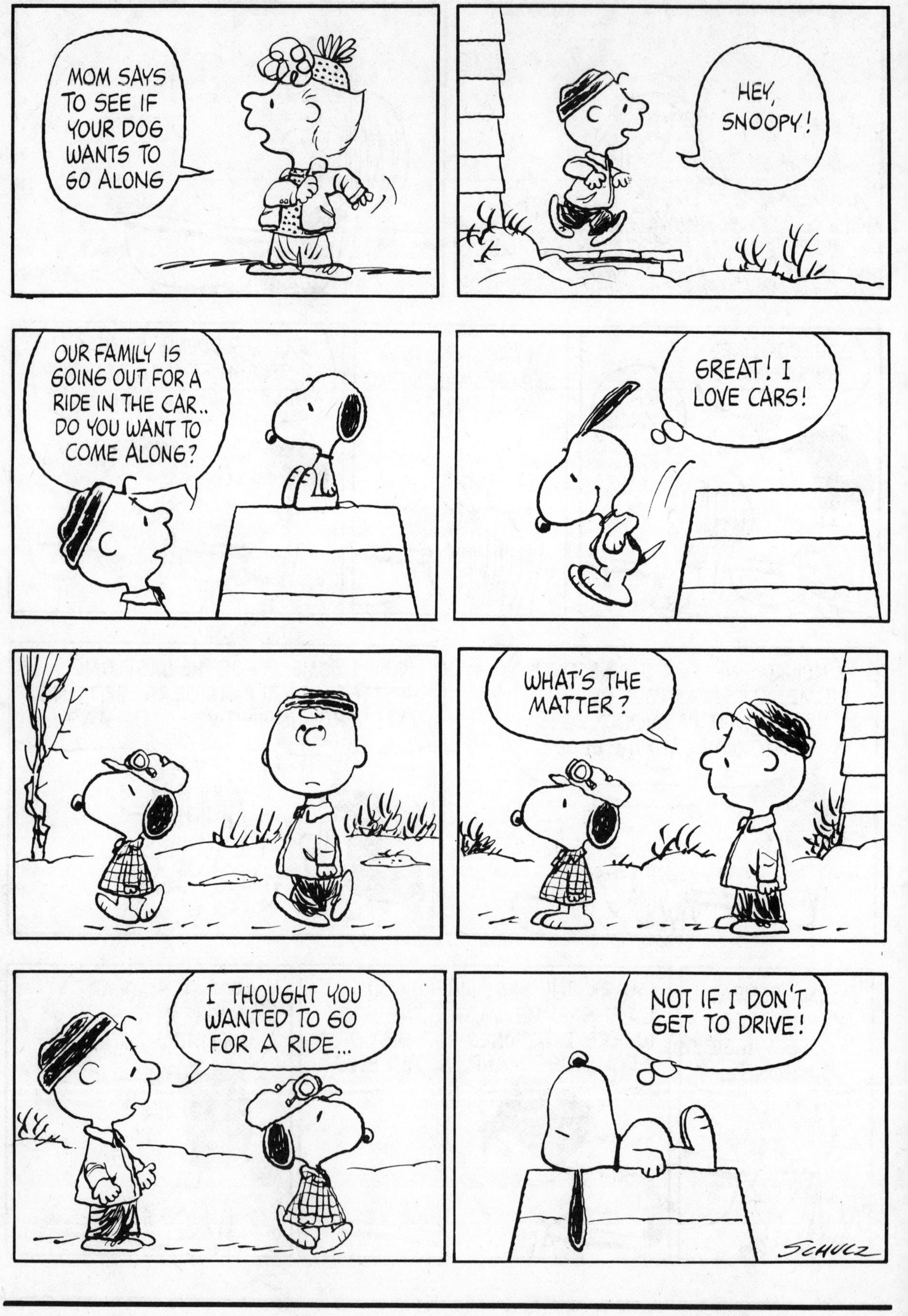
MOM SAYS TO SEE IF YOUR DOG WANTS TO GO ALONG
HEY, SNOOPY!
OUR FAMILY IS GOING OUT FOR A RIDE IN THE CAR.. DO YOU WANT TO COME ALONG?
GREAT! I LOVE CARS!
WHAT'S THE MATTER?
I THOUGHT YOU WANTED TO GO FOR A RIDE...
NOT IF I DON'T GET TO DRIVE!
SCHULZ